Fantasies:

Black Satin
The Pleasures of JessicaLynn
Slow Dancing

Other Books by Joan Elizabeth Lloyd
Available From Carroll & Graf Publishers:

The Love Flower
Velvet Whispers
Midnight Butterfly

FANTASIES:

Black Satin
The Pleasures of JessicaLynn
Slow Dancing

By Joan Elizabeth Lloyd

Carroll & Graf Publishers, Inc.
New York

Carroll & Graf Publishers, Inc.
A Division of Avalon Publishing Group
19 West 21st Street
New York, NY 10010-6805

Library of Congress Cataloging-in-Publication Data is available

Manufactured in the United States of America

ISBN: 0-7394-4354-2

Contents

Black Satin

Chapter 1

"You sent for me, Miss Gilbert?" the man said. Although he looked about forty, paunchy, with a neatly trimmed moustache, he was dressed in a traditional boy's school uniform: short navy pants, white formal shirt, a green-and-navy plaid blazer, and white, knee-length socks. Incongruously, he also wore Gucci loafers with small tassels on the vamp.

"I certainly did, Bobby," Miss Gilbert said. She sat behind an antique desk that she had previously moved to the center of the large, beautifully furnished living room. As arranged, she was dressed in a high-collared, long-sleeved white blouse fastened with a classic cameo at the neck. Her straight black skirt was pulled primly over her knees, covering most of her sheer hose. Her grey hair was swept up and pinned into a bun on the top of her head and her rimless glasses were perched on the end of her nose. She stared at Bobby over the top of her spectacles. "I'm afraid you're in serious trouble."

As Bobby looked at the floor he could see her heavy, black sensible shoes with their thick heels. Although the sound was muffled by the plush carpet, he could see her toe tapping rhythmically. "Yes, ma'am."

"I've seen the results of your exams and they're totally unsatisfactory." Miss Gilbert picked up a ruler from the desk and smacked it into the palm of her hand.

"Yes, ma'am," Bobby said, his knees shaking and a bulge forming in the front of his shorts.

"Do you know what that means?" Again the ruler smacked her hand, her long slender fingers wrapping around the wooden slat.

"Yes, ma'am." Bobby's palms began to sweat and his breathing accelerated.

"Tell me, exactly." She smiled. Smack, smack.

"It means that either you'll tell my parents or. . . ."

"Or what, Bobby?" Smack, smack.

"Twenty?"

"There were three failures," Miss Gilbert said. Her index finger stroked the edge of the ruler slowly.

Bobby's eyes followed the bright red nail back and forth. "Th, th, thirty," he stammered.

"Yes, I'm afraid so." Her finger kept sliding from one end of the ruler to the other. "Thirty." Smack. "It's your choice."

"You can't call my parents," Bobby said. "My father would kill me." Inside he smiled. His father had been dead for almost five years but that didn't matter. This dialogue had been honed over many encounters. Sweat tickled his underarms.

"Then we know what it will be, don't we?"

Silently, Bobby pulled off his jacket and shirt revealing a slightly over-weight body and hairless chest. Nervously, he ran his hand through his thick, dark brown hair and wiped a light film of sweat from his face. He dropped his hands to his sides and waited for the instructions he knew would come.

Her voice conversational, Miss Gilbert said, "That's good. Now drop them."

His fingers were barely able to unzip his fly as Bobby opened the uniform pants and let them drop to the floor around his sock-covered ankles.

"What are you waiting for?" Miss Gilbert said.

Trembling, he slipped his fingers into the elastic waistband of his white cotton drawers and started to pull them down. As usual, the task was made more difficult by the size of his erection. He pulled the shorts out over his hard cock and down so they fell and joined his navy blue uniform pants on the floor.

"Well," Miss Gilbert said, rising from her seat behind the large maple desk and staring at his cock. "I can see that dickie is anxious for what is next." She rounded the desk and tapped the end of the ruler against Bobby's hard cock. She reached across the desk and picked up an Ace bandage. She wrapped the wide elastic around Bobby's hard cock, attaching the first turn with a metal clip. Then she wound the stretchy fabric around his hips, then over his now-bulging erection. Around and around, she encased the area from Bobby's waist to his crotch in the stretchy fabric.

Bobby could barely contain his excitement. The first few times they had played out this scenario, he had come inside the elastic before they could get to the best part. By now he had developed some self-control. He bent his arms on the bright green blotter-covered surface and placed his forehead against his crossed wrists, his gold Tourneau watch showing the exact time and date.

"Now, Bobby," Miss Gilbert said, "you know that you must count for me and thank me for not calling your parents." She tapped the ruler against his shins, still covered by the white socks. He moved his legs back and spread them apart.

Swoosh. The first slap of the ruler fell across the elastic over his ass. It didn't really hurt but rather made his cheeks vibrate. "One, Miss Gilbert and thank you."

Nine more swats fell across his buttocks. Now the entire area covered by the Ace bandage tingled. "Ten, Miss Gilbert, and thank you." He knew what came next, but it didn't make it any easier.

With little warning, the eleventh swat fell across the back of his bare right thigh. Miss Gilbert made sure that it stung and left a slight red mark.

"Eleven," Bobby said, "and thank you Miss Gilbert." By the twentieth swat, the backs of both well-muscled thighs were bright red and sore.

"I think we'll wait for the last ten for a short while," Miss Gilbert said. She tapped the back of Bobby's neck and he raised his head. She put the ruler on the desk where he couldn't help but stare at it. "Are you very sore?" she asked innocently.

"It's not too bad," Bobby said. His legs were on fire but it wouldn't do to admit it.

"I'll make it better for you," Miss Gilbert said. Carefully, she unwrapped the elastic bandage from around his body and touched the deep indentations it had left. "Poor baby," she said, running a long fingernail over one particularly deep groove on one cheek. Holding the end of the pink stretch material still encasing his cock, she ran the tip of her tongue over the groove in his skin. As she yanked at the end of the material, Bobby's cock pulled toward her. She released the material and it snapped back. Alternately pulling and releasing the bandage, she continued to lick the marks on his ass.

As she straightened and looked toward his cock, she could see drops of sticky fluid oozing from the tip. "Is it hard not to come?" she asked sweetly.

"Oh, yes, Miss Gilbert," Bobby said.

"Well, we can't have you disgracing yourself, can we?"

"No, Miss Gilbert."

Still playing with the end of the elastic, she pulled at his cock and smiled. "You know the penalty for premature ejaculation, don't you?"

"Yes, Miss Gilbert." It happened occasionally. The last time they had been together, he had come like a fountain, spurting semen all over the desk. He had been forced to clean up the mess and had gotten ten extra swats from the ruler. He had come again then, but had been disappointed with his performance, his lack of fortitude. This time, however, he was sure he had enough self-control to finish.

Miss Gilbert unwound the elastic from Bobby's cock, put the roll down, and picked up the ruler. "You've been very good today," she said. "Should we reduce the punishment to twenty-five?"

As much as he might like to decrease his suffering, he wanted to continue to test his endurance. "No, ma'am," he said. "I need to be thoroughly punished."

Swat number twenty-one was a stinger, just hard enough to burn his now-bare ass. "Thank you Miss Gilbert. That was number twenty-one."

By number twenty-eight, Bobby's ass was as red as the backs of his thighs, but he stayed bent over the desk and took it.

Miss Gilbert knew what was expected now. For swat number twenty-nine she raised her arm as it would go and brought the wooden ruler down as hard as she could.

It hurt terribly, but Bobby didn't move. "Twenty-nine and thank you Miss Gilbert."

She heard Bobby's deep breathing and knew he was trying not to cry out. She raised her arm one last time and administered the final swat as hard as she could.

"Thirty and thank you Miss Gilbert." Bobby stood up, his hands at his sides, his erection enormous.

"Are you sure you've learned your lesson?"

"Oh yes, Miss Gilbert, and thank you. I'm ready for the rest of my punishment now."

Miss Gilbert went into the bathroom and returned with a large bath towel which she spread over the desk. She tapped the ruler across Bobby's inflamed buttocks and he moved so the fronts of his thighs pressed against the desk. "I'm going to watch you now. That's the rest of your punishment, you know. Show me what a bad boy you are," she said, her voice smooth and soft as cream. "Show me how you rub your dickie when no one's looking. Show me."

Bobby watched Miss Gilbert round the desk and sit down in her chair. He saw her ice-blue eyes riveted on his cock, still striped by the small folds that had been in the elastic. He hesitated. This was still the worst and best part.

"Bobby," Miss Gilbert said, "I want you to play with yourself so I can see. I want to watch everything. Now, wrap your hand around your dickie and rub." When he still hesitated, she picked up the ruler and snapped, "Now!"

His hands shaking, Bobby took his cock in his hands and began to rub.

"Wait," Miss Gilbert said. "I have an idea." She opened the desk drawer and pulled out a tube of lubricating gel. "Hold out your hands."

Slippery stuff. This was new, Bobby thought, a deviation from the ritual. But it was wonderful. She had guessed what he wanted without his having to tell her anything. That was what made her so special. He held his hands out, palm up, in front of him, and Miss Gilbert squeezed a huge glob of slippery goo into one hand. "Now rub," she said.

It feels so cold, he thought as his hands surrounded his hot cock. The moment he touched himself, he was lost. He closed his eyes and slid his fingers up and down his cock.

"Open your eyes you naughty boy," Miss Gilbert snapped. "I want you to see me watching your hands play with your cock." When he didn't obey immediately, she snapped again, "Now! Do it!"

He opened his eyes and looked into her face. Her eyes were riveted on his hands stroking his cock. It was sensational. It only took a moment until spurts of come erupted, falling on the white surface of the towel. His knees almost buckled, but he held on, enjoying the afterglow of one of the best orgasms of his life.

Miss Gilbert sat, unmoving, until Bobby swept up the towel and disappeared into the bathroom. Fifteen minutes later, she was sitting behind the desk reading when Bobby emerged from the bathroom, dressed in a grey pinstriped suit, light blue shirt, and paisley tie. He wore black socks and the Gucci loafers.

Without another word, he checked the time on his gold watch, put a handful of bills on the green blotter, and left the room.

The slam of metal against metal, the impact of her chest against her car's shoulder belt, and Carla's "Oh shit," came almost simultaneously. She shifted the car into park and stared out through the windshield. "Where the hell did he come from? There wasn't anything there a second ago," she said aloud, slumping against the seat. The front bumper of her six-year-old Ford had put a significant dent in the passenger-side rear quarter panel of a classy, gleaming dark blue Cadillac. "Oh God," she moaned. "Oh God, why me?"

Several pedestrians and a bicyclist had stopped to gawk at the tableau. Carla's car was blocking the sidewalk, halfway out of a Kinney underground garage between First and Second Avenues on East 53rd Street, an upscale Manhattan neighborhood. The Cadillac, which had been heading west across 53rd, sat in the road, the front of Carla's car resting against its side.

With a deep sigh, Carla climbed out of her car and watched the driver of the Cadillac emerge. As the woman stood up, Carla stared. The driver was a tall, slender statuesque woman with dark blond hair twisted into a perfect French knot. As the classically beautiful woman stared at her through dark, tortoiseshell sunglasses, Carla self-consciously ran her palms down the thighs of her comfortable, well-washed jeans.

The more Carla studied the woman, the more stunning she looked. The woman removed her designer sunglasses and shaded her eyes from the afternoon sun. She had perfectly arched brows over deep blue eyes, a long slender nose, and coral lips. Carla thought that she looked like Grace Kelly at her best.

Carla ran her fingers through her shoulder-length, brown hair, and tucked an errant strand behind one ear. "I'm terribly sorry," she called as the woman closed the Cadillac's door. "I can't imagine how this happened." Now that's an inane statement she thought.

Carla had been so happy when her doctor's visit had confirmed that all her worries had been needless. The lump in her breast had turned out to be nothing but a fluid-filled cyst. She had been so relieved after a week of suspense that she had almost run to the garage, bailed her car out, and started for home. Why was she going home? She wasn't really sure. The kids were still at school and her mom and dad were both out for the day. And anyway, she hadn't told her parents or her three boys about the lump. No need to worry anyone, she had reasoned. Unfortunately, that meant that she now had no one with whom to celebrate.

As Carla watched, the blond walked around the joined vehicles, calmly assessed the situation, and shook her head. God, Carla thought, I had to hit someone like her. The woman wore a classic dark red Donna Karan suit, a matching red-and-white patterned blouse, and perfectly coordinated Robert Clergerie pumps. She adjusted a gold, red, and white Hermes scarf over her shoulder with long, slender, perfectly manicured fingers. "Oh dear," the woman said, her voice soft and well modulated. "I'm so sorry."

"You're sorry?" Carla said.

"Of course," the woman said. "I was going a bit too fast and I wasn't watching where I was going." The woman hesitated, staring. "Wait. It couldn't be." She continued to stare. "Carla?"

"Excuse me?"

"Carla. You're Carla MacKensie."

"Carla Barrett," she answered. "But I was Carla MacKensie before I married. Do we know each other?"

"It's Veronica. Ronnie Browning, now Talmidge."

"Ronnie? It can't be." Carla and Ronnie had been roommates at Michigan State and had graduated together fifteen years before. During their three years together they had shared everything: field hockey, the debate team, the drama club and even, unintentionally, a few boyfriends.

Ronnie's laugh was a full rich sound. "I'd know you anywhere. You haven't changed a bit." She looked down. "I guess I've changed a little since then."

Carla remembered the moderately attractive brunette with wire-rimmed glasses and little makeup whom she had loved like a sister. "Have you ever! You look sensational." She smiled ruefully. "And you're right, I haven't changed. Unfortunately I look pretty much like I did fifteen years ago: Medium brown and average, average, average." Carla looked Ronnie over carefully. "What in the world have you been doing for the last fifteen years?"

"More than you can possibly imagine." Ronnie looked at the two cars and waved her hand. "You know, this seems relatively minor. Listen. Where were you off to?"

"Minor?" There had to be thousands of dollars worth of damage. You couldn't have an accident that didn't cost thousands these days. "I was going home to Bronxville—where I live now."

"That's silly. Now that we've found each other let's not lose track again. Why don't we park here and have lunch? We can catch up on all those years. And anyway I'm starved."

"Weren't you going somewhere?"

"I have an appointment at two," Ronnie said, glancing at her gold Cartier watch, "but that gives us over an hour, and there's a great little Italian place down the block."

When Carla hesitated, Ronnie's voice dropped. "Please. I'd love the company and we have so much to catch up on."

The parking lot attendant ran up waving his hands, trying to clear the entrance way. "You'll have to move these cars," the uniformed man yelled.

Ronnie's voice was soft, yet authoritative. "If you'll wait just a moment, Tom, we'll be out of the way." She turned to Carla and said, "I'm in this neighborhood a lot. I used to park here all the time but I've found a less expensive place around the corner."

As Ronnie returned to her car, Carla climbed into her Ford and backed up. The cars separated and Carla noticed that the damage to the Cadillac was less than she'd expected. Just a nasty dent and some chipped paint. She'd have to examine her car, but since the bumper had been the point of contact she thought it should be okay.

"Over here," Tom said. "Back it right over here." He waved Carla into one parking space and Ronnie drove into the one next to it.

As she climbed out, Ronnie said, "We'll be a few hours, Tom." She leaned into the passenger seat to grab a fashionable bag that Carla knew had to be either a Fendi or a great knockoff and slung the chain strap over her shoulder. Carla reached through the open passenger window of the Ford and grabbed her ersatz leather purse and camel-colored wool jacket. She slipped her arms in the sleeves and buttoned the blazer over her denim-blue-and-white striped shirt.

"Oh, Carla, this is so wonderful," Ronnie said. She looked at the front end of Carla's car. "Not bad," Ronnie said. "Looks like you got out of this little accident with almost no damage at all."

Carla nodded and wrapped her arm around Ronnie's waist. "I'm so glad I ran into you." She laughed. "Literally."

"Me too. This way." Ronnie led Carla under a small awning that proclaimed the restaurant to be The Villa Luigi. As they entered, Carla inhaled the enticing odor of garlic, oregano, and olive oil. They were shown to a quiet table in the back. "Give us a bottle of your Ruffino and some garlic bread," Ronnie told the waitress who seated them. As she left, Ronnie laughed. "Remember the night we got a gallon of jug-red and drank it with an entire package of Oreos with Double Stuff?"

"All I remember is how sick we were the next morning. I had to hold onto the floor to keep from falling off."

"And I puked my guts up for over an hour." The two women laughed. "Tell me what's new with you now," Ronnie said.

Carla took a deep breath. "Well, I was married for almost nine years but Bill was killed in a car accident almost five years ago."

"I'm so sorry."

"Well. . . . Bill wasn't exactly Prince Charming. He drank too much and was not a nice drunk. I had been thinking about a divorce for a year before his death."

"Kids?"

"BJ—that's Bill Junior—is thirteen, Tommy's eleven, and Mike's ten. Three boys. Where did I go wrong?"

"I remember that you wanted ten kids, all girls. And you never wanted to work."

"Never work? God, imagine thinking that being a mommy wasn't work."

"So you're a mommy full time?"

"Fortunately Bill left me pretty well provided for. That, and I sell a little real estate. I got my license about two years ago and I put what I make away for college for the boys. Sometimes I think I should work more, what with the boys in school all day and my folks right next door, but I can't think of what I could do, college degree or no college degree." Carla put her napkin in her lap. "English literature. A useful degree if ever there was one. Anyway, what about you? Married? Where do you live?"

Carla waggled her left hand under Carla's nose. The wide gold band on her third finger flashed. She also wore a thin band of diamonds on her index finger and a heavy free-form gold ring on the middle finger of her other hand. "Jack's an independent geologist who does consulting for a number of oil companies. It's a combination of lots of travel and a house full of computers. He's only home about one week a month." She heaved a sigh. "Unfortunately, no kids. I found out early on that I couldn't have any and neither of us wanted to adopt. We live in Hopewell Junction, in Dutchess County, almost two hours north of here. What were you doing in town, by the way?"

"Doctor's appointment."

Ronnie jumped in. "Nothing serious, I hope."

"Nothing. A lump in my breast that turned out to be a benign cyst."

"I'm glad." She squeezed her friend's hand.

Carla was touched. Ronnie was someone with whom she had always shared everything. It felt good sharing now. "So, Ronnie, I couldn't help noticing the quality of your wardrobe. And the new Cadillac. Jack's obviously doing well."

"Well enough. But the Caddie's mine."

"You work?"

Ronnie smiled in a way that puzzled Carla. "Yes, I work." She paused, then continued. "And I take occasional courses in creative writing at NYU. I've even had a few articles published."

"That's great." The waitress brought their wine and a basket of bread dripping with butter, garlic, and herbs. When she had poured them each a glass and left, the two women picked up their glasses and tapped them together.

"To work in all its forms," Ronnie said mysteriously, then laughed.

Puzzled, Carla drank.

For the next hour, Carla and Ronnie caught up on everything that had happened since they lost touch after graduation when Ronnie traveled in Europe for a year. As the two women finished espressos and the last of the bottle of wine, Ronnie looked at her watch. "I hate to say this, but I have to run. Someone's meeting me at two. But let's get together next week. Noon. Why don't we meet out front and eat somewhere else? And, don't worry about the damage to my car. I'll let my collision coverage take care of it." Carla took the check, added a generous tip, and split the amount. After settling up, the two women stood and Ronnie reached out and hugged Carla. "God, I've missed you."

For each of the next three Mondays the two women lunched in the same neighborhood: at a Chinese restaurant specializing in Peking Duck, an Indian hole-in-the-wall that made the best mulligatawny Carla had ever tasted, and today at a sushi bar where Carla sampled raw fish for the first time. Over ginger ice cream and green tea, Ronnie suggested their next meeting place. "I'd like you to see my place," she said. "Let's have lunch chez moi next week."

"In Hopewell Junction? I guess I could. You'll have to give me directions."

"Not Hopewell Junction. Around the corner." With an enigmatic smile, Ronnie gave Carla an address on East 54th.

"I don't get it, Ronnie. You have an apartment right here?" She saw Ronnie nod, then pause. "No wonder you know all the good spots to eat. Have you got a secret life? Tell me everything."

"Next week I promise you'll know all." As Ronnie left for her usual two o'clock meeting, she added, "I'll arrange to have the whole afternoon free. We'll talk."

The address that Ronnie had given Carla led her to a small, three-story brownstone on East 54th. Carla climbed the four steps to the entrance and rang the bell. Ronnie opened the door dressed in a soft grey wool long-sleeved jumpsuit, her dark blond hair loose around her shoulders. A pair of large, free-form silver earrings and a silver herringbone choker were her only jewelry. Carla was glad that she had chosen to forgo her usual jeans and had worn a dark green wool suit with a beige raw silk blouse.

The two women bussed cheeks, and Carla followed Ronnie through a small vestibule and into a beautifully furnished living room.

"Some fantastic place," Carla said as she looked around. Everything was done in black, white, and shades of grey. The sofa was overstuffed, covered in black leather banded with leather straps secured with heavy metal buckles. It was accented with throw pillows in black-and-white stripes and plaids. The two comfortable-looking soft chairs were white jacquard fabric with identical black-and-white pillows. A fluffy white rug covered the center of the floor; Carla could see the original highly polished inlaid wood where the rug ended. The walls were covered with a soft silver-grey silk and the windows were draped in a slightly darker grey damask. End tables of black lacquer held white-based, modern lamps that filled the room with light.

Vases and pots of flowers placed on tables and pedestals around the room provided the only color. Roses, chrysanthemums, and geraniums added their hues to blooming cactuses and unusual blossoms that Carla didn't recognize. Several hanging baskets of living blooms hung from hooks in both the walls and ceiling. One wall was all windows with a decorative but highly functional iron grill outside. The opposite wall contained a long, white, glass-fronted wall unit filled with books of every kind, from popular novels to poetry to volumes on natural sciences and history. The other walls held black-and-white Ansel Adams prints and other, smaller black-and-white photographs by artists Carla didn't know. At one end of the room sat an antique maple desk.

Carla whistled. "Holy cow." Through her real estate wanderings, she had learned enough to appreciate the class and expense of the decorating.

"Just a little hideaway," Ronnie said, laughing.

"Little? Either you inherited a small fortune, your writing is doing extremely well, or Jack indulges you and your 'little hideaway.'"

"Or 'D' none of the above." Ronnie handed Carla a champagne flute and filled it from an already opened bottle of Dom Pérignon. She clinked her glass against her friend's and, with an enigmatic smile, said, "To 'none of the above.'"

They drank. "Okay," Carla said, "give."

"I think we know each other well enough for me to show you my photographs. Sit down." She motioned toward the sofa and Carla picked up a photo album covered in black satin and sat down next to her friend. When she opened the album Carla saw a picture unlike anything she had expected. A statuesque brunette posed, wearing a black leather and chain bathing suit-like outfit. The links draped over her naked breasts, the supple leather caressed her hips and belly. On her hands she wore soft, elbow-length, black leather gloves and her legs were covered with thigh-high patent leather boots with five-inch heels.

The woman's wavy, auburn hair hung softly across her chest with one curl surrounding an erect dark brown nipple. In one hand she had a short, black leather riding crop. Her makeup was heavy, with bright red lipstick and exaggerated eyeshadow and liner. "I don't get it," said Carla.

"Turn the page."

The picture on the following page was of a woman with pale white-blond braids that hung down in front of her dress. She was turned slightly sideways, looking shy and vulnerable and dressed in a puffed-sleeve pink dress, an adult version of the dress a five-year-old girl might wear, with a fluffy full skirt over several petticoats and a wide sash tied into a large bow which peeked out from behind. Her white ankle socks were neatly cuffed and her black patent leather maryjanes gleamed. Her face, artfully made up with soft rouge and pale pink lipstick, looked youthful and familiar. As Carla examined the face more carefully, she gasped. "That's you." She flipped the page backward. "So's this."

"Turn the page."

The pictures that followed were all of Ronnie in various costumes: a harem girl with a transparent veil covering the lower half of her face, a prim grey-haired woman in a white high-necked blouse and sensible shoes, a voluptuous female pirate wearing short shorts that showed the half-moons of her ass peeking beneath and a blouse unbuttoned to the waist, and a woman in a black satin teddy standing over a man whose arms and legs were secured to the frame of a brass bed with lengths of heavy-link chain and padlocks.

"Phew. Ronnie, I'm amazed here. Okay, fill me in."

"I call the album Black Satin and it's really a menu. Selected people get to pick their . . . shall we say entrée and I supply the dessert."

"You're trying to tell me that you're a hooker."

"I'm a very selective, high-priced prostitute."

Carla was flabbergasted. She had expected something unusual. After all Ronnie had never been mainstream. But this? What could she say?

Ronnie spoke, her voice a bit tentative. "No condemnation? No 'how could you?'"

"I'm too much in shock to say much of anything. But, of course, your life is your own."

Ronnie smiled. "And it's wonderful. I enjoy every bit of my secret existence."

"What about Jack?"

Ronnie smiled. "I think he knows what's going on. He travels and I know that he entertains himself while he's away, and so do I."

"What about AIDS?"

"I thought about that a lot when all this began. Many of my friends— that's what I call them, my friends—don't want actual intercourse. They want oral sex, toys, and/or mutual masturbation. And those who do want to have intercourse must wear condoms."

"What about oral sex? Isn't that risky?"

"Not as risky as unprotected intercourse, but yes, it is. I thought about it a lot at the beginning, and I decided it was a risk I was willing to take."

"How in the world did you get involved in this?"

Ronnie leaned back and put her feet on the coffee table. "How, indeed."

Chapter 2

"I guess it all started just over three years ago," Ronnie explained. "You have to understand that Jack and I have always had an open relationship. I guess you'd say we were swingers. We both enjoy sex a lot and find that outside activities actually enhance what we have."

"You mean . . . with other people?"

Ronnie chuckled. "Yes, both of us were. And it didn't bother me at all. I loved the idea that someone else was making Jack happy, particularly since he was—and still is—away so much. And back then he'd come home with new ideas, toys, sexy lingerie." When she saw Carla's expression, Ronnie added, "Put your eyebrows down, Carla. You remember I was always the experimenter."

"I remember some of your experiments. Like Oreos and peanut butter. Go on."

"Well, the only strict requirement that Jack and I had, and still have, is that no one has intercourse without a condom. Period."

"Weren't you jealous?"

"I can say truthfully that I'm not jealous. I can't speak for what goes on in Jack's mind, but for me, not a bit. Anyway, because of his traveling, Jack and I spend at least three weeks out of every month apart. We are always very careful with each other's feelings. We talk often, and I'm sure that Jack has no objections to what I'm doing, although he doesn't know all the details. I have no problem with his flirtations. And they're just that, flirtations. Nothing serious, just lust and good sex. For me too."

"If you can really handle it. . . ." Carla paused. "I'm not sure I could."

"I don't actually know of many who can, but Jack and I seem to do okay."

"You were telling me how this thing," Carla waved her hand around the luxurious room, "got started."

"Jack and I were having dinner with a business associate of his, TJ Sorenson of American Oil and Gas Products." Ronnie closed her eyes. "It was Christmastime about three years ago. I remember that there were tiny trees and red candles on the tables."

"What a meal," Jack said, settling back with a cup of espresso. "I've never been here before but you can be sure I'll come here again."

"I discovered Chez Martin several months ago," TJ said, "and I keep hoping that no one else will. I read the restaurant columns and am relieved every time I find other places discussed. So far no reviewer had found Chez Martin. I'm particularly glad I could share it with you. You're two of my favorite people." TJ Sorenson was about fifty, with a head full of white hair and a bushy white moustache, which he stroked with one index finger when he was thinking. An old-time wildcatter, TJ's eyes were the color of cornflowers with deep lines at the corners from squinting in the bright sun for dozens of years. He was a handsome man, with the outdoor look of someone who spent a great deal of time in the sun, wind, and weather. He didn't look old enough to have a grown son, a married daughter, and three grandchildren.

"Thanks so much, TJ," Ronnie said. "I'm so full I could burst." She took a sip of her white crème de menthe on the rocks and gazed at the two men, both looking mildly uncomfortable in double-breasted suits, white shirts, and ties. Although he looks great in his usual jeans and sweatshirt, I love how Jack looks in a suit, Ronnie thought. And the slight grey at the temples of his carefully combed dark brown hair makes him look more like a banker than an oil explorer.

"I'm glad you're so satisfied, because I have an ulterior motive for inviting you tonight." TJ stroked his moustache. "I would like to ask you a favor and I'm not entirely sure how to do it."

"Just ask," Jack said. "You've been so great to me for all these years, I'll be happy to help if I can."

"Well," TJ said, "I need both of you to agree, although it's really Ronnie's favor."

Ronnie's head popped up, her blond hair brushing her shoulders. "Me?"

TJ sighed. "Let me explain. First of all, I hope you don't mind that Jack has told me about your delightfully original relationship."

"Of course not. Jack and I are not ashamed of our lifestyle." Ronnie stroked Jack's hand lovingly. "We love each other and have fun as well." Jack winked one grey eye and nodded.

"You two seem to have figured out something that works for you and you know how much I like you both."

Ronnie rested her elbows on the table and studied the older man. TJ, who had recently been promoted to executive vice president of American Oil, had been Jack's first boss. The two men had hit it off almost immediately, and as TJ climbed the corporate ladder, Jack climbed with him. Several years earlier, when Jack formed his own geology consulting firm, TJ had given him moral support and had seen to it that American Oil put him on retainer. Jack and Ronnie owed him a lot.

In addition to their business relationship, the two men had become friends. In the early days, TJ and Jack had traveled together on oil drilling expeditions, often spending weeks at a time in the field, living in a tent, and actually wielding a pick and shovel. In the years since TJ had become office-bound, Jack and Ronnie had dined occasionally with TJ and his wife Alice, most recently one evening the previous summer on the Sorensons' new forty-foot sailboat.

When TJ seemed at a loss as to how to continue, Ronnie said, "Whatever is bothering you can't be that terrible. Why don't you just come out with it?"

"Right." He sipped his cognac. "It's my son. You met Tim last summer on the boat. What was your impression of him, Ronnie? As a woman. And be honest."

She remembered TJ's son. He had been on his way somewhere but had paused for a moment to make small talk. She recalled an awkward young man who seemed uncomfortable with her. "He's a nice-looking guy, as I remember," she said, hedging. "How old is he now?"

"He's twenty-four. Tell me what you think of him as a person."

"I hardly spent any time with him," Ronnie said. "But he was charming, seemed to know the right thing to say but I guess he seemed a bit distant, a bit difficult to get to know."

"He's shy with women because he's had a few bad experiences. And now he's much worse. He was engaged, you know."

"No," Ronnie said. "I didn't know. You said *was?*"

"I did. The bitch did a number on him. I think she was more interested in my money than in Tim. Anyway, about a month ago, when he seemed to be losing interest, she lost her temper at our dinner table one evening. There were several other couples, their friends and ours, and Clarisse had been drinking. Something snapped, I've no idea what. But whatever caused it she read him out and, among other things, told him he was a lousy lover. I think her exact phrasing was that he couldn't give a nymphomaniac an orgasm."

"Oh shit," Jack said. "He must have been devastated."

"He was. Fortunately Tim and I have an honest relationship and we've talked at length since then. He doesn't want anything to do with Clarisse, but he admits that she might have a point about his sexual prowess. He told me that he feels inadequate and awkward as a lover. I told him that good sex takes two and that maybe he and Clarisse just weren't compatible, but he's really down on himself. We talked about finding a prostitute to, you know, teach him about women and sex, but he didn't want anything like that. Too impersonal, too clinical."

"Am I starting to see a plan here?" Ronnie asked.

"I hope so," TJ said. "I know and trust both of you and I need someone to teach Tim about women. Ronnie?"

"I'm flattered and I'd like to help. But I won't do anything without his knowledge," Ronnie said.

"Of course not." He looked from Ronnie to Jack. "If you two agree, I'll talk to him. I mentioned you recently and he remembers meeting you last summer. As a matter of fact, I think he was impressed, said you were a knockout, as I recall. I don't know whether that's the good news or the bad."

"I think it would be wonderful for Tim," Jack said, his charming grin revealing even, white teeth. "Ronnie's just the right woman to teach a young man about love and sex. She's terrific." He squeezed his wife's hand.

"So you're both willing?" TJ said.

"If Tim wants to, I'm certainly willing," Ronnie said.

Later that night, Ronnie and Jack lay in bed, naked, propped up on several pillows. "That's quite an assignment," Jack said, "teaching a young man about sex."

"I know," Ronnie said. "It's a bit daunting."

"Nonsense," Jack said. He tangled his fingers in Ronnie's hair. "Any man who looks at your full lips will want to kiss you." He pressed his lips against hers. "He'll want to use his tongue to play with yours." He opened her mouth with his tongue and stroked the inside. "He'll want to touch your face." He ran the pads of his fingers over Ronnie's forehead, cheeks, and nose. "And close your eyes with his lips." He kissed her eyelids.

"Maybe you should teach him," Ronnie said. "You do things so well."

As his hands made her skin burn everywhere they touched, Jack said, his voice hoarse, "Will you tell me every detail? Will you demonstrate to me everything you taught him?" His breathing was rough as his hands found her wet center.

"I may not share exactly what we do because that seems very private. But I'll make up something delicious," Ronnie said, wrapping her legs around her husband's waist. "But for right now, just fuck me good."

They were both so hot that their mating was frantic, tangling their bodies in sheets and pillows. He pounded into her hard and screamed when he came. Her orgasm wasn't far behind.

Tim called Ronnie about a week later. "My dad told me about your conversation," he said without preamble. "I'm really embarrassed about all this."

"I'm a little uncomfortable too, Tim, but I gather that this type of thing is common in Europe. The older woman educating the younger man."

Tim's hollow laugh echoed through the phone. "That doesn't help and anyway, you're not that much older."

Ronnie laughed. "It doesn't help me either, but I'd love to spend time with you, if you'd like. We could talk and do whatever you want, nothing more."

Ronnie heard Tim take a deep breath. "I think I would." He paused. "Maybe we could have dinner at that place Dad took you to. Like next Tuesday evening?"

Ronnie had been dreading a long dinner during which she and Tim would have to make pleasant conversation. It sounded awful. "You know, let's pass on dinner," Ronnie suggested. "Let me meet you at your apartment at about eight. We can talk and see what happens from there."

"I could pick you up." Ronnie could hear the hesitancy in his voice.

"I'd prefer to meet you, if that's okay." No long drive with awkward silences.

"Sure. Ronnie?"

"Yes."

"I'm terrified and mortified."

"Don't be. We'll only do what makes both of us comfortable. Okay?"

"I'll see you Tuesday." Tim gave Ronnie directions to his apartment.

"Okay. I'll see you at eight o'clock. And Tim, wear those tight, over-washed jeans you were wearing that evening last summer. I remember how good they looked on you."

"Yeah," Tim said, his voice a bit lighter. "Sure. I will." He hung up.

Ronnie drove to the apartment complex the following Tuesday and grabbed a heavy camel wool coat from the back seat. She wore a deep red, button front, man-tailored shirt and jeans, with her bare feet stuffed into soft leather loafers. She had on almost no makeup and had pulled her hair into a ponytail. Although she was in her early thirties she looked younger and less threatening. Only her lingerie was intended to tantalize, a dark red demibra and matching thong-style panties.

Her palms sweaty, Ronnie parked her car, found her way to Tim's apartment, and rang the bell. It took a moment before she heard footsteps.

"Hi," Tim said as he opened the door. Ronnie was surprised at how much he had changed in the few months since she had last seen him. Although he had been twenty-three that evening on the boat, he had still had some of the gawky teenaged angles and hollows to his body. No more.

"You've grown up," Ronnie said as she looked him over slowly and appraisingly, enjoying the way his body now filled out the navy blue knit shirt he wore. His shoulders were wide and his hips narrow. Lord she loved muscular shoulders and she longed to run her palms over his upper arms, feel them around her. That would have to wait, however. Right now Tim's fists were clenched at his sides and the open ingenuous smile that she knew could warm his ordinary-looking face was hidden beneath his nervousness.

Tim was terrified. When he and his dad discussed Clarisse's ugly comments, and Tim had reluctantly admitted that even before that evening he had begun to doubt himself. He'd been a normal teenaged stud, seducing several members of his high school class, then having several longer-term relationships in college. But with Clarisse it had been different. As the months of their relationship passed, it took longer and longer for him to arouse her. He tried to be considerate and give her the time she needed but after prolonged foreplay, once he finally got inside, he came so quickly that Clarisse complained that Tim always left her unsatisfied. The last few times they had slept together, he'd been unable to get an erection at all. "Don't you have a clue about women?" Clarisse had shrieked late one night. "All you want to do is fuck. Stick it in and to hell with the woman." She'd laughed at him. "Now you can't even get it up." His brain understood what was going on, but his soul had doubts.

The scene at his father's dinner table had been a humiliation for Tim and for several weeks he had gone straight home after work and shut himself in his apartment. After almost a month his father had showed up at his door and sat him down for a serious talk.

At first Tim had been appalled by his dad's suggestion of hiring a prostitute, but when Ronnie's name came up, Tim's interest had been piqued and his body had reacted. Although he'd only met her the one time on the boat, he'd spent many nights fantasizing about her long blond hair and great body. TJ had explained about Jack and Ronnie's unusual relationship, and Tim had agreed to the outlandish plan.

Now Ronnie was here and Tim was panic-stricken. This was all a terrible mistake. As Tim saw the corners of her mouth turn up, he asked, "What are you smiling at?" Her eyes were roaming all over his body, making his skin prickle. Was she going to make fun of him and of this ridiculous idea?

"Nothing. It's just that you've matured and I enjoy looking at you." She would tell him later, in detail, how hunky he'd become. Instinctively Ronnie knew that he wasn't ready.

Tim was nice looking, with sandy brown hair and eyes the color of toast. As Tim nervously ran his long, delicate fingers through his hair, Ronnie thought about how those hands would feel on her skin. Nice, she thought warming to her task. Very nice. And despite his nervousness, he had a sexy way of looking right into her eyes that made Ronnie tingle. "May I come in?" she said, noticing that he had worn the jeans she'd suggested.

Tim stepped back and let Ronnie brush past him into his apartment. God, he thought, she smells so good. "I'm glad you came." His face reddened and he looked mortified as he realized his accidental double entendre.

"You know, Tim," Ronnie said as Tim shut the door, "we're going to drive each other crazy if we don't relax." She placed a light kiss on his cheek and dropped her coat on a chair.

"Yeah," he said with a sigh. "I've been jumpy as a cat all day." He rubbed his hands down the thighs of his jeans. "I'm not sure this was a good idea."

"It was a wonderful idea and we'll just talk for a while. Nothing you don't want. Okay?"

Tim looked at his shoes, then looked at Ronnie. God, she was so sexy. He nodded.

Suddenly Ronnie was completely comfortable. Tim was a genuinely nice human being. "There's nothing to be jumpy about. Have you got anything to drink? I think we could both use one."

"I've got a bottle of champagne."

"Great. Got any orange juice? We could make mimosas."

"Sure. Good idea. The OJ's in the fridge."

"Any brandy?"

"There might be a bottle in the closet to the right. Why?"

"To make the perfect mimosa," Ronnie said, crossing to the tiny kitchen, "you should add a shot of brandy." Ronnie retrieved a container of juice and rummaged through the liquor closet until she found a bottle of Triple Sec. "This'll do," she said. Returning to the living room, she saw that Tim had half-filled two champagne flutes with champagne. He quickly added an equal amount of juice, then she topped each off with a shot of Triple Sec.

"To the evening," Ronnie said, touching her glass to Tim's.

Tim stared into her eyes over the rim of his glass, unaware of the sensuousness of his gaze. "Yes. To the evening."

Not too fast, Ronnie told herself, tearing her eyes from his face. She wandered. "Nice place," she said. They stood in the large living room which was comfortably furnished with a cream-and-navy rough-textured sofa, a matching lounge chair, and modern wooden coffee and end tables. The walls were covered with photos, mostly landscapes, taken all around the world. One that particularly intrigued her showed a market scene of stalls stacked with merchandise and aisles filled with over-tired tourists. Although the photo was in black and white, it conveyed all the colors of the scene. "Where's this?"

"Cairo," he said. "I was there two years ago with my dad."

"And this?" The picture was of a river with houseboats littering its shores.

"Amsterdam."

"Wow," she said, honestly impressed. "Did you take all these pictures?"

"Yeah. Photography has been a love of mine since I was a kid."

"These are terrific."

"Thanks. I've converted my second bedroom into a darkroom and I do all my own developing and enlarging."

Ronnie walked slowly around the room studying the black-and-white photos. "These are really very good. Do you ever do portraits?"

"Sure." He pulled out an album and proudly showed Ronnie several skillfully taken photographs of women. He pointed to one, a slightly over-made-up woman in her early twenties with an expression that, despite the smile, seemed disapproving. "That's Clarisse, my ex-fiancée. I wanted to mount this photo on cardboard and use it as a dart board, but it's too good a picture. You know, it's funny. Now that I think about it, this was one of the few times I ever saw her smile when it wasn't for effect."

Ronnie laughed. "From what your father told me, the dart board idea sounds like a good one."

Tim hesitated, then joined Ronnie's laughter. "You're right. But it truly is a good picture of her." He studied the photo. "Actually, she's never looked that good."

Ronnie kicked off her shoes, settled onto the sofa, and patted the seat next to her. "Sit here and we'll talk." As he sat down, she asked, "Would you be interested in taking some pictures of me? I'd love to have a good portrait to give Jack for our anniversary."

"Sure. That would be great. I'd really enjoy it."

"Have you ever considered taking portraits professionally? The ones you showed me were really good."

"Do you really think I could do this for money?"

"You never know. Maybe the ones I have in mind will be the start of a new career."

While they made small talk Ronnie felt the alcohol warm her body and knew that it would be easing Tim's fears as well. When there was a lapse in the conversation, she slid down so that her head rested on the back of the sofa. She handed Tim her glass and asked, "Would you like to kiss me?"

Tim put their two glasses on the table and said, "I think I would."

Ronnie wrapped her hand around the back of Tim's neck and gently pulled him toward her. She framed his face with her hands as he touched her lips with his. Gently, teasingly, she moved her mouth over his, nipping his lower lip with her teeth. "Ummm, nice," she purred.

Tim sat back. "This is so awkward. I don't know what to do with my hands. Maybe this isn't such a good idea." He looked away.

"We don't have to do anything you don't want to," Ronnie said, "but I'll be very disappointed."

Suddenly annoyed with the whole thing, he looked at her and snapped, "I don't need charity."

Ronnie stood up, unzipped her jeans, and slid them to her knees. She grabbed Tim's hand and pressed it against the crotch of her panties. "What do you feel? Am I hot and wet for you? Does this feel like charity?"

Her heat warmed his hand and her wetness made his fingers damp. She wanted him. Really wanted him. He looked into her eyes and saw desire burning there. Oh Lord, don't let me back out, he prayed, both to himself and to Ronnie.

She pulled his hand away from her crotch and held it while she slid her jeans back up and sat back down on the sofa. "I want you," she said softly, her gaze never leaving his eyes, "but I'll stop if you really want me to." She raised his hand to her mouth and placed a kiss on the end of each finger. "Should I stop?"

"No," he moaned.

She flicked her tongue over the tip of his index finger. "Then let's pretend that this is your cock." She drew the tip of his finger into her mouth. "Can you feel it? Does it feel good?"

He certainly could and it was unbelievably erotic. Electricity sparked in his groin, hardening his penis. "It feels very good." The words came out as part breath and part groan.

"Good. Then close your eyes and let me suck you." Tim closed his eyes and let his head fall onto the back of the sofa. It would be all right. Millimeter by millimeter she pulled Tim's index finger into her mouth, licking and nipping at the tip. She moved to the second finger and sucked it, then the third and then the pinkie. She lavished attention on each finger of his other hand in turn, until heat radiated from his body.

"This is how much I want you," she whispered. She took his hand and rubbed the palm against one erect nipple. This was wonderful. She could use his hand to touch herself exactly the way she wanted. She pressed and rubbed, arching her back and reveling in the sensations caused by his hand on her breast. Despite her hunger, however, she went no further, wanting Tim to take some of the initiative.

Soon touching Ronnie's breast through her shirt wasn't enough for Tim. He wanted to kiss her, to touch and taste her. He licked his lips and stared at her mouth. "I want you." Hesitant to do anything to break the mood, yet unable to resist any longer, he leaned forward and brushed Ronnie's lips with his. Suddenly he needed to devour and be devoured. He moved his head so he could delve into her warm mouth. He couldn't get enough of her.

Ronnie had never been kissed so thoroughly. "Oh Tim," she sighed, wrapping her arms around his neck. They kissed for a long time, as Ronnie slowly stretched out on the sofa and pulled him over her so that his body covered hers.

"Too many clothes," Ronnie whispered when they paused for breath. As Ronnie removed her blouse and tossed it on a chair Tim stood up and pulled off his shirt. His body was just as beautiful as Ronnie had anticipated. When he stood and started to unbutton his jeans, Ronnie stopped him. "Not yet." She stood up and moved so close to him that her lace-covered breasts brushed the sparse hair on his chest. Slowly she ran her hands over his well-developed shoulders. "When you opened the door I knew your body would look like this," she murmured. "So beautiful."

"I go to the gym a couple of times a week," he said, breathless. "I lift."

"You certainly do," Ronnie said, sliding her palms over his chest and down his back. "Your body is wonderful."

Tim unhooked Ronnie's bra and freed her breasts. "So is yours."

Ronnie slid Tim's hands down her ribs. "Pick me up," she said. "I want to feel you move."

With Ronnie's palms on his upper arms, Tim tightened his hands on her waist and lifted. "I love the way your muscles move under your skin," she said, kneading Tim's biceps.

"And I love your tits," he said, holding her so her breasts were level with his mouth. He took one nipple and drew it into his mouth.

Her hands roaming over Tim's smooth shoulders and back, Ronnie let her head fall back, exposing her smooth, white throat. Tim took the invitation and lowered her slightly so he could nuzzle her neck. Holding her easily with her feet inches off the floor, Tim licked Ronnie's pulse points and nibbled at the tender spot where her neck joined her shoulder. "You taste so good," he moaned.

He set her down gently and continued kissing her neck and shoulders. Soon neither of them could stand, so they quickly removed their jeans and underwear and stretched out on the sofa. "This feels so strange," Ronnie said, rubbing her back against the rough texture of the sofa's fabric. "It's actually erotic."

Tim rubbed his arms over the material. "I'll never think about this sofa the same way."

"I want you, you know." Not giving the flash of panic she saw a chance to blossom, Ronnie reached for Tim's already-hard cock. She unwrapped the condom she had dropped on the table earlier and slowly unrolled it onto Tim's hard cock. "Cold?"

"Yes," he said. "And very exciting."

"Let me share it." She rubbed the end of his cold, wet prick over her wet pussy. "Ummm, it is cold. And I'm so hot for you." She positioned his erection between her inner lips and arched her back. His cock drove into her. "Hold still and let me," she said, squeezing her vaginal muscles and watching the pleasure clearly visible on Tim's face.

She turned and pushed him back so his head rested against the back of the sofa and he was half sitting and half lying. "Hold still and just feel." She sat on his lap and impaled herself on his shaft. She used her thighs to raise her body, then drop, over and over, altering the speed and depth to suit her desires.

"Oh Lord," he moaned. "I'm going to shoot."

"Not yet," Ronnie said as orgasm built deep within her. "Hold completely still and feel, but don't come." When she felt him twist, she snapped. "Don't move and don't come!" He opened his eyes and stared at her. Slowly a smile spread over his face and he nodded.

She settled in his lap barely moving, his cock deep inside of her. "I'm going to come and I want you to share it." She took Tim's hand and touched her clit. Waves of pleasure started at her toes and deep in her belly and washed over her body ending in her pussy. "Feel," she yelled.

Her orgasm clutched at his cock, drawing his climax from him. "Yes. Now!" she groaned. "Do it." He thrust upward once, twice, then came, hard. Almost without movement, their mutual orgasms continued for long seconds. Ronnie collapsed pulling Tim with her and they dozed, tangled together.

Later, Tim stretched. "That was amazing."

"It certainly was. You were perfect."

He sighed and smiled. "We were perfect. I never knew making love could be so wonderful. Can we do this again sometime soon?"

"As long as we don't get confused. I enjoy fucking you, and we're friends. But that's all. Jack and I have a special thing and I love him very much."

"I understand. I can keep everything in perspective. Okay?"

"Okay. And you'll take some pictures of me sometime?"

"I'd love to."

An hour later, Ronnie arrived home to find Jack waiting for her. "How did it go, love?" he asked.

"It was fabulous and I think very . . . how should I say it . . . educational. How are you?"

"You know, I'm surprised at how I am. I'm great, and horny as a goat just thinking about you with that boy."

Ronnie grinned. "Well, we could go upstairs and work off that excitement." She walked over to Jack's chair, knelt between his knees, and unbuckled his belt. As she unzipped his fly she brushed his hard cock. "Or maybe we could stay right here." She separated the sides of the fly in his shorts allowing his hard cock to spring forth. "What's your pleasure?"

"You're my pleasure," Jack said softly. "So much pleasure."

Ronnie made a tight ring of her index finger and thumb and slowly slid that ring down the length of Jack's cock. With her fingers tightly encircling the base of her husband's cock, Ronnie licked the tip with the point of her tongue. Then she kissed the tiny hole in the end. "Your cock is so hard—like warm velvet over steel." She sucked the end into her wet mouth and slowly slid the length of it into her throat.

Jack watched his wife's head bob in his lap, unable to control the frantic excitement bubbling inside him. His hips bucked and his hot come tried to rush through the tight ring of her fingers. "Oh babe, let me. I'm so horny."

"Let you come?" she said, letting her breath cool Jack's wet cock. "Release my fingers?"

"Yes."

She sucked in his cock and then pulled back. "Say please."

"Please, babe."

Ronnie released her fingers and took Jack's entire thick cock into her mouth, sucking and flicking her tongue over the tip. Almost immediately hot come filled her mouth. As fast as she swallowed, some thick liquid escaped from the corners of her mouth.

When Ronnie had licked all the stickiness from Jack's cock, she sat back and said, "Now, let's go upstairs and we'll make love nice and slow."

Jack grinned his agreement.

Three days later, Ronnie stormed to the door, waving an envelope, as Jack arrived home. "You'll never believe what came in the mail today."

Jack could tell she was furious. "Calm down babe, and tell me what happened."

"TJ sent me a check for three hundred dollars and a thank-you note for the evening I spent with Tim."

"So why are you so angry?" Jack said, dropping his briefcase on the hall table.

"I didn't do this to get paid. I feel like a whore."

"But he was going to pay a prostitute anyway. Why shouldn't you take the money?"

Ronnie released her breath. "I am not a whore."

"No one said you were."

"But doesn't this make me one? Sex for money."

"Stop being judgmental," Jack said walking into the kitchen. "You had fun, Tim had fun, and TJ was delighted with the way everything turned out. And Tim's a better person because of your help. Right?"

"Yeah, but. . . ." She was flustered.

"Don't but me. How can this be wrong when no one's been hurt?"

"But I'm not a . . ." Ronnie paused.

"Hooker, call girl, prostitute, whore?" Jack said. "Words. Just words with all kinds of bullshit behind them. Stop using labels and think. Was anyone hurt?"

"No."

"You performed a service, and did it well. Right?"

"Yes."

"So you should be rewarded. Of course, you could send the check back. . . ."

"I could."

"But you don't want to. So the end result is that you had fun and got paid for it. A dream job."

"I guess I never thought of it that way." She dropped into a chair. "God, I did have fun."

"And so did we that night, if you remember." He groaned loudly and pressed a hand against the small of his back. "Our acrobatics almost put me out of commission for good."

Ronnie laughed. "You're right, you know. I am being silly." She stared at the check. "Three hundred dollars for having a good fuck. Seems almost too good to be true."

"So buy yourself something extravagant. Buy some sexy lingerie and gift wrap your gorgeous body for me."

"I could squander this. It's like found money."

"Yes, it is. You know," he paused, "my clients are sometimes out-of-town visitors who need to be entertained. Dinner, a show, intelligent conversation, and afterward . . . well, that's between the client and his date. If you think you'd like to earn some extra money. . . ."

"Prostitution?"

"Fun and games and a little cash on the side. And only if you want to."

"How much cash on the side?" she said, amazed at how excited she suddenly was by the idea.

"I've never been involved directly, but from what I understand they pay anywhere from three hundred to one thousand dollars per evening. For adult entertainment."

Ronnie's eyes widened. "One thousand dollars???"

Jack nodded.

"I'm flabbergasted. For doing what we've been doing anyway. Would you be okay with it, me with other men?"

"Well, if you'll tell me afterward a little about what happens, the idea turns me on."

"I won't violate any confidences, you understand."

"Of course not." He saw the gleam in Ronnie's eye. "Interested?"

"I think I might be."

He took her arm. "This conversation has made me horny. Wanna practice for your new profession? Or I could conduct your preemployment physical."

Ronnie headed for the stairs. "Last one to the bedroom has to sleep in the wet spot."

Chapter 3

"And that was how this began," Ronnie told Carla. "Tim took these pictures of me, you know."

"He really does great work," Carla said.

"He does, doesn't he? He's got a few girlfriends now, and he's marvelous in bed. He loves women, and it shows in his photographs."

"I love happy endings."

"Me too."

"And this works for you, this call girl thing?"

"It does. I make a nice living and I meet fascinating people."

Carla had a thousand questions. "Have you ever had a bad experience? You know, someone who gets abusive and wants something you don't want to do, that sort of thing?"

"No one has ever gotten out of line. I screen my friends very well. They're all recommended by other friends. I never give out my address until I'm satisfied they're safe and I have a private, unlisted phone number. And I never answer that phone. I let the answering machine take a message and I call back or I hear who it is and then pick up. Our first date must begin with dinner somewhere nice. I can size someone up quickly and if I don't get good vibes we part right then."

"Have you ever had an evening go wrong?"

"I've had several men who wanted things I wasn't willing to do," Ronnie answered. When Carla raised an eyebrow, she continued, "One man wanted me to urinate on him as he masturbated and another wanted to give me an enema."

When Carla made an ugly face, Ronnie said, "Don't judge. These activities give them sexual pleasure and that's their business. And some of the things I enjoy would turn others off. But sometimes I have to tell a customer that his fantasy won't work for me." Ronnie's smile was warm. "The urination guy was a really nice man, actually, and he offered me more money. I explained that money wasn't the issue and I suggested that he find someone else. We finished our meal and spent a pleasant hour discussing movies and he paid for dinner. I never saw him again."

"Any others?"

"A man named Harry was recommended by an old friend. We had dinner and talked about his fantasies. He was heavily into control and he wanted to dominate me, run things, and spank me when I was naughty. That would have been very difficult for me, since I'm a dominant personality myself." She laughed. "I never play with anyone when I can't have some fun too."

"Control?"

"Lots of people have fantasies that revolve around power and control. This guy wanted to be in charge of all the action. Actually he had another interesting fantasy. He wanted to have me take a pretend pill that would render me incapable of resisting anything he wanted to do. And there's another man who wanted to tie me to a bed. Not my thing either."

Carla felt a jolt of electricity flow through her body and directly into her pussy. The control fantasies sounded wonderful to her. "From the look on your face," Ronnie said, "I think we've found something you'd enjoy. Should I give you a phone number? He'll pay a thousand dollars for one night."

"Holy. . . . Not yet," Carla said, realizing that she was more than a little interested in Ronnie's work.

"Hmmm. I don't have to be psychic to guess what you're thinking, darling," Ronnie said, "but you realize that this isn't for everyone. You have to have strong, good feelings about yourself and you have to enjoy sex. The money is just an extra added attraction. In my mind, the fact that the money is secondary is what makes me an entertainer, not a whore."

"Listen," Carla said, glancing at her watch, amazed that it was already after three. "I have to get home and I have a lot of thinking to do. What day next week works for you?"

"I'll be away next week." Ronnie laughed. "A friend has invited me on a cruise. Delicious food, wine, dancing, cavorting under the Caribbean skies, the works." She winked. "And I get twenty-five hundred dollars for little old me."

Carla whistled. "Holy shit."

"Mmmm. And he's a doll. Really an interesting man."

"Why you?" How could she ask what she wanted to know without it sounding like an insult? "I don't mean you're not great, you understand, but why. . . . well, you know."

"He's got the funny idea that no 'nice girl' would like the kind of cavorting we do." She settled back. "Actually, the entire cruise is devoted to dominance. It's an annual event and there's a whole group going. We've taken an entire separate area of the ship. I will be his Mistress Ronnie for the week and he'll be my sex slave. I've got a bunch of special toys and outfits for both of us."

"Have you ever done anything like this before?"

"We met two years ago on this very cruise. Another woman and I swapped slaves for an evening and Bob enjoyed being with me so much that we repeated the trip last year and will again next week. We play during the year as well." She flipped to the photo of the grey-haired school marm in the sensible shoes and smiled. "Bobby's a very difficult student."

"I'm speechless." Ronnie shot Carla an understanding glance.

"Let's see. The following week the boys are home from camp and we're going to a lake in the Adirondacks with my folks."

"Then I'm away," Ronnie said. "Jack and I are going to Disney World, of all places, for two weeks in August. I've never been there and despite all the warnings about the heat I'm like a kid looking forward to the rides and the parade of lights. And we'll siesta after lunch, of course. Jack and me, an air-conditioned room, and a king-sized bed."

"You and Jack have a good thing going, don't you?"

"Yeah, we do. It's just this damn *blasted* business of his. He's gone more than he's home. But we have two weeks of sun and fun to look forward to and I, for one, intend to make the best of it."

"It looks like we won't see each other until September."

"I'm afraid so. You know, I'll miss you."

"Me too."

Ronnie checked the tiny date book she kept in her purse. "Okay. How about the day after Labor Day? Lunch here."

"That sounds great." The two women bussed cheeks. "You're quite something," Carla said.

"So are you. And I'm so glad we found each other again."

"Me too," Carla said. "Me too."

During the month that Ronnie was away Carla did a lot of thinking. She was intrigued and titillated by the idea of Ronnie's business and the prospect of joining her was never far from Carla's mind.

With the boys in camp, Carla spent the first week at home, pretty much alone, cleaning and shopping and fantasizing about being tied to a bed with a handsome man standing over her, watching her useless struggles. One morning she lay in bed until after nine, dreaming about being under some man's power, letting him do whatever he wanted without being able to resist him. With that picture in her mind, she slipped her hand between her legs and rubbed her clit until she came.

She spent the second week in the Adirondacks with her three rambunctious boys and her parents. They had a wonderful time together, swimming, horseback riding, playing softball and frisbee, and eating everything in sight, while blaming their astounding appetites on the mountain air. And every man she encountered became the center of a fantasy in which she was a paid courtesan. Carla spent the entire vacation in a state of frustrated sexual excitement.

More than once she looked at her three high-spirited sons and thought about their future. All three were exceptionally bright and all would be able to select from the best colleges. The question was would she be able to afford it. There was money set aside, but would it be enough? Or was money merely an excuse to do what excited and intrigued her? What did it matter? She had made up her mind and she knew it.

Trying not to lie too much, she talked to her mother one evening about the possibility of spending more time with her grandchildren. "I've spoken about my old college roommate Ronnie," she told her mother one evening over coffee after their return to Bronxville.

"How in the world did you find Ronnie?"

"I literally ran into her." Carla told her mother the story of her accidental encounter with her old friend, reassuring her that the medical scare had been really nothing.

"And how is Ronnie?" Mrs. MacKensie asked. "I remember the vacation she spent with us. She was such a lovely girl."

"She's hardly a girl now," Carla said. "She's married and she owns her own business."

"Your father and I were always sure she'd go far. She seemed like such an intelligent girl."

Carla smiled to herself. "I wanted to talk to you about that. She wants me to join her business part time. It'll mean extra money and I could use it for the boys' college fund. The costs are getting astronomical." From upstairs, she could hear the laughter that always accompanied her father's efforts to settle the boys in bed.

"What kind of business?"

"It's a service business of some kind. Public relations. I don't know many of the details but it will involve entertaining clients in the city some evenings."

"That's wonderful dear," her mother said. "You need some other interests in your life besides your sons."

"It would mean that you would have to stay with the boys more often. A few nights a week and occasional weekends."

"Weekends? How come? Not that I mind, you understand."

"God only knows," she answered, "but Ronnie warned me about some out-of-town stuff. I don't know how often, but from time to time."

"That's great," Mrs. MacKensie said, laughing. "Force me to spend time with the boys. Twist my arm."

Carla laughed as she always did with her mother. "Thanks, Mom."

"And maybe you'll meet someone nice at one of those meetings. Maybe your friend Ronnie knows a nice man for you."

Carla laughed harder. "Mother please." When her mother raised an eyebrow, Carla said, "Okay. Maybe she does. I'll keep my eyes open."

"And if a date keeps you in the city, like overnight. . . ." She winked. "Just give me a call and I'll see to the boys."

An early September heat wave baked New York City and the humidity that hung over the metropolis caused Carla's short-sleeved rayon blouse to stick to her back. She walked up the brownstone's front steps and rang Ronnie's bell. "Come on in," Ronnie called from inside. "It's open."

Carla walked into the foyer and heard, "Lock it behind you, will you? Then come into the kitchen."

"Sure," Carla called, throwing the deadbolt.

Carla walked to the back of the building and into the large, airy kitchen. Ronnie already had lunch laid out on the table: a green salad, a bowl of crab salad, and a cold pasta with basil. Crisp rolls nestled in a napkin-covered basket and a bottle of white wine stood opened beside two crystal glasses.

"Oh, Carla," Ronnie said, hugging her friend, "I've missed you."

"Me too. How was Disney World?"

"Sensational. The rides were a thrill, the lines were short, and the siestas were . . . athletic." She picked up a small package wrapped in silver paper. "I hope you don't mind, but I bought you a present."

"A present? I didn't think to get you anything, I'm afraid."

"I didn't expect that you had," Ronnie said. "But I saw this and couldn't resist."

Carla tore off the paper and opened the small box. Inside was a pewter figurine of a dragon with his wings spread, his head thrown back as if roaring. He perched on a faceted crystal globe, his talons buried in the transparent ball.

Ronnie watched Carla lift the four-inch-high dragon so that the light turned into rainbows within the crystal. "The dragon is for fantasy," Ronnie said. "And for dreams that can be made to come true."

"You know that I've decided to join you in your business don't you?"

"I knew a month ago when I watched your eyes light up. Actually, I probably knew when we met again that first afternoon. After all, we were roommates for three years and I knew you very well then." She poured wine into the two glasses and raised hers in toast. "To fantasy. And to making fantasies come true for everyone involved."

"To fantasy," Carla said sipping the crisp white wine.

Over lunch Carla told Ronnie about her week with her boys and her parents. "How are your folks?" Ronnie asked. "I've always loved your mother. And your dad's a stitch."

"They were always fond of you too. They asked to be remembered to you and want you to come up for dinner some time."

"I'll do that."

"And how was the cruise?"

"I'd rather tell you about the entire week some other time," she said. "It's a little early in your education for that story."

"Was it that shocking?"

"Not for me. Trust me for a few weeks," Ronnie asked and Carla demurred.

After lunch, Ronnie said "I think it's time for you to have a look around upstairs."

Ronnie and Carla put the dishes in the dishwasher, then climbed the lushly carpeted stairs to the master bedroom. It was softer and more romantic than the downstairs, done in pastel pinks and warm, spring greens. The lounge chair was upholstered in a pink-and-green floral with green piping to match the bedspread and drapes. The oriental carpet contained the same shades of green, and together with half a dozen plants, gave the entire room a warm and comfortable aura. "I entertain in here when romance is at the heart of the encounter," Ronnie said. "I also sleep here sometimes when I'm stuck in the city."

"This is a wonderful room . . . soft and loving somehow."

"That's exactly the way I designed it. We'll need to coordinate, but you're free to use it whenever you want, for whatever you want. I have a cleaning woman who comes regularly so you don't even have to tidy up."

"Are you sure about my using your place . . . this room?"

"Despite the homey feeling, this is my working space, not where I live. Let me show you what I mean." Ronnie opened the door to a huge walk-in closet. "On this side," she said waving one hand, "are everyday clothes, the usual suits, dresses, blouses, things like that. Shoes are underneath." She looked Carla over. "I would guess we still wear the same size, so take your pick whenever you need something you don't have. I try to keep the two parts of me completely separate so I don't wear my personal clothes during business. You might feel differently."

Carla admired the collection of expensive clothes. She didn't need to examine the labels to know that Ronnie only chose the best. "Isn't this overkill? So many outfits."

With a smile, Ronnie said, "I love clothes and now I can indulge myself. Anyway, I do a lot of entertaining and traveling. It's surprising how many men want a well-dressed, well-educated companion to decorate their arm at a luncheon or business dinner."

"You mean like in *Pretty Woman?*"

"Exactly. Sometimes without any sex at all." She turned and indicated the other side of the closet. "This is the evening stuff."

Carla was stunned at the number of designer dresses: chiffon, lace, sequins, and satin in a variety of colors and textures. Her fingers strained to pull each garment from its hanger and try it on. At the end of the clothes rod hung a deep rose silk jacket, a full-length black satin coat, and two faux furs. "You're ready for anything, aren't you?"

"You have no idea." Ronnie crossed the room and opened the door to a second closet. "Play clothes," she said. Inside hung an assortment of costumes. Carla recognized some of them from the photograph album Ronnie had shown her. The pink little-girl dress and the leather-and-chain outfit hung with a leopard-patterned leotard, three leather dresses with multiple zippers, and several see-through lace bodysuits.

"On each hanger," Ronnie explained, "are all the items necessary for that persona. Besides the clothes and underwear, I have coordinated jewelry, perfume, extra makeup, whatever's needed, all in a plastic bag on the hanger. With one or two there's even a wig, should you care to wear it. I love the wigs; they make me feel like a different person. Feel free to use anything, just put the stuff back in its place. Sometimes I need to dash into the bathroom and change quickly so I like to have everything ready."

Carla whistled, long and low.

Ronnie opened the drawers of the wide dresser and showed Carla dozens of slips, bras both with and without cutouts so nipples could show through, satin and lace panties, silk teddies in a dozen colors, and garter belts with stockings. "Try anything on and wear whatever fits your mood. Or you might want to wear nothing at all under your evening clothes. There are few things more arousing than telling a man that you're not wearing underwear, and then going out for an evening. But everything's replaceable so if anything gets torn or whatever," she winked, "we'll get new."

When Carla looked as though she didn't understand, Ronnie said,

"Sometimes a man wants to tear clothes off or cut them off slowly and dramatically."

As Carla gazed into the drawers, she couldn't imagine a piece of lingerie that Ronnie didn't own. She picked up a cellophane package. "Panty hose?"

"Even panty hose," Ronnie said. "I have one friend who loves to pull them off of me, very slowly and lick each part he uncovers. Another friend likes to cut a hole in the crotch and have my legs—in the panty hose—wrapped around him. And, now that I think of it, I had a friend about two years ago who liked to wear them himself. He'd put a pair on before we went to dinner. He claimed they sweetened the anticipation and from the way he attacked me when we got back here, I don't doubt it at all."

Carla tried not to be shocked. She had read about transvestites but she'd never thought to meet one. "Woman's clothes?"

"First of all, he wasn't a transvestite," Ronnie said, as if reading her friend's mind. "Several men I know like to wear satin undies under their business suits. The slippery fabric feels good against the skin and it's a sexy little secret.

"Secondly, don't judge. There's nothing wrong with an activity that consenting adults enjoy in private, or, for that matter, in selected public locations. I learned that first time with Tim that labels are for people with small minds."

"You're right, of course. And I'm not being judgmental, just naive."

"Fair enough."

On the side of the closet opposite Ronnie's costumes were outfits for men: a Robin Hood-style green vest and tights, a black outfit that looked like it was designed for a second-story man, a silver lamé top and pants that had been cut to resemble a knight's armor, and a white shirt and short pants combination. "For a naughty little boy," Ronnie explained. Carla struggled to not let her amazement show.

Eventually they returned to the living room. "I want you to go slowly," Ronnie said when the topic turned to Carla's new career. "I'd like to see you build your sexual and sensual awareness little by little. And I've got just the place to start."

"You have?"

"Um-hmm. Rick. I'm due to call him in," she glanced at her watch, "five minutes."

Carla looked a little flustered. "Now? Oh God. I thought I was ready for this," she said. "Suddenly I'm not so sure."

"Don't worry, I wouldn't do anything for your trial run that you couldn't back out of at any time. Nothing is mandatory. But Rick is the perfect place to start. I call him and we make love over the phone."

"Phone sex? Like 1-900-suck-me-off?"

"Something like that. And don't make fun of it. Talking about sex and describing lovemaking is very erotic, very exciting, and leads to some delicious orgasms." When Carla hesitated, Ronnie said again, "Trust me?"

Carla relaxed. "I do trust you. It's just that phone sex conjures up such awful visions. A sweaty body jerking off while some impersonal bimbo talks and files her nails at the same time."

"It's not like that with me. Not at all."

"Of course not," Carla said.

"Before I call Rick—or Mr. Holloway as I call him on the phone—let me tell you about him. Rick's a happily married man who's involved in some kind of financing business on Wall Street. Like so many of my friends, Rick believes that his wife couldn't be interested in the things we talk about. Every now and then I'm tempted to phone his wife and somehow get her to talk to him. I think he'd be surprised. But, of course, I wouldn't do anything like that. My friend's lives, outside of our relationship, are strictly off-limits. I've never even seen Rick."

"Never?"

"Nope. One of my friends suggested that he call me. He did and we talked in private for an hour. I discovered that he likes to listen to sexy talk, sexy stories, things like that. He'd tried those 900 numbers but never found one he really liked. He has now."

"I assume you get paid."

"Sure. He leaves a message for me once or twice a month. The message tells me what time to call him back. He'll be sure to be in the middle of the office where he's surrounded by people. After we talk, he sends me a check for a hundred and fifty dollars. Now, I'll call first, then I'll tell you to pick up. Yes?"

"I guess. But I don't want to eavesdrop."

"You won't be. Let me take care of everything. I know Rick very well and he'll enjoy this conversation immensely."

While Ronnie dialed Carla settled deeper into an overstuffed chair and tried to prepare herself for what was to come. As hard as she tried, she couldn't imagine what would happen.

"Good afternoon," an efficient-sounding female voice said, "Mr. Holloway's office."

"Mr. Holloway, please," Ronnie said. "Mr. Black's office calling."

"Thank you. One moment please."

Joan Elizabeth Lloyd

Although she was on hold, Ronnie held her hand over the mouthpiece. "Okay, Carla, you can pick up now."

"Are you sure this is okay, Ronnie? After all the man's paying good money for this phone call. He's not doing it to expand my education."

"Not only am I sure it's okay," Ronnie answered as Carla picked up the extension phone and draped her legs over the arm of the chair, "but I'm going to tell him that you're listening."

"You aren't," Carla said.

"I know just what he likes. This plays right into his fantasies. Knowing that you're listening will heat things up for him. You can't imagine how much I enjoy knowing I can make him hot just by talking. He gets hot and so do I. I think you'll find it very erotic also."

"Mr. Holloway here," said a deep, resonant voice. Carla watched Ronnie curl up and tuck her feet under her.

"Mr. Holloway," Ronnie purred into the phone, "this is Mr. Black's office. Can you talk?"

"Of course not," Mr. Holloway answered.

"That's good. How many people are within earshot?"

"About six."

"Can they see you? I mean your entire body," Ronnie said, "not just your head."

"Just the upper levels," he answered.

"Than I want you to move. I want you to be where, when you get all hard and swollen, everyone could see if they knew where to look." When there was no sound at the other end of the phone, she asked, "Have you moved?"

There were shuffling sounds, then he answered, "I have." Carla could hear office noise in the background.

"Good. I have a little surprise for you today."

"You have?"

"Say hello dear," Ronnie said, waving at Carla.

"Hello darling," Carla said, dropping her voice a full octave and letting lots of breath escape as she spoke.

"Who's that?" the surprised voice said.

"That's Snow White," Ronnie said. "She's listening to everything we say. And she's never heard anything like this before. She's going to listen as you get excited. You won't be able to hide from her."

"Snow White?" he whispered. "Oh shit." His voice trembled as it resumed its normal timbre. "What's your associate like?"

"Oh, she's beautiful. Would you like to hear about her?"

"That's a fine idea. Let's discuss that."

"Well," Ronnie said, closing her eyes. "She's tiny, only about five feet tall, and she's got wide, sky-blue eyes and lots of long red hair. Her skin is like a soft ripe peach and her mouth is painted with bright red lipstick."

"That's fine," the business-like voice said.

"Her hands are tiny but she has long fingernails. You know how they're painted?"

"Of course."

"Certainly you do. They've been polished so they're shiny and bright red, like her lips. And she's wearing a white dress, cut low across her bosom so the tops of her nipples are just hidden beneath the lacy edging. Her cleavage is so deep and inviting that your hands itch to bury themselves between her large breasts. The dress is tight over her ribs and there's a full skirt with a dozen stiff petticoats. She's wearing very high-heeled sandals that are held to her feet with lots of tiny straps."

"That sounds like a fine arrangement," Mr. Holloway said.

Carla was blushing listening to Ronnie's description. She was also getting very aroused.

"And she's wearing long white gloves," Ronnie continued. "Her fingers aren't covered so you can still see her red fingernails, but white satin starts at her palms and extends up way past her elbows." She paused. "Can you see her?"

"Certainly. I need to know more about how the deal will proceed."

"Well, she's listening to me and getting very excited."

Carla was surprised at how excited she really was becoming as Ronnie described this imaginary Snow White. Her body was responding. She wanted to loosen the jeans that constricted her.

Carla could hear movement at the other end of the phone, together with the clack of keyboards and the occasional jangle of a telephone. "Is that true?" the man's voice said.

"Yes," Carla said, strangely no longer embarrassed. "I'm very excited. My thighs are open and I'm getting wet." Ronnie opened her eyes and nodded her approval.

"Wonderful," Rick said. "It sounds like the arrangement is working well."

In the distance, a woman's voice interrupted. "Mr. Holloway. Can you take Mr. Malone on line two?"

"Not right now," Rick said. "Tell him I'll call back."

"You mean you can't take another call right now?" Ronnie chuckled.

"Not a chance," Mr. Holloway said. "Our business is more important. Where were we?"

"You'll have to refresh my memory," Ronnie teased.

"Shit," the voice whispered. "Okay, we were talking about the irrigation project."

Carla laughed. "Yes we were. I was telling you how wet I am."

"Snow White is just waiting for you, Mr. Holloway. Are you hard enough for her?"

"Certainly. What about the rest?"

"Well, Snow White is wearing pantalets trimmed with white lace. They're getting wet in the crotch as her pussy gets hotter. Should we have her take them off?"

"A fine idea," Mr. Holloway said.

"Take off your pantalets, Snow White," Ronnie said. "Hold the phone so Mr. Holloway can hear your clothes come off."

Carla raised an eyebrow and Ronnie nodded. Carla stood up and pulled off her jeans, holding the phone so the man at the other end could hear the rustle of each leg as she pulled her feet through. "Did you hear that?" Carla said. She heard the man's breathing, then continued, "I'm now naked under my dress, but I'm pulling my skirts down so you can't see or touch. . . . yet."

Ronnie made an okay sign with one hand. Carla was continually surprised at how easy and enjoyable this was. And Ronnie got paid for this?

"It's about time you got to the meat of the proposal," the man's voice said.

"Honey," Ronnie said, "it's your meat I'm proposing."

Holloway's deep laugh echoed through the phone line. "I'm not used to this kind of work being amusing. I guess that's why I like doing business with you," he said.

"Does a laugh make your cock any softer?" Ronnie asked.

"Of course not," he answered.

"Good. Now, where were we? Oh yes, Snow White is sitting on her throne, one leg draped over each arm, her skirts pulled down between her spread legs. Can you see her?"

"Uh-huh."

"She reaches down and dips her red-tipped fingers into the sweet valley between her breasts and pulls first one, then the other, out of the bodice of her gown. Her nipples are sensitive and deep pink. She pinches them so they're hard, like large pebbles. She tweaks at one with her nails and rubs the satin palm of her glove over the other. Tiny pains and satiny pleasure. She switches pinching and stroking, going back and forth until her tits are aching."

Carla massaged her breasts, feeling exactly what Ronnie was saying that Snow White felt.

"Is your cock aching too, Mr. Holloway?" Ronnie asked.

"Most assuredly."

"Is anyone looking at you right now?"

"As a matter of fact yes. Just a moment please." The two women heard Mr. Holloway shift the phone. "What is it?"

"I need your signature so I can get this into Express Mail by three o'clock."

There was some shuffling, then Mr. Holloway said, "That's done."

"Your poor cock," Ronnie said. "It must be hurting. Your balls too. And you can't do anything about it or everyone will see."

There was a barely audible groan.

"Wonderful," Ronnie purred. "Now, as Snow White sits on her throne, her pussy gets so itchy that she had to reach down and touch it. Can you see her? She's sitting with her legs spread wide apart. She slowly pulls up her skirt and slides her fingers up the inside of her creamy thighs. Do it, Snow White," Ronnie said, looking at Carla. "You know you love to have people watch you."

Carla stroked her pussy through her panties. She was soaking wet. She knew that if she caressed herself just right she would climax immediately but she found that she wanted to wait and continue to amuse Mr. Holloway. And, amazingly enough, she liked the fact that Ronnie was watching her.

"Mr. Holloway?" Carla said softly.

He cleared his throat. "Yes?"

"I'm right here, scratching the insides of my thighs with the tips of my long red nails. Now I'm using one nail and touching my clit, just brushing it, flicking it. It's so good."

"I bet if you play with it, you'll come," Ronnie said. "Right Snow White?"

"Oh yes," Carla groaned. "I want to come."

"That sounds acceptable to me," Mr. Holloway said.

"Stroke your cunt, Snow White," Ronnie said. "Put the phone near your cunt and let Mr. Holloway hear your fingers moving."

Carla held the phone close to her pussy and slid her fingers under the crotch of her panties. She knew just how to touch herself because she'd done it so many times in the past five years.

"Yes," Ronnie said. "I can see you with my eyes and Mr. Holloway can see you in his mind. Rub it harder."

"Yes," Carla whispered, panting. She was so close. Just another moment.

"Rub it faster, Snow White," Ronnie said. "Can you hear her, Mr. Holloway? Hear how close she is to coming? Hear her breathing, how fast it is? She's going to come . . . right now!"

Carla let out a low moan as she spasmed. She held very still and reveled in the waves of pleasure that washed over her body.

"Does your cock hurt, darling?" Ronnie said into the phone as Carla slowly recovered from one of the best orgasms she'd had in a long time.

"I think that will work out nicely," Mr. Holloway said. "I have to go now."

"Are you going into the bathroom to take your big hard cock in your hand and massage and fondle it until you spurt hot come all over?"

"I think that will be enough for now," he said, laughing. "Otherwise it won't go well for any of us."

"Right," Ronnie said, laughing too.

"Thank you darling," Carla said into the phone, her breathing not yet back to normal. "That was wonderful."

"I'll speak to you soon," Mr. Holloway said. "And thank you for your help in this matter. I'll handle it from here." As he hung up, everyone was laughing.

Chapter 4

"Oh, Lord," Carla said, curling up in her chair. "If that's what it's like all the time then I'll be both exhausted and delighted." Strange, but she wasn't embarrassed by Ronnie watching as she came.

"It is if you want it to be. You understand most of my rules and know that I stick by them, no matter how much money is involved."

"Spell them out again."

"I never do anything I don't think I'll enjoy and I make it clear to my friends that I always have the right to call things off at any time, as do they. That's part of the reason for having dinner with a new acquaintance before our first encounter. Doing what I do takes trust. Everyone must have the right to say stop and we always agree on a safe word."

"Safe word?"

"I usually use 'popcorn.' At any time, if anyone says that word, everything stops. Immediately. And if I can't trust my friends to obey if I say it, and to say it if they want to stop, it's no deal."

"Why is it important that they say it too? You're the one who needs a way out."

"Not really. Take men who enjoy being dominated. If I can be sure they'll use the safe word, I can do anything that takes my fancy. I describe what I'm going to do if it's the first time and I don't have to worry about going too far. The safe word is there so they can yell, 'Please stop,' and know I won't, but be sure I'll stop when that's what they really want."

"That sounds reasonable," Carla said, still catching her breath after the phone call.

"Also, no heavy drinking, although a glass or two loosens things up. No drugs of any kind and, as you know, I insist that my friends use condoms. He can have seventeen blood tests or whatever, but condoms are mandatory. Period."

Carla nodded. Everything that Ronnie said seemed, if anything, overly cautious.

"You're still interested, aren't you?" Ronnie said.

Carla took a deep breath. "After that phone call," she said, "more than ever. But I'm a little apprehensive about where to start."

"I have a suggestion," Ronnie said, stretching out on the sofa and crossing her long legs at the ankles. "An old friend called me a few weeks ago. His name's Bryce and I've known him for over a year."

Carla had learned in college that Ronnie's particularly delightful, slightly mischievous smile meant that she was deeply involved in hatching an inventive plot. When Ronnie didn't continue, Carla said, "And. . . ."

Ronnie picked up the glass of wine from the table next to her and took a sip. "He's had an ongoing fantasy about wedding nights and seduction. He's heavily into romance, music, wine, all that." Carla could see the dreamy look in Ronnie's eyes. "He's also into a bit of control, which I think you'll find irresistable. And he's dynamite in bed, a deliciously creative man who gets his satisfaction from giving as well as taking pleasure. We've spend some memorable nights together."

"He sounds too good to be true. Is he married? And if he is, why does his wife let him out of her sight?"

"His wife died several years ago and part of the reason he plays with me is that he's surrounded with matchmaking friends who bombard him with suitable women. I think that, when he's with me, he's comfortable. We have wonderful times together, great sex, and there are no strings, no commitments." Ronnie smiled. "I hope you don't mind but we talked about you."

"You knew that I was going to do this, didn't you."

"You're not expert at hiding your feelings, and I know you pretty well."

Carla smiled and pulled on her jeans. "You certainly used to, and after that game we just played with Rick Holloway, you know me even better."

Ronnie laughed. "True. Anyway, I think he'd be a wonderful first time for you. He'd love it and, I can guarantee, so would you."

"It sounds like he's *your* friend."

"He's a special man, but he's just a friend. And I think you'd enjoy being together."

"But. . . ."

"Listen, Carla. I don't know whether you should do this at all. I understand myself and I've been doing what I do for almost four years. I love it."

"I know you do. I've given this entire situation a lot of thought and, well, it titillates me. I've told you that I don't know much about off-center sex, but I know that I want to find out more."

"And, of course, you can call things off at any time and go back to Bronxville and sell real estate," responded Ronnie. Each woman wrinkled her nose.

The phone rang and Ronnie and Carla listened as the answering machine picked up. "This is Black Enterprises. Please leave a message at the sound of the beep, and thanks for calling."

"Hi, Ronnie and Snow White, this is Rick Holloway. You're probably both listening right now so I wanted to tell you that I feel great. I'm in my private office right now and I'm sending you a check for three hundred dollars. I hope to talk to you both again soon. And Ronnie, thanks for knowing exactly what would increase the fun even before I did. Take care." He hung up.

"He really liked it," Carla said, still surprised at the power of the spoken word.

"He sure did. And you had a lot to do with that."

"I thought he usually paid a hundred and fifty dollars. He said he's sending three hundred."

"He's paying double. I guess he's sending half for me and half for Snow White." Ronnie pulled out her wallet and handed Carla three fifty-dollar bills. "That's your share."

Carla stared at the money in her hand. "This has to be immoral, illegal, or fattening. Maybe all three."

"Well, it's certainly not fattening and, as far as I'm concerned, it's not immoral. I don't think you can have a crime without a victim and none of my friends is ever a victim." She sighed. "Actually, some claim that what we do together makes them better lovers at home, either more creative or less demanding. However, it is prostitution and that's illegal . . . but what the hell." She sipped her drink and gave a mock salute. "Anyway, Bryce would love to spend an evening with you—your virgin experience, as it were."

Carla's hands trembled. "Now that I'm actually going to do it, half of me can't wait and half is scared to death."

"That's exactly the fantasy that Bryce wants. He loves the scared little girl and the initiation part of this. And you can say stop at any time. Bryce knows the rules. So, if you're sure. . . ."

Carla took a deep breath. "I am."

"Good. I'll give you his number and you can call him, make your plans. He'll take you to dinner, dancing, then to a hotel room."

"Not here?"

"You know you can use the house any time, although we'll have to coordinate carefully. But Bryce likes the idea of neutral territory. He's got oodles of money and he can afford the best. By the way, as a present to him, I think we should forgo the fee for this one night."

Carla chuckled. "I'm glad. Somehow it seems more honest for my first time." As she lifted her wine glass, her hands shook. "I'm nervous."

"Good." Ronnie handed Carla a piece of paper. "Here's his number. Call him right now, while you're in this mood. Use the phone in the spare bedroom."

Carla stood up and looked at the paper in her hand. "Bryce McAndrews—555-6749." She walked into the spare bedroom, picked up the cordless phone, and settled on the bed.

With shaky fingers, she dialed the number.

"Hello."

"Is this Bryce McAndrews?"

"Yes."

"This is Carla."

His voice was suddenly soft and warm. "Ronnie's friend?"

"Yes." She had no idea what to say.

There was a warm laugh and Bryce said, "Are you free Friday evening?"

"Yes." Shit, Carla thought. Why am I so tongue-tied?

"I'll pick you up at Ronnie's place and we'll have dinner at an intimate restaurant I know. They have a small dance combo. I hope you like to dance. Leave everything to me. Just be ready about seven. Okay?"

"Okay." Her voice shook and Bryce was intrigued.

"You have no idea how I'm looking forward to meeting you, Carla."

"Me too," she said softly.

Bryce's laugh was infectious. " 'Til Friday," he said, then he hung up.

"Until Friday," she repeated into the silent phone.

For the next few days, Carla was a wreck. She drove her children to and from cub scouts and swimming lessons. She cooked dinner, watched TV, and visited with her parents, all the while quaking inside with a delicious excitement that she was amazed no one noticed.

Thursday, on a whim, she had her nails done. She'd passed Plaza Nails often and had occasionally thought about treating herself to a manicure. Always before, however, the cost had stopped her. If I want to stay home with the boys and not work full time, she had told herself as she walked passed the door toward the supermarket, I've got to be a little careful.

As she drove past the mall on the way to Little League Thursday afternoon she gave in to temptation. It's an investment in my career, she told herself. Anyway, I have Rick's three fifties in my wallet.

So while the boys were at practice, a manicurist named Micki, who didn't stop talking for an hour, lengthened Carla's nails with linen wraps and glue then polished them in a soft lavender shade called "Lilacs in the Spring." As Carla left, Micki told her to come back in a week for a glue manicure, whatever that was.

"Hey Mom," said Mike, her youngest son in the car going home. "You've got stuff on your nails."

"I decided to have them polished," she said, glancing at her nails for the dozenth time. "Looks snazzy, no?"

"I guess," Tommy said, "but it'll be hard to make pizza dough." Practicality was Tommy's hallmark. "They'll get all ookey. We are having your pizza tonight, aren't we? You promised."

"Of course. I promised."

Thursday evening after pizza, Carla spend several hours standing in front of her closet debating exactly what to wear. After her call to Bryce, she and Ronnie had rummaged through Ronnie's closet in the brownstone, but nothing in Ronnie's wardrobe made just the right statement. As the boys did their homework and watched TV, Carla put on, then took off at least a dozen combinations, selected then reselected like a schoolgirl preparing for her first date. "I'm an idiot," she muttered, throwing a beige, summer knit dress on top of the growing pile on her bed. She picked up the phone and started to dial Bryce's number to call the whole thing off. "God, this is really stupid." Then she put the phone down. "I can always call it off during dinner."

She hung everything back up, then closed her eyes and pulled a blouse from its hanger, coordinated it with a linen suit and stuffed all three garments in a tote bag to bring with her. Then she sat on the bed, pulled the items back out, folded them neatly, added a pair of low-heeled pumps and put everything back into the bag.

She gazed into the mirror, brushed her shoulder-length hair and shook her head slowly. Should I go down to the city early and have my hair done? she wondered. Somehow that didn't feel right. She had no idea why her nails should look better than her hair but it seemed wrong to have some fancy hairstyle. "Shit," she said aloud, "this is ridiculous. I'll worry myself to death at this rate." She stuffed a strand of hair behind one ear and went to tell the boys that it was bed time.

The following afternoon Carla packed an overnight bag for each of her boys.

"Are we staying at Gramma's?" her 13-year-old asked.

"Yes. For tonight."

"Got a hot date, Mom?" BJ asked as she packed.

"Where did you get that idea?" she asked, taken aback.

BJ put his fingers to his temples and closed his eyes. "I see all and know all," he chanted. When Carla raised an eyebrow he continued, "Well, Mom, new nails, an overnight visit Gramma and Grampa. I'm not a kid, you know. I watch TV." When she continued to stare at him he continued. "It's okay with me. Mothers need some fun. Oprah and Donahue say so. I'll be nice to Gramma and watch Tommy and Mike."

Her kid was watching talk shows and telling her that mothers needed fun. She playfully swatted his bottom, then stuffed Mike's PJs into his bag.

On her way into the city, Carla stopped at a local mall on a whim and bought a pair of large pearl-drop earrings that matched her outfit perfectly but differed from anything she owned. With the new jewelry in her purse, she arrived at the brownstone at about five. Since Ronnie was in Dutchess county Carla had the place to herself.

She wandered upstairs, filled the oversized tub, poured in a large scoop of bath salts and, while the water ran, put a Sinatra cassette into the tape player. While the crooner's familiar voice filled the room, Carla settled into the deep tub and leaned back, letting the light spicy scent relax her. She spent an hour in the water, adding hot whenever it became too cool. She fantasized about the evening and what Bryce would look like. She pictured him undressing her slowly, touching and stroking her. She could imagine him whispering in her ear, telling her how beautiful she was. She almost felt his hot body entering her and slowly loving her.

When she finally emerged from the tub her skin was soft and deep pink all over, and her nipples and pussy tingled. Part of her wanted to stimulate herself to orgasm, just to take the edge off, but she didn't. The edge fit right in with the fantasy that she and Bryce were creating.

At six-thirty, she put on a white, lacy bra and matching panty, an stylish white garter belt and stockings and a white satin half-slip. Then she slipped into the full-sleeved gold silk blouse and mid-thigh, off-white linen skirt she had brought and slipped her feet into her pumps.

She snapped on the earrings she had bought and looked at herself in Ronnie's mirror. As she had suspected, the earrings set off the blouse perfectly, but felt so alien to her that she pulled them off. After looking at her reflection for a moment she slowly put them back on. In for a penny, she thought, in for a pound.

She sat at Ronnie's dressing table and applied makeup, wishing that she knew enough about cosmetics to be able to do something different with her face. She examined her new long fingernails, then drummed them on the dressing table just to hear them clack. She brushed her brown hair until it shone and pulled it back behind one ear with a gold comb. She stood and stepped back so she could see herself in the full-length mirror. Not bad, she thought, not bad.

Ronnie had told her that if and when Carla wanted, she could have a makeover session with an old friend but Ronnie had also assured her that Bryce would prefer the natural Carla. Ronnie had several spray bottles of scent on her dressing table and Carla selected Opium, dabbing it sparingly on her neck and in her cleavage.

Trying to shake off her nervousness, she looked at herself one last time, grabbed her jacket and carried it downstairs, arriving in the living room just as the doorbell rang.

She took a deep relaxing breath, dropped her jacket on the back of the sofa, and opened the front door.

With a lazy gaze, Bryce looked Carla up and down. "You look splendid."

Carla stared at Bryce and for a moment was unable to move. Carla was dumbstruck. He was gorgeous. Tall and slender, Bryce McAndrews had carefully styled iron grey hair and deep hazel eyes that made Carla shiver as they took in her entire body. His charcoal grey suit was carefully tailored to show off his broad shoulders and flat stomach and his light blue shirt perfectly matched the small design in his Italian silk tie.

Bryce's full lips slowly curved upward indicating that he appreciated what he saw. "I've been looking forward to this evening ever since Ronnie told me about you," he said, "but now that I've seen you. . . . Well let's just say this is going to be a some evening."

Carla stepped aside and Bryce walked to the sofa, picked up her jacket, and held it out for her. As she slipped her arms into the sleeves, he leaned down so his lips were beside her ear. "You smell sensational. This was worth waiting for," he whispered. He placed a feather-light kiss in the hollow below her left ear, then stepped back. "Let's go."

His shiny black Porsche occupied a no-parking zone in front of the brownstone. He opened the door for Carla and, as she climbed in, he gazed at her long shapely legs and the shadowy cleavage between her breasts. "Ummm," he murmured. "Nice all over."

During the drive to the West Side, Carla learned that her date had four sons, all grown. She and Bryce talked easily about their children. It was so comfortable and Bryce was so charming that occasionally Carla forgot the purpose of the evening and where they were going to end up.

"It's just like a real first date," Carla said hesitantly as Bryce drove.

He softened his voice. "It certainly is. And I like it like that. Relax and let me make it good for you."

"I'll try," she said, startled that she had voiced her feelings.

"Are you really nervous?"

"Yes," Carla admitted, clasping her hands in her lap to stop them from shaking.

"Good. A little scary expectation is just the right spice. Let me tell you about our evening. We're starting at a little restaurant called the West Side Club. They have great food, a fantastic wine list, and a three-piece combo for dancing. You do dance, don't you?"

"I used to love it," Carla answered honestly, "but I haven't danced in a long time."

"Like good sex, it's something you never forget." Giving her no time for a rejoinder, Bryce deftly pulled the black two-seater into the space in front of a long maroon awning. Immediately a uniformed doorman rushed around to open Carla's door. "Thank you, Marco," Bryce said, "but I'll assist the lady." Marco stepped aside as Bryce rounded the car.

Carla took Bryce's extended hand and, as she climbed out of the car, felt Bryce scratch her palm with one fingernail. Shivers skittered up and down her spine and the area between her legs grew warm. She looked over at her escort but he was busy giving his keys to Marco. Hand in hand, they walked into the depths of the darkened restaurant. "Ah, Mr. McAndrews," the maitre'd said unctuously. "I have your table all ready."

Without a word, they were led to the side of the room. Because of the expert placement of potted plants and lacy screens, each table seemed to be in its own private alcove. Bryce seated her. Almost immediately the waiter brought a cooler with a bottle of white wine already chilling. Proudly he showed Bryce the label.

"I hope you don't mind," Bryce said, "but I made a few arrangements in advance. Of course, if you'd prefer a mixed drink, or red wine, the waiter can bring you whatever you want."

"White wine will be fine," Carla said.

"Good. This is a Portuguese Vino Verde that I particularly like." The waiter poured a sip for Bryce, who tasted it and nodded. "Don't freeze the poor wine," he said as the waiter poured for Carla. "Take the cooler away and just leave the bottle on the table."

"As you wish, sir," the waiter said.

Carla sipped. "This is excellent," she said. "I've never had a Portuguese wine before. You have great taste."

Bryce gazed into Carla's eyes over the rim of his glass. "If you put yourself into my hands for the rest of the evening, you'll see what good taste I really have."

Bryce ordered dinner for both of them. Through fresh asparagus and thin slices of Smithfield ham, poached salmon with dill sauce and tiny boiled potatoes, they talked about inconsequential things from the music they enjoyed through books and movies to vacations. Since Bryce had traveled extensively both for pleasure and business, he regaled Carla with tales of the sites he'd seen. With Carla's agreement Bryce ordered lemon sherbet and Irish coffee for dessert.

As she finished her sherbet and sipped the heady brew, Carla realized that she hadn't had such an enjoyable evening in many years.

Music began. "Dance with me," Bryce whispered. He took Carla's hand and guided her to the tiny wooden dance floor. He held her gently, his right hand placed correctly in the small of her back. Carla realized immediately that he was a sensational dancer, gliding effortlessly across the small space. Several other couples joined them and, as the floor became more crowded, Bryce held her closer, his mouth against her ear, his left arm pressing lightly against the side of her breast.

"You're so graceful," he said, rubbing his forearm against the side of her bra and the flesh underneath, "like an angel in my arms."

Carla swallowed hard and remained silent. Although she knew that this was to be her initiation into the world of recreational sex, she felt like a woman on her first date with a dangerously attractive man.

"I love holding your body close," Bryce whispered. "Your breasts are so full and your hips fit perfectly against mine." His breath on her ear caused a tingling at the base of her spine. "You're so responsive," he continued, "that I'll bet you're getting hot already."

For some reason, Carla needed to deny what he was saying. It was like a seduction, not an assignation, and somehow it was important not to be easy. When she took a breath to deny her feelings, Bryce interrupted, reading her thoughts. "You can deny it all you want but your body radiates sexual heat." He flicked the tip of his tongue in her ear, then nipped at her earlobe.

She shuddered, telling him about herself as accurately as she could have with words.

"Yes. You want me," he whispered. "But resist as well. It makes it all the sweeter to know that later I will hold you in my arms, naked and open. I'll overcome all your resistance and control your body with your own hunger."

He put his finger under her chin and lifted her face so she had to look into his eyes. "You'll want me so much that you'll beg for it." He tucked her against him and continued dancing, holding her close. No one else on the floor could possibly know about Bryce's erotic whisperings but Carla felt as if everyone was watching her.

They danced for a few more songs. Carla felt Bryce's hand sliding over her silk blouse. "I want your body to know exactly what's to come." His hot breath tickled her ear. "We're going to leave in about fifteen minutes. One or two more dances should be just right."

Carla realized that Bryce's planning and take-charge attitude would turn some women off, but the control that Bryce was exercising was driving her crazy. After the first few years of marriage, she had called most of the sexual shots. Bill would have been content with quickies, but Carla had wanted more. Frequently she would wear an alluring nightgown or a teddy and, when Bill responded, she would tell and show him what she wanted. She had enjoyed the sex, but would have preferred not to be in charge.

"I want you to do something for me," Bryce said a few minutes later. "Go into the ladies' room and take off your bra. I want to dance with you and feel your unrestrained breasts against my chest. I want to be able to look down the front of your blouse and see your nipples. Do it for me, Carla. Do it because I want you to and because it will make you a little less secure."

They walked to their table and Bryce gave Carla a tiny push toward the ladies' room. "Please," he whispered. The wine and the Irish coffee made her brave and daring. Not giving herself time to think, Carla walked to the bathroom, closeted herself in a stall, and removed her bra. She put the bit of silk in her purse and rebuttoned her blouse. She looked down, then smiled and unbuttoned the blouse's top two buttons.

She walked out of the stall and checked her appearance in the large mirror. Nothing showed from the front or side but, as she looked down she could see her full breasts and her hard, erect nipples. She smiled and walked back toward the table, enjoying the sway of her breasts and the brush of her nipples against the silk of her blouse.

"Nice," Bryce said as he watched her approach. He met her on the dance floor and took her in his arms. As they danced, he looked down. "Your breasts are magnificent," he whispered. "Your nipples are a dark, dusky pink. Are they so hard that they hurt?"

Carla had never been asked such sexual questions by a man before. She cleared her throat, unable to speak.

"Tell me. I insist." When she remained silent, he repeated, "I insist. Say to me, 'My nipples are so hard that they hurt.'" He slid his hand into her hair and turned her face up. "Say it, angel."

Certain words were hard for her to say; they always had been, even with her husband. Talking directly about sex and the anatomical parts involved had always been difficult for her. "I do hurt for you," she murmured.

"What hurts?" he said. She was silent. "The word 'nipple' is difficult for you to say isn't it? I can tell from your body's reaction. Your palm is damp and your hand is shaking." She tried to look down, but his hand remained tangled in her hair. "I don't care whether you want to or not," he said, his lips almost touching hers. "You will do as I say. Say 'My nipples hurt for you.' "

"Oh God. My nipples hurt for you." Carla could barely stand. The thrill and humiliation of saying that word made her knees weak. Fortunately Bryce held her tightly, supporting her.

"Oh yes. I like this. Let's continue this discussion somewhere else." Quickly he paid the check and guided her to the door. They walked a block in silence, the cool air clearing Carla's head a bit. They climbed the stairs to the door of an undistinguished building and Bryce unlocked it. "A very private place," he said as they went inside. "It's owned by good friends of mine who let me use it when they're away, which they are for the entire month of September."

Carla was aware of little as Bryce put her jacket away and guided her to the stairs that lead to what she assumed was the master bedroom. They stopped about three quarters of the way up. "Take off your blouse," Bryce said. "Right here."

She looked at him. Shouldn't he undress her? Removing her own clothes seemed so forward. Remembering why she was here, she realized her feelings were ludicrous, but they were her feelings none the less.

"Do it," he said, softly. "Be what they used to call a brazen hussy for me because I tell you to."

Slowly, Carla unbuttoned her blouse and pulled it off. "Yes," he said. "Your tits are magnificent, so hungry for my touch." He saw that the harsh language made Carla's hands shake and he smiled. "Tits. Say that word. Say 'My tits are so hard for you.' " He could see the muscles in her throat working as she swallowed. When she hesitated, he made it sound like an order. "Say it, Carla!"

"My . . . tits. . . . are hard for you."

"That's a good girl," he whispered. He walked up a step so that his mouth was level with her chest. "Hold your beautiful tits so I can suck them. Hold them for me."

It was both scary and liberating for Carla. Bryce was making her do things she wouldn't do herself, and she felt both compelled and freed. She slid her hands beneath her heavy breasts and lifted them so that the swollen nipples were level with Bryce's lips.

"Good girl," he purred. He flicked the tip of his tongue up and down over Carla's left nipple. Then he bit it, gently. "Is that good?"

"Mmmm, yes," she murmured.

He moved from side to side, from nipple to nipple, licking and biting until both breasts were swollen and reaching for his mouth. He turned her, urged her up the stairs and into the large bedroom. He moved to the bedside and turned on a small lamp, bathing the bed with soft light. "Your skin glows," he said.

Carla stood and dropped her blouse, watching Bryce watch her. Suddenly she realized how good it felt to have someone look at her naked body the way Bryce was looking at her. She was a sex object, and glad of it.

Bryce flipped the covers aside, sat on the edge of the bed, and leaned back on his elbows. "Strip for me, slowly."

Carla smiled and slowly unzipped her skirt, a bit less embarrassed knowing how she was pleasing him. She stepped out of her shoes, pulled her skirt and slip down and let them fall around her feet. She stood, wearing only her garter belt and matching stockings and her sheer white panties.

"Take off the panties," Bryce told her, "but leave on the rest. I want to see your pussy-fur surrounded by white lace."

Words like pussy made her tremble as she removed her panties. She stood and watched Bryce's gaze wander slowly over her body. "Nice?" she asked.

"Lovely," he said. "But you're a little too calm. You're getting too comfortable. Let's heat things up a bit. I want you to massage your breasts while I watch. Pinch your nipples."

When she did as he asked without much hesitation, he said, "Exhibiting your body doesn't make you shiver the way I want you to. What seems to tantalize you is saying those words." As he watched her blush he knew he'd found the way to make her hotter. "Say to me, 'My pussy is wet for you.'" When she remained silent he laughed. "You'll need to learn to say those things so I'll have to train you. Walk over here."

Bryce sat up as she walked to the side of the bed. When she started to sit down, he said, "Not yet. I want to make it difficult for you to stand up." She sighed and stood between his knees. "Now," he said, "when you're a good girl and do as I say you'll get your reward." He slid his finger into her wet pussy, touching her erect clit, then pulled his hand back.

"And when I don't?" Carla asked.

"You'll have to just stand there and wait. Understood?"

Carla nodded.

He leaned forward and blew cool breath through her pubic hair. She shivered and he said, "Good. Now say, 'Play with my pussy.'"

"Oh God," she said, feeling her juices soak her crotch. "It's so good when you touch me."

"Like this?" He caressed her clit again.

"Yes."

He pulled his hand back. "Then ask for it."

"Touch me."

"No. Not good enough," he said. "I told you what to say."

"Play with my . . . . pussy."

"Good girl." He slid one finger between her swollen lips. He could feel her muscles react to his touch. "Do you want more?"

Her hips were moving involuntarily. "Yes. I want more."

"Then say, 'Put your fingers into my pussy."

She was going crazy. She wanted everything. "Put your fingers in my pussy," she said.

When Bryce saw that Carla was shaking so much that she was about to fall, he said, "Lay down and spread your legs so I can see your beautiful pussy."

She stretched out across the bed and parted her legs. "Aren't you going to take your clothes off?" she asked.

"Not yet, angel, not yet. We're not finished with your lessons yet. We have to continue to increase your vocabulary. You've learned to say 'pussy' too easily. Say 'cunt.' Say 'Finger-fuck my cunt.' "

Oh God, she thought. I can't say those words. She swallowed hard and shook her head.

"Such a bad girl," Bryce said when she remained silent. He leaned over and roughly spread her legs wider. Then he blew a stream of air on to Carla's cunt and watched as her skin quivered. He flicked his practiced tongue over her exposed clit, then blew cool air again. "Say 'Finger-fuck my cunt.' "

It was torture. The alternate warm and cool sensations were driving her wild. She reached toward her pussy but Bryce grabbed her hands and held them at her sides. "Oh no. You can't relieve yourself that easily. Only I can give you what you want and you're going to have to ask for it."

She wanted his fingers inside her. Mindless with desire, she said, "Please. Finger-fuck me. Put your hand inside my cunt. Please."

"Oh yes, baby." He inserted first one then two fingers into her cunt and spread them to fill her. He pulled out, then rammed them inside. With his other hand he rubbed her clit until both of them felt the ripples of Carla's first orgasm.

"Don't stop," she screamed. "Oh God, don't stop."

"I won't angel," Bryce said, feeling the orgasm roll over her entire body. "Let go. Let it devour you."

"Yes, yes, yes." She spasmed for what seemed long minutes. When she calmed, he stood and pulled off his clothes. His large, fully erect cock stood straight out from his groin. Hungrily she watched his hand stroke the smooth, hard flesh.

"I love the way you watch my hands," he said. "Do you want to touch me?"

"Yes. Let me touch you. Let me take you in my mouth."

"Ahh," he said. "You like sucking cock. Tell me."

"Yes. I want to take you in my mouth." She sat up, watching his cock.

His hand slid over his hard penis, to the tip then pulling back to the root. "Say, 'I want to suck your cock.'"

Those words again. Carla could feel her body tighten. "I want to. . . ."

"Tell me."

"I want to suck your cock."

He leaned over and held his hard cock against her lips. "Open for me angel," he said. "Suck me into your mouth."

When she pulled him into her mouth he let his head fall back. She was good, giving him exquisite pleasure. Her mouth was slippery and hungry and her tongue slid all over his smooth flesh. She pulled back until the tip of Bryce's cock rested against her lips. "Say 'I want you to suck me'," she said, grinning.

He laughed, then said, "I want to fuck your cunt." He pushed her backward on the bed, slipped on a condom, and drove his large penis into her steaming pussy. Her stocking-covered legs wrapped around his waist and her hips bucked. Over and over he drove hard into her body.

"Yes, angel. Oh yes," he yelled.

"Hard inside me. Don't stop," she cried.

They came, first Carla, then Bryce. Still entangled, they rested for a few minutes.

"That was unbelievable," Bryce said later. "I'll tell you something you aren't going to believe. It's never been any better."

"Ummm," Carla said. "For me either."

"You're a desirable woman. And from what Ronnie told me, you're going to get to channel your charms into a productive business."

"Yes, I am. And I now know that it's going to be okay. I had almost forgotten how much I love fucking." She laughed. "I can even say 'fucking' now, thanks to you."

"Next time we'll have to find something else to play."

"Next time?"

"Certainly. I'm not letting something as good as you get away. And next time I'll happily pay for your attention."

"You don't have to pay me. This is too much fun."

"If you intend to go into business, your first lesson is not to give it away," Bryce warned. "And I hope you'll enjoy it every time with every man you're with. Especially me."

Chapter 5

Carla and Ronnie had lunch together the following afternoon in Ronnie's living room. "From your contented look," Ronnie said, swallowing a bite of grilled mushroom, "I assume Bryce did right by you."

"He sure did. It was wonderful."

"I'd love to hear all the details," Ronnie said, "But I don't want you to tell me anything that makes you uncomfortable."

With a laugh, Carla said, "That's very funny coming from you and considering the business we have in mind."

"You still have the right to be uncomfortable about things. You give up no rights here."

"I know, and thanks." Carla proceeded to tell Ronnie about the previous evening, chapter and verse.

"This tendency you have to be submissive could be a profitable addition to our business. You know that I tend to be the dominant one and I have many friends who enjoy playing with me. But lots of men like to be the master. Well," Ronnie said, spearing a shrimp with her fork, "we'll figure that out as time goes on. First, I'd like you to think about changing your appearance. Making yourself look more sophisticated. I'd love to get you an appointment with Jean-Claude."

"The Jean-Claude? The one who works with all the stars?"

"That's him. And he's done pretty well for himself since he and I first met," Ronnie said. "He did a makeover for me a long time ago, when he was still a hairdresser named Jimmy and I was still relatively monogamous. He did my hair, taught me how to use makeup, how to select the most becoming clothes, the works. I recommended him to my friends. He'll do wonders for you."

"Am I that bad?"

"You are perfect for the supermarket and the PTA but not quite right for men who want to take you out and show you off. Like last evening. In addition to how it will make you feel, it makes a man feel potent if the woman he's with makes other's heads turn."

"I guess you're right." Carla crossed the room and looked at herself in the antique mirror that hung over the maple desk. She lifted her long brown hair and turned left and right to study her face. As usual she wore only rouge, grey eyeshadow, and lipstick. Her earrings were simple gold hoops. "Do you think Jean-Claude could do something with me?"

"You bet." Ronnie looked sheepish, then said, "As a matter of fact, you're due at his studio in about an hour."

Carla's laughter was immediate. "You were so sure?"

"What woman could resist putting themselves in the hands of a talented, gorgeous Frenchman with the soul of a lover."

"Does he know about you and this?" Carla said, waving her arm around the lavish room.

"Actually he's a good source of referrals," Ronnie said. "He works around celebrities and he occasionally meets someone who wants discrete company."

"You've entertained celebrities? Here?"

Ronnie sighed. "Russell Street was here just last month."

"I'm impressed," Carla said. "Russell Street."

"Don't get star struck. Eventually you may entertain someone famous, but what they want as much as anything else is a companion who'll enjoy cavorting without the trophy-collecting mentality that groupies are known for."

"Well," Carla said, "if I'm due at Jean-Claude's, I'd better take a quick shower and wash my hair. Are you coming too?"

"I wouldn't miss it for the world."

Jean-Claude did wonders. He cut Carla's hair short so it formed a soft frame around her face and rinsed in a slight reddish highlight. He and Ronnie spent an hour showing Carla how to put on her makeup and select clothes that would best accentuate her lovely figure. Together they tried earrings and necklaces on Carla to see which complemented the shape of her face and her large brown eyes. Jean-Claude's manicurist did her nails in a bright shade that Carla thought of as hemorrhage red.

Finally, when she studied herself in the mirror, Carla was thrilled. Her eyes appeared larger and her cheekbones seemed higher. Dangling gold earrings made her neck look longer and the teal scarf Jean-Claude had draped around the collar of her white blouse brought out the pink in her cheeks.

"Remember when we . . . uh . . . ran into each other that morning last summer?" Ronnie said with a wink. "You described yourself as medium brown and average, average, average?"

"I did, didn't I."

"And now?"

Carla gazed at herself in the mirror. "Well, I have to admit that I'm not half bad."

"Not half bad indeed."

When Carla arrived home late that afternoon, her boys just stared. "Hey Mom, what's with the new hair and stuff?" Tommy asked.

"I had a makeover. My friend Ronnie suggested it. Do you like?"

"Heck no," Tommy said. "You look like a model or something, not like a mom."

"Yeah," her youngest chimed in.

"I think I'll take that as a compliment."

"Cut it out you guys," BJ said. "Mom's looking for a man. It'll be good for her, dating and all." He patted her on the arm and Carla suddenly realized that her thirteen-year-old son was almost as tall as she was. "It's okay, Mom. If you find a nice man, I'll explain it to these guys."

"Thanks, BJ," she said, completely nonplussed, "but I'm not looking for a man. I just want to look nicer for my business meetings."

"You know as well as I do," BJ said, "that grown-ups need a partner. Hormones and all that."

"Oprah again?"

"Yeah. And we learned about that in sex education."

Carla tried not to laugh.

"Will you still cook and stuff?" Tommy asked, his eleven-year-old mind not yet taking it all in.

"Of course. If you'll let me get into the kitchen we'll do Barrett-burgers for everyone."

Three days after Carla's session with Jean-Claude, Tim Sorenson maneuvered his station wagon into the parking space that appeared unexpectedly when a van pulled out from right in front of Ronnie's door. He sat for a moment, thinking about his assignment: to take photos of Ronnie's friend Carla for an album like Black Satin. Ronnie had told him a lot about the woman he was about to meet and he was confident that he could do a professional job.

Since his first evening with Ronnie, Tim had come a long way. He'd managed to tell his father that his working life wouldn't revolve exclusively around the oil business and, to his dad's credit TJ had taken the news just fine. Although he still worked at American Oil and Gas Products with his father, Tim now also viewed himself as a photographer. His work had appeared in several photography magazines and two of his views of the California coast were appearing more and more frequently in photo stores. Clients wanting Tim to do portraits had to book him three months in advance.

More important, thanks to Ronnie, Tim had discovered the joy of sex, to borrow a famous phrase. His new vibrancy showed in his work. Women seemed more beautiful, men more robust. His first serious photographic assignment had been the nearly two hundred pictures he'd taken of Ronnie for her album. During that photo session they'd made love in ways Tim hadn't dreamed of and they'd been together several times since. He now considered himself a sexual sophisticate. And he loved it.

He climbed out of the driver's seat and unloaded cases from the back of the wagon, stacking lenses, camera bodies, and video equipment. He also pulled out a nylon bag filled with goodies he'd gathered after his long conversation with Ronnie about Carla. He walked up the steps and rang the doorbell with his elbow.

When Carla answered the door she saw a wholesome, appealing looking young man standing on the stoop, his hands filled with black leather cases. Tim held the handle of a blue nylon gym bag with his teeth, which muffled his words. "Catch the top one," he mumbled. "It's going to fall."

The case toppled from the stack and Carla neatly caught it, tucked it under one arm, and snatched the bag from his teeth. "You certainly come prepared," she said.

"Over prepared, one might say. May I come in? This stuff's heavy."

"Sorry," Carla said, stepping away from the door and holding it open with her foot. "Come on in."

As if familiar with the house, Tim walked directly into the living room, dumped the cases on the leather sofa, and extended one hand. "Hi. I'm Tim, as you already know, and you're Carla."

Carla shook his hand and was charmed by the warmth of both his grip and his open smile. As Tim sat on the sofa and unsnapped his cases, Carla settled next to him and curled her feet underneath her. "Nice to meet you, Tim."

"Me too. I've talked about you with Ronnie and I've got some dynamite ideas about this shoot."

"You and Ronnie talked about me?"

"Sure. She helped me get a handle on what kind of pictures you want. I hope you don't mind."

"I don't. What did she tell you?"

"Just that this is your first venture into this . . . uh, business . . . and that you want shots for your album. I've got ideas about that but, if it's fine with you, I'd like to keep them to myself for the time being. Anyway, what do you think of Ronnie's album?"

"Impressive." Carla thought about the erotic photos of Ronnie and wondered whether she'd be comfortable enough with this stranger to pose like that. She twisted her fingers in her lap. "Ronnie looks so great."

"Yeah, they did turn out well. But I had a good subject." Tim studied his new subject more closely and muttered aloud as he thought. "Great eyes, fabulous cheekbones, great skin so there'll be no problems with closeups."

Carla squirmed under Tim's scrutiny, glad of the job that Jean-Claude and Ronnie had done with her. She ran her fingers through the cap of soft waves and nervously licked her lips. Tim's smile was warm and understanding and since his manner was both professional and friendly, she began to relax.

"I'm sorry you're nervous," Tim said. "I think you'll find the nervousness wears off quickly once we start."

"I hadn't realized how anxious I was about this. I really don't know exactly what to do."

"Don't worry about that. It's my job. Would you stand up?"

Carla stood, her hands hanging awkwardly at her sides.

"Relax," Tim said. "You're going to be great." Long legs he thought. A great body, magnificent breasts. He decided to take a risk. Either he was going to get terrific, sexual pictures or he was going to blow it before he even took one shot. "I can see your nipples through your shirt," he said softly. "Any man would want to suck them." He watched her body react and knew just how to get the attitude he wanted.

Carla was a bit surprised by the language coming from this stranger, but excited too. Although they shocked her, she realized his raw words also aroused her.

"Can I get you a drink or something?" she asked.

"Actually I'd like to get started, if that's okay. This light is wonderful and I'd like to get a few head shots right here before we do anything else."

Carla used the mirror over the desk to touch up her makeup. "Where would you like to start?"

Tim shoved a chair toward the window, adjusted its position several times and said, "Sit here and let's see." Carla settled into the chair but Tim shook his head and pulled her to her feet. He moved the chair slightly and sat her back down again. "Yeah. That's nice," he said finally.

Heeding Jean-Claude's advice, Carla had selected a simple kelly green tank top and black palazzo pants. She added a gold chain with large open links and oversized gold earrings. As she settled in the chair, she fluffed her short hair and Tim watched the sunlight coming through the window catch the reddish highlights. She had used three shades of eyeshadow, liner, and mascara as Jean-Claude had shown her and, with the addition of rouge and lipstick, she had been pleased with the results.

"You look smashing," Tim said. "Now turn your head this way and tip your head." He spent several more minutes peering through the lens of his camera and adjusting the tilt of Carla's head and the angle of her shoulders. He also set up a video camera on a tripod, aimed at her chair.

"Video?"

"Sure. You'd be surprised how many men will enjoy watching you on tape, knowing that you're in the room with them, naked and willing."

"I never considered that but I'm getting an education quickly. Does Ronnie have a video?"

"Several. I'll shut it down if you don't want it."

Carla stared into the video camera's eye and found that being on display was exciting. Go the whole way? she asked herself. Who am I fooling? Damn straight I will. "Leave the camera running. It's fine."

When Tim had her positioned to his satisfaction, he said, "Now close your eyes." When she did, he said, "Picture yourself lying stretched out on your back on a blanket in a secluded clearing in a forest. The sun is beating down and heating your face. Can you feel it?" When she started to nod, he said, "Don't nod, just tell me. Is the bright sun hot on your skin?"

"Yes," Carla said softly raising her chin to the warmth.

"Now open your eyes." When she did, Tim snapped off several pictures, capturing the soft, dreamy look he'd wanted. "Close them again. You're still lying in that clearing in the forest but now you're naked. You can feel the sun on your entire body, on your shoulders, your belly, your breasts." He paused and watched her face. "Open your eyes." He snapped several more pictures. "God, the camera loves you," he murmured.

"More?" Carla said, her voice husky.

"Close your eyes." She complied and he continued. "A man walks out of the forest. You can't see him because your eyes are closed, but he's tall and very good looking, with a great body and soft hands. He's wearing a pair of faded blue jeans and nothing else. You don't have to open your eyes to know that he's looking at your body, but you're not nervous. The heat of his gaze adds to the heat of the sun. He's staring at your breasts and he can see that your nipples are getting hard. Although you're pretending to be asleep, he knows, Carla. He knows you're excited. He knows that he's making you excited." When Carla opened her eyes, Tim snapped again, then told her to move one arm and retilt her head and took several more shots. With the sound of the clicking in her ears, Carla stretched and extended her arms over her head, making love to the camera.

"Close your eyes. It's important that the man believes you're sleeping, so when he stretches out next to you on the blanket you stay still and keep your body relaxed. He just stares at you for a moment, then brushes his fingers through your pubic hair just touching your love button. You remain motionless, wanting him to continue.

"Although you don't move, he knows how wet you're getting." Tim picked up a different camera and snapped a few shots of Carla with her eyes closed. He didn't know whether it was her expression or the line of her body, but she was radiating sex and he wanted to capture it. "You want to move your hips to deepen his touch, but you don't want him to know how he's affecting you, so you remain absolutely still, pretending that you're still asleep."

Carla was there, in the clearing in the woods. Tim's voice had transported her and she could actually feel the sun on her body, feel fingers probing and exploring the secret places of her body. God, she thought, he's really turning me on. I'm going to explode.

"Keep your eyes closed and pull off your tank top and your bra," Tim said.

Carla removed her clothes without hesitation. She was no longer nervous or embarrassed. Both Tim and the cameras seemed erotic and right.

When Carla was naked to the waist, Tim repositioned her in the chair so shafts of sunlight illuminated her shoulders and breasts. Her eyes were still closed as Tim moved back behind his camera lens. "Beautiful. Let your head fall back against the chair." He kept snapping as she moved, each pose a sensual invitation. "Now, he's still touching your clit and you're still pretending to be asleep. His fingers caress each fold and part your lips. You're so wet that his finger slides easily into your body."

Tim watched Carla's body react to his story. He knew that she was having a difficult time holding her hips still and he smiled as he watched her through his lens. "He adds a second finger, then a third, filling you completely." He saw how puckered her nipples were and added this to his story.

"Your nipples are so hard and tight that you think you'll die if his mouth doesn't take them. You slide your hands up your ribs and hold your magnificent tits out for him to suck. Offer them to him, Carla. Don't speak, but offer him your hard, tight nipples."

Carla's body tightened and she did as Tim asked. She flattened her hands against her belly and slid them upward, lifting her full breasts and offering their rosy tips to the camera. When Tim asked her to open her eyes, she still envisioned an attractive man lying next to her on a blanket in the sun.

"So good, Carla," Tim said, trying to resist the lure of his own sensual story. He wanted to take the breasts being offered into his own mouth, but he knew that would come later. For the moment, he kept repositioning her, snapping pictures as the video camera hummed in the background. He finished his second roll of film and changed to a third while Carla stood up and removed the rest of her clothes.

Ronnie had told Tim a lot about Carla and he had come prepared. He took a large piece of satiny soft leather from the nylon bag he'd brought and spread it on the chair. "Sit back down," he said, "and close your eyes again. Feel the leather against your skin." As she moved her naked body against the soft surface, Tim knew he'd been right. Leather would take Carla to the next level of sensuality. "Feel it, smell it. Fill your senses with it. Put your right leg over the arm of the chair and slide your ass forward. . . . Yes, that's right." Her pussy was wide open and shining.

Carla was in a sexual daze. She'd never dreamed that the smell and feel of leather could arouse her so. She felt she was going to climax, but everything about this experience was soft and gentle. She didn't understand it, but then she didn't have to.

"Go with it. Fly with the feelings. The blanket in the forest is made out of leather, soft, black, fine-grained leather. It's becoming warm from the sunshine and the heat of your body, and the man is rubbing a corner of it over your legs, your arms, your belly. There's no sound, except the rustle of his movements. You're unwilling and unable to move. You just lie there in the sun absorbing the sensations. Open your eyes." Carla opened her eyes, and Tim snapped several more pictures.

"He's stroking your clit faster now. It tightens your lower belly." Tim watched Carla's body and saw the tiny movements he'd been waiting for. "Do you want to touch your pussy, Carla? Are you so hot that you want to rub yourself while the man watches, while the camera watches?"

Carla had never wanted anything more in her life. "Yes," she whispered.

"Then do it," Tim said. "Touch your pussy. Make yourself come."

Carla touched herself, one hand on her breast and one in her pussy. She rubbed and probed until the tightness in her breasts and her pussy became almost pain.

"Rub it just right," Tim said. He moved around, snapping pictures of Carla's hand on her breasts, her fingers working in her cunt, her face as she strained in pleasure.

Carla heard the click of the shutter and felt Tim's movements around her. To her surprise, it added a new dimension to her excitement. She opened her eyes and watched the camera as it watched her. She moved so Tim could get a better view.

"You're close now, and you want to come," Tim said, taking the video from the tripod and aiming so it captured Carla's body and hands. "You like the camera watching you. You love it that I'm watching you. I can see everything. I'm going to record you as you come. Anyone who sees the pictures will see you getting off. Tell me when you're going to come. Tell me, Carla."

"Now," she said. "Oh yes. Now! I'm going to come right now! Watch me come." Waves washed over her. She moved her fingers around her pussy touching the right places with exactly the right rhythm. She drew the orgasm from her body, bit by bit, savoring every spasm, making it last as long as she could. Tim alternated between the video and his still cameras, taking dozens of pictures and long moments of tape.

While Carla recovered, Tim fused with his camera equipment. "Unbelievable," Carla said. "I was really nervous about this, but you're amazing. You've come a long way since you and Ronnie met."

Tim chuckled. "She told you about that?"

"I'm sorry. I hope that doesn't embarrass you."

"Not at all. That was the opening to a whole new world. She's wonderful, you know."

"I know." Carla sighed.

Tim handed her a glass of water and she took a long drink as her breathing returned to normal. "If you're recovered, why don't we go upstairs and try on some of the costumes for your album photos." He picked up the piece of leather and threw it over his arm. "And I think you should use a black leather cover on your book. Leather seems to turn you on."

Carla nodded her agreement. "I never realized it, but you're right."

Naked but unembarrassed, Carla climbed the stairs with Tim behind her. "You've got great legs," he said, "and a nice tight little butt. I like the way you walk around nude. You don't parade, yet you don't hide either."

"I used to walk around without clothes a lot but with three inquisitive boys, I don't get much chance to anymore."

Tim squeezed past her and shot a few snaps of her walking up the stairs. "God, you've got a great body," he said. "I love taking pictures of you."

She put her hands behind her head and raised her elbows.

"You've got the most beautiful tits I've ever seen," he said.

In the bedroom, Tim opened a closet and pulled out an evening dress. It was a column of royal blue silk with classic lines and a high neckline in the front. "I've seen Ronnie wear this and I'd like to see you in it," he said. "You should wear primary colors, bright greens and blues. Red would look terrific on you, and black and white of course. Stay away from too much yellow and orange. It won't go with your skin."

"You've got quite an eye," Carla said, selecting a pair of tiny bikini panties from a drawer. "That's exactly what Ronnie and Jean-Claude said."

"I hope you don't mind if I pick out a few things for you," Tim said, flipping through the dresses.

"Not at all." She looked at the high-necked dress hanging on the closet door. "But isn't this a bit tame for our photos?"

"Wait until you see it on."

As Carla reached for a bra, Tim shook his head. "No bra. You don't need it."

"You're the boss," Carla said. She pointed to a large jewelry chest that stood on the makeup table. "What do you suggest with this dress?" While Tim rummaged through the extensive collection of costume jewelry, Carla picked up the hanger and took a better look at the gown. From the front it looked almost demure, but the dress had no back. It was cut low enough to reveal the line between her cheeks. As she slipped it over her head, she said, "I'll have more cleavage in the back than in the front."

"That's the idea. That's the first dress I ever photographed Ronnie in."

"It isn't in the album," Carla pointed out.

"I know. I kept that picture for myself. I have it in my bedroom. I may keep the one I'm about to take too."

"Do you have fantasies about her?" she asked, fluffing her hair.

"Not any more. I did for a long time after our first meeting. Now we're just good friends. We fuck now and again and I take her to an occasional party, but that's about it." Tim had selected a pair of large silver-and-diamond dangle earrings and he handed them to Carla.

"They look like chandeliers," she said.

"Try them."

Carla stood in front of the mirror and clipped on the oversized earrings. Tim was right again. They accented the dress perfectly. "Change your makeup," he said. "More eyes and a darker lipstick."

Carla quickly adjusted her makeup as Jean-Claude had taught her to and suddenly she was a seductive woman of the evening. "Brilliant," she said.

"Brilliant is right," Tim said. He posed her with her almost-naked back to him, looking seductively over her shoulder. He snapped several pictures. "Now we come to album photos," he said, opening Ronnie's other closet. "Which of these says you?"

"I don't know. Which do you think I should wear?"

"Not my decision. For the album you need pictures of fantasies that you would enjoy acting out with a friend. That's a very personal decision." He reached into the closet and took out the pink little-girl dress. "This fantasy is about the older man who likes to make love to virginal little girls. You wear white socks and mary-janes, white cotton under-shirts and underpants."

Carla smiled as she put it on. Tim photographed her sitting on the edge of the bed with her hands folded in her lap and knees locked together, looking a bit scared.

"This," he said, holding a short wedding dress and a veil, "is a similar fantasy, deflowering a wedding-night virgin." She dressed and Tim snapped that outfit as well.

They continued for over an hour, with Carla portraying a cheerleader, an aerobics instructor, a bikini-clad nymphet, and a harem girl. When Tim suggested the stern teacher costume, Carla demurred. "I don't think I'm the dominant type."

"Ronnie is," Tim said, "and I have some very sexy shots of her with a whip in her hand and a man wearing nipple clamps licking her pussy."

"I never saw those."

"She has some particular pictures for special friends."

"Should I have a special album? I can't see myself with a whip."

"I know that. But I have a different idea. Come with me into the other room," Tim suggested.

"What other room?"

"Ronnie's playground. She told me she hasn't shown it to you, so let me."

"Should I wear anything special?" Carla asked removing her costume, a nurse's uniform with a starched cap.

"Just your beautiful skin."

Tim opened the door to the other bedroom and let Carla precede him. As she entered the room she gasped. Almost cave-like, it was darkened with wood-paneled walls and heavy velvet drapes. As Carla looked around she saw that the room resembled a dungeon with eyelets, chains, and bondage equipment proudly displayed on every wall. There were three differently shaped wooden benches with hooks and straps attached and two cabinets filled with items Carla didn't recognize. A huge brass bed dominated one end of the room. As shocked as she was, Carla also realized that she could hardly breathe.

Tim walked in behind her and wrapped his long fingers around one wrist, holding her tightly. "Exciting?"

"Yes," she whispered.

"Ronnie thought as much. I took several rolls of film in here with Ronnie dressed all in leather brandishing whips and paddles. But I don't think that's you, is it?"

Carla shook her head. She was picturing herself held down or chained, restrained and helpless with a man standing over her enjoying her vulnerability. Tim took her other wrist and held her arms against her sides. He put his mouth close to her ear. "The word is 'popcorn,'" he breathed, rubbing his fully clothed body against her back. "Say the word and I'll stop whatever I'm doing. And let me give you some advice. Never play in here without a safe word. And never play with anyone you don't trust to honor it. Understand?"

"Ronnie and I discussed that. I understand."

"Say 'popcorn.'"

"Popcorn."

Tim released her hands and moved away. "Now, stand here and look around the room while I get my camera. While I'm gone, picture yourself strapped into each piece of equipment, unable to escape. From now on, don't speak unless I ask you a direct question. And don't move!"

The last was an order, one that Carla had no intention of disobeying. She looked around and studied each device. She imagined herself restrained in a few but she had no idea what many were for or how they worked. She didn't care. Her palms were sweating and she was struggling to get air into her trembling body.

"Good girl," said Tim reentering the large room. "You're so excited, you're ready to burst. That's very good. Come here." As Carla walked across the thick dark grey carpet her feet sank into its soft lushness. "Give me your arm." Carla held out her arm and Tim fastened on a tight leather wrist band. He looped a ring attached to the band over a hook on the wall and took a picture of her hand and arm.

"You know you can unhook yourself any time you want." Tim's voice caused a heat wave to wash over her. "But you want to stay there. You want me to restrain you. That's excellent." He fastened an identical strap around her other wrist and one around each ankle. The rings attached to additional hooks on the wall so her arms were held out from her shoulders and her legs were spread about two feet apart.

As the camera snapped, Carla imagined how she looked, fastened to the wall, controlled and helpless. God she was hot. If she could just touch herself. . . . But she wouldn't move, couldn't move.

Tim walked over and kissed her full mouth. Then he slid his finger across her hip until it was against her clit. "You want to come? Just like that?" He stopped. "No. Not yet. I want to play a while." He put the camera down. "After Ronnie and I had been together a few times, we discovered that we both have a love of dominance. I want to be in control. I want to be able to tease. I want to do anything and everything without any protest. Do you want to play with me?"

Carla nodded. At that moment she wanted to be dominated by him more that she'd ever wanted anything else.

"Do you remember the safe word?" he asked.

"Popcorn," Carla said.

"That's good. Now, a few questions. And I want honest answers. What if I hurt you, just a bit?" He pinched her nipple and twisted it hard.

It was so sudden that Carla cried out.

"Good or bad?"

Carla paused, then admitted, "Good."

Tim grabbed a handful of her hair and dragged her head back. He kissed her mouth, grinding his face against hers. She responded, pressing against him as much as her bound body would allow. "A true playmate," he said, unhooking her limbs from the wall. He pulled her over to a wooden bench, adjusted the length of its legs, and laid a leather spread over it. "This has been a fantasy of mine for a long time, but Ronnie is too dominant herself to really enjoy this. Lie down on your back."

Carla did, feeling and smelling the leather. "Inhale," Tim said. "Smell your own aroma." Carla breathed deeply and knew the scent of her arousal. She was so hot that she doubted it could get any better, but each time Tim spoke, it did.

"Here's something else for you to enjoy." He slipped a leather blindfold over her eyes.

The darkness was total. Being unable to see made her more aware of her other senses. She heard the rustle of Tim's clothes as he moved around the room. She smelled leather and sweat and sex. She rubbed her hands over the leather, appreciating its rich texture.

"Don't move," Tim said. Carla could hear the camera and imagined this scene as it would appear to those thumbing through her own 'special' pictures.

"Now slide up until your head hangs off the end. There's a pillow that will support your neck and let your head hang down gently." She slid along the leather until her neck rested on the pillow and heard snaps as Tim fastened her arms and legs to the bench. "These aren't hooks, they're padlocks," he said. "I want you to struggle to get free."

Carla experienced a moment of panic as she pulled at the locks. She had to test Tim's words. "Popcorn," she said.

Tim fumbled with the first lock until her right arm was free. "Refasten it," she said. "It's all right."

"I was afraid that I'd gone too far," he said. "I was seriously disappointed."

"Don't be. I just needed to be sure."

"Of course you did."

Tim quickly relocked her wrist. "Now struggle. I want to see your body strain, unable to get free."

She pulled at her arms and legs. The bindings didn't hurt at all, but she was, nevertheless, completely helpless.

"Beg me to let you go."

She heard the hum of the video camera. "Please." She knew that she could say popcorn at any time and he would let her go. She could also beg and plead and know he wouldn't release her. Her head angled downward was making her a little light-headed but it was fantastic. "Please let me go. Oh god, please."

"Oh no, baby. Not a chance." Then his hands were on her face, gently feeling around the blindfold. He slipped a finger into her mouth and she sucked as he worked it in and out.

"I want you to understand exactly what I'm going to have you do," Tim said. "This bench is at just the right height." What had to be his naked cock slid over Carla's cheeks. "You're going to suck me good." He withdrew the finger from her mouth and replaced it with his hard erection. Carla gasped as Tim forced his large member into her mouth, but she quickly started sucking as he fucked her mouth. "Too good, too fast," he said, pulling away from her greedy mouth.

She again heard a rustling then a buzzing. "Hear that?" he said. "That's a vibrator and I'm going to make you come with it. I'll be in control of your body. You won't be able to resist. You'll come when I want you to and only when I'm ready."

Carla jumped when she felt the buzz against her nipple. Jolts of magic electricity bounced around inside of her, stabbing her in the breasts, the belly, and in her hungry pussy. She wanted nothing more than for Tim to fuck her, any way he wanted, but she sensed that her resistance was part of his fantasy and she wanted him to have it all. She knew instinctively what to say.

"Oh stop," she said, "please stop. It's torture."

"It's exciting to beg, isn't it? And to know you can't sway me. And I love to hear you plead for mercy, but there will be none." He placed the tip of the vibrator deep in her armpit.

Carla was afraid it would tickle, but it didn't. It just excited her more. "I can't take it. No more, please."

"There's so much more," Tim said. He moved the vibrator until it was rubbing the insides of Carla's thighs. "Want it against your cunt?"

"No. Don't."

"I will. And what's more you want me to. It's so embarrassing to admit that you want me to fuck you with this vibrator, this artificial buzzing cock that can give you such pleasure."

"Oh god, no."

Tim was in heaven. This was his favorite fantasy and it was better than he had dreamed it would be. And he was taking it as far as it would go. "I think you'd better ask me to fuck you."

"No."

He teased Carla's cunt, touching her swollen lips, then stopping. Sliding the vibrator through her thick wet juices, then moving it back to the inside of her thigh. "I can make you crazy with wanting. Admit that your pussy needs to be fucked. Say it."

"Yes, do it," Carla said, slipping out of character. "Fuck me good."

Tim inserted the penis-shaped vibrator into Carla's pussy and strapped it in place with a piece of leather that was connected to the bench. "Now suck my cock," he said, walking around to the head of the bench and laying his cock against her mouth.

Carla became pure sensation. She sucked and lapped as the buzzing filled her demanding cunt. Tim came quickly, unable to resist the pull of Carla's mouth. She swallowed as he pumped until he thought he would never be able to come again. He pulled his exhausted cock from Carla's mouth, knowing that she hadn't come yet. "Do you want to come now, baby?" he asked.

"Please. Help me."

"Of course," he spoke reassuringly. He knelt between her legs and flicked his tongue back and forth against her clit. "Yes," she screamed. "Don't stop."

He didn't and Carla climaxed, shuddering and bucking against the straps holding her wrists and ankles. Tim pulled the vibrator from her sopping pussy, unfastened the straps and carried her to the bed.

"I've never experienced anything like that before," Carla said.

"It was great for me too," Tim said. "Maybe when I've developed the pictures, we could get together again to look them over . . . and whatever."

"Yes." Carla sighed. "Lots of whatever."

Chapter 6

Carla stretched languidly on her bed and, knowing her friend would still be up, dialed Ronnie's number in Dutchess County from the private phone she'd had installed in her bedroom. It was not quite eleven in the evening and, once the boys were in bed, Carla had soaked in a hot tub for almost an hour. Despite the predictable romance novel she had read, she had been unable to relax. She was confused about the following evening, her first with her new black leather album.

Wrapped in an old velour robe, socks, and a pair of Garfield slippers that her boys had gotten her the previous Christmas, she listened to the phone ring.

"Hello," Ronnie answered.

"Hi, it's me."

"Hi. What's up?"

"Well. . . ." Originally it had felt odd to discuss the business of sex with her three boys sleeping just down the hall, but after a few late-night phone sessions with Ronnie the whole thing felt almost normal. "A man named Max called and I called him back. He says he got my number from you."

"He did. When my friend Bert called and told me he had a friend, I suggested you. You've got to get your feet wet at some point, so to speak. I hope that giving him your number was okay."

"Oh sure it was. He left a message on my answering machine. And now I'm excited, but also nervous. What if I'm not good enough? What if he doesn't get his money's worth?"

"He will. I assume you two talked and you feel comfortable with him."

"Of course. He sounds nice and he's never been with a . . . someone like me before." She giggled into the phone. "I think he's more nervous than I am."

"He probably is. You'd be surprised how anxious some men get. But that can add to the anticipation."

"I know. Part of me is so keyed up I'm ready to come if someone looks at me crooked. But part of me is worried."

"You'll be fine. And if something feels uncomfortable, just tell him. If he's unwilling to do anything else, give him his money back and say good night."

"He says he wants to see my album. He's obviously heard about yours."

Ronnie snuggled deeper under her covers. She had been watching TV in bed, naked, and now she slithered over her satin sheets, feeling the smooth fabric against her skin. Talking about sex always made her horny. "Is your album ready?" she asked.

"I met with Tim yesterday and we looked over the pictures he took. He does marvelous work. Some of those photos made even me hot. I bought an album. It's black leather."

"Great. Satin and leather."

"Max said he's looking forward to a creative evening. How do you broach the subject of fantasy?"

"It's different each time," Ronnie answered. "Some men just want straight fucking and you don't have to use the album at all. Most men who call me, and who will call you, have been referred by someone else, someone who's enjoyed the fantasies that I've created. Let's face it. I'm expensive and you will be too. Someone who just wants a good lay can get that for a lot less money. So our kind of friends, or clients as you call them, want something out of the ordinary, something that they can't get at home. I guess creative is as good a term as any."

Carla shifted the phone to a more comfortable position on her shoulder. "But how, exactly, should I begin things? I can't just say, 'Want to act out a story,' can I?"

"You probably won't have to. Most of the time new friends will know about your album from whomever recommended them. They may even have decided on a fantasy. Some, will never have thought about role playing, and those are the most fun for me. Once you get past a man's initial shyness, play-acting can be the greatest sexual turn-on there is. Gets them outside themselves. They can do anything, be anyone, and no one's judging or censoring."

"You're still not answering my question. How do you start things happening?"

"Okay. Let's take the first man I played with after I put together my album." Ronnie shifted the phone to the other ear, settled back, and stared at the ceiling, remembering Tory Palluso.

Ronnie introduced herself to the maitre d' at La Bon Nuit and he efficiently guided her to a quiet section off to one side of the busy restaurant. As she slalomed between tables of two or four expensively dressed diners, she had a moment to look over Mr. Palluso who, she saw, was sitting on a chair opposite the banquette, hesitantly sipping a glass of red wine.

Tory Palluso was about forty-five, Ronnie guessed, with a receding hairline and wire-rimmed glasses. To his credit, his dark hair wasn't combed over the top to disguise his balding pate, but was neatly trimmed and styled. From several tables away, he didn't appear to be a good-looking man. His granite-hard profile and pointed chin, heavy black eyebrows and matching moustache seemed overwhelming.

As Tory looked up and saw her moving toward him, Ronnie smiled and nodded. He looked straight at her and she was struck by his eyes—so bright blue that if not for his glasses she would have thought he was wearing colored lenses. Both his smile and his unusual eyes made his face surprisingly appealing.

As he watched the beautiful woman making her way to his table Tory thought, she doesn't look like a call girl. But Frank had assured him she was the best. If she was as good in bed as she looked, she was going to make him regret that he only got to New York two or three times a year.

"You're Ronnie," Tory said.

"Tory," Ronnie said, extending her free hand, "I'm so glad to meet you." The maitre d' pulled out the table and Ronnie settled herself on the banquette. She set the package she was carrying down next to her.

"Wine?" he asked. When she nodded, he asked, "Red or white?"

"Red."

"I looked at the wine list and they have a nice Burgundy, if that's okay."

"That will be fine," Ronnie said. She had barely gotten comfortable when the waiter brought the wine. When Tory nodded the waiter opened the bottle and nearly filled her long-stemmed glass. "To an eventful evening," Ronnie said, lifting her glass toward Tory.

"Eventful," Tory said as his glass touched Ronnie's. "A superb way of thinking about things." He sipped. "You're lovely."

Ronnie smiled. She had selected a soft chiffon scoop-necked dress in a shade best described as cantaloupe and worn it with a triple-strand pearl necklace and pearl drop earrings. A matching triple-strand bracelet and a gold watch showed off her long, slender fingers. On a whim she'd had her nails done that afternoon in a frosted shade the exact hue of the dress.

"Thank you," she said softly, and raised an eyebrow. Tory's dark suit was carefully tailored to hide the slight paunch she had noticed as he stood up and he wore a monogrammed white on white shirt and conservative paisley tie. Everything about him bespoke pride in his appearance and money enough to indulge it. "You're not bad yourself."

Through a savory vegetable pâté, a crisp green salad with a peppercorn vinaigrette dressing, veal with capers served with a wine, lemon, and butter sauce, and julienned vegetables, they talked about business, family, and other ordinary things. Over an apple tart with a delicate, thin crust they discussed politics. They agreed more than either had expected.

Over napoleon brandy and espresso, Tory finally broached the reason for their dinner. "We have a mutual friend," he said, suddenly hesitant. "Frank Morrison."

"I know," Ronnie said. "He gave you my phone number."

"Right."

When the silence became awkward, Ronnie said, "Do you want my company for the rest of the evening?"

"I enjoyed our dinner. You're a highly intelligent and knowledgeable woman, for. . . ." He stumbled over the end of the sentence and swallowed hard.

"For a hooker." Ronnie laughed. "Don't be embarrassed. I'm not. I love what I do and I love fulfilling men's fantasies, which, I gather, is what you want."

"My wife is a wonderful lady, don't get me wrong."

Ronnie interrupted. "Why don't we agree not to mention her for the rest of the evening. Tonight is for a little adult entertainment. Maybe, one day, you'll see fit to share some of your desires with her. I'll bet she'll be more receptive than you'd imagine, but that's neither here nor there. Let's discuss you."

"I want something unusual. Frank said you and he played out a fantasy of his. He wouldn't tell me about the specifics. 'Too personal,' he told me. But from the grin on his face, he must have enjoyed it tremendously."

"Do you have a fantasy in mind that you want to act out?"

"Not really. Frank said you'd have suggestions."

"I have something here that may help you decide." The tables on either side of them had long since been vacated, so Ronnie motioned for Tory to sit beside her on the banquette. She picked up the package she had carried into the restaurant and placed it on the table. From a large black-satin drawstring bag, she withdrew a photograph album with a black satin cover and placed it in front of Tory.

She placed her hand on the closed book. "In here are fantasies, scenes that we can play together. Look through the book and I'll describe each fantasy." She handed Tory a flat, black-satin envelope about four inches square, with a black tassel tied to one corner. "When you find something you'd like, put my fee in the envelope and use this bookmark to hold the page. Then we'll go back to my house and play."

Hands trembling with expectation, Tory took the envelope and opened the cover of the album. The first photo was of Ronnie dressed in a black satin bustier with matching garter belt and stockings. "That's Marguerite, the stripper," Ronnie explained as Tory gazed at the first picture. "She'll strip very slowly for you."

He turned to the next photo. Ronnie was dressed all in green. "That's Maid Marian. She's been in love with Robin Hood for months, but they've never had time to be together."

Tory lifted the album page and turned to the next photo. "Nita's a harem girl. You were very brave in battle and saved the sultan's life. He's allowed you to pick one girl from his harem and she's yours for the evening. She's been very well trained in the arts of love."

She continued as Tory turned pages. "That's the Princess Mellisande. She's not allowed to have intercourse until her marriage, but she satisfies herself, and most of the guards in the castle, by masturbating while they watch, then bringing them to climax with her mouth."

The next shot was of Ronnie in her bed, dressed in a nightgown, holding a sheet up against her breasts. "And that's Bethann. She was asleep in her bed when a burglar broke in. At first, he wanted to steal her jewels. Now he just wants her body."

He turned the page again. "That's Miss Gilbert. She's the headmistress at an exclusive boy's school and, if you want to meet her, she'll explain your punishment for being a naughty boy in class."

For picture after picture, Ronnie explained fantasies to Tory. The last dozen photos in the album were explicit pictures of Ronnie, guaranteed to ignite the most selective viewer. Ronnie stood as Tory turned back to the beginning to review the photographs. "I have to use the ladies' room. I'll be a few minutes so look through the book and select. Of course, you could make up your own fantasy or we could just go back to my place and make love."

"Not on your life. I've never had a chance like this."

When Ronnie returned from the ladies room, Tory had her coat over his arm. He helped her into it, then handed her the book. She opened to the page he had selected and removed the satin envelope. "Nita will please you in every way," she whispered as she slipped the five hundred-dollar bills into her purse.

The ten-minute cab ride was the longest Tory could remember. Ronnie's stocking-covered legs were just inches from his and he longed to run his fingers up the inside of her sweet thighs. He held himself back. This night was going to be something extraordinary. He was going to let Ronnie dictate the speed. And he would savor every minute.

Ronnie had initially been reluctant to use her brownstone, worrying that one of her friends might get out of hand, either during an evening of pleasure, or afterward. But she quickly realized that her customers had more to lose than she did if the police became involved.

The cab let them off in front of her house and they quickly made their way inside, then up to the bedroom. "There's a bottle of champagne in the fridge," she said, pointing to the small wet bar in the corner of the room, "and glasses just above. Pour some for each of us and make yourself comfortable. I'll just be a moment." She took a hanger from the closet and disappeared into the bathroom.

Five minutes later Ronnie emerged from the bathroom. "Sir Knight," she said softly, "I'm Nita. The Sultan has told me of your bravery and I'm honored you picked me for your evening."

Tory just stared. Her halter top was made of light-blue gauze so sheer that it allowed glimpses of her nipples. A veil of the same material covered the lower part of her face. Matching harem pants rode low on her hips, flared at the legs and gathered tightly at the ankles. Through their sheer fabric Tory saw a dark triangle of hair at the junction of her thighs.

Nita's feet were bare, and she wore long earrings and bracelets on her wrists and ankles, all with tiny bells that tinkled as she moved. Her head was bowed and her long blond hair was covered with a soft blue, gauzy veil. A golden chain hung around her bare midriff. Covering her navel was a dark blue jewel.

"I hope I please you," she said softly. "You have only to indicate how I may serve you and your wish will be my command." She crossed to stand in front of him and slid her hands up his silk shirt, sliding her jacket off his wide shoulders.

"Will you dance for me?" he asked.

Ronnie put a tape in the player and the room filled with rhythmic, exotic music. Sinuously, Nita undulated around the room, turning down lamps, and lighting candles and sticks of incense. As she twirled, she removed the veil covering her hair and slid its soft folds across Tory's face. At one point, she stood in front of him, placed the veil over his head and kissed his lips through the sheer fabric, the bells continually tinkling.

When he reached for her, she danced away, trailing the veil over his skin. She held the transparent fabric under her breasts and lifted so the unrestrained twin mounds stood out from her chest and jiggled as she moved, covered only by thin layers of gauze. She thrust her chest into his face but, when he went to kiss one nipple, she danced away.

Near then far, close, yet not quite close enough. The fragrance of her eastern perfume filled Tory's head and he longed to taste her mouth. When next Nita danced close, he grabbed the scarf that covered her face and wrapped it around her body, trapping her swaying bottom.

Nita leaned over and licked Tory's upper lip with the tip of her tongue. Back and forth, her tongue danced over his mouth as her bottom swayed against the imprisoning scarf. Each time he would have pressed his lips tightly against hers, she moved slightly away, allowing only the lightest of touches of mouth against mouth.

"More," he growled. "Kiss me, woman."

Nita's mouth was so close to Tory's that her breath cooled his wet lips. "Your wish," she breathed, "is my command." She pressed her mouth against his and her tongue requested entry. Greedily, he opened his mouth and swirled his tongue against hers. For long moments, their lips and tongues joined in fiery combat, plunging, then drawing back.

While they kissed, Nita opened the buttons of Tory's dress shirt and tugged it from his body. She removed her mouth only long enough to pull his undershirt over his head and finally she ran her hands across his chest so the hair slid between her fingers. She scraped one nail down his skin.

He was on fire, yearning to devour this woman who was his for the evening. When he let go of one end of the scarf she slipped away, teasingly moving around the room. She turned her back, then took off her top. Naked to the waist, Nita held up a scarf and twirled. Tory got quick glimpses of her full breasts, their large darkened nipples standing out from the soft white skin.

Without taking his eyes from her body, Tory stood, removed the rest of his clothes, and tossed them aside. "Your staff is fully ready, my lord," Nita said, staring at his erect cock. "Shall I take it in my mouth and show you how much pleasure I can give you?"

He dropped into the chair. "Oh yes, Nita, but just a little. I will have better uses for my staff."

She knelt on the floor at his feet and brushed her hair across his loins, combing her hair with his cock. The sensation was so exquisite that he was afraid he would come without her ever really touching him. When she finally placed a light kiss against the tip of his erection, it took all his concentration not to climax right then.

Nita flicked her tongue over the end of Tory's cock, licking the sticky pre-come fluid. Then she pursed her lips and sucked his purple cock head into her mouth. She took it in as deeply as she could, then pulled back, her head bobbing up and down in his lap.

"No, not yet," he growled. He stood, put on a condom, grabbed her around the waist, and pulled her harem-pants down. He turned her so she was facing away from him, bent her at the waist and plunged his cock into her wet pussy from behind. Over and over he drove into her until he moaned with his release.

Ronnie hadn't actually climaxed, but she was strangely satisfied, sharing Tory's pleasure. She reached between her thighs and cupped his testicles, squeezing and milking all the thick fluid. His body bucked as the last of his orgasm flowed into her.

When Tory collapsed, Ronnie got a warm, wet face cloth from the bathroom and leisurely washed his penis and testicles. She squeezed his cock and satisfied herself that there was, at least for the moment, no arousal left in him. She never left anyone unsatisfied.

He stood up, stretched, and looked at the clock beside the bed. "That was great, but I'm afraid I have to go now," he said.

"You have my number," Ronnie said, "and there are many other pictures in my album."

"I don't get to New York often," he said sadly, buttoning his shirt. "But when I do, you can be sure you'll hear from me."

Ronnie shifted the phone to the other ear. "I see Tory two or three times a year," she said to Carla, "and he's very generous." Carla heard Ronnie's short laugh. "Last time, in addition to paying me, he brought me a magnificent gold bracelet with a tiny bell on it."

"Do you always play the same scene with him?"

"Not always, but we come back to Nita more frequently than any other fantasy."

"Thanks for the story," Carla said. "That makes it much easier for me to deal with Max."

"Well, good luck tomorrow night," Ronnie said. "And most important of all, have fun."

"I will. Believe me, I will."

When she first saw Max, Carla had to smile. He looked like the stereotypical mountain man, about thirty-five, with almost black hair, a rugged build, and a full, bushy beard and moustache. "You're a great looking woman," he said without preamble. "Nice body, good bones."

"Thank you," Carla said, her nervousness quickly disappearing. "And you're very handsome yourself."

He fluffed the beard that was long enough to cover the first two buttons of his open-necked shirt. "You mean this," he said as she put her napkin in her lap. "I think it's ridiculous that a man spends ten or fifteen minutes each morning scraping a dangerously sharp instrument over his face. When I graduated from high school, I stopped shaving."

"I guess that means that you don't work in the grey flannel world of corporate America."

His laugh was as booming as she had expected. "You're right. I'm a maverick and proud of it. I own my own business, Sheridan Plastics. Hell, I am Sheridan Plastics. Built it myself from the get-go, you might say. Now some guys in pin-striped suits want to buy me out for an amount of money that has more zeros than I had dollars when I started. And I can sell or I can tell them to go to hell. It doesn't matter to me."

"Are you married?"

He saddened. "Unfortunately, just when life was getting good, Marie died. Auto accident. It was real fast so at least she didn't feel anything."

"I'm sorry."

"It was almost eight years ago. Now I just like to have fun. Nothing serious, mind you. Just fun. What do you want for dinner?" Max asked.

"You selected this place and you seem to know your way around. What do you suggest?"

"I love a good steak and this restaurant serves the best in town."

"Sounds great to me," Carla said. Recently her life seemed to be a gustatorial war between nouvelle cuisine and peanut butter and jelly. She looked up as the waiter held his pencil poised. "Sirloin, medium rare with a baked potato and a salad."

"Good choice," Max said to the waiter. "Do that twice. And let's have a bottle of Chateau Margeaux. I think you have a 1964 hidden away." He turned to Carla. "The Margeaux is a bit light for a steak, but it's excellent."

"Very good sir," the waiter said.

"You're full of surprises," Carla said. "I would have taken you for a beer type of guy. Or even bourbon."

"I was—still am—but I've learned to appreciate a good wine. I also enjoy ordering the most expensive bottle on the menu."

Carla laughed loudly. She found she really liked this unusual man.

"I understand you have children."

They spent the next hour in pleasant conversation. As the meal neared its end, Carla considered the problem of how to bring up her album but, as Ronnie had predicted, Max saved her the trouble.

"I'd like to see your pictures."

Nonplussed, Carla reached down and opened a black leather attache case that sat near her feet. "How did you know about the album?" she asked as she placed the book on the table.

"I guess that's called Black Leather. Bert told me about Ronnie and her book, Black Satin. I assumed you would have some photos too. That's why I called you. Now, be a good girl and get lost. I want to look at this in private. Oh and take off that bra. I like tits that jiggle."

Carla burst out laughing. "Anything you say." She went into the ladies' room and, inside a stall, took off her bra. She was glad she had worn her teal-blue knit dress and only a half-slip. Max would be happy at the way her breasts bounced. When she arrived back at the table, Max was looking at a picture of a woman in a slinky negligee. "I want to wear something like this," he said, not the least embarrassed. "And I want you to fuck me in the ass with a dildo."

"You certainly know what you want," Carla said, completely surprised by the nature of the request.

"I most certainly do. Can we play?"

"Of course." Ronnie had told her that she had lingerie in larger sizes and had shown her the love toys. "I can't guarantee that exact outfit, but I'm sure I have something you'll like."

"That's okay. And by the way, you have great tits."

Max dropped a handful of bills on the table and almost dragged Carla to a taxi. In the bedroom of the brownstone, Carla put her coat and Max's away and went through the bureau drawers. She pulled out a black nightgown with a deep vee front and back and thin straps over the shoulders. She placed it across Max's lap. "How about this?"

His huge, calloused hands slid over the delicate fabric. "It's beautiful."

Carla found another, a peach-colored satin lounging set with feathery trim. "Or this?"

Max held the black gown in one hand and the peach in the other, rubbing the slippery material between his fingers. In another drawer Carla found a bright red teddy that had long attached garters and panties to match. As she handed the pieces to Max, she saw his eyes light up. "Do you have stockings?" he asked.

"Of course." Seeing Max's expression she said, "You've obviously selected this one?"

"Definitely." He stood up and quickly removed all his clothes.

Carla tried not to think about how much hair Max had all over his body and how the undies he had selected would look. She was afraid she would giggle. When she looked at his face, however, she quieted. He was mesmerized and his body showed clearly that he was extremely excited. Anything that excites a man like this can't be bad, she thought.

"Will that thing fit around my waist?" Max wondered, pointing to the bustier.

"Well, let's try." Carla stretched the silky red lace teddy around his waist and threaded the laces through their eyelets.

Max let his head fall back and closed his eyes as the silk caressed his skin.

Carla fetched a pair of thigh-high red stockings. "Sit on the edge of the bed and I'll help you put these on." Max sat and Carla scrunched one nylon on her thumbs. "Raise your foot," she said, kneeling on the rug. Slowly, she took his foot in her hand and slid the nylon up the arch. Inch by inch, the sheer red material covered first his ankle, then his calf, his knee, and his hairy thigh. His cock was rock hard as Carla fastened the stocking to the garters.

Max held his breath and trembled as the second stocking inched up his leg and Carla snapped the garter in place. "Soft," she said, sliding her hand down his nylon-covered leg. "Very smooth."

He lifted her hand from his leg. "Not yet," he said through gritted teeth. "I want to feel the rest of the outfit."

"Of course," Carla said. She slid the bikini panties over his large feet and up to his knees. "Now stand up." Agonizingly slowly, Carla pulled the panties over his engorged cock, then stroked his body through the cloth. Up and down his legs, across his chest, up and down his cock. Her hands were everywhere, their touch muffled by the various fabrics.

Max's breathing was ragged. This was better than it had ever been for him. He stood, his eyes closed, his body quivering, as he tried to retain control. He realized that Carla was no longer touching him. He opened his eyes and saw her, still completely clothed, holding a slender penis-shaped dildo in her hand, stroking its length.

"You know what I'm going to do now, don't you?"

He could no longer remain standing. He collapsed, curled on his side, on the bed. "I know."

Carla sat behind him and applied a generous amount of lubricant on the flesh-colored rod. "You know where you need this?"

"Yes."

She pulled the panties to one side and slid the dildo easily into Max's ass and replaced the nylon. "Now, that's done and held in place firmly. Stand up."

"I don't know whether I can."

"You can and you know it."

Max stood up, almost unable to control his body. It was taking all of his strength not to come. But when she milked his cock with one hand and rotated the end of the dildo with the other he was done. Semen soaked the front of the panties, drenching Carla's hand. It seemed hours and still he came, Carla handling his cock in front and twirling the dildo in back. When his body was empty, Max dropped back onto the bed.

Carla sat beside him until his breathing had almost returned to normal. Then she withdrew the dildo from his body, washed it and put it away in the toy drawer.

"That was marvelous," Max said, turning on his back and watching

Carla move around the room. "Just marvelous." He sat up. "Help me off with this stuff."

Carla carefully removed the clothing, then slid a new pair of red satin panties up Max's legs and over his limp penis. "Leave them on under your slacks and think of me as the material rubs your cock."

"Hell, Carla, you'll have me hard all the time."

"That's the idea. Your cock will be hard and you'll remember me."

With a quick laugh, Max pulled on his slacks over the red panties. "I just hope I don't have to pee before I get home. Someone in a men's room might see this red stuff and get the wrong idea."

"Or the right one."

"You're quite something, lady," he boomed. "I'll be calling you. And I've got a lot of friends. I hope you're not overly booked."

"I'll make room. Any friend of yours will become a friend of mine."

As Max left, Carla noticed that he was walking just a bit differently, enjoying the slither of the red silk under his slacks.

About a week later Carla received a note in the mail. "Max told me about you. The plumber will be at your apartment at six o'clock on Tuesday evening the 27th." The note was signed "Gene." The only other thing in the envelope was five hundred dollars in cash. Later, Carla got a phone message from Max saying that a friend of his named Gene would drop her a note soon.

Carla was at the brownstone at six on the selected evening, dressed in a pair of tight, white denim pants and a snug-fitting plum-colored polo shirt that accentuated her bralessness. When the doorbell rang, she opened the front door and faced a muscular, if slightly overweight, man of medium height. He wore a pair of stained coveralls and carried a toolbox. "I'm Gene," he said, "and I'm here to fix your kitchen faucet. Max said your plumbing wasn't usually a problem."

Carla almost giggled. "My plumbing is usually fine," she said. "But that kitchen sink has been giving me a terrible time recently."

"Let's check it out." Gene followed her the kitchen and proceeded to actually dismantle the faucet while she watched. "Okay, lady," he said, "I'm going to need some help here."

"What can I do?"

"Most things, I'd imagine," he said, grinning. He had disconnected the faucet and fastened a huge pipe wrench around some connection at the back of the sink. "But right now I need you to hold this wrench."

Carla replaced his hairy hands on the wrench with her own. "Now pull hard," he said, "and hold tight. If you let go, we'll have water everywhere."

Knowing nothing about plumbing, Carla had no idea what this man had done, so she pulled on the wrench with both hands. "Don't let go," he warned again. As he stood up, he brushed against Carla's breasts which, since she was bent over the sink, were hanging heavily against her shirt. "Nice melons, lady," he said, squeezing one of the heavy globes.

"Hey," she said, "cut that out."

As she started to straighten, he said, "Don't let go of that pipe or it'll make old faithful look like a garden sprinkler."

"Shit," Carla said. She had no idea how much of this was fantasy and how much was reality. Not ready to take a chance with Ronnie's kitchen, she held onto the wrench.

"I'm glad you understand," Gene said. He squeezed her breast, weighing its fullness in his hand. "Nice big tits," he said, nodding. "Fill the hand, and then some. I love titties that are more than a handful."

"Will you let go," Carla snapped.

Gene backed up and, behind her, Carla heard tools banging around in the toolbox. "Here we are," Gene, the plumber, said. Carla heard a loud snipping sound. Suddenly her polo shirt was being cut up the back and across the shoulders. With a yank, she was naked from the waist up. "That's better," Gene said.

"Now wait a minute," Carla said but Gene silenced her with a pinch of one of her swollen nipples. "Ouch."

"Be a good girl," Gene said, "and don't let go of that pipe." He leaned over and bit her earlobe. "If you say 'Uncle,' I'll stop. Understand?" he whispered. Carla nodded.

With both hands holding the wrench tightly, Carla tried to wiggle away from the plumber's hands, but she had almost no room to maneuver. He pressed his body against her back and his rough palms cupped her heavy breasts and pressed them against her ribs. As he held her, he thrust her lower body against her buttocks, jabbing her with what felt like the largest cock ever.

"That's for later," he said, his laugh warm, moist waves against her ear. Again he backed up and rummaged in his toolbox.

Suddenly Gene draped heavy, cold lengths of chain over her shoulders and wrapped it around her ribs and under her breasts. "That's cold," she shrieked, as he fastened the chain in the back.

"And this is warm," he said, leaning into the sink and sucking one nipple into his mouth.

The contrast between his hot mouth and the cold chains was tantalizing. She started to relax and loosen her grip. "Don't let that go," he said. "I mean it. It'll drown us both."

"Shit," she hissed again.

Gene pulled one nipple while he nursed on the other. He moved around to the other side and exchanged his hand for his mouth. He was rough and both his mouth and hands were painful, hurting yet exciting and soothing all at once. "Am I hurting you?" he asked, pinching her left tit hard.

"Ouch! Yes, you're hurting me." Carla looked down and saw a bright red mark. She knew that she would say 'Uncle,' but she wasn't anywhere near needing to. Quite the contrary. She felt wonderful.

"Good," Gene said, unzipping her jeans and pulling them down. Automatically Carla lifted her bare feet so he could pull the pants off, leaving her dressed only in her panties and several lengths of chain. Gene slid his hand down her belly and into her panties. "You're hot for me," he said, his fingers pulling her wet pubic hair. Carla couldn't deny what was obvious to the touch. "I have just the right tool to use and it's not the one you think."

He pulled something from his toolbox and Carla felt something slender, cylindrical, and cold wiggle into the narrow crevice between her legs. "The right tool for every job," Gene muttered. He slid the dildo deep into Carla's pussy. In and out he fucked her with it, moving the slender object around so it touched every inch of her insides.

Her knees weak, Carla had to be reminded not to let go of the pipe. "Hold on to that wrench, lady. Hold on." He pulled her panties back up to keep the dildo in place while he undressed. Since she couldn't let go of the wrench that held the disconnected pipe, Carla backed up as far as she could and arched her back.

She worried about how to insist on a condom without ruining the fantasy, but, as if he had read her mind, she heard the telltale ripping of the condom wrapper. "Don't you worry about a thing. I wouldn't do any job unprotected."

Gene held his large cock in one hand and moved aside the crotch of Carla's panties with the other. With little warning, he pulled out the dildo and rammed his huge cock into Carla's soggy pussy. He was enormous, stretching Carla's body almost to the point of agony. But not quite. The sensation of being so full drove Carla to climax quickly. With a loud scream she came and soon thereafter Gene spurted come deep into her.

When his breathing was more normal, Gene took the wrench from Carla's hands and disconnected it from the sink. No water spurted out. As she dropped on a kitchen chair, Carla watched Gene efficiently reassemble the faucet.

"Nice plumbing," Gene said, packing his wrenches in the toolbox and gazing at Carla's body. "Very nice plumbing."

"And the tools you used were absolutely perfect for the job," Carla said, still puffing.

"I'll be back if you have any more trouble."

"Any time," Carla said. Gene zipped up the front of his coveralls, picked up his toolbox, and left.

Chapter 7

Over the next few months, Carla and Ronnie established a routine. Carla didn't want to be away from her sons any more than was necessary, so she limited her encounters in the city to Tuesday and Thursday evenings and the occasional daytime frolic that didn't keep her from being home when the boys arrived from school. Ronnie used the brownstone other evenings and occasionally on weekends. Every Monday Ronnie and Carla met for lunch, sharing stories and deepening their friendship.

By Thanksgiving Carla had developed a clientele consisting of about a dozen men who regularly perused her album and played out their fantasies with her. A special favorite, her first customer Bryce McAndrews become a regular visitor to the brownstone on 54th Street. At least twice a month, he and Carla got together, ate at a four-star restaurant, and attended a Broadway show or a concert at Lincoln Center. Once they had spent an hour at a Benjamin Britton concert that they both hated. They left after the first selection, when they discovered their mutual dislike of any music composed in the twentieth century. Most evenings they ended up in the paneled room, although occasionally they parted without making love at all.

One afternoon in mid-December Bryce called and told Carla that he wanted to act out an especially elaborate wish of his. He'd make all the arrangements for the following Tuesday and he asked her to leave the brownstone at seven-thirty that evening, setting a key beside the front door, then come back at exactly eight o'clock.

Carla left at the appointed time, had a cup of coffee at a little restaurant on Second Avenue, then returned to the house filled with mounting expectation. Bryce seemed to understand her desires more and more and their appetites matched perfectly. She walked into the front hallway and heard his familiar voice. "Up here," he called from the second bedroom.

When Carla walked into the room, the entire atmosphere had changed. Bryce had replaced the dim lighting with strong, 100-watt bulbs and all of the exotic equipment that could be concealed was out of sight. Bryce wore a white lab coat and had a stethoscope draped around his neck. "Thank you for being so prompt, Miss Barrett, and I'm sorry you haven't been well."

It took only an instant for her to slip into the part and only slightly longer for her to be wet and trembling. "It's been a difficult time," Carla said trying to suppress her growing flush.

"I understand completely." Bryce handed her a light blue paper smock exactly like the one she had worn at her last doctor's appointment. "Step into the bathroom and put this on. I'll be ready for you in a moment."

As she took the smock from him, Carla noticed a narrow, padded table covered with a strip of plain white paper, set up in one corner of the room. Her knees wobbled. Did he know about her "playing doctor" fantasy or was this his own erotic dream? It didn't matter.

In the bathroom it took Carla only a moment to strip off her clothes and put on the smock. "Nothing but the smock," Bryce's voice said through the bathroom door, "and have the opening in the front. I'll need to examine all of you."

Timidly she walked from the bathroom. She realized that the room smelled of antiseptic. "That's a real doctor's examination table," Carla said.

"Of course," Bryce grinned. "And this is a real doctor's office. Now, Miss Barrett, lie down."

She stretched out on the table and the doctor put a pillow under her head. "I hope you're comfortable," he said. "Are you nervous?"

"Maybe a little," Carla said. Barely covered by the scratchy paper gown, she felt exposed, despite the fact that Bryce had seen her nude a dozen times.

The doctor picked up a pencil and pressed the point gently against her upper arm. "There," he said. "I've given you something to relax you. Now let's discuss your symptoms. Any loss of appetite?"

"Unfortunately none that I've noticed."

Bryce ran his hands down her sides. "You've nothing to worry about, Miss Barrett. You have a beautiful body. Any difficulty sleeping?"

They continued bantering for a few moments, then Bryce said, "Are you less anxious? I hope so. That injection I gave you should thoroughly relax you. Your arms should feel very heavy."

The sound of Bryce's voice flowed through Carla's body like warm honey. Although he'd used no real medication on her, she felt almost liquid as she melted into the table. "My arms are very heavy."

"And your legs too. As a matter of fact it's getting very hard to move at all. It's a nice, floaty feeling, but you know you can't move. Close your eyes."

Carla did, slipping further and further into the scenario Bryce was enacting.

"Good girl," he said. He took out some cotton and a bottle of alcohol. He soaked the cotton and pressed it against Carla's upper arm.

The cold was surprising and the smell was enough to transport Carla more deeply into the scene. "That's cold," she whimpered.

"Yes," Bryce purred, "it is. And you want to move away from the cold but you can't. As a matter of fact you can't move at all." He moved the still-wet cotton to the inside of Carla's calf. She wanted to pull away but she couldn't break through the haze of the fantasy. Or she didn't want to.

"You're not frightened, but you can't move. The medicine I gave you is a special blend of exotic drugs. You can see and hear and feel, but you can't move, can't speak, can't resist anything I want to do to you.

"First, your breasts." With almost medical objectivity, he pressed and prodded at her flesh and pulled at the nipples. "Your tits get firm," he said. "Good reaction to stimulus." He used a pair of tweezers to pinch one erect nipple. As Carla's body winced, he said, "That must hurt a bit. It's too bad you can't move. And you can't move, can you?" He used the tweezers to lightly pinch tiny pieces of skin all over her body, nodding as her body reacted. "Very good," he said.

Carla gazed at Bryce but said nothing.

"Next is the temperature test." He reached behind him and picked up a glass full of ice. While Carla watched, he picked up a cube and held it so the icy water dripped on one breast. As the drop trickled down her white skin, he licked up the water with the tip of his tongue. Drip, lick, drip, lick, he alternated ice water and the heat of his tongue. She became accustomed to the routine and closed her eyes. Suddenly the frozen cube pressed firmly against her left nipple. "Owww," she yelled, her body jerking.

"Don't try to move," Bryce said. "It's impossible to overcome the effect of the shot I gave you and it is very harmful to your body when you try to resist. Just hold still and I'll finish the temperature test." He dropped the cube back into the glass and placed the flat of his tongue against her almost-frozen dark-pink bud and held it there as the warmth seeped back into her skin.

"Good," he said as Carla's body relaxed, "you've done very well with this test." He opened the bottom of the gown and slid his fingertips up the inside of Carla's thigh until he reached her cunt. "So wet," he chuckled. "You are excited by these procedures. That's very interesting."

Excited by these procedures? Carla was certainly excited by these procedures, but it was humiliating to know that Bryce could reach between her legs and tell how aroused she had become.

"Let's see. What else excites you?" he said. "I know. Words excite you. Let's just test to see which ones exactly." Keeping one hand on the springy fur between Carla's legs, Bryce leaned close to her ear and whispered, "How about when I tell you that your pussy hair is so soft? Yes. Your cream is flowing so those words must work." He rubbed the wetness around, stroking her clit. "How about when I say 'Your titties are standing up, waiting for my mouth'?" He sucked her upright nipples and continued to agitate her cunt. "What if I tell you that my balls are heavy and my cock is hard, waiting to slide into your pussy? Soon I'll place the tip of my dick against the opening of your greedy slit and push it in ever so slowly."

Carla was lost in a sensual fog, her eyes closed, giving herself to Bryce, hearing his voice and feeling his fingers between her legs. Tremors began deep in her belly and she knew that his manipulation was going to bring her to orgasm.

"You're close to coming," Bryce said. "But I don't want you to just yet." He stopped and got another ice cube. "Let's cool you down a bit." He maneuvered the frosty cube over Carla's pussy lips.

"Oh God, stop," Carla said, forgetting that she supposedly couldn't speak.

"You know the word to use," Bryce said, removing the ice cube, "if you really want me to stop."

"Yes. I do, Bryce," she said, warmth flowing back into her chilled lips. Then she added, "Doctor, please don't do that."

"It's no use asking me to stop," he continued. "The doctor has to do these sexual tests. It's purely scientific."

He's making me crazy, Carla thought. "Please no more." But she wanted more. As much more as Bryce wanted to give her.

Bryce rubbed the cube lightly over Carla's clit, watching her arousal decrease. "Good girl," he said. "Your reaction to this test is excellent." He pushed the cube into Carla's cunt, then pushed two fingers in after it. "You feel hot and cold at the same time," he said. "The sensations must be driving you crazy."

"Ummm," Carla said. Cold water from the melting ice trickled down Bryce's fingers and ran from her cunt down over her ass.

"Maybe you're getting hot enough for the final test," Bryce said.

Final test?

With two fingers buried deep inside of Carla's pussy, Bryce took his other hand and explored the rim of her tightly puckered hole. Then, with both hands moving he leaned down and flicked his tongue over her clit. Fire blazed to and from all the sensitive places he was touching. Hot and throbbing, Carla released, screaming. Every muscle in her lower body spasmed.

"Your body is clenching my fingers," Bryce said, his face buried in her pubic hair. "Come baby," he purred, his hot breath restoking the fires in her pussy. "Keep coming." He drew his fingers from her cunt and quickly moved around the foot of the table and parted the sides of his lab coat. He wore nothing underneath and his arousal announced itself.

As he stood at the foot of the table his cock was at the height of Carla's pussy. He slipped on a condom, then pulled her legs so she slid down the table. He parted her thighs so her soaked cunt pressed against the tip of his cock.

Her juices were still mixed with melted water from the ice. "Not too fast," he told himself, gritting his teeth against the desire to slam his body into hers. "Make this last." His body shook and sweat ran down his chest as he fought for control. He rubbed his sheathed cock against Carla's overheated flesh, then pressed just the tip into her.

She was more excited than she had ever been, yet, because she had already climaxed once, she was able to experience all the nuances of Bryce's body. She could hold herself at a level just below climax, slipping into the ecstasy whenever she wanted to. He opened her inch by inch with his cock, slowly filling her. Occasionally she squeezed her inner muscles and smiled as Bryce shuddered.

When he was fully inside, Bryce stood still for a moment savoring the sensation of being encased in pulsating velvet while the tip of his cock was slightly cold from the remains of the ice. Carla wrapped her legs around Bryce's waist, then pushed her cunt against him driving Bryce's cock still deeper. He could hold still no longer. With panting breaths he clenched his ass muscles and let his body thrust into the slick heat.

"Oh yes," he cried as hot bursts of semen exploded from his penis. "Oh Carla yes." He collapsed, his upper body lying across hers, both breathing hard and trembling. She shuddered as her muscles pulled at him.

Long minutes later they were calmer. "Oh doctor," Carla said with a giggle, "your tests are so educational."

"Zertainly," Bryce said, imitating a thick German accent. "Ve try to be zo zientific." They lay together until Carla's leg began to fall asleep. She moved slightly and Bryce's satisfied cock slipped from her body. As Bryce stood up, he said, "Okay, last one to the shower has to scrub the other, all over."

They made love again in the shower, steaming water pouring over their soapy bodies as Bryce pounded into Carla's cunt from behind.

When he was dressed, Carla said, "You have no idea how much fun our evenings are for me." She stretched on the bed watching his eyes rake her naked body.

"Me too," Bryce said, kissing her on the tip of her nose.

As usual on their evenings together, Carla had arranged for her parents to stay with the boys so she could sleep in the city. "You could stay here tonight," Carla said, reluctantly. Although Bryce still paid her for their evenings together they were also lovers and she sometimes wanted to spend the night with him. But staying here together felt wrong, somehow. Too comfortable. Too married.

"No, but thanks. We both like things just as they are." He counted out five hundred dollars and put it on the table. "No strings."

Carla smiled. "Right," she said, playfully swatting his now-clothed behind. "Let me know when you want to get together again."

"Will do," Bryce said as he walked toward the bedroom door. "Call you soon."

The Village Tavern, known affectionately in Greenwich Village as the fat-factory, was not one of Carla's usual restaurants. It specialized in mammoth hamburgers, great steaks, forty-five varieties of beer, and desserts covered with real whipped cream. Patrons joked that an ambulance stood by at dinner time in case of a heart attack.

The two men who sat at the table in the back of the Village Tavern were not Carla's usual type of client. As she studied them she saw that, except for the fact that one man wore rimless glasses, they looked as alike as two men who weren't related could. Both men were of medium height and build with ruddy complexions and weathered skin. Both men appeared to be in their thirties, with well-muscled arms and upper bodies. Their heads were together and they were deep in conversation.

As Carla approached, the darker of the two obviously said something funny and both men roared. "Which is Dean and which is Nicky?" asked Carla dropping into an empty chair.

Both men looked at Carla, and looked and looked. Carla smiled easily, enjoying their frank admiration of her white cotton man-tailored shirt, western vest, and tight-fitting, stonewashed jeans. She wore a multicolored zuni fetish necklace and matching earrings and had applied little makeup. The two men were silent for a long moment, then spoke simultaneously.

"He's Dean."

"I'm Dean." They laughed together, a warm sound that made Carla imagine how nice it would feel to be so close. "Timmy wasn't kidding when he told me you were a knockout," Dean said. "Until you got here, Nicky and I had been wondering whether this was a dumb idea. Now I think we've done real good."

"Tim told me that you two had some recent good luck," Carla said. Tim Sorenson had called Carla and told her that Dean Gerard and his friend Nicky Romano wanted to employ her for an evening. Except for vouching for Dean's character and setting up the meeting, Tim would tell her nothing else.

"We won fifteen thousand dollars in the lottery. Seventy-five hundred each."

"I've never met a lottery winner before," Carla said. "Congratulations."

"Thanks," Nicky said. The waiter arrived and Dean suggested a German beer that Carla had never heard of. When Carla nodded, Dean held up three fingers and the waiter disappeared.

"Tell me a little about yourselves," Carla said, aware that she was treating them like a pair rather than two individuals.

Dean did the talking. "We both work for the city department of sanitation. Sometimes we toss garbage cans and sometimes one of us drives a truck. In the winter we shovel and plow." No wonder they have such great arms, Carla thought. "We've been doing this for almost fifteen years and we met our first day on the job. Nicky and me are a team."

"Married?"

"Dean is, I'm not," Nicky said. "Not any more."

"And how do you know Tim?" Carla asked. "He told me almost nothing when he called."

Dean took a breath and pushed his glasses toward the bridge of his nose. "I've known Timmy for many years. We met in a beginner's photography class and we've kept in touch ever since." Dean looked at Carla. "I know, I don't look like a photographer but I've been into picture taking since I was a kid."

The waiter put their beers on the wooden trestle table in front of them and listed the specials of the day.

"I'll have the double lamb chops, medium rare, french fries, and a salad with roquefort dressing," Carla said. In for a penny. . . .

"A woman after my own heart," Nicky said. "Make that two."

"Three," Dean said and the waiter disappeared. "You know, this is all a bit strange," he continued, "so let me get to the point and explain what I have in mind. Timmy told me that you're a call girl."

"Dean, that's not a nice thing to say," Nicky said. He turned to Carla. "Sorry, Carla. This is kind of awkward."

"It's okay," Carla said. "I enjoy having sex and fulfilling men's fantasies and I do it for money. I guess that makes me a call girl."

"Fantasies," Dean said. "That's what Timmy said. And I've had a fantasy for as long as I can remember. I want to direct a movie."

"A movie?" Carla said.

"A movie. Just a short thing. Nicky's going to be the male star and we want you to be the girl star."

Carla had a moment to consider the proposal as the waiter arrived with the most enormous chops she had ever seen. When he was gone, Carla took a bite. "Fabulous," she said. "Tell me more about this movie."

"I love to watch X-rated movies and I've always wanted to direct my own," Dean said. "I want to do one that's better than the crap that's out there."

"Don't get us wrong, Carla," Nicky said. "We don't want to sell it or anything. We just want to make it and then watch it ourselves."

"I've never been in a movie," Carla said. "It might be fun. But I don't want to go to my local theater and see my name in lights or my naked body on the screen."

"Of course not. That's not at all what we have in mind," Dean said. "Hey Nicky, can you picture the guys we know watching you naked."

Nicky got a strange look on his face but Carla decided to go along with the idea. "If Tim says that you guys can be trusted, it's fine with me."

"That's terrific." They spent the rest of the meal discussing the film's almost meaningless plot.

As the three finished gigantic pieces of apple pie with homemade vanilla ice cream, Dean reached into his pocket and withdrew an envelope. "For your time," he said. "I hope it's right. Timmy told us about your usual fee, but there are two of us and . . . well. . . ."

Carla put the envelope into her purse without looking inside. "I'm sure it's fine," she said. "Now, where to?"

"I've taken a suite in a hotel," Dean said. "Nicky knows where. I've set up lights and some fancy video stuff I rented but let me have one final check and get ready." He glanced at the dinner check and put a few bills on the table. "You two wait here for a few minutes, then follow along. Come into the room together and we'll take it from there."

Nicky raised his hand to his forehead in a mock salute. "You got it, boss, Mr. Director, sir." He turned to Carla. "I hope this works out."

Carla and Nicky talked for ten minutes then made their way to a suite in the Gramercy Park, an older hotel in the low twenties. As they approached the door, Nicky said, "You know what we're doing?"

"I guess," Carla answered. "It's a little loose."

"We'll fake it." Nicky knocked, then inserted a key in the lock and opened the door. Carla entered and saw the camera, filming their actions. She turned to Nicky, waiting at the door. "I had a nice evening," she said, working herself into the part she was playing. "I enjoyed myself a lot."

"Me too," Nicky said. They were supposed to be coming back from their first date. "Can I come in for a nightcap?"

"I'm kind of tired," Carla said.

"I won't be long. I just don't want the evening to end yet."

Carla and Nicky walked into the sitting room of the two-room suite that Dean had rented. It was done in cream and gold, with accents of light blue and grey. The heavy ivory drapes were tightly drawn and all the lights were lit, supplemented with two bright spotlights aimed at the sofa.

Nicky closed the door and leaned against it. "You know I want you," he said. "Your gorgeous body has been driving me nuts all evening."

Carla's character was supposed to be reluctant, but persuadable. "But we hardly know each other," she said.

"Do you believe in love at first sight?"

Carla laughed. "I believe in lust at first sight."

"Oh sugar," Nicky said. "Let me make love to you."

"Cut," Dean said. "That's great. Let's move to the sofa. Now Nicky, let's say that you and Carla have been making out. Kiss her good, then show me how you get her to start undressing and how you begin touching her."

"This is really weird," Nicky said.

"It's kind of fun," Carla said. "I like being directed, told how to act." She sat on the ivory upholstered couch, ruffled her hair, and extended her arms. "Come here and convince me."

Nicky looked at Dean, shrugged, and sat beside Carla. He kissed her tentatively, brushing his lips against hers. He stroked her hair back from her temples and kissed her forehead. "Hey, Nicky," Dean said. "I don't have endless film. Let's get serious."

"This is making me really uncomfortable," Nicky whispered, his lips against her cheek.

"I understand," Carla answered *soto voce*. "It can be weird having to perform."

"All right," Dean said, "cut. When you whisper I can't hear you. Listen. I gotta take a leak. You two figure out the rest of the show and I'll be right back."

When they were alone, Nicky said, "This seemed to be a terrific idea when Dean dreamed it up. Now, I'm afraid I won't be able to . . . you know. Those guys in the movies are so well hung and seem to get it up whenever. . . ."

"It'll be okay."

"Oh it's not you. I just don't think I can perform on command."

Carla unbuttoned the top button of her shirt, took Nicky's hand and stroked it softly over her breast. "I won't let you embarrass yourself. I promise."

Nicky slid his palm over Carla's erect nipple. "You're very sexy," he said.

"Hey, I've got an idea," Carla said, sitting up. "Let's make Dean tell us exactly what he wants. Move for move. We do nothing unless he tells us to. That sounds extremely sexy to me. And no pressure on either of us."

Nicky took a shaky breath. "You mean that he calls all the shots?" He paused. "Actually, that sounds sexy as hell."

Dean had returned and overheard Nicky's last sentence. "You want me to tell you guys what to do?"

"Right," Carla said. "It's hard to pretend to be part of some story and get turned on at the same time."

"Hummm. Being the director for real. It sounds kinky. The audio will pick up what I say." He paused to think it through. "Telling you to suck and fuck . . . sounds hot."

"Not fucking," Carla corrected. "Making love. Touching, stroking, kissing, licking, you tell us everything. And remember that if we're not hot and ready to fuck when you say so your movie has no final scene and it isn't our responsibility."

"I love a challenge," Dean said. "Okay with you, Nicky?"

"Just so long as you understand that if I don't get hard, it's your fault, not mine."

"Okay. I like this. Let's go into the bedroom." Quickly, Dean moved his lights and video equipment into the bedroom. "Lie on the bed, Carla," he said, "and Nicky beside her." The two did as they were instructed, stretching out on the satin bedspread. "Nicky, kiss Carla on the mouth and slide your hand onto her tit."

Nicky leaned over Carla and gazed into her eyes for a moment. "This really is a turn-on," he said as his lips pressed against hers. He spread his palm over her right breast and kneaded the soft globe. He kissed her mouth, then moved his lips to her ear. "That's right, lick her," Dean said, and Nicky swirled the tip of his tongue into Carla's ear. As he licked, he hummed softly and Carla could feel the vibrations through her entire body.

She twisted, giving Nicky better access to her ear as his hand brushed back and forth against the fabric of the front of her shirt. "Unbutton her blouse," Dean said.

The remaining two buttons came undone easily and Nicky slipped his hand inside. "Pull the blouse open so I can see her undies. I love those shots of breasts in tiny brassieres." Carla was glad she was wearing a palepink lace demicup bra. They'd have their money's worth and more, as much as she could provide.

Dean moved around the bed, peering through the lens of the camera. "Yes," Dean exclaimed. "Beautiful. You've got such great nipples that I can see them through your bra. Don't you agree Nicky?"

"I certainly do." He rubbed her breasts through the lacy fabric.

"Suck one nipple through the lace and make it hard," Dean said and, as Nicky followed his instructions, Dean rounded the bed and crawled across to get a close-up of Nicky's lips on Carla's erect nipple. When he could resist no longer, Dean put the camera down and sucked Carla's other nipple. Two mouths on her breasts was unbelievably erotic.

A little shaky, Dean returned to his camera. "No, no. Mustn't lose my objectivity," he said. "I want to make this good so I can watch it over and over." He positioned himself at the foot of the bed. "Carla, I think you should take Nicky's shirt off, very slowly. And kiss and lick his chest as you do it."

She opened Nicky's shirt and rubbed her hands over his lightly furred skin. She kissed his flat nipples as she eased his plaid shirt from his shoulders. "And yours too, Carla," Dean said. As Carla shrugged out of her shirt, Dean sighed. "Great boobs. Shit, see how they overflow the cups of that tiny bra?" Carla heard the whine of the zoom lens as Dean came in for a close-up of her right breast.

Suddenly, Dean turned off the camera. "I just realized that we're missing a great opportunity here," he said. "Anyone see a TV?"

Seeing none, Carla said, "There must be one. Maybe it's in that wall unit. Why?"

Without comment, Dean found the large-screen TV and connected some wires from the camera to the back. "Now watch. Nicky, suck her nipple again." As Dean started the camera, the picture of Nicky's mouth appeared on the screen.

"Oh God," Carla said. "That's wild."

"Right. You get to star in your own X-rated movie and watch it at the same time. Nicky, feel up her breasts so she can watch your hands massage her."

Carla found it amazingly exciting, feeling Nicky's hands on her body and watching it happen on the screen at the same time. "Okay, take the bra off." Nicky unclasped the bra and dropped it on the floor. There, in full color, were her breasts, with Nicky's dark-skinned hands covering them. "Suck and bite them. Lick them until the nipples are real tight."

Nicky's mouth covered Carla's breasts, softly pulling them to tight peaks. Carla watched the TV screen as Dean moved the camera around, getting different angles of Nicky's mouth and Carla's breasts.

"Cut." Carla smiled as she sensed Nicky's reluctance to stop what they were doing.

"Take the rest of your clothes off, Carla," Dean said, "so I can get some shots of your sweet pussy." She pulled off her jeans and panties and stretched out on the bed, with Nicky beside her. "Now, Nicky, get her wet." He turned his back to adjust his video.

Nicky ran his hand up the inside of Carla's thigh and tentatively touched her lips. "She's already soaked," he said, surprised.

"You make me horny," Carla whispered. She reached down and squeezed the ridge of hot flesh that pressed upward against his belly beneath his jeans. She winked. "You seem to be horny too."

Dean turned the camera back on and focused the lens on Carla's breast. "Spread her legs, Nicky. I want to see your hand on her pussy." The camera panned slowly down her ribs and belly until her cunt filled the screen.

Carla turned and looked at the TV. She had never seen herself like this, open and waiting, ready to be filled, with Nicky's dark, blunt fingers playing idly with her pussy hair. It sent a jolt of pleasure shooting into her depths. She saw Nicky's fingers slide toward her swollen lips and, when he touched her, she could both feel it and see it. It was the most intense sensation she could remember.

Without being told, Nicky pulled off his clothes while the camera watched. His erection was rigid and thick, jutting from a nest of black hair in his groin. Carla smiled. Arousal was no longer a worry for him. She reached out and wrapped her hand around the engorged organ and pulled it until Nicky was sitting on the bed beside her. She turned so her ass was in the air and her head was in his lap.

"I'm going to make you come," she said softly. "And you're going to watch. Look at yourself."

Nicky stared at the TV screen and watched Carla's mouth on his cock. He was both feeling and watching a beautiful woman kissing the head of his cock, then pursing her lips and sucking him into her waiting mouth. He closed his eyes and reveled in the sensations.

When Nicky started to lose control, Carla wrapped her fingers around the base of his erection and squeezed his cock and balls tightly, preventing him from climaxing. She wanted Dean to have great pictures, ones that Nicky would be proud of. Higher and higher Carla forced Nicky, her head bobbing in his lap, sucking his cock yet keeping him from coming.

Finally she looked at the camera and said, "Every good porno flick has a come shot and Nicky's going to be the star of this one." She breathed hot air on the end of his cock while she grasped the shaft with one hand and kept the fingers of the other around the base. "Are you going to watch your own climax?" she asked Nicky.

Dean panned to his friend's face and watched as Nicky's eyes opened and stared at the screen. The camera returned to his cock, covered by Carla's hands. "Watch, baby," she said. "Watch your cock as you shoot beautiful come on my tits." She licked the length of his erection, making the hard shaft shiny and wet. She rubbed just a bit more, then, as his semen boiled from his balls, she released her hold on the base of his cock and moved so his come spurted on her breasts. The camera recorded as thick gobs of goo covered her large tits.

"Shit, Nicky," Dean said as semen erupted from Nicky's cock. "I didn't know you were such a stud. Maybe we should show this to the guys." Finally, Nicky collapsed onto the bed, exhausted.

By the time Carla returned from the shower, fully dressed, Dean had returned all the camera equipment to the cases and Nicky was dressed. "We're going to watch the tape," Dean said. "Are you going to stay?"

"No, I don't think so. I already know how it ends."

While Dean fiddled with the VCR, Nicky walked Carla to the door of the suite. "Thanks," he said. "I doubt that Dean will be able to keep that film to himself and now I'll get some kind of reputation with our friends. I hope you don't mind if your face shows a bit."

"Not at all, as long as it's just your friends. After all, a stud like you should be able to show off a little."

As Nicky watched Carla walk toward the elevator, he said, "Hey Carla, thanks again."

Dennis Stanton was an old friend of Ronnie's and they had spent many enjoyable evenings together. Tonight, however, he had something very unusual in mind and since the evening's entertainment wasn't exactly her taste, Ronnie had suggested that he call Carla. When Carla heard about the engagement, and, of course, the fee, she agreed quickly.

A stretch limo arrived in front of the brownstone at exactly eight o'clock. Dennis helped Carla inside. A man of about fifty, Dennis had deep chocolate-brown eyes and dark hair with wings of silver at the temples. He wore a magnificently tailored midnight-blue tuxedo with a matching tie and cummerband.

"It's nice to meet you," Dennis said softly, sliding the partition window up to prevent the limo driver from overhearing. "It's a short drive to where we're going, so let me get right to the point. Ronnie said she told you what I want."

"She did, but explain again. I want to be sure I understand everything."

"I belong to a sort of unofficial sex club. There are about twenty of us, all men, some married, some not. Once a month we get together and indulge our shared passions. Some men bring women, paid or otherwise, and some don't. The women, of course, must be of a particular type."

"I know. Submissive."

"Exactly. And if you know Ronnie, you know that that's not her."

Carla smiled and nodded. She couldn't picture Ronnie bowing her head and submitting meekly while men used her body. To Carla, however, it sounded irresistible.

"Anyway," Dennis continued, "I've never brought a woman to one of our partices . . . until tonight. If you're willing, of course."

"I am, as long as condoms and safe words are agreed to in advance."

"They are," Dennis said. "No whips or anything like that, except with the permission of the woman involved. The word 'Yellow' is a temporary safe word, in case you want to stop things for a minute, say if you're cold or your foot's asleep. 'Red' is an absolute stop and anyone disregarding it is asked to leave our club and is not allowed back." His soft smile made him look a bit like Cary Grant. "Every member values membership too much to risk banishment so should you say so, everything stops. Is that all right with you?"

Carla took a deep breath and nodded. It was hard to reconcile Dennis's handsome, open expression with the dark nature of the evening's entertainment, but as she thought about the sex party she was about to attend, she shivered.

"Good. From now on you will follow my directions without question. You will keep your eyes downcast and speak only when spoken to. Do you agree?"

Carla started to answer, then decided to begin her part immediately. She looked at the floor of the limo and nodded.

"Good girl," Dennis said. "Are you wearing the clothes I sent you?" When she nodded, he said, "Then take off your dress."

Quickly, Carla pulled off her navy knit dress. Beneath it she wore a tight, crotchless, dark blue satin teddy with openings at the front of each breast so her nipples were exposed. Old-fashioned dark blue-and-white lace garters held up her blue net stockings and she wore very high-heeled blue satin pumps. She placed her dress on the seat beside her, folded her hands in her lap, and stared at Dennis's shoes.

"Very nice," Dennis said, staring at her scantily dressed body. "Your clothes will be here waiting for you when we return." He looked her over carefully then continued, "You really are gorgeous and you seem to have the proper attitude." He pinched one of Carla's nipples hard and, although she winced slightly, she didn't make a sound or look up. "Yes indeed," Dennis said. "I will be proud to present you to my friends."

She knew it was silly but Carla found she was pleased that he thought her worthy of the evening's entertainment. "Now," Dennis said, "a few additions." He buckled a leather cuff with a large metal ring attached around each of Carla's wrists and ankles. A slightly narrower cuff went around her neck and Dennis turned it so the ring was in the back. He attached a short chain to the ring and let it fall, cold and heavy, down her back between her shoulder blades to her waist. "Now," he said, "remember 'Red' is the safe word." He took a small padlock from his pocket, drew her arms behind her back, and locked the rings on her wrist cuffs to the end of the chain. Carla wasn't in any physical discomfort, but, with her arms secured behind her she was awkward and off balance.

"Good," Dennis said, as the car pulled to a stop. He buttoned a long, full-length, royal blue evening cape around Carla's shoulders and, as the chauffeur held the door, they got out. Carla quickly realized that despite her immobilization, to a bystander she looked like any woman might, going to a formal function.

Her head lowered, she moved her eyes from side to side and realized that they were entering the lobby of a very exclusive hotel, although she wasn't sure which one. They entered the 'Penthouses Only' elevabor. Dennis said, "Only members and their ladies will be permitted up here. We've taken the entire floor for the evening."

The elevator doors swept open onto a small vestibule. Her eyes on the carpet, Carla followed Dennis through the only open door into a large living room.

"Ah, Dennis," a man said. "I see that you've brought a young lady for us. Wonderful."

Something about the gathering made Carla shiver with expectation. Although she'd read about them in magazines, she'd never believed that clubs like this really existed.

"Gentlemen," a man said, tapping a tiny hammer on a miniature gong, "now that everyone's here, the meeting will come to order. Bring the women forward."

Dennis propelled Carla to the center of the room where she stood, eyes downcast, with two others. One woman was a statuesque blond with light blue eyes and dark red lips and the other a petite black woman with very short fluffy hair and skin the color of taffy. The women were dressed in capes similar to Carla's, each in a different color. Carla looked around as best she could without raising her eyes and estimated there were about a dozen men, of varying ages and physical types, all in formal attire.

"Do the women know the correct forms of address?" the leader asked. He was of Mediterranean origin, with very dark hair and eyes and olive skin.

"Not mine, sir," Dennis said. "I felt it was your place to instruct her."

"Ladies," the leader said. "For tonight I will be your king and you will address me as 'your majesty' or 'sire.' "

"Yes, your majesty," Carla said. She heard the other woman say the same thing.

"All the other men will be addressed as 'my lord.' "

"Yes, sire."

"Obedience is your most important function. You will follow the orders of any man here, without question. The safe words are 'Red' and 'Yellow.' Have these been explained?"

Carla heard voices assuring the leader that the women had been told. "You understand that you must use these words if you feel any discomfort, either physical or mental. I emphasize the word must. If we find that you've been too polite to use the safe words when you should have, then everything will stop and you'll be escorted home. And that would be a shame."

"Yes, sire," Carla said.

"Now, will the gentlemen who brought our gifts for the evening please unwrap them." With a flourish, the capes were pulled from the three women's shoulders. Carla could see that the other women were cuffed and chained the same way she was and dressed in teddies, stockings, and shoes that matched their capes.

The leader started with the blond, whose cape and teddy were a soft rose. "Vivian," he said, "you're as beautiful as ever." The leader raised his right arm and slapped her hard on her naked ass.

"Thank you, sire," she said, a small smile playing around the corners of her mouth.

"For the two new men here tonight," the leader said, "let me explain that Vivian likes her pleasure a little rough. Sometimes she deliberately disobeys commands and must be disciplined. Those who enjoy that type of play may want to stay with her for the evening."

He moved to the tiny black woman. "Shanna," he said, "we haven't seen you for quite a while. And I see that you've cut your hair."

"Yes, sire. I sincerely hope you approve."

He tangled his fingers in her short fluff, dragged her head back, and kissed her hard. "I do," he said finally. "Down." Shanna clumsily fell to her knees despite her chains and pressed her forehead against the leader's shoe. "As you see, Shanna is very well trained and will gladly do whatever she's told to. We are all happy to have her back with us this evening."

He turned to Dennis. "This one is new. Thank you for bringing her." To Carla he said, "Do you have a name?"

Carla looked at Dennis from the corner of her eye and when he nodded, she said, "Carla."

"Carla what?"

She knew he wasn't asking for her last name. Softly, without lifting her eyes, she said, "Carla, sire."

"Very good. Very good indeed." He turned to the men gathered around. "Blindfold them."

Someone tied a soft cloth firmly around Carla's head. She heard the rustling and shuffling of people moving around, and the hum of lowered voices. Suddenly someone pinched her left nipple, which was proudly standing out through the opening in the front of her teddy. She gasped, but didn't move. "Nice," a voice said. Then several hands slid over her breasts, legs, and buttocks, the sensations heightened by Carla's lack of sight. "Very nice," another voice said.

Carla recognized the leader's voice. "Mark, I assume that you and Harry want to take Shanna." There was a pause, then he continued, "Good. Take her into room two. Paul, take Vivian across the hall."

"Thank you," a man's voice answered.

"I want to break in our newest guest myself," the leader said. "The rest of you," he laughed, "pick your pleasure. You have three lovely ladies from which to choose."

Carla was flattered at having been chosen by the leader. She had no idea how many other men were in the room. Someone thrust one finger between her legs. "She's very wet," a man said.

"Wonderful," the leader said. "She's a lovely piece, Dennis. You've done an excellent job."

"Thank you. Shall I undress her for you?"

The leader must have nodded because someone loosened the laces of the teddy and the garment fell from her body. Hands were everywhere, probing, stroking.

"She has the most fantastic boobs," a voice said. "May I have them?"

"I see no reason why not, Chet. Prepare her." Carla's hands were unlocked and a belt was buckled tightly around her waist. Her wrist cuffs were refastened above her elbows and then attached to rings at the sides of the belt. Her upper arms were now efficiently attached to her sides, leaving her lower arms free. Then she was pressed down until she was lying face up on a pad on the floor. Someone quickly spread her legs and fastened her ankle cuffs so she was held wide open. Hands checked to be sure that her blindfold was still in place.

"Thank you," the man called Chet said. Chet straddled her waist and squeezed her full breasts. "These are so big and full," he whispered. "I must have them." Hands rubbed something cool and slick all over her chest.

"Chet's in heaven," a voice said.

"If he's not careful he'll come before he's even started," the leader said, laughing.

"A hundred says he'll come in under two minutes." Carla heard a mix of voices.

"Hold them," Chat said, oblivious to what was going on around him. He grabbed Carla's wrists and pressed her hands against the sides of her breasts. "I said hold them!"

Carla had no idea what he wanted, but held her mounds the way Chet's hands showed her. Suddenly, she felt Chet's hard cock thrusting between her tits. He was fucking her breasts, driving his cock so hard that on each stroke it pressed against her chin. Now that she understood, Carla held her breasts tightly together, making a narrow channel for Chet's hard cock. He bucked against her breasts until he screamed and spurts of come covered Carla's chin and chest.

"One minute, forty-two seconds." There was a round of applause.

Almost immediately, Chet was lifted from Carla's body and damp cloths whipped over her chest and face. "You have great tits for fucking," the leader said. "How's your mouth?"

"I hope I am worthy, sire," Carla said, licking her lips.

"Open for me," he roared. When she did, he filled her mouth with his erection, pressing it all the way into her throat. The velvety length slid in and out of her mouth. She sheathed her teeth with her lips and tightened around his shaft.

"He'll come even faster than Chet," a voice said.

"Squeeze my balls, bitch," the leader snapped, and Carla did as she was instructed, tonguing and sucking until the leader came. She eagerly swallowed every drop.

"My Lord, she's a great little cocksucker," the leader said when he regained his voice. He rubbed her wet pussy. "And she's loving it all." Low voices said things that Carla couldn't quite hear. Then she heard the leader's voice. "Dennis. Since you brought her, you may play first."

Play?

"If you have no objections," Dennis said, releasing her arms, "I'd like to remove her blindfold."

"If you like." When the cloth was removed from her eyes, Carla blinked several times, then glanced around the room from where she lay on the pad. Her ankles were being held open by two men who sat so they had a full view of her wide-open pussy. Another man sat on a chair, intently watching her face. The leader lay near her hip, his head propped on his hand. She couldn't see Dennis until he walked around to her other side, something in his hand.

"Carla, darling," he said. "I have some toys for us to play with." Dennis opened a large black-and-red lacquered box and showed Carla the contents. Inside, a collection of dildos was arranged according to size. The smallest was about as slender as her pinky, the largest almost two inches around. "Let's see how much you can take." He inserted three fingers into her wet pussy, then selected the next to the largest dildo.

It looked too big to ever fit inside her, but as Dennis slid it into her waiting body Carla realized that she was filled completely. "Yes, that's just right."

Carla swallowed hard, trying not to lose control in front of all these men. She saw Dennis select a dildo about the size of his thumb from the other end of the collection. "How's your ass?" he asked.

"Virginal," was the only answer she could think of.

"Fantastic," the leader said. "Dennis, you're a lucky man."

As Dennis spread some lubricant on the dildo two men slid Carla's body forward so her knees were bent. One of the men rubbed cold, slippery gel around her rear hole, then Dennis pushed in the slender dildo until the flange at the base rested against her cheeks. Another man pulled a thin piece of fabric mesh from the belt in the back, and stretched it between her cheeks and across both dildos to anchor them securely in place. The mesh snapped to connectors at the front of the belt.

"How do you feel? Tell us, Carla."

"Strange. Filled, yet empty. Wanting. . . ."

"Ah, Dennis," the leader said. "A gem." There was a round of quiet applause, either for her or for Dennis.

Dennis reached into the box and pulled out a pencil-shaped rod. Suddenly, a humming sound filled the room and, as Carla watched, Dennis knelt on a pillow and inserted the wand through the mesh and into the dildo in her cunt. Shafts of pure pleasure coursed through her body and her hips bucked as much as her shackled ankles would permit. "Ahhh," she cried.

Dennis moved the dildo so the pulses touched every inside part of her. As one dildo pressed against the other, the vibrations flowed from her cunt to her ass. Dennis withdrew the rod, then slid the vibrating tip around her pussy, through her soaked folds "Watch her," he said, "as I make her come."

"We will," the leader said. "I love it when a woman loses control."

Watch her come? It was humiliating, but erotic. She closed her eyes. "No," Dennis said. "Watch us as we watch you. I command your body and I can make you come whenever I want. All these men will be watching you and they'll know exactly when you lose control."

One man unzipped his pants, took his erect cock in his hand, and fondled his straining shaft. He caught Carla's eye and grinned, licking his lips.

"Are you ready, gentlemen?" Dennis asked.

"Ready, Dennis."

"Good. Carla, I'm going to make you come now, and you have no choice. We're all going to watch your hips buck and see your face as your climax fills your body. We will all know that you cannot resist."

Oh God, Carla thought. She was so hot that her entire body was quaking. Although it didn't feel right to want to be so controlled, she knew that he was right. She would come and Dennis knew it.

Dennis fitted the vibrator into the dildo in her ass and slowly moved it in deeper. "Now, Carla. Come for us." He rubbed her clit. "Keep your eyes open and watch these men come as they see you lose control."

She couldn't help it. She screamed as one of the strongest orgasms she had ever experienced took over her entire body.

"Oh fuck," a voice yelled. Carla looked up at the man stroking his cock and saw semen spurt from the tip and spatter on his hand and his pants legs.

Dennis turned the vibrator off, but left it inside Carla's body. He pulled down his pants and shorts and threw them on the bed. "Touch your pussy and make your hand wet." Carla did and Dennis took her slippery hand and placed it on his cock. "Hold your hand still so I can fuck it. Do it for me, Carla."

She held his cock in her hand and squeezed. Dennis moved his hips, forcing his erection through her tight fingers. Although she didn't move her hand, she tensed her fingers in rhythm, milking the come from his cock. "Oh that's so good," he said, groaning. "But it's too fast." Carla enjoyed rushing him, forcing him to come as he had forced her. She knew just where to press and squeeze. When he came she could feel the pulses throughout his cock.

The leader reached over, unsnapped the mesh, and pulled the dildos from Carla's passages. "Turn her over," he said, and the men quickly removed her shackles, turned her, then replaced her bindings so that she lay face down on the pad. The leader placed a pillow under her hips so her rear was in the air, then parted her cheeks with his fingers and rubbed more lubricant around her puckered hole. "So. You have never been fucked in the ass," he said, unrolling first one, then a second condom over his cock. Although he wasn't very large, Carla was afraid.

"No, sire," Carla said, tensing. She had always been a bit leery about anal sex and, so far hadn't been asked for it by any of her clients. Dildos were one thing, but she was unsure that she wanted to go this far. The leader watched her face as she considered.

"I won't come inside of you," he said, gently, "and I'm always very careful."

Although she had climaxed, Carla was still excited and intrigued by the idea of being fucked in a new way. She knew that she could call things off whenever she wanted so she deliberately relaxed her muscles and closed her eyes.

Sensing her agreement, the leader pressed his slick covered cock against her anus. As her body tensed and relaxed, he pushed, slowly forcing his hard penis into her rear passage.

"Oh, sire," she whispered. "That's so strange."

"It is good?"

She hesitated. "Yes, sire."

When he was as deeply inside as he could get, the leader took his index finger and rubbed her clit.

Blazing heat slashed through her body and orgasm took control again, her rear muscles clenching rhythmically on the leader's penis. "Yes! Yes!" Her orgasm went on and on, until she had no more to give.

"Ahhh," the leader said, pushing against her as she came. "Wonderful." He pulled his still-hard cock from her body, peeled off one condom, had his men turn her, and then he plunged his sheathed cock into her pussy, slamming it into her until he suddenly screamed, and spasmed inside her.

Later, when they had all cleaned up and were ready to leave, the leader kissed Carla deeply. "You were a marvelous addition to the evening's entertainment, darling. We'll be sure to let you know when we meet again. Please feel free to join us, whether Dennis can attend or not."

"Thank you, sire," she said, wrapping her dark blue cape around her naked body.

Dennis held her around the waist. "If she can be here, sire, you can be sure I'll bring her."

Carla smiled as she stepped into the limo.

Chapter 8

Ronnie and Carla were in the sunny kitchen of the brownstone finishing the last of a pint of chocolate-mint frozen yogurt. Falling snow created miniature drifts on the railing outside the living room window.

"Is something bothering you?" Carla asked.

"Jack's home."

"That's great," Carla said. Ronnie's husband had been overseas for the last month. "Isn't it?"

"Oh it's wonderful to see him, if only briefly." Ronnie put her dish on the coffee table and was silent.

"Come on, give," Carla said. "Trouble?"

Ronnie took a deep breath. "No, not really. Not anything I can put my finger on. It's just that, after what you and I do here, sex with Jack seems so ordinary."

"Ordinary?"

"You know. We fuck quickly and hungrily, and then he talks about business: oil, rock formations, three-dimensional computer models, helicopter surveys, whatever. We never talk about us, really. Our lives."

"That's part of the problem of being apart so much. You have so little day-to-day contact that you live in different places. Mentally, I mean. When my folks lived in Florida briefly a few years ago, my mother used to insist that I call at least once a week. She said that when you talk frequently all the everyday stuff is important, but when you only talk occasionally, it's hard to find anything worth mentioning."

"That's true, I guess. It's also the sex."

"No rushing across airports and fucking in the back seat of the car?"

Ronnie's laugh was warm and rich. "Lots of that. We're good together but it's just ordinary, somehow."

"That figures."

"Huh?"

"Of course sex with Jack is ordinary, unless you work hard at it. Everything we do here is exciting, first times with new people, new fantasies, toys, games, whatever. But it's just the same old Jack. Nothing new."

"I guess."

"Have you ever played fantasy games with him?"

Ronnie thought. "Not recently."

"Well, take your own advice. Do what we always suggest that our clients do. Let your mind wander. You're one of the most skilled women I know at reading other men and their sexual desires. Read yours and his, for a change."

"You know, you make a lot of sense."

"Of course I do. I've learned from an expert. Do the two of you have time tonight?"

"Unfortunately, no. Not for a month or so. He's gone again."

Ronnie looked so forlorn that Carla quickly changed the subject. "You know, I've had quite an education over the last three months so now I think it's time for you to tell me about that wild cruise you went on last summer."

Ronnie licked the last of the yogurt from her spoon and dropped it into her bowl. "Yes, I suppose it is. Okay. You make coffee and I'll tell all."

They wandered into the kitchen and Carla got the coffee from the fridge. While she set up the filter, Ronnie started her tale.

"It all began almost four years ago with Bob Skinner. He looked through my album and when he found the picture of me in that stern teacher outfit, he reacted immediately. We came back here and I disciplined naughty little Bobby who couldn't get his lessons right.

"A few weeks later, he selected the photo of me in that leather outfit holding the whip, and said, 'Would you be her for me, ma'am?' In that scenario, he calls me Mistress Ronnie. We've played both those fantasies frequently and he really gets off by being slapped around and made to do things."

"And that's what you did on the cruise?" Carla said, pouring water into the coffee maker. "Be Mistress Ronnie and whip him?"

"We discovered very early that it's not the pain that turns him on, although Bobby loves it when Miss Gilbert hits him with a ruler. Mostly he loves to feel powerless, to know that he must submit to all of my demands without question. He's hard all the time until I let him come.

Some women don't let their subserviants come at all, but I make sure that Bobby climaxes every time we're together. Eventually."

"I'm so curious," Carla said, settling at the country kitchen table across from Ronnie, the room filling with the smell of brewing coffee. "Tell me about the cruise. How do they set it up? Aren't there other people on the boat?"

"Two couples started this group," Ronnie explained, "and they set up each cruise. We use the same ship, the *Atlantic Voyager* each year. It's small and they set aside a special area for just us, off-limits to the rest of the passengers: a private dining room, secluded deck space, and so on. And our cabins are in a roped-off area. The crew knows what we do and only those who've agreed to ignore what goes on work in our section." She sighed. "That caused an unusual situation this time, but I'll get to that later."

"How many people go on this cruise?"

"There are usually about thirty couples, most like Bob and me, a dominant mistress and her servant. A few are men with submissive women. We use common sense and rules, like you and I do with our customers. Everyone gives and gets pleasure and that's all that matters to any of us."

Carla nodded. Since she had gotten into power and control fantasies, first with Bryce and then with Dennis and the sex club, she had a much better understanding of the intense eroticism of dominance and submission.

"Some of the couples are into heavier activities than Mistress Ronnie and Bob. Some get into heavy pain and whips, shoe licking, and other things that Bob doesn't enjoy. But each of us knows our partner's tastes and we cater to them, and to ourselves. And we always use safe words."

"Are there many . . . professionals like us there?"

"Some are part-time relationships like Bob and mine, and some are married couples or partners who live together and are into dominant fantasies either full- or part-time. But both partners enjoy their roles and love the chance to submerge themselves in eroticism for a week."

"Okay," Carla said, pouring the steaming coffee into mugs. "Tell me everything."

"When we first arrived, Bob unpacked and put away our clothes while I wandered around our area of the ship. I ran into several women I remembered from the previous year and we sat on deck and discussed a few special activities we had planned. I have to tell you that talking about the upcoming week got me going. I couldn't wait to return to the cabin. When I arrived at our stateroom Bob was prepared."

* * *

"Everything's ready, Mistress," Bobby said as Ronnie walked back into the spotless cabin. He had arranged the closets carefully and Ronnie's clothes were all hanging or neatly folded. He had put his few outfits in a bottom drawer. He had set out two lightweight paddles on the small table. Several brown-paper-wrapped packages sat on the dresser where he had been instructed to put them. He had no idea what was inside but knowing Ronnie's creativity, curiosity made his cock hard.

"Very nice," she said and Bobby glowed with pride. "Are you ready as well?" Ronnie asked. She was dressed in a soft pink sleeveless blouse and a full deep blue peasant skirt. She wore high-heeled sandals over her bare feet. Her toenails, like her fingernails, were painted deep red.

"Yes, Mistress," he said, staring at the floor. Ronnie circled Bobby examining his outfit. He had changed since arriving on shipboard and now wore only a pair of extremely tight black spandex shorts that enclosed his erect cock. He had fastened a leather collar around his neck and he wore a green band around his right bicep signifying his servitude. His feet were bare and he stared at his naked toes.

Ronnie patted the giant bulge in the front of his shorts. "My goodness. Have you been thinking about the mysterious packages? Have you been wondering what's inside?"

"Yes, Mistress."

"Well, you'll find out." She patted his groin again. "And you'll be glad."

"Thank you, Mistress. Is there anything you desire of me?"

"Yes. I think I'll let you pleasure me before dinner."

"Thank you, Mistress. How would you like me to do that?"

Ronnie glared at him. "You shouldn't have to ask. You should know how to please me by now." She walked to a small chair and sat down. "After you've done your job, you'll have to be punished for your lapse of understanding."

Bobby knew that there was no way that he could have guessed how to please Mistress Ronnie at that particular moment, but the punishment was part of the excitement. And anticipating the punishment was another. But now he would give his mistress pleasure and there was nothing better than that.

"Down," she said and Bobby got down on his hands and knees and crawled toward her. "I need my feet massaged."

Carefully Bobby removed each of Ronnie's shoes and placed them under the table in the corner of the room. Then he sat at his mistress's feet and pressed his fingers deeply into her arch, which he knew she loved. He massaged each foot and calf, then paid careful attention to each toe until his fingers ached. Slowly Ronnie relaxed. "Mistress, may I go further?" he asked, knowing better than to look her in the eye.

"I think so," she answered, excited by Bobby's submissive behavior. "But first, take off my panties." When he reached for her undies, she added, "With your teeth."

He looked startled, but quickly addressed himself to the task. "Yes, Mistress," Bobby said. He rolled Ronnie's skirt up around her waist and, as he grasped the elastic of her bikini panties with his teeth, he could smell her musky aroma. She wanted him and that made him happy. He jerked at the elastic.

"Ouch!" Ronnie said, slapping him sternly on the shoulder. "Be gentle!"

"I'm sorry, Mistress." He pulled at the waistband gently, shifted to the other side, and pulled again. Ronnie moved her rear so he could slowly maneuver her panties over her hips, down past her knees, and off. Bobby picked up the wisp of dark blue silk with his teeth and placed it neatly on the bed. He gazed at Ronnie's cunt, newly shaved and now exposed for his viewing. There was something demanding about a shaved pussy and it excited Bobby so much that his cock became even more uncomfortable inside the tight shorts. But, of course, he knew that that was not Mistress Ronnie's concern.

Bobby massaged Ronnie's calves and thighs, reveling in both her relaxation and her building sexual excitement. "Mistress may I?" he asked, flexing his cramped fingers.

Ronnie shifted her hips to the edge of the chair and nodded. Bobby stroked the inside of each thigh, approaching but not touching her bare pussy. He brushed his mistress's outer lips with the tip of his finger, then with the tip of his tongue. "Please, Mistress."

"Please what?"

"Mistress, may I lick your clit?"

"All right," she purred.

Bobby knew how to please his mistress. He licked and sucked like a man possessed, his tongue and fingertips everywhere at once. He slid two fingers deep into her pussy and sawed them in and out. When he added a third finger and simultaneously sucked her clit, her muscles spasmed almost immediately. "That's so good," she moaned. "Don't stop."

He smiled. She knew he wouldn't stop until he had given her all the pleasure it was possible to give. He licked and stroked, adjusting his movements to her excitement level. Leaving his fingers quietly inside Ronnie's body, Bobby soothed her until she was calm, and then pulled his hands away.

"May I get you a glass of water?" he asked.

When she nodded, he opened a bottle of spring water he had placed in a bucket and poured her a glass.

"That was very good," Ronnie said, taking a long drink and patting Bobby on the head like a pet. "But there's still the matter of your punishment."

"Yes, Mistress."

"Since your tongue was so talented, you may pick the instrument you prefer."

"Thank you, Mistress," Bobby said, picking up a Ping-Pong paddle and handing it to Ronnie. "My pants, Mistress?"

"You may leave them on," Ronnie said.

Without another word, Bobby lay across his mistress's lap, his spandex-covered bottom ready for Ronnie's skillful application of the paddle. "Since I'm in a very good mood," she said, "I think ten will suffice for the moment."

"Thank you, Mistress."

The first three were light slaps and, with the covering of the tightly stretched shorts, Bobby felt only a general tingle. The next three were heavier, making his body jerk slightly with each one. Swats number seven and eight were harder still, stinging his ass and forcing his hard cock against Ronnie's thighs. Ronnie pulled the spandex down and administered the final two swats with all her strength on his bare cheeks. She pulled the stretchy fabric back up and patted his inflamed bottom.

"Mistress, please," Bobby said, his body quivering.

"Please what?"

"Please, I want to come. I'm so excited."

"Are you my good boy?" Ronnie asked, moving so her thighs rubbed his swollen member.

"Yes, Mistress."

"What if I say no?" She usually denied him any release for several hours. The women liked their slaves to be constantly erect, anxious to please in order to be allowed to climax.

"Oh sweet Jesus," Bobby said, sweat forming on his forehead.

Ronnie reached underneath him and squeezed him tightly. "Is that better?"

"Yes, Mistress," he said, although both of them knew it was not.

"You may come," Ronnie told him.

"My shorts?"

"Too bad. After you spurt they'll be all sticky inside." She smiled. "Of course, for the rest of the day, as you move, you'll be reminded of my generosity."

"Thank you, Mistress."

"Touch it yourself."

Standing in front of Ronnie's chair, Bobby rubbed the length of his rock-hard cock through the tight elastic fabric. When she sensed that he was almost ready to climax, Ronnie picked up the paddle and swatted his ass. He came, screaming.

For the rest of the afternoon, Bobby followed Ronnie around, sitting at her feet as she lounged with other women, fetching drinks and snacks for her and her friends, and watching the way the other women treated their slaves. He was so lucky, he realized, that Mistress Ronnie knew exactly what he liked.

That evening, at dinner, he cut Ronnie's meat and fed her, waiting until she was finished with her meal before he ate anything. The cruise ship staff discretely ignored the goings on, although one busboy stared longingly at Ronnie.

After dinner, three of the women and their slaves put on a show. The men danced, slowly stripping, then one of the men was whipped by the other two under the direction of the women.

Bobby took part in a contest to see which of four naked men could hold out the longest against the sexual teasing of a woman who looked like an in-the-flesh Barbie Doll, with huge breasts and a tiny waist. The woman whose slave lost the contest and spurted semen all over the stage dragged the hapless man back to their cabin for what would undoubtedly be a long lesson in self-control. Ronnie praised Bobby for his ability to restrain himself and, as a reward, let him fuck her with a large dildo.

The following morning, Bobby unwrapped the packages Ronnie had brought. Inside one he found a flanged anal plug and in another a harness to both control his cock and keep the dildo in place. Ronnie lubricated the plug and filled his ass with it. Using the many buckles, she fitted the harness so that it held his balls away from his body, showed off his erect cock and held the dildo deep inside his ass. For the entire afternoon, he wore nothing else so that everyone in their part of the ship could examine his body and discuss his excitement level.

About four days into the cruise, Bobby was feeding Ronnie lunch when she noticed the busboy staring intently at her. He was in his late teens and of medium height with shoulder-length sun-bleached blond hair held with a rubber band at the nape of his neck and pale blue eyes that seldom left her hands. As she thought about it, Ronnie realized that he had been watching her since the week began. As he stared, she quite deliberately poured the contents of her water glass into an empty cup beside her and when Bobby tried to refill it, she waved him away.

"Young man," she said, pointing at the busboy, "I need more water."

The other two couples at the table stared at her, obviously curious as to what was going on.

"Certainly," the busboy said, fetching the pitcher. When Bobby looked crestfallen, Ronnie said, "I know you like serving me but don't worry. You'll be rewarded later." She pointed to an area on the floor beside her chair and Bobby sat down.

As the busboy arrived with the water pitcher, Ronnie said, imperiously, "Pour very slowly and don't spill a drop."

"Yes, ma'am."

"You've been watching me," she said as the young man poured the water, his hand unsteady.

"Yes ma'am." The glass was about half full.

"Don't stop pouring," she said, unzipping the front of his black slacks. His hard cock sprung free, sticking out lewdly. She wrapped her hand around it and held tightly. The busboy's hand began trembling so much he spilled water on the table. "You spilled," Ronnie said.

"I'm terrible sorry, ma'am," the young man said.

"What's your name?" Ronnie asked, still holding his erection.

"Mike," he answered, gazing at Ronnie's filled water glass.

"Well, Mike, you've been very careless." Ronnie looked at the other two women and their subservants, all of whom were watching the scene before them intently. "What should we do with careless workers, Mike?"

"They should be punished."

"I agree," Ronnie said. "What are your duties for the rest of the afternoon?"

"I'm off duty at two and I don't have to serve again until dinner."

"Oh, you'll have to serve again before that." Ronnie glanced at her watch. Quarter of two. "Good. Report here to me at two-oh-one sharp."

"B-b-but I have to change out of my uniform. That will take at least five m-m-minutes."

"Two-oh-one. And I don't like to be kept waiting." She gave his hard cock a final squeeze.

Zipping his pants, Mike scurried away.

"May we stay and see the show?" one of the women asked.

"Of course," Ronnie said. The two women moved to the far side of the table, their men at their feet. Ronnie's heart was pounding. She particularly enjoyed the thrill of a first encounter with a man who wanted to be dominated. She looked at Bobby, sitting quietly at her feet. Since he was paying for the week, she had to be sure this was all right with him. "Yes?" she whispered. From the smile of his face, she knew it was fine.

Precisely at two-oh-three, Mike arrived in the small dining room dressed in jeans and a sweatshirt. His breathlessness was a result of either running from the kitchen or his excitement. Ronnie purposefully looked at her watch. "You're two minutes late."

"I did the best I could."

"Let's understand a few things. First, I am Mistress Ronnie and you will always address me that way."

Mike rubbed the palms of his hands down the thighs of his slacks and swallowed hard. "Yes, Mistress Ronnie."

"Good. Second, you will never look me in the eye. Your gaze must never be above my waist." Mike's eyes dropped. "Third, you will never wear anything from the waist up or the ankles down in my presence unless I expressly tell you to." When Mike didn't move, she added, "Is there any problem with that?"

"No, Mistress." As rapidly as he could, he pulled off his sweatshirt, kicked off his shoes, and dragged off his socks.

"I love the look of bare toes. Wiggle yours for me." He did.

"Have you ever been with someone like me before?"

"Yes, mistress." He hesitated and Ronnie motioned for him to continue. "Her name was Mistress Gail and she was my neighbor for a few months about a year ago. We were together only a couple of times."

"Good enough. Then you understand what is expected." Ronnie reached out and grabbed Mike's crotch. "Why me?"

Mike trembled. "You're very strong, and very beautiful. . . ."

"And . . . ?"

"And you treat your slave the way I'd like to be treated."

Ronnie removed her blouse and Mike stared at her bra, which had zippers up the center of each cup. "Unzip me with your teeth."

Hesitantly, Mike knelt down and took the tab of the left zipper between his front teeth. He pulled gently until one puckered brown nipple poked through the opening. "Bobby," Ronnie said, "the other."

Bob quickly complied. Ronnie placed one hand on the back of each head and forced one mouth to each breast. "Suck," she said, "and maybe I'll reward the one who does the best job." Ronnie leaned back, submerged in the sensation of two mouths on her body. "Nice," she said. "You are each doing a fine job."

Ronnie looked at the two other women who had been intently watching the performance. Each of them had bared her breasts and had her slave servicing her nipples.

"Bobby," Ronnie said, waving the two men away, "you know how I like my pussy licked. Instruct Mike on the proper procedure." She slid forward on the chair until her hips were at its edge. When she parted her thighs, the two men saw that she wore no panties.

As Mike knelt between her spread legs, Bobby said, "See how wet she is. Doesn't she smell fantastic?"

Bobby showed Ronnie's newest servant how to stroke her inner thighs, flick his tongue over her swollen lips, and use his fingers to give her maximum pleasure. "Now," Bobby said, pointing to her clit, "rub her right there, just hard enough to make her feel it."

"Ummm," Ronnie purred. "So good."

To Bobby, this situation was unique, and incredibly erotic. He was not quite a servant, but not a master either. And he was anxious to show the newest slave how to satisfy his mistress.

"You're doing well," Bobby said, slightly jealous of Mike's ability to please. "She likes three fingers in her pussy if she is going to come." He hesitated. "Mistress. May I touch you as well?"

Ronnie nodded and Bobby took one nipple in each hand and pinched the swollen tips. With Bobby's hands on her tits, Mike's tongue lapping her pussy, and his fingers deep inside her cunt, Ronnie came. Her body jerked so hard that the two men had to struggle to stay connected.

"Oh, splendid," Ronnie said when her breathing returned to normal. She smiled at the two other women, each of whom was having her pussy serviced. "Are you very horny?" she asked her slaves.

"Yes, Mistress," they said in unison.

"Then strip. Quickly."

When they were naked, she said, "Face each other." The two men stood, close enough so that their erections were almost touching. "Now, hold each other's cock."

When they hesitated, Ronnie ordered, "Do it now!"

With a groan, each man reached out and wrapped his hand around the other's cock. Ronnie remembered a conversation she had had with Bobby several months earlier when he had admitted to the dark fantasy of holding another man's cock and being held by him as well. She had decided to make it come true for him.

"Mistress, please don't make me do this," Bobby said. His body, however, said that, rather than stopping, he wanted to be forced.

"Quiet," Ronnie snapped, looking at Mike carefully. "And you, Mike?"

He bowed his head and whispered, "I will do whatever gives you pleasure. If it gives you delight to watch me do this, then I can only obey."

"Then, Mike, make Bobby come."

"Please no, Mistress," Bobby said.

Ronnie stared at him and raised an eyebrow.

"I'm sorry, Mistress," Bobby said.

"Good. Now you will both do as I say. Make each other come while I watch."

The two men stood, stroking each other's cock, watching their hands, their breathing hard and ragged. "Concentrate," Ronnie said and the men did.

"Cup each other's balls and fondle them. Use both hands!" As the small group watched, the two men acted out their hidden desire.

It took only moments until each man spurted semen on the other's hand. One of the women cried out her pleasure as her slave drove her to orgasm. The other climaxed silently.

"The rest of the cruise was delightful," Ronnie told Carla, sipping a fresh cup of coffee. "Mike spent each of the remaining afternoons with a different woman.

"How did you know about Bob's desire to touch another man?"

"He'd told me once, when I forced him to reveal his darkest fantasy, and his body language that afternoon was more than eloquent."

"You always seem to know how to find that extra bit of spice. How do you do it?"

"I've no idea. I guess I read my friends well." She tapped her forehead. "And I remember everything."

"I hope, someday, I'll be that good."

"You will," Ronnie said. "You will."

Jeffrey DeLancy III was an extremely dignified looking man in his mid forties with eyes that were almost navy blue and carefully trimmed, salt-and-pepper hair, beard, and moustache. A corporate attorney visiting New York, his three-piece suit was immaculately tailored and he wore a heavy gold ring with three channel-set sapphires on the ring finger of his right hand. When they met, Carla had commented on his well-developed body, and he had told her that he played racquetball and tennis as often as he could.

Now, as Carla returned from the ladies' room, Jeff was staring at the picture of the nightgowned woman clutching her bedclothes to her breast and staring, terrified, at someone just behind the camera. As Carla sat down he slammed shut the book. "Let's go back to your place," he said, picking up his coffee cup, then setting it down without drinking any. "This fantasy business is silly."

"We can go if you like," Carla said, "but I think there's something you want to tell me."

"I don't think so." He signaled the waiter for the dinner check.

"Jeff," Carla said, placing her hand over his, "tell me. That's what I'm here for."

"We both know what you're here for. So let's get to your place and do that."

"You don't have to tell me what's upsetting you," Carla said, "but I doubt that it's as bad as you think it is." Jeff sat silently staring into his coffee. "I saw which picture turned you on. That's Bethann and she was asleep when the burglar broke in. Do you know what he's going to do?"

Jeff's hand trembled under hers as she continued her story. "He's going to hold her down, feel her struggles, force her to bend to his will. She's afraid that she will be unable to fend him off." She was as excited by her recitation as Jeff obviously was.

"You're talking about rape," he said.

"Yes. But this is fantasy rape, not intended to actually hurt or do anything that Bethann's not willing to do."

"Fantasy rape, real rape. It's wrong however you define it."

"You know, nothing that goes on only in your mind is bad."

Jeff slowly raised his eyes and looked at Carla. "I wish I could believe that."

"You've got a fantasy. You want to rape a woman. Well not rape exactly. You don't want to really hurt her, just have her pretend to resist so you can subdue her. Force her. Right?"

The waiter arrived with the check, took Jeff's credit card, and disappeared.

"More people than you might imagine have rape fantasies," Carla continued. "As a matter of fact, I've always wanted to be ravished. Held down so that I couldn't move."

Jeff gazed into Carla's eyes. "You mean that, don't you?"

"I really do. While I was having that picture taken, I was thinking about the man who would tear off Bethann's clothes."

"Will Bethann fight the burglar?" he asked softly.

"She'll fight very hard."

"She'll know that he won't really hurt her, but she'll fight anyway? Struggle and try to get away?"

"Yes," Carla whispered. "Let's just be clear about two things. First, 'popcorn' is the safe word. If either of us says that, everything stops. And second, you'll use a condom even if it's out of character."

Jeff looked into her eyes, believing that this might actually happen. "Popcorn. Everything stops." He pulled out his wallet and slipped five crisp one-hundred-dollar bills into the black leather envelope. "I understand."

They traveled to the brownstone in silence and Carla motioned to Jeff to wait downstairs. She ran to the closet then back downstairs and handed

Jeff some loose-fitting black sweatpants and a black turtleneck shirt. "When the light goes out, Bethann will be in bed, asleep. There has never been a burglary here, you know, but Bethann has always been worried."

Carla hurried back upstairs and pulled off her clothes. Knowing that many men have fantasies about ravishing a woman, she and Ronnie had adjusted several pieces of lingerie by clipping a few threads to make them almost fall apart if someone yanked. She slipped on a specially prepared kelly green charmeuse short gown, climbed into bed, pulled the sheets up to her chin, and turned out the light.

Minutes later she saw a dark form slip through the doorway. Light suddenly filled the room and a hand pressed across her mouth, forcing her against the mattress. "Don't scream," the voice hissed. His other arm snaked across her belly, pinning her down. "I just want your jewelry."

She struggled, trying to get free but he was too strong. But she had to be sure he understood the rules. "Popcorn," she mumbled. Reluctantly, he eased the pressure against her mouth and stood up. Carla stared into Jeff's eyes, deep blue against his black turtleneck. "You understand."

He nodded and she smiled. She slid across the bed, away from him. "Don't hurt me," she whimpered. "I'll tell you where all my jewelry is."

He watched her heaving chest. "I've changed my mind," he said in a menacing tone. "I've decided I don't want your jewelry. I want you."

"No, please," Carla said, getting into her part. Even pretending, the danger felt incredibly real and exciting. Her heart pounded as she grabbed the sheet and held it against her breasts.

Jeff crossed the room and theatrically closed the door. "You're not getting away," he said, "but you can try, of course."

"Don't hurt me," Carla said in a tiny voice.

"I won't hurt you unless you resist." He grabbed Carla's wrist and dragged her across the bed. He tangled his hand in her short hair and pulled her head back.

Carla's eyes widened. His hand in her hair hurt, but the discomfort excited her. She tried to twist her head to avoid Jeff's mouth which was slowly descending on her, but his hold in her hair allowed her almost no movement. She used her fists to pound on his chest, but it was like hitting a board. His mouth captured hers and molten heat flowed through her lips. Somehow it wasn't just a kiss, it was possession.

Jeff climbed onto the bed and straddled Carla's hips, effectively pinning her to the bed. He leaned forward, pressing his forearms on hers and holding her head with both hands in her hair. "You're mine," he growled, "whether you want it or not."

"Please, let me go. I won't tell anyone you broke in here." Real tears pooled in the corners of her eyes. "Please."

"Not a chance, lady," Jeff said. His mouth moved over her face, licking her eyelids and nipping at her earlobes. "I can do anything I want and you've got no way to stop me." He grabbed the front of her green nightgown and pulled. The fabric parted easily, leaving Carla naked.

She had to get away. She relaxed for a moment, then with a burst of energy, she arched her back and pulled her arms free. As Carla lay on the bed panting Jeff suddenly needed to get out of his clothes. He pulled the dark turtleneck over his head and tossed it on the floor. His pants and shorts followed and, erect and huge, he climbed back on top of his victim. "You've had enough time to contemplate what's going to happen."

Again Jeff grabbed her wrists and held her arms above her head. He devoured her mouth, forcing his tongue inside to duel with hers, rubbing his naked, lightly furred chest sinuously against her chest. "Nice," he rumbled. He released her wrists and held her head as he kissed her face and neck.

"No," Carla yelled, dragging her fingernails across Jeff's back. "Let me go."

"A regular wildcat," he said. He used the weight of his body to pin Carla to the bed, then slapped her hard across her thigh.

His handprint stung, but it also increased the heat in her groin. It was hard to fight against being raped when being possessed by him was exactly what Carla wanted.

Again and again he slapped her until his hand began to sting. "Had enough?" he asked.

Carla nodded, blinked hard. "Just don't make me . . . you know. I'm a nice girl. I've never been with anyone but my husband. Don't force me. Please."

"Ah," Jeff said, "but I will do just that." He slipped on a condom, then held his hard cock at the entrance to Carla's pussy. Sensuously, he rubbed it against her clit. "You say you don't want me," he said. "I'm a rapist, forcing you to accommodate me, but your body is wet. You must be very evil."

"I'm not wet. I don't want you." She struggled, dragging her fingernails down Jeff's back and across one shoulder. Bright red tracks appeared down his skin.

"Your body says different." He guided his turgid erection to her opening and pushed. "And you can't stop me anyway." He pressed his hips forward and drove his cock into her. "You're wet and wide open so I can fuck you." His fantasy was so real that he lost control, pounding into his victim until he arched his back and spurted semen deep inside of her in shuddering pulses. Panting, he collapsed on top of her.

Carla stroked his back and ran her fingers through his hair. "That was so good," she whispered.

"It was unbelievable," he said, his body limp and exhausted. The scratches on his back stung. He rolled to one side and Carla walked, naked, to the bathroom. She returned with some antiseptic and applied some to his back and shoulder.

He looked at the welt on one side of his chest. "I'll enjoy looking at that for days," he said, running one finger over the mark.

"I'm glad. I was afraid of doing damage."

"And I'm really sorry if I hit you too hard."

"You didn't."

Jeff put his clothes on. "Thanks for a fantastic evening," he said. "May I call you again?"

"Of course. Bethann will always be here, as well as any other women you want to be with."

"I'm glad. You'll be hearing from me."

As the winter waned, Carla and Ronnie spent one day every week sharing experiences, since they were the only ones with whom they could discuss their flourishing business. Each Monday Carla packed her boys off to school, tidied the house after the weekend, and then drove into the city. Ronnie discovered R & R's Gourmet Take-out and each week she picked up a luxurious luncheon, usually a pasta salad and one of the unusual breads for which R & R's was famous. When she returned to the brownstone, she selected a bottle of fine wine from the cellar and made sure that it was the proper temperature.

One Monday, after a particularly sumptuous meal of prosciutto and cantaloupe, rottini and mushroom salad, and crusty, hot sesame bread, Carla and Ronnie slipped off their shoes and stretched out at opposite ends of the living room sofa, their bare feet on the coffee table. "That was a particularly good Sauvignon Blanc," Carla said.

"You know, six months ago you wouldn't have known it was a Sauvignon. You've grown, you know."

"I know. Every now and then I say something to my mother and she gives me that look. You know the 'I didn't teach you that so how could you possibly understand it' look."

"Oh yes, I know it well." She sipped her second glass of the full, flavorful wine. "Carla, I have something I'd like to discuss with you."

"Sure, shoot." Carla set her glass down and her body became more alert.

"Occasionally one of my friends makes a request that I'm not sure I can fulfill." She toyed with the stem of her wine glass.

"Are you getting coy with me?" Carla asked.

"No, but this is a bit unusual and it involves you." Heat flushed Ronnie's cheeks.

"You're blushing. I don't believe it."

Ronnie laughed. "Neither do I. Anyway, I've been getting together with one friend every month or so for years. He enjoys selecting erotic stories from magazines, scenes from novels, things like that, reading them to me, then acting them out. He's very creative and I've learned a lot from him and his stories." She sipped her wine.

"You're working up your courage, Ronnie. I can tell. Just remember there's nothing you can ask or tell me that will change our friendship."

"Thanks. He read me a story about two women involved in a torrid love scene. In the story, a man first watches, then joins in their lovemaking."

"Oh," Carla said, suddenly uncomfortable.

"I realy didn't know how to broach the subject to you since we've never even mentioned that type of sex. If it turns you off, let's drop it right now."

"You obviously didn't say no to him or we wouldn't be discussing it now."

Ronnie sighed. "No, I didn't."

"Have you ever been with another woman?" Carla asked, in a small voice.

"Yes," Ronnie said. "In college. Although we were roommates, even you didn't know."

"No," Carla said, surprise showing in her voice. "Who?"

"Remember Evelyn Sage?"

"The gorgeous blond with the tremendous eyes and great skin. She had the most fantastic breasts as I recall. I always wondered whether they were hers or silicone."

Ronnie laughed. "She was fantastic looking all over, wasn't she? They were her own. Anyway, we had been in several of the same classes and we got together to study on occasion. Somewhere during our junior year she casually mentioned to me that she thought I was very attractive and she wondered whether I felt the same way about her. One thing lead to another, and another, and another. Anyway, we had been together only a few times when I met Sid."

"I remember him. You and he got pretty heavy for a while."

"We certainly did. He was into skin. Used to love to give me back-rubs with scented oils. But while we were dating, I didn't see Evelyn and by the time Sid and I broke up, she was with someone else."

"Did you enjoy it with her?" Carla asked.

"Very much," Ronnie answered. "It was new and different and very sensual. I've been with several women since then, always brief flings. I assume you've never done anything like that."

"Never," Carla said, sipping her wine. "This is hard to admit but I guess I've always been a little curious."

Ronnie looked Carla in the eye. "I'd love to show you but I don't want it to spoil our friendship."

"Would it?" Carla asked, now curious at the prospect.

"I don't know. I hope not. But if anything ever feels wrong, just tell me and I'll stop."

"Isn't that what we tell everyone before we play?"

"I guess so." Ronnie put her glass on the table, then leaned over and whispered in Carla's ear. "It will be wonderful. I've fantasized about you. In my fantasy you're here just like this."

Ronnie's breath on her ear made Carla's heartbeat speed and her breathing deepen. Her doubts dissolved and she relaxed.

"Close your eyes and just feel." Ronnie watched Carla's eyes close. "Good. Like that. Don't move. Just feel." Ronnie touched the tip of her finger to Carla's mouth and saw her lips part. "Your lips are so soft. So moist and smooth." She touched Carla's teeth and brushed her nail against Carla's tongue. "Does that tickle?"

Carla was awash in sensations. Nothing sexual had happened but her body tingled and her pussy was swollen. But she was in no hurry. She pursed her lips around Ronnie's finger and sucked lightly.

"Oh yes," Ronnie whispered in Carla's ear. "Suck my finger." She allowed Carla to draw her finger into her mouth, then pulled it slowly outward. In and out, mimicking the fucking motion that they had both experienced so often in the past. The rhythm was primitive and deeply sexual. Ronnie pressed the tip of her tongue into Carla's ear, echoing the rhythm the two women had established.

Carla had never imagined that such simple things could be so deeply sensual. She was sucking Ronnie's finger as her friend fucked her ear with her tongue. Suddenly her blouse was in her way. She wanted her breasts free.

Carla reached for her buttons but Ronnie stilled her hand. "Don't move at all. Let me be in charge of everything." With a nip at Carla's earlobe, Ronnie pulled her finger from her friend's amorous mouth and unbuttoned her blouse. "Your nipples are so swollen. Are they uncomfortable under your bra? Do they want to feel my hot mouth?"

"Oh yes," moaned Carla.

Ronnie parted the front of Carla's blouse and stroked her palm over her friend's erect nipples through the satiny fabric. "I can feel how hard they are. Do you like my hand?" When Carla moaned again, Ronnie continued, "It's real, isn't it? You want more, I know that. Your heart is pounding and you can't seem to get air into your lungs."

Ronnie leaned over and took one nipple in her teeth. Although the sensation was diminished somewhat by her bra, the nipping drove Carla wild.

"I like it that this bra fastens in the front," Ronnie said. "I can unfasten it without you moving. And I don't want you to move, even a little." With a deft flick of her fingers, Ronnie unclipped Carla's bra and separated the cups so her breasts were free. "Such beautiful breasts, baby," Ronnie whispered. "I've seen you naked many times, and each time I've imagined how your gorgeous nipples would taste."

Ronnie cupped Carla's large breast, weighing the handful. "Heavy and ripe. And hungry. Flesh can be hungry, you know, needing my touch." She drew her fingers from the outside of the breast in her hand to the pink center, pulling at the nipple. She repeated the motion over and over until Carla thought she would go mad from wanting.

"I want you," Carla said, "and need you."

"You need me to do what? Give you pleasure? I'm doing that. Need me to increase the heat? Oh baby, yes." Ronnie leaned over and licked one erect nipple with the flat of her tongue. Then she drew back and blew on the wet tip. Alternately she wet the tight bud, then cooled it with her breath. "Is that driving you wild?" she asked as Carla's hips began to move.

"You're making me crazy," Carla murmured. "My pussy is going to explode."

"No, it's not and that's the wonderful part. Your pussy will get hotter and hotter but you won't come until we're ready. And it'll be so intense I'll be able to feel it, share it with you." Ronnie quickly pulled off Carla's jeans and panties, then removed her own clothes. "I want to be naked like you are."

Carla reached out to touch Ronnie's naked skin. "Not yet," Ronnie said. "This is for you. I don't want you to do anything at all. Another time you can touch me but this time is just for you." Carla's hand dropped to the sofa. "That's a good girl. Just feel."

Ronnie licked Carla's nipple again, then drew it into her mouth. She sucked hard, causing a tightness to flow from Carla's breast to her pussy. It was as though the sucking made a path through her body and Carla could feel the pull between her legs.

"Is your pussy wet?" Ronnie asked.

"Yes," Carla murmured. "I'm so excited I don't know what to do. I can almost reach my climax, but not quite."

"I can reach it for you," Ronnie whispered. "Now spread your legs so

I can see your magnificent pussy. Spread them wide. Put your feet on the edge of the table and open your knees for me."

Carla did what Ronnie's deep throaty voice told her. She opened her body as Ronnie moved so she was on her knees on the carpet between Carla's spread legs.

Ronnie watched Carla's soaked pussy twitch with excitement. How long could she keep her friend on the edge of climax without letting her over the edge? There was so much pleasure she could give. She bent her head to one side and allowed her hair to brush the inside of Carla's thigh. She allowed the strands to slide over Carla's white skin, tickling and stimulating. Ronnie blew a stream of air at the other thigh.

Carla was going crazy. She was sure she would fly apart in a million pieces and she didn't think she would even feel the explosion. "You're torturing me," she whispered, reaching for Ronnie's head to force it between her legs.

"Don't do that, baby," Ronnie said, replacing Carla's hands at her sides. "Hold still and let me show you how good this can be. Be patient."

"It's making me crazy."

"Is it bad?"

Carla hesitated. "No. It's wonderful."

"I promise I won't make you wait too long." She used one finger of each hand to part Carla's outer lips, then slowly explored her folds with her tongue. "You taste delicious," she said, continuing her exploration. Then she found Carla's clit with the tip of her tongue. "You can come soon," she said, flicking her tongue over the swollen bud. "And your climax is going to be so big I'm going to share it with you."

Ronnie took one finger and slid it into Carla's pussy, while she slid her other hand between her own legs, rubbing and circling over her clit. A second finger joined the first in Carla's pussy. As she filled her friend's cunt she flicked her tongue back and forth over her clit as she fingered herself.

"Oh God," Carla screamed. "Oh God."

"Let it come, baby," Ronnie said. "Don't say anything. Concentrate on what I'm doing to your body. Don't move. Hold perfectly still so you can enjoy my fingers and my tongue." She blew hot air over Carla's inner lips. "Yes. Share your climax with me." Her tongue licked and her fingers drove in and out.

Pressure built in Carla's belly. Waves of pleasure began to crest. "Don't stop," Carla cried. "Don't stop." Ronnie continued tonguing her friend's clit. Then she shifted her licking to her inner lips, around her fingers. She used the fingers to spread Carla open, then licked all the flesh her tongue could reach.

And then Carla came. The spasms continued, longer than Carla had thought possible. It was a different kind of orgasm than any she had ever experienced. It wasn't the hard, fast kind she had when she masturbated, nor was it the kind she had with her pussy filled with a man's hard cock. It was deep inside, and wonderfully different.

Ronnie slowed her movements until Carla's body calmed. She collapsed onto the sofa, took Carla's hand and gently guided it to her own hot cunt. "Rub gently, just the way you like to be touched." Carla moved so she could watch her fingers while they explored and massaged Ronnie's hot, wet flesh. Ronnie held Carla's hand and used it to bring her to orgasm. "Like that," she cried, "just like that." Gales of pleasure overpowered her.

The living room was quiet for a time, then Ronnie said, "Oh God. That was amazing."

"It was magic," Carla said. "Different somehow."

"I know," Ronnie said, her breathing calming. "But it doesn't detract, at least for me, from heterosexual sex. I enjoy that as much as I ever did."

"I'm glad you said that," Carla said. "I was afraid that you'd be insulted if I did. This was a treat, but I still like men."

"If the situation arises, would you be interested in doing that while someone watches and participates?"

"Yeah, I think I would. You know how I enjoy being watched. Being the passive one makes me crazy."

"And I enjoy calling the shots. We're made for each other and for this business."

"Well," Carla said, "I guess that's settled." She picked up her wine glass. "To new experiences. Especially ones that pay well."

Ronnie took a big swallow of her wine. "Salute."

Chapter 9

Over the months, Ronnie had visited Carla's house in Bronxville many times. With no family of her own, she had become Aunt Ronnie to the boys, and Carla's parents had taken her into the fold. Every time the subject of their business came up, the two women would sidestep any questions, saying only that they were in the public relations field, working for corporate clients, and doing very well.

One evening, while the boys were in their rooms, ostensibly doing their homework, Ronnie and Carla relaxed in the living room of Carla's modest house. "I envy you," Ronnie said, wistfully. "Sometimes I wish Jack and I had kids."

"Sometimes I wish I could lend them to you for a few months. Did BJ thank you for his birthday present? Ronnie, getting him his own phone was really extravagant. The bills may be exorbitant."

"He did thank me, and the bills won't go over a fixed amount that he and I have already agreed on. And I love doing it for him. By the way, don't tell Mike, but I'm getting him his own TV for his birthday next month."

"You're too much. You miss having your own children, don't you?"

"I do. But I often think that Jack and I wouldn't have made good parents anyway. We're too self-centered. We enjoy our creature comforts, like quiet and privacy."

"God knows, you get little of either with three growing boys in the house. How is Jack?"

"He's good. He's in the used-to-be Soviet Union, somewhere that ends in 'istan,' I think. I talked to him just a few days ago."

Carla saw the wistful look on Ronnie's face. "You miss him."

"Yeah, I do. I sometimes wish that he'd give up the traveling. Maybe we'd have a real life."

"Would you give up the business if he was home every evening?"

"I don't know. What about you? You and Bryce see a lot of each other. Are you two getting serious?"

"I don't know that either. He was here last weekend."

"No! With your parents and the boys?"

"Yup. We spent the day ice skating with the kids, then had a big family dinner." She laughed. "I thought my parents were going to start making wedding plans right then and there. My mother's talked to me several times since. 'He's well-off and he likes the boys' she keeps saying."

"And. . . ."

"And nothing. He's a nice man and we have great times together." She lowered her voice. "Both in and out of bed. But that's not enough to build a life on."

"Give in time," Ronnie said.

"I have lots of that. And besides, I'm having too much fun in *public relations*."

A few weeks later Carla and Ronnie double dated for the first time. Glen Hansmann was an executive with a motion picture production company. Ronnie had entertained him several times, to their mutual delight. About a week earlier, Glen had called and left his name on her answering machine.

"Ronnie, babe," he told her when she called back. "I know I've asked you this several times, but any chance of a double date? My friend Vic O'Keefe is in from the west coast and I'd love to do dinner with you and a friend. You understand. Some dinner and entertainment."

"I do have a friend. Her name's Carla and her fee is the same as mine."

"That's super," Glen said, "and the fee's no problem. Is next Tuesday evening okay?"

"I don't know whether Carla's available," Ronnie said. "But if she's around that evening I see no reason why it wouldn't work."

"Good. Check with her and call me back. And if she's anything like you, I can't wait."

Ronnie called Carla immediately and explained the situation. "How would you feel about a double? I don't know what they'll want, but I think we're ready for anything. And it's a Tuesday."

"It sounds fine. Hang on and let me check next Tuesday." Carla flipped pages in her appointment book. "Believe it or not, next Tuesday is the only night I have free for the next month. It must be fate."

Glen Hansmann was not at all what Carla had expected. He was in his late forties, soft spoken and rather sweet, with light eyes and a dimple in his chin. His shoulder-length dark brown hair curled just above the collar of his light blue dress shirt. Carla noticed that his hands were beautiful, long slender fingers with perfectly manicured nails. Other than a functional wrist watch, he wore no jewelry.

Vic O'Keefe, on the other hand, was a Hollywood cliché. His tan was too perfect, accented by the laughter-created crinkles of lighter skin at the corners of his eyes. He wore a ruby ring on his right hand and a heavy good-and-steel Rolex watch on his left wrist. His voice was too loud, as was his tie, and he spent the first hour of the evening trying to impress the two women, dropping names and discussing all the exotic places he had been. At one point Carla caught Ronnie's eye and their expression spoke volumes about their long evening ahead.

Finally, Glen had had enough. "Vic," he said when the man paused for breath, "you're not usually like this. Remember that these girls are ours for the evening. You don't have to impress them." His fingers drummed on the tablecloth.

Vic was quiet for a moment, then looked apologetic. "I'm really sorry. I guess I'm so used to Hollywood types that I'm out of practice with real people. I know the arrangement. It's just that you two are so attractive I forgot."

"That we're bought and paid for?" Ronnie said, a slight edge in her voice. The evening threatened to become a disaster.

With a disarming grin, Vic said, "Open mouth, insert foot, and take a giant step. I'm really not a bad guy, you know." His rueful smile seemed genuine. "How about we just forget my gaucherie and start again." He stood up, walked around the table, and sat down again. "Hi, everyone. My name's Vic."

Slowly a smile spread across Ronnie's face. "Hi. I'm Ronnie."

The remaider of the sumptous meal sped by, fueled by good conversation and easy humor. As the foursome sat over coffee Vic said, "Okay, what's the difference between a tire and three hundred used condoms?"

"I give up," Ronnie said, "what?"

"A tire is a Goodyear. Three hundred used condoms is a great year." Everyone laughed. "You know, I can't remember when I've enjoyed a dinner more," Vic continued, looking at his watch. "And Glen and I have arranged a special surprise that we hope you'll like."

"Absolutely," Glen continued. "We've gotten the private use of the spa, pool, and hot tub at Vic's hotel for the rest of the evening. It usually closes at nine o'clock, but I slipped the concierge a little cash and can pick up the key at the desk."

"Sounds like fun," Ronnie said, checking her watch, "and it's already nine-thirty. We're ready if you are."

The two couples, Ronnie with Vic and Glen with Carla, traveled to Vic's hotel. The three waited while Glen picked up the key to the spa. Together, the four slipped through an unmarked door into a back hallway. Giggling, they followed Glen through another door and found themselves in a workout room filled with exercise equipment. "Nice," Carla said. "This is some facility."

"Let's try some of it out," Vic suggested. Quickly, the men were out of their suits and down to their shorts. "Undies only," Vic called so Ronnie and Carla stripped to their bras and panties. "Have either of you ever done circuit training?" he asked, staring at the two beautiful bodies magnificently displayed in bras and panties.

"I do aerobics, when I have the time," Carla answered.

"And I'm a confirmed couch potato," Ronnie added.

"I can show you how to use this stuff. I work out a lot," Vic said.

Ronnie looked over Vic's well-developed body, his wide shoulders, heavily muscled arms, flat stomach, and tight buns and she smiled. "I'm sure you do."

Carla walked behind Glen and ran her hands over his muscular back. "I'll bet you've seen the inside of a gym too," she whispered against the back of his neck. She smiled as she felt his muscles tense and his back straighten. "From time to time," he said, sucking in his stomach.

Vic tapped the seat of an arm-exercise maching. "Let's see how you'd look on here," he said to Ronnie. She sat on the seat and Vic placed her arms on the padded upper armrests. "Now, press down," he said, "then release very slowly. It works your biceps and triceps." As she pressed, he watched her chest muscles swell, lifting her breasts. As she reached the bottom of the machine's travel, he reached out and brushed his fingers over Ronnie's nipples. Smiling, she released her pressure and allowed the machine to return to its starting position.

Glen showed Carla how to lie on her back on the platform of the leg-press machine. He positioned her feet about twelve inches apart on the footrest and showed her how to use her quadriceps to straighten her legs. Several times he adjusted the weights so it took only a moderate amount of strength to extend her legs. "Now," he said, "try to hold your legs straight." Once she had her legs straight, she locked her knees to hold the foot support as far from her body as she could. Glen slid a stool next to the machine, sat down, and rubbed his fingers against the crotch of her panties.

"Hey," Carla said, giggling, "that makes this much more difficult."

With the soft warmth spreading through her body, she had to concentrate on keeping her knees locked.

"Yeah, it certainly does." He placed one hand on each of her thighs, pressing his palms lightly against her skin. "Okay. Now release and press." As Carla relaxed, then extended her legs, Glen felt the tension in her muscles under his hands. Carla's body shined with sweat as she continued to do leg extensions.

Ronnie moved from the arm machine to a device Vic called an adductor. Vic sat her down on the padded seat and, spreading her legs at a forty-five-degree angle, placed her legs in the supports. He fiddled with the weight setting. "Try to close your legs," he said.

Ronnie used all her strength to try to press her thighs together. "Not a chance," she said.

"Good," Vic said. He walked around and knelt between her widely spread legs. He yanked at the tendrils of pussy hair that escaped around the crotch of her panties and heard her gasp. Quickly, he soothed the smarting skin, then pulled her hair again. Ronnie gave up trying to force her thighs together, closed her eyes, and relished the sensations that Vic was causing. "Makes you crazy, doesn't it?"

"God, you know it." Ronnie shuddered.

Vic grinned. "I certainly do." He pressed his mouth against the crotch of her panties and nipped at the flesh and fur beneath. His hot breath warmed her lubricating pussy.

"See what Vic's doing?" Glen said to Carla. She turned and watched Vic's face buried between Ronnie's legs. "Now straighten your legs," Glen said. Carla's thigh muscles were getting tired but she pressed the footplate. Glen cupped one hand against her cunt and tweaked her nipples with the other. Carla wanted to sink into the erotic pleasure, but she had to concentrate to keep her knees locked. "Shit, Vic," Glen said, "I never imagined the uses you can put these machines to."

"Enough for now," Vic said, lifting Ronnie's legs from the adductor machine. "I'm for the hot tub."

Glen helped Carla stand and stretch and after a few minute's walking, her legs felt stronger again.

The foursome walked into the dimly lit pool and hot tub area. Glen stopped beside the steaming water and wrapped his arms around Carla. While caressing her back, he pressed his lips against hers, flattening her full breasts against his powerful chest.

Vic and Ronnie sat on a bench and Vic caressed Ronnie's face with his fingers and his lips. For long minutes, the two couples kissed, adding fuel to the building sexual fires.

Finally, Vic pulled away from Ronnie and flipped the controls for the air and water jets. "Last one in the hot tub is a rotten egg," he said. Still in their underwear, the four slowly settled into the bubbling water, hands and mouths exploring as they moved.

Glen unfastened Carla's bra and tossed the wet fabric across the tiled room. He bent his head and licked the top of Carla's half-submerged breast. "You taste of chlorine," he said.

Ronnie placed one hand on Vic's shoulder and whispered into his ear. "You do exactly what Glen does. Watch very carefully and imitate him, move for move." She felt his back tighten and then the tell-tale trembling for his shoulders.

Vic looked at Glen and saw his friend's tongue laving Carla's breast. "It feels weird to watch."

"Do it to me," Ronnie said. Vic removed Ronnie's bra and slid his tongue over her skin.

Glen lifted Carla's breast and his mouth reached for her nipple. Carla deliberately settled more deeply into the water so that, when he attempted to take a rosy crest into his mouth, he got a face full of bubbles. They giggled and wrestled until Glen had his arms wrapped around Carla's ribs and she was floating, her breasts out of the water.

Vic was kissing and nuzzling Ronnie's neck when Ronnie whispered, "Look what they're doing now, Vic. You're really not watching carefully enough." She reached down into the swirling water and squeezed his cock, hard.

"Ow," he cried, his breath caught in his throat. The pain seemed to make his cock harder.

"Then pay more attention."

Quickly, Vic repositioned Ronnie's body and suckled her breast, his breathing fast and ragged. Ronnie smiled, knowing that she had found the best way to give him pleasure.

Still supporting her upper body on one arm, Glen lifted Carla's legs onto the tiled edge of the tub. He bent her body at the hips until a jet of warm water shot directly against her swollen lips. "Oh God," she cried. "That's wonderful."

"I want you to play with the water too," Ronnie said to Vic, "but I want it to spray against your cock. Kneel here." She moved his knees onto the ledge and pressed her hand into the small of his back. His erection was now directly in the stream of another warm-water jet. "Oh shit, baby," he hissed. "I'll come if you keep doing that."

"And if you do," Ronnie said, "we'll just have to start again." She held Vic's body in the water stream until she felt him shudder. She reached around and held his cock as he came in the water, his semen feeling thick and gooey through his cotton shorts.

Carla was about to climax as well. Glen sucked on her breast and rubbed his finger against her rear as the water pulsed against her cunt. It was so quick and so intense that her orgasm took her by surprise.

"Oh baby," Glen purred. "You're hot as a pistol. I want to fuck you good, but I've got no rubbers."

"Sit up here," Carla said, patting the edge of the tub, "and let me take care of you." As he climbed up, she pulled off his shorts so that, when he was seated, his cock stuck straight up from his lap.

"Look at that hard cock," Ronnie whispered into Vic's ear, feeeling him getting hard again. "Do you know what she's going to do?"

"Yes," he murmured.

"Well, you're going to watch. Have you ever watched a woman suck cock in person? So close you can touch her?" Vic shook his head. "Good," Ronnie purred. She and Vic moved beside Carla in the water. "Now watch very carefully," Ronnie said. "Watch her mouth as she gives Glen pleasure."

Carla licked the hollow behind Glen's knee, then kissed and bit the inside of his thighs while Ronnie kept up a running commentary in Vic's ear. "She's licking his leg," Ronnie said, scratching her fingernail up his skin. "Right here."

Carla slipped her hand between Glen's thighs and tickled his heavy balls. Ronnie did the same with Vic, while saying, "I'll bet his balls feel tight and hard. See his cock? It's hard and throbbing." Ronnie pulled Vic's shorts off under the water and placed the wet garment on Glen's knee. "Hey Glen," Ronnie said. "I just want you to know that Vic is naked under the water and I'm holding his cock."

Carla wrapped her hand around Glen's cock. "Like that?" she asked Ronnie.

"Just like that."

"And if I slide my fingers right to the end?" Carla asked Ronnie.

"I'll do the same to Vic's cock under the water."

"And when I squeeze his balls?"

"Yeah," Ronnie sighed.

Glen and Vic groaned simultaneously. Carla stroked the sensitive flesh between Glen's balls and his anus. "His ass is very tight," she said.

"Vic's is too, but I think a finger will fit. The hot water makes it easy." Ronnie rubbed his tight hole, then slipped the tip of her finger inside.

"No," Glen groaned. "It will hurt."

Since she knew that Glen knew the safe word, Carla realized that he didn't really want her to stop. "Yes, it will hurt," Carla whispered, "but it will feel so good." As Carla's finger invaded Glen's ass, she said to Ronnie and Vic, "Look how hard it makes him. His cock is twitching and moving all by itself."

Glen was so excited by Carla's hands and her voice that he knew he should be ashamed at her vivid descriptions of his body's reactions but he was too far gone to care. Carla kept her finger just inside of him, not moving.

Vic felt Ronnie's finger slide depper into his rear. "Vic's able to tolerate more of this," Ronnie said, "since he came just a little while ago. I'm sliding my finger farther inside him. I can slide in and out, rubbing the sides of his channel. I'm fucking his ass and he's trembling. His cock is getting very hard again."

Carla looked at Glen's face, knowing it was difficult for him not to come. She flicked her tongue over the tip of his penis, licking the sweet drops of pre-come she found there. "Ummm, he tastes good." She pursed her lips and sucked the end of Glen's cock into her mouth.

"Look, Vic," Ronnie said, her finger still deep inside his ass, "Carla's got Glen's cock in her mouth. Touch her head as she sucks. Do it."

Barely coherent, Vic reached out and cupped the back of Carla's wet head. "Press," Ronnie said. He pressed her head and she sucked Glen's cock deeper into her mouth. "Release," Ronnie said and Vic relaxed his hand, allowing Carla's head to release Glen's cock. "Again," Ronnie said and Vic pressed Carla's head.

Glen watched as Vic pressed Carla's mouth up and down on his cock. It was the most erotic thing he'd ever seen. He held himself as tightly as he could, trying to keep himself from coming too fast but it was impossible. He filled Carla's mouth with his semen.

"Good baby," Ronnie said to Vic. "You did so well that you deserve a reward." With her finger still deep in his ass, she pressed him upward until his hard cock was sticking from the water. "Make it good for him, Carla," she said and Carla squeezed her large breasts around Vic's cock. He climaxed right then, spurting into the air above the water. "Oh fuck," he yelled.

"What about you?" Glen said to Ronnie. "You didn't come. Neither of you did. I mean you two should. . . ."

"Would you like to watch Carla and me?"

Silently, Glen and Vic stared at the two women. Ronnie climbed out of the tub and sat on the side, her feet in the water. "Come here, baby," she said to Carla.

Eagerly, Carla buried her face in her friends furry muff and licked and sucked the delicate flesh. "Is she hot?" Vic asked tentatively.

"Oh yes," Carla said. "Feel." She took Vic's finger and held it against Ronnie's pussy. "You too," she told Glen.

The two men fingered Ronnie's pussy until she was ready to come. "You know what she'll enjoy?" Carla said. "She loves having her tits sucked." With Glen's mouth on one breast and Vic's on the other, Carla flicked her tongue over Ronnie's erect clit.

"Do it good!" Ronnie yelled. "Oh yes. Do it so good!" Her entire body contracted as her orgasm roared through every part of her. "Oh yes, it's so good."

Later, the four lay silently on towels on the tile. "I think there are seismographs as far away as California that registered that." Ronnie laughed.

"I've never had a more satisfying experience," Vic whispered.

"Oh yeah," Glen added. Glen and Vic held a quick, whispered conversation. "Look, I think I can convince the folks on the west coast that Vic has to stay another week. Can we get together over the weekend? The four of us?"

Carla thought about it. She didn't usually spend weekend time away from her children, but BJ and Tommy each had a sleep-over and she was sure she could leave Mike with her parents. And she was flattered. Every time a client called her again, she felt wonderful. This was the ultimate compliment, to her and to Ronnie. These two men wanted a repeat performance.

"I think I can arrange it," Carla said.

"Me too," Ronnie agreed.

The following Saturday evening, the four gathered in Vic's room at the hotel. Glen and Vic sat on the sofa in the sitting room of the luxurious suite and Ronnie and Carla each occupied a soft chair. They were all dressed casually, the men in slacks and sport shirts, Ronnie in a soft rose wool skirt, a matching sweater, and high black patent leather boots, Carla in black slacks and a royal blue silk blouse.

"We've already ordered room service for the four of us," Vic said. "Glen and I have talked a lot about this evening and we've got a few exciting ideas."

Carla stretched her long legs in front of her and said, "Like what?"

Glen opened a bottle of champagne and poured four glasses. He handed two to Vic and kept two in his hand. "Vic and I loved the way Ronnie took control that evening. It was erotic, being told what to do, where to look. So, for the moment, we've decided to be in charge. We'll do everything, take care of you for the evening. You just relax and do as you're told." He held a glass near Carla's lips. "Have a sip," he said as he tipped it. As she drank, she saw Vic hold a glass for Ronnie.

As they finished the first glass of champagne, a white-jacketed waiter arrived and wheeled a table to the center of the sitting room, opened leaves on the sides, and arranged plates of food. "The main courses are in the warmer under the table," he said, showing Vic how to open it. "And be careful. The plates will be hot."

Vic added a large tip, signed the check, and closed the door behind the waiter. "We're going to play a game," Glen said. "We're going to make you guess what you're eating." Ronnie and Carla felt blindfolds placed over their eyes. "First course," Glen said.

Glen pressed something cold and smooth against Carla's lips. "Open," he said, "and stick out your tongue." He placed a round object on Carla's tongue and she drew it into her mouth. "A grape," she said.

From across the room she heard Ronnie say, "A piece of cheese."

"Good. Both right." Carla ate several more cold grapes, followed by some of the cheese that Ronnie had been enjoying.

Carla felt something spread on her lips and when she licked off the creamy substance she knew immediately. "Blue cheese dressing."

"Mine's italian," Ronnie said.

Carla chewed crunchy bits of lettuce, cold, crisp slices of cucumber, and tomato wedges, all coated with dressing. Then Glen whispered, "My finger's are all gooey. Lick them off, will you?"

As Glen placed one finger at a time against Carla's mouth, she used her rough tongue to lick off the dressing. She drew each of his fingers into her mouth to suck off the last bits, then Glen wiped her mouth with a soft napkin. "Thirsty?"

"Yes," she said. Glen held the champagne against Carla's lips and she drank.

"I hope you like oysters," he said, pressing the slippery morsel against her lips.

"Love them," Carla said, as the slippery bite entered her mouth. It was not in the least sexual, but the entire experience was sensual and being blindfolded enhanced the sensations.

"Want a drink?" Glen asked.

"Yes," she said. She felt Glen's lips, wet and cold, press against her mouth. A trickle of cool liquid flowed from his lips onto hers. Drinking from his mouth made the champagne extra bubbly and it tickled her tongue.

"More?"

"Ummm, yes," she said and they shared a few more swallows.

Vic and Glen fed the two women the main course, sole almondine, tiny roasted potatoes, and petit pois with pearl onions.

"What's for dessert?" Ronnie asked, her voice sensual and hoarse.

Vic took some chocolate mousse in his fingers and pressed it against Ronnie's mouth. Slowly she sucked each finger, and heard Carla doing the same thing.

"What about you?" Ronnie asked. "Did you get some dessert?" She pulled off her blindfold, scooped up a handful of mousse and held it for Vic. He smiled at her and ate from her palm, licking up the last of the chocolate. "That was nice," she said, "but you missed a spot." He licked the mousse from her thumb.

Glen removed Carla's blindfold and she offered him some mousse from her fingers. When the mousse was gone, the two women went into the bathroom to wash up while Glen and Vic put the table outside the door.

Carla ran a comb through her hair as Ronnie freshened her lipstick. "You know, Carla," Ronnie said, "they're waiting for something."

"I agree. You're always so quick about these things. Do you know what they want?"

"I think they want me to take over as I did last time. Is that okay with you?"

"Sure. If you don't know what turns me on by now, no one does."

"Have you ever gotten into pain as pleasure?"

"Once or twice," Carla said. "I've been slapped a few times, once until I had to tell the guy to stop."

"Bad?"

"Not really," Carla said. "As a matter of fact, until it got to be too much, it was very erotic."

"Great. Are you willing to give it a try if things go the way I think they will?"

"Sure. Are you certain that this is what they have in mind?"

"I'm not, completely, but I've developed a sixth sense over the years. I'll go slowly and read the signs. Just remember the safe word."

Carla nodded. "I'll use it if I need to."

They went back into the living room. "Carla, pour everyone another glass of champagne," Ronnie said. "You two," she said to the men, "sit down."

The two men dropped into chairs while Carla poured wine. "You've called the shots so far," Ronnie said. "Now it's my turn." When neither man answered, Ronnie knew she had been right. "Each of you close your eyes. Picture the rest of the evening. Play it in your mind like a movie—picture it exactly as you wish it would happen. Now, Glen, you first. Tell me precisely what you see." When Glen hesitated Ronnie said, "Do it now."

"This is very difficult."

Carla walked behind Glen's chair, cradled the back of his head in the valley between her breasts, and glided her hands down the front of his shirt. "I know it is, baby," she murmured. "Tell me. Are we making love? Are we fucking good?"

"Yes, but before. . . ."

"Tell me, baby." She bent over his shoulder and placed her ear next to his lips. "Whisper it to me."

"Ronnie's making me do things to you." The words exploded from his mouth and his body shook.

"What things? Tell me, baby," Carla whispered.

When he was silent, Ronnie said, "You must tell us, Glen. Do it."

"Oh Carla. Ronnie's forcing me to spank you. And she's forcing Vic to watch everything."

Ronnie knelt in front of Vic, whose eyes were still closed as he fantasized about the evening. She placed her hands on his thighs. His body would tell her even if his words didn't. "What do you see, Vic? What are you doing?" When he was silent, Ronnie continued. "You must tell me." She had heard what Glen said. "Am I making you watch? Are you getting hard?" When he remained silent, she continued, "Am I spanking you, too?"

"No," he whispered.

Ronnie knew there was something else, but Vic was unable to tell her what it was. "Vic, put your mouth close to my ear. Now, whisper. Say, 'Please don't make me . . .' and end the sentence."

She felt him shudder as he whispered. Now she knew. "It's all right, baby," she said. "I'll make it all right."

Carla stared at her friend. She had no idea how Ronnie sensed the things she did, and got men to admit to their darkest sexual fantasies, but she felt the level of tension in the room increase moment by moment.

Ronnie stalked to the closet. She took out a wooden coat hanger and slapped it on her high boot. She pulled off her sweater and skirt and revealed a tight black satin teddy and black stockings. She settled comfortably on the couch, one ankle resting on the opposite knee. She slapped the hanger against the leather as she spoke. "Glen and Vic, shirts, shoes, and socks off. Now." The two men hurried to comply.

Ronnie's boots, Carla realized, hadn't been an accident nor had the underwear. Somehow Ronnie had known. "Vic, sit here," Ronnie said, indicating the spot on the sofa next to her, "and Glen, close your eyes and stand facing Carla. Now, touch Carla's face. Describe it to me. Tell me how it feels and smells and tastes."

Glen gazed into Carla's eyes, then closed his eyes and touched her face. "Her skin is so smooth. She smells of perfume, exotic and eastern."

He licked her cheek. "Her skin tastes of salt and spice." He ran a fingertip over her lips. "Her lips are soft and warm."

"Now, Glen, open your eyes and undress Carla. Do it slowly and describe her body for us as you do. Blouse first."

Glen slowly unbuttoned Carla's blouse and slipped it from her arms. "Her skin is smooth and pale. There are no marks from the sun anywhere, just white skin." He touched his tongue to the pulse of her neck. "Her neck is slender and she tastes and feels smooth under my tongue."

"Do you want to take her bra off? Taste and feel her tits?"

"Yes," Glen whispered.

"Then do it."

Glen unfastened Carla's bra and took it off. "Her breasts are gorgeous. I saw her body last week, but I never realized how beautiful her tits were." He filled a palm with one large breast and lifted. "They're heavy and fill my hand. Her nipples are delectable," he grazed her areola with his tongue, "and so soft."

"Do they get hard if you suck them?" Ronnie asked, idly rubbing her hand over Vic's chest.

Glen drew one tight tip into his mouth and pulled. "Yes. Hard and warm."

"Use your champagne to flavor them," Ronnie said.

Glen smiled and picked up his glass. He slowly trickled cool liquid down one breast, then licked it off her erect nipple. "Vic," Ronnie said, "the other one."

Vic jumped up, dribbled champagne down Carla's other breast, and sucked it off. Carla's breath caught in her throat and her knees wobbled. Pleasure knifed through her.

"Vic," Ronnie said, tapping the sofa with the coat hanger, "over here." Again he sat beside her. "That's good," Ronnie said. "Now Glen, pull off her slacks and panties."

Glen unzipped Carla's pants and pulled both slacks and undies off in one motion. "Tell us about her body, Glen," Ronnie said.

"Her stomach is flat and her belly button is very deep." He flicked his tongue into her navel. "Tastes smoky. And I can smell the aroma of her cunt."

"Feel her pussy. Is she ready for fucking?"

Glen ran his fingers through her pubic hair. "Yes, she's steaming."

"That means we're ready for the next part." Ronnie got up and turned one of the chairs from the dinner table to face the group. "Sit there, Glen. And Carla, you know what you must do. As they say, assume the position."

Glen sat on the chair and Carla lay across his thighs. He stroked the gorgeous globes laying so invitingly across his lap, delightfully crushing his erection. "Spank her on one cheek, hard." Glen raised his hand and brought it down on Carla's bottom.

"Again." He did. "Again."

After a few minutes, Carla whispered, "Popcorn."

"Oh, poor Carla," Ronnie said. "Her poor ass is so sore. Glen, make it feel better."

Glen stroked Carla's flaming bottom, caressing each cheek softly. "Does she feel good?" Ronnie asked.

"Yes, very soft and very hot."

"Does her hot bottom make you hot as well?"

"Absolutely," he said. "I want to fuck her."

"Not yet!" She reached down and held Glen's cock. "Neither Carla nor I have climaxed yet. Lie on the floor."

When Glen was stretched out on the carpet, Carla impaled herself on his erection and Ronnie crouched over his face. As his cock serviced one woman, his mouth serviced the other. Vic squeezed Ronnie's breast in one hand and fingered Carla's clit with the other and the two women climaxed almost simultaneously, then Glen screamed and came.

"You've been so patient," Ronnie said to Vic. "Now you get your reward." She snapped her fingers and Vic stretched out on the sofa. Carla licked one side of his fully erect penis and Ronnie licked the other. The two women licked in perfect unison, until thick come spurted from Vic's member.

Vic looked at Ronnie and smiled. "Holy shit."

"Precisely," Glen said.

Later, as Ronnie and Carla were leaving, Vic and Glen stood at the door. "Next time I'm in town?" Vic said.

"Love to," Carla said.

"Just give me a call," Ronnie said. "You both know the number."

Chapter 10

"I got a catalog in the mail a few weeks ago," Bryce said to Carla as they entered the paneled room one evening in early spring. "And I did some shopping." He put a large cardboard box down on a wooden bench.

From the expectancy in his voice, Carla assumed that he wasn't talking about new shirts or remaindered books. "And . . . ?"

"And I bought us a few new toys. I know Ronnie has a bunch of stuff here, but I wanted some things of our own. Why don't you get undressed?" As Carla took off her clothes, Bryce opened the box and pulled out his first purchase, two pairs of handcuffs. "Come here." He kissed Carla firmly, cupping her firm buttocks and squeezing her cheeks. He nibbled on her neck, then fastened one cuff to each wrist. "Now let's see. . . ."

Carla had a general idea of what was to come. She and Bryce played here often and several of their fantasies had become regular games. They had learned to easily communicate their desires. Often an evening started with one fantasy and veered off in another direction midway through. But, no matter what scene they enacted, they always ended up truly satisfied.

Bryce backed Carla against a wall and fastened the cuffs so her widespread arms were stretched over her head. "Nice. I love to see you like that, exposed and vulnerable." He took a sip of his wine. "Tonight, you need to learn a new sexual lesson."

"And what might that be?" Carla asked, her body already wet and hot, ready for whatever Bryce wanted to teach her.

"Patience," he said.

"What's that supposed to mean?"

"Tonight I'm going to see how far I can push you. It's a game that we're both going to win. As they say so dramatically in those romance novels you're so fond of, 'I'm going to make you beg for me.' "

"I'll beg right now. I want you and you know it. And you want me too."

"Of course I do, but tonight is a contest. I want to make you want me like you've never wanted anything before. I want to push your need as high as it will go, tear it down, and push it higher still."

"This isn't supposed to be an endurance contest," Carla said.

"An endurance contest might be fun." Bryce took out his wallet, counted out ten one-hundred-dollar bills and placed them on the bed. He pulled a timer from the bag and set it for fifteen minutes. "I'm putting this right here," he said as he set the timer on a bench. "If you can hold out until it goes off, the money is yours."

"This is nuts," Carla said, intrigued. "You already paid me for the evening."

"I know that, but this is a wager. I'll bet you that I can make you so hot that you'll say, 'Fuck me,' before the timer goes off. Of course, if you should climax you lose."

"Why are you doing this?" Carla asked, truly puzzled.

"I love making love with you," Bryce said, "but I've always felt that you're so busy giving me pleasure that you never reach your own limit. I want to extend you, push you to the ultimate." He grinned at the beautiful woman spread-eagled against the wall. "Is it a bet?"

"Let's get this straight. If I can keep from asking you to fuck me until that thing bings, I win a thousand dollars?"

"Yup."

"And if I fail?"

"You get the best damn fuck you've ever had."

"That sounds too good to pass up."

Bryce slid his hand up the inside of Carla's thigh, past the top of her stocking, and brushed the crotch of her panties. "You're soaked already," he said, rubbing her crotch lightly. "Want me to fuck you right now?"

"I can wait," Carla said, feeling the electricity that always jolted her body when Bryce touched her. She liked Bryce a lot and would have dated him without the money, but he always insisted on paying. He tried to explain that it made it easier for him. And whether or not she truly understood his reasons, she knew that he could afford their frequent rendezvous and Carla enjoyed watching the boys' college fund grow.

Bryce pressed his fully clothed body against Carla, entwined his hands in hers, and placed his mouth against her ear. He traced the tip of his tongue across her sensitive skin and whispered, "Remember, just say

'Fuck me' whenever you're ready." He bit the tip of her earlobe, then kissed a fiery path along her jaw and down the pulse in her neck.

"You'll have to do better than that."

"If that's a dare," he said, "I'll take you up on it." He opened the box and pulled out a jar. "This is called Slippery Stuff," he said, opening the jar and tasting a bit. "Strawberry." He rubbed some of the goo on Carla's nipples, then withdrew another package from the box. "These are nipple suction cups. I thought about getting clips, but I know you don't enjoy real pain and those things hurt. But these, well according to the package," he said, reading the cardboard, "these are supposed to 'create the erotic sensation of love-sucking.' Let's see."

"That's not fair," Carla said, heat rising through her belly.

"It's my game and I decide what's fair." He held the silver-dollar-sized suction cups where she could see them, then attached one to each already-erect nipple. "Are they right? Do they feel like my mouth?"

"Not really," Carla said, "but they're exciting just the same."

Bryce's fingers danced over her breasts as the suction cups enhanced the sensation. "They make your skin blush," he said. "Want to stop?"

Carla's hips moved of their own volition, but she said, "Not a chance."

"Good." He pulled another cardboard-and-plastic-wrapped package from the box. "Here we have a pair of 'Vibrating Ben-Wa Balls.' It says, 'Guaranteed to give maximum vaginal or anal pleasure.' You'll be happy to know that I even thought to bring batteries." Agonizingly slowly, Bryce put batteries into the control pack, then inserted the one-inch balls deep into Carla's vagina. "Now, let's see how this works." He pushed the slider so the balls hummed.

Vibrations filled her body. "Shit, Bryce," Carla said. "Oh God."

"One more thing," Bryce said, pulling another toy from the box. "An anal plug." As he unwrapped the plastic, he continued. "We've played with these before, but this is our very own, just made for your sweet little ass." He held the almost-two-inch-wide dildo in front of Carla's face. "See how big it is?" He rubbed the thick phallus through the over-sensitive valley between her breasts.

"That won't fit inside of me," Carla said, squirming. The vibrations still filled her cunt and the suction on her nipples made them almost unbearably sensitive.

"Let's see," he said. "Make it wet." He pressed the tip against Carla's lips. "Open," he snapped. Carla took the thick plastic cock into her mouth and slid her tongue over the plastic.

"Good," Bryce said. "I wonder how this will feel pressing against those vibrating balls in your pussy." It took only a little pressure to insert the dildo into Carla's rear.

"Oh God," Carla screamed. "Too much."

"Don't forget that if you come, you lose."

Carla gritted her teeth, trying to think about cold showers or trips to the dentist. It didn't help.

Suddenly, the timer sounded and Carla sighed.

"Good girl," Bryce said. "You win. Now, how about double or nothing for another fifteen minutes."

Carla's eyes were glazed and she was unsure whether she could last much longer. "Done," she said, deciding she could hold out, or at least try.

"Wonderful." He stood up and took a video tape from his jacket pocket. "This toy's a little unusual. Do you remember two men with whom you made a movie several months ago? Dean and Nicky."

"I remember," she hissed through gritted teeth. She was on fire and it took all of her concentration not to surrender to the pleasure.

"Well, when you told me about it I was curious. I called Tim who put me in touch with Dean and he made me a copy." He brandished the unmarked video cassette. "Now I want to watch it."

He turned on the TV and slipped the tape into the VCR. Familiar images appeared on the screen. For several minutes Bryce rubbed his hands over her body while, on the screen, Nicky kissed her as she lay on the couch of the hotel suite. As the scene changed to the bedroom, Bryce's hands became more demanding. Suddenly, almost angrily, Bryce removed the toys from her body, unfastened her wrists, and almost dragged her to the bed.

Bryce pulled down his jeans and briefs and forced his cock into her mouth. "Do me just the way you did him. Hold my cock with your free hand just like that."

Carla squeezed the base of Bryce's cock and his sac the way she had Nicky's, effectively keeping him from climaxing. Watching the TV screen, she sucked his erection. "Now," he cried and she released her hand so his hot semen could fill her mouth. As he came, the film ended.

Moments later, the timer sounded again. "You win," Bryce said, burying his face in her muff. "Come for me, baby." He licked her clit and fucked her cunt with his fingers until she, too, came.

Although her orgasm was wonderful, Carla was disappointed that Bryce has given up the game so easily. As he lay silently beside her she knew that something was wrong. "Tell me," she said softly, wrapping her arms around his waist and placing her head on his shoulder.

"Nothing."

"Bryce, that's not fair. If there's something you don't want to talk about, that's fine, just say so. But don't insult me by saying that nothing's wrong."

Bryce sighed and stroked her hair. A few moments later he said, "Seeing you like that bothered me in a way I didn't expect."

"I'm sorry that it upset you."

"I guess I care about you more than I thought I did. It surprises and scares me." When Carla remained silent he continued, "Would you consider giving this all up?"

"What?"

"I suddenly realize that you mean more to me than I thought and I'm suddenly very bothered by the thought of you with other men."

"But. . . ."

Bryce placed a finger across her lips. "Let me finish. I've spent a few days with your parents and your boys and I like all of them very much. If everything works out, eventually we could get married. You know that I'm very well-off, financially, and I'd make sure your boys' college was provided for. You wouldn't need to do this to earn money."

"But that's not the reason I do this," Carla said. "Sure, the money's nice, but I really enjoy giving pleasure and discovering new games in bed. And when the men that I'm with discover that their darkest fantasy isn't really so terrible, well, it makes me feel so valuable."

"We have fun together and there's nothing we couldn't do together, in or out of bed."

Carla patted Bryce's hand. "I know that, but this is what I want to do right now."

"But I love you. I want you to be part of my life forever."

"Love?"

"Of course. I guess I didn't realize it until now." He kissed her. "I love you," he whispered against her lips. "I guess it just takes a jolt like that movie to make me realize it."

"Oh Bryce," Carla said, pressing her lips against his. "I love you." But I love this too, she said to herself.

"Think about it. Please."

The following Monday morning, Carla and Ronnie sat across from each other in the living room of the brownstone. "Bryce proposed last Thursday," Carla said.

"That's great." Ronnie jumped up, wrapped her arms around her friend, and squeezed Carla. "What did you tell him? Should I break out the champagne?"

Carla sighed. "I told him that I loved him, but now I don't know. I think I said it because he did. Of course I'm very fond of him, but I don't know whether it's love. His offer is tempting: security, affection, and good sex. But although he told me he does, I don't think he loves me, at least not yet."

"What makes you think that?"

"Well, for one thing, we haven't spoken since last Thursday. You'd think that he'd have called over the weekend. I think the 'I love you' was sort of an afterthought, that his sudden decision to get serious is about me and this business. I think the thought of me with other men bothers him a lot."

"If he loves you, it would."

"Jealousy and possessiveness aren't love. Jack loves you and he understands. I think what Bryce is saying is 'I want you to love me so much that you'll give up fucking other men for money.' " Carla told Ronnie about the video that precipitated Bryce's proposal. "Bryce is a wonderful man, but the more I think about it, the more I realize that I'm not in love with him. Maybe some time in the future, but not now. And I enjoy what you and I do."

"I know."

"It's a tough decision."

"I don't think it would be a difficult choice if you really loved him."

"You may be right."

"I've got a similar problem," Ronnie said. "Jack's home."

"Great. For how long this time?"

"He's back for good. He got in late Saturday night, so excited and he wanted to surprise me. He's gotten an offer from a computer software house to develop a program about geological formations, three-dimensional modeling. He got a small advance and will get a nice royalty deal when it sells. His old boss, TJ Sorenson, has wanted him to come back here for a long time but there wasn't enough work to offer him a full-time position. Now Jack's sure that he can arrange a three-day-a-week slot with TJ, and spend the rest of his time at the computer."

"Ronnie, that's great!"

"I guess."

"What does that mean?"

"I've made a life for myself here, with our business and all. I don't know if Jack will want me to stay at home all the time and I don't know whether I want to give this up. And sometimes wonder Jack and I have enough for a full-time life. It was always easy to believe that we still had something between us when he was gone most of the time."

"You've told me often enough that your sex life wasn't very adventurous."

"Yeah. Hot and hormonal, but predictable. We fucked like bunnies all day yesterday, but I've come to enjoy the creative side of our work."

"Does he know the details of what you do? The fantasies and all? Have you ever showed him Black Satin?"

Ronnie shook her head.

"Maybe he'd be interested in meeting one of your characters."

"You think? It's silly but it's easier to share that side of me with a stranger than with my own husband."

"From all you've told me about Jack, he may be no different from some of our clients. He may have fantasies in his mind that he can't share with you. Maybe you should give him the chance."

"And maybe you should do some thinking about Bryce. I've known him for years and he's a very special person."

"You're changing the subject."

"I know but the comment's still relevant."

"I've got a date with a new guy tomorrow night. I somehow think that it will help me clarify things. And you need to have a good heart-to-heart with Jack."

Since Carla enjoyed making a bit of an entrance, she usually arrived slightly late for dinner with a client. So it surprised her when she was seated at a table in Vinnie's Waterfront Cafe, a well-reviewed yet inconspicuous seafood restaurant overlooking the Hudson River and her client wasn't there waiting for her. She placed the leather case that contained her album on the floor beside her feet and ordered a glass of club soda with a piece of lime. As she sipped, she gazed out through the wide expanse of glass at the river with the lights of the boats making patterns on the rippled surface.

Almost fifteen minutes later, Carla glanced up and saw a man weaving his way toward her. Gil, he'd said his name was. Just Gil. He had refused to tell her his last name and that was all right with her. He had been recommended by a client she'd been with many times.

As he approached, she realized that he was unusually tall and incredibly thin. He really does look like a bean pole, she thought. He's maybe six-six and he couldn't weigh more than one fifty. Carla extended her hand. "Gil," she said as she took his tentatively offered hand, "I'm Carla."

"Nice to meet you," he said. He sat down quickly and took a long swallow of the glass of water already waiting at his place. "Sorry I was late. Unavoidable."

Carla watched her newest client intently. His hands were never still. He put his glass down and fiddled with his napkin. When it was neatly in his lap, he picked up his fork and twirled it in his long slender fingers. "You sounded nice on the phone," he said, his words quick and clipped, "but I'd like to make this perfectly clear. I don't want to talk about my wife or my marriage. I won't talk about my job and I've given you a phony name so you won't be able to trace me."

Carla tried to keep her smile warm yet impersonal. If she had any desire to find out who he was, her friend Ed, who had vouched for him, would tell her anything she needed to know. But why should she? A man's personal life was his concern. "I have no intention of trying to find out who you are, Gil. I'm here because you called me."

"Yes, yes I did," he said, putting his fork down and picking up his water glass. His nails were bitten down to the quick and his cuticles were chewed and scabbed over in a few spots. He wore a casual shirt and tan slacks, an outfit that unfortunately made his almost emaciated body look even thinner. "As I told you on the phone, I have these needs that no one would understand so I decided to hire a hooker." He looked at Carla, stylishly dressed in a pair of black wool slacks and a long-sleeved, kelly green silk blouse, and his mouth tightened. "I'm sorry. You're not really a hooker."

"I am a hooker and I enjoy it. Do you know where the word hooker comes from?" When he was silent she continued. "During the Civil War a general named Hooker brought women along with his army to keep the troops happy between battles. Hooker's Women, they were called. That's what I do, after all. Keep the troops happy. And what's wrong with that? Sex is fun."

The corners of Gil's mouth turned up for a moment, then his lips returned to their original thin line. "I don't want to talk about sex either. That is, not yet."

"That's fine. Tell me what you like to do in your spare time. Do you like sports?"

"You mean do I like basketball," he snapped. "A tall guy like me has to like basketball, right?"

"Ouch," she said softly and Gil had the good grace to look chagrinned. "I thought no such thing. I'm just trying to make small talk. Wow, you've got quite a chip on your shoulder."

Gil's shoulders slumped. "I guess you're right. I'm sorry."

The waiter interrupted. "May I get you a drink?"

"Sure. What have you got on tap?"

The waiter listed several brands and Gil and Carla each ordered a Sam Adams.

"I'm sorry," Gil said as the waiter disappeared, "about my remark before. You hit a sore point and I'm very strung out."

"I wouldn't have noticed," Carla said, taking his dinner knife from Gil's hands and placing it back on the table. "Want to talk about it?" Carla had realized long before that part of her job was being a counselor, friend, and confidante. So many of her clients had problems and no one to talk to about them.

"They used to call me Zip in school."

"Zip?"

"I was already over six feet tall in junior high and I weighed under a hundred pounds. The kids used to tease, 'Stick your tongue out and you'll look like a zipper.' Thus the nickname Zip. I lifted weights but it didn't help."

"You are what you are."

The waiter arrived with their beers and they each took a long drink. "I understand you're a college graduate," Gil said.

"Unusual for a hooker. Right?" Carla winked and Gil smiled ruefully. "Touché," he said.

"I went to Michigan State and majored in English Literature. You?"

They spent the meal talking and quickly discovered that they had similar taste in movies and books. They had both vacationed in St. Martin and both lamented the commercialism of what had once been a quiet island with great French and native island food. They also shared the same taste in restaurants and each had a quiet little out-of-the-way spot to recommend. They had completely different opinions of the current administration and argued hotly over a recent cabinet appointment.

Over coffee, Carla decided it was time to get to the reason for the dinner. "Not that I'm not enjoying our dinner," Carla said, "but maybe it's time to get slightly more serious. What lead you to call me?"

Gil picked up a sugar packet and turned it over and over in his long fingers. "I have needs. You understand. I have things that pound on my brain, fantasies that I have when I'm with my wife. You know, in bed. It's gotten so I never really make love to her but always pretend she's someone else or that I'm someone else."

"She wouldn't be interested in playing out these fantasies with you?"

"Of course not. We've been married for twenty-four years. She's not that kind of woman."

Carla let that remark pass. "What kind of fantasies?"

He jumped up as the packet in his fingers burst open and sugar poured into Gil's lap. When he was seated again, he said, "I was talking to Ed, you know, like guys talk, and he told me about you. That you fulfill fantasies. That's what I need. Someone like you."

"I'm happy to oblige," she said, "but you'd be surprised what your wife might enjoy if you gave her the chance."

"Don't talk to me about my wife," Gil snapped. "I know her better than you do."

So many men came to her with the same story. And so many of them were wrong. Carla's sigh was inaudible. It wasn't her job to educate her clients, just to please them. "I won't say another word about your wife," Carla said.

His gaze was fixed on the corner of her leather case. "You have a book. Ed told me about it."

Carla pulled her album from its case and handed it to Gil. "Ed probably told you how this works. There's an envelope inside." When he nodded, she rose and picked up her pocketbook. "I'll freshen up and be back in a few minutes."

Gil opened the cover.

When Carla returned from the ladies' room Gil was staring at one of the pictures. She glanced over his shoulder as she took her seat. "Gil?" He was a million miles away. "Gil?" she said again. His eyes cleared and she caught his eye. "That's Sally. She's twelve and she really likes candy." She could see Gil's Adam's apple bobbing up and down.

Suddenly, Carla knew exactly what he wanted and although she'd never been Sally before, she could think of several ways to enhance the experience. She could see his fantasy playing, like a movie, behind her eyes. "I know where she lives."

Gil held the book with one hand and his fingers fiddled with the tassel of the now-filled black satin bookmark. He suddenly pulled out a credit card and dropped it onto the dinner check. The waiter whisked it away and returned with the receipt which Gil signed, his finger still in the album marking Sally's photograph.

It took the cab almost fifteen minutes to arrive at the brownstone. Carla showed Gil into the living room, then disappeared upstairs.

Ten long minutes later Gil stood in the center of the room. "Gil," Carla said as she walked down the stairs.

He turned and stared at the little girl in the pink party dress who walked toward him. Her face was freshly washed and she wore no makeup or jewelry. "Hi," the girl said, hugging a large doll under one arm. "My name's Sally. My mommy says that I should always call my elders by their last name. May I call you Mr. Smith?"

Gil could only nod, his hands still for the moment.

"Can I have that?" Sally said, taking the book from Gil's tight fingers. "Thanks," she said, her voice slightly higher pitched than usual. She placed the book on the desk at the side of the room. "Do you like my new shoes?" She stuck out one foot then polished the shiny tip by rubbing it up and down Gil's trouser leg. "My mommy lets me wear them on special occasions."

Gil cleared his throat. "They're very nice," he said, dropping onto the sofa.

"Wanna play a game Mr. Smith?" she asked. "We could play with my doll." She bent over and put the doll on the sofa beside Gil. As she bent, her short skirt allowed a clear view of her white cotton underpants.

This is a grown woman, a prostitute, Gil told himself. But oh Lord she even smells of baby soap. He rubbed his sweating palms on his trouser legs. "I'd love to play a game." He saw the candy dish on the end table next to him. "There's some candy here," he said, trying to say the right thing to make this fantasy go on and on. "Would you like some?"

"My mommy only lets me have candy on special occasions. Is this a special occasion?"

"It certainly is," Gil said, slowly slipping into the fantasy. She was a hooker, but she was a little girl and he wanted her as he'd wanted nothing else in his life. "If I give you a piece of candy will you do something that will make me happy too?"

"Okay, Mr. Smith," Sally said. Gil handed her the dish and she selected a Hershey's Kiss. Slowly she removed the silver paper while Gil watched her very move. Reflexively he wet his lips as Sally stuck out her pink tongue and licked the surface of the chocolate.

As she watched his eyes on her hands and tongue Carla was happy that she'd taken an extra minute to remove her nail polish. He wouldn't realize how much thought had gone into creating Sally but he would get tremendous pleasure out of playing with her. "Thanks for the chocolate," she said, popping the morsel into her mouth, but deliberately leaving a chocolate stain at the corner. She slowly licked her lips, missing the stain.

"You've got some chocolate on your mouth," Gil said. "Come here." He took her arm and used his handkerchief to wipe the brown goo from her mouth. He pulled her close and placed a feather-light kiss on her lips.

"I can do a dance for you," Sally said, bouncing up from the couch. Anticipation was the best part of the game.

"That would be nice," Gil said, disappointed that she had moved away.

Sally put a tape in the player and whirled around the living room, flipping her skirt so Gil could catch glimpses of her undies. "Sometimes," she giggled, "I do this without my panties. The wind feels funny when I twirl. Wanna see?"

Gil could only nod, his fingers playing with a fold in the sofa's leather. Quickly Sally pulled off her panties and twirled. In her ten minutes upstairs, Carla had run an electric razor over her groin and now her crotch was clean as a baby's. "Wheee," she said, landing on the couch as if dizzy. "It's all tickly." Since Gil was silent, Carla continued to lead him through the fantasy. "If you give me another candy, I'll let you touch where it's tickly."

A bit dazed, Gil handed Carla the dish and she selected a carmel. She unwrapped it and popped it into her mouth. As he watched, she chewed the sticky candy slowly, moving it around her mouth with her tongue. She inserted a finger into her mouth and pulled a glob of candy free. "Now I'm all sticky," she said. "Wanna lick?" She pointed her finger at his mouth and reflexively he opened and sucked her finger inside. She pulled just hard enough to create suction, then allowed him to draw her finger back in.

He flicked his tongue around her nail, sucking at the sweetness. "Wanna touch my tickly part?" she asked as she withdrew her finger.

"Yes," he groaned. She lifted her skirt, took his hand and brushed his fingertips over her freshly shaved and lotioned flesh. "Oh Jesus," he moaned, rubbing his palm over her now-hairless mound.

"You moaned, Mr. Smith. That's too bad. You must be hurting." She patted the bulge in his pants. "When I hurt, mommy takes all my clothes off and puts me to bed. Like this." She whisked her dress off over her head and pulled off her shoes and socks. She stood before Gil dressed only in a white cotton undershirt, stretched to its limit by her large, unrestrained breasts. "You should take your clothes off if you're sick."

He stood and removed his shirt, folding it carefully and placing it on a chair. He pulled off his slacks and straightened the creases with quick, efficient motions. His shoes and socks followed, then his underwear until all his clothing was folded and stacked in a neat pile. He stood in the middle of the living room, naked, with his long, slender erection poking straight out from his body like a large thorn on a long, skinny branch. His fingers stretched across his flat abdomen, twisting and untwisting.

"Wow," Sally said, "you look different from me. You've got that thing sticking out. Can I touch it?" Without waiting for Gil to answer she cupped his prick and slid it through her hands. "It's very long and very hard," she said. She touched, examined, and stroked his cock and balls as though she'd never held one before. "What does it do, Mr. Smith?" she asked, her voice high pitched and a wide-eyed innocent expression on her face.

He pulled back, unsure of his ability to control his body for long. "I'll show you, if you want."

"Can I have candy when you're done?"

"Of course," he said, barely able to keep the quaking from his voice.

He sat on the sofa and pulled the little girl so she stood between his knees. "But first I have to make you ready." The insides of her thighs were like the softest silk as his fingers tickled their way from her knee to her smooth, hairless crotch. She was already wet and his cock and balls were on fire with his need for her.

"Come here." He pulled her so that she was kneeling astride his lap, straddling his cock. "Sit down right here and you'll understand."

She opened a foil package she'd taken from the end table and unrolled the condom over Gil's cock. "A little girl is always prepared." Without any delay, she sat on his erect cock. "That way? Is this what that's for?"

Gil rubbed the sides of the cotton undershirt. Avoiding her large breasts, which would have ruined the fantasy, he bucked and arched as she bounced in his lap. "God, yes," he cried as an orgasm deeper than any he ever remembered overtook him. "Sally!"

Ten minutes later they were still in the same position and his hands had been quiet for the entire time. "Can I see you again?" he whispered.

"You have my number," Carla whispered, rising and handing Gil a wad of tissues. "Call me anytime."

He dressed quickly and, reliving the evening over and over, he left. Carla gathered her props and walked upstairs, considering. She was pleased at how deeply Gil had gotten into his fantasy. She had given him a wonderful evening and had earned five hundred dollars as well. It's amazing, she thought. I become part of almost every fantasy I play and so far I've enjoyed them all. She pulled off the white cotton undershirt and threw it and the rest of Sally's clothes into the hamper.

In the bathtub, she held the massager hose and played the spray over her freshly shaved pussy, thinking about Sally and Gil. It took only a few moments for her to climax. Bathed and relaxed, Carla climbed into bed.

Ronnie had always called her customers friends and now Carla realized why. These men were her friends, if only for one evening. She liked all the men she had been with and got tremendous pleasure out of satisfying them and, in doing that, satisfying herself.

No, she thought, a smile lighting her face. Although I like Bryce a lot and his offer is flattering, I don't want to give up the pleasures that I've found with my friends. At least not yet.

If Bryce could continue their relationship as it had been, that would be wonderful. And if he couldn't, then they would have to go their separate ways. She would miss him dreadfully, but not enough to make her give all this up.

She snuggled down, pulled the satin comforter up around her ears, and quickly fell asleep.

* * *

In Hopewell Junction, Ronnie sat in her living room with Jack, sipping a glass of diet Pepsi. She had just finished telling her husband about the lifestyle she, and now Carla, had established. "I enjoy helping my friends understand that their fantasies are not very different from the dreams that we all have at one time or another."

"I know what you were involved in, of course," Jack said, "but I had no real idea how much there was for men to experience."

"It's fun, Jack," Ronnie said, "and men pay me a great deal of money to share their fantasies with me."

"Are you going to continue in the business?"

"How do you feel about it?"

"Now that I'm going to be in New York full time," Jack said, "I guess I'd be upset if you spent time with other men. Of course, I'd love to meet Carla. You two seem to have become such good friends."

"We certainly have. But if I gave up the business, what would I do all day to keep from being bored crazy?"

"I was thinking about the amount of writing that is connected with my job. There are going to be manuals and guides and scads of documentation. I'll hate that part and you'd be so good at it."

"But what do I know about geological models?"

"Hey, babe. You've got a college degree in writing and you're very bright. I'll teach you how the model works and you can explain it on paper to the users. I know you—you'd pick up what you needed to know very quickly."

"You really think so?"

"I'd like you to give it a try."

Ronnie winked at her husband. "I think I'd like that."

"And you'd give up the business?"

"Only if I can play with you."

"Play with me?"

"Men have been paying me a lot of money to play fantasy games. Wouldn't you like that? Some different ideas to spice up our sex life."

"I guess we've never done much off-center stuff. But it's always been good just the way it is."

"I know that. But variety is wonderful. Don't you have a fantasy that you'd like to act out with me?"

"I don't know. Like what?"

Ronnie reached into a paper bag she had put beside the couch and pulled out the black satin album. She slid over next to Jack, placed the book on his lap, and opened the front cover.

"Is that you?" Jack said. He turned the page. "That *is* you. Holy shit."

Ronnie smiled and cuddled against her husband. "That's Marguerite, the stripper." He turned the page. "And that's Nita, the harem girl, and on the next page is Miss Gilbert, who enjoys disciplining naughty students. And there are many more. Wanna play?"

"Holy shit," Jack said, turning another page. "Holy shit."

The Pleasures of JessicaLynn

Chapter 1

"Steph, it's Jessie." Thirty-six-year-old JessicaLynn Hanley kicked off her high heels and stretched out against the mountain of pillows on her king-sized bed. She crossed her stocking-clad ankles on the paisley bedspread and, holding the cordless phone between the pillows and her ear, unfastened the thin gold bracelet she had just bought.

"I thought about you a lot today," Jessie's best friend Stephanie Carlton said from a thousand miles away, "and I was hoping you'd call. Is it done?"

"Done," Jessie said, glancing at her watch. "According to my lawyer, for three hours and seventeen minutes I've been a legally separated woman. All the papers neatly signed by the judge. It's over." Through surprisingly misty eyes, she glanced around the tastefully decorated room in which she had slept for the last nine years of her marriage and the fourteen months since Rob moved out.

"You knew this day would come," Steph's soft voice said. "Weren't you prepared?"

"Oh, I guess I was," Jessie said, taking a large swallow from the can of diet Pepsi she had grabbed on her way upstairs, "but, I guess I wasn't quite as ready as I thought I was."

"How do you feel about everything now?" Steph's voice was filled with concern.

Jessie let out a long breath. "Mixed emotions. I thought about Rob a lot this afternoon and, hell, he's still the person I spent all those years with, thinking we were happy. Part of me is sad, like something died." She shook her head. "Of course, most of me still wants to shoot the bastard." She closed her eyes and the moment that changed her life played behind her lids like a movie.

It had been more than a year since she had arrived at her husband's dental office late one afternoon with swatches of fabric for new chairs for the waiting room. His receptionist had left for the day, so Jessie had wandered back toward his private office where he often worked late getting his paperwork in order. As she glanced into the main operatory, she had been greeted by the vision of her husband's bare ass, muscles clenching, back arching as he crouched over the contour dental chair and drove his cock into his recently hired twenty-two-year-old dental assistant. "Harder Robby baby, harder," the girl had been screaming. "Fuck me good. Fill me up."

Snapping back to the present, Jessie said, "You know, Steph, all I could think of when I walked in on the two of them fucking was the old joke about the voluptuous woman who goes into the dentist's office. After a brief exam, he tells her that she needs quite a bit of very expensive dental work. 'Oh fuck,' she says. 'Okay,' says the dentist, 'just tell me which cavity you want me to fill and I'll adjust the chair.' "

Jessie enjoyed her friend's deep husky laugh. During their senior year at Ottawa High in Ottawa, Illinois, Steph, her steady boyfriend and now husband Brian, Jessie and Rob had hung out together. They had gone to the drive-in in LaSalle in Rob's father's Pontiac and pretended to watch the latest movie, shared burgers and fries at Bianchi's or the Root Beer Stand, and planned their futures.

"Wall Street," Brian had said, over and over. "I'm going to make millions and then Steph and I will get married and have a dozen kids."

Immediately after graduation Brian, true to his dreams, had moved to New York and had made a great deal of money as a commodities trader. He had sent for Steph and they had married and moved to Westchester County. Unfortunately, their only child, Theresa, had been killed at the age of nine. She had been riding her bicycle near the elementary school when a drunken driver ran his car onto the sidewalk and struck the child.

"I'm going to be a doctor or dentist and make scads of money," Rob had said from the driver's seat of the Pontiac. "I'll join the country club and play tennis every Thursday afternoon." And Rob had done just that; gone to college and dental school while Jessie had worked to support both of them. Insisting that he wouldn't make a good father, Rob had also decided that the couple would have no children.

Through the years, though a thousand miles apart, Steph and Jessie had kept in touch and had remained close. Jessie had even visited the Carltons' home in Harrison occasionally.

"It's good to hear that you haven't lost your sense of humor," Steph said.

Jessie sat on the edge of the bed and began to pull the pins from her carefully arranged titian French knot. An attractive, green-eyed redhead, she had freckleless ivory skin and a slender figure with ample curves in all the right places. "My funny bone is still intact. Actually, I feel a little sorry for the jerk. I get weekly reports from some of our old supposedly well-meaning friends who think I need blow-by-blow accounts of their comings and goings, pardon the pun. I understand that he's going to marry the bimbo. She has the brains of a thumbtack and giggles all the time, but you know all the stories about the seven-year itch. Rob always was a bit slow. It took him thirteen years to feel it. I hope they'll be very happy, snarl. I'll retract my claws now." Jessie's voice dropped. "Anyway, maybe she's good in bed, better than I ever was." Jessie was amazed at the knot of bitterness that was lodged in the pit of her stomach. She and Rob hadn't had a volcanic sex life but she had been content. Content. What a horrible word to describe a sex life.

"Do I hear a note of self-pity?" Steph asked. When her comment was followed by a long pause, she continued, "Cut that out, Jessie."

"I know. It's just that I thought we were happy. I feel duped, somehow." She stood up and walked to the window, overlooking the backyard. She raised the sash and inhaled the fragrance of freshly cut grass. "And suddenly I feel very lonely, very foreign here."

Steph changed the subject quickly. "Are you changing your name back?"

"No. I thought about it, but so much of my business life is under the name Hanley that I'm going to keep the name. And, after all, it's so much easier to pronounce and spell than Florcyk."

"Lord knows you're right about that," Steph said. "Remember, in school, how we always waited for the teacher to get to your name the first day. No one could ever say it right."

Jessie smiled. "Remember Mr. Honeywell? He never did learn to pronounce it. He got as far as Fler-cuck and called me that all year." Jessie pictured their senior English teacher. He had held all the girls spellbound with his sensual reading of eighteenth-century English poetry.

"God, he was something," Steph said with a small sigh. "I still get the hots just thinking about him. He had the greatest buns in those tight jeans he wore."

"A tight, flat rear and that fantastic bulge in the front. We speculated for hours about whether he wore padding in his shorts." Jessie smiled. She hadn't thought sexy, outrageous things like that in years, and, she suddenly realized, she missed it.

"And what about men in your life?" Steph asked. "Are you dating yet?"

"Yes and no. There's a guy I've known for a few months. We've been to dinner a few times in the past few months and I think he's interested."

"And you? How do you feel?"

"I don't know. Maybe I'm not ready yet. Steve, that's his name, Steve's sweet and kind and thoughtful. But I feel, I can't explain it, sort of closed in."

"So come back here and stay with Brian and me for a few weeks or longer." Steph had been trying to convince Jessie to visit for months. "You're selling the house so you have to move anyway. Let someone in your office handle the arrangements and get the hell out of town for a while."

"Oh, Steph, I wish I could."

"Why can't you?"

"I have responsibilities here."

"Like what?"

"Like the office." Jessie owned Ferncrest Realty, a small but success-ful real estate agency specializing in newly built town houses. "And sell-ing the house. Packing, organizing, you know."

"You've told me over and over that the office runs like clockwork. I'm sure you hate to admit that it can get along without you, but it can and it will. And how will it feel showing strangers through your house, know-ing that they're criticizing your landscaping and your wallpaper? You don't need that right now."

Jessie looked down at the backyard. She remembered planting most of the red, white, and pink azaleas that blazed in full bloom along the foundation. "I know that, but I don't mind selling the house. It was always too ostentatious for my taste. Rob was the one who wanted a big, showy house in which to entertain. His lawyer told me that he wanted to keep it, buy me out but I told him no. I won't have Rob and bimbette living here." Her eyes misted as she stared into the master bath and took in the new fix-tures she and Rob had had installed just a month before 'the event.' "I just can't bear that."

"I understand, Jessie. If, God forbid, anything like that ever happened to Brian and me, I wouldn't want him to live here either."

"Everything has two sides, you know, and sometimes my feelings change from minute to minute. There's a big part of me that still feels the history in here. So much entertaining: the bridge games, the country club crowd that Rob wanted so much to be a part of, barbecues on the deck." Jessie tucked the phone between her ear and shoulder and, with all the pins now removed from her long, red hair, combed her slender fingers through the strands and rubbed her scalp. "That's all over now."

"So, why stay there? Come to Harrison and stay with us. You know this huge old place has plenty of room. You could have the entire end of the house you had when you were here two years ago. All the privacy you could want, and all of my company you can stand."

"Oh Steph, it sounds so tempting."

"I wish you'd come. Harrison has so much to offer you, especially at this point in your life. It will be like old times. Girl talk, movies. We can lounge by the pool and talk about life, love and good sex, not necessarily in that order."

"What about my life here? I've got to find a place to live."

"Do it later. You don't want to make any long-term decisions right now anyway and you can certainly afford to dump most of your stuff. Put things you really want to keep in storage and split." Jessie paused, so Steph continued, "It would be so great. You and me, on our own near the big city. Nobody gleefully keeping you up to date on Rob's escapades. Just Broadway plays, expensive restaurants, museums, Bergdorfs, Bloomingdales, Saks, Lord & Taylor's, the works."

"Not too many restaurants," Jessie said, running her palm down her flat stomach. "My figure couldn't stand the calories."

"Calories are overrated." Steph stopped suddenly. "Whoa. Wait a minute. Was that a yes I heard?"

Jessie flopped back onto a stack of pillows. "Why the hell not? For a couple of weeks anyway."

Steph squealed like the girls had when they were kids. "Wonderful. I never believed you'd actually agree."

"Are you sure you're not regretting your offer now that I've said yes?"

"Of course not. It will be great. I don't mean to push my luck but how soon can you get here?"

Jessie giggled and pulled her datebook from her bedside table. She flipped the pages. "Okay. It's May seventeenth." She planned out loud. "Give me a month to get a few arrangements made. Make it six weeks. I'm selling most of the furniture anyway, so all I have to do is sort out some personal stuff. God, the amount of crap one collects in nine years."

"Just pull out what you want and let Rob sort out the rest. Since you're there, you get first dibs."

"It's all in that long-discussed separation agreement anyway. Now let's see." She planned out loud, her pencil tapping the dates on the calendar in her book. "The house goes on the market July first. I'll put a few things in storage, pack a couple of bags. . . . How about I fly out June twenty-fifth. That's a Sunday. I'll plan to stay for. . . ."

"Leave your return open. Maybe I'll be able to convince you to stay for the whole summer."

"Okay. No return just yet." Jessie wrote 'Go to Harrison' across the space for June twenty-fifth, then slammed her datebook shut and dropped it onto the bed. "Oh Steph, thanks. Now that I've made the decision, I feel so relieved. I guess I didn't realize how much this divorce has taken out of me."

"Well I did, and I'm delighted that you've finally made the right decision."

The two women talked for another half an hour, and, after she hung up, Jessie pulled off her clothes and soaked in a hot bath. Then, after a dinner of pasta, salad, and a glass of Beck's Dark, she collapsed into bed and slept through the night for the first time in weeks.

Later that evening, in her bedroom in Harrison, Stephanie stretched out beside her husband Brian. "I can't believe I actually talked her into coming out here. It will be so good for her."

Steph was Jessie's physical opposite, tall and angular with long legs and a slender, tight figure. She had recently had her almost-black hair styled into a shoulder-length bob that framed her conventionally pretty face. She needed almost no makeup to highlight her doelike deep brown eyes, cute turned-up nose, and full, sensuous lips.

Brian rubbed his palm over his wife's naked hip. "What about us? You know. How much does Jessie know about the way we live?"

"Not much yet, love," Steph said, sliding her fingers through the heavy black hair on Brian's chest and gazing into his unusually pale, blue eyes. "But she will, soon enough. It will be an enlightening experience for her."

"I've always had the feeling that there was so much more to her than Rob ever saw. The jerk. While we were making out in the backseat, I used to listen to them in the front."

"You're kidding," Steph said, caressing her husband's flat stomach with the tips of her fingers. "I was always too busy trying to control your hands, or pretending to, to pay attention to anything else."

"Oh, I just heard bits and pieces, before and after. He always satisfied himself but I had the feeling that he didn't pay much attention to whether Jessie was satisfied or not."

"Tell me the truth," Steph said. "You always had the hots for her, didn't you?"

Brian's breathing quickened. "She was a sexy little number. I know there's animal sensuality hidden beneath the surface, fighting to get out through all that carefully orchestrated facade. I'd love to be the one to let it out."

"You and she never made it?"

"Unfortunately, no."

Steph wrapped her long fingers around Brian's hard cock. "There's still hope, you know."

"I know, babe," he said, sliding his index finger over her wet inner lips. "I know." Brian rolled his wife onto her back and slammed into her until they both came, screaming.

After a long and delightfully uneventful flight from Chicago, Jessie walked down the long corridor at Newark Airport and grinned as she saw Steph waving. Just outside the security gate, Jessie dropped her carry-on bag and the two women hugged. Jostled from all sides, they moved out of the line of deplaning passengers. "You look tremendous," Steph said.

"You like?" Jessie said, turning so Steph could appreciate her new navy linen pantsuit and pale pink tailored blouse. "I went shopping yesterday. I'm new from the skin out." She lifted one foot and waggled it to show off her new navy low-heeled opera pumps. "And from the top down."

"You look fabulous," Steph said, "but I'm disappointed. I wanted to take you shopping myself. You need jeans, shorts, T-shirts, things like that. And, although I lead a denim kind of life most of the time, you'll need a dress or two."

"We will shop until we drop, to coin a phrase," Jessie said, settling the strap of her suitcase on her shoulder. "I only bought a few things and I brought my checkbook and my credit cards."

"You're doing okay, financially, I gather."

"I'm doing just fine. The business is thriving despite the economy and Rob, under mild duress, was very generous, bless his pointed little head."

"Are you getting alimony?"

"We hassled for a while. His practice nets him in the low six figures but I just wanted payment for the years I spent putting him through dental school so he could drill his bimbo."

"Bitter, darling?" Steph asked, raising one eyebrow.

Jessie sighed. "I have my moments. But on to better topics. What do we have planned for the next week or so?"

"I thought you might want to relax for a few days. Become a vegetable. So I arranged my schedule so that I'm at the gift shop at the hospital Monday and Thursday, but for the rest of the week, I'm yours." Steph had been working at the shop at the hospital for several years and, since her arrival, it had become a profitable business for the small local institution.

"You like working at the hospital. I wish I had something like that, something that made me feel good about myself."

"So do it. When you get back. . . . No, I won't talk about you going back to Illinois. It'll spoil my good mood."

"And how's Brian?"

"He's great, working hard and playing hard. He's got a tennis game this afternoon, but he said to give you a kiss and tell you he'd see you at dinner."

"God, I'm so glad to see you," Jessie said, hugging her friend again.

The two women walked toward the baggage claim area stopping occasionally to hug again. "How much luggage did you bring?" Steph asked, matching her stride to her friend's.

"Only one large suitcase with some essentials and enough clothes to hold me for a few days. I didn't want any leftovers." She heaved a great sigh. "The house is ready to go. And I do mean go. It's well priced and should sell quickly. And the office is better organized than I'd like to admit."

In the baggage claim area, they spotted the illuminated sign for the flight from Chicago and reached the edge of the carousel just as it started to move. "We're looking for a beige tapestry suitcase with brown trim," Jessie said.

As they watched, the first bag over the top of the chute and onto the turning plates was Jessie's. "That's never happened to me before," Jessie said, her mouth hanging open. "My suitcase is usually so far down the line that almost everyone has already left."

"Well," Steph said, "it's an omen." She hefted the bag from the moving platform. "Good luck and good things are coming."

"Oh, I hope so." Jessie fumbled in her purse for her baggage stub. "Sometimes I'm so up, excited about starting a new phase in my life." She looked her best friend in the eyes. "Then, at other times, I'm so down. Rob and I were comfortable and good together. I knew what he was thinking and he knew. . . ." Her eyes began to fill. "It's so final."

"None of that," Steph said, linking her free arm with her friend's. "Only good thoughts will be permitted."

Jessie shook her head and a wisp of hair fell from her French knot. Impatiently she stuffed it into one of the bobby pins that pulled her hair tight against her head. "Right. Only good thoughts."

They arrived in Harrison and had just pulled Jessie's suitcase from the trunk of Steph's BMW when Brian drove up the long driveway, honking the horn of his Lexus and grinning through the windshield. He pulled to a stop, jumped out of the car, and enveloped Jessie in a giant bearhug. "Oh, JJ," he said, reverting to Jessie's nickname from their days in high school. "I'm so glad to see you."

"Me too," she said, hugging him back. "I'd almost forgotten the days of being called JJ. You're the only one who calls me that anymore. It takes me back."

"If you hadn't been so hooked on Rob, I would have jumped you back then and Steph would have had to find someone else."

"You are so full of it, Brian," Jessie said, laughing, swatting him on the ass. "You should have been born Irish."

"Okay, okay, so I exaggerate a bit. But I am glad to see you."

Jessie pushed Brian to arm's length and looked him over. Although he was not particularly tall, Brian was a big man, with large hands and feet and an open, ingenuous smile that lit up his ordinary-looking face. His tennis whites accentuated his oversized arms and legs, all covered with heavy black hair. His skin was heavily tanned, making his eyes look even paler than she remembered. She hugged him again, enjoying the feel of a virile man after so many months alone. "You look fantastic, sir," she said, a bit embarrassed by the erotic thoughts his tight shorts aroused. "And happy."

Brian reached out and draped his arm around his wife's shoulders. "Happy doesn't describe it." He pecked Steph on the cheek, then said, "When's dinner? I'm starved."

"Everything's in the fridge and ready to go. You get the fire started and I'll show Jessie to her room."

"Will do. I'll start the grill, then take a quick shower. Dinner should be ready in less than an hour."

Just over an hour later, the three friends were filling their plates with rare steak, a rice pilaf that Steph had just removed from the microwave, and a crisp green salad with tiny shrimp and bacon bits. "I hope you're not watching your calories," Steph said. "At least not for today. I decided that in honor of your arrival I would make all the things I don't ordinarily eat. To hell with cholesterol."

Brian uncorked a bottle of California Cabernet and poured some into each glass. Jessie looked at the label on the bottle. "Stag's Leap. 1984. Very nice wine."

Brian lifted his glass. "For a very nice lady and her new life. To JJ." His eyes locked with Jessie's and, after a moment, she looked away.

This is silly, Jessie told herself. It feels like he's flirting with me. It only goes to show that I've been celibate too long. He's my best friend's husband, for heaven's sake. She shook it off and spent the rest of the evening chatting amiably with Steph and Brian.

The following day Jessie unwound. Between Brian's job and Steph's stint at the hospital, Jessie saw nothing of either of them. Content to be alone she sat beside the pool until her skin turned a luscious shade of soft apricot, read a romance novel, soaked in a bubble bath for an hour in the oversized jacuzzi-tub in her bathroom, and generally exorcised Rob from her consciousness.

She saw Steph briefly late that afternoon. Jessie had grabbed a container of yogurt from the fridge and was sitting at the table in the kitchen, eating with one hand and holding her book open with the other.

"Hi, Steph," she said, looking up from her book. "What's up? How was your day?"

"The day was great, but I now have a delightful idea. Brian got two tickets for a concert tonight from some client and we can easily get a third. Very last minute. It's the Julliard String Quartet. Brian and I love them and we don't get to hear them very often. How about us both joining him in the city? Dinner, the concert? It would do you a world of good."

"I'm not a concert kind of person, Steph. All that music, particularly after a good dinner, just puts me to sleep. You go, and have a great time."

"But we haven't spent any time together. You've been alone all day."

"And I've enjoyed every minute of it. Go and enjoy your concert. I want to get to bed early anyway. All this relaxing is making me tired." To emphasize her drowsiness, she yawned. "I don't want you to feel you have to entertain me. I do just fine on my own."

"I feel so guilty. But we're best friends and I'll trust you to be honest. So if you're sure you don't mind I'd really like to see this. And the next two days, and Friday as well, are ours. Shopping. Bloomies maybe?"

"Done. See you in the morning."

The next morning, dressed in jeans and a white tank top, Jessie sat in a long white lounge chair in her favorite room in the Carltons' house. Jessie knew that, when Steph and Brian had bought the house a dozen years before, the room had been an open flagstone patio overlooking the pool, shaded at each end by a huge red maple. The couple had immediately seen its potential and had enclosed it with louvered windows and white wood. They had furnished it in white wicker and cluttered it with dozens of pillows in primary colors.

Once the room was constructed, Steph had worked with a florist, learning everything she could about houseplants. She decorated the room with carefully selected specimens, and then tended them with loving care. One end contained cactuses, many blooming with either flowers or colored globes. The other end was all greenery, with ivys, ferns, and a six-foot-high fig tree. In the center, where there was sun most of the day, Steph had put florals with several plants in bloom at all times—African violets in exotic shades, orchids and lilies, anything that caught her fancy. One section was her hospital. The owner of the florist shop frequently gave Steph plants that weren't doing well, for her to nurse back to health.

She spent time almost every day misting, watering, pruning, and removing dead blooms.

Jessie had gotten up early that morning and, although it was only eight-thirty, she was sitting and reading, a cup of fresh coffee at her elbow. As she read, she suddenly became aware of sounds from the pool. She shifted her position and peered through the leaves of a deep orange hibiscus. She couldn't believe what she saw.

Not twenty feet away, beside the pool, Steph lay, stretched out on a lounge chair, dressed in only the top of a tiny black bikini. The bottom of the suit lay on the concrete beside her chair. Her legs straddled the cushions and a man lay between her thighs, his head buried in her pussy. "Ummm," Jessie heard Steph mumble. "That's wonderful." As Jessie watched she became aware of a smooth, tanned back and a tight, tiny ass. She realized that the head that bobbed in Steph's lap was blond. It was not Brian.

Jessie could hear slurping sounds and moans. Wanting to turn away yet fascinated, Jessie watched through the leaves and blossoms.

"Oh Tony," Steph moaned. "Do that more." Her legs trembled and her fists clenched and unclenched. "Yes, just like that." She reached behind her back and untied the top of her bathing suit to free her breasts. As the young man lapped, she pinched her nipples and squirmed. Jessie saw Tony hold Steph's hips still as his mouth worked its magic. Jessie's body throbbed and she could almost feel Tony's tongue as it brought Steph closer and closer to orgasm.

"Oh baby," Steph yelled, "don't stop!"

Jessie wiggled her hips to scratch the itch that grew between her legs. She clenched her vaginal muscles as Steph yelled, "Now, baby. Stick me now!"

Tony plunged two fingers into Steph's body. His arm worked like a piston as Steph's hips thrashed. "Yes," she screamed. "Yes!" As she clutched the arms of the lounge chair and arched her back, the man could barely keep his face against her cunt and his fingers pistoning.

Jessie could almost feel her friend's orgasm and, as she heard Steph's heavy breathing slow, Jessie snuck back into the house and up to her room.

What the hell was that all about? she wondered as she closed the door to her room and dropped onto the bed. She took a few deep breaths to calm her excited body, then propped her head on the pillows. Steph had been a bit wild as a kid, she remembered. She had dated several boys before she met Brian and had told Jessie in great detail about one particular gymnast who finally convinced her to go 'all the way' in the backseat of his father's Oldsmobile. "Boy," Steph had told her, "his gymnastics aren't limited to the gymnasium."

Jessie shook her head. I never thought she'd cheat on Brian like this, she thought, her eyes filling. What is it about sex that makes good people like Steph and Rob do such impossible things, lie and cheat? What is it about sex?

It was after ten when Jessie heard a light knock on her bedroom door. "You up?" a voice whispered.

Jessie wiped her eyes, composed her face and, trying not to look as upset as she felt, said, "Sure. Come on in."

"Well, good morning sleepyhead," Steph said. She had changed into a pair of tight-fitting jeans and a short-sleeved, navy-blue shirt.

"Good morning yourself," Jessie answered, not totally successful at keeping the edge from her voice.

"What's wrong, Jessie?" Steph said. "You sound upset."

"Nothing's wrong," Jessie said. "Just a bit cranky this morning."

"Don't kid me, babe," Steph said, plopping onto the edge of the bed. "Something's up." When Jessie was silent, Steph dropped the novel Jessie had been reading onto the bed beside her. "I found this in the plant room. Does this have anything to do with your mood this morning?"

Jessie picked up the book and put it on the bedside table. "I must have left it there last evening."

"Don't, babe. You never were a very good liar. You saw Tony and me earlier, didn't you."

Jessie blushed, but remained silent.

"You're embarrassed. I can understand that, but what Tony and I did was just clean, honest fun. He comes to tend to the pool and, occasionally, he tends to me as well. It's really nothing."

"Nothing?" Jessie spat. "What about Brian? I'm sure he wouldn't think it was nothing if he knew."

"Of course he knows," Steph said softly. "Come on downstairs. Let's get some coffee and I'll explain everything. I was going to tell you about things before this, but I haven't gotten a chance."

"What things?"

"Coffee first. I need some right about now. I promise I'll tell you everything."

Fifteen minutes later, the two women sat in the plant room, each with a fresh cup of coffee and a toasted english muffin. The coffeepot sat on a warmer near Steph. As she munched on her muffin Jessie's lay untouched on the plate beside her. They had not spoken a word.

"Okay, Jessie," Steph said with a long sigh, "let me try to explain." She sipped her coffee. "About three years ago, Brian was infatuated with a single woman in his office. He told me about it and, for a while, telling about what it might be like if they ever got together made for wild times in bed. Finally, I asked him if he'd like to actually be with her. You know, make love. He said yes."

"He told you that he wanted to go to bed with another woman?" Jessie was horrified.

"There isn't a man on this earth who hasn't thought about doing that at one time or another. Brian was just honest enough to admit it. He would never lie to me and I knew that he wouldn't do anything without telling me."

"And you allowed him to be with someone else?"

"Allowed is an interesting word. I hate to think that I'm in charge of his sex life. I gave it a lot of thought and I decided that I wanted him to be happy. I guess I'm very strong because I didn't feel threatened. It wasn't that kind of thing. He wasn't in love with her, just in lust."

Jessie laughed and started to relax. "In lust. That's an interesting way to put it."

"Well, that's really what it was. Haven't you ever felt that pull, that almost irresistible urge to jump into some man's pants?" When her friend was silent, Steph continued, "You, my love, haven't lived. It's a great feeling, even if you never get to do anything about it."

"I guess I've got no sex drive," Jessie said softly. "And no sex appeal either."

"Bullshit," Steph said. "You just haven't discovered them yet. Anyway, getting back to Valerie. That was her name, Valerie. I never saw her, but Brian described her to me. Tall and shapely, with big, soft tits and great, long legs. But it wasn't her body that turned Brian on. It was her obvious attraction to him. Her eye contact, smiles, movements."

"He told you all that?"

"He described everything in detail afterward, in bed. And the telling got him so hot that we fucked like bunnies."

Jessie shook her head. "I don't believe it. You lay in bed discussing another woman fucking your husband."

Steph nodded, silently letting Jessie absorb what she had heard.

Jessie picked up her muffin and took a bite. "Amazing. How long did it last?"

"He was only with her for about two months, then it all wore off for both of them. So much of being in lust is the expectation, not the actuality. Reality is frequently a letdown."

Despite her amazement, Jessie was fascinated. "You still haven't told me about this morning."

"Give me time," Steph said. "It's a long story. It was several months after that and Brian and I had spent an evening playing Boggle with Lara and Hank Cortez, friends of ours from Scarsdale. Have you ever played Boggle? It's a word game and it's lots of fun. Your score is based on the number of words you can make that no one else wrote down. Well, everyone had had quite a bit to drink and, toward the end of the evening, we had gotten very silly."

Chapter 2

"I have only one word left," Hank said. "Pussy." He grinned at Lara and licked his lips. "Anyone else have pussy?"

"Not me," Brian said. "I haven't had any good pussy in quite a while. Except Steph's, of course, but a wife's pussy doesn't count."

Hank refilled the wine glasses and then threw the letter-dice again. "Cunt," Hank said, triumphantly pointing out the word among the letters before anyone had had time to write anything. "And look. You can make *suck* and *fuck*."

Lara giggled and squeezed Brian's arm. "Such nice words, don't you think?" She looked up at Brian and blinked.

Brian looked at Steph, then stroked Lara's face. "Very nice words."

"I've got an idea," Hank said. "Let's play strip-Boggle. The winner is the one with the most dirty words and everyone else has to take off one article of clothing." He looked at Brian and Steph. "Game?"

Hank was not a particularly good-looking man but the twinkle in his eye and his delightful sense of humor made him attractive. Steph had always been interested in him, but had never before thought about doing anything about it. "Want to?" Brian whispered into Steph's ear.

Steph thought a minute. Yes, she really did. She gave a tiny nod. "Okay, let's do it," Brian said.

After six rounds of the game, the men were down to their socks and shorts, and Lara, who had won three of the rounds, was still wearing her blouse and underwear. Steph had a particular love of delicate undies, and was glad she had worn a black, demi-cup bra with matching lace panties, which, by now, was all she was wearing. "You are one gorgeous woman," Hank said, admiring the way Steph's small, yet soft breasts filled the tiny cups. "I knew you'd be sensational without clothes."

"Not without clothes yet," Steph said. "I'm not wearing any less than I'd be in a bikini."

"I know, but it's knowing that it's not a bikini that's such a turn-on," Hank said.

Brian was gazing silently at Lara's legs and the dark shadow he could make out through the crotch of her white nylon panties. She also still wore her short-sleeved, flowered blouse. "I feel I've been gypped," he said to Lara. "You're still decent."

Lara lowered her head and looked up at him through her lashes. "I'm afraid you won't have the same thrill. I haven't nearly the body that your wife has. As a matter of fact, I'm so flat-chested I don't usually wear a bra. And I've certainly got my share of stretch marks from the babies."

Brian reached over and brushed his hand down the front of Lara's blouse, feeling her erect nipple rub his palm. "I bet you're beautiful under there," Brian said. "Will you take the blouse off, just for me?"

Lara looked at her husband and raised one eyebrow.

"Does everyone understand where this is going?" Hank asked. When everyone nodded, he said, "Then why don't we separate this party. Lara, you and Brian can have the bedroom and Steph and I will take the guest room." He rubbed his knuckles down Steph's cheek. "I want this lady all alone."

As Brian stood up and took Lara's hand, Steph swallowed hard. She was suddenly terrified.

"Baby," Brian said softly, looking at his wife and immediately sensing her discomfort, "this isn't a command performance. It's supposed to be fun. You look like a deer caught in the headlights. Talk to me."

"Did you and Hank set this up? I don't think it's as spur of the moment as it might appear."

"We talked about it," Brian admitted. "Hank has had the hots for you for a long time, and I know he turns you on. It's kind of like me and Valerie. I think we will all get pleasure from this evening, but if you don't want to we can leave right now."

Steph looked at Lara. "What about you? Did you know about this?" Although the question sounded accusatory, her voice was soft and gentle.

"Hank and I have done this sort of thing a few times. It's a game, fun and harmless. We have our rules, of course. Things only happen if everyone's willing and anyone can call things off at any time. And, of course, condoms at all times."

Steph giggled nervously. "Where have I been while all this has been going on?" she asked. "I always thought you two were so conservative."

"Shows how much you know," Lara said. She smiled and squeezed

Hank's hand. "We have a few friends who like to play the same games we enjoy."

Steph took a swallow of her wine and looked at Brian. "You want to do this, don't you?"

"Only if you do."

Hank took Steph's hand and placed it gently on the crotch of his shorts. "I want you very much, and I'd love to show you how good it can be with someone new."

Steph sighed, torn between the indignation she ought to feel and the excitement that was making her pulse pound. Deciding that she did indeed want this, she relaxed her arm and let Hank use her hand to stroke his cock. She smiled and looked from Lara to Brian. "Why don't you two go upstairs. I need a few minutes to get comfortable with this and I think Hank is just the one to help me do that."

Arm in arm, Lara and Brian went upstairs and Hank, clad only in his shorts and socks, sat on the tweed sofa. "Why don't you come and sit beside me?" Steph moved to the couch and sat with a few inches of space between her and Hank. "Baby, I've wanted you for a very long time, but I can wait until you're ready. I want to touch you and hold you. I want to make you wet and hot."

Steph sighed and leaned her head on the back of the sofa. Without touching her, Hank rested his head beside hers and spoke softly. "You know what I'd like to do? I'd like to take off that bra and watch your nipples get hard. I'd like to lick them and then blow on the wet skin. Your nipples will get as hard as tiny pebbles."

Hank watched Steph's body relax, then warm to the sound of his voice. "Then I'll take one nipple between my thumb and index finger and pinch it, hard. You'll think it should hurt, but it won't. It will make your pussy twitch and you'll have a hard time keeping your legs together. While I'm pinching one, I'll take the other in my mouth and bite it gently."

Steph's eyes closed as Hank continued. "I'll alternate, pinching one nipple and sucking and biting the other. Can you feel it, Steph? Can you feel my fingers and my teeth on your breasts? Tell me. Can you?"

"Yes," Steph said, squirming, unsuccessfully trying to keep her body still.

Hank moved his mouth closer to Steph's ear, his hot breath adding fuel to her fire. "Oh yes, I know how you feel." He grasped the snap between the cups of Steph's bra and unclipped the fastener. As he separated the sides, freeing her breasts, her hard, erect nipples reached for Hank's mouth. "Like this," he purred, pinching Steph's left nipple. "And this." He pinched the right. "And this." He leaned over and nipped at her pebbled breast. "So delicious."

When Steph reached out to touch Hank's arm, he gently pressed her hand back onto the back of the sofa. "This is entirely for you. I want you to lie there and just enjoy. I've wanted to do this for so long."

Her voice hoarse and breathless, Steph asked, "What exactly did you imagine?"

He leaned close to her face, his breath hot on the side of her neck. "I imagined breathing into your ear and watching you shiver with pleasure." He caressed the skin on her cheeks and forehead with the pad of his index finger. "I imagined stroking your face and touching your lips with the tip of my tongue." He licked the sensitive skin around the edges of her lips until it was almost torture for Steph not to rub the ticklish spot. He brushed his tongue along the joining of her lips until her mouth opened. "And I dreamed of tasting you." He pressed his mouth against Steph's until their tongues found each other and played deep inside the sensual depths.

"Oh, baby," Hank purred when they separated. "I knew it would be this good."

Steph opened her eyes and gazed at Hank. She should be ashamed of what was happening, but she wasn't. She was revelling in the sensations and in the knowledge that this wasn't her husband. This was a sensual man who wanted to make love with her. In the small part of her brain that was still capable of coherent thought, she realized that it was okay. No, she corrected herself. It was wonderful. She smiled.

"Oh yes, baby," Hank said, almost able to read her mind. "Let me make love to you. Shall we go upstairs to where we can be more comfortable?"

Steph stood and, barefoot, wearing only her tiny, lace panties, she followed Hank upstairs to the guest room. While he ripped the spread off the bed and heaped the covers on the floor, she stood in the center of the room now eager to let Hank make love to her.

Hank turned and allowed his gaze to roam over Steph's almost-naked body. "I can't believe this is really happening," he whispered.

"It is happening," she purred, feeling sexual power and strength flow through her.

When she started to pull the tiny wisp of lace down over her hips, Hank knelt and took her hands. "Let me do this the way I've fantasized." Then he pressed his mouth against her flat belly, flicking his tongue into her navel. He slowly lowered her undies and inhaled her fragrance. He helped Steph step out of her undies, then nudged her legs apart to make it easier for him to touch and taste and smell her.

He reached his tongue between her legs and pressed it against her swollen clit. He felt her legs tremble. "So excited," he whispered, standing and scooping her into his arms and gently laying her on the cool sheets. He crawled between her spread legs and lowered his face to her cunt. He blew hot air through her pussy hair, further inflaming her, then brushed his chin lightly against her fur, just barely touching it, watching her hips buck and reach for him. "Tell me now, baby. Tell me how hot you are."

"Oh God, Hank, I need you so much. I want you."

"And I want you. My cock is so hard that most of me wants to climb onto you and fuck you until we both come. But I'm going to wait. I'm going to give you more pleasure than you think you can stand." He brushed her pussy with his finger, then slid the length of her slit, parting her lips but not entering.

"That's torture," Steph moaned. She raised her hips but Hank kept his fingers just touching her.

Hank's laugh was deep and sexy. "Yes. It certainly is." He pressed just a tiny bit harder so his finger penetrated only a small way.

"Oh God," she moaned. "Oh God."

Hank tightened his tongue and flicked the tip over Steph's hard, swollen clit.

With his breath on her skin, his tongue stroking her nub, and his finger rubbing her pussy lips, Steph could hold out no longer. "I'm going to come," she cried.

As he felt her body begin to spasm, Hank forced three fingers deep into her body and sucked her swollen clit into his mouth.

Waves of liquid heat pulsed through Steph's body, filling her belly and cunt. He seemed to know just how to rub and lick, when to make it hard and when to stroke. Her orgasm continued for what seemed like hours.

"Hold on to it and don't let it down," Hank said as he climbed over her quivering body.

Steph wasn't sure what he meant, but she concentrated on not relaxing, on reaching for more of the glorious sensations and not letting them ebb. When Hank plunged his fully erect cock into her soaking passage, it triggered more spasms of erotic pleasure. He thrust into her over and over until he climaxed and she came again.

"Lord," Hank said as his breathing returned to normal. "It was even better than I dreamed."

"It was fantastic," Steph said.

Back in the kitchen in Harrison, Jessie listened to her friend's story with increasing amazement. When Steph sat back on the kitchen chair,

Jessie was silent for a long while. "I'm flabbergasted," she said finally. "I'm . . . I'm . . . I don't know what I am."

Steph stared into her empty coffee cup. "Horrified? Disgusted?"

"No, of course not." She got up and poured a fresh cup of coffee for herself and her friend. On the way back to her chair, she give Steph a quick hug. "Not horrified or disgusted. Surprised and, I guess, a bit curious. Can I ask you a few questions?"

"Of course. This wasn't intended as a monologue. I wanted you to know. For lots of reasons."

Jessie remembered the picture of Steph, draped over the lawn chair. "This obviously wasn't the only time."

"Actually, Brian and I are now what you would probably call swingers. We have a wonderful life together, but we also have other relationships." When she saw Jessie's eyebrow go up, she said quickly, "None serious. Just playtimes."

"You have people you go to bed with and Brian does too? Like a lover? It's not just the occasional couples swapping partners?"

"That's exactly what I mean." Steph wasn't sure how much Jessie was ready for so she decided just to react to questions for a while. "Right now I have two men with whom I get together from time to time, and Brian is currently seeing a wonderful woman, a systems designer in the computer department at his office."

"The mind boggles," Jessie said, then giggled. "That's how it all started. Boggle, I mean."

Steph let out a deep breath. She hadn't been sure of Jessie's reaction but she had wanted very badly for her best friend to understand. "You're okay with this?"

Jessie reached across the table and took Steph's hand. "I'm fine with this, as long as it works for you and Brian. It was the lying that upset me so much before. But you don't lie to each other. This is all very new to me, but I love you both and you seem very happy." She pulled back and grew thoughtful. "I guess I never thought about women who make love to other people's husbands."

"Hold it," Steph said. "I never make love to anyone who is married, unless the wife knows what's going on. No lying. That's my first and most important rule. No lying. To Brian, to the man involved, or to wives. Period."

"No lying," Jessie said softly.

"In my mind, that's the cardinal sin, the commandment, if you will, that Rob broke with his bimbo, as you call her. He lied to you and he probably lied to himself. It's the dishonesty that makes me want to wring his scrawny neck."

"I guess I never looked at it that way, exactly. For me it was two things. The dishonesty, of course, but it was also the fact that I obviously wasn't good enough for him in bed." Jessie's eyes filled and she looked down.

"Bullshit!" Steph put a finger under Jessie's chin and gently raised her head so the women were looking into each other's eyes. "Listen to me good, JessicaLynn Hanley, you're not good or bad in bed alone. If you and scrawny-neck didn't make it together, it was a mutual failing. Individuals aren't good or bad at making love. Only couples are."

"Yeah, but . . ."

"No 'yeah but.' You're a warm, caring person and you're as good in bed, or as bad, as the chemistry and communication between you and the man you're with." As she looked into her friend's face, she continued, "Don't look at me like I just told you that the earth was flat. It's true."

"But Rob told me. . . ."

"Rob isn't the sexpert of all times, you know. Besides, was he ever with anyone else beside you?"

"He says that bimbette was the first," Jessie said, snuffing.

"What about before you two got married. Was there ever anyone else?"

"No. The first time for both of us was in the front seat of his father's Pontiac." Her face softened. "He almost came on my jeans trying to get them open."

"So what makes him the ultimate judge of sexuality? Certainly not experience."

"I don't know. If I were being brutally honest, I'd have to admit that it wasn't very good. He used to give me a shot of alcohol to 'loosen me up.' He said I was uptight and needed to relax." Her voice dropped and she wiped a tear from her cheek with the back of her hand. "He said I was frigid."

"He can say anything he wants, Jessie, but he can't make you believe it. And I don't believe it."

"But I don't think I've ever had an orgasm."

"And whose fault is that?"

Jessie's head jerked up and she was silent for a minute. "I never thought about it that way. You mean there might not be anything wrong with me?"

"Probably not. You're healthy. No physical problems. No drug abuse. You probably weren't excited enough to come. I read something a while ago that has stuck in my mind. Someone wrote that a man flames like a match and a woman heats like an iron. That timing requires some coordination. It takes a woman twenty or thirty minutes from a cold start."

"A cold start." She laughed. "That's an unusual way to put it. It makes me sound like an auto engine on a winter morning."

"Is that such a bad analogy?"

"Maybe not. I was always a cold start. I came to dread sex."

"Make that forty-five minutes to warm up," Steph said. "Jessie, relax. You're fine. It's scrawny-neck I want to kill."

"Thanks for that, Steph. You always were a good friend."

"And I still am. Let's table this topic for the moment, get dressed up and do some outrageous damage to your credit card at Bloomingdales."

Jessie took a deep, shuddering breath. "Good idea. You've given me lots to think about, and I'd like to continue this discussion another time."

"Any time, babe. I love to talk about sex."

Steph and Jessie spent the afternoon shopping. At first, Jessie selected outfits that were conservative and concealing. At one point, however, Steph convinced Jessie to try on a low-cut, Indiansilk sundress with a very full, soft skirt. When her friend came out of the dressing room, Steph grinned. "You look wonderful." The dress, in shades of soft peach and rose, complemented Jessie's red hair and sun-warmed complexion.

"I do? Isn't it a bit much?" She yanked upward on the neckline, trying to minimize her deep cleavage. "I mean isn't it a bit young for me?"

"Young? Come on. You're thirty-six years old. That's young enough for almost anything, except maybe being proofed at a bar. I think you look terrific, and with a little makeup. . . ."

"Don't get carried away." She swung back and forth in front of the mirror watching the skirt move with her body. As she watched herself, her smile broadened. "But although it's not my usual, I do like this dress."

"Now you need shoes to go with it," Steph said to Jessie's back as she disappeared back into the fitting room. "And a new bathing suit and a few other things I can think of."

When they arrived home, the two women dumped their purchases on the sofa and adjourned to the plant room with two glasses and a bottle of California chardonnay. When they had settled into long chairs side by side, and sipped some wine, Jessie reopened the earlier topic. "I guess I've digested some of our conversation of before. Now I'm curious. How did Brian react to your first encounter with Hank?"

"He was pretty quiet for a day or so, then, in bed a few nights later, he asked me all about it."

"He wanted the gory details?"

"Not specifically, but he wanted to know whether I enjoyed it and whether I came."

"Did you tell him? I mean, weren't you worried that he'd be jealous or something."

"Jessie," Steph said, turning to fully face her friend. "I will never lie to Brian. That's the bottom line. If he doesn't like something that happens we can change the rules but I will never lie. I told him it was wonderful. To me, lovemaking isn't a contest. It's not who's better than whom at this or that. It's pleasure for the sake of pleasure and that's all it is. And, of course, there's never a substitute for first times in bed together. It's the greatest kick in the world."

"Wow. That's quite an attitude."

"I guess, but it's one that Brian and I share completely. We have a deal that if something makes one of us uncomfortable, either about what we are doing ourself or what the other is doing, we talk about it and decide how to rearrange things, if necessary."

"Has he ever been jealous? Have you?"

"Once in a while one of us becomes obsessed with someone for a short time. But it's always hottest at the beginning and eventually it all cools."

Jessie hesitated. "Am I cramping your style?"

"Of course not. There are a few couples in the neighborhood who get together for fun from time to time and we will, either with you or without, in the near future."

"Me?"

"Yes, you. We've found quite a few honest, open kindred spirits." She smiled. "You know, some people who claim to be openminded have said to me, 'Just don't tell my wife the details. I don't want her to know about. . . . ' Honest my foot. They have more secrets than the FBI. We don't find that type of person very congenial."

"Hey, girls, your lord and master is home," a voice yelled from the front hall.

"Hi lord and master," Steph yelled back. "Bring a wineglass. We're killing a bottle of chardonnay and need an accomplice."

"Let me change and I'll be right in."

"You really found the best one," Jessie said wistfully.

"I know I did. But he didn't make out badly in the deal."

Jessie's head snapped up. "I didn't mean. . . ."

Steph laughed. "Of course you didn't. You know you could talk to Brian about all this too."

"Talk to Brian? I'd be too embarrassed."

"Nonsense. He can tell you better than I can how he feels about it all."

"I don't think I'm up to discussing this with him just yet."

"Do you mind if I tell him that we talked?"

"I guess not. It's just so, I don't know, so intimate."

"That it is. And try not to treat him differently because you know what's going on."

"That will be a tall order. I never dreamed there was a tiger under that teddy bear."

At that moment, Brian walked in, wearing a pair of form-fitting swim trunks and carrying a wineglass. The two women burst out laughing. "Okay," Brian said, filling his glass, "what's the joke?"

"We were just talking about what could be hiding under your teddy bear exterior." Steph took a minute to control her laughter. "Then you walk in in those tight little nothings you're wearing and we know you can't hide a thing."

Brian looked down at his body with its heavy black hair. "Okay, ladies, now I'm insulted. Teddy bear indeed. I've always wanted to be a centerfold." He posed with his arms flexed. "A sex symbol. Like Burt Reynolds."

"You're my sex symbol darling," Steph giggled.

Brian walked over and gave his wife a kiss on the top of her head then started toward the pool. "Thanks," he said over his shoulder. "I'll just take this teddy bear body and go for a swim. Join me?"

"Sure." The two women followed Brian to the pool and while he swam laps, Jessie and Steph talked about gardening.

As he swam, Jessie watched Brian's shoulders. He always did have great shoulders, she thought. He fools around. With other women. She watched his huge hands cut through the water. Now stop that, she told herself as a warm flush spread through her body. That's Stephanie's husband you're leering at. But, she said to herself, he fools around with Steph's permission. Interesting.

The following day was Wednesday, matinee day in Manhattan. Steph knocked on Jessie's door and Jessie called, "Come on in." She stood in her bra and panties, rummaging in the dresser drawers for a clean polo shirt.

"Good," Steph said, one hand buried in the pocket of her flowered terrycloth robe. "I caught you before you got dressed. Put on your best city duds, I've got a treasure." She raised her hand and waved a small white envelope. "*Phantom of the Opera.* This very afternoon. Two tickets, row eight."

"Oh Steph. I've wanted to see that show for ages." She slammed the dresser drawer and opened the closet door. "City duds. How's the outfit I arrived in?"

"Just fine," Steph said, looking at her watch. "I'd like to make the ten o'clock train. We can lunch someplace nice, then go to the theater. I'll give Brian a call and he can meet us for an outrageous dinner."

"Sounds terrific."

The day was perfect. The weather was unusually temperate for New York in late June, temperatures in the high seventies and low humidity. The two women window-shopped, ate a quick lunch at Twenty-One, and enjoyed the theater. Brian met them at Le Cirque and the three spent hours gorging themselves on fine food and memorable wine. After dinner, Jessie snuck out to the maitre d' and secretly gave him her credit card. When Brian asked for the check, the waiter nodded toward Jessie. "The madam has already taken care of it."

"Jessie, you shouldn't have."

"That's to say thank you for everything. You're the best friends anyone could ever have and I'm grateful."

Brian stood up, walked around to Jessie's chair and gave her a soft kiss on the cheek. "You're our best friend and we love you." He slid the tip of his finger up the nape of Jessie's neck, ending just below her tight French knot. A shiver slithered down Jessie's spine.

Thursday, Steph spent the day at the hospital and, since Brian had a business dinner, the two women ate in the kitchen, dressed in shorts and T-shirts. "Oh lord, Steph," Jessie said as her friend pulled a casserole dish out of the oven. "Franks and beans. I haven't had franks and beans in . . . gosh, since we were in high school. Rob always said that beans gave him gas and he always watched his fat intake so franks were out."

"So? You never made some just for you?"

Ruefully, Jessie shook her head. "You don't have any of that brown spiced bread we used to have, do you?"

Steph pulled the cylinder of deep brown, spicy bread from the microwave. "Only ze best for ze madam," she said in a bad, mock French accent.

Over coffee, Steph said, "Jessie, I'd like to invite some friends over to meet you on Tuesday night. That's the Fourth of July. Just a few couples we know and particularly like. I think you'll like them too."

"Couples you and Brian fool around with?" As soon as the words were out of her mouth, Jessie regretted them. "I'm sorry."

"That's okay. And the answer is yes and no. I'd like to invite three couples, nice normal everyday folks, one of whom we've swapped with, two we haven't. I challenge you to figure out which couple we've swapped with. I had intended to invite two single men so you wouldn't find the evening so couples-oriented but one of them, a wonderful man named Gary, is out of town. You will get to meet him too, eventually. He's a very long story, but suffice it to say that he gives the best parties. You'll have to attend one with us some evening. I know you'll like the other man I've invited. Eric Langden's a doll, divorced and gorgeous. And no, I've never been with either Gary or Eric. Exactly."

Jessie let that final remark pass, for the moment. "Are you trying to fix me up?"

"Frankly, yes. But not fix you up with someone specific. It's just that you should have some fun now. It's been over a year and Rob's past history. It's time for the next phase of Jessie's life."

"I don't think I'm ready for that yet, Steph."

"For what? All I'm planning is a nice evening with nice people. Period. No sex, nothing kinky. No future plans unless you want some. No awkward foursomes. Just people. And no Jessie and Rob. Just Jessie."

"Just Jessie." She nodded. "Okay. Sounds wonderful."

The long holiday weekend sped by. Tuesday afternoon, Steph and Jessie sat chatting in the plant room. "By the way, Jessie," Steph asked, "what are you wearing this evening?"

"I thought I'd wear that same navy linen suit. Why? Is it too dressy?"

"Well. . . ." Steph hesitated. "May I make a suggestion? I'd love to see you wear that print dress we bought last week."

"Oh no, Steph. Not for tonight. It's so, I don't know, so flamboyant."

"But it's a party and that light, pretty party dress will make you feel like a party. And anyway, what's wrong with a little flamboyance? Let's look at this as a coming-out party for a new Jessie, a JessicaLynn party."

"That's silly."

"It is not silly. Let's look at it this way. If you decide to leave sometime soon—and I'm not for one moment suggesting that you should— you'll never see any of these people again. If you stay, they'll have met the new you and I'm sure they'll love you as much as I do. Let's create a new look for you to match your new life."

"Oh Steph, I don't know."

"I know you very well, JessicaLynn Hanley, and somewhere inside you a little JessicaLynn-voice is saying, 'Do it. Have some fun for a change.' Another, louder Jessie-voice is saying, 'That's ridiculous. Be yourself, conservative and proper.' Tell that Jessie-voice to stuff it and let JessicaLynn out."

Jessie laughed. "You do know me well, don't you. That's exactly what's going through my brain. I would really like to be JessicaLynn, fun-loving party-girl, but on the inside I'm still Jessie, proper and restrained." When Steph didn't respond, Jessie raised an eyebrow. "The flowered dress?"

"The flowered dress."

"The strappy sandals we bought to go with it?"

Steph nodded, then added, "And no tightly organized French twist. Wear your hair softer, maybe even loose."

"But that's not me," Jessie protested softly.

"It's JessicaLynn."

"It's JessicaLynn," she whispered. "Okay. I'll wear the dress and the shoes, but I don't know about the hair."

"Yippee. JessicaLynn gets to come out and play."

The party was scheduled for eight o'clock so the three friends had a bite to eat around six. Then Jessie went to her room, took a long shower, and scrubbed her long red hair until it squeaked. She wrapped herself in a towel, then wandered into the bedroom, opened the closet door and stood before the full-length mirror. Her fine, soft hair was already drying and flowing softly around her shoulders. The summer sun had turned the ivory skin on her face, arms, and legs a soft peachy color.

She hadn't really looked at herself in years, so Jessie took a deep breath and dropped the towel. Her figure was softer and more rounded than it had been in high school. Her breasts were high and full, her nipples deep smoky-pink. Her hips were wide enough to accentuate her small waist. Her legs were long and shapely. She smiled. I should be thinking about my thick thighs and my not-too-flat stomach, she thought. But JessicaLynn wouldn't do that.

She put on a white lace bra and panties, added a short half-slip, and then she was ready for the dress. Jessie took the hanger from the closet and, without looking in the mirror, pulled it over her head and zipped it up. She looked down and all she could see was the deep shadowed valley between her breasts. She wiggled her hips and pulled up at the neckline. "I can't do this," she said. Then she glanced up and looked at her reflection. "Wow," she said.

The dress was perfect. It hugged her upper body and cascaded in soft flowing lines over her hips and thighs. The skirt fell to just below her knees and below her short slip it was slightly translucent. She looked five years younger than she had looked a half an hour before and, she admitted to herself, she felt ten years younger.

She struggled with the tiny straps on her sandals and finally got them adjusted to her satisfaction. Again she looked at herself and grinned. "Okay, JessicaLynn, what about this hair?" Part of her wanted to put it into her traditional French twist but she stopped herself. She brushed it until it was soft and dry and pulled it back from her face. She tried a ponytail at the back of her head, then one at the nape of her neck, and finally one on top of her head. None of them were right. She pulled it one way, then another. Nothing looked the way she wanted.

She almost surrendered and put her hair up in her usual style when she remembered a long silver-colored comb she had once pushed into the fold of her twist. She found the comb in the bottom of her cosmetic bag and used it to pull one side of her hair back behind her ear. "Oh my God," she muttered as she saw the sexy woman in the mirror. "Is that me?"

It is if you want it to be, JessicaLynn said in her mind.

But is this the conservative midwesterner you've always been? Jessie asked.

No. And so what? JessicaLynn answered.

But what would Rob think?

Out loud, JessicaLynn said, "Who gives a fuck!" She dusted her cheeks with blush, pencilled on a line of eyeliner, and colored her lips with a coral lipstick. "Well, JessicaLynn, here goes."

Chapter 3

Jessica walked into the kitchen where Steph and Brian were doing a few last-minute things for the party. They had bought several party platters at the local gourmet food store and, while Steph filled a bowl with mixed nuts, Brian was dropping fresh fruit into the blender. Steph was wearing a white cotton halter-top dress with a navy belt and sandals. Brian wore identical colors, a white short-sleeved shirt, white duck slacks with a navy belt, and navy deck shoes.

"Did you two dress to match on purpose?" Jessica asked.

At the sound of her voice, Brian and Steph turned. "Holy cow," Steph said while Brian just whistled long and low. "You look fabulous."

"Now I see what I've always known," Brian said, staring. "You are not only a lovely looking woman, you're sexy as hell."

"JessicaLynn," Steph said, "you're amazing."

"JessicaLynn?" Brian said.

"We decided that the person you've seen for the past week is Jessie, but it's time to let her sensual alter ego out." Steph waved her arm at the gorgeous woman standing in the doorway. "This is JessicaLynn."

"Actually, I'd prefer to be Jessica for the moment. I'm not yet ready to become JessicaLynn but this," she swirled her skirt, "isn't Jessie either."

"Okay, what's this name thing you two have got going?" Brian asked.

Jessica motioned for Steph to explain. "Jessie lives in the midwest. She's a bit conservative and sexually repressed."

"Steph!"

"Well, she is," Steph said.

As Brian laughed, he asked, "And JessicaLynn?"

"She's a swinger. She loves sex and games and fun." Steph gave her husband a peck on the cheek. "Like us, darling."

Brian looked at Jessica and, after a moment, said, "You're telling me that you're halfway there."

"Not yet. I am telling you that I'm trying to open my mind to everything. But it's a slow process."

"Okay, Jessica it is," Steph said.

"Well, lovely lady," Brian said, crossing the kitchen and wrapping one bearlike arm around Jessica's waist, "I like your new name and your new attitude. Will you dance with me?" He swept her into his arms and they twirled around the kitchen.

"You know, Brian," Jessica said, laughing, "I never knew you were such a good dancer."

Brian pivoted, raised his arm, and let Jessica twirl underneath it. "You never gave me a chance." They danced into the living room and, gazing into her eyes, he bent her over his arm in a deep dip.

"You're flirting with me," she said, moving from his embrace.

"And why not?"

"Your wife, my best friend, is in the kitchen. Remember her?"

"Of course. But I know she told you about our unusual relationship and I've wanted to hold you for a very long time." As he watched the confusion flash over Jessica's face, Brian said, "Haven't you ever thought about how it might feel to be in my arms?"

At that moment, the doorbell rang, signalling the arrival of the first guests. "Saved by the bell," Jessica said.

"One last thing. I would never make you uncomfortable, JJ, I mean Jessica. You know that. I'll back off any time you say. But you're sexy and attractive and I enjoy playing with you, wherever it leads."

Jessica smiled as she heard Steph's footsteps in the hallway. "I understand, but it does make me a little uncomfortable." When Brian looked crestfallen, Jessica added, "But it's a nice discomfort."

As they separated, Brian ran his fingertip up Jessica's spine, then walked toward the hallway to greet their guests.

As the first couple walked into the living room, followed almost immediately by two more, Jessica remembered Steph's words. *I challenge you to figure out which couple we've swapped with.* As she was introduced to each, Jessica had to admit that she had no idea who Brian and Steph had slept with. All six people were delightful, bright, interesting, and interested.

Chuck O'Malley worked at the same brokerage firm as Brian and his wife Marcy was the vice president of an international bank. They had a married daughter who was expecting their first grandchild in two months.

"Of course," Marcy said as she settled in the living room, "I'm only going to be a grandmother because I had Betsy when I was six years old."

"I know," Chuck said, "and Betsy's only nine now."

"Right!" Marcy said, giggling. "That makes me. . . ."

Chuck snatched the drink Brian offered before Marcy could take it. "That makes you only fifteen and too young to drink."

Pete Cross worked at General Foods as a research chemist and his wife Gloria was deeply involved in local politics. They had five children, ranging in age from seven to eighteen, and regaled the group with tales of their adventures in parenthood.

Steve Albright was the biggest, blackest man Jessica had ever seen. At six foot six, with skin that was almost blue, he was an imposing figure. In contrast his wife Nan was five foot one with cafe au lait skin that was stretched to its limit by her eight and a half months of pregnancy. Steve was a junior partner in a prestigious Wall Street law firm and would be a full partner before he was thirty-five. "Our first," Steve said, lovingly rubbing his wife's belly.

"And, if this pregnancy is any indication," Nan said, easing her body into a soft chair, "my last. I waddle like a duck, I sleep sitting up and I haven't seen my feet in six weeks. I've finally had to stop working, too." Jessica's ears had perked up when she learned that Nan had worked for a local real estate agency and would go back to work part-time after the birth of the baby.

"I've been wondering," Steve added, "why they call it morning sickness. Nan's been nauseated since day one, all day."

"I think they call it morning sickness because it starts in the morning," Nan said, sipping the glass of club soda Steve handed her and nibbling on the saltine crackers she always kept at hand. "But only a couple of weeks to go. The doctor says that little Stevie's right on schedule."

"You know it's a boy?" Jessica said, her envy obvious to Steph.

When Jessie and Rob had married, she had wanted several children. Over the months and years, Rob had talked her out of it. 'We want so many things. Travel, freedom. Kids would just get in the way,' Rob had said. Jessica gazed wistfully at Nan's enlarged belly.

"It's a boy. Steven James Albright Junior." She beamed at her husband. "But the doctor also said that he's already over seven pounds. Another two weeks and he'll never be able to get out the old-fashioned way."

Steve winked. "He got in there the old-fashioned way."

Over the laughter, Nan cocked her head to one side, paused, then said, "Oooohhh, yes. I remember. That sex thing. It used to be very nice, back when such a thing was possible."

"Don't give us that," Steve said. "We've found ways. Oral sex has never been as pleasant."

"Oral sex is always pleasant," Gloria said.

"And we found the most delicious goo in a sex catalog," Pete added. "I hate the ones that taste like fruit juice. This one's cinnamon. Very spicy."

Gloria winked. "Just like me."

Jessica was amazed with the openness of the talk about sex. Rob had always found the subject distasteful, so it never came up in conversation with their friends.

As the group chatted in the large living room, the doorbell rang again. That must be Eric, Jessica thought, her palms damp. Not a date, Jessica told herself. Just a man coming to a party.

Eric Langden was about six feet tall with iron-gray hair and a well-trimmed, iron-gray moustache and beard. An architect, he had been divorced for five years. The group was obviously comfortable together and they all made an effort to draw Jessica into the conversation.

Over rum and fruit drinks that Brian whipped up in a constantly whirring blender, they talked for several hours about everything from world tensions to real-estate prices, from television shows and movies to crabgrass. When she stopped to think about it, Jessica realized that she hadn't had such a light, tensionless evening in a long time.

"By the way, did anyone see Sally Jessie this afternoon?" Nan asked, sipping her club soda.

"Most of us have to work," Marcy said. "And anyway, since when have you been interested in the adventures of dysfunctional families airing their dirty little secrets in public?"

"I'm practicing to stay home for a few months at least. You have to watch at least two hours of talk shows and an hour of soaps each afternoon to keep your daytime TV certification. Actually, there's not much else on."

"So which dirty little secret did Sally Jessie reveal today?" Steph asked. "Transvestite lesbian cannibals?"

"People who've had plastic surgery on their penises," Chuck said.

"Women who've been fucked by Elvis's ghost."

"Couples who've been abducted by alien polar bears."

"A family of seven who've lived at the bottom of a well for three years."

"All right," Nan said, holding up her hands. "Take pity on the pregnant lady, will you? The show was about sexual fantasies and it got me thinking. They had couples dressed up as their favorite fantasy. One was a pirate and his captive, one was an Arabian guy with his harem girl, you know. The nice thing was no one had a Barbie and Ken shape or anything. They were just regular people and very free with their conversation."

"Sounds kinky," Chuck said with a leer. "Like Gary's party. Remember?"

"Who could forget that night?" Marcy said. "But that was before you guys moved here," she said to the Albrights.

"We've heard about Gary's parties," Steve said, patting his wife's belly. "We're not up to that yet."

When Jessica looked particularly puzzled, Steph winked at her and said, "It's a long story. I'll tell you at length sometime."

"Actually, Sally Jessie was interesting. God I hate to hear me saying that. Talk shows and interesting in the same sentence. Ugh. But anyway, some of the people discussed how difficult it had been in the beginning to tell their wife or husband about their fantasy."

"It must be for some people," Steph said seriously.

"These days I fantasize a lot," Nan continued. "I think it's lack of good sex that does it. And I know it would be hard for me to share the details with Steve. I was just wondering whether any of you have fantasies and whether you tell each other."

"You know," Marcy said, "now that you've admitted to having fantasies that you haven't shared, Steve will force all that sexy information out of you." She twirled a nonexistent moustache. "Force you to tell all the yummy details, all those sexy four-letter words."

Steve and Nan looked at each other, their look saying, 'We'll talk later.' "I guess he will," Nan said. "But now I'm curious. Do you have fantasies and have you shared them?"

As Brian poured another round of fruity drinks, he said, "I've shared most of mine with Steph, but I've kept one or two secret."

Steph jumped in, "You have?"

"Yes. Telling a fantasy and acting it out, as we have, is delicious. And yes, we've acted a few out so you guys can all eat your hearts out. But it also takes the erotic edge off of it somehow."

"What's your favorite fantasy?" Nan asked Steph and Brian.

Steph answered, "He likes to pretend that he's kidnapped me and taken me to a cabin deep in the woods. That way he can have his way with me in private."

"Oooo, yummy," Gloria said, winking at her husband.

"Would you like me to abduct you?" Pete asked. "I could have my way with you and you couldn't object."

"Why do you suppose so many fantasies revolve around being made love to forcibly?" Nan asked. "I've always thought it was evil somehow."

"Rape fantasies aren't about rape," Brian said. "They're about power.

I love to have Steph under my control. That way I feel free to do some of the things I might not otherwise. I can demand. But I also know that Steph will let me know if I've gone too far."

"And I enjoy being under Brian's control," Steph said, sipping her drink and enjoying the buzz she had developed. "I don't have to worry about my reactions, what I'm supposed to be doing. I can lay back and enjoy things."

Jessica sat there enthralled. She had never heard people admit to having sexual fantasies before, much less discuss the plot. "You sure do speak your minds," she said softly.

"I'm so sorry, Jessica. Are we embarrassing you?" Nan said quickly. "You fit in so well with us that I forgot that you're new to this little group. We're pretty open-minded."

"And openmouthed," Steve added.

"I'm not really embarrassed." Jessica paused then added, "Yes I am, but it's a fun embarrassment. And I'm fascinated by the way you all talk about this stuff so freely."

"Didn't you and your ex talk about sex?"

"Rob? Not a chance. I think his only fantasy was to have a larger dental office. Sex for him was a routine. Releasing his precious bodily fluids. He wasn't the creative type."

"That's sad," Eric said. "How can you understand what you like and don't like unless you try different things?"

His look lingered on Jessica's face a bit longer than was necessary. She could feel the tingle deep in her body. "I never really thought about it. I guess we were pretty 'missionary position' and totally noncreative."

"My ex and I had a dynamite life in bed," Eric said. "It was out of bed that we fought like cats and dogs."

"How about you guys," Nan asked, turning to Chuck and Marcy. "Any sexual fun and games you'd like to share?"

"Actually," Marcy said, "Chuck has the greatest hands. He gives the most interesting massages." Chuck blushed and silently munched on a cracker and brie. "I guess," Marcy continued, "that we'd show up on Sally with me dressed in a towel and Chuck in a white uniform."

"Pete and I have a fantasy too," Gloria admitted. "We haven't acted it out, but we like to turn out all the lights and. . . ."

"Hey, babe," Pete said. "Aren't we going to have any secrets left?"

"Not a one. We're among friends. We tell a story in the dark. He's a doctor and I'm his unsuspecting patient."

"Babe . . ." Pete warned.

"Okay, okay. I'll say no more."

"Have you ever actually acted it out?" Nan asked.

"So far, no," Gloria said. "But now that you mention it. . . ."

"This conversation is making me very hot," Pete said. "Anyone for a swim?"

"Not me," Nan said, rubbing her belly, "but I'll sit by the pool."

"I turned the heater on just before you folks got here," Brian said. He turned to Jessica. "Suits are optional. Some wear them, some don't. Dealer's choice."

"I think I'll put a suit on," Jessica said, "if that's okay. I'm not that liberated yet."

"You won't be upset if I don't, will you?" Brian asked.

"I don't think so. If I am, I'll look the other way."

In her room, Jessica pulled her three bathing suits from the drawer. The one she had brought from Ottawa, a one-piece floral print, held her in in all the right places. Too conservative and definitely Jessie. She held up the bikini that she and Steph had bought on their recent shopping trip. It barely covered any of her. She dropped it back into the drawer and compromised on a one-piece black suit that mock-laced up the front and left a panel of barely concealed flesh from waist to cleavage. As she wiggled into the suit, she realized that she was slightly drunk, totally relaxed, and very aroused. Her nipples were hard and showed prominently through the tight black fabric.

This sexual tension was a revelation. Poor old Rob, she thought. He would never do anything like this. He missed a lot, and so have I. Well, she told herself, maybe he experiments with bimbette. You know, I really hope he can. She shook her head. I must be mellowing, but I do hope he's getting some good sex. I know I will get mine, eventually. Maybe sooner, rather than later. She fluffed her hair and, barefoot, she ran down the stairs.

When she arrived at the pool, all the patio lights were out with just the underwater lights to illuminate the soft mist rising from the water. Nan was stretched out in a lounge chair with Gloria and Pete sitting in chairs on either side of her. Everyone else was in the water and through the choppy surface it was impossible to tell who had clothes on and who didn't. Steph and Steve were involved in a splash fight at the shallow end, with Chuck egging them on. Brian, Eric, and Marcy were hanging onto the ladder at the deep end, talking. Jessica found herself looking at Brian's muscular shoulders and wondering what he looked like without a bathing suit.

Jessica walked to the deep end and dove cleanly into the eight-foot-deep water. She came up beside Brian, facing the side of the pool, holding on to the edge. "The water's perfect," she said, pushing her sopping red hair out of her face.

"So are you in that bathing suit. I could rape you right here," he whispered, pressing his obviously naked body with its ridge of hard male flesh against her side. "You look so sexy." He released the pressure of his body. "But I won't rush you. I just want you to know that our time will come, eventually, if I have my way." He let go, pushed Marcy under the water and together they swam to the other side, leaving Jessica with Eric.

"That suit looks terrific," Eric said, moving nearer. "It's actually more sensual than being nude." When she was silent, Eric continued, "I'm sorry if I come on too heavy. You're new to this crazy life we have here. But we're just free spirits and we do what feels good and doesn't hurt anyone else. I won't embarrass you, but I would be less than honest if I denied that you turn me on."

Remembering that Eric had been divorced for several years, she asked, "Were you and your wife swingers?"

"We had occasional flings, with each other's knowledge, of course. We were very creative in the bedroom."

"If you'll pardon me for asking, what caused your breakup?"

"Money, mostly." He pulled himself from the water and sat on the edge of the pool while Jessica remained in the water next to his ankles. As water sluiced from his torso she admired his body, substantial in his brief red trunks. "I made some, she spent more. She always wanted me to do things that made more money, I wanted to do things that made me happy. When I was offered a new job with a large architectural firm in the city at an unseemly increase in salary, she begged me to take it."

"You didn't want to?"

"Not really. Commuting was not my idea of how to spend three hours a day. And that job would have also meant weeks, even months travelling. I had commuted and travelled before and it took too much out of me. That's why I took the job in Scarsdale in the first place. It was a small firm but we created some wonderful buildings.

"So we argued about the job. She whined about all the things she wanted out of life. I tried to explain that all I wanted was to stay in Scarsdale, enjoy my ten-minute drive to work, and have enough money to do the things that were important to me. And that wasn't a big house, a maid five days a week, and trips to Europe several times a year."

"What is important to you?"

"I love my kids. They're boys, twins, and they were fourteen then. I liked being able to get to their soccer games and parent conferences. She wanted them in a private school. I like tennis and golf. And I like my friends." He looked around the group. "I wanted to have something left at the end of the day, not get up at the crack of dawn, work, come home, eat, fall into bed so I can get up with the roosters and do it all again."

"And your wife wanted you to take the city job?"

"She demanded. She gave me the 'If you loved me' bit and I thought about it and discovered that I didn't love her. At least not enough to do everything the way she wanted. So we split. We still see each other occasionally, though not as much now that the boys are in college. I miss them, especially since they're spending their summer together in Colorado. Anyway, Marilyn lives in Hartsdale, in a large condo I bought her, and I think she's happy. But her happiness isn't my responsibility anymore. It took me a long time to realize that nothing I did was going to make her happy anyway."

"That's a very grown-up attitude," Jessica said.

"How about your divorce. Was it very difficult?"

Jessica told him about Rob and bimbette. "I find I'm becoming less bitter day by day. Being here has opened my eyes a lot."

"And, if you'll pardon my asking, was your sex life really as boring as you alluded to before?"

Jessica sighed and sipped the drink Brian had set on the edge of the pool for her. "I guess so. I'm not sure how much was his fault and how much was mine."

"Why does it have to be anyone's fault?"

"Not fault, exactly, but I'm just not responsive enough." Why in the world had she admitted that? Now he won't be interested. She looked at the glass in her hand and put it down. And she realized that she wanted Eric to be interested.

"Did he tell you that?" When she nodded, he said, "A sensual woman like you? He has to be a jerk."

Jessica laughed and, bobbing in the warm water, moved slightly away from the side of the pool and kicked her legs. "Thanks for that. But why do you say I'm sensual? What do you know about me?"

"I know that your nipples are hard and it's getting difficult for you to hold still." When her cheeks pinked, he said, "And you're blushing. I love that." He grinned. "I know this is sudden, but could we get together one evening soon?"

"Is this a proposition, sir?" Jessica said, flirtatiousness coming easily from somewhere deep inside her.

"Maybe. I have to admit that I'd love to teach you how sexy you really are, but let's start with dinner. It can progress as quickly or as slowly as we like from there. Or not at all, if that's what we decide."

Jessica smiled. This man was making a pass at her and she was revelling in it. "I'd love to have dinner with you."

"Friday? I can pick you up here at about six?"

"Friday it is."

* * *

"Did you have a nice evening?" Steph asked as she and Jessica tidied up the kitchen. They could see Brian, a towel around his waist, wandering around the pool area, stuffing plastic plates and glasses into a large black garbage bag.

"I had an amazing evening," Jessica said. "Your friends are terrific people. I like them all so much."

"I knew you would. They're the greatest."

"Okay. I think I'm ready for the big revelation. Which of them have you slept with?"

Steph laughed. "Couldn't tell, could you."

"Not a clue. Everyone's so open and sexy. I'd sleep with any one of the guys."

"So, my dear, would I. However. . . ." She stuffed a large platter into the dishwasher. "Okay, okay," she said, catching Jessica's look. "Steve and Nan only moved here about a year ago and they were trying desperately to get pregnant. We discussed our lifestyle with them, and they were tempted. Isn't he the most gorgeous thing? Makes me sweat just to think about those arms around me. Anyway, they didn't want to confuse things. I hope, after the baby's born. . . ."

"You're right about him. He's got the greatest body."

"That's my Jessica talking. I think Jessie's long buried."

Jessica sighed. "You may be right. What about the others? Who did and who didn't?"

"Pete and Gloria discussed it and decided that they didn't want to risk the jealousy that they were both afraid would surface. They tried swapping once, many years ago, and Pete particularly found it very hard to deal with the thought of someone else making love to his wife. They go to most of the parties but they stay together."

"So you've been with Chuck and Marcy."

Steph just grinned as Brian walked up behind her and wrapped his arms around her waist. "The four of us," Brian said, "spent a weekend in the Adirondacks together last January. Get Steph to tell you about it sometime. It was incredible." He nibbled his wife's neck. "Just incredible."

"Certainly was," Steph agreed. "And, by the way, I also spent a creative evening with Gary about six months ago. I was sorry he couldn't come tonight. He's the sexiest man I know, with the exception of Brian, of course."

"Is he very handsome?"

Steph thought about it. "Actually, not at all. He sort of reminds me of Ichabod Crane. He's about six foot two or three and probably doesn't weigh one fifty. Long legs, long arms, sort of like a stork. He wears mismatched clothes that hang on him. He always looks like he's just lost fifty pounds and his wardrobe hasn't caught up."

"But you said. . . ."

"I said sexy and attractive, not handsome. There's a big difference."

"Like . . . ?"

"He listens when you talk and concentrates like you're the only one in the world who matters at that moment. He touches you, accidentally on purpose, if you know what I mean. A hand on your shoulder as you sit down, or a palm in the small of your back to guide you through a doorway. And he looks at you like he wants to make long slow love to you all the time."

"Where was Brian all this time, while you were out with Gary?"

"I was here," Brian said, walking through the large sliding glass door. "It doesn't have to be a couples thing with us. I've had my . . . adventures too. Solo. It's really okay with us."

"And what did you think of Eric?" When Jessica blushed, Steph continued, "Did he ask you out?"

"We're having dinner on Friday," Jessica said softly.

"That's great," Brian said. "He's one of the nicest people I know and you two should get along well."

"I liked him a lot. He's bright and so open about things."

"Well," Steph said, "I'm beat." She closed the dishwasher and turned it on.

Jessica glanced at the clock on the microwave. "Holy cow. Is it really after one?"

"Yup," Steph said. "Time sure rushes by when you're having fun."

Brian grabbed Steph by the arm and dragged her toward the sliding glass door. "Let's go out by the pool so I can ravish you before bed."

Steph giggled. "Weallll suh," she laid on a thick southern accent. "What kahnd of a girl do you tahke me foah?"

"I know what kind of girl you are," Brian said, still tugging. "That's why I want to take you out to the pool."

"Nighty night, Jessica," Steph said as Brian dragged her out the door.

"Good night, folks," Jessica said. "I love you both."

Brian blew her a kiss and he and Steph disappeared into the darkness.

Upstairs, Jessica pulled off her bathing suit, took a quick shower, and collapsed onto her bed. Despite the late hour, she couldn't sleep. Images of the people she'd met that evening and an image of herself so different from anything she could have imagined a few weeks before crowded her brain. Finally, she dropped into an exhausted slumber.

In her dream she rode on a merry-go-round. The calliope played random notes that didn't combine into anything she recognized, but surrounded her and filled her head with erotic music. Multicolored lights winked and flashed in a primitive rhythm.

She was gloriously naked. The snow-white horse rose and fell between her thighs, cool against her heated flesh. She leaned forward and pressed the cool metal bar against the valley between her breasts, against her flaming forehead.

As the merry-go-round turned, Jessica closed her eyes and let the wind blow her hair until it flew behind her like the tail of the horse she rode. Up and down the horse moved, carrying her with it.

Suddenly, there was a man seated on the horse with her, the fronts of his thighs against the backs of hers. She felt the prickle of the coarse hairs on his legs against her delicate skin. Just ignore him, she told herself. But she couldn't. When she started to turn to look at him, he placed his hands gently on the sides of her head, effectively preventing her from seeing who he was. When he lowered his hands to her waist, she didn't try to turn again. Around and around they rode, his hands on her waist and his thighs against her legs.

Gradually, he leaned forward until the length of his chest pressed against her back. Hands splayed on her belly, he used the tip of his tongue to tickle the hollow just behind her right ear. Holding her against him, he bit the tip of her earlobe, then sucked it into his mouth.

As the erotic power of his mouth held her against him, he slid his hands up to cup her aching breasts. He filled his hands with them, weighed and massaged them. Jessica looked down and admired the contrast between his dark fingers and her white skin. She watched in fascination as the hands kneaded her soft fullness and moved ever closer to her fully erect nipples. Squeeze me, she whispered to herself. Pinch me. Make me feel you.

"I will," the man's voice breathed into her ear. "I will give you everything you want. But at my pace." He caressed her breasts lightly. "Just ride the horse. Feel the wind in your face. Close your eyes. Feel." His fingers reached her nipples and he held the left between his finger and thumb. "Feel." He pinched and pulled, causing a sensation that was almost pain.

Erotic heat knifed through her body, stabbing deep into her secret spaces. Don't stop, she thought. Oh God, don't stop. She wanted to tell him, say it out loud, but she couldn't. The words echoed in her head.

"You don't have to say it," he whispered. "I won't stop." One hand pressed her belly and forced her buttocks to cradle his mammoth erection. The other hand shifted to her right breast, grasping it tightly and twisting.

"You're hurting me," Jessica said, not sure whether it was true.

"No, it doesn't really hurt although you think it should. It gives you pleasure; hot demanding pleasure. It makes you hungry. So hungry that you are being devoured by it. Aren't you?" When she remained silent, he moved his hips so his cock slid more deeply into the crack between her cheeks while his fingers worked on her nipple. "Aren't you?"

"Yes," she sighed. "Oh yes."

He shifted his hips and lifted her body. Suddenly his cock was touching her hot, moist entrance. "You want this," the voice whispered, the heated breath tickling her ear. "But you'll have to take it."

Between Jessica's thighs, the merry-go-round horse continued its unrelenting up and down movement. She supported her weight on the stirrups and held herself above his cock. Her thigh muscles quivered from the effort of holding herself up.

"Take it," he whispered. "Let your body go. Take what you and I both know you want."

Yes, she admitted to herself, she did want this. Slowly, she lowered her body so she filled herself with his cock. The merry-go-round went faster and faster and with each note of the calliope the horse rose, carrying him deeper inside. She rode him, synchronizing her movements with the rhythm of the horse. Her mind splintered, sensations darting from the fingers on her nipples to his mouth on her neck to his cock, filling, caressing. Faster and faster she rode until she was a bubble about to burst.

And burst she did, a million colors surrounding her. The lights of the carousel flashed, penetrating her lowered eyelids. She screamed, but then couldn't get her breath. She flew, then plunged with the horse and the man beneath her, the wind unable to cool her body. On and on they rode, climax after rending climax, until she collapsed.

Jessica awoke in a pool of sweat, the sheets tangled around her naked body. Her breathing was rapid and her heart pounded. She could almost hear the music and see the lights. She lay in the darkness until her body calmed, then took another shower. Afterward, she climbed back into bed and slept dreamlessly until morning.

Thursday evening Eric called and he and Jessica talked for almost an hour. "About tomorrow evening," Eric said. "If you agree, there's a concert at a place I think you'd enjoy called Caramoor. There'll be a small jazz group playing in a part of the estate called the Venetian Gardens. I thought we'd have a little picnic on the lawn before the music."

"That sounds lovely."

"Great. Wear jeans and something long-sleeved. It's supposed to be cool and it does get a bit buggy. I'll bring the dinner and the bug spray and pick you up around six."

"I'll see you then."

Jessica flopped back onto her bed. She was both jittery and excited, looking forward to the following evening with a combination of terror and delight. Okay, she thought, jeans. She mentally flipped through her small collection of clothes and selected a soft buttercup-yellow silk shirt. Should I take a jacket? It's only a picnic. But it might get cool later in the evening. But I might look pretentious. Sneakers? Maybe loafers? Or what about sandals?

That night and most of the next day while Steph was at the hospital, Jessica selected, discarded, and reselected. She sat in the garden room and tried to read, only to get up and pace around the pool. "This is ridiculous," she said aloud. "I'm acting like a kid on her first date." Then she grinned. "I am a kid on her first date."

At about four o'clock, she soaked in a tub and managed to relax for a short while. Then she put on the clothes she had selected, changed her shirt, then changed back. At six o'clock, Jessica was dressed in the outfit she had first selected, yellow shirt, soft, well-washed jeans she had had for many years, tennis shoes, and socks. Then, at the last minute, she added a fitted denim vest.

She put her hair up, then held a pair of earrings near her ears. She discarded them and picked another pair, which she also dropped back into the drawer. Something bigger, she thought. But it's only a picnic. Maybe no earrings. She settled on a pair of medium-sized wooden hoops. She gazed into the mirror, smiled, added blush and lipstick and hurried downstairs, glad the house was empty.

As she heard Eric's car in the driveway, Jessica stood inside the front door debating whether to open it and walk outside or wait for him to ring the bell. You're jumpy as a cat, she said to herself, turning the knob in her right hand and pulling the door open. Eric stood with his hand poised above the doorbell.

God, he's sexy, she thought as he stood, openly appraising her. He was dressed in tight jeans and a white tennis sweater with the sleeves pushed up to the elbows, showing off well-muscled forearms. He wasn't gorgeous and she doubted that anyone would stop in their tracks and stare at him. But there was a gleam in his eyes as he looked her over that created a small flutter deep in her belly. His eyes lingered on her breasts as they pressed against the silky fabric of her shirt, then wandered lower to her narrow waist and full hips.

"Very nice," he said. "Although I've seen you in a bathing suit, I still enjoyed speculating about the way you'd fill out your jeans." As she colored, he continued, "You're blushing again." He used the knuckle of his index finger to raise her face, then he dropped a light kiss on her lips. "It's sort of virginal. I love it." Then he took her elbow and guided her out the door.

Together they walked toward the driveway where Eric's vintage BMW 2002 was parked. Bright red with slick black leather upholstery, it was in mint condition. "That's some car," Jessica commented.

"I love old BMWs. I found this one about a year ago and I had it restored. It cost more than buying a new one and it's silly of me, but I get a kick out of it. Drivers of these old cars flick their lights at each other in recognition and I like that kind of camaraderie."

Jessica stroked the supple leather seat beneath her, silently wondering how he could afford to 'restore' a classic car like this one. Did architects make that kind of money?

Eric and Jessica passed the next twenty minutes in comfortable conversation, driving along the tree-lined roadways of Westchester County. They arrived at Caramoor, passed through the big iron gates and drove to a grassy parking area. He helped her out of the car and, arm in arm, they walked along the dirt pathways toward a small picnic area. Before they arrived at the tables, however, Eric turned into a small area of lawn surrounded by a low hedge. In the middle was an old fountain, now filled with flowering plants.

"By the way," Jessica said, her stomach reminding her that she hadn't eaten since breakfast, "you're not carrying any basket. I thought you mentioned dinner."

"I did."

They approached a large plaid wool blanket spread on the lawn under a large maple tree, set with fine china plates, full settings of silverware, and crystal champagne flutes. Each place setting was accompanied by a white linen napkin and a red leather seat cushion.

But it was the man who stood beside the blanket who caught Jessica's attention. He was immense, probably over two hundred and fifty pounds, but well muscled with a long golden ponytail and a heavy gold hoop in one ear. He looked like he might have been a football player or a prize fighter, with gigantic hands and a face that looked like it had taken a punch of two in its time. Beautifully groomed, the man wore tan slacks and a forest-green polo shirt. He was obviously waiting for the lady he would share his feast with.

"Isn't that lovely," she said to Eric. "What an elegant presentation."

"Why thank you," he said, approaching the blanket. "I'll tell Timmy you're impressed."

As Jessica turned to Eric, puzzled, the man near the blanket said, "There you are, sir. I was afraid the food would get warm."

"Not to worry, Timmy," Eric said. "I know better than to keep one of your sumptuous meals waiting." He turned to Jessica. "Jessica, this is Timmy Whitmore. He's my right-hand man and my chauffeur when I want one. He's in charge of my house and he's the best damn cook in the county."

Timmy inclined his head slightly. "It's nice to meet you Ms. . . ."

Totally nonplussed, Jessica answered automatically. "Hanley. It's Jessica Hanley." She turned to Eric who looked sheepish. "Didn't you say you were a modestly well-off suburban architect who used to argue with your wife about money?"

"I did, didn't I. I know that I owe you an explanation but can it wait until after dinner? Timmy's meals are always works of art and he gets very huffy if his food isn't presented just so."

"Of course it can wait," Jessica said. "But you'll have to give me a moment to adjust." Eric held her arm as she settled onto one of the leather cushions.

With a flourish Timmy pulled two plates from a hamper a few feet away and set one in front of each of them. Artfully arranged on fresh lettuce and watercress were half a dozen of the largest shrimp Jessica had ever seen, with a dollop of dill sauce and a few small toast-rounds on the side. "Good grief, Timmy," Eric said. "These shrimp look like they should have saddles."

"I know," Timmy said, looking downcast and a bit irritated. "I tried to get U12s but all they had were U5s. They're really too large to be as tender as I'd like, but the man in the fish store swore that they were superb. If they're not. . . ."

Eric tasted one. "Well, Timmy, your man was right. They are delicate and crisp, cooked exactly right. Not chewy at all."

Timmy beamed, the smile giving his singularly unattractive face an appealing glow. "Thank you sir."

Feeling like she was in the middle of a James Bond movie, Jessica speared a shrimp with a slender shrimp fork and tasted, then dipped the shrimp into the sauce and took another bite. "These are delicious," she said and watched Timmy's smile grow still wider. "I make cold shrimp often, but with cocktail sauce with extra horseradish, or a cold mayonnaise. I've never made anything like this sauce. It's wonderful."

"Thank you. I've met only a few people who appreciate shrimp with mayonnaise," Timmy said.

While they ate in silence, she watched Timmy deftly open a bottle of Dom Perignon and fill two flutes, each half full. "This meal is delightful," Jessica said as she lifted her glass.

"And the company is a perfect complement," Eric whispered, holding her gaze until her hand shook. He lifted his glass and touched the rim to hers, enjoying the single clear note it produced. "To an enjoyable evening, the first of many I hope."

"To an enjoyable evening." She sipped the wine, knowing she was already intoxicated.

When they had finished their shrimp, Timmy whisked the plates away and replaced them with larger, prearranged dinner plates. "I made cold smoked breast of duck with a chilled pasta primavera." Moving with surprising grace for such a large man he placed a sauceboat on the blanket. "There's a light vinaigrette for the duck." He placed small bread plates, each with two tiny hot rolls, beside Eric and Jessica. Jessica was amazed that the surface of each butter pat was covered with a tiny staff and notes of music. "These are beautiful, Timmy," she said.

"I enjoy doing that. You might call it a hobby of mine."

"That's along with cake decorating and baking the most delicious breads you've ever tasted."

"Actually, I once worked as a food stylist on photos for a cookbook," Timmy boasted, removing the champagne glasses and replacing them with white wine glasses. "I have a sauvignon blanc from Chili, 1992. It will go perfectly with the duck and was very reasonable."

"Timmy haunts the local wine stores."

"I found this one at Zachy's actually. It was so well priced that I bought us a case," Timmy said.

"Jessica?" Eric asked.

"If Timmy recommends it, how can I argue?"

Timmy beamed as he uncorked the wine and poured a small amount into Eric's glass.

"Anyone can find a good fifty-dollar bottle of wine," Timmy said. "I can find a good bottle of wine at under ten dollars. What do you think?"

Eric tasted and nodded. "Right as usual."

Beaming, Timmy handed Eric the cork and half-filled each glass. "Keep the cork," Eric said, handing it back to Timmy, "and you can recork the bottle before you leave. If we finish even half of this wine, I'll never be able to drive home."

As they ate, they made small talk. "Do you know why the host breaks the wine cork?" he asked.

Jessica took a sip of wine to moisten her dry mouth and tucked her legs underneath her. "I always wondered why the waiter hands it over, but I didn't want to sound as unsophisticated as I felt so I never asked."

"Most of these rituals are left over from the dim past when there was a real need for precautions. Now it's mostly just snobbery and uptight people who like to make a simple glass of wine into a Japanese tea ceremony." He reached out and Timmy handed Eric the cork which he in turn handed to Jessica, his fingers lingering on hers. "You'll notice that the imprint of the winery is on the cork, with the year." He laid the cork in Jessica's palm, rubbing the rough surface along her skin. "In the olden days unscrupulous people used to fill an empty bottle with jug wine, then recork it and sell it as the expensive stuff. So, rather than break the expensive bottle so that wouldn't happen, they broke the inexpensive cork."

"Oh. That makes sense." She held the cork under her nose. "Why do they smell the cork?"

"Before wine was sterilized, pasteurized, and otherwise purified, occasionally bad yeasts would get into the vats and, instead of fine wine, you'd get fine vinegar. Actually the word vinegar is from the French, *vin* meaning wine and *agre* meaning sour. And if the wine was sour, you could smell it in the cork." Eric smiled. "These days, wine is never sour and there's no need to smell the cork. The only ones who sniff it are those who want everyone to think they know something." He reached over and wrapped his long fingers around Jessica's then slowly drew the cork from her hand.

As his fingers slid from her hand, Jessica's breath caught. She gazed at the attractive man who sat across from her, then looked at her plate. She lifted a small forkful of the duck to her mouth and tasted it, unsure of whether she'd be able to swallow. To break the tension she was feeling, she said, "This is very unusual, Timmy. I really like it."

"I'm so glad. I didn't know anything about you or your taste in food, so it was difficult to plan the meal."

"Well, Timmy, I'm easy. I enjoy tasting new things and I can't imagine anything that you created that I wouldn't like."

Eric gazed into her eyes. "I'm glad you enjoy trying new things, Jessica."

The food turned to cardboard in her mouth and she sipped her wine to moisten her lips. Although it was difficult for her to eat with Eric's hot gaze on her, she couldn't insult Timmy so she finished every bite along with two glasses of wine.

"I'm so glad the meal pleased you, Ms. Hanley," Timmy said as he removed the plates and the wine glasses. "I have a triple-crème blue cheese and fruit for dessert. There's coffee and I've taken the liberty of opening a 1971 Chateau D'Yquem. It will go superbly with the cheese and fruit. The pears are especially good." Leaving the platter with the fruit and cheese, china mugs for coffee beside the filled carafe, the decanter, and new glasses for the sauterne, Timmy efficiently packed everything else in a hamper. "I'll be leaving, now. I've left a small basket over there," he pointed, then lifted the heavy hamper as though it weighed nothing. "Everything should fit quite nicely."

"Timmy," Eric said, stretching out on the blanket as people wandered through the gardens around them, "you've done a wonderful job, as usual."

"Thank you, sir," he said, "and it was so nice meeting you Ms. Hanley."

"Thank you for the wonderful meal, Timmy," Jessica said. "I don't think I've ever had better."

"Good night," Timmy said and walked toward the exit with a surprisingly light step for such a big man.

Chapter 4

"Try the cheese with the sauterne," Eric said. He cut off a bit of pear, spread a small amount of cheese on the morsel and held it in front of Jessica's mouth. She ate from his fingers and he quickly handed her the wine. "Close your eyes and drink this so the tastes are in your mouth at the same time."

When she had sipped the thick, deep yellow liquid, he asked, "What do you taste?"

"Cream and pear and . . . pineapples." She opened her eyes, amazed.

He took a bite of pear and cheese, then sipped his own wine. "Pineapples. Wonderful. A few years ago, someone introduced me to the combination of sauterne and blue-veined cheese. There's a strange synergy. The whole taste is so much more than the sum of its parts." He spread another bit of cheese on another piece of fruit and offered it to Jessica.

She took it from him, placed it on her tongue, and sipped the sauterne. "It is wonderful, but if I have much more to drink, I'll be incoherent." She dropped onto her back on the soft blanket.

Eric took the glass from her hand. "I certainly don't want you incoherent. I want you to be fully aware of everything that happens."

"And what is going to happen?" Jessica asked, the words out of her mouth before she could stop them.

Eric grinned and licked a tiny crumb of cheese from her lower lip. "Everything and nothing."

"What does that mean?"

"Everything means that I'm going to spend the rest of the evening seducing you with wine and food, music and evening breezes and me."

"And nothing?"

"Nothing means that as much as I want to, and, I hope, as much as you will want me to, I'm not going to make love to you tonight."

"Why not?"

"Because I want you to anticipate how wonderful it will be with us when I undress you and touch you and lick every inch of your skin. I want you to wonder how it will feel when I slide, ever so slowly, into your body and feel your hips reaching for me, unable to wait any longer.

"Then I want you to think about it in the cold, sober light of day. Sex for the sake of sex. Not love, just desire. Then you can decide whether that is truly what you want."

Jessica sighed and closed her eyes. Her thighs were trembling and her heart was pounding. She did want him. Badly. She felt a tickling on her neck and reached up to brush it away. As her hand dropped she felt the tickling again. She slowly opened her eyes and saw Eric, his face close to hers, a blade of grass in his hand. "I know what I want right now," she whispered, unable to stop the words.

"Maybe you do. But I know what we're not going to do. It's important to me that we don't make love because of too much wine or too long since the last time." He saw the disappointment on Jessica's face. "Oh lord," he said, smiling. "This is going to be a long and singularly frustrating evening." He tossed the grass aside and sat up. "I owe you an explanation. About Timmy and all."

Jessica sighed and partially shook off the cloud of desire that surrounded her. She sat up and poured herself a cup of steaming coffee. She looked at him and lifted a cup. When he shook his head, she put the decanter down and added milk to her coffee. "Okay. Tell me."

"Marilyn, my ex-wife, must be, in some ways, the unluckiest woman in the world. When we split, I was, as you put it, a humble architect. I made eighty thousand a year, a nice salary but not enough for her, so she went looking for greener pastures. Maybe there was a deeper reason. But money seemed to be all she thought about."

"Don't tell me you won the lottery or something."

"Let me give you a little background." He sipped his sauterne and watched the people wandering past them. In the far distance he could hear the sensual sound of a clarinet tuning up. "My father took off when I was seven. I think my mother was glad to see him go although it meant that she had to work. He was a heavy drinker, a gambler, a womanizer, and a general pain in the ass. He was never abusive, or anything like that. It was just that he was totally unpredictable. Rich and expansive one minute, poor and depressive the next. He wouldn't come home for days, even weeks at a time. Then he'd arrive home like the prodigal son, frequently reeking of perfume. Of course, at the time, I idolized him, thought he was the greatest, especially when he arrived with his arms full of presents."

"It must have been a tough life for you."

"My mom was a very sane, down-to-earth woman and I was a very happy child in spite of my on-again, off-again father."

Jessica smiled. "You were lucky."

"I guess I was. One evening, my dad arrived home after almost two weeks, and told my mom that he was leaving for good. He packed his things in an old black-and-white suitcase and disappeared. My mom cried for about a week, then pulled herself together and made a good life for herself. She had worked in a local nursing home as an aide and discovered that she enjoyed helping older people. So she put herself through nursing school, then made enough to put me through college. She died the year after I graduated."

"She sounds like a nice woman."

Eric's face softened. "She was the best. Anyway, about a year after Marilyn and I split, I received a visit from a lawyer. My father, it turns out, had done okay for himself. He'd ended up in Vegas and amassed a small fortune. Before he died, he had a will drawn up leaving everything to me. There was a letter from him for me, too. He tried to explain that although he didn't consider himself a bad man, he had been a terrible husband and a worse father and that we had been better off without him. He said that he had spent a lot of years broke and then started a run of luck and had gotten some money together. He hired an investigator who learned that my mom had died and that I was doing very well on my own." Eric ran his long slender fingers through his iron-gray hair.

"Personally, I think he didn't contact me then because we had almost nothing in common except some genetic material. I don't remember him as a bad father, but that's the way he thought about things. I'm just sorry that my mother didn't live to know that he still thought about us. Anyway, I inherited everything. Including Timmy."

"Including Timmy?"

"He was my father's bodyguard, and, I gather, he needed one. He was in some pretty ugly businesses with some pretty nasty people. My father won Timmy, who had spent a few years as a professional wrestler, in a poker game almost ten years before he died. His old manager put up his contract in lieu of five thousand dollars. Fortunately for both my father and Timmy, the manager's full boat, aces over sixes, wasn't as good as my father's four deuces.

"Timmy's a gem and a thoroughly nice man. He was unquestionably loyal and able to take care of himself and my father, particularly in my dad's final months which, I gather, were lousy. Timmy won't talk about those years and the things my father was into. He says it's a closed book now that he's dead. And I guess it is."

"How could he leave Timmy to you?" Jessica asked. "It sounds like some kind of indentured servitude."

"Not at all. My father got to know Timmy very well. Although he left him a generous amount of cash in his will, my father left Timmy something more important. One section of the will guarantees him a job with me for as long as he wants. And that's all he wants. I guess he's like my mom. He wants to take care of someone the way he took care of my father, and he stays because he wants to. He keeps the money my dad left him in the bank. 'For his old age,' he says."

"Your dad sound like a very perceptive man."

"He was."

"And Timmy's cooking?"

"That had been a hobby of his for many years. He used to cook for my father, who taught Timmy to enjoy fine food and good wine. After my father's death, Timmy told me that he had always wanted to study seriously so I encouraged him to take a year to study at the Culinary Institute. Now, as you've gathered, it's more than just a hobby—it's a passion."

"That's quite a story."

Distant strains of jazz filtered through the evening air. "The music's starting," Eric said, stretching out on the blanket. "They discourage listening from here rather than going to the terrace, but I bought six tickets and made a special plea to the staff so they'll leave us alone."

Jessica stretched out beside Eric, her head buzzing with the wine and the music and the feel of Eric's fingers entwined with hers. Together they watched the sky darken and the stars appear while they listened to an erotic baritone saxophone. From time to time, Eric would lift Jessica's hand to his lips and kiss her knuckles, or nip one fingertip. As the first half of the concert ended, he sucked her index finger into his hot mouth and swirled his tongue around the tip.

To calm her fluttering stomach, she said, "With this inheritance of yours, do you still design buildings?"

He chuckled. "Getting too hot for you?" He sucked her finger again, then answered, "Sure. I like to be productive and I don't know what else I'd do. I do one or two projects each year, overall design, not the bathroom fixtures or landscaping. I keep my job within strict limits. I never take on a project that will occupy more time than I want to give, leaving the rest of my time for the parts of my life that give me joy." He bit the tip of Jessica's finger, then swirled his tongue around the palm. "How about you? What was your family life like as a kid?"

Jessica struggled to concentrate enough to answer his question.

"Dull. I was born and brought up in Ottawa, Illinois, a small town near Chicago. Steph and I went to high school together and that's where she met Brian and I met Rob, my ex-husband."

Jessica tried to gently withdraw her hand from Eric's but he held her fast. "Tell me about him. He must be some kind of idiot to let something as gorgeous and sexy as you get away."

"I don't mean to make him sound like a total jerk," Jessica said, finally pulling her hand away from Eric. "We met in high school and he knew precisely what he wanted out of life, so it happened. Dental school and a very busy practice in Ottawa."

When Eric took her hand again she sighed and didn't try to pull away. "I gathered from your conversation Saturday night that you and he weren't setting the world on fire in the bedroom."

Jessica laughed softly. "No, we weren't. Most of our problems in bed were probably due to inexperience. We were both virgins or close enough for government work when we met and there never was anyone else for either of us. Not until bimbo."

"He found a sweet young thing?"

Jessica told him about finding Rob in his office that afternoon so many months before. When he laughed at her version of the story, he apologized. "Don't apologize." she said. "Now, looking back on it, it was pretty funny. At the time, however, it seemed my life had ended."

Eric propped himself up on one elbow and slid the tip of his tongue across Jessica's lips. "And how does it seem now?"

Jessica reached up, cupped the back of Eric's head and smiled as she touched her lips to his. "It seems like it might have been the best thing that ever happened to me." When she felt his mouth on hers, it was soft and warm and incredibly exciting. They kissed for a long time, savoring the taste and feel of each other's lips and tongue. Eric stroked Jessica's side until she longed for the feel of his hands on her breasts.

As the second half of the concert began, Jessica lay on her back on the blanket with Eric, who propped himself on his elbow, gazing down at her. "Even though you can barely see me in the dark, you make me self-conscious when you look at me like that," she said.

"Uncomfortable?"

"A little."

"Good. You make me uncomfortable too. All I can think of is how much I want you."

Jessica closed her eyes as Eric continued, "Do you know how it will be with us? It will begin with a glow, soft and warm and gentle. Slowly it will build until it will blaze with fire too hot to touch but too sweet to resist." His hand lay on her flat belly, fingers widely spread. "I can feel your muscles tighten when you're excited. Like now." He placed his mouth beside her ear, his breath tickling her. "I can tell you some of the things we're going to do. Would you like that?"

She groaned. "Tell me."

"First, I'll unbutton your blouse. Wear a blouse next time so I can open each button and lick your skin as I expose what's beneath the material." He ran his finger down her breastbone to the first button of her blouse, then up to the hollow of her neck, feeling her shiver.

"Then I'll open your bra so I can admire your beautiful breasts. I've seen them in my dreams, full and white with hard, dusky brown nipples. They'll be so hard and hungry that I won't be able to resist taking one in my mouth. They will taste of your skin, spicy, tight little nubs. I'll use my teeth and you'll try to pull away from the slight pain, until it turns to hot pleasure flowing through your body." He slid his hand lower, until his fingers rested between Jessica's thighs.

"Then I'll slide your bra and your slacks off until you're wearing only your panties. Have you ever been stroked through the silk of your panties? It slightly muffles the sensation, making it softer, and more delicate." He felt the heat of her body through the crotch of her jeans and slowly rubbed. "I'll rub you there, slowly, back and forth, back and forth until you're filled with such heat that it's hard for you to breathe." He rested his head on his upper arm and used his now-free hand to draw her hair from the comb that held it. "I'll run my fingers through your deep red hair, both here on your head and between your legs."

Jessica tried to draw air into her lungs, but she could only tremble and respond to Eric's touch. The rhythmic pressure of his hand between her legs was becoming almost torture. She wanted him inside of her, to fill her and satisfy the unending hunger he was creating. "Oh Eric," she whispered.

"You'll be so wet and slippery that I'll want to slide my fingers into your body. Maybe one finger, deep inside, maybe two or even three, filling you completely. And you'll be moving your hips, trying to capture my fingers, pull them in deeper."

As he rubbed her body through her jeans, Jessica felt the pressure build somewhere deep inside and flow through her groin and thighs. It grew hotter and hotter, like a fire consuming, yet not satisfying. "So good," she moaned.

Eric placed Jessica's hand over his between her legs. "Feel me rubbing you."

She rested her hand against his and felt the movement of his fingers. "Oh God."

"I'll keep stroking you until you want me more than you've ever wanted anything in your life. My cock will be so hard that it will hurt, but I'll wait until I feel your muscles tense and your back arch like it is now. Yes, baby, let it go. Come for me, baby. Do it."

The fire inside of Jessica's belly smoldered into life. She ignited hot and white, flames roaring in her ears. As she started to moan, Eric covered her mouth with his own, filling himself with her climax. Despite her writhing, Eric managed to keep his fingers between her legs, draining her of the remnants of her orgasm, drawing the final notes from her now-quieting body.

"Oh my God," Jessica breathed, shaking her head in amazement. "Never. . . ."

Eric grinned. "Never what?"

"Never before like that." She tried to catch her breath.

His eyes widened. "You mean no one's ever touched you like that. Your husband never. . . ."

Jessica reached up and pressed her fingers over Eric's lips. "I've never climaxed like that before." As he started to ask more questions, she kept his lips still with her finger. "Give me a sip of coffee and I'll try to explain. Let me catch my breath."

Eric poured Jessica another cup of coffee, then cooled and diluted it with lots of milk. She took the cup in a still-trembling hand and drank the contents. Then she dropped back onto the blanket. "Rob and I were into very simple sex. He loved my breasts. He said they got him hot just thinking about them. When he wanted to make love, which was two or three times a week, although much less frequently toward the end, he'd take off my pajama tops, suckle until he was excited and hard, then we'd do it. You know, missionary position."

"Nothing creative?"

Jessica chuckled. "Being creative wasn't Rob's strong suit. And I didn't know any better. Until now."

A grin split Eric's face. He'd done it for her. "Oh, Jessica. Making love to you is so good."

"It will be."

"It was. What do you think we just did? That was making love just as surely as fucking is. Making love is sharing all the sexual pleasures we can. And there are so many."

Eric became aware that the air was silent. No music. He sat up and looked around. Clusters of people were ambling toward the parking lot. He glanced at his watch. "Good grief, it's almost midnight. Time to get Cinderella back to her castle."

Together they packed the remains of the fruit, wine, and coffee in the hamper, folded the blanket, and placed it on top of the lid. Eric and Jessica each took a handle and they walked back to the car in silence, through the soft summer evening.

When Eric dropped her off at Steph's house, Jessica said, "I don't know what to say, Eric."

"I'd like to invite you to my house, but you need to make a decision before then. In the light of day and with a clear understanding of what it means."

"And what does it mean?"

"It means that I want to share some wonderful pleasures with you. I want to make love to you for several hours, then relax and make love again. It doesn't necessarily mean that I want to spend the rest of my life with you or that I want to be with you and you alone. That's very important. I like you and I want to fuck you until we're both exhausted."

"It's hard for me to grasp. Sex for the fun of it. Like tonight."

"Sex for the fun of it." He thought about it. "That's exactly right. Sex for the fun of it. Think about it, Jessica. I'll call you in a few days."

"I won't be able to think of much else."

Eric leaned across the gearshift lever and placed a soft kiss on Jessica's mouth. "Good night, sexy lady."

"Good night, Eric."

In her room, Jessica stripped off her clothes and climbed into bed. Sleep, however, was impossible. She lectured herself all night.

Sport fucking, she told herself. That's all it is. Fucking because it feels good seems so . . . sinful. But yet so wonderful. For once, my sexual world is filled with light and pleasure.

Am I in love with Eric? No, she argued, I'm not. Would it make it easier if I believed that I were? Yes. And no. I'm infatuated. That's what it is, and it feels good. And I want more of his lovemaking. It's like I have a new toy and I want to play with it.

And what's wrong with that.

By morning, she had debated, argued, vacillated, and finally arrived at the conclusion that she wanted to make love with Eric just because it would feel good. And, for once in her life she was going to do something for herself, just because she wanted to.

Steph and Brian were out for the day and Jessica needed an outlet for her new feelings of freedom. She called a rental car company that specialized in sports cars and asked them to deliver a tiny red Alfa Romeo convertible. When the rental agent asked how long she'd be keeping the car, she told them that she had no idea. "Just give me the weekly rate for two weeks and I'll call a few days before the end of the second week and let you know." She gave them her credit card number and hung up.

Two hours later, when the man arrived with her car, she drove him back to the agency, then put the convertible top down, pulled the rubber band from her hair and spent the rest of the morning driving around Westchester County. With the radio turned up loud and the wind in her hair, she felt fifteen years younger than her thirty-six years.

She drove to the Bronx Botanical Gardens and wandered the grounds, stopping to smell the flowers. She ate a hot dog at the Old Snuff Mill, then, realizing she was starving, ordered and ate another, this one smothered in sauerkraut and pickle relish. She drove up to the Bear Mountain Bridge, found a place to park at the Westchester end and walked across and back.

On her way home late that afternoon, she stopped at a delicatessen and picked up a pastrami sandwich with cole slaw and Russian dressing and a sour pickle. Back at Steph's she sat in the kitchen and devoured every bite, washing it all down with three Samuel Adams Dark Beers.

Then she dialed Eric's number. When she heard his voice, she said, "It's Jessica."

"Well, hello," Eric said, his voice tentative. "I didn't expect to hear from you."

"I didn't expect to call, but I wanted to thank you for last evening." She told him about the car she'd rented and the day she had spent. "I feel so good, I just had to thank you. It's like my life is just beginning."

"I'm so glad to be part of that."

"I feel a bit awkward, but I wanted to ask when we can get together again."

"You're sure you understand everything?" Eric said.

When Eric spoke, Jessica could hear the smile in his voice. "I know that what we did last evening felt wonderful and I want to explore," she said. "I'll probably chicken out several times before I see you again, but in my heart of hearts, I know that this is what I want. And, of course, I've had three beers and I'm smashed."

Eric laughed. "I don't want to take advantage. Are you really drunk?"

"No," Jessica admitted. "But it's a good excuse to let go and do what I want."

"Can I pick you up in half an hour?"

She glanced at the clock. It was 7:30. "I'd like that," Jessica said, smiling.

"I'll see you at eight o'clock."

Jessica hung up the phone and giggled. "I've got a date and I know what I'm going to be doing." Her body sang and her mound throbbed. "Jessica," she told herself aloud, "you're a piece of work."

She took a two-minute shower, then put on a short-sleeved red blouse, a pair of white slacks and white flats. She brushed on a bit of blush, lipstick and left her hair loose. She had just left a note on the kitchen table, telling Steph and Brian that she was out and she didn't know when she'd be back when she heard Eric ring the doorbell.

Jessica opened the door and Eric filled the opening. He was wearing the same soft jeans he had worn the evening before, this time with a tailored, navy-blue polo shirt.

"Oh Lord," he said, staring at her, "I feel like a starving man gazing at a gourmet feast."

"You're looking at me like I'm the blue-plate special," she said, squirming.

"Am I embarrassing you?"

"A bit. But I like the way you look at me." She grabbed her purse and closed the door behind her.

"Can we take your car?" Eric asked. "It's warm and I'd love to drive with the top down."

Jessica fumbled in her purse and found the keys. She tossed them to Eric who opened the passenger door for her. Then he climbed into the driver's seat and started the engine. "Do something for me," he said. "Take off your bra."

Jessica paused for a moment, then turned away from him. She unbuttoned her blouse, unhooked her bra, and wriggled it off. She rebuttoned the blouse, feeling the fabric brush across her erect nipples. She stuffed the bra in her purse, snapped her seat belt, and lay her head back against the headrest.

"Nice," Eric said. "That belt falls just in the right spot, right between your luscious breasts." He reached over and traced the belt with his fingers. "Unbutton the blouse so you can feel the wind on your skin."

Jessica gave him a questioning look. Then she opened the buttons and spread the sides so the red fabric just covered her areolas. The canvas of the seat belt was cold against her bare chest.

"Oh yes," Eric said. "We're going to have everything." He tuned the radio and, as they drove out of the driveway, Frank Sinatra's voice filled the warm night.

During the five-minute drive to Eric's house, Jessica closed her eyes and let the sensuality carry her. The wind was cool on her naked skin, the radio mellow. The air smelled sweet, of summer flowers. She was almost disappointed when they drove up the driveway of Eric's house. As the car stopped, Jessica couldn't believe the building in front of her. "You designed this?"

"Yes." The building seemed to be made of rock and glass, lean and low to the ground, almost growing out of the earth. Although the rooms appeared square, each one was at an angle to its neighbor, gently slanting roofs complementing each other. It was a strange harmony of unusual shapes, softened by lots of hundred-year-old maples. "It was an idea of mine that I adapted to this piece of land. You can't see much from here but there's a rocky pool with a little waterfall on this side," he pointed, "and woods in the back. Real woods. We cut down only one tree."

"I want to see it during the daytime. It must be magnificent."

His laughter was deep in his throat. "Some say yes and some think it's ugly. I like it and I'm all that counts." He ushered Jessica inside, through the darkened living room, up the stairs, through the master bedroom, and into the master bath. He lit a small oil lamp in the corner and began to light candles.

"Oh my," she said. The room was dominated by a huge two-person tub that nestled in an alcove surrounded by a redwood-and-tile ledge covered with pots of ferns, interspersed with dozens of glass containers of clear oil with wicks floating inside. Eric poured bath oil into the tub and turned on the tap. Then he lit each candle and they both watched as shadows danced and flickered on the walls and ceiling. The scent of greenery with a hint of flowers filled the room. "Lavender," Jessica whispered.

"Just a wisp, one candle. And, from now on, every time I smell it, I'll think of you." He lit the last candle, turned to a wine bucket he had placed beside the tub and picked out the bottle. He lifted Jessica's right hand, turned it palm up and cupped it in his large hand. Then he poured a tablespoon of cold wine into her palm, leaned down and licked it up with his rough tongue.

Then he filled his palm and held it out to Jessica. She held his hand in hers and slowly licked the wine from his skin. She slid the tip of her tongue down his index finger, then nipped at the tip. She was wanton. She was brazen. She was free.

"Oh, baby," he groaned as she nibbled on the end of his finger. "I thought you were new at this."

"I am," she whispered. "I'm just learning."

"You learn too well," Eric said, pulling his hand away. "I want to take it slowly. Very slowly. I want us to savor every step, every pleasure."

Jessica wanted to take it all slowly, but her body ached for what she knew would happen. She was excited, her body and soul reaching for something she knew she could have at last. She took a deep breath and stepped back. She looked behind Eric and saw the mountain of bubbles threatening to overflow the huge tub. "Eric," she whispered, "we're about to have a minor flood."

Eric turned around and grabbed for the taps, turning them off just before the water sloshed over the edge. "A long time ago I covered the overflow drain with tape so I could fill this beast as high as I liked. I've never lost track of time before." He released the drain to allow a little water to empty from the tub.

"Thank you. I take that as a compliment."

"Oh, believe me, it is." He filled two wine glasses and handed one to Jessica. "Sorry about the plastic, but I won't have glass in here."

"I like the cups we used a moment ago better," she said, raising the glass to her lips and looking up at Eric through lowered lids. She was flirting. She was playing. She tried to control her grin, but didn't succeed. "Oh God," she said, "I'm so happy."

"And a bit drunk?"

"Just enough."

Once a few inches of water had drained from the tub Eric replaced the stopper. "Our bath awaits." He pulled off his shirt, pants and shorts, kicked off his shoes and stepped into the bubbles.

Jessica saw only his back, smooth and firm with tight buttocks and well-muscled legs. He had just a little extra weight, enough to make him look soft and inviting. He kept his back to her, fussing with a few more candles.

Now she had to undress. Can I do this? Can I take off my clothes in front of a man I've known for less than a week? Quickly, while his back was turned, she pulled off her clothes, stepped into the water and sat down, covering herself with bubbles. This makes no sense, she thought. I've made a decision, I've licked wine from his palm and nibbled on his fingers. Why now am I afraid of his seeing me naked?

"Can I turn around now?" Eric asked.

"You knew?"

"Jessica, my sweet, your mixed emotions are written all over your lovely face." He turned, settled into the warm water, took her hand and held it. "I want this to be your decision all the way. I want you to want me and want my lovemaking. And I want you to explore all the things that give you pleasure. I will never knowingly embarrass you, although it might happen without my realizing it, I'm afraid."

"Thank you for understanding my confusion."

"I want you to promise me something. Some things we do will make you want to laugh. Silly stuff. And if you want to laugh, do it. I want this to be fun. Some things we might try will make you a bit uncomfortable and some discomfort is very exciting. But if we ever do anything that makes you want to stop, you must say so. Immediately. Just say 'Eric, stop' and I will. Promise me."

"I promise."

Eric placed a palm on each side of Jessica's face and gazed into her eyes. "If I can be sure that you will tell me to stop, I can do so many things we might enjoy."

"I do promise, Eric."

They were facing each other in the giant tub of warm, bubbly water. Holding her face in his palms, he caressed her with his gaze, softly sweeping from her sea-green eyes to her lips to the sensual line of her throat. "So lovely," he whispered, stroking her cheeks with his thumbs. "Half of me wants to grab you by that gorgeous red hair of yours, throw you down on the floor, and fuck you until we're both exhausted, the other half wants to savor this and make our loving last all night."

She remained silent, enjoying the warm, sensual web he was spinning around her. Slowly all worries about how briefly she'd known Eric ebbed. She wanted him to make love to her. It was that simple. She picked up a cake of soap and lathered her hands. She placed her palms on his shoulders and made lathery circles on his biceps. She felt him lower his hands into the water as she spread lather onto his upper chest. Smooth, tight skin covered his well-developed muscles.

As she slid her slippery hands up the sides of Eric's neck, she watched his head fall slowly backward, exposing his throat to her caress. There was something so intimate about the motion that she smiled and rubbed her thumbs along the line of his jaw. She closed her eyes and her hands returned to his chest, swirling through the soapy lather. "Mmmm. You feel so hard and smooth." Rob has curly chest hair, she thought, then pushed the thought aside.

She opened her eyes and found Eric looking at her. "I told you before that your face tells all. Were you thinking about your ex-husband?"

Without stilling her hands, she said, "Yes. But he's gone now."

"No he's not," Eric said, "and that's okay. He's the only man you've ever been with and it's natural that you should think of him right now. I don't mind."

"He's a fool."

"That may be true, but he's your only measuring device." Eric reached under the bubbles and cupped her breasts in his hands. "I, on the other hand, have had enough experience to know that you will be a sensual delight." He rubbed his thumbs over her nipples and felt them contract until they were tight under his fingers. "We will learn to share so many pleasures." He leaned forward and placed a soft kiss on Jessica's lips. Then he soaped his hands and rubbed the lightly scented lavender soap over her shoulders and upper arms. "Your skin is so soft." He increased the size of the soapy circles until his hands slipped under the water and caressed her breasts.

Jessica let her head fall back, soaking in Eric's touches as she soaked in the water. Her ribs, her underarms, her neck and arms, she felt Eric stroke them all. Then he lifted one of her hands out of the water and carefully soaped each finger, sliding his fingers between hers. Then he dipped the hand into the water and sucked the tip. "You taste soapy," he said. He picked up his wine glass and poured a bit of the cold, clear liquid over her fingers, then drew each, in turn, into his mouth. "Delicious," he whispered. He repeated the ablutions with her other hand.

"I'd like to make love to you right here," he said, "but we need to shower off first."

Puzzled, Jessica looked at him. "They always do it in hot tubs in movies."

"In movies, the actors aren't really covered with soap, that might irritate your tender body. In addition, let me show you something about hot water." He stood up, water and bubbles pouring from his slight belly.

Jessica couldn't help gazing at his penis, small and flaccid. I am a failure, she told herself. Rob was right. I am frigid.

Laughing, Eric said, "Hot water and too much wine. Not you, my love." He lifted her into a standing position and sluiced water and soap from her body with the flats of his hands. "Definitely not you." He caught the drop of soapy water at the tip of one breast with the tip of his tongue.

Jessica shuddered, not sure whether Eric was lying to save her from embarrassment. She watched Eric pull a shower curtain across the open side of the alcove, release the tub's drain, and reach for the shower controls. Suddenly the alcove was filled with soft, warm spray, coming from shower heads in each corner at once. "It's like a soft summer rain," she said.

"There are several settings, but this one is designed for moments like this." As water drained from the tub, warm water poured over their bodies and Jessica turned her face to the spray, rinsing off all traces of soap. "Done?" Eric asked.

"Ummm," she purred.

Eric turned off the water, opened the curtain and wrapped Jessica in a thick, thirsty bath sheet. As she rubbed her hair, Eric, a towel around his waist, walked out through the connecting door. Slowly, as she watched, candlelight began to dance on the walls of the bedroom.

Without giving Jessica time to think, Eric returned, swept her into his arms, and carried her to the bed. He spread a dry towel on the satin spread, laid her on it and stepped back, feasting on her naked body. "God, you're lovely." He nipped her toes and kissed his way up her shin.

Jessica looked at the wavy gray hair on the man who was quite purposefully making love to her. It wasn't Rob. It was Eric. Then she felt Eric's hot breath on the hair between her legs and she couldn't think anymore. Reflexively, she pulled her knees together.

"Oh, baby," Eric whispered. "You're so sweet." He pulled her legs open and blew a cool stream of air on the hot flesh between her thighs.

"But. . . ." She willed her muscles to relax, but they wouldn't.

"Rob never kissed you here?" he asked.

"No." Her voice was barely audible.

"Does it feel bad?"

"I don't think so. Just odd."

He lightly rubbed his index finger over her clitoris. "And this?"

Her mind was filled with colors, swirling reds and purples, oranges and bright sulfurous yellows. "God no. It feels . . . indescribable."

"How about this?" He surrounded her clit with his lips, swirled his tongue across it, then sucked it into his mouth. As he felt her body tighten, he slid two fingers into her drenched pussy.

The sensations were too much for Jessica. The colors exploded, pinwheels and kaleidoscopes, angles and shards of color and light. "Eric," she screamed, arching her back and clenching her fists. "Eric."

"There's so much more I want with you," Eric said, "but I can't wait right now." He unwrapped a condom, unrolled the latex over his engorged penis, crouched between Jessica's legs and pressed his cock against her opening. "Feel that?" he said. "Feel how hard for you?" He slid it into her passage, a bit at a time. "Feel how it fills you, stretches you? Feel how I want you." When he had filled her completely, he held still above her, balanced on the heels of his hands. "Open your eyes, Jessica. Look at the man who wants you beyond everything right now."

Jessica opened her eyes and looked at Eric, his face tight as he held his body in check for one last moment. She watched the control in his passion-clouded eyes. That passion and control is for me, she thought. A small smile curled the corners of her mouth. He was holding back. He was controlling his excitement. She clenched her vaginal muscles and squeezed the cock that filled her.

"Oh baby," he groaned, pulling back, then plunging deeper inside, giving in to the needs of his body.

Jessica's last coherent thought was that she had caused him to lose control. She, Jessica. One-time frigid wife of Rob the asshole. Oh lord, I've missed so much. But not anymore. Then waves of an incredibly intense orgasm overtook her.

Chapter 5

They lay together on the bed, and dozed for almost an hour. When she opened her eyes Jessica found Eric gazing at her. "You're staring," she said, a grin spreading across her face.

"I guess I am. I knew you'd be wonderful, but I didn't expect to be overwhelmed."

Jessica giggled. "I'm overwhelming, am I?"

"Jessica, you're priceless and wonderful. Not only do I get the joy of making love with you, but I get the delight of watching you discover yourself. What more is there?"

Jessica turned and propped herself on her elbow. "This takes a bit of getting used to," she admitted. "I guess I've been told that there was something lacking in me for so long that it's hard to grok that it wasn't true."

"Grok?"

"My word, actually Heinlein's, for something that's even deeper than just understanding. It's like someone telling you that the world really is flat and that round was just propaganda."

"You've got an unusually honest way of looking at things."

"Maybe I do. It's just that here and now, I find it necessary to put some things into words for which there aren't really words."

"Ummm." Eric took her hand. "Can I tell you something very personal, Jessica?"

Was he going to reject her? Tell her she really was frigid? Fearing the worst, Jessica tightened her abdominal muscles, closed her eyes, and nodded.

Eric barked a single laugh. "Oh baby, don't look so stricken." He kissed her fingers. "I just want to say that I'm starved. I was so excited when you called that I never ate dinner."

Jessica let out a long breath, then cocked her head to one side. "Me too." She rolled over on her back and grinned, sliding her arms and legs over the sheets like she used to as a child when she and her friends made snow angels. Life was fun.

Eric got them each a fluffy, terrycloth bathrobe and, laughing like schoolchildren, they ran down to the kitchen. Jessica walked into the white Formica room and gasped. It was larger than her living room in Ottawa.

"I know," Eric said. "It's ridiculous. But it's Timmy's playground and I let him design it when I built the house."

"I can see that," Jessica said, gazing at the wide counters, hanging baker's racks, and masses of cabinets and closets. There was a six-burner stove, a microwave, a conventional oven, and a convection one. Eric crossed to the industrial-size refrigerator that dominated one end of the room and opened the double doors. "You know," he said, reaching for a slice of strawberry cheesecake, "one should really eat healthy stuff, especially after good sex."

"One certainly should," Jessica said, looking over his shoulder at the second shelf, which held a plastic container of something that appeared to be chocolate pudding.

Eric put the cheesecake on the counter, then grabbed a jar of peanut butter and a loaf of bread from the refrigerator. "Good choice," Jessica said, grabbing the pudding, then shutting the door with her hip. "Got a toaster?"

"You're kidding. Toast and peanut butter was always my favorite. I haven't had it since Timmy arrived."

"And where is he tonight?" Jessica asked, inserting two slices of white bread into the toaster.

"I gave him a quarter and sent him to the movies." When Jessica laughed, he admitted, "Actually, Timmy lives in the guest house on the far side of the garage and I saw him earlier, just getting back from a day with friends in Jersey. When you called I asked him to stay away from the house for the evening." He winked. "Timmy said to say hello to you."

Blushing slightly, Jessica said, "He knows? About us? About this?"

"He knows that I find you exciting and that I intended to do something to scratch the itch, yes."

The toast popped up and Jessica put the two slices on a plate and put two more into the toaster. She handed the plate to Eric who slathered chunky peanut butter on each piece. "You know what goes with toast and peanut butter?" he asked.

"What?"

"V8."

"We must be long-lost twins," Jessica said, smiling. "When I was in high school on my way home I would stop at the store and get a loaf of bread, a jar of Skippy, and the oversized can of V8."

"Actually," Eric said, getting glasses from an upper cabinet, "you were much healthier than I was. I'd usually get a bag of potato chips, a container of sour cream, and a box of onion soup mix. That and a bottle of Pepsi and I was set for the afternoon. Peanut butter and V8 were for bedtime."

"Were you into sports or after-school activities?"

"I went to elementary and junior high school in Manhattan." Eric pulled out a large can of juice and filled two glasses with thick, red liquid. "There wasn't much of that sort of stuff to do. Then I went to Bronx Science High School, mostly eggheads with a calculator in their pocket. I guess I was a bit of a nerd."

"I was the artsy type back then," Jessica said. "Before I met Rob, I was into writing, both short stories and, of all things, poetry."

"Why do you say 'of all things' like that? What's wrong with writing poetry?"

"Nothing, really. I just wasn't the type."

"And why not? What type writes poetry?"

"People with things worth saying. Important things about life and love."

"Nonsense. People write poetry because they want to write poetry. Even I wrote some at one time. Did you write good poetry?"

"Oh lord. It was very free-form, sophomoric stuff filled with suppressed desire. You know, now that I think back, it was probably sexual frustration, pure and simple. In most of my images, two lovers raced toward each other across a flower-filled meadow. That sort of thing." The toaster popped and Jessica put a piece of toast on top of each peanut-buttered one.

"Ummm, suppressed sexual desire. I like that. But now that it's not suppressed anymore, you'll just have to write some erotic poetry and attend one of our evening readings."

"Readings?"

"You know there are several people, including a few whom you met at Steph's party, who make up a very enlightened group. We sometimes get together and read erotic literature out loud, and sometimes Gary tells a story."

"I've heard about Gary. Steph told me he gives great parties. She didn't elaborate."

"He does, and he has the money to indulge in all his hitherto suppressed sexual desires. He has the most wonderful imagination and has no reticence about using it to plan outrageous gatherings."

"Erotic readings?" Jessica smiled.

"Don't laugh. At one of his parties, Gary turned out the lights and we all lay around on the floor while he told erotic fantasy tales. There was a lot of suppressed desire when he was done, I'll tell you, although it didn't remain suppressed for long."

Jessica took a bite of her sandwich and chewed for a minute. This was still all so new to her. "Ummm," she said. "Good peanut butter." Her words came out muffled through the mouthful.

"You make a hell of a sandwich," said Eric. Sensing her need to digest more than the peanut butter, Eric let the conversation veer off in a different direction. They shared their companionable meal, then pigged out on chocolate pudding and Timmy's best strawberry cheesecake. When they had put the dishes in the dishwasher, Eric said abruptly, "I think it's time for me to drive you home."

Nodding, Jessica said, "I think I understand." Eric had made the rules and they both were keeping their new-found intimacy within tight boundaries.

When Eric grinned, Jessica continued, "But we'll see each other soon, I hope."

"That's the difficult part. I'm sorry to say that I have an assignment that requires my presence in San Francisco. My job only demands that I be on site occasionally, but this is one of those occasions. I found out today that I have to leave first thing tomorrow so I can be ready for Monday morning. Then I'll work all week and red-eye back Friday night. The timing stinks."

"Yeah. It does," Jessica said, disappointed that they weren't going to see each other for a week. Sexual freedom felt like her new toy and she wanted to play with it. "We can talk on the phone, though."

"Of course." He told her the name of his hotel and they arranged for her to call. Then he hugged her and they went back upstairs, located their clothes and dressed in silence. As they climbed into Jessica's car, Eric said, "We need to be totally honest from the outset. Sex can be good with anyone who has an open mind and a desire to please."

"I know. But I have just come to terms with extracurricular activities with you."

"Extracurricular activities. That's one way to put it. Just remember, however, that you have no curriculum any more. Play. Have fun. Rob is history and good riddance."

"To bad rubbish."

It was almost one in the morning when they drove into the driveway and parked next to the Carltons' two cars. Eric kissed her hard, then quickly climbed into his own car and drove away.

Jessica gazed after him, then turned. She walked over to Brian's car and stopped, resting her hand on the cold hood. "Extracurricular activities." She slid her hand along the highly waxed surface, then walked into the house.

Stephanie found Jessica the following morning, sitting in the plant room staring into space. "Morning, Jessica," Steph said.

Jessica looked up. "Morning," she said, a strange look on her face.

"We saw Eric's car when we got in last evening," Steph said, "and I got your note. Wanna tell me about it?"

"Eric and I went back to his place."

"And. . . ."

Jessica burst into delighted laughter. "And wow and double wow. It was sensational. Lights, colors, bells, whistles, candlelight, and peanut butter."

"Peanut butter?" Steph settled into the chair next to her best friend.

"Oh, Steph, I'm so glad I came to Harrison."

"So am I. Are you and Eric an item? He's a really nice man and Brian and I are very fond of him."

"Not exactly an item. Not that way. We understand each other. We make love like rockets and supernovas, but it doesn't mean anything more than that."

"Sounds like you're a different person than you were when you left Illinois."

"Well," Jessica giggled, "I know I'm not in Kansas anymore. God, who's been hiding orgasms all these years. I think mine registered on the Richter scale at one point."

Steph leaned over and hugged Jessica. "I'm so happy for you. Maybe we should send scrawny-neck and bimbette a blow by blow. Pardon the expression."

"I don't even want to think about Rob. You know, though, I feel kinda sorry for him. He has no idea what he's missing."

"Are you seeing Eric tonight?"

"That's the sad part. Even as we speak, he's winging his way to the west coast. Some big job he's got to work on."

"Oh, Jessica, that's too bad. How long will he be gone?"

"Til the end of the week, he thinks. We have a date for next Saturday."

"That's great. Eric's a wonderful guy." Steph looked at her watch. "Okay. It's almost nine and Brian's still in bed. What shall we do today?"

"Let's drive around, have a high-calorie lunch, and pick up guys."

"JessicaLynn Hanley, I love you." Her voice dropped. "There's a party a week from Saturday at Gary's. Not just couples but it *is* a swinger's get-together. Fun and games, and I do mean games. Interested?"

"Being with Eric has opened up a whole new world for me. I want to explore. But I'm not ready for an orgy, I'm afraid."

"Not an orgy at all. These swingers' parties are very tightly controlled because not everyone is interested in the same thing."

"Controlled how?"

"Well, for example, the living room and kitchen are off-limits for any hankypanky. They're safe zones where people who don't want to play or haven't decided yet can gather. That way no one will ever be embarrassed by something they don't want to see or do. There are pieces of colored yarn on or beside every door. A black ribbon on the door means off-limits. Like, if we had a party at my house, your room would be off-limits. A red ribbon on a door means the room is occupied, stay out. Like that."

"Sounds like you've thought this through."

"We have. And we've made mistakes and learned. We want to have a good time and not hurt anyone."

Jessica thought a moment, then smiled. "I don't know whether I'm ready for something like that yet. Maybe. I assume that, if you guys go, they're all nice people. No weirdos."

"The only new faces will be people personally endorsed but mostly it's the same people. Like the ones you met here last weekend. And then there are very specific rules about safe words."

"Safe words?"

"We use 'cease and desist' for an absolute stop. If anyone says 'cease and desist,' whatever is going on that involves them must stop. Immediately. And you must use that phrase if things get uncomfortable. No martyrs or endurance contests. We use 'time out' for things like, my foot itches or my arm is cramped."

"I don't get it. Why don't you just say stop?"

"If you say stop, no one knows whether you really want to stop or not. It can be fun to say, 'Please no' or 'Don't do that' without worrying that someone will actually stop. Control games can be very exciting."

"Control games?"

"You're just beginning your sexual education. Let's leave control games for a graduate-level course. Suffice it to say that dominant and submissive fantasies have been around for centuries and can be a lot of fun to play out."

"I always thought you were so suburban yuppy, so conservative."

"Shows how much you know."

"You know what I'd like to do today, really? Let's drag Brian to the Bronx Zoo."

"I haven't been to the zoo in years. Great idea. Then seafood for dinner. I know a great spot on City Island." Steph stuck her head out into the hallway and yelled at the top of her voice. "Hey Brian, get dressed, you bum. We've got the day all planned."

The following Tuesday morning, Jessica stretched out on the bedspread in her room at Steph's. The room was cool, with off-white, grasscloth wallpaper, green and off-white sheets and a dark green flowered comforter. The carpeting was thick and a deep forest green, giving the room the look of a forest glade.

Since she wanted to be free to say anything to Eric she picked up her cellular phone and dialed The Stanford Court, Eric's hotel in San Francisco. The switchboard connected her immediately. After only one ring, a sleepy voice answered. "Hello?"

"Good morning, Eric. You did say I should call you at this ungodly hour." Jessica could hear the rustling of Eric's body as he moved around in bed three thousand miles away.

"Good morning. And yes, this time is fine. I have to get up anyway and what better way is there to be awakened?"

Eric told Jessica that his job was going well. "I should have no problem getting back by the end of the week. How about you? What have you been doing?"

Jessica told Eric about her time with Steph and Brian, trying to put her feelings into words. "It's like someone just lit a lamp in a part of my life that I didn't know existed."

"Well, I'll be sure to have my flashlight with me at all times so I can illuminate more dark corners."

"It's so much more than sex. It's me. I'm free to do and say things I haven't done or said since I was in high school. I didn't realize how much of my life I've lived with the feeling that Rob was looking over my shoulder, judging me."

"It must be wonderful to feel so liberated."

"And, of course, it's all that good lovemaking we did. The only problem now is that my mind seems consumed with thoughts of you and your gorgeous body." As the picture of Eric's naked body flashed across her mind, she realized that he wasn't really well built at all. He was soft and a bit overweight. But he was sexy and attractive and a total turn-on.

"I'm glad you think I'm gorgeous, although it does make one wonder about your eyesight. By the way, what are you wearing?" Eric asked.

"That's a question out of left field. I'm wearing shorts and a polo shirt. Why?"

"Well, I'm not wearing anything, and I want you the same way. Put the phone down and take your clothes off." When there was silence, Eric added, "Please."

"This is silly."

"Come on. Pull the shirt off over your head, take your bra off and get out of those shorts and underpants."

Jessica giggled, then complied. She cradled the phone against her ear and lay back down on the bed. "Okay. I've taken my clothes off. Why?"

"Because we're going to make love."

"Three thousand miles apart?"

"Yes, three thousand miles apart. Stretch out on the bed and close your eyes. I'll close mine. What are you lying on? A bedspread? A quilt?"

"A comforter."

"Okay. Feel the cool, smooth cloth on your back. Feel it on your buttocks and calfs, on your heels. Stroke the comforter with one foot and feel the smoothness against your sole. Can you feel it?"

"Yes."

"Is the window open or do you use the air conditioner? It was pretty cool when I left."

"It is cool and I have the window open."

"Good. Feel the air that is coming in the window. Feel it against your skin, all over. Listen to the birds and the leaves rustling. Smell the green smell of the grass and the trees. Part your lips and breathe in through your mouth. Now run your tongue around your lips and taste the cool air. Feel the coldness as you breathe in again."

Jessica did as Eric asked. She had never been as aware of all the sensations around her.

"Lick your thumb. Taste your own skin."

She did, feeling only a tiny bit silly. "It's tangy, spicy kind of."

"Good. Now put your fingertips on your breast bone, right between your beautiful breasts. Stroke up and down, from your throat to your belly. With my eyes closed I can imagine that I'm watching and touching you."

Still feeling awkward, Jessica placed her fingertips against her chest and stroked her skin the way Eric wanted her to.

"Are you doing it?"

"Yes," she said softly.

"Does it feel good?"

"Yes." It did feel good. Soft and gentle.

"Jessica, have you ever touched yourself, explored your body?"

"I shower every day," she said, laughing nervously.

"That's not what I mean and you know it. When I was a kid, I touched my body, rubbed my cock, discovered the things that felt good. It was hard not to because all the feel-good parts were right out there, aching to be touched. I think every boy knows those places, if not before puberty, then about twenty minutes after. But, somehow, I don't think girls do. Did you ever touch yourself like that?"

"No," she admitted. Jessica could hear more rustling through the phone. Eric was obviously moving around in bed.

"How can you know what will feel good when a man touches you," he said softly, "if you don't know yourself? How can you help him to find the feel-good places if you don't know where they are?"

"I never thought about it."

"Well, you will now. Let's find out together. Swirl your fingers over your right breast. Your fingers feel the soft skin of your tit, and your breast feels the rougher texture of your fingers. Don't touch the areola, just the soft white skin. Are you doing that?"

"Yes," she whispered, torn between the erotic sensations and the feeling that she shouldn't be doing this.

"And it feels good. Don't answer that. Just indulge me for a few minutes. Just do as I ask without thinking. Now, slide your fingers up your side, to your underarm. Are you ticklish?"

"Not really."

"Good. I know that feels good, but we're looking now for places that make you hot. Slide your fingers over your neck and behind your ears, then across your face. Touch yourself."

Jessica was doing exactly what Eric was asking of her and it did feel good. Her skin tingled and she felt more alive, somehow.

"Now slide your fingers back to your breast. I know how sensitive your nipples are. If I close my eyes I can see them getting hard and tight. Fondle them and make them hard. Squeeze and pull. Make it feel good."

Jessica sighed, and touched her right nipple. She felt it contract and become more erect under her fingers. She dropped her hand and took a breath, about to tell Eric that this was ridiculous. Then she stopped herself and put her fingers back on her nipple. "It does feel good. It does."

"I know it does. And it makes other parts of your body feel good too. You are becoming aware of the heat between your legs. You don't really want to think about it, but you can't help it. Your mind keeps travelling to the tightness low in your abdomen and you can feel the area between your legs swell and get hot and wet. Slide your fingers down your belly and make large, swirling circles. Use your palm."

Jessica could hear him chuckle and she smiled. "What are you laughing at?"

"I know what's going on in your brain right now. Part of you wants to explore, wants to find out what mysteries are hiding between your legs, waiting to have the light shone on them like the lights we turned on a few nights ago. But part of you is still, wondering whether nice people do things like this. You're brain is yelling words like 'masturbation' and remembering all the things your mother told you would happen if you touched yourself."

Jessica nodded. "She said I'd spoil it for lovemaking with my husband. She told me that if I touched myself, then I would always need that kind of stimulation in order to become excited. It would become a habit. Therefore I would never get any pleasure from relations with my husband. It sounds so uptight when I say it out loud now."

"Lots of people believe it. But, if you never know your own body and what gives you pleasure, then how can you ever help a man to know how to please you?"

Jessica was still sliding her palm over her belly. "Men were just supposed to know."

"Yeah. Right. That's been the bane of men's existence since we lived in caves. Don't help us, just expect us to know. No wonder sex becomes tedious."

"I guess that's not really fair."

"No, it's not. But it's a very common attitude. I enjoy making love and I've made love to lots of women. It's a unique experience when I find someone like you and I can introduce you to all kinds of exciting new activities, but I also like it when a woman knows her body and what she enjoys." His voice dropped and softened. "What do you enjoy, Jessica?" Without giving her time to answer, he continued, "Do you like it when the ends of your fingers brush the springy hair between your legs? Do that. Just brush your bright red bush very lightly."

Jessica did as Eric asked. She had washed herself every day in the shower, but this was different. She never thought about her body in the shower. Now she could think of little else.

"Part your knees. Let your legs open wide. Feel the cool air on the hot, wet skin that's probably never felt cool air on it before."

"That feels strange," Jessica said, "forbidden somehow."

"I can hear your mother now. Keep your knees together. It's not ladylike to allow anyone to even think about what's between your legs." As if sensing her feelings, Eric said, "No, no. Don't slide them closed. Keep them spread wide apart. Reach between your legs and touch the hair there."

"How do you know what I'm thinking?"

"You're a sensuous woman who's never had any opportunity to revel in her sexuality, in her body. This is all new, exciting, and a little scary. Am I on the right track?"

"Actually, it's very exciting and very scary."

"Good. Scary is exciting, too. Are you touching yourself?"

Jessica's fingers just grazed the hair between her legs. She knew she got wet, but she'd never actually felt it before. God, it felt good, both on her fingers and on her swollen lips. "Yes," she whispered.

"Touch yourself more. Let yourself explore. Feel. Your body is slick, and rubbing it makes you want things you've never allowed yourself to want before. Are you touching all the crevices and folds? Tell me, Jessica, are you?"

Jessica was sliding her fingers into places she'd never touched for pleasure before. And it felt so good. Her outer lips were open, giving her access to the areas within. Her inner lips were covered with slippery wetness. She found that some places felt better than others. "Yes," she answered.

"This will be more difficult for you, Jessica, but I want you to touch your clit. You've been avoiding touching that part, but your clitoris can give you intense pleasure. Slide two fingers into the fold between your outer lips and find that hard, swollen little nub of nerve endings. Slip one finger on either side and stroke back and forth. And shut off your mind, except for the parts that feel and hear. Just rub. And if you find a spot that feels particularly good, rub more. Find the places that make your toes curl and your back arch. Find the places that seem darkest and most erotic. Stroke yourself, baby. Do it for me."

Jessica touched her swollen clit. Torn between the intense pleasure and the feelings left over from her past life, she did as Eric's voice told her to. She rubbed. And she rose higher and higher. It became easier and easier to touch the places that gave her the most pleasure. She closed her eyes.

Eric's voice was husky as he continued. "Let me tell you what I'm doing while you're touching yourself. I've got my hand on my hard cock and I'm squeezing and stroking it. I'm caressing my balls, then holding my cock."

Knowing that Eric was touching himself made what she was doing seem less dirty somehow. This was part of a mutual experience.

"Remember how it felt when I touched you? Reach for those feelings. Do things that bring you closer to those swirling colors you told me about. Touch just the right places. Pretend that those are my fingers, if you need to, but feel the erotic intensity growing."

"Oh yes, Eric. It feels so good."

"Don't stop. Prop the phone against your ear and take the other hand and use your index finger to rub your slick inner lips. Rub the opening of your slit. If you want to, slide one finger into your body. If that doesn't feel good, don't do it."

"It all feels good."

Jessica heard Eric chuckle. "You're magic, baby," he said. "Feel the orgasm coiled inside you, waiting for you to release it. Find the places that tighten that coiled spring. Find them. Use them. Wind it tighter and tighter."

Jessica was burning. She rubbed her body with both hands, and squirmed on top the comforter. She rubbed her feet on the material and arched her back. She found a tiny ball of light and touched the places that made the light grow. Higher and hotter, she didn't want to stop. Her slippery fingers offered her ecstasy and she reached for more. The light changed from soft yellow to white and grew brighter. Suddenly it exploded, enveloping her in heat and brightness. "Oh," she said, her breathing hard and fast. "Eric."

For long moments she was filled with lava, reaching every nerve in her body. She was lost in it, yet aware of every sensation. Never before had anything like this ever happened while she was alone. And somewhere a tiny part of her was sad for all the lost opportunities.

"I came with you," Eric whispered. "God, that was great."

Jessica laughed. "It certainly was." She looked at the clock on her bedside table. They had been on the phone almost forty-five minutes. "Look at the time," she said.

"Time flies when you're having fun. But I do have to get to work. And a shower is most definitely necessary now."

Jessica lay on the bed, limp and smiling. "This is all so incredible," she whispered.

"Unfortunately, I have to get up," Eric said. "But you lay there until you want to move. And don't think. Feel. And when those thoughts about what's right to do and what isn't surface, and they will, tell them to get stuffed."

"Yeah. Get stuffed. I'll do that."

"I'll call you when I know my schedule."

She needed to tell him one last thing. "There's a party at Gary's a week from Saturday. Steph invited me to go."

"Great. Gary called me and I'll be there too. But even if I weren't going to be there, you'd have a wonderful time and get to explore the new you."

"But, you'll be there?"

"Yes. And I want to make love to you in every way possible, in every place possible. I want you to explore your new-found sexual understanding with others, too. Meet new men and make love if they turn you on. Women too, if that gives you pleasure. You're a new person, Jessica."

"I don't think I'm ready to do this alone."

"I'll be back on Friday and, if you're free, we can see each other Saturday night. By then, I'm sure you'll be more comfortable with the new you. Okay?"

"Great." Jessica took a deep breath.

"I'll call you later in the week if I can."

"Okay," she said, disappointed that he didn't say that he'd definitely call tomorrow. "Don't work too hard."

"Jessica, have a terrific week, and don't play too hard." They both hung up.

It was almost eleven when Jessica wandered into the kitchen. Brian was standing at the counter, pouring Cheerios into a bowl. "Good morning, JJ."

"What are you doing here?"

Grinning, Brian said, "I live here."

"That's not what I meant and you know it. Why aren't you at work?"

"Day off. I'm allowed, you know. Even us Wall Street types get time off for good behavior." He leered at her long legs, exposed beneath her brief denim shorts. "Or bad behavior."

Jessica blushed and sat down at the table.

"JJ, I'm sorry," Brian said, sitting across from her. "I don't ever mean to make you uncomfortable. Steph told me about you and Eric and I understand how you're feeling right now. I know Eric well enough to be sure that he's told you that he's a free-spirited guy with a girl in every port."

"He has, of course."

"This is all new and strange. You've suddenly realized that men are attracted to you and, if you wanted, you could enjoy more than dinner and a movie together." He reached across the table and took Jessica's hand. "And, you've never thought of me as anyone but Steph's husband. However, I am attracted to you. I won't deny that. Just understand that I will never knowingly do anything to hurt you. If I tease you a bit, or make a remark, it's because I care about you as a friend and as an attractive woman. Okay?"

Jessica smiled warmly. "Yes, Brian, I do understand."

"And I want to make love to you in seven different positions."

Jessica's laughter filled the sunlit kitchen. She looked at Brian for a moment, then added, "And maybe you'll get your wish, eventually."

Brian stood up and retrieved his bowl of cereal. "You give an old man hope," he said.

"Old, my foot," Jessica said. "You're exactly three months older than I am, if I remember correctly."

"But I'm several decades more experienced."

Jessica shook her head ruefully. "I certainly do have a lot of catching up to do."

Brian raised his hand high in the air. "I'll help," he said, waving the hand around. "Ooooh, oooh, pick me."

"Good morning, everyone," Steph said, interrupting the conversation. "What are you volunteering for so enthusiastically?"

"Never you mind, snoopy," Brian said. "That's between JJ and me."

"Sorry I asked." She grinned and kissed Brian on the cheek, then hugged Jessica good morning. "What should we do today?"

"I'd just like to lounge around the pool," Brian said. "And I've got a few errands to run. And how about some tennis later?"

The threesome spent the remainder of the morning beside the Carltons' pool then made chef salads for lunch. Late that afternoon, Jessica watched as Steph beat Brian in two sets of tennis at their country club. The two opponents were laughing together as they walked back to where Jessica sat beside the court with a diet Coke in her hand. Sweat dripped from their bodies, soaking their tennis whites. "I'd say six-four, six-two is a thorough trouncing," Steph said. "And that doesn't happen often."

"I was distracted looking at JJ's legs in those tiny shorts," Brian said. "She kept crossing and uncrossing them at just the wrong moments." He groaned. "And when you decided you needed more sunblock on your thighs I double-faulted three times in a row."

Jessica stretched her long legs in front of her and ran a finger up the inside of one thigh. "If you can't take the distractions," she said, then winked at Steph, "tough."

Brian whacked his wife on the arm. "Did you plan this?"

"Well . . ." the two women said in unison.

"JessicaLynn Hanley," Brian said, grinning, "you're becoming entirely too frisky."

Jessica grinned. "Thanks," she said. "And I'm not *too* frisky, but I am just right."

"You sure are. Okay, I'll meet you ladies in the bar in fifteen minutes," he said. "Gotta shower and shave." He walked toward the men's locker room.

"I'll meet you there," Steph said, handing Jessica her racket.

While Steph and Brian took showers, Jessica settled at a tiny table in the bar and ordered a Bloody Mary. As she nibbled on a piece of celery, a man of about forty leaned over the table. He was wearing crisp white tennis shorts and a light blue soft-collared shirt with a tiny Donald Duck stitched above the left breast. "You're Steph and Brian Carlton's friend JJ, aren't you? From the midwest."

"Yes," she said, warily.

"I thought it might be you. Brian described you several times. My name's Cameron Hampstead, but everyone calls me Cam. I work in the city and I ride Metro North with Brian. When I saw him yesterday, he mentioned that he and Steph had a tennis date this afternoon." He held out his right hand and Jessica placed hers in it. His palm was warm and soft, his grip strong.

"Hmmm," Jessica muttered. "And I thought this tennis game was spur of the moment." Aloud Jessica said, "And how did you recognize me?"

"Brian's described you as a gorgeous redhead with green eyes."

"Oh," Jessica said, a bit nonplussed.

He looked at the other chair at the small table. "May I?"

"Sure," Jessica said, not totally comfortable with being picked up in a bar, despite the club's exorbitant annual dues.

He sat down and placed his racquet and tote on the floor beside him. "I guess this is where I'm supposed to ask you what your sign is, or something inane."

Totally puzzled, Jessica's head snapped up. "Excuse me?"

"I'm sorry, but this isn't my usual thing."

"Okay, you've lost me. What isn't?"

"Picking up women in bars. Brian told me yesterday that he and Steph would be here with you today and he suggested that I might meet you. He thought you and I would get along splendidly."

"He set this up?"

Cam smiled ruefully. "He did. He's a big fan of yours and, I suppose, of mine too. I guess he thought we'd hit it off."

"I'm very embarrassed," Jessica snapped. "I really don't need Brian fixing me up."

"I'm so sorry. I know he meant well. I'm the one who botched this." There was a slight trace of an English accent in Cam's voice, which had gotten more pronounced as the conversation progressed. "This was a really bad idea."

As Cam rose to leave, Jessica placed her hand on his, where it rested on the table. "This is dumb and awkward," she said, somehow warming to Cam's openness, "but not an entirely bad idea. Brian's intentions were good and your only fault is one that I suffer from as well. Honesty. Let's start again."

His grin lit Cam's ordinary-looking face. "Thanks." He sat back down.

"Hi." Jessica extended her right hand. "My name's Jessica. Jessica Hanley. Nice to meet you."

Cam's grin widened still further and he took her hand. "Mine's Cameron."

"Cameron. That's an unusual name."

"It's a family name." He deliberately broadened his accent. "Very British and all that. Actually, I hate it. Cam's much better."

"Well, Cam, until recently, people called me Jessie, and only Brian calls me JJ. Right now I prefer Jessica."

"Jessica it is." Cam ordered a glass of cabernet. "What takes you into the city on the train with Brian?"

"I'm in advertising. TV commercials. Lots of pressure, lots of late nights and coffee. Lots of famous people being temperamental and thinking that they know my business better than I do. And lots of sponsors who think they know my business better than I do."

"Sounds awful."

Cam smiled ruefully. "It does, doesn't it. To be truthful, I love it."

Jessica liked Cam's grin and she matched it with one of her own. "Someone has to," she said.

Over the next five minutes, Jessica told Cam briefly about her divorce and her extended visit to Harrison.

"I was married briefly," Cam said, "but my wife was killed in an auto accident." When Jessica looked distressed, he added, "That was almost fifteen years ago. I guess that I've idealized her over the years, and I just haven't found anyone since that I wanted to spend my life with."

Brian arrived at the table dressed in navy shorts and a plaid sport shirt, pulled up a chair and dropped into it. "Well, Cam, fancy meeting you here."

"I told her, Brian," Cam said. "Everything."

"Uh-oh." He looked a bit sheepish. "I got caught. I'm really sorry, JJ."

"You should be," Jessica said, wanting to make him suffer for a few minutes. "You made both Cam and me very uncomfortable."

Brian picked Jessica's hand up from where it lay on the table. He kissed her fingertips, one by one. "Am I forgiven?" He gave her an I'm-too-cute-to-be-mad-at look. "Please?"

Jessica burst out laughing. "Okay. I'll forgive you. But just this once. From now on I'll select my own friends."

"I agree," Steph's voice said from behind Jessica. "When Brian told me about this. . . ."

"She didn't know in advance," Brian said, jumping in to keep his wife in Jessica's good graces. "I told her between our two sets. Honest."

"Hi, Cam," Steph said. "I'm glad to see you, even under these circumstances." She cuffed Brian on the arm. "You're impossible."

Brian grabbed Steph's arm and pulled until she plopped into his lap. "I'm entirely possible," he said. "And you love it. Am I forgiven?"

Steph wriggled into her own chair. "Buy me a club soda and I'll think about it."

"Jessica? Forgive me?"

"Well. . . ."

The four talked for about half an hour, then Brian glanced at his watch and said, "It's almost six-thirty. If I haven't entirely turned you two off about each other, I'd like to suggest that the four of us have dinner together. Cam?"

"I'd love to join you all for dinner. But only if Jessica has forgiven both of us for our subterfuge." He looked at her. "Have you?"

There was a boyish, attractive quality about Cam, Jessica thought. He's charming and good company. She thought briefly about Eric, then said, "I'd like that." She looked down at her bare legs. "I'm obviously not dressed for anything fancy."

"I know a great place for Texas-style barbecued ribs and chicken," Cam suggested. "It's up-county in Yorktown. A place called Rattlesnake's. And they have an appetizer platter with things called rattlers that will cook the fillings in your teeth."

When Steph looked dubious, Cam added, "Not everything is hot, but I happen to like chili peppers."

"Sounds good to me," Jessica said. "And I don't mind having my teeth rattled occasionally."

"Really?" Brian leered, waggling an imaginary cigar, Grouchostyle.

"Sounds good to me too," Cam added, holding Jessica's gaze a fraction too long.

"Okay, you two," Steph said, wanting to bail her friend out of a potentially uncomfortable situation. "Enough of the double entendres. You're embarrassing the two refined ladies at this table."

"Where?" Jessica said. "I only see two grown women and two attractive guys, one of whom you're married to."

Both Cam and Brian beamed. "Thank you, Jessica," Cam said.

"Rattlesnake's, it is," Brian said.

After getting directions to the restaurant, they separated. Steph and Brian drove away in Brian's Lexus and Jessica and Cam in Cam's Toyota. After half an hour of good conversation, Jessica and Cam met Steph and Brian in front of the restaurant and they were shown to a table in front of a wide window. They ordered beers and, while the other three looked at the menu, Cam ordered the Rattlesnake PuPu appetizer platter.

When the platter arrived, they ordered a barbecued chicken and a rack of baby back ribs, deciding to share. Cam gave the other three a guided tour of the enormous plate of appetizers. He pointed to a shapeless lump, breaded and fried. "This is a popper, a hot pepper filled with cheese and deep fried, and this is a rattler, a shrimp stuffed with a hot pepper. Warning!"

Jessica picked up a rattler and bit off a small piece. Her mouth flamed almost immediately. "Holy cow," she said, grabbing a taco chip from the pile of nachos and stuffing it into her mouth. "These do smart a bit."

"How about the wings?" Steph asked.

Brian bit one and answered, "Just at the borderline of your heat tolerance. I think you'll like it."

Stephanie did, and the rest of the meal as well. When the check arrived, Cam laid his credit card on the tray. Jessica reached for her purse. "Brian, Steph, and I have agreed," she said. "We split checks." She wondered how Cam would react, and in her mind, it was a test of sorts. Would he be gracious?

"Okay, if that's what makes you comfortable," Cam said. "About twenty each ought to do it."

Jessica pulled a twenty-dollar bill from her wallet and handed it to Cam. Without fanfare, he tucked it into his pocket.

As they left the restaurant, Jessica walked with Cam toward Brian's car. "I'd like to take you to dinner," Cam said. "Would you like that?"

Jessica linked her arm in Cam's. He was charming, and refined, and, she admitted to herself, without any overt effort, very attractive. "I would, very much."

"Would tomorrow night be too soon? I could pick you up about six. I know an Indian place that makes the best shrimp vindaloo. It will sizzle your tail feathers."

"I haven't had my tail feathers sizzled in a while. I love vindaloo."

Again, Cam's smile lit up his face. "Six it is." Jessica nodded as she climbed into the backseat of Brian's car. "See you tomorrow," she said.

Cam leaned in through the open door and kissed Jessica lightly on the mouth, then ran his tongue across her upper lip. "Till then."

As they drove south, Brian said, "Hey, JJ. I hope I'm forgiven. I guess it was a bit sneaky."

Jessica pictured Cam's face. "You're forgiven, but no more. Okay?"

"Okay."

Chapter 6

The following day, Steph joined Jessica at breakfast. After some small talk, Steph asked, "Have you ever considered having your hair done? Maybe getting a body wave?"

"That's out of left field," Jessica responded. She ran her fingers through her long hair and tucked a strand behind her ear. "Actually, I wanted to cut and soften it a few years ago, but Rob thought it was pretentious so I dropped it." She made a face.

"I'd love to see you shorten it, and give it some soft waves."

"What brought this on?" Jessica asked.

"I've got a hairdresser appointment this morning and I was wondering whether you'd like to come along and maybe do something a bit experimental. Something more Jessica and less Jessie."

Jessica thought about her long, straight hair, which she now wore either in a ponytail or just hanging loose down her back. She fluffed out the sides, which fell back against her face. "I don't know. How about if I join you, and consider my options later?"

John's of Harrison was an incredibly opulent salon. Ten full-time operators cut, styled, blow-dried, and colored the hair of Harrison's rich and pampered. When anything new was considered for any of its slightly spoiled patrons, five-foot five-inch John Matucci bustled over and discussed the changes at length. No one, absolutely no one, would make a move without John's specific approval. Several women put off stylings if John wasn't at the salon.

When Stephanie and Jessica arrived, the salon was only half full. A woman in a pink and gray jumpsuit hurried over. "Good morning, Ms. Carlton. We were expecting you. As you can see we're not very crowded so we can do as much as you'd like today."

"As much as you'd like?" Jessica muttered.

"You'll see," Steph said, turning to the perfectly groomed reception-ist. "Gina, I'd like to introduce my friend Jessica Hanley. She's from my old hometown, here visiting for the summer."

"Ms. Hanley. How nice to meet you. Will you have time for anything today? You have magnificent skin," Gina said. "Maybe a facial?"

"Jessica, John's does massages, body wraps, waxing, just about any-thing you could want."

"Sounds delightfully decadent," Jessica said.

"Have you thought about your hair? Maybe a soft wave?" Steph asked.

Gina reached out and took a strand of Jessica's hair and rubbed it between her fingers. "Such wonderful hair. With a light rinse and loose wave, you'd be spectacular." She lifted one of Jessica's hands. "And won-derful long fingers. How about a manicure and an herbal hand-wrap?"

"Gina, down girl," Steph said. "She's just visiting. Don't go over-board."

Gina leaned over so her face was close to the two women. "John's here today and he's even got some time." She leaned even closer to Jes-sica's ear. "I could fit you in."

Jessica sighed and smiled. "Okay. What the hell. Tell John to do his worst."

"But, he will do his best," the woman said, unused to Jessica's ban-tering.

"Of course. It will be his best." Jessica and Steph laughed, then got ready to be pampered. While Jessica's hair was rinsed with a gentle high-lighter then waved, she had an herbal wrap on her hands, a manicure, a facial, and an hour-long massage. When Steph replaced her on the mas-sage table, she said, "Isn't that the most hedonistic thing you've ever done?"

"God, Steph," Jessica admitted. "I've never had a massage before. That's heaven."

"Imagine how it would feel if a man did it on his bed, with his hands awakening all those feelings in your body, then satisfying all those hungers. God."

Jessica felt the prickling between her legs. "I'll bet it would be unbe-lievably erotic."

While the manicurist massaged Jessica's feet, filed off the calluses, and applied bright red polish to her toenails, Jessica nibbled on a light tuna salad with melba toast.

When John combed out her hair and blew it dry Jessica was delighted with the subtle difference in her appearance. He had shortened her hair until it fell just at her shoulders, longer in back and waving loosely around her face. He had enhanced her existing style without making any dramatic changes. "What do you think?" the talented, officious salon owner asked.

"It's just lovely," Jessica answered, truly impressed by the improvement. "I look years younger."

"Lovely? Of course not. John does not do lovely." He seemed to refer to himself in the third person frequently. "John does magnificent. John does terrific. But lovely?"

Steph walked over. "John, it's sensational."

Jessica quickly agreed. "Yes, of course John," she said, trying not to laugh. "It's magnificent."

John smiled, and tried to look humble without success. "Thank you Ms. Hanley, Ms. Carlton." He took Jessica's hand and guided her from the chair. "And such soft hands." He kissed her knuckles.

Steph and Jessica settled their exorbitant bills with their credit cards and left the shop, giggling like schoolgirls.

Cam picked her up that evening and commented on how nice she looked in tight beige slacks and a soft off-white silk blouse. She wore her hair loose and it now flowed softly around her face.

"You look different," Cam said. "Softer."

The curry was terrific, hot enough to awaken every nerve in her mouth, but not so hot as to deaden her taste buds. They shared tales of past curries, compared life in England and Ottawa, Illinois, favorite movies, TV shows, and books. As they sat over rasamalai and spiced tea, Cam said, "I'm sorry to say that I've got to end our evening early. I've got an impossible job to finish that will take the rest of the week and all weekend."

"I'm sorry too," Jessica said. "When is it due?"

"Tuesday morning, at eight a.m., come hell or high water."

"Oh Cam, I'm sorry. You should have called and cancelled tonight. I feel so guilty."

Cam covered her hand with his. "Don't. I wanted to see you again and it was worth whatever time it took. I'm just sorry that we can't continue this evening. With final revisions and everything, I should be off the hook by the middle of next week. Could I interest you in a drive out to Connecticut for dinner? The traffic might be awful, but I know a place that has the best steamers and makes flounder that's so fresh. . . ."

"I'd love to, Cam." She was seeing Eric on Saturday, now Cam next week and the party the following Saturday. God, she felt good.

"Great. I'll call you at the beginning of the week and we'll set a definite date."

Cam drove her back to Steph's and helped her out of the car. As she stood up, he took her in his arms and softly pressed his lips against hers. They kissed for a long time, exploring each other, pressing their bodies tightly together, feeling the soft, yet building arousal. When he pulled away, Cam said, "If I keep doing that, I'll throw you into the car, take you back to my place, and ravish you in the driveway."

Jessica kept her arms around Cam's neck. "You would, would you?" she said, savoring her slightly aggressive feelings. She wanted him and they were both adult, single and capable of making their own decisions. Then she pressed her mouth against Cam's and kissed him for another long minute. "A bit more of that and I might let you."

Cam flashed her his most charming smile. "You're quite a woman, Jessica."

"And you're quite a guy, Cam. Thanks for dinner."

"Till next week?"

"Till next week. Call me when your job's finished."

Jessica turned and walked into the house, happier than she had been in a long time.

The following morning she called Eric. After a few pleasantries, she said, "I had a date last evening."

"Great. Have fun?"

"Yes. I did. It's a whole new thing, this dating."

"I'm happy for you, Jessica."

When she told him about her day at John's he asked, "Are you gorgeous? More so than when I left?"

"You know, I feel gorgeous and I've never felt like that before. I feel like men might want to look at me, might find me attractive. That's a new thing for me." She laughed. "I also had a massage. What an experience."

"If we're still on for Saturday, I'll give you one of Eric's patented massages, no holds barred."

Jessica felt heat flow through her body. "I'd like that," she said huskily. "Then could I give you one?" She had never explored Rob's body and now she found that she wanted to touch all of Eric's.

"That sounds like an offer I can't refuse." He picked up his watch from the table beside his bed. "It's after nine-thirty there. Are you still in bed?"

"Yes," Jessica said. She stretched, liking the feeling of cool sheets against her naked skin.

"Well, I need to know something. When I give you that massage where would you like me to touch you?"

"Where?"

"Where. Exactly."

"Oh, just everywhere," Jessica said, suddenly shy.

"Your breasts? Touch them and see whether they would like that."

Jessica pressed the palm of her hand against her breast and felt her swollen nipple fill her hand. "Oh yes."

"And you'll want me to rub your thighs and your beautiful ass. Then I'll rib your clit until you come. It won't take long, will it?"

Without thinking, Jessica slipped her hand between her legs and found her swollen, wet clit. She rubbed long and slow, then harder and faster. "No," she whispered. "It won't take long at all." She felt the familiar tight knot in her belly.

"Are you rubbing where it feels so good, baby?"

"Yes," she moaned.

"Don't stop. Stroke and touch. Do exactly what feels best. Reach out for the orgasm and pull it closer. Use your mind to see your fingers as they rub and give you pleasure."

Jessica reached for the climax and drew it closer and closer. As it flowed up her thighs, she tensed her legs and arched her back slightly. "Yes," she groaned and it overtook her. "Yes." It filled her, swirling in hot shards of orange and gold. It came so hard it almost hurt. She gritted her teeth and felt it curl her toes.

After a short silence, Eric said, "You did it, didn't you. You gave yourself pleasure. You were responsible for your own orgasm."

Jessica caught her breath. "I guess I was."

"I hope you've recovered from those feelings that Rob stuffed you full of."

She smiled. "Not entirely, but it's hard to feel frigid when a man can make you come over the phone."

She heard Eric's rich laugh. "True enough. Saturday? My place? Timmy's wonderful dinner, then whatever?"

"Yes. What time?"

"I'll come get you at about six-thirty, if that's okay."

"Great," she said, feeling her languid body sink into the mattress. "See you then."

The rest of the week sped by. As had become a habit, Thursday afternoon she called her office in Ottawa and talked at length to Vivian Whitman, her second-in-command and, next to Steph, her best friend. She made a few necessary business decisions and was gratified to learn that everything was running as smoothly without her as it did when she was there. "Viv," she said, "you make me feel unnecessary."

"Jessie, we all love you and we want you to take this time off. We're deliberately not bothering you with anything but the most important stuff." Viv's voice lowered. "Are you having any fun?"

Jessica could picture the slightly overweight black woman who, right now, had her head bowed with the phone tucked between her shoulder and her ear. One hand would be cupped over her mouth, as she always did when she was being conspiratorial.

"Oh lord, Viv," Jessica said, "I'm having more fun than I could have imagined." Leaving out the more lurid details, she told her friend about Eric and about Cam. "I feel attractive and sexy and free."

"That's great. I'm so happy for you."

Jessica could hear a note of sadness. "What's wrong, Viv?"

"I guess I'm scared you won't come back. I miss you." Viv and Jessie had become friends several years before although Rob had always declined offers to have dinner with Viv and her husband.

"I miss you too, Viv," Jessica said.

"Dates are not coming out of the woodwork here. Nice men are in short supply, as you may remember. I'm just afraid you'll decide to stay in New York."

Jessica felt uncomfortable with Viv's correct assessment of Ottawa, Illinois. It was a bit dull. "Any nibbles on my house?"

"We've gotten several repeat visits, but no offers yet. I'll call you if anything appears promising. Oh, and by the way, your ex seems to have dropped out of sight. Do you know anything?"

Jessica found that she wasn't hurt by the mention of Rob's name. Now, she was angry. "Not a thing, and I really don't want to either."

"Sorry."

"Don't be. And I didn't mean to sound waspish. I hope he's happy. Remember the line from *Fiddler on the Roof*? 'May God bless and keep the tsar . . . far away from us.' That's how I feel right now. They should be happy, and invisible." Jessica could hear Viv's giggle over the phone lines.

"Lord, I do miss you, girl."

"Me too, Viv. Talk to you next week."

"Till then."

Eric picked Jessica up that Saturday evening and they sped to his house. As they drove up the driveway, Jessica was struck by the way the low-slung, strong, rugged, rough-hewn house matched Eric's looks and personality. She glanced at his angular chin and close-cut, granite-gray beard and said, "The house fits you."

"Thank you." He stopped the car and pulled up the emergency brake.

"I didn't really see it the last time I was here. I was a bit distracted, if you remember. I'm awed by how perfectly your house suits you. It's beautiful."

"Thank you. And don't be awed. That's what I do for a living, you know."

"I didn't know you were so good."

"I'll bow modestly and admit that I'm damn good. Actually what I'm good at is finding out what people are and what they want." He rested his head on the headrest. "I get people to paint me a picture of the way they see themselves, then I design a frame to put that picture into."

"I've been selling real estate for a long time and I'm hard to impress." She waved her arm to take in the house and the subtle landscaping. "This impresses me."

"Thanks." He got out, rounded the car and opened the door for Jessica. "Very non-politically-correct."

Jessica extended her hand and Eric grasped it. "Very," she said as she unfolded herself from the tiny car, "and I like it." Without releasing his hand, she stood very close to Eric's body, looking into his smoky-gray eyes. The day was hot and humid, but it couldn't match the heat radiating from her body and Eric's.

He raised her hand to his lips and, without releasing her gaze, he swirled his tongue around her palm. Then he pulled a length of thick dark-gray yarn from his pocket and tied it around Jessica's wrist. "You may not remember from your last trip here, but my bedroom is decorated in shades of gray, from the palest hue, which looks almost white, to the deepest shade, the color of the ocean in a storm. This," he finished the knot, "is the color of the sheets on my bed. Tonight, you will be there, with your red hair spread on my pillow, your green eyes clouded with passion, your body needing me."

Jessica swallowed hard, around the lump in her throat.

"And you know what you'll be doing?"

"What?" she croaked.

"You'll be begging me to fill you up. And I won't. I'll tease you and drive you crazy."

"Oh."

He grinned. "But we have to have dinner first. Timmy's been expecting you." He aimed her at the front door.

They walked down a short hallway and through a formal dining room dominated by an oak table that could seat twenty. The chairs were upholstered in a soft rose damask and the deep plush carpeting was a richer shade of the same color.

"Ms. Hanley," Timmy said as they entered the kitchen. "I'm so glad to see you again."

"I'm glad to see you, too, Timmy, but could you call me Jessica?"

"Okay, Jessica," Timmy said, opening the refrigerator door. "You spoke about liking cocktail sauce with horseradish so I gambled that you'd also like Bloody Marys. Was I right?"

"Timmy, you're a mind reader. I love Bloody Marys, extra spicy."

Timmy withdrew a pitcher from the refrigerator and filled two glasses. He garnished the drinks with stalks of celery and thin slices of tomato and onion. "Actually," Jessica said, lifting the celery from the drink, "I like Bloody Marys but I love celery." She bit off a chunk and chewed loudly. "Aren't you having one, Timmy?"

"If I drink before I cook, I don't cook."

Eric patted Timmy on the shoulder. "Occasionally Timmy and I share a bottle of wine or something before dinner. First, the rolls don't get made, then the salad bites the dust. By the time dinner arrives, it's meat and pasta."

"Yes," Timmy said, "but I thought you were usually too sloshed to notice."

"Too true," Eric said. "What's for dinner tonight?"

"I've made a cold cucumber and yogurt soup, chilled chicken breasts with white grapes and watercress, and tabbouleh."

"What's tabbouleh, Timmy?" Jessica asked.

"It's a middle eastern salad made from bulgar, tomatoes, parsley, lemon, and olive oil."

"Bulgar's wheat, isn't it?" Jessica felt Eric ease around behind her. While she talked, he pulled the back of her blue-and-white-striped shirt out of the waistband of her white linen slacks.

"It is wheat, but I have no idea exactly what's been done to it."

Jessica felt Eric insinuate his index finger into the back of her pants and stroke the top of the crack between her buttocks. She swallowed then she said, "That sounds delicious."

"Oh," Timmy said, "it's so nice to have an appreciative audience."

As Eric's fingers lightly brushed the skin in the small of her back she sipped her drink, wanting him to stop, yet not moving away. As Timmy turned back to the refrigerator, Eric licked a wide swathe from her collar up to her hairline. She smiled as she remembered her debate about whether to sweep her hair up to the crown of her head with a silver comb and a narrow blue silk scarf.

"I like your hair up," he said, his breath hot on her ear, "but I want to see how it looks with its new styling."

"Would you like to have your soup now?" Timmy asked, oblivious to what was going on.

Eric tucked Jessica's shirt back in loosely and said, "I want to show Jessica the back. Let's say fifteen minutes?"

"Everything's served cold this evening, so take your time. I'll have soup ready whenever you like."

With Eric's warm palm in the small of her now-covered back, Jessica walked through a gigantic living area, cleverly divided into several seating groups. "Oh Eric, this is fantastic," she said, clearly awed. Although each area had a different pattern to the furniture—florals in one area, stripes in another, solids in a third—the areas were held together by the consistent use of southwestern shades of soft rose, sand, and slate blue. "I would have thought you more the chrome and glass type."

"I went to Tucson about five years ago and fell in love with the country, the people, and the ambiance. I had already built the house, so it's very steel, rock, and glass outside and soft and plushy inside."

"I know a lot of people like that," Jessica commented.

Eric smiled. "Now that I have it the way I want it," Eric said, "I don't use the house much, except for an occasional party."

"But you wouldn't sell this," Jessica said. "It's a part of you."

"I don't feel that way about things, I guess," Eric said, "but it would be a shame to leave this. I would, though, as long as I felt that I was leaving it in good hands." He led her through a sliding glass door and into the backyard.

A flagstone patio about fifteen feet wide ran the length of the back of the house. The area was edged with a three-foot-high wall of natural rock with water gurgling out at intervals into small pools and a six-foot-high waterfall at one end. Shrubs and low ground covers grew in crevices in the rocks and half a dozen large trees closed the area in. To Jessica it looked like an oasis out of an Arabian Nights fantasy or a secret cove on a tropical island. It should be tacky, she thought, but it isn't. It's glorious. Jessica looked around, taking in the beauty of the secluded spot. The air was heavy and humid, filled with the sweet aroma of distant flowering plants. "It's beautiful." A soft breeze brushed her face as Eric stood behind her.

"I pictured you here," he whispered, his fingers deftly unbuttoning her top. "I saw you naked, like some kind of jungle creature, wild and wanton." He unfastened the last button and pulled her shirt loose from her slacks. He took the drink from her hand and put it on a small wicker table. Then he removed her shirt, unhooked her bra, and slid it off her arms.

Jessica stood still, letting the warm breeze pucker her nipples and whisper over her skin. She closed her eyes and let her head fall back as Eric pulled the scarf, then the combs from her hair. She felt the soft mass cascade to her shoulders as Eric buried his fingers in the soft red strands. "You smell wonderful."

His hands were all over her body, touching, moving, dancing. He moved around until he was facing her, then he cupped her breasts and buried his face in the curve of her neck. "Just as I dreamed it would be," he purred. He stepped back and let his fingertips trail toward her nipples. "But not yet," he said.

When she felt him pull back, she opened her eyes, a silent question on her face.

"I want this evening to be filled with sensual pleasures. And I want it to last." He handed her her top, keeping her blue lace bra in his hand.

"I understand," she said. She slipped her arms through the openings and buttoned a few buttons. When he handed her her scarf, she tied it in her hair at the nape of her neck.

"Now feel your nipples against the soft fabric of your blouse." He lifted the end of the scarf and brushed it over her cheek. "Feel everything. Smell everything. Taste everything. We are going to make love all night." He kissed her softly, then led her back into the house.

They ate dinner in a small dining area adjacent to the kitchen. The table was oyster-colored Formica and the place mats and napkins followed the southwestern feel of the living room. The soup was cold but it cooled only a bit of her internal heat. The chicken was delicious, and the salad was the perfect complement. Eric poured each of them a glass of cold, crisp chablis, but she drank only a little. She was gently buzzed and didn't want to get any more so.

Throughout the meal, they talked about unimportant things. He amused her with stories of his travels and some of the unusual people he had designed for. She countered with tales of the weird couples for whom she had tried to find houses.

Although they laughed and shared and nothing overtly sexual was mentioned, a soft, sensual haze pervaded everything they did. Occasionally Eric would reach across the table and tug gently on the yarn around her wrist but she needed no reminders. The picture of her on Eric's bed was never out of her mind.

When they were finished with the main course, Timmy removed the plates and brought simple bowls of fruit sherbet for dessert. He placed a plate of chocolate truffles and tiny butter cookies in the center of the table. He poured coffee into their cups and put the pitcher on the table. "Unless there's anything else you want," Timmy said, "I'm going to go watch the Mets game."

"Nothing else," Eric said. "Who are they playing?"

"Los Angeles. Actually, I'm dying to see that Japanese phenom who's pitching for the Dodgers. Nomo."

"I've heard of him," Jessica said. "He's being considered for rookie of the year, but he's hardly a rookie. He's played for a dozen years in Japan."

"I'm impressed," Eric said. "I didn't know you were a baseball fan."

"When you live within spitting distance of Chicago, it's either the Cubs or the White Sox. I'm a Cub fan, myself, although I only watch games on TV."

"Maybe we can watch together some time," Timmy said.

"That would be fine," Jessica said. "Are you a Mets fan? We can watch a Cubs/Mets game and we can scream during alternate innings."

"I'm not a real rooter in that sense. I watch any sport and any team," Timmy said. "I just enjoy good competition."

"Timmy will watch anything from arm wrestling and surfing championships to chess and gymnastics. We watch a lot together on the weekends."

"Good night, Ms. Hanley." He caught himself, and said, "Good night Jessica. It was nice to see you again. And I'd love to watch the Cubs with you sometime."

"Good night, Timmy. Enjoy your game."

As Timmy left, Eric said, "We'll enjoy our games too." He took the spoon from her sherbet. "First game, no spoon."

"No spoon?"

Eric dipped his finger into the sherbet and extended it to her. She smiled, then licked the cold sweetness from his fingers. Then she scooped a dollop of sherbet and put it into the hollow of her hand.

Eric grinned as she held out her hand and he licked it from her skin with long, slow laps. "You taste heavenly."

Licking sticky sherbet from each other's hands, they ate their dessert. Eric poured them each a cognac, then they walked back onto the patio. As Jessica stood in the middle of the patio, Eric removed the scarf from her hair and held it in front of her at eye level. "May I?"

When Jessica looked puzzled, he lay the scarf across her eyes. "I want you to feel, not see. May I?"

Jessica thought only a moment before nodding. Eric tied the scarf across her eyes, then removed all her clothes, leaving only the yarn around her wrist. Jessica felt him lift first one foot and then the other to remove her sandals.

"Feel how cold the stone is on your feet," he said, stroking her insteps. "You're so beautiful," he said, sliding his hands up her legs.

"Your legs are long and shapely, your thighs white and soft." He brushed his knuckles over her red pubic hair. "Red, like fire. Do you burn for me, Jessica?"

"Oh yes," she moaned. She felt him take her hand to lead her across the stones. Jessica hesitated. She couldn't see. What if she spoiled the mood by stubbing her toe or doing something equally awkward. She didn't want to ruin this.

"Trust me," he said softly.

"But. . . ."

He placed a finger against her lips. "Just trust me. Nothing will spoil this." He picked her up in his arms and carried her to the edge of the patio and sat her on the cold stones. Then she felt him take one of her hands and dip it into the cold water of one of the pools. "You're all sticky," he said, carefully rubbing the sherbet from each finger. He did the same with her other hand.

Then, when both her hands were cool and wet, he took her palms and placed them on her breasts. Cool water ran down her ribs in tiny rivulets, tickling her sides. She struggled to hold on to the mood but, as Eric dribbled water onto her belly, she started to laugh.

"Ticklish?" Eric said, laughing with her.

"Not usually, but right now, yes," she said, worried that she had ruined the mood.

"Good. Laughter is necessary." He licked the droplets of water from just below her belly button and she giggled again. Then he suckled at her right breast and heat stabbed through her, making her as hot as she had been. He took her nipple in his teeth and bit gently, just hard enough to make her squirm. "Like that," he said. He took one finger and slid it into her, rubbing the sides of her slick, hot channel. "And that." He withdrew, stood and lifted her into his arms. "Oh yes." He moved her body so her hip rubbed against the bulge in his slacks. "Come upstairs with me. I want you in my bed."

Still blindfolded and naked, Jessica felt herself carried through the house and up the stairs. "I've been dreaming of you in my bedroom all week." Eric set her down on the floor and said, "Sit down, love."

He placed her hand on the edge of his bed and she sat on the smooth slithery sheets. She felt the bed sway just a bit as she settled onto it.

"If you were as excited as I was last weekend, you were too excited to notice that this is a water bed and particularly delightful to make love on. And the sheets are satin, cold and slippery. Lie back."

She stretched out on the cool fabric and spread her arms and legs, moving to intensify the feel of the satin. "Ummm," she purred.

"Now I want to play."

Jessica felt something soft and velvety rub lightly up and down her arm. "That's a rose," Eric said. He brushed the flower across her face and she could smell its light fragrance. She felt the flower caress her breasts then her shins. "Don't move," Eric said when her hips began to move. "Just hold completely still." The flower was gone. "This is a piece of fur from the collar of an old coat." He rubbed the fur over her skin, touching her underarms, the insides of her thighs and the backs of her knees. When her hips moved, he said, "No, no. Don't move."

"But I want to move. It's very hard to keep still."

"That's part of this lesson," Eric said. "You must keep your body completely still. You can't see, you can't move, just feel. Nothing more. Concentrate."

Jessica held still despite the increasing difficulty of controlling her body. Now that she knew what she craved, the heat and orgasmic excitement, she wanted it. She needed it. She reached for it, but Eric skillfully kept it just out of reach.

"You're getting so aroused," he purred. "Your pussy is an open and hungry mouth. But I'm not ready to fill it just yet."

"Yeeooow," Jessica yelled as she felt something icy pressed on the hot, swollen flesh between her legs.

"That's an ice cube." Eric laughed deep and warm. "Hold still."

"I can't," she said as she squirmed to get away from the freezing cube. When she felt the ice being removed from her clit, she took a deep breath and willed her body to relax.

"You know that this is a game we're playing. I'm going to tease and play and you're going to hold perfectly still while I do."

"If it's a game, then what do I get if I win?" Jessica asked, giggling at the sheer joy of it all.

"If you win, you get the best fucking you've ever had."

"And if I lose?"

"Then I get to fuck your brains out."

Jessica laughed. "Then I guess it's important that I win."

She felt Eric press the ice against her right breast and take her left nipple in his mouth. The contrast between the cold and the heat drove her crazy. After about a minute, he switched, placing the ice against her warm breast and his hot mouth on her cold one. It's strange, she thought with the small, coherent part of her brain. The pleasure is the now, the feelings, the eroticism, not the anticipation of the fucking that will come later. It was a revelation for her. It's the journey, not the destination.

Eric took a deep breath and removed Jessica's blindfold, as though he sensed the change in her attitude. She looked at him and grinned.

"You understand what I'm trying to teach you now, don't you?"

"Yes. I always thought foreplay was just to get ready for fucking. But foreplay is fun just for itself."

"You get an 'A' plus. Okay, next lesson. What gives your body pleasure?" When Jessica hesitated, Eric continued, "I've touched you, caressed you, kissed you, made love to you. And I've taught you to do the same. What, exactly, gives you pleasure?"

"That's really hard to talk about."

"I know, but I want you to tell me."

"I like it all."

He made a rude noise. "Cop-out."

"I like it when you kiss me."

Eric leaned over and licked Jessica's lower lip. He slowly inserted his tongue into her mouth and played with the tip of her tongue. He nipped at her lips and sucked her tongue into his mouth.

Heat flowed through her body. A moment before she had been relaxed but now she was tense and wanting. She reached up and held his head against her mouth.

He pulled back, took her wrist, and pressed it back against the sheets. "No hands. You're still under my orders not to move."

"Orders?" she said, the word causing heat to knife through her belly.

"Yes, orders. Now, that last answer was also a cop-out, but I enjoy kissing you too so I'll let it pass. Tell me where you like to be touched, where you want me to kiss you." She remained silent, so Eric said, "Is it difficult to say the words? Do you like it when I suck your tits?"

The crude word again sent waves of heat through her. "Yes," she whispered.

He licked her erect nipple, then said, "Tell me." A smile spread across Eric's face. "Makes you hot, doesn't it. Those words. Okay, first show me with your hands. Hold your tit for my mouth." He placed her hand on the underside of her breast and lifted, holding it upward for his mouth. He drew the hard tip into his mouth and sucked. "Say *tit*," he said as he blew cool air on her hot dusty-rose areola. "Say it."

"Oh baby," she moaned. "Please."

He couldn't resist her and he took her flesh in his mouth, laving and sucking it. "Where now?" he said.

Jessica took his hand and pulled it down, pressing his fingers against her swollen vulva, rubbing, kneading. "Please," she cried. "Oh God, please."

"You want my fingers in your pussy?"

Pussy. The word increased her excitement. The power of the words. She wanted to say them. She wanted to be forced to say them. She wanted. "Yes," she said, her breathing ragged and harsh. "I want your fingers inside me." Saying them felt so forbidden, so dirty, so good. She took a breath. "I want your fingers in my pussy."

Eric moaned, then plunged two fingers deep into her cunt, sawing in and out, fucking her with his hand. "Yes, baby, take it," he cried.

"Eric," she said, looking at his face, "fuck me." She saw it all, including the effect her voice was having on him.

He unrolled a condom onto his stiff erection and climbed over her. She grabbed his cock and rubbed it over her clit. The power to give pleasure, to excite, to drive him as crazy as he was driving her. It was intoxicating. She wanted to touch him, to drive him a little crazy too.

She placed her palms against his lightly furred chest and stroked his skin. As he moved, she caressed the skin over his contracting muscles. She wanted to touch his soft belly, and she did, sliding her hand lower and lower until she heard his harsh intake of breath.

"You'll kill me doing that," he groaned.

"But it will be worth dying for," she said, his passion making her bolder. She found his hard cock and did what she imagined would feel good. She laid his shaft in her palm and stroked the length of him.

"Oh, Jessica," he moaned and she revelled in the giving, exploring his excitement. She grew bolder, finding his sac and cupping his heavy testicles. She squeezed his cock and watched his face contort with pleasure. She wanted and needed and took. She placed the tip of his cock against the opening of her cunt, slid her hands to his buttocks, and pulled him into her.

The power of it was as enlightening as it was exciting. She moved with, then against him. They varied their rhythm, first fast, then slow and languid. He pulled out, then drove into her. He slid to the opening of her sheath, then slid in, inch by teasing inch. He was quiet inside of her, then pounded hard and fast.

Finally, she felt him tense and he reached between their bodies and rubbed her clit. "Yes," she screamed, "now, do that, yes. Do that." They came almost simultaneously, but the orgasm was only the culmination of the pleasure, not the pleasure alone. It wouldn't have mattered if she hadn't come, she realized with amazement. There were so many climaxes before her orgasm.

"It's so wonderful," she said later, running her hand up his side. "I never realized until now."

"Well," Eric said, panting, "I'm afraid I've created a monster."

Jessica propped herself on her elbow. "You have, you know. You certainly have."

Chapter 7

"Tell me about Gary," Jessica asked Steph the following Tuesday morning over breakfast.

"Gary Powell is quite a story," Steph said. "When he was in his early twenties he invented some kind of computer chip. I have no clue what it did, but it did it faster than anything else. So he started a manufacturing company and made a bundle. I mean a real bundle." She sipped her coffee. "About three years ago, someone offered him a couple of gazillion dollars for the firm, lock, stock, and patents."

"Obviously he took it."

"It was more than that somehow. He took the money and dropped out. Of everything. He was, and still is, mind you, single and very interesting. Although he's not especially good looking, he's always been sexy as hell. Now he's that and rich as Croesis as well. For a while mothers would invite him over to meet their eligible daughters, run into him accidentally at parties, whatever they could do to lure him into the family. Him and all that money."

"And . . . ?" Jessica said.

"Nothing. He owns a huge estate in Scarsdale. It's on about fifty acres with tennis courts, three pools, a ten-car garage. The landscaping is gorgeous, and you know how I feel about flowers.

"The house has to be seen to be believed. He gutted an old inn, and had the entire thing rebuilt. Actually, now that I think about it, Eric designed the inside. It has a dozen guest bedroom suites, three entertainment rooms, a main kitchen and two auxiliary ones for people who stay over and want to make breakfast or what-have-you."

Jessica let out a long, low whistle.

"And the house has twenty-two bathrooms."

"Does he still work at the company?"

"That's the amazing thing. When they bought him out, they offered him a seven-figure salary to stay on as CEO, but he turned them down flat. He took his money and he decided to enjoy it. He travels, spends time in the city, dines at the best restaurants, sees shows and goes to concerts, sometimes with a woman on his arm, sometimes by himself." Steph laid her hand on Jessica's arm. "Get this. He even learned to ride and keeps a stable of thoroughbreds. He flies his own plane and goes to Boston for lunch. But he gets his jollies throwing parties."

"How do you mean?"

"He throws lavish parties and spends money like it's water. One party was a masked costume ball. He prepaid for everyone to rent costumes from one of the biggest Broadway distributors. We all went down and took our pick. Lord, that was some party."

"I'm impressed. Does anyone else give parties like that?"

"We all agreed early on not to play can-you-top-this. We all have the type of party we want to and leave the conspicuous consumption to Gary.

"Once he rented a yacht for an evening and we went out into the lower harbor and partied. Another time he flew us all to a private Caribbean Island for a weekend. He'd had the whole place set up with tents, food, wine, even a dance floor. Warm breezes, good champagne, and free love. For another weekend, he took over one of those hedonism resorts, the ones with the champagne-glass-shaped hot tubs in every room."

"You're kidding."

"He's a hedonist, with the money to indulge himself. The costume party was the one during which Brian and I first discovered one of our favorite pastimes."

"Don't tell me you discovered sex. I remember you and Brian in the backseat of a certain Pontiac."

"Not sex but a new and particularly exciting way to enjoy it."

"So tell me everything."

Steph raised an eyebrow. "I think you're ready to hear the next install-ment in my sexual education. I remember it so clearly, even though it was two years and many parties ago."

"We have to dress as our favorite sexual fantasy," Steph said.

"For what?" Brian said absently.

"For Gary's party a week from Saturday. It's a costume thing and we have to dress as our favorite fantasy." She turned the invitation over and there were the names and addresses of one costume shop in Manhattan and one in White Plains.

Brian looked up from the current issue of *Time* magazine. "My favorite sexual fantasy? In costume? I don't think so." They sat at the dinner table over dishes of fresh fruit and cups of coffee.

Brian's tone seemed harder than usual. Steph looked up at him. "Why not?" she asked, curious.

"I don't have many sexual fantasies but the ones I have are mine and I don't share. And certainly not in dumb costumes." He looked back down at his magazine.

"We've never talked much about sexual fantasies. I assume you have a few."

"Enough," he growled.

Ignoring his harumphing, Steph pushed a bit harder. "Come on, tell me. Chasing Heather Locklear around Melrose Place maybe? Or making love in the bathroom of a 747? Tell me. Please?"

"No."

Stephanie sensed that he was protesting too hard and might enjoy talking about his desires. She poured two glasses of brandy, walked to Brian's chair, pulled the magazine from his hands, and plunked herself in his lap. She handed a glass to Brian and said, "Come on."

"This is dumb," he said, sipping the drink Steph had handed him. "If you want me to tell you a fantasy, you have to tell me one of yours. And not one of those lightweight backrub or bubble-bath fantasies either. I assume you have a few, don't you?" he said, mimicking her question. When she was silent for a moment, he continued, "See. It's not easy to just tell someone that secret."

"I thought we didn't have secrets," Steph said, standing up.

"We don't," Brian said seriously. "Not real secrets. It's just that fantasies are personal. It's risky to tell someone that you want to, oh let's say make love in the pool."

"We've done that," Steph said.

"Don't pick nits with me. You know what I mean."

"Actually, I do." Steph was thoughtful. She did have some fantasies that she'd never shared with another soul. She was sure that if she said them out loud, everyone would know she was really perverted. Several vivid pictures flashed through her mind and her eyes glazed.

Several moments went by, then Steph snapped back to the present. She looked at Brian and found him staring at her. "You were a million miles away," he said. "Fantasies?" Steph's cheeks turned pink. "Holy cow," Brian said. "You're blushing."

Steph giggled and covered her face with her hands.

Brian picked up the two brandy glasses and said, "Follow me."

Steph followed him up to the bedroom. He placed the glasses on his bedside table, then placed one hand on each of his wife's shoulders and pushed her over backward onto their bed. He turned out all the lights, then stretched out beside her. "You know, I must admit that I'm so excited by this fantasy idea that my cock is almost painfully hard."

Steph propped herself up on one elbow, reached over and started to unzip Brian's jeans. He placed his hand on hers and removed it from his crotch. "Not yet." He hesitated. "This is really tricky," he said with a sigh, "but part of me wants to share a fantasy I've had for a long time. If I tell you one of mine, will you tell me one of yours?"

"Phew. This got serious in a hurry." She dropped onto her back.

"It's not serious, just intense."

"Why now, after all these years?"

"You started this, you know. And now we're playing with other people and, without realizing it, I've played out some fantasies with them. But part of me wants to play out a fantasy with you." Steph could hear his voice brighten. "Of course," he continued, "part of me is scared as hell."

"Scared I'll think you're weird?"

"Exactly."

"Scared to say it out loud? Because I'll think you're perverted?" When he remained silent, she added in a small voice, "Me too."

Brian rolled onto his side and kissed his wife softly on the lips. "Nothing you could tell me could make me think you were weird, at least any weirder than I already know you are."

"And nothing you could tell me would ever, ever make me think less of you. I promise," Steph said.

Brian took her hand and rolled onto his back in the dark. There was a long silence while each considered the new ground they were treading on. "Why don't I tell you a story," Brian said finally. "Let's see how far I get."

"Okay," Steph said.

"Once there was a young man. He was in his late twenties and he was the janitor at an all-girls high school. It was one of those schools where the girls all wear uniforms. You know the ones." Brian dropped her hand and lay not touching his wife.

"Sure," Steph said softly, trying to encourage what she knew was a difficult revelation. "Maybe the uniforms were blue-and-green plaid skirts and crisply starched white blouses."

"Yeah," Brian said. "Just like that. And this janitor, maybe his name's John, he likes to listen to the girls giggle. Most of the time they forget he's even around and they talk about their dates and boys and things like that."

Steph thought about taking Brian's hand, but didn't. She didn't want to do anything that might interrupt.

"John's particular favorite was a girl named Missy. She was all blond and blue-eyed, with a great body, only partly concealed by the dumpy clothes she was forced to wear. He would slowly sweep the floor and watch her as she talked about her dates. He'd watch her mouth and her hands and her hips and her large breasts. More and more, he became fixated on her breasts. He had to see them.''

When Brian lapsed into silence, Steph encouraged, "Go on.''

"Anyway, although he never wanted to really hurt anyone, over the months he decided that he had to see her, have her all to himself. So one afternoon he drove along the route he knew she took home every afternoon. He saw her up ahead, her cute tush swaying as she walked. He pulled his car to a stop beside her.''

Brian took a deep breath. " 'Hi, Missy,' he said to her. 'Need a lift?' 'Oh hi, John,' she said back. 'Sure, if you don't mind. I just live a few blocks from here.' So she comes around to the passenger side of the car and opens the door.''

Brian was silent for a long time. Steph took his hand in the dark. "This is really difficult for you. You don't have to tell me any more.''

"I know I don't," Brian said. "And a lot of me wants to stop, but part of me wants to tell the story. God, telling it makes me horny.''

"Want to get naked?" Steph asked.

"You know, it's funny but it's easier to do this with clothes on and in the dark.''

Steph rolled against Brian's side and pillowed her head on his shoulder. "Okay. Missy's climbing into John's car so he can drive her home. Except I don't think he's going to drive her home. Is he?''

"No. He lives in a remote part of town, in a house where they won't be disturbed. That's where he's going to go.''

"When does she catch on that they're not going to her house? What does she do?''

"Well,'' Brian said, slipping back into the story, "he's planned this all very well. He's got the car's seat belt rigged so it's really tight and doesn't release. Missy throws her books and stuff into the back and sits down in the passenger seat. John reaches over and pulls the seat belt over her, trapping her hands at her sides. He snaps it into the holder and speeds away.''

"It takes a minute before Missy realizes that she's in trouble.''

Steph slipped into the fantasy. " 'Let me go,' Missy says, squirming, unable to get loose. 'What are you doing? Where are we going?' What does John answer?''

"John is silent. He's enjoying her struggles. He likes to watch the way her breasts are separated by the seat belt and how they move as she wriggles. 'I'll scream,' Missy says. 'Don't bother,' John says. 'With the windows closed and the heater on, no one will hear you.' "

"So eventually they arrive at John's house. Missy is thinking that she'll get loose when he tries to take her into his house, but he's thought all that through very well. He gets out, comes around to her side and, before she can yell, he's tied her hands behind her and put a scarf into her mouth so she can't scream."

Steph wanted to give Brian the option of a cooperative scenario. "Maybe she's only pretending to struggle. Maybe she has enjoyed watching him watch her all along."

Steph could feel Brian thinking about her option. "Oh yes," he said, "maybe that's right. She's a little tease and enjoys making the boys sweat before she lets them have her."

"Maybe," Steph said, "but she'll never let John know that."

"He wants her to fight, but it's comforting to know it's all an act."

"You know, I always wanted someone to kidnap me," Steph whispered. "And ravish me while I fought as hard as I could, knowing that I couldn't win." It had become so much easier to share her fantasy, too. It was the sharing that made it all right.

"Really?" Brian said.

Steph took Brian's hand and pressed it against her crotch. Even through the denim of her jeans, he could feel the wet heat.

"I never suspected," Brian said.

"Will you continue the story?"

"Sure," Brian said, his voice stronger. "John carried Missy into the house, placed her on the bed, spread her legs, and tied her ankles to the bedframe. He tied her arms to the headboard, wide apart."

Steph spread her legs and arms on the bedspread. "Turn on the light," she whispered.

Brian flipped the switch and looked at his wife, spread-eagled on the soft rose bedspread.

"Like this?" she whispered.

Brian drew a ragged breath. "Just like that, except she was tied."

"Was she?" Steph said softly. "How?"

"Shit, baby," Brian said, trembling. "Are you serious?"

"Tie me down, then tell me more of the story." God, she wanted this. It had been a fantasy of hers for as long as she could remember.

Brian pulled several stockings from Steph's dresser and awkwardly tied her wrists and ankles to the head- and footboards of the bed. Then, for a long time, Brian stared down at his wife. What had started as a small, risky story had turned into something far more intoxicating. Although she was still fully dressed, Steph looked so vulnerable. "Are you okay? Is this all right with you?" he asked hoarsely.

Steph wanted even more. "Am I allowed to speak?"

Brian looked as if she had ignited him. She had asked his permission to speak. "Tell me," he said.

"I am much more than okay. I'm so turned on I could come just listening to your story. Tell me more. Show me what John did in that remote house."

Brian swallowed hard. His voice was trembling. "John had Missy tied to the bed, but she still had her uniform on. He was prepared for that, though. He had a big pair of scissors and he slowly cut off all her clothes."

"Did he do it very slowly? Did he watch her face as she slowly revealed her body? Did she tremble as his fingers touched her bare skin?"

"Oh yes," Brian said. "He mostly liked looking at the white cotton underwear she had to wear under her uniform."

"I'm not wearing anything like that," Steph said, "but there's a pair of scissors in the hall closet." When Brian continued to stare at her she nodded. "Do it," she whispered.

He hurried to the closet and returned with the scissors.

"What did he cut off first?" Steph asked.

"He started with her socks." Brian worked around the stockingties and cut Steph's socks off.

"What do you see?" Steph asked as Brian gazed at her ankles.

"Those ties around your legs are the most erotic things I've ever seen." He looked into her eyes. "Next he cut her pants."

"I've got other jeans," Steph said. "And these are old anyway."

Brian smiled and started at the cuff of her right pant leg. He cut up to her belly, then repeated the process with the other pant leg. Then he connected the openings by cutting across just above her pubis. He looked at her tiny black-lace panties, then touched the crotch. "You're soaked," he said, incredulous.

"What did John do next?" Steph asked.

Brian unbuckled Steph's belt, cut up the front of her pants and pulled them open. With less hesitation, he cut up the front of her black sweatshirt, then down the arms until she lay in the tatters of her clothing, wearing only her bra and panties.

"Does he like what he sees?"

"John likes what he sees. Missy struggles, knowing what John has in mind. As she moves against the ropes that are holding her body wide open for him, he watches her breasts and her pussy, knowing they are his for the taking."

Steph pulled against the stocking holding her limbs. She writhed, her breathing uneven, her nipples pressing against the lace of her bra. When Brian reached underneath to unhook her bra, she said, "Cut it. Cut it off of me."

Brian cut the thin strip of fabric that connected the two cups, then the straps above them. He feasted his eyes on his wife's luscious body.

"God, baby," she said, "you're making me crazy. What next?"

A slow smile lit up Brian's face. "John did things very slowly. He liked to stretch out every part." Brian reached down and rubbed the nylon-covered flesh between Steph's legs. He found her swollen clit and rubbed and stroked until her hips were bucking beneath his hand. "He also had a few surprises for Missy. He had prepared for a long time for this moment."

Brian went into the bathroom, rummaged in the closet for a moment, then found an old plastic toothbrush holder. He washed it, then brought the phallus-shaped instrument back into the bedroom. He and Steph had never played with toys, but this was his fantasy and he would know it if he went too far. From the look on Steph's face, he suspected that she was hot enough for almost anything.

He stood next to the bed, brandishing the bright red phallus. " 'I'm going to fuck you with this, Missy,' John said. 'And you can't prevent it.' John pulled her panties aside and rubbed his toy all over Missy's pussy." Brian took the scissors and cut the sides of Steph's panties and pulled the fabric free. The he rubbed the red plastic through the soaked folds of her cunt. "Then John slipped the toy inside."

Steph felt the cold plastic invade her body. She was beyond any coherent thought. "God, Brian, make me come."

Brian rubbed her clit with one hand and fucked her pussy with the plastic cock with the other. "Missy fought the orgasm," he said, "but John kept fucking her. Missy didn't want to come but John had complete control of her body." Brian bent low over Steph's bush. He knew just what his wife liked. "When he ate her, she couldn't hold it back." He slid the plastic in and out of Steph's pussy while his mouth sucked her clit.

Steph screamed, unable to control what was happening to her. She climaxed in a blaze of heat and clenching muscles. Usually her orgasms were sharp and short, but this one went on and on and Brian wasn't letting her body calm. She felt him rub and suck until finally she shrieked, tightened all her muscles, came again, then became limp.

Brian quickly untied Steph's wrists and ankles, then stripped off his clothes and stretched out beside her.

Steph's hand found his hard cock and her fingers wrapped around it. "You're so hard," she purred, "and so big. I'll bet Missy would be impressed." She squeezed. "But she couldn't use her hands if she was still tied up, could she?" She got onto her knees and, still trembling from her violent climax, clasped her hands behind her back and lowered her mouth toward Brian's cock. "All he could do would be to hold her hair, bend her head back, and force his cock into her mouth." Steph pursed her lips around Brian's cock and sucked it deep into her wet mouth. Up and down she bobbed, sliding her tongue and cheeks over his slick erection.

"Shit, baby, I'm going to come."

"Do it," Steph said.

"But. . . ."

He had never come in her mouth before but now she wanted it all. "Do it," she said, fucking his cock with her mouth. In only moments, he spurted deep into her throat. She had always been afraid it would make her gag, but, although it tasted strange, it didn't bother her at all. She swallowed some and let the rest of the thick fluid flow down her husband's penis. Then she lay her head on his stomach and wrapped her arms around his waist.

They gazed at each other silently, then burst out laughing. "That was not to be believed," Brian said.

"I'll bet people in the next county heard me scream."

"Was that really a fantasy of yours?" he asked quietly.

"Yes," Steph admitted. "I've always wanted to be ravished."

"Why?"

"I don't know. I guess I like someone else to be in control. You can put layers of psychological gobbledygook on it, but I just like it. Wow, did I like it."

"Me, too, baby. Me too."

Steph finished telling Jessica the story. "I guess that's quite an admission, friend to friend. But I do love to be play-raped. Brian and I do that often now."

Jessica was silent for a long time.

"Are you shocked?" Steph asked, suddenly afraid she'd said too much.

Jessica grinned and patted Steph's hand. "Not at all. I'm sorry for my silence. I'm just thinking about my own fantasies." She chuckled. "Rob would be mortified to hear me say this, but I would lie in bed after we'd made love, frustrated and angry. I'd wish that he would do things to me, things that at the time I thought were dirty and weird. Let me tell you that I never even masturbated while we were married, but it would have helped at those moments. But I'd fall asleep remembering a scene in a movie I saw once. I was snapping past the Playboy channel late one night. I didn't even have the courage to watch the damn thing, although I was curious. But as I snapped past, a woman had a man on a leash and was ordering him to do things to her."

"Like what?" Steph asked.

"You know, the funny thing is that I was never sure what. Now, however, I've got a few ideas." She shook her head to clear her thoughts. "Did you go to that party?"

"Believe it or not, we found a schoolgirl uniform in my size, just like the one in Brian's story. And we got a pair of coveralls for him, and a mop and bucket." She smiled dreamily at the memory. "We came home from the costume shop and, although he couldn't cut the clothes, we did the next best thing. He tied and untied me until he stripped me naked, then we fucked and fucked. . . ." Steph squirmed in her seat.

Both women took deep breaths. "I wasn't sure about going to this party before but now I'm really looking forward to it," Jessica said. "Does it have a theme?"

"That's right. I got the invitation last evening, but I forgot to open it." Steph fetched the small square envelope and ripped it open. "Story-tellers," she read, "have existed for thousands of years. In days of old they told tales of bravery, sacrifice, beauty, and devotion. More recently they tell of submarines and crime. The kind of story I like best tells of love and desire. So, for Saturday night, if you like, write an erotic story for us to share. Make it as hot as you like, as hot as I'd like. Submit it anonymously or sign it. Read it yourself, or I'll read it. I've already written one about an alien couple making love to an earth person, but of course you can pick your own subject. Have fun writing and I'll see you Saturday."

"What an interesting idea for a party," Jessica said.

"I love the idea of a story about making love with an alien. Are you going to write one?"

"I might just," Jessica said. Ideas were whirling in her head. "But I've never written anything like that. I've never even read anything like that, except for Hollywood novels."

"Come upstairs with me a minute." Steph and Jessica went to the master bedroom where Steph opened her closet and pointed to several large stacks of books and magazines. "My collection."

Jessica stared. There were copies of x-rated magazines, books of erotica, books of sexual advice, even books devoted to sexual games and fantasies. Steph pulled several out of the pile and handed them to Jessica. Then she added a few magazines to the stack. "Read."

"Wow."

"But I'm warning you that this stuff," she patted the magazines, "gets you very excited. Do you have a date with Cam tomorrow night?"

"He called last evening. He's picking me up about three tomorrow and we're driving to Connecticut."

Steph smirked. "You'll be eager to see him, I'm sure. And, when you're ready to try writing a story, Brian's laptop computer's in the den."

"Can I take it upstairs?"

"Sure. Plug it in in your room. I'll use the one downstairs."

Jessica giggled. "I'm going to do a lot of reading, then we both can write something deliciously outrageous?"

"I think we must."

It was late that night and Jessica lay in the dark on her bed. A wide shaft of moonlight colored the room in a soft blue. Steph's story had fascinated her, opening new realms for her fertile imagination, as had the books she'd read all afternoon.

So much was possible. She could do anything, be anyone. It was as if someone had opened an entire area of her mind and thousands of pictures poured out. Pandora's box was open.

She looked at her body, glowing in the moonlight. She played Steph's story through in her mind for the dozenth time. It had become as familiar as if she had lived it. She was tied to the bed, helpless, not responsible for anything but taking pleasure. In the fantasy, however, she was also Brian, having someone under her control. She closed her eyes and thought about several stories she had read. Pieces moved, separated and reformed. Pictures, images, positions. I am JessicaLynn, she thought, in control of myself and my sexual destiny. She thought about her ideal partner in this new world.

He was tall, in his mid twenties, with sandy hair and deep blue eyes. He had a gorgeous body, honed by hours of daily heavy manual labor. His muscles were well developed and, because he worked without a shirt, his skin was heavily tanned, smooth, and hairless. When he lifted heavy two-by-fours his muscles rippled and sweat trickled down his chest and disappeared in the waistband of his jeans.

He worked for her, constructing an addition to a house she was selling. His crew had left for the day, but he remained to finish a small piece of work. His name was Walt.

As Jessica lay on the bed a soft breeze wafted across her naked skin and she smiled. Yes, she thought, his name is Walt.

"Ms. Hanley," Walt called from just outside the kitchen door, "I'm done for today."

JessicaLynn was dressed in a pair of short-shorts and a tank top that left little to the imagination. She had been aware of Walt's stares but she had been waiting for just the right moment to take advantage of the situation.

"How about a cold drink?" JessicaLynn asked.

"That would be great," he said. "Thanks." He walked into the kitchen and sat down at the table as JessicaLynn put a glass of iced tea in front of him. "It's really shaping up," he said, his gaze moving from her nipples to his hands.

"Yes," JessicaLynn said. "It's coming along nicely. You do excellent work."

"Thanks," he said, finding his eyes more and more drawn to her breasts.

"You look very warm. I'm sorry the air conditioning isn't working properly yet." She walked around behind him, leaned over his shoulder and took his frosty glass from his hand. "This might help." She wiped her finger through the beads of condensation on his glass, then down Walt's spine. "Better?"

His only answer was a quick intake of air.

JessicaLynn placed the cold glass against his overheated back and, when he jumped, placed the flat of her tongue against the cold spot. "Sorry," she whispered, "I didn't realize it would be so cold."

He turned in his chair and looked up at her, the obvious question in his eyes.

"Yes," she said, "but my way." She paused, watching passion darken his eyes. "You can leave at any time. But, for as long as you stay, you will belong to me. And it will be the most fantastic time of your life."

"That's all right with me," Walt said softly.

"In which case, you will obey the following rules. You will call me Mistress and speak only when you are spoken to. Do you agree?"

"Yes."

"Yes?"

"Yes, Mistress."

"You will do as you are told without hesitation. If anything is distasteful you may say, 'Only if you wish it' and I will reconsider. Do you understand?"

"Yes, Mistress."

"And you will not be restrained in any way. At any time you may leave. If you do, however, you may not return to me for this, just to work on the house. You will do what you do willingly. Do you understand?"

"Yes, Mistress."

JessicaLynn cupped her right breast through her tank top, extending it to Walt. "Suck," she said. When he reached out to wrap his arms around her waist, she added, "No hands."

Walt leaned forward and took the fabric-covered nipple in his mouth. He sucked and licked until the material was slick with his saliva. JessicaLynn backed away. "Enough. I'm going to change now, and you will sit here." She watched his fists clench and unclench. She reached down and pressed her palm against the fly of his jeans. "And that is mine. You may not touch it without my permission and I do not give my permission. Do you understand?"

"Yes, Mistress," he said.

JessicaLynn pulled the tank top off over her head, exposing her naked body to Walt's eager gaze. "You will be able to do wonderful things that will excite both of us, but only if you behave."

"I will, Mistress."

"You know," JessicaLynn said as she headed toward the kitchen door, "I like that eager look in your eyes. I like knowing how much you want me. You'll do anything to have me, won't you?"

Walt sighed. "Oh yes, Mistress. I'll do whatever you want."

JessicaLynn smiled. "Of course you will." She walked out and upstairs. While she changed clothes, she thought about Walt, sitting in the kitchen, waiting for her hungrily.

As Jessica lay on the bed in her moonlit room, creating the scene in her mind, she slid her hands over her ribs and up to her full breasts. He's so hungry, she thought.

When JessicaLynn arrived back in the kitchen she was wearing a tight black-leather teddy with metal studs and openings and covered with chains and hooks in various places. Her breasts were uncovered, as was her pussy. Her matching high-heeled leather boots came to just below her knees and she wore narrow, buttersoft black leather straps around her wrists and a wider one around her neck. She had several matching straps in her hand. She walked to within a foot of Walt and watched his eyes.

He stared, his gaze moving slowly from her out-thrust nipples to the tangle of red hair that peeked out through the open crotch. He looked at her face, now made up with heavy eye shadow and liner and deep crimson lipstick, then lowered his gaze to the floor.

"Do you want this?" JessicaLynn asked.

"Oh yes, Mistress," he said.

She reached out and ran her hand over his smooth, rock-hard chest. "Nice," she purred. She fastened a leather collar around Walt's neck and one around each wrist. "You're not restrained in the usual sense," she said. "But these straps mark you as my possession. Strip."

Clumsily, his hands shaking, he pulled off his work boots, socks, jeans, and shorts. His cock was fully erect, rising from a thatch of sandy hair.

JessicaLynn handed him a leather jockstrap. "Put this on."

Walt stared at the tiny garment, then down at his enormous cock. "But. . . ."

JessicaLynn raised one eyebrow.

"Yes, Mistress," Walt said, pulling the garment on and stuffing his cock into it as best he could.

"Now," she said, "you like sucking my tits, don't you?"

"Oh yes, Mistress."

JessicaLynn placed two kitchen chairs about two feet apart. "I want you to kneel, one knee on each chair."

Walt scrambled to obey. With his knees widely separated, the awkward position left his jockstrap-covered cock and balls exposed.

"Clasp your hands behind your back." Walt did.

JessicaLynn moved so her erect nipple touched Walt's cheek. When he turned to take it into his mouth, she backed up. "No," she said. "Move only when you are told to." He turned back and she rubbed her nipple over his cheek, his chin. She watched as he licked his lips, but made no other movement. She heard his thick, heavy breathing, saw his thighs begin to shake with the exertion of his strained position. Finally, she brushed her nipple against his lips and he opened his mouth slightly. "That's fine," she said. "Open your mouth but don't move unless I tell you to."

He did and JessicaLynn rubbed her erect nipple over his teeth and tongue. "Such a good boy," she said. "You may lick it."

She felt his tongue lave her flesh, gently caressing. "Suck," she said, needing him, wanting him.

He was like a man first starved, then given a feast. He sucked and licked, pleasuring first one breast, then the other. The erotic sensations were so intense, JessicaLynn felt as if she could come just from the feeling of his mouth. But that wouldn't do at all.

Jessica opened her eyes and looked down at her moon-bathed body, naked and so hot. Her hands played with her nipples, pinching them and making them hard and tight. She felt the heat in her belly and slid her hand down, tangling her fingers in her red bush. She found her flesh warm and moist as she had several times in the past few days. She knew now where to touch to give herself the most pleasure. She touched those magic places.

"Enough," JessicaLynn snapped. She grabbed Walt's crotch and squeezed his cock. "You're very good at that. It pleases me."

"I'm so glad, Mistress. I like giving you pleasure."

JessicaLynn smiled. "Are your legs tired?" She ran her hand down one steel-hard thigh, straining from the difficulty of holding himself up for so long with his knees separated.

Walt hesitated, then said, "Not if it does not please you, Mistress."

JessicaLynn patted his pouch, then said, "Come inside."

Walt took a moment to stretch his aching thigh muscles, then followed JessicaLynn into the living room. His feet sank into the thick carpeting and he watched her stretch out full length on the black leather couch, one foot on the back and one foot on the floor. She snapped her fingers and pointed so he knelt at her side at the level of her knees.

She handed Walt a comb. "I like my bush looking nice," she said. "Comb it nicely."

He used the comb so the teeth just touched her skin, caressing her with the plastic.

"And I like my thighs to be very soft." She handed him a bottle of baby lotion. As she watched intently, he filled a hollow in his palm. When he took some on his fingers, she added, "It must be warmed first."

He held the lotion in his cupped hand until it was body temperature, then rubbed it into her thighs with long, powerful strokes. He rubbed the lotion into every inch of her skin, raising her legs so he could stroke the backs as well.

"Is it all to your pleasure, Mistress?" Walt asked.

JessicaLynn reached down, ran a finger through her dripping cunt, then extended it for Walt to lick. "Do I taste good?" she asked.

He sucked her finger. "Oh yes, Mistress."

"Would you like to lick my pussy now?"

"May I please?"

JessicaLynn nodded and Walt lay the flat of his tongue against her clit, pressing gently. She placed her hands on his muscular shoulders and felt the play of his muscles beneath his skin as he caressed her with his mouth. "Yes," she said, "right there. Lick it and suck it good."

Eyes glazed in the moonlight, Jessica's hand slid through her folds, rubbing her clit. She inserted one finger of her other hand into her waiting cunt, filling herself, driving herself higher. In her fantasy, she came, yet in her bedroom she wanted more, and she now knew what it was.

As spasms rippled through JessicaLynn's cunt, Walt filled it with his fingers, pumping, rubbing, spreading. He licked, sucked, rubbed, and caressed until her body was drained of every ounce of her climax. She lay, panting, while Walt watched her. "That was very good," she purred. "But there's more. You watched me come, now I get to watch your pleasure too."

Walt looked a bit startled.

"Haven't you ever touched yourself with someone watching you?"

Walt paused a moment, then said, "No, Mistress."

JessicaLynn stared at his swollen crotch. "But you're so excited, you want to come very badly, don't you."

Walt groaned. "Oh yes, Mistress."

"Well then, you'll have to do it yourself." She pointed to the leather jockstrap he wore. "Take that thing off."

She smiled as she watched his hesitancy. She loved his embarrassment. "There are no shackles on you. You know where the door is. But, if you want to stay, take that off."

While his eyes remained staring at the floor, he wriggled out of the leather garment. He stood, trembling, his engorged cock jutting from his body.

"Pull that glass table over here," JessicaLynn said, indicating a chrome and glass coffee table in the corner of the room. Walt pulled the table near the sofa. "Now kneel," JessicaLynn said. When he knelt on the soft carpeting, his cock was just above the level of the table.

JessicaLynn reached out, placed her hand on top of his cock and pressed it down against the cold glass. "Feel good?"

"Yes, and no, Mistress. I like your hand on me, but the glass is very cold."

"You take the good with the bad," JessicaLynn said. She stroked his cock, keeping it pressed against the table. She could feel him twitch, almost ready to come. She pulled her hand back. "But I said I wanted to watch you. Touch it yourself."

Hesitantly, Walt touched his cock with one hand. "Wrap your fingers around it, rub it with long strokes." She grabbed the lotion. "No wait, hold out your hand." She filled his palm with lotion. "Now do it."

JessicaLynn watched his face as he drifted deeper into his own sensation. She could see as his pleasure took precedence over his embarrassment. "Use both hands," she said.

His other hand joined and they rubbed and squeezed. "Oh," he moaned. He was lost. Spurts of thick come erupted from his cock, splashing onto the table.

"That's a good boy," JessicaLynn purred. "A very good boy."

In her room, Jessica couldn't hold back anymore. The vision of a man masturbating while she watched drove her over the edge. She gave in to the spasms that filled her body, feeling the rhythms that filled her. She sighed audibly, long and low as her body continued to climax. She touched the spot that extended the climax and trembled, panting, the picture of Walt coming filling her mind.

When she was calm again, she thought about her fantasy. She wondered whether it was best to keep this idea in her mind. No, she decided. If she had the opportunity, she would act this one out. But with whom?

Chapter 8

"I guess I've always found sex to be a bit of a letdown for me," Cam said as he and Jessica walked, hand in hand, along the water. They had driven to a small strip of beach in Fairfield, Connecticut, after a sumptuous dinner at a local seafood restaurant. They had removed their shoes and walked across sand still warm from the heat of the day, to the water's edge. Cam had rolled up his pant-legs and now walked calf-deep in salty foam, with Jessica on his left, only ankle-deep.

"A letdown?" Jessica said. Jessica had been puzzled by the fact that, although this was their third date and Cam talked about how sexy she was and how much he wanted her, he hadn't made a serious pass at her.

"I've dated lots of women, don't get me wrong, and I've been to bed with many of them. But it hasn't been, well, you know, skyrockets, the earth moving, that sort of thing. From what you've told me, you seem to have found that in the past few weeks, and I'm envious."

"I guess I thought that you men had it easy. You're always ready, willing, and able and you can do what you want in bed."

"Not so. I spend most of my time worrying about whether I'm making my partner happy."

"Haven't you ever had anyone ask for what they want? Wouldn't that make it easier for you?"

"Sure it would," Cam said, standing still and gazing out over the ocean, watching the sky darken. "But not many women are willing to do that. Or at least I haven't found any."

"Take a big risk with me," Jessica said, holding Cam's hand tightly. "Describe to me your perfect sexual evening."

"Phew," Cam said. "That's really difficult."

"I know it is, but it may just get you what you want. Is the risk of telling me worth that reward?"

Cam took a deep breath and let it out very slowly. "I don't think I can."

"Okay," Jessica said, holding Cam's hand tightly. "Let me try to help. . . ."

Interrupting, Cam started walking. "This is going too far," he said. "Let's just walk and enjoy the evening."

"Stop," Jessica said. "Stand right there." Jessica felt the tightening of Cam's hand as he stopped in his tracks. "That's better," she continued. "Now, I really want to know what you're thinking because I think there's something very wonderful here. Do you trust me?" Cam nodded. Jessica leaned over and kissed Cam on the cheek. "I'm going to say a few things and, if what I say excites you, squeeze my hand. Okay?"

"This is really silly," he said.

"Scary is more like it," Jessica said, noticing that Cam's erection was now clearly visible under the fly of his navy trousers. "Will you trust me?" Cam remained silent, so Jessica continued. "You said you would enjoy making love to someone who told you exactly what to do to give them pleasure. What if a woman was very clear and forceful about what she wanted? What if she told you how to give her pleasure?" She felt Cam's hand tremble. "What if she went further? What if she ordered you to do things?"

Releasing her hand, Cam turned his back to Jessica and stared out to sea.

Jessica stood behind him and reached around his waist. Since he wasn't much taller than she was, she moved her mouth close to his ear. She deliberately switched from 'she' to 'I.' "What if I told you to take both of my hands in yours?"

Slowly, Cam's hand covered hers, his fingers interlocking with hers. Jessica's breathing quickened. This was her fantasy, and, it seemed, his too. She was going to make the decisions. She had read so much about it but had never actually experienced anything like this. Should she go slowly? Should she jump right in? In for a penny . . . she thought.

"Cam, unzip your pants." When he hesitated, she whispered, "Do it."

"But. . . ."

"No talking," she snapped. "Do as you're told."

Jessica could feel Cam's body tremble and he moved his hands slowly to his fly. Ever so slowly, Cam pulled his zipper down. Jessica reached for his cock, which peeked through the opening in his clothes. "Touch it," she said, moving to his side so she could see his hands. "You know you want to, Cam." With a groan, he moved one hand toward his erection, then dropped his hand and again turned his back.

"It would give me great pleasure to see your fingers wrapped around your cock," Jessica said, placing her hands on his shoulders and turning him to face her. "Do it to please me."

Cam looked into her eyes and Jessica watched the battle raging within him. Then Cam's shoulders dropped and his facial muscles relaxed as he gave in to what was happening. He took his cock in his hand and held it. "Oh yes," Jessica said. "You're so beautiful and so excited. Nothing has ever felt like this before, has it?"

"No," he whispered.

Jessica took his free hand in hers. She had to ask him for confirmation one last time. "You don't have to tell me anything with words, but tell me with a squeeze of your hand. Is this what you wanted?"

Jessica felt Cam's hand squeeze hers.

"This is a fantasy of mine, Cam," Jessica said, clearly able to see how excited Cam was. "You're going to be mine for tonight. But I don't want you so hot that you're in pain. Do you know what would please me? I want to see you come. Right here, right now."

Cam looked stricken. "I can't."

"Oh yes, you can," Jessica said. "You know you're so close now that if you slid your cock into my pussy you would come immediately. Close your eyes if you need to and think about pleasing my demanding pussy." She touched Cam's hand, and the hard cock within. "Tightly," Jessica said. "Hold it and think about my pussy. Later tonight, you'll know how wet it gets, how it feels, how it tastes." She felt his free hand twitch. "Tasting me. Is that what you want? Then I'll order you to lick and suck me until my juices are flowing into your mouth."

She watched Cam's eyes close and his hand begin to stroke his cock. "Maybe I'll sit in a chair and order you to your knees in front of me. . . ." Cam's cock erupted, spraying thick fluid into the ocean water. "It's so beautiful to watch you come."

The two were silent for a few minutes as Jessica pulled a tissue from her pocket and handed it to Cam. When he had cleaned himself off, he mumbled, "I don't know what to say."

"Don't say anything. But watching you has made me so horny that I want you right now," Jessica said. "Is there a nice motel nearby?"

They drove to a small motel in town and Cam registered for them. He drove around back and used the key to open the door to room 203. It was a standard room, with a double bed, several chairs, a table and a long dresser. Jessica walked inside. "Close the door," she demanded, "then I want to see all of you. Take off your clothes."

Clumsily, Cam stripped off his slacks, shirt, and shorts.

"Now stand there while I look at you." Jessica walked around Cam's naked body, slapping his hands when he started to cover his limp penis. "Keep your hands at your sides," she said. She ran her hands over his shoulders and back, soft, with an extra layer of fat under the skin. She took a handful of his buttocks in each of her hands and dug her fingers into the soft flesh, pulling the cheeks slightly apart. She smiled as she felt him quiver. There were so many things she wanted to try, but one step at a time. She walked around and stood, facing him. Because he had climaxed only a half hour before, his cock was still soft.

"There are so many things I want you to do to pleasure me," she said. "But I need to be sure of one thing. If I do anything, or ask you to do anything that doesn't make you feel good, tell me. Say 'Please no,' and we'll stop. Promise me."

"I promise," Cam whispered.

"Unbutton my blouse." Slowly and awkwardly, Cam pushed each silver button on Jessica's gray silk blouse through its buttonhole. "Now unhook my bra." He worked at the center-front clasp until the fastening parted. "Do you want to see them? Touch them? Lick them?" God, she wanted him, but she was enjoying extending her pleasure by making both of them wait.

"Oh yes," Cam said, his eyes glazed.

"I like gentle fingers and soft lips," Jessica said as Cam parted the sides of her bra, exposing her breasts. Softly, reverently, he swirled the pads of his fingers over her skin. He traced the line between tanned skin and creamy white flesh.

Jessica cupped her right breast and held it up. "Suck."

His lips touched the tip of her nipple and shots of electricity stabbed through her body. She pulled back and dropped into a chair. She pointed to the floor and Cam knelt beside her chair. "Yes," she purred, "suck my tits."

Hungrily, Cam's mouth pleasured her breast, kissing, sucking, tasting. She wanted more, and suddenly realized she didn't have to wait until he decided what to do. She could ask for anything she wanted. "Pinch this one," she said, guiding his hand to her other breast. "Harder. Make me feel it."

"But I'll hurt you," Cam said.

"That's not your decision. You do as I ask."

"Oh yes," he sighed.

He pinched her nipple, driving heat through her. "Enough," she said, standing. "Undress me."

She stood, stepped out of her shoes and Cam quickly removed her blouse, slacks, and underwear. When she stood in the middle of the motel room, gloriously naked, she watched Cam's hungry eyes as he looked at her. "Do you like what you see?"

"Yes," he groaned. "And I like what you're doing."

"That's good," she said. "Very good." They were both learning, she realized, each trying to find the ideal place for this fantasy to go. "Is there anything particular you want to add to this?"

"Yes," he said.

"Tell me."

"I want to be able to see it all," he said. The closet doors in the vanity area were mirrored and, slipping out of his submissive role for a moment, he opened first one then another. Soon he had a three-sided, floor-to-ceiling, mirrored area in which his naked body was reflected over and over. He pulled a chair over, repositioned it a few times, then nodded. "If it pleases you," he said softly.

"Oh it does," Jessica said, as she seated herself in the chair. She could see her cunt for the first time between her widely spread legs. Watching in the three mirrors, she slid her fingers through her springy hair, then pointed to the floor between her feet. Cam sat. "Very nice," she said. "We can both watch everything." As Cam stared at Jessica's wet, swollen pussy lips, she asked, "What do you see?"

"I see that your body likes what's happening."

"It does," Jessica purred. "It wants you to touch and watch as you do it."

Cam's fingers slid up the insides of her thighs, and Jessica saw them reflected over and over in the mirrors. She slid her hips forward and pushed Cam's head against one leg to improve her view. She guided Cam's fingers to just the right spots. "Rub here, very slowly. Yes. Faster now. Oh yes." She revelled in being able to tell Cam exactly what she liked.

"I want your mouth," she said, suddenly. "Lick just where your fingers have been. Lick with the flat of your tongue. Yes. Like that. Now suck my clit into your mouth and flick your tongue over it." She was soaring. She closed her eyes, then opened them so she could see Cam's moving head reflected in the three mirrors. Would she let him bring her off this way, with his mouth? Was that what he wanted? But this wasn't for him. It was for JessicaLynn. "Put two fingers inside me," she said. "Fuck me with your hand. Hard. Now."

He did and, only a moment later, Jessica came, her fists tangled in Cam's hair. "Don't stop," she yelled. "More." As her orgasm continued she felt Cam's fingers continue their rhythmic fucking while his mouth worked its magic. She spasmed for what felt like hours, then, as her orgasm ebbed, she told Cam to stop.

He laid his head against her belly and said, "I've never felt a woman climax like that," he said. "I could feel the sensation on my hand." He looked up at her and grinned. "It was truly remarkable."

"It certainly was," Jessica said. She looked down at Cam's cock, surprised that he wasn't erect.

Cam's laughter warmed her. "I got a great deal of joy from your orgasm," he said, looking at his limp penis, "but I'm not as quick to recover as I once was and I came less than an hour ago. I'm not ready to make love so soon again."

"I've learned a lot recently and the most important thing is that we *have* been making love. For hours."

"Yes," Cam said. "We have, haven't we."

They stretched out on the bed, pulled the quilt over themselves, talked and napped. Later, they touched and stroked each other, free now to share what gave each of them pleasure. When Cam's hard cock finally slid into Jessica's waiting body, it was a completion to an evening of loving.

Hours later, as Cam's car pulled into the Carltons' driveway, Cam said, "I hope we can see each other soon again."

"Me too. How's your schedule?"

They made plans for the following week and Cam promised to consider new ways that he would like to make love. "Think about something totally outrageous," Jessica suggested. "Then, if it turns me on, we can do it. If not, we'll think of something else."

Cam smiled and kissed her. "With you, this all seems so possible."

"It's all possible," Jessica said, climbing out of the car. "Everything's possible and most things are probable between us."

All day Friday, Jessica worked on an erotic story for Gary's party. She wrote, edited, printed, but wouldn't let anyone read it. When it was as good as she thought it could get, she printed it, without her name on it. "Did you write a story?" she asked Steph Saturday morning over coffee in the plant room.

"Brian and I coauthored one about an alien and a human. We only wrote a few paragraphs at a time. I think we fucked more yesterday than we have in ages."

"At least you had someone to work out your frustrations on."

"You can borrow Brian any time, you know."

"You say that, but it feels weird."

"Eventually, you and Brian will find the right time and the right place. If and when it feels right, you'll know it's fine with me."

"I guess," Jessica said, patting her friend's hand.

"So we each have a story for tonight," Steph said. "Do I get to read yours?"

"Not a chance. I've mentally chickened out several times already, and almost threw it away twice. But I've now decided that Gary can read it at the party tonight. Probably."

Steph laughed. "Brian and I agreed that we'd allow Gary to read ours too. But, even though it's fiction, it's so personal, somehow."

"Yeah. I know what you mean. What are you wearing?" Jessica asked.

The two women discussed the party, then, when Brian returned from a tennis game, the three friends spent the day anticipating the evening to come.

"And you must be Jessica," the tall, almost emaciated-looking man said as he took her hand. "I've heard a lot about you." His eyes held Jessica's.

She inhaled deeply. "And I've heard a lot about you, too." Gary had deeply set eyes and hard, angular features. He's almost homely, Jessica thought, fleetingly, enjoying the heat that his gaze engendered.

"Hello, Gary," Steph said from behind Jessica. "We're here too. Remember us?"

Gary's laugh was rich and deep. "I do remember you," he said, dropping Jessica's hand, grabbing Steph by the waist, lifting her up, then sliding her down the length of his body. He placed a deep kiss on her open mouth, then set her down. He reached for Brian's hand and clasped it warmly.

"Jessica," a voice from the living room called, "it's so nice to see you again."

Jessica remembered Marcy from Steph's party. "It's good to see you too," she said, walking into the enormous living room, comfortably decorated in shades of soft blue, toast, and ecru and filled with comfortable chairs and sofas. Plants softened the otherwise masculine aura and a heavy tweed carpet, overlaid with small patterned area rugs, covered the floor.

"Great news, guys," Marcy said to the three newcomers. "Steven James Albright, Junior weighed in at eight pounds fourteen ounces."

"Fantastic," Steph said. "When did Nan have the baby?"

"Late this afternoon," Marcy announced. "Steve is already saying how considerate his wife was. She woke him about six this morning and the baby was born at five. Eleven hours of labor with no lost sleep and no midnight rides to the hospital."

The room filled and, when everyone had a drink in hand, Marcy said,

"To Steven James Albright, Junior." The dozen or so people touched glasses and drank. It was an interesting group. Besides Marcy and Chuck and Pete and Gloria whom she knew from Steph's party, there were three other couples, all between thirty-five and fifty. Jessica considered her previous notion of what swingers would look like. This slightly conservative group wasn't it.

The doorbell rang yet again. "Sorry we're late," a female voice said. "The baby-sitter was late."

Steph leaned over and whispered to Jessica. "Hank and Lara. You remember I told you about them." When Jessica didn't immediately connect, Steph said, "The Boggle game? My first outside activity?"

"Ah yes," Jessica said, looking at the balding man who entered the room, followed by his laughing wife. "I do remember." Steph quickly introduced Jessica to the newest arrivals.

Finally Eric arrived, looking particularly attractive in a black sport shirt and white slacks. Heat flowed through Jessica's body at the sight of the familiar grin. God, he's sexy, she thought. Eric, as if reading her mind, winked.

"Steph," Jessica said softly, "doesn't Gary have a date?"

"Sometimes he does and sometimes not," Steph explained. "Sometimes he does a threesome with another couple. And, of course, couples form, dissolve, and reform during one of these evenings. I can guarantee that I won't spend the evening with Brian, and Gary won't end up alone. It's whatever anyone wants."

Jessica gazed at Eric, who was talking with another couple, then wondered where Gary would end up. "Are there any people here who don't play?" she asked.

"Not tonight," Steph answered, looking around, "although Pete and Gloria won't swap, at least not yet. But they get really excited nonetheless, and take a bedroom and make love all night."

"Anyone who wrote stories," Gary said, "put them on the mantel within the next half hour, with or without a name. Then we'll have my dramatic reading. I've written a fantastic piece of pornography, by the way. Maybe I can even get it published."

"Modesty was never your strong suit, Gary, my love," Marcy said.

"How can you be modest when you're as terrific as I am?" Gary answered.

For the next half hour, the party was not unlike many that Jessica had attended with Rob. People talked about everything from politics to the weather. They ate crab puffs, shrimp in pastry, miniature bacon and spinach quiche, and lamb riblets. Eric made her close her eyes and fed her a roasted green chili stuffed with goat cheese. Some drank champagne, others a soft, Chilean merlot, and still others fruit and rum. A few of the guests drank soft drinks. Jessica slipped away from Eric for a moment, took her story from her purse, and put it on the mantel, with several others.

At about nine o'clock, Gary got everyone's attention. "Okay, reading time. Everyone cuddle up with someone, or some ones, and I'll turn out most of the lights."

People pulled pillows into the middle of the floor, others stretched out on sofas, or sat one atop another in chairs. Gary turned out most of the lights, leaving only a small spotlight shining on the chair in which he sat. Eric had pulled several pillows together and he and Jessica lay side by side, holding hands.

Gary cleared his throat. "Okay, I thought I'd read mine first, just to loosen things up." In a low-pitched, mellifluous voice, he began to read.

THE ALIENS

Louise lay in bed, unable to sleep. She kept thinking about the strange incident at the pool today. The couple who had come over and sat beside her as she dangled her legs in the water were two of the most attractive people that she had ever seen. They had asked her questions about herself that were so personal that she would not have answered them if asked by anyone else. But somehow, after talking with them for only a few minutes, she had felt completely comfortable with the intimacy of their questions. Although she had never met them before, she had felt their warmth, their caring, and their seemingly genuine interest in her. When they got up to leave, Louise had felt an almost overwhelming urge to go with them. Now, lying in bed, she was creating the most wonderful fantasies about them as she stroked herself beneath her nightgown.

As she slid her fingers between her legs, Louise became aware of a glow outside her bedroom window. As it grew brighter and brighter, she became frightened and jumped out of bed to see what was happening. Suddenly she was engulfed in a glowing light that rendered her powerless, unable to move. She felt hands pull her nightgown over her head and lift her into strong, muscular arms. Although she was still afraid, she also realized that the hands and arms that held her were gentle. She somehow felt certain that they would not hurt her and she felt most of the fear flow from her.

Louise opened her eyes to find herself lying on her back on a table in a brightly lit room with bare walls. Her wrists and ankles were bound to the corners of the table by a material that was both the softest she had ever felt and totally unyielding. Strangely, although she should have been uncomfortable, the table was the most restful thing she had ever been on. It molded itself perfectly to her body, firm, yet softer than down.

Suddenly Louise became aware of the couple from the pool, standing, looking down at her. They were wearing long robes of a transparent, shimmering material that seemed to flow over their bodies like a glowing liquid. It was also obvious that they wore nothing underneath.

"Where am I?" Louise asked.

"You wouldn't understand," the man replied, in a voice so warm and soothing that Louise found herself relaxing despite her fear and the strangeness of her surroundings.

"We're not going to hurt you," the woman said in a low, throaty voice. "I am called T'Mar and this is P'Lan. We're from a place that's very far away, but we have learned from long contact with the people of your planet that we're a lot like you. We have been sent here to study the ways our two races are the same and explore the ways we differ. Our particular field of study is sexuality."

"We have been observing your people's mating rituals," P'Lan said. "In many ways, it's similar to our ways of lovemaking. But we prefer small groups rather than pairs. And we have certain sexual abilities that your people don't seem to have. The experiment that we are about to do is designed to find out whether our abilities have sufficient stimulative effects to permit mating between your people and ours."

Louise realized that she was going to be the subject of a sexual experiment and she was helpless to do anything about it. But, she realized that she felt more excited than frightened.

"I'm going to touch your breast," T'Mar said. "You will feel a sensation, but it will not hurt. Just relax."

The woman slowly brought her hand toward Louise's body. Instinctively, Louise tried to move away, but she could not. The woman kept her hand open so that the palm of her hand touched Louise's nipple. Louise's body jolted against her restraints as a sensation instantly made it contract and turn hard. The sensation in her nipple was echoed by an instant feeling of wetness between her legs. As T'Mar placed her other palm on Louise's other nipple, then cupped both of her hands over Louise's breasts, Louise felt an incredible pleasure and heat spread through her. An electric tingling combined with an irresistible need overwhelmed her, and her body bucked and strained against the restraints. She could feel wetness flow between her legs.

T'Mar removed her hands from Louise's body and, as Louise relaxed, smiled down at her. "Now you know what the restraints are for," she said. "They're not to keep you from escaping. Just to prevent you from hurting yourself when we stimulate you."

Louise's head was spinning. All fear was now gone. All she wanted now was to be touched again by this wonderful creature.

Suddenly Louise realized that P'Lan had been watching her while she was being touched by T'Mar. He had seen her naked body writhe and had heard her moan with pleasure. Through his flowing robe, she could see that his erection was not unlike those of the men she had made love with in the past, although thicker and longer. She felt her face turn hot as he gazed into her eyes and smiled knowingly. His face said that he knew she ached to experience his touch. Without realizing what she was doing, Louise spread her knees slightly.

P'Lan tried to explain the wondrous sensations Louise had just experienced. "In your world, there are creatures that use electric currents for defense or for capturing prey. On our world, our bodies are able to generate electric currents also, but we use it only for sexual stimulation—as part of our mating ritual." His eyes conveyed a loving warmth as he continued. "We are going to stimulate you in various ways. If you look around, you will see that you are surrounded by machines that will record your body's reactions to our probing. The only difficult part for you is that you will not be allowed to climax until we have completed our experiment. Now, we want you to just relax."

Relax? Louise's body tensed in anticipation of what she was going to feel. She watched the woman move toward the head of the table and the man toward her legs. Suddenly she felt a warm glow and soothing vibration as the woman began to stroke her temples and forehead. Just as she began to calm, she was jolted against the restraints as the electricity from P'Lan's fingers touched her inner thighs. The calming warmth of the hands on her head only intensified the sexual intensity of the burning pleasure as the man's fingers stroked the bare backs of her knees and the entire length of her naked inner thighs, stopping only when he reached the crease. She gave herself up to the pleasure and whimpered as she felt his hand move over her mound and caress her.

T'Mar bent forward and Louise could see her breasts through the shimmering robe. She slid her hands over Louise's breasts until her robe touched Louise's face. Suddenly Louise realized that the robe was not a solid material. It was warm and flowed across and around T'Mar and over Louise's face like water. As the robe flowed over her nose and mouth, Louise could feel the woman's nipple touching her mouth. The electricity sent a burning pleasure over her lips. Instinctively, she opened her mouth and began to suck the woman's pillow-soft flesh. She felt a warm, electrically charged fluid enter her mouth and felt the hot pleasure spread down her throat just as the man's fingers began to stroke the insides of her labia and her clitoris. Desperately she sucked the woman's tit and felt the electricity of the woman's hands caressing her body. She cried out as the man inserted fingers deep into her cunt and she helplessly strained against the restraints, begging T'Mar to let her come. "Just a little longer," the woman crooned. "It will be over soon."

Finally P'Lan looked at the woman and said, "I think we have almost all the data we need. We'll just do the anal stimulation study and then we can give her relief. But you had better hold her. The restraints may not be sufficient."

As Louise began to tremble, T'Mar came alongside the table and stretched out across Louise, belly against belly, breast against breast, leg against leg, pinning her entire body to the table. Louise felt bathed by the warm liquid flow of the woman's robe over her skin, and T'Mar gently spoke into Louise's ear. "Because of the intensity of the erotic stimulation, this part will be difficult to bear but we will soon be finished."

Louise's entire body tingled where the woman pressed against her, and the woman's nipples burned as they pressed against Louise's breasts. Suddenly she felt P'Lan's finger slide between her legs and under her until it touched her anus. With no hesitation, he plunged into her ass and the burning need that filled the entire lower part of her body made her shriek and press upward frantically against the woman who was holding her down. With the man's finger still in her ass, Louise felt the woman slide her hand down between Louise's legs and plunge her fingers into Louise's cunt. For a few seconds there was no electricity, just the sensation of both her ass and her cunt being filled. Then T'Mar crooned in her ear. "Are you ready, Louise? Do you want to come?"

"Please, please," was all Louise could whimper.

The woman looked at the man and in a low, gentle voice said, "Now."

Suddenly Louise shrieked and strained as the electric current from the invading fingers melded into a flame of molten heat and she felt the sensation of her throbbing clitoris spread to every limb, every vein of her body. She felt her cunt contract against T'Mar's fingers and her sphincter contract around P'Lan's hand as wave after wave of orgasm wrenched her body. Moments later she was enveloped in a warm glowing light. And then there was darkness.

Since that day Louise searches the sky every night. She loves to masturbate under the stars, pretending that she is being made love to by aliens. Most people think she's crazy. . . .

Eric's hand had been teasing Jessica's nipple while Gary read the story and now she was squirming, anxious to wrap her legs around his waist and drive his cock into her hungry cunt.

"I do love that story," Gary said. "It makes me so hot to read it." He looked around at the assemblage of hungry bodies. "Don't leave yet. I have other stories and no one's allowed to satisfy hungers with anything except strawberries until I'm done."

Jessica had a flash of Eric rubbing a strawberry on her hot, swollen tissues, then pushing it inside and sucking it out.

Gary's laugh was a deep, rich, highly erotic sound, and, as if reading her mind, said, "And you can't do that either. At least not until I'm done."

"You, dear sir," someone said, "make the Marquis de Sade look like a wimp."

Gary laughed again and Jessica wondered how that laugh would feel rumbling against her nipples as she held him. "Good," he said. "That's exactly what I had in mind." He picked up a second set of pages. "This one was written by Steph and Brian and, at first glance, it looks like another alien story."

Jessica looked across the room and saw Steph sitting on the floor with Marcy and Chuck, then found Brian stretched out near a woman named Angela.

Gary cleared his throat. "This one is called 'Assimilation.' "

"What have you got?" I asked, looking through the observation glass at the humanoid who had been brought in from sector seven. His back was facing the glass as he sat on the bench in the middle of the sterile room. I could see that he didn't look like any of the inhabitants we'd encountered from the planets in this part of the galaxy. All I had been told was that the alien had walked into sector seven almost one solar day ago and had come to our facility willingly. The report said he seemed to be waiting ever since. Waiting for what? We had no idea. I knew that the research team had been monitoring him since his arrival here, trying to determine his level of intelligence.

"Hi Libby," said Dirk, our chief scientist. "We're not sure what he is. He appears to be a humanoid, but he hasn't responded to any language we've used. He's six feet tall, weighs about two-hundred pounds, and by his build, we're assuming most of that is muscle. His skin looks leathery and he seems to have no hair anywhere on his body." He continued reciting the notes off his clipboard as we walked around the corner to view him from another angle.

"We've been referring to him as male," Dirk continued, "but as you will notice, he has more than one phallus." From the angle at which I was observing, I couldn't make out what Dirk was referring to.

"Has anyone gone in?" I asked, looking at the alien's face from the side. It was smooth and round, giving him an almost human look, except that he had no eyebrows and his eyes were widely spaced, giving him a curious expression.

"No," said Dirk. "We were waiting for you." I was in charge of the research lab and authorized all first-contacts with aliens.

"I'm going in," I said, taking off my clothes.

"Are you crazy?" yelled Dirk. "He could snap you in half in a minute."

"You can use the force shield if I run into problems," I said, pulling off my jumpsuit.

"Do you really need to take off your clothes?" he asked as I handed him my jumpsuit. "It's a little disconcerting."

"Thanks, Dirk, but you know how this works. Tell them I'm going in." I was used to being naked in front of the research team. Throughout our space travels we had found that most civilizations did not wear any type of clothing and it had become a standard practice to take off ours when we interacted with any non-humans.

Dirk looked at me as he pressed a button on the neck of his jumpsuit and spoke into the tiny mike. "Libby is going in to observe. Be ready with the force shield in case she has problems."

I opened the door slowly and the alien turned to look at me. His eyes were peaceful and I saw no tension in his body. I let the door close behind me and entered the room. He was only a few feet away from me when I stopped.

"Hello," I said, smiling at him. "Can you understand me?"

He stood up slowly and turned to face me. My eyes immediately dropped to his groin and I stared at the unique combination of sexual organs. He did not appear to have any testicles, but instead had one penis in the front and a longer one hanging behind it.

He held his hands palm outward in front of him, extending them to me. Looking down at my hands, he nodded for me to raise them. He was only a foot away from me and I swallowed hard as I held my hands toward his.

"Be careful Libby," I heard Dirk say through the intercom.

Our fingers touched and I could suddenly hear his thoughts and feel his emotions. "I am many people, called by many names," he said with his mind. I looked in his eyes, and my thoughts told him my name was Libby.

"Where am I?" he asked telepathically. I told him our galactic location. He explained that he had found our outpost after his ship had been hit by a meteorite. He was a scientist, exploring the galaxy, studying and learning. Then, ever so slowly, his eyes lowered to my breasts and I could feel his sexual need increase.

"Are you okay Libby?" I heard Dirk ask.

"Yes," I said back. "He's communicating telepathically through his fingers."

I could hear his thoughts as he asked me if he could touch my body. I nodded yes and he dropped one of his hands and slid it down my chest until it stopped at my breast. The nipples I had noticed on his chest slowly inverted and started making a sucking sound as he moved his hand from one of my nipples to the other.

I looked down and saw the front penis had extended itself. His hand slid down my stomach and touched the hair around my pubis. When his finger slid between my legs and touched my clit, then rubbed my soaked vagina, I shuddered.

He brought his hand back up and touched his wet fingers against mine. The intensity of his sexual hunger flashed through my body as he stared into my eyes. I felt myself being pulled toward him and I took two steps nearer.

"Are you sure you're all right?" said Dirk over the speaker.

"Yes," I said, keeping my eyes on the alien.

We were standing face to face and he slowly lowered our hands to our sides, keeping our fingers touching at all times. He leaned toward me and, as my nipples touched his inverted breasts, like tiny mouths, they drew them in. I couldn't believe the sensation of the leatherlike suckers on my breasts.

Over the sound of my pounding heart I heard him tell me not to be afraid. He wanted to join with me. The magnetic pull was so strong that I was soon spreading my legs as he pushed his knobby penis inside. I let out a gasp as I felt it slide deeper, moving in and out even though he was standing completely still. Little knobs around the penis-shaft pulsated against my vaginal walls as it pushed in and out. Soon tiny lips appeared above his penis, locked onto my clitoris, and started sucking.

"Libby!" I heard Dick yell. "What's happening?"

"Oh God!" I said, trying to keep my knees from buckling. "I'm getting fantastically fucked!"

"Do you want us to stop him?" yelled Dirk.

"No!" I yelled. The sensations were magnificent and I most certainly didn't want them to stop. I felt something touch my buttocks and I suddenly realized that his secondary penis had extended itself up to my anus. He heard the panic in my mind and somehow made me relax with his thoughts. His rear penis felt wet and oily as it touched my rear opening, then slowly inserted itself into the hole. It pulsed against the thin wall in unison with the one in my vagina. I wasn't sure how much longer I could stand there. My knees were buckling.

His eyes were intense as he stared at me, but no other visible signs indicated what was going on. His breathing was normal even though I was visibly panting. I tried to move my hands away, but he gripped them and held them tightly against my buttocks, holding me still against him.

His penises were moving in and out seemingly with a life of their own and the lips around my nipples and my clitoris were increasing the pressure of their sucking. I could feel an orgasm building inside of me but I heard him tell me to wait. Then, as he pressed his forehead against mine, a jolt of pure pleasure shot through me that set off a chain reaction. I came. I tried to scream but no noise escaped my lips. I suddenly understood that, despite his physical immobility, he was sharing my orgasm as we stood frozen against each other.

The climax pulsing through my body wouldn't stop and I wondered how long it could go on. "Much longer," I felt him say. Instead of deflating, his penises became harder and pumped in and out faster than before. The sucking became more intense against my clitoris and my nipples, and I felt my legs give out. His arms held me securely as he braced my body against his. Our foreheads still touching, wave after wave of orgasm continued until I thought I could take no more.

"It's time," I heard him say in my mind.

"I don't know what you mean."

"It's time to become one," he said.

"One?"

"Follow the orgasm." His pumping became harder, faster, increasing the sensations. I could hear Dirk yelling at me, but now I couldn't respond. I was drawn further and further back into his mind with each wave of the orgasm until I saw myself standing next to him. I was somehow inside his mind. It was warm, soft, and unbelievably peaceful as I flowed within him. I watched my body go limp in his arms.

Dirk and two others came running in and pulled the body that had been me out of the room. Then Dirk ran back in, his face filled with rage, and pointed a laser gun at me.

"Wait Dirk!" I said holding up my hand. "It's me." I could hear my voice coming out of the alien's body.

"What do you mean it's you, Libby? What happened?"

"We joined, Dirk," I said. "I'm now a part of him." I now understood everything, and it was wonderful. I watched Dirk drop to the bench and stare at the alien, at me, at the one that was us.

"This is why he travels the galaxy. Every time he mates," I explained, "he incorporates the mind and spirit of the person into him, me, us. I have become part of some complex entity. In addition, when he joins, he takes a body part he needs to grow. He chose my voice because he didn't have one." I/we reached over to pat Dirk's hand and he jumped up off of the bench and bolted toward the door.

"I'm sorry Libby," Dirk said. "I have to consider this for a while."

"I understand, Dirk," I said. "I need some time to adjust as well. But don't be angry or afraid. It's the most miraculous feeling I've ever had."

Chapter 9

After Gary had read several more stories, he said, "I have one more." Jessica knew it had to be hers. "It's called 'Educating Paul' and," Gary grinned, "it doesn't seem to have anything to do with aliens." Feeling the now-familiar tightness she placed her hand on Eric's thigh as Gary began to read.

It was a bright sunny day and, since Paul's parents were away for the weekend, he was all alone in the house. Although he was a reasonably attractive seventeen-year-old boy, he was painfully shy. Girls thought that he was snobby and aloof and generally avoided him. On his rare dates, he was clumsy in his sexual approaches, and usually did not get very far. He was still a virgin.

As he usually did when his parents were away, Paul had taken advantage of the rare period of privacy by pulling out his collection of erotic pictures and masturbating. It was a treat to be able to spread out his collection of magazines and pictures without having to hide or worry about being *caught*. As he gazed at the pictures of beautiful naked women, he tried to imagine what it must feel like to be touched by one, to feel a girl's tongue against his tongue, to suck a girl's nipple and to feel his hard cock slide deep into her cunt. His cock was rock-hard as he lost himself in his fantasies.

Suddenly he heard the doorbell. Shit, he muttered to himself. He remembered his mother telling him, "I've asked the Jacksons next door to check on you while we're gone." But he had seen the Jacksons drive away about an hour ago. When the bell chimed again he decided to ignore it. Whoever it was would think no one was home and leave him alone. Then he heard the front door open and a woman's voice call, "I know you're home Paul. I saw you through the window."

Paul immediately recognized the voice. It belonged to Terry, the Jacksons' twenty-one-year-old daughter. She had been away at college all year, but she must have come home for the summer. Terry had flaming red hair, long legs, and was gorgeous. Although she was the subject of many of Paul's fantasies, Paul had never had the nerve to talk to her.

"My folks asked me to check up on you," Terry called, as Paul heard her close the front door behind her.

Quickly, Paul shoved his magazines and pictures under his pillow and started to throw on his clothing. Paul wondered what she had seen through the window.

"I'll bet you're in your room," Terry called.

Paul met her at the doorway to his room. They faced each other, Paul's clothing in disarray, his face flushed and Terry dressed in a sundress that displayed the tops of her ample breasts. Her skirt came to mid-thigh and her legs were bare.

Terry smiled at him and looked at the rumpled bed. "Well, it's a good thing I came up to check on you," she said, teasingly. "What have you been doing?"

"Nothing," Paul mumbled, not knowing what to say.

Terry brushed past him, her breasts grazing his arm, and walked over to the bed. Paul's arm felt as though 1000 volts of electricity had gone through it at the point of contact. Sunlight streamed through the window onto Paul's pillow and the corner of the magazine that protruded from beneath it.

Terry slowly reached over and pulled out first one magazine, then the others, along with pictures that Paul had hidden under the pillow. She sat down on the bed and smiled as she slowly leafed through everything. Paul stood and watched, unable to move. "I guess now I *know* what you've been doing," she said with a grin. "But looking at pictures isn't nearly as exciting as looking at the real thing. Come over here," she ordered.

Now trembling as much from excitement as embarrassment, Paul walked over to Terry and looked down at her as she sat on the edge of the bed. Her skirt had ridden up almost to her hips and the sight of her bare thighs and her nipples poking against the thin material of her sundress was making Paul's cock so hard that it was forming an obvious lump in the front of his pants.

"Come closer, Paul," Terry said, her voice low and throaty as she looked directly at the crotch of Paul's pants. She spread her knees apart. "I want you standing right between my knees."

As Paul stood between her legs, Terry calmly and efficiently undid his belt and pulled down his pants and underpants. Then she carefully began to fondle his swollen cock and balls. "What a big cock," she said, stroking the length of its shaft with her right hand while cupping and gently squeezing his balls with her left. Looking up at him she said, "I saw you looking at my tits. I'll bet you're thinking about what it would be like to suck them. Aren't you?"

Paul felt his face get red and the trembling of his body increase.

"And, I saw you looking at my legs. I'll bet you want to touch them. Have you ever put your hand between a girl's legs, Paul?"

Paul's throat was so tight he could not reply.

"Well, I think it's time you learned a few things. Such a big, beautiful erection shouldn't be wasted." Her fingers danced over his skin from his anus, across his balls to the tip of his cock. Suddenly she removed her hand. "It will be all over too quickly if I keep doing this," she said. Terry reached out and took Paul's right hand and gently pressed it against the front of her dress.

The feel of her nipple and the softness of her breast burned the palm of Paul's hand. He found himself gently squeezing her breast.

"That's very good," Terry said. She removed his hand and slipped the straps of the sundress over her shoulders, lowered the top, then put Paul's hand back on her naked breast. She guided his hands as they roamed across the softness of her bare tits.

"I want you to kneel between my legs now," Terry said. As Paul kneeled, Terry cupped her right hand under her right breast and sliding her left hand around the back of Paul's neck, pulled his face toward her tit. "It will taste so good, Paul," she crooned as Paul opened his mouth.

As Paul sucked, he felt Terry stroke the back of his neck. Her breathing quickened and he heard small sighs and felt her nipple harden in his mouth as he sucked and licked. After a little while, Terry pulled his head away and gave him the other tit. As he sucked and gently bit her nipples, Paul began to stroke Terry's legs and the inside of her thighs. He felt her spread her legs wider, inviting him to explore.

"Don't be afraid, Paul," she encouraged. "It feels wonderful there." As he sucked her tits, she gently took his right hand and slowly guided it deeper into the cleft between her legs. She wore nothing under the dress and soon Paul felt the hot, soft wetness of her mound. He heard Terry sigh as she guided his middle finger along the center of the heat and moisture. He felt the lips separate and then his finger was stroking the slippery insides of her labia.

Terry held Paul's head tightly against her breast, and demanded,

"Suck it good, baby, suck it good." She was groaning and her hips were pressing against his hand. With her hand, she guided his finger to her swollen clitoris. "Can you feel that?" she asked him.

"Yes," Paul replied breathlessly, releasing her nipple from his mouth.

"Well, I want you to lick right there. Flick your tongue across it."

Paul hesitated.

"Now do it like a good boy," she ordered, pressing Paul's head down toward her lap, and spreading her legs even wider. "That's such a good boy."

Paul inhaled Terry's wonderful musky aroma as he buried his head between her legs. She tasted delicious when he ran his tongue along the length of her crack then began to suck on the knob of her clitoris. As he licked Terry's cunt and clitoris, she whimpered with pleasure. His balls and cock were aching for Terry to touch him again and he knew that now the slightest touch would make him come. He had never been so excited.

Suddenly Terry's naked thighs clamped hard against the sides of Paul's head and her hand pressed his face hard against her cunt. She cried out as her hips began to press rhythmically against his mouth. After a short while she relaxed, then placed her hands on the side of Paul's face and guided his face away from her.

"Did I do something wrong?" he asked, puzzled, looking at Terry sitting on the edge of the bed, bare-breasted with her dress bunched up around her hips.

"Definitely not," she smiled. "You gave me a wonderful orgasm. And now it's time for your reward. Take off the rest of your clothes."

Paul stepped out of his pants and underpants, still bunched around his ankles, then pulled off his shirt while Terry pulled off her dress and, completely naked, stretched out on the bed with her legs spread. She held out her arms. "Come here, baby. It's time to fuck me."

As Paul positioned himself between her legs, Terry gave his cock one long stroke, then guided it to her pussy. For the first time, Paul felt his cock slide deep into the ripeness of a woman's cunt. Looking down at her face, he saw her smile as he slowly withdrew then again pressed his cock into her until his naked hips were grinding against hers. Suddenly he was out of control. He pounded his cock as far into her as he could, over and over, until, with a shriek, clutching her naked body, he felt himself spurt deep inside her.

Terry and Paul spent a lot of time together that summer. Sometimes Terry would be the *teacher* but, since Paul learned quickly, sometimes, he would do the *teaching* and Terry would pretend to be a virgin. Paul was sad the day Terry returned to college, but, over the years, he found many other girls he could teach and be taught by.

"And that, ladies and gentlemen," Gary said, "is the last of our wonderful stories. There are drinks and food for any who want them, and you know your way around the house."

"Good stories."

"That last one was your story, wasn't it?" Eric asked softly, his mouth close to Jessica's ear.

"How did you know?"

"I could tell by the tenseness of your hand on my thigh and generally in your body." His hot breath on her neck made her quiver. "Which person were you when you wrote it," Eric continued, "the student or the teacher?"

"Sometimes I was one, sometimes the other. I was feeling what each of them felt at the time."

"And right now, which are you? Or are you something else entirely?"

Jessica propped her chin on her palm. She was excited and curious about all the things she had yet to experience. "Actually, I'm open for almost anything. The more I read and the more I experience, the more interested I become. There were a lot of things in the stories that Gary read that I've never done."

"That's what I had hoped you'd say." Eric walked over to Gary, whispered something in his ear, then returned. "Gary has a special room downstairs. I'd like to show it to you."

"Special?"

"He and I designed it when we redid the house. It's full of toys and equipment to play with." Eric took a deep breath. "I've got another question. How do you feel about Gary?"

"He's very nice, why?"

"Look at him," Eric said, directing her gaze to the tall, angular man still draped over his chair. "Think about his hands on you, my mouth sucking you while he does enticing things to your body. Does that sound exciting?"

Jessica looked at Gary, who was talking to another couple. She watched his long hands move as he talked and thought about them on her skin. She thought about two men making love to her at once and her knees shook and her hands trembled. She felt herself swell and moisten. "Yes," she said hoarsely.

"I'd like to invite Gary to join us. Would that be all right?"

"Yes," she sighed. "Is it all right with you?"

"Gary and I go way back and we, shall we say, understand each other. I'd like to share your pleasure with him."

Jessica nodded and watched as Eric approached Gary again. As they spoke, Gary turned to look at Jessica and his gaze travelled all over Jessica's body. A smile spread over his face, then he winked. Jessica couldn't help but return his grin. She trusted Eric completely and, without having exchanged more than a few sentences with him, she found she trusted Gary as well.

Gary mouthed 'Are you sure?' and Jessica nodded. Gary winked again, then said something to Eric, who returned to her.

"Gary will be along in a little while. He has a few host duties to attend to. Let me show you the downstairs."

Shaking with excitement, Jessica followed Eric down a flight of carpeted stairs into a large entertainment room. There were both a pool table and a ping pong table, several pinball machines, two television sets, and an octagonal card table with eight chairs. In addition, there were several comfortable seating areas and a fully stocked bar. Surprisingly, the room was empty.

Answering her question before she asked it, Eric said, "Most of the guests prefer the comfort of the bedrooms upstairs. The room I told you about is used only on special occasions, or with special people."

"Oh," was all Jessica could say.

They crossed the large open room and Eric used a key to unlock a door, almost totally hidden by cleverly designed panelling. "Remember that if anything makes you uncomfortable you have to say so." Eric opened the door and flipped on the lights.

Jessica stared. Two opposing walls were upholstered in white leather and the other two walls and the ceiling were mirrored. Eric turned the dimmer switch so the recessed lights gave the room a soft glow. In the center of the room were several benches of differing heights and shapes and a few chairs. The floor was covered with a thick white carpet. Eric crossed the room and pulled a small handle in one of the leather walls. A closet door opened. "Would you like to pick something to wear?" he asked her.

Jessica looked into the closet. On one side hung stretch-lace cat suits, teddies, stockings, garterbelts, and bras in every color. On the other were leather outfits, collars, masks, hoods and, on the back of one door, whips and paddles of every description. Jessica was awed.

"You aren't into the whip stuff, are you?"

Jessica looked saddened. She momentarily thought about saying what she thought Eric wanted to hear, but then remembered her promise. "I don't think so. Are you?"

"When the moment is right I enjoy giving pain. But only when it's pleasure for my partner."

Jessica swallowed. "I don't know."

"Then the answer is no. It must be pleasure for you yourself, not pleasure because it excites me."

Jessica smiled weakly. "I know. But if something gives you. . . ."

"It won't please me unless you enjoy it. Enough said. Now, pick something fun to wear. And think about who you want to be for a few hours. Do you want to be the one in control?"

Eric turned his back and Jessica rifled through the clothes. She selected a navy-blue teddy with matching stockings. As she pulled off her clothes she thought about what she wanted for the evening. "Shouldn't this be a mutual decision?"

"It will be. I need only one thing from you and that's who do you want to be?"

As Jessica pulled the left stocking on, she said, "I don't know."

"Okay. Let's do this. Let's pretend it's one hour from now. Tell me about how you feel. Are you excited?"

Jessica pulled on the second stocking, sliding her fingers up her leg, feeling the springy nylon hugging her legs. Still having a difficult time sorting out her feelings, she said, "Oh yes."

"Are you watching me as I try to get free of my bonds, or are you tightly bound?"

Almost unable to pull on the teddy, she took a deep breath and said, "I'm bound." She adjusted her clothes, stepped into her shoes and walked up behind Eric's back. She rested her head against his shoulder and said what was in her mind. "I want to be crying for help, knowing no one will help me."

Eric turned and took her in his arms. He pressed his pelvis against her and Jessica could feel his excitement. "Can you feel what that idea does to me?"

Jessica giggled. "It's hard to miss."

"Okay. We need safe words. Rather than 'cease and desist' which I'm always afraid someone will forget, let's use 'red' and 'yellow.' Red if you want me to stop *for any reason*. I mean any reason. Yellow for 'I need a moment to catch my breath,' or 'My foot's asleep.' Is that okay?"

" 'Red' and 'yellow'. I think I can remember that. Are we really going to do this?" Jessica was incredibly excited.

Eric kissed her deeply. "Oh yes. We certainly are." He stepped back. "Mmmm. I love you in that outfit." He ruffled her hair, which fell loosely at her shoulders. "Now," he said, "we have to talk about the rest of the evening. First, do you trust me?"

"Absolutely."

"Let me tell you about Gary. He's a dominant. That means that he enjoys being in complete control of his sexual experiences. He likes to give the orders and have them obeyed without question. Do you think you could enjoy letting someone else control everything?"

Jessica thought about the story that Steph had told her about being tied to the bed and having Brian 'have his way with her.' "I think I could really get into that. I've sorted a lot out."

"Good. Tell me."

"Well," Jessica said, trying to put her feelings into words, "I've fantasized about being in complete control and it makes me a bit uncomfortable. It bothers me that I might not be giving my partner complete pleasure. I don't much like that responsibility. When I tried it, it was satisfying, but. . . ."

"And giving up complete control? Does that excite you?"

"The idea does, but I don't know about in reality."

Eric wrapped his arms around Jessica's waist and pulled her toward him. He slid his fingers into her hair, cradled her head, and pressed his lips against hers. After a long, hot kiss, he said, "I love your honesty. I would have worried if you had said anything else. Do you remember what I told you about the words 'red' and 'yellow?'"

"Yes."

"And do I have your promise that you'll speak up if anything disturbs you. Anything at all?"

"Yes." Jessica shivered. She assumed that Gary was going to join them, somehow giving orders about what they were going to do, all three of them. God, she was excited at the prospect. "And Gary's going to join us?"

Eric's smile was warm and caring. "Yes. And thanks. I've been looking forward to this ever since we first got together. I'm going to tell him that we're waiting. Would you like something to eat? Some wine, maybe?"

Jessica took a deep breath. "A glass of wine would be nice."

"I'll only be a minute."

While Eric was gone, Jessica prowled the room. There seemed to be several doors of varying sizes concealed in the leather paneling. She touched one of the three benches, and found the white leather covering to be butter-soft and supple, with lots of foam padding beneath.

Every time she looked up, it was almost impossible not to look at herself, reflected on both walls, then rereflected again and again. She ran her fingers through her hair, fluffing it out, giving it a wild, almost animal appearance. When the door behind her opened, she jumped. Eric walked back into the room, a drink in each hand. Jessica took a glass from Eric and took several swallows. She heard the door open again and turned.

"Jessica," Gary said, looking at the teddy and stockings she wore, "you look enchanting."

Jessica stared. Gary's angular, slightly mussed appearance had been radically altered. He now wore a pair of skin-tight, black leather pants that disappeared into a pair of thigh-high, black leather boots. His slender upper body was covered by a matching black leather vest, and his hands were covered with leather gauntlets. All he needed, Jessica thought, was a sword and a scarf around his head and he would be the stereotypical pirate. Ichabod Crane had been replaced by Jean LaFitte.

"Eric says that he's told you about my sexual preferences."

"He has."

"And you're willing to be mine for the rest of the evening. With or without Eric?"

Jessica looked at Eric, whose smile reassured her. "Yes," she said.

"Wonderful. Eric has told you the safe words. Now the rest of the rules. First, you will do whatever I ask without question. If what I ask, or what I do, makes you uncomfortable you will use a safe word. If I can be sure of that, I can do anything I want."

"I understand," Jessica whispered.

"I like to be addressed as 'sir' at all times."

Jessica looked at Gary's boots and said, "Yes, sir."

Gary grabbed a handful of Jessica's red hair and used it to pull her head backwards. He captured her mouth, driving his tongue into the dark, moist depth, tasting, probing, inflaming. He let her go and stood up while Jessica caught her breath.

"Eric," Gary said, "she's magnificent. We shall have a delightful evening. Now, fix her clothes."

"Yes, sir," Eric said. He went to the closet and got a pair of scissors from a drawer. He cut the cups from the teddy, just above the underwires, and then cut across the crotch both front and back, and removed the small panel of fabric. "Gloves, sir?" Eric asked.

"Yes," Gary said.

Jessica watched as Eric opened another drawer and pulled out a pair of long, fingerless gloves. He handed them to Jessica. As she pulled them on, she noticed one side of a zipper ran up the inside of each. When she had the gloves on, Eric pulled her arms behind her and somehow zipped the two gloves together. Now Jessica's arms were imprisoned, held behind her, forcing her breasts forward. She felt a moment of panic.

"Test them, Jessica," Gary said. "Try to pull your arms out. Get used to the fact that you belong to me now. Be afraid of the helpless feeling, then let it go. Release yourself to me and to all the new pleasures you will feel this evening." He walked up to her, cupped her chin and looked into her eyes. "If you can't let go of the fear, tell me and we'll stop now." He continued to gaze into her eyes. "You will feel no more fear, just intense, tightening pleasure."

Jessica felt the fear ebb. She wasn't afraid. As the panic faded, it was replaced with a flood of heat through her body. She looked into Gary's eyes and smiled. "No fear at all," she whispered.

"Oh God, Eric," Gary said, "she's perfect. Eric tells me you're not turned on by pain."

"I don't think so, but I've never thought about pain as pleasure before."

Gary took one of Jessica's nipples between his thumb and index finger and twisted, hard.

Jessica gasped.

"Good or bad?" Gary asked as he released the pressure.

Jessica looked down at the hard, deep brown point that extended from her breast. The pain had been erotic and had made her very wet.

Gary pulled off one of his gauntlets and slid one finger between her legs. He laughed when she trembled at his touch. "You're soaking, Jessica. I may try a little light pain and I think you'll enjoy it. If you don't, you know I'll stop any time."

Jessica smiled as her trust in the two men increased. She could completely let go. It was a level of freedom different from any she had experienced before.

"Eric, release her hands for a moment," Gary said, and Eric unzipped the glove-connection.

"Offer your tits to me, Jessica," Gary said.

Jessica slid her hands up the sides of the satiny fabric of the teddy until she cupped one breast in each hand. "It's JessicaLynn, sir," she said.

"JessicaLynn it is. And what a tasty morsel you are." He leaned over and drew her erect nipple into his mouth. He motioned to Eric who suckled at her other breast.

The intensity of the sensations was almost too much for JessicaLynn. "Oh my God," she whispered.

When the two men stood up, Gary said, "You spoke without my permission, JessicaLynn. I understand that this is all new to you, but independent actions are not allowed."

JessicaLynn looked at the floor. It was hard not to smile, but in her most serious voice, she said, "I'm sorry sir."

Gary took one nipple in each hand and twisted. "I'm sure you are."

The feeling that started in her nipples and stabbed through her belly wasn't pain. It was molten fire, irresistible and unquenchable.

"Eric," Gary said, "refasten her arms." Eric did. "And let's begin with the chair."

Eric reattached the gloves behind her back, then opened a panel and pressed a button. A strange-looking chair attached to a sliding platform glided into the room. "Sit down, my dear," Gary said.

The chair had wide, leather-covered arms and legs and virtually no seat. There was a ledge around the border of the seat-space and, when JessicaLynn sat on it, it supported her weight but left her cunt exposed. It was an excitingly vulnerable position. Quickly Eric attached her lower legs and her thighs just above the knee to the chair with wide elastic bands. Then, with her arms behind her still encased in the gloves she felt Eric pull a wide elastic band from behind the chair around her ribs and fasten it in the front with velcro. It encased most of her upper body, but left her breasts exposed and available.

"My god, you're a succulent piece," Gary said. "What size would you estimate, Eric?" Gary asked.

What size for what?

"The queen or the rook, I'd guess," Eric said, handing a large box to his friend.

Gary opened the case and showed the contents to JessicaLynn. "I bought this on a trip overseas a few years ago. These are handcarved phalluses. Notice that there are eight smaller ones, then two of each of three larger sizes, one each of the large and the largest, here." He pointed and JessicaLynn suddenly smiled. "You've guessed," Gary continued. "It's a chess set made up of dildos."

"Amazing," JessicaLynn said, then added, "I'm sorry for speaking, sir."

"You do show the proper respect, and I like that so I'll excuse it one last time." He lifted one of the larger phalluses and showed JessicaLynn a notch around the base. From a drawer in the base of the box, he withdrew a holder with a large ring attached then fitted the phallus into the holder. The holder created a small flange around the base of the phallus, with a ring attached. "You see? Isn't this clever? This is the rook." He held it in front of her face. "Now I want your mouth to experience what your delicious little pussy will feel in a few minutes. Open."

JessicaLynn opened her mouth and sucked the cool smooth wooden cock into her mouth. Gary moved it in a fucking motion as she sucked. As she started to close her eyes, Gary said, "You will look at me at all times. You may look me in the eye or you may watch in the ceiling."

Jessica's gaze strayed to the ceiling. She saw herself, bound, half naked, as Gary fucked her mouth with the dark dildo. She saw Eric stroking Gary's shoulder with one hand and her breast with the other.

Gary looked up. "Oh yes. That's quite a sight, isn't it." He held Jessica's head and forced her eyes to lock with his. "But, when you're being fucked by me or by Eric, I want you to look into my eyes."

JessicaLynn looked deeply into Gary's eyes and saw his excitement. Out of the corner of her eye she could also see Eric, standing, fully clothed, at Gary's side, obviously enjoying the tableau as Gary pistoned the dildo into and out of her mouth.

"Yes, that's fine," Gary said, pulling the large phallus from Jessica-Lynn's mouth. He tipped the chair back slightly on its rear legs and, to her surprise, it remained at that rakish angle, her head resting against its raised back. "Yes, this chair does some wonderful things. I had it built to my specifications." He caressed JessicaLynn's wet pussy, then slipped the large dildo into her.

She was full. She arched her back, trying to pull the smooth, cool wooden dildo farther into her body. She squeezed her vaginal muscles, hugging the penis inside of her.

"Too small," Gary said, removing the dildo from her body.

She felt bereft and yearned to be filled again as Gary removed the queen from the phallic chess set. He connected the holder, then handed it to Eric. "You do the honors," he said.

Eric slowly inserted the larger dildo into JessicaLynn's body, stretching her almost to the point of pain, but not quite. She groaned and it took a tap under her chin from Eric to remind her to look Gary in the eyes.

Gary pulled a slender strap from the elastic cincher at the small of JessicaLynn's back, ran the end through the ring on the end of the dildo-holder, then fastened it to the elastic in the front. The large wooden phallus was now imprisoned deep in her body, filling her, stretching her, but unmoving.

JessicaLynn didn't want the dildo to remain quietly in her body. She wanted it moving, fucking her. She moved her hips, trying to move the dildo, trying to satisfy the growing craving.

"No, my dear," Gary said, "that won't help. That's part of the fun of this. Like that woman in my story, you will climb higher and higher and get no satisfaction until I decide it's time." He smiled and stroked her thigh. "Oh I love to see a woman's pleasure pushed to its limits." He turned to Eric. "Strip," he said. "Then give yourself to me and don't move."

JessicaLynn watched as Eric quickly removed his clothes. His erection stuck straight out from his body like the branch of a great tree. Gary cradled Eric's cock in his hands, then ran his fingers up and down the length of it. Despite Gary's order for her to watch only his eyes, Jessica-Lynn stared at the soft look of pleasure on Eric's face, then at his huge erection. She wanted that cock for herself, to hold and stroke it. She was envious of Gary's freedom to use his hands to give pleasure.

Gary looked at her. "You want this, don't you?"

"Yes, sir."

She watched Eric's head fall back, his arms hanging limply at his sides. "I can deny you your pleasure," Gary said to her. "I can give him satisfaction this way." He caressed and petted Eric's cock. "But you've been so good, I'll let you. Suck him."

Quickly, Gary tipped the chair farther back until JessicaLynn's mouth was level with Eric's cock. "Eric, don't move your hands." Eric moved so his cock brushed JessicaLynn's lips. Gary held it and stroked her mouth, cheeks, and chin with the wet tip. "Open." JessicaLynn opened her mouth and Gary pushed Eric's cock inside.

She felt so complete. With Gary's hand on the back of her head, JessicaLynn caressed Eric's cock with her tongue. She trapped it between her tongue and the roof of her mouth and moved her head slightly so it rubbed the rough surfaces. She couldn't get enough. When she again started to close her eyes to savor the sensations, Gary tapped her cheek and she gazed into his eyes as Eric, unable to hold back any longer, erupted, groaning and ejecting semen deep into her mouth.

As Eric continued to pump his hips against JessicaLynn's mouth, Gary tapped on the end of the dildo, causing heat to ripple through her body. When he reached under the slender strap and touched her puckered anus, JessicaLynn almost came. But she knew that Gary wouldn't let her. Not yet.

When Eric's cock was finally small and soft, he withdrew. Gary filled a bowl with warm water and used a soft cloth to wash his friend's body as JessicaLynn watched. When everyone was calmed, Gary said, "I think we need the pawn, too."

JessicaLynn had no doubt what he had in mind. She was frightened for a moment as she stared into Gary's eyes. She took a deep breath, then let it out slowly. It was all right.

"Good," Gary said, knowing what she had been thinking. He opened the chess box again and pulled out one of the smallest dildos and fit it into another holder. With deliberate slowness he took out a jar of lubricant and slathered it over the dark wood. "You know where this is going, don't you, JessicaLynn?"

JessicaLynn swallowed, then said, "Yes sir."

"Have you ever had your lovely ass fucked before?"

"No sir."

Gary grinned. "Wonderful. That's an added pleasure for me." Gary unfastened the crotch-strap and wiggled the end of the dildo, still buried deep in her cunt. He said, "Eric, hold this and move it just a bit. I want her right at the edge."

Eric held the ring on the end of the dildo and rotated it slowly in JessicaLynn's pussy. "Ohhh," she moaned.

"Let's let her come when I do this." Eric nodded. "That way she'll always associate having her ass fucked with a good, hard climax." Gary rubbed the slippery dildo against her anus, then slowly pushed the tip inside.

JessicaLynn felt her body tighten. "No," she said. "Don't."

"You know the words," Eric said.

"Red or yellow," Gary said.

"Oh please don't."

Both men laughed. "She knows how to increase our pleasure, doesn't she?"

Whether it was increasing their pleasure or not, it seemed important for her to protest, although she wanted to be filled more than she could have imagined. "No more, please."

Gary pushed gently and suddenly JessicaLynn's body opened to the new invasion. She felt the dildo slide into her ass while Eric withdrew the one from her pussy, then pushed it in again. The pleasure was too much. "Yes," she screamed. "Do it, do it, do it."

Gary nodded. "Watch me as you come, JessicaLynn," he said as Eric fucked her cunt with the large wooden phallus. "Look up."

She climaxed violently, watching her body writhe in the mirror on the ceiling. Heat and light blazed through her. Eyes on the ceiling, she felt the two penises continue to fuck her. Over and over she came, her pleasure almost too much to take.

When she was finally calm, Gary put the dildos aside and kissed her deeply. "I like to come in someone's hand," he said. He unfastened the cincher and freed JessicaLynn's arms. "I want both of you to touch me."

He unfastened his leather pants and his cock sprang free. Gary moved close to the chair and JessicaLynn took his cock in one hand. Eric wrapped his hand around hers, fingers intertwined, all touching Gary's penis. "Watch our hands," Eric said to Gary.

Eric spread a gob of lubricant on their hands, then the ten fingers formed an elongated tube. Eric placed one hand in the small of Gary's back and pushed his cock into the slippery passage. As the two hands massaged Gary's cock, he grabbed each by a shoulder, bucked his hips and came, spurting thick fluid on the arm of the chair. "Yes," he growled.

Later, having showered and redressed, Gary guided Eric and Jessica-Lynn to the front door. "That was quite an experience," she said.

"I hope you enjoyed the evening, JessicaLynn," Gary said.

"I did," Jessica said. "Tremendously. And out here, I'm still Jessica."

Gary kissed her deeply. "I understand," he said. "And I'll tell Brian and Steph that Eric drove you home."

"They're still here?"

"I think so," Gary said, pointing to their Lexus in the driveway.

Jessica grinned. "I hope they are having as wonderful an evening as I did."

"I'm sure they are," Gary said.

Eric helped Jessica into the car and started toward the Carltons' house. "Are you sure that wasn't too bizarre for you?"

"If you had asked me yesterday, I would have said that it would be. But it was all terrific."

They drove up the driveway and Eric helped Jessica out of the car. "I'll call you," he said as she found her key in her purse.

"I'll look forward to that." Jessica unlocked the door and walked inside.

Chapter 10

Jessica slept until after eleven the following morning, then showered and dressed in a pair of white cotton slacks and an olivegreen camp shirt. She wandered downstairs, both eager and a bit reluctant to share her experiences with Steph.

"Good morning," Steph said as Jessica carried a cup of coffee and a toasted English muffin into the plant room. "Did you enjoy the party? I lost track of you after the stories but Gary said that Eric had driven you home."

"I had an incredible evening," Jessica said, settling into a lounge chair. "And you?"

"Let's just say it was incredibly satisfying."

"Where's Brian?" Jessica asked.

"He had a tennis date at noon so he just left."

"Oh," Jessica said, nibbling at her muffin. "This is almost as awkward as going to the party in the first place. Part of me wants to tell you everything, and hear about your evening, and part of me is. . . ."

Steph's head snapped around. "Not ashamed?"

"Absolutely not. Not ashamed at all. Just a bit embarrassed. I did things last evening that I didn't know existed a month ago. Hedonistic and more damn fun than I've ever had. Are you ashamed of anything you did?"

"Not in the least," Steph said. "But, it was unusual."

"I'd love to hear about your evening," Jessica said, "but only if you want to tell."

"Tell me about yours first."

"Well, let me begin with the fact that JessicaLynn was in her glory." Jessica spent almost half an hour telling Steph about her adventures in

Gary's special room. Except for an occasional 'You're kidding' Steph was silent.

When Jessica was done, Steph said, "Oh Lord, that sounds so terrific. I'm shaking just thinking about it."

"I'm excited just talking about it. It was the most intense orgasm I've ever had."

"What about you and Eric? Is this getting serious?"

"I hope not. I care about him a lot. I love the time we spend together, in and out of bed. I enjoy Cam too, and Gary is a wonderful lover and I'm hoping he'll call and we can continue some of the adventures we began last night. I'm not ready to even consider something exclusive and I don't think Eric is either."

"You amaze me, Jessica," Steph said. "I never would have expected this from you. You were so serious, so married."

"I always thought so too," Jessica said. "But that was the Jessie inside of me. Now that I've grown and become Jessica, I realize that there are so many wonderful things to try. Do you want to tell me about your evening? You don't have to, you know."

"I know that, silly. But I'd like to tell you. It's a bit offbeat. It seems that we both had a new experience."

"You mean that you did something last night that you've never done before? From all you've told me, I didn't think there was anything left."

"Oh, there are things I've never done and some I never want to do. But last night I got to try one of those secret things that tickles your mind but you never believe will actually happen."

"So tell all," Jessica said, refilling her coffee cup, then Steph's.

"Well," Steph began, "during the storytelling, I was sitting with Marcy and Chuck. You remember that I told you that Brian and I spent an adventurous weekend with them in the Adirondacks last winter. Well, halfway through that story about the teenaged boy, he whispered in my ear, 'What are you doing after the show?' "

"What did you have in mind, Chuck?" Steph answered.

"Marcy and I have been talking about you."

"And . . . ?"

"Later," he said, turning back to Gary.

Later. The word echoed in Steph's mind. She and Chuck had been together a few times as part of a foursome with Brian and Marcy, and she had always found him to be a talented and intuitive lover. He always seemed to know what she wanted, sometimes before she knew herself. And he had no hesitation about doing the unusual.

After Gary finished the final story, Steph, Marcy, and Chuck talked.

She noticed Eric and Jessica walk to the stairs toward the downstairs play-room. Steph felt Chuck's hand on the back of her neck, but decided to wait until he was ready to explain about the rest of the evening.

Finally, he said, "When we spent that weekend together last winter, I got some feelings about you." Steph remained silent. "My relationship with Marcy has changed since that weekend." Chuck reached over and lifted Marcy's hand from her lap. He held it so that Steph could see the heavy gold bracelet she wore. "Marcy belongs to me, now, body and soul." He fingered the tiny gold charm on the bracelet. Steph looked more closely at the tiny gold object and saw that it was a tiny pair of handcuffs. "She does what I want, when I want, and she loves it."

"May I?" Marcy asked.

"Of course," Chuck said.

"It's wonderful. At work I have two secretaries, three private phone lines, and a stack of incoming information that I have to digest each morning." Marcy was vice president of a medium-sized, international bank. "I make decisions that involve tens of millions of dollars every day. But when I get home Chuck tells me exactly what he wants me to do to please him."

Steph was surprised. Marcy had always been a no-nonsense type in her early fifties with salt-and-pepper hair cut in a short businesslike style. Ever organized and efficient, she had been the one to orchestrate their reservations and transportation for their weekend away.

Chuck picked up the story. "Remember that evening when the four of us made love on the floor in front of the fire?"

"How could I forget?" Steph said, memories of naked bodies flashing through her mind. She pictured a particularly exciting moment when she held Brian's cock in one hand and Chuck's in the other.

"At one point, I ordered Marcy to jerk me off, and she did. When we got home, we talked and discovered this mutual need, hers to serve, mine to give the orders." He ran his fingers through the wings of silver hair above his temples. "It changed everything."

"We've been together several times since," Steph said. "You never shared this before."

"I know," Chuck said, "but we had to get completely comfortable with it ourselves."

"Are you two happy?" Steph asked.

The smile that lit Marcy's face was dazzling. "I've never been hap-pier. It's the perfect life for us right now. The kids are long gone and we can play to our hearts' content in the house."

"You're the first person we've told about this," Chuck said.

"I'm honored," Steph said, getting genuine pleasure out of the fact that these two people chose to share their discovery with her. "I have the feeling that there's more to this revelation than just information."

"We want you to join us this evening," Chuck said. "Just the three of us." He paused, then said, "I told you before that I had a feeling about you." Again he ran his fingers through his hair. "I think you might enjoy following my orders for an hour or so." He grasped Steph's wrist in one hand and his wife's in the other. He tightened his grip. "I brought a few toys for us to play with, if you're willing."

Steph's heart was pounding. She looked down at the hand encircling her wrist, then at Marcy.

"I would enjoy it too," Marcy said.

With a smile, Chuck said, "I can feel your pulse and your heart is racing. The idea excites you, just as it excites Marcy and me. Play with us. Say yes."

"Yes," Steph said.

Marcy got a small paisley tote bag from the hall closet and the three of them climbed the stairs. They found a bedroom with a red ribbon beside the door, tied it around the doorknob to indicate that the room was occupied, then went in and locked themselves inside. "This is a fantasy come true," Chuck said as he set the bag on the desk in the corner. The room was masculine, with navy, red, and white bedding, a red rug, and white wallpaper with a thin navy stripe. Chuck switched the radio to a music station and stretched out on the bed. He interlaced his fingers behind his head, sighed and said, "Okay, ladies, I would like to see a bit more of you both. Take off your clothes for me, slowly and sensually."

Steph realized that her decision to wear a sleeveless black sundress that zipped up the back hadn't been a wise one. In order to unfasten it, she would have to twist her arms into an awkward, very unsensual position. Chuck read her mind as he often seemed to do. "Marcy, help Steph undress."

Marcy's red silk blouse hung open, revealing a shiny red waist cincher. She walked around behind Steph, found the tab on the zipper and stroked Steph's back as she pulled the zipper down.

Steph had never been caressed by a woman before. She liked the smooth soft feeling of Marcy's fingers. She felt Marcy slide the dress from her shoulders and guide it down over her hips. She stepped out of it and Marcy draped it over a chair.

"Turn around, Steph," Chuck said.

Steph turned to face him, knowing that her choice of undergarments had been much better than her choice of dress. She wore a black-lace demi-bra through which her dark brown nipples showed prominently. Her black-lace bikini pants matched it, as did her thigh-high lace stockings.

"I had almost forgotten how beautiful your body is. Now you, Marcy," Chuck said, not moving from his regal position on the bed.

Marcy removed her blouse, then opened the full-length zipper on her black skirt. It parted and she put both garments aside.

"It's latex," Steph said, gazing at the tight red waist cincher that raised Marcy's full breasts and squeezed her body tightly. The garment went from halfway down her breasts to just above her black bush. Long garters down the front and sides held up her red stockings.

"Yes," Chuck said, "it is. And it's very tight. Sometimes, when we go out, I make Marcy wear it. She feels it all the time and it reminds her of me. Show her the chain," he added.

Marcy reached into her pussy-hair and showed Steph a thin gold chain that attached to the cincher front and back, stretching tightly between her pussy lips. "Every time she walks," Chuck said, "a special gold loop rubs her clit. It keeps her wet for me at all times. Move your hips for me, Marcy."

Marcy swiveled her hips hula style and Steph could see her knees tremble as the loop rubbed her clitoris. "Not too much," Chuck said and Marcy became still.

"Stand face to face," Chuck said and the two women did as he said. Because they were of similar height, they stood eye to eye, breast to breast. "Closer," he said and they moved so their nipples touched, Marcy's bare, Steph's barely covered by the lace of her bra. "Oh yes," Chuck said, "I've dreamt of this."

Steph looked into Marcy's eyes, soft and kind and almost loving. "I've dreamt of this too," she heard Marcy croon. She felt Marcy reach out and touch her hair, caress her cheek, run her fingertips over her eyebrows and lips. Marcy's hand slipped behind Steph's neck, drawing her close. She pressed her soft, warm lips against her friend's.

Her lips are so much softer than a man's, Steph thought, her breath sweet, her touch ever so gentle, like a butterfly caress. She sighed, then sank into the kiss, matching lip for lip, tongue for tongue. Steph's hands held Marcy's face as their lips changed position to draw forth every nuance of sensation. Steph felt Marcy's hands slowly make their way down her upper arms to rest on the sides of her breasts. Featherlight fingers teased the lace, then slipped inside to flick the erect nipples beneath.

"Have you ever been with a woman before?" Chuck asked softly, not wanting to break the spell of the moment.

"Not until now," Steph said.

"Nor has Marcy," Chuck said. "But we've talked about it and I know that Marcy has fantasized about being with you."

That remark gave Steph a strange, warm feeling deep in her belly. She smiled, and Marcy returned her grin. The women separated.

"Marcy," Chuck continued. "Pull off Steph's panties, then get the vibrator from the case." As Marcy complied, Chuck said, "I know each of you has masturbated with a vibrator before, and I've watched Marcy make herself come. Now I want to watch you pleasure each other. Steph," he said, taking her wrist, "lie here." He positioned her on the bed, arms over her head, legs widely spread, then lay beside her, his body in the opposite direction, his head close to her pussy, his fully dressed lower body level with her head.

Steph was liquid inside, filled with heat and longing. She made small purring sounds to assure both Chuck and Marcy that she was anxious to continue.

"I can smell your juices," Chuck said, sliding one finger through her bush. He brought the finger to his lips and licked. "And I always did like the way you tasted." Steph felt the bed move as Marcy joined them. "Marcy, think about what gets you hot, then do it to Steph."

Steph heard a click, then the hum of the vibrator. Suddenly a bolt of heat speared through her as the cool plastic tip of the vibrator touched her inner lips. Like an expert, Marcy slid the humming machine around Steph's cunt, touching all the sensitive places, driving Steph closer and closer to orgasm. When Marcy rested the vibrator against Steph's clit Steph cried, "You're going to make me come!"

"Finish her with your mouth," Chuck said, taking the vibrator.

Steph felt Marcy's warm lips draw her clit into her mouth. The sucking and a finger, she didn't know whose, penetrating her slit drove her over the edge. Sharp contractions of pleasure knifed through her, making her scream as she came.

Chuck pulled his clothes off and lay on his back, motioning to Marcy who mounted him, filling herself with his cock. Chuck took Steph's hand and placed her fingers on Marcy's clit. "Hold still," he told Marcy. Then to Steph he said, "She likes to be rubbed right here," he said, holding Steph's fingers against his wife's sopping pussy. Steph rubbed, feeling Marcy's clit swell under her touch.

"It's hard to hold still," Marcy groaned.

"Another moment," Chuck said, releasing Steph's hand. "Do it," he told her. "Make her come the way she made you come."

Steph probed, inserting her fingers between Chuck's pelvis and Marcy's. She could feel Chuck's cock as it filled Marcy's body. She rubbed, watching Marcy's face, sharing her increasing excitement. She explored, reaching every part of Marcy's cunt she could. Hearing

Marcy's sharp intake of breath Steph knew she had found the spot. She rubbed and stroked until Marcy moaned and her body became rigid.

Steph was surprised that she could actually feel the tiny muscle movements of Marcy's climax.

"I love to feel you come when I'm inside you," Chuck said. "Now for me," he moaned. As Marcy rode Chuck's cock, Steph reached between Chuck's thighs and tickled his balls. As she sensed his approaching orgasm, she rubbed the band of flesh between his balls and his anus. He roared, arching his back and holding Marcy's bucking hips tightly against him.

"Jesus," Jessica said as Steph finished her story. "It must have been sensational. I'm a wreck just hearing about it."

"It was remarkable," Steph said. "I never suspected that making love with a woman would feel so different."

"I don't know how I'd feel. I don't have many hang-ups left, but that one. . . ."

"If you are exposed to the possibility sometime you'll decide then. I didn't think I could do it before last evening either."

"Will you do it again?"

"Same answer. If and when the time comes, I'll decide."

"It was quite an evening for both of us," Jessica said.

"It certainly was."

The weeks sped by. Jessica spent time with Eric and Cam, learning about them and about herself, growing and changing. One morning in August, Jessica joined Steph for one of their frequent mornings in the plant room.

"Steph," Jessica said, "I'm going back home for a few days."

"Just a few days, I hope," Steph said, her face showing her unhappiness.

"Just a few days for now, but I can't stay here forever, you know."

"Sure you can, if you want to. You can get your own place and I'm sure there are dozens of real estate agencies that would be glad to have someone with your talent."

Jessica hugged her friend. "I'm sure that's true. I could make a life here. That's part of the reason I'm going back, Steph. I don't know where I belong anymore or what I want do to or be for the rest of my life. I've seen and experienced so many things and it's all confusing the hell out of me right now."

Steph looked bemused. "I can imagine that," she said.

"Actually, I talked to my friend Viv, you know, the woman in my office. There are several people seriously interested in buying my house and she thinks that my presence might just push one to make an offer. She also thinks I might get close to my asking price."

"That would be great, babe," Steph said. "One less thing to think about."

"And Viv also said that Rob has been asking for me. He and bimbette split."

Steph looked incredulous. "You're not thinking of seeing the louse when you go back?"

"Actually, I am. I loved him for a lot of years, and I think seeing him might help me sort out my feelings for Eric and Cam and who and what I am."

"You're a big girl now, Jessica, but just be careful. You've changed a lot over the past month. You're not the same woman who loved Rob for all those years."

"I know that, but I have to do this, Steph."

Three days later, Jessica disembarked at O'Hare Airport from an early morning flight and rented a car to drive to Ottawa. The air was hot and steamy, but it smelled like home, the breeze filled with the odors of farm and fields. Despite the heat that dampened her underarms and caused a tiny trickle of sweat to run down between her breasts, Jessica rolled down the windows of her rented Ford and a grin spread across her face as she approached her home.

She wanted her house to stay perfect-looking so Jessica had made a reservation at a local motel. Since it was barely noon, however, she decided to stop at the office. Ferncrest Realty occupied a small house on a side street in Ottawa. Jessica pulled her rented car into the small lot in front of the building, got out and straightened her tailored white blouse and navy linen pants.

"Jessie," three women squealed as she walked through the front door into the cool, cozy sales area. "You look sensational," one said. "I love your hair," a second said. "Oh Jessie," Viv said, standing quietly behind her desk, "we missed you."

After the three women hugged Jessica they filled her in on the details of the past weeks. "Well," Jessica said when they finished, "things seem to have gone very well. You can't even tell I was gone."

"We knew," Kathy, a short, round, and bosomy agent said. Kathy had a knack for knowing exactly what a potential buyer was looking for. Once or twice a month she could be heard on the phone saying, "I have three houses to show you, but after the first, you won't want to see the others. I've found one that's perfect for you." Usually it was and Kathy made a good living for herself and her ailing husband.

"We missed you a lot," Marie, the second woman, said. She was tall and appeared slightly anorexic but she had a charm that made her beautiful. Viv would giggle as she relayed all calls for 'the lovely tall, skinny woman with the great smile' directly to Marie. "Are you back to stay?"

"I think I still need some time," Jessica said. "But you are doing so well without me that maybe I'll just stay gone."

"You're not serious," Viv said. Warm with her friends, but shy with strangers, Viv was Jessica's best friend in Ottawa. She had tried selling early on, but had found that her strength was in organization and paperwork. She kept everything running smoothly and each time she took a vacation, the office took weeks to recover.

Several phones rang simultaneously, and Marie and Kathy directed their attention to their customers. Jessica crossed the office and dropped into the comfortable chair beside Viv's desk. "I don't know what I'm going to do in the long run," Jessica said with a sigh. "The liberated life has been fantastic. Hot, heavy and very exciting, in all ways." Jessica spent the next half hour telling Viv some of the details of her weeks in Harrison. Viv's eyes widened at her descriptions of Cam and Eric, and widened still further as Jessica shared some of the details of her adventures.

"It must seem really boring here," Viv said, sadly. "We're so low-key we look forward to the next issue of *Cosmo*."

"How would you know anything about the sexual adventures of the average Ottawa citizen?" Jessica said. "You and that husband of yours have been monogamous forever."

"True. And I like it that way." She looked abashed. "I didn't mean that the way it sounded."

"Of course you didn't," Jessica said, sitting forward in her chair. "Anyway, let's order pizza and talk about my house."

Over slices of pizza the four women discussed the people interested in buying Jessica's house. "I hope you don't mind, but knowing you were coming in today, I arranged to meet the MacDonalds at the house at three. They're so nice that I really wanted you all to meet."

"Great," Jessica said. "Let me drive over and return this rental car, pick up my car, and I'll meet you there."

At quarter of three she drove up the driveway of the house that she and Rob had shared for nine years. It had been just this time of year when she and Rob had finally moved out of their tiny apartment, having saved enough for a down payment. As she crunched across the dry lawn she remembered how they had danced around the empty living room the day they closed, knowing that their few pieces of furniture wouldn't make a dent in the lavish space. They had made love right then, in the middle of the bare bedroom floor, she remembered. Marie pulled up with the Mac-Donalds's car right behind.

For the next hour, Jessica wandered through the rooms with their carefully chosen furnishings, showing the MacDonalds all the advantages of the house. "I love your furniture," Mrs. MacDonald said wistfully, "although it will be a long time before we can afford anything this nice." The couple was in their late twenties and Mrs. MacDonald was quite obviously pregnant. "The only thing I would change is that your husband's den would make a great nursery"

"That's the perfect place for it," Jessica said, smiling at the young woman. Jessica liked the young couple more and more as they toured the outside. She and Carol MacDonald shared a love of azaleas and they spent five minutes discussing fertilizers and acidifiers before Mike Mac-Donald dragged them back to the driveway.

As they walked, behind the young people's backs, Marie winked at Jessica and gave her the thumbs-up sign.

"Darling," Mike said, "let's think about it and we can call tomorrow."

"That will be fine," Marie said.

"And listen," Jessica said on the spur of the moment, "I was planning to sell all the furniture but I think that, if you decide to make an offer, we can come to some understanding about the contents too." She suddenly liked the thought of the charming couple eating breakfast at her table or storing their clothes in the matching dressers in the bedroom. And a baby. . . .

Carol MacDonald wrapped her arms around Jessica's neck, bumping her pregnant belly against Jessica's flat one.

"You'll really like it here," Jessica said as Carol climbed into the couple's seven-year-old Nissan. "It's a good house."

The MacDonalds left, followed immediately by Marie, leaving Jessica to wander the grounds, glad she had hired a yard service to keep things tended. As she arrived back at her car, she saw a familiar black Honda Del Sol speed up the driveway. Her heart pounded as Rob got out, stood and stared. "Jessie, my god, you look wonderful. What have you done with yourself?"

Jessica fluffed her shorter hair and straightened her back. "Hello, Rob. How have you been?" He hadn't changed a bit, she realized. He looked exactly the same as he had when she had last seen him, his sandy brown hair carefully blown dry, his short beard and moustache neatly trimmed. He was wearing his uniform: gray slacks, a light gray shirt, tiny-print paisley tie, and a navy blazer with gold buttons.

"I've been the same, but you . . . You look stupendous." He enveloped her in his arms and hugged her close. Jessica stood stiffly, not yielding to the familiar embrace. Funny, she said to herself, the things you notice. He still smells of Old Spice.

"I know," Rob said, backing away. "I've been a louse. The whole thing with Suzanne."

Suzanne. Jessica had forgotten her name. She tuned back in to Rob.

"That's all over. I guess it was some kind of midlife thing. I don't know what could have made me do something so dumb."

"I don't know either," Jessica said dryly.

"I've missed you something fierce, Jessie," he said, "and I'd like to see you now that you're back."

"First of all, I'm not back. I'm just here showing two wonderful young people the house. They remind me of us years ago, except she's pregnant." When Rob remained silent, Jessica continued, "And by the way. How did you know I would be here?"

"I've been driving past here several times a day. Viv let it slip that you'd be coming back to show the house and I wanted to see you." He hugged her again.

He smelled so comfortable that this time Jessica hugged him back automatically.

"Oh Jessie," he said. "It's so good to have you back."

"I use the name Jessica sometimes, now," Jessica said.

"Jessica? Nah. You're not the Jessica type. You're my Jessie." He looked at his watch. "Look. I've got a patient at five, but he's the last for the day. Meet me at The Grotto for dinner." When Jessica hesitated, he smiled his most charming smile. "Please? We've got a lot of catching up to do."

The Grotto. Their place. She hadn't been there since about a week before the infamous bimbette-in-the-dental-chair incident. "Okay, just for dinner."

Rob leaned forward and pressed a quick kiss on Jessica's lips. Without thinking she kissed him back. "I'll see you about six," he said, sprinting toward his car.

Puzzled by her reaction to her ex-husband, Jessica drove to the motel, registered and found her room. As she hung up the few clothes she had brought she wondered. Have I been wrong about him all this time? Have I been wrong about myself? She pictured Eric and the erotic room, then Cam and his deliciously subservient attitude. Was this all her own midlife crisis? Was it something she had had to prove to herself? Something that wasn't real?

She showered, dressed in a conservative white summer dress and paisley shawl and met Rob at the Grotto. Hector, the owner of the family-style Spanish/Italian restaurant, greeted them like long-lost relatives and indicated a quiet table in the back. "I'll get you a bottle of Rioja on the house. I'm so happy to see you Dr. Hanley, Mrs. Hanley. It's so good to see you two together again." He hustled away.

"Together again?" Jessica whispered to Rob.

"I called when I got back to the office and reserved our special table. I guess he just assumed."

"A powerful assumption," Jessica muttered as Rob possessively took her elbow as they made their way between the tightly packed tables.

They sat and, when Hector returned, Rob ordered for both of them without looking at the menu. "We'll both have the gazpacho, we'll share an order of the roasted peppers with anchovies and, for the main course, we'll have linguini with your lemon and dill pesto."

"Hector," Jessica said, "didn't you used to make a garbanzo bean salad with an herb dressing?"

"Of course, Mrs. Hanley. Shall I bring you some?"

"Please," Jessica said. She hadn't had that salad for many years.

"Jessie, you know that gives me gas."

"Then don't have any," Jessica said, glaring. "I'd like some."

"Well, oh yes. Of course. Then you should have some," Rob said and Hector disappeared. "Now," he continued, leaning across the table and taking Jessica's hands in his. "Tell me about your little vacation in New York."

Jessica pulled her hands back, then told Rob a severely expurgated version of her last few weeks.

Looking surprised, Rob said, "You seem to have enjoyed yourself with Steph and Brian. It's good for you to get some of that, you know, carrying on, out of your system. One needs that sort of thing. It should help you to understand my Suzanne silliness."

"Silliness?" She swallowed the rest of her comments as Hector brought the wine and the gazpacho.

"Tell me about the shows you saw," Rob said as they ate their soup.

She told him about *Phantom* and he smiled enviously. "I wish I had been there," he said wistfully. "Maybe next time."

Jessica almost choked on her soup. Next time? "How's your practice going?" she asked, changing the subject yet again.

"Oh it's about the same." He brightened. "Actually I've gotten at least a dozen new patients. . . ."

Jessica sat back and looked more closely at Rob as he chattered on. He was wearing a different shirt. The one earlier had been pale gray while this one was pale blue, carefully ironed, with a different small-patterned tie that was so like all his others. She tuned out his conversation and just looked at him. It was as though there were two images, superimposed. One was the Rob of high school, young, charming, and a bit daring, with dreams of their life together. He was arrogant but enthusiastic. Then, as Jessica forced that image aside, there was an older Rob. Still sure of himself and arrogant, but with a hard edge that robbed his face of any of its previous boyish charm.

She brought herself back to the present when Hector arrived with their peppers. "These aren't totally skin-free," Rob said, covering his annoyance with a smile. "Your kitchen staff is slipping."

"I'm so sorry doctor," Hector said. "I'll replace them immediately for you."

"Don't bother, Hector," Jessica said. "They're just fine. If there's a bit of peel on one, I'll take it."

"Jessie," Rob said, "I'm paying good money for this and it should be perfect."

Jessica patted his hand, a placating gesture that was surprisingly familiar. "It's fine Rob."

Hector placed the plate of garbanzo salad beside Jessica's water glass. "I'm sure you'll enjoy this too, Mrs. Hanley."

Rob looked dubious, but said nothing.

During the rest of the meal, they talked about trivialities. Rob handed his credit card to Hector and signed the receipt. As they were leaving, Rob again took Jessica's arm. "I'm so glad you've missed me as much as I've missed you."

"Did I say that?" she asked.

"You don't have to say it. I know you've been lonely. I can see it in your eyes. And I understand why you went to New York. You thought it was all over between us."

"Is that why?" Jessica found she was gritting her teeth.

"Of course, Jessie. What we had was good and," he draped his arm across her shoulders, "we could have it again."

Jessica thought about how she had once longed to hear those words. She almost laughed. He was such an ass. How long had he been like this? Was this the Rob she had been married to?

"I know you've been as hungry for me as I've been for you." He hugged her to his side and smothered her breast with the hand that had been loosely on her shoulder until a moment ago. He kneaded her flesh, then grasped her hand and pressed it against the crotch of his slacks. "See what you do to me? Let's go back to the office and I'll remind you of how good it used to be."

What an idiot, she thought. I can't believe him. She was so astonished that she didn't move for a moment, during which he continued to knead her breast with one hand and use her hand to stroke his erection with the other. "Remember?" he whispered in her ear.

She remembered. She remembered all the evenings he had insisted she have a shot of bourbon to get her relaxed enough for his lovemaking. She remembered him sucking on her nipples, then spitting on his palm to make his cock wet enough to penetrate her not-yet-excited body. She remembered his lectures about how she should read a few books about how to be better in bed. She remembered it all.

Slowly, a smile crept across her face and she nodded imperceptibly. Then she squeezed his cock. "I remember," she said. "Let's go back to your office. That's a wonderful idea." She walked to her car. "I'll follow you there."

On the short ride to Rob's dental office Jessica turned the radio up loud and sang along to several old Beatles songs. As she pulled into the parking space next to Rob's car, she smothered the urge to laugh. She had all her plans made.

Holding hands, they went up to the second floor in the elevator and Rob used his key to open the glass door to the plush outer office. His face was flushed, his breathing rapid as he flicked on the lights. He quickly loosened his tie and unbuttoned his shirt.

"Let's go in the back," Jessica said, noticing that he never had changed the fabric on the chairs in the waiting room. They seemed even shabbier to her now. She glanced at the glass door to the hallway, then at Rob. "It's too public here."

"Of course, Jessie. Whatever you want. Oh babe, you turn me on."

They walked back toward the operatory where she had stumbled upon him humping bimbette all those months ago. "You know, Rob," she said, "I've changed a lot since we were together."

Rob was panting, pulling his shirttails out of his slacks. "I'm sure you have."

"I like to take charge of lovemaking now."

Rob flipped on the light in the operatory, threw his shirt on the counter, and turned to Jessica. "You do?"

She realized that she had accidentally alluded to her other lovers, but he didn't pick up on the slip. If he wanted, he could believe for another minute or two that she was pining for him. "I like to do all kinds of wonderful things." She reached underneath the waistband of his slacks and grabbed his cock. "I've learned all kinds of new ways to have fun." She squeezed and Rob groaned. "Let me show you." As Rob stood in the middle of the room, stupefied, Jessica unzipped his pants and pulled them off, along with his shorts, shoes, and socks. Kneeling, she took his cock in her mouth and sucked, looked up through her eyelashes at his wide eyes.

"Oh, Jessie. Oh God, Jessie." His fists clenched and unclenched at his sides.

"It's Jessica," she said, pulling off his shirt. "How about playing with me?" She pushed him, now totally naked, into the dental chair. "You just watch." She turned her back and slowly unzipped the back of her dress. "It unzips just like this, all the way down." Her voice was low and throaty. She turned and lowered the front of the dress until it fell at her feet. Her gaze never left his eyes as he stared at her breasts, half exposed in her white lace and satin bra. She pinched her nipples, making them hard and pointed.

"Jessie," Rob moaned, "you're making me crazy."

She lowered first one shoulder strap, then the other, lifting her breasts out of their cups, then, finally, unfastening the clasp and dropping the tiny garment on the floor.

"Do you want to touch? You always did love my tits." She walked over to the side of the chair. When he reached out to grab her tits, she held his hands. "No, no. My way, Rob." She took his hands and pressed the palms against her erect nipples and watched his head fall back against the headrest of the chair.

"You've got the greatest tits. And you feel so good," he groaned.

"Do you want a taste?" She placed his hands in his lap and moved closer to the side of the chair.

"You know I do. I want to suck you as much as you want me to," Rob said.

"You have no idea," Jessica said, rubbing one erect nipple across his cheek. When he reached for her, she said, "I said my way. You're very grabby. Maybe we should do something about that." She opened a drawer in one of the rolling cabinets and pulled out a roll of adhesive tape. She placed Rob's right forearm on the arm of the dental chair and taped it down tightly.

"This isn't like you, Jessie."

"I know, but it's like Jessica. And it makes you excited, doesn't it?" His cock was enormous, bobbing in his lap as he moved.

"Oh yes," he said.

She taped his other wrist, then wrapped tape around the chair, then around his thighs and ankles. "That's much better." Jessica massaged her breasts while Rob watched, pulling at the nipples until they stood out from her white flesh, firm and tight. Then she slid her hands under the front of her lacy panties and buried her fingers in her wet pussy. She was hot, but not for the reasons Rob was thinking. She loved this. He was hers. He was all hers. And she could do what she now realized was what she had wanted ever since getting off the plane that morning.

She rubbed her pussy until she could hold back no longer. Watching Rob's eyes on her hands and seeing his cock twitch, she came, shuddering, standing in the middle of his operatory. "Good," she purred. "Very good."

"I don't believe this." He struggled, but couldn't move. His cock stood up in his lap, a tribute to Jessica's power.

"I've changed a lot in the past few months," Jessica said, slowly putting her clothes back on. "And this evening has been a revelation." She zipped her dress, slipped back into her shoes and picked up her handbag. "You, my darling ex-husband, are a jerk. You're worse than that, because you had me convinced that I was the one who was sexually incomplete. You had me convinced I was frigid. Remember all those 'discussions' we had? Remember how you threw that word at me? *Frigid*." She stared at his lap. "Your cock doesn't think so." She went into the receptionist's area and returned with several sheets of paper from the copy machine. "I was hoping that your receptionist still smoked so she'd have these." She brandished a pack of matches.

Rob struggled to get his hands free of the tape that held them against the arms of the dental chair but neither his arms nor his legs would move.

"I was going to leave you here until morning, but you might get sick or something and I wouldn't want anything to happen to you, Robby baby." She twisted the paper tightly into a torch, then struck a match and lit it.

"What are you going to do, Jessie?" Rob asked.

"You never will understand that it's Jessica. JessicaLynn. And by the way, are you still doing the dental work for that fireman's organization?" When he didn't answer, she nodded. "I thought so. Try explaining this." She waved the smoking torch under the smoke detector. As the alarm started, she said, "It should be only a few seconds until the sprinklers go off and then about two minutes later the fire department will arrive." She grinned. "Bye-bye, Robby, baby."

As she crossed the reception area, water started to gush from the sprinklers. She shook her head like a wet puppy and laughed as she walked down the single flight of stairs. She sat in the car for a few minutes, and watched as two fire engines pulled up. Still laughing, she drove back to her motel and booked a flight back to New York for the following day.

At nine-thirty the next morning, on her way to the airport, Jessica stopped by her office. "The MacDonalds made an offer," Marie told her as she walked through the door. "Only five thousand below your asking price, but I don't know how much higher they can go. I think they're pushing their ability to get a mortgage now, with the new baby and all."

"You know," Jessica said, thinking about Eric's reaction to the house he had built, "I've made a nice profit on that house and I like that couple so much. Take their offer and offer them most of the contents for another five thousand."

"Five thousand? You're nuts. You spent twenty times that on the furniture."

"I know. But they liked it and I want them to have it. I just want the right of first refusal if they sell any of the contents."

Marie shook her head. "If you're sure, Jessie."

"I am."

"Jessie," Viv called. "Telephone."

"I didn't even hear it ring." When she went to pick up the extension on Marie's desk, Viv said, "Pick it up in your office, why don't you."

With a quizzical look at her friend, Jessica walked into her office and lifted the receiver. "Jessica Hanley."

"Jessie," a gravelly male voice said, "it's Steve. Steve Polk."

"Steve, how are you?" She pictured the tall, bespectacled man in his early forties with whom she'd had dinner several times the previous spring.

"I'm fine. I've missed our dinners together. How has New York been for you? Replenishing?"

"Very. A good way to put it. How did you know I'd be here this morning? I'm leaving at noon."

"I asked Viv to call me. I really have missed you. It's too bad you're leaving. I was going to invite you to lunch today."

He sounded so disappointed that Jessica smiled. "Listen. I was going to rent a car and drop it at O'Hare but, if you can get away, how about driving me to the airport. We can talk on the way." A successful local contractor, he might be able to take some time off.

"Great. I'll pick you up in fifteen minutes."

"Meet me in front of the municipal lot next to Hertz at . . ." She looked at her watch. "Make it ten o'clock."

She hung up and walked back to Viv's desk. She leaned over and placed both palms on her friend's blotter. "Have you and Steve been conspiring?"

Viv grinned. "Maybe just a little. I wanted you to remember that Ottawa does have a thing or two to recommend it."

Jessica leaned over and kissed Viv's cheek. "Thanks babe. You're right. I need to figure out a balance to all this."

"Oh, and by the way. Did you have anything to do with the craziness at Rob's office last evening? The fire department responded. Then they had the cops and lord knows who else."

Jessica winked. "Did he get into trouble?"

"Nah. The fire chief wasn't happy about the false alarm, but he want upstairs, and then, I understand, he came back down laughing."

Viv came around her desk and the two women hugged. Then Jessica bade farewell to Marie and told both women to say goodbye to Kathy, who was out showing houses to a young man who had just been hired by a large local computing firm.

Jessica drove to the municipal lot and put her car in a special section for long-term parking. When she exited the lot, Steve was waiting for her. They embraced, then he took the suitcase from her. "I missed you more than I thought I would."

They had been friends for about six months and things had never gone any further. Suddenly, her arms around Steve's muscular body, Jessica began to wonder what he would be like in bed. Down girl, she told herself.

On the way to the airport, they talked and Jessica remembered why she had liked him so much. He was comfortable, never pushing her, seemingly content to wait until she felt ready to move things to a more personal level.

"How long will you be gone this time?" Steve asked.

"I don't really know. I'm going to coast for the rest of the summer, then make some decisions around Labor Day."

He concentrated on the view out the front window of his car. "I'm worried that you won't come back."

"You're the second person who's said that to me."

"We're not New York here," he said, speeding East on 180, "but I just want to be sure you remember that there are things here for you, too." He placed a hand on her knee. "All kinds of things when you're ready for them."

Jessica felt her heat rise. There was certainly no doubt that he was propositioning her. How long had he been suggesting this? She had no idea, since she wouldn't have been aware of his offer two months previously. She patted his hand. "I understand, Steve. I really do."

An hour later, as she took her suitcase from Steve in the parking lot, she said, "I'll stay in touch. And keep the fires warm for me for a while, will you?"

Steve leaned over and kissed her gently. "For you, certainly."

She walked toward the terminal with a happy spring in her step.

"How was your trip back home?" Eric asked the following evening. He and Jessica were sitting on the flagstone deck sipping Timmy's extra-spicy Bloody Marys.

Jessica started to laugh. Over the next half hour, she told Eric the story of her encounter with Rob. "You're a pisser, woman," Eric said. "I admire your style."

"Thanks. You know what the last straw was? He kept calling me Jessie. He refused to understand that I'm a different person now, and that it went much further than a name. But the name was a symbol of everything, somehow."

"Well, Jessica, you're too much."

"Thanks, Eric," Jessica said. "But, despite Rob, I am seriously thinking about moving back to Illinois after Labor Day."

Eric was silent for a few moments, then he said, "I'd like you to stay here."

"Part of me would like that too. But this is an interlude, a piece of another world. I feel like I belong in Ottawa. Anyway, I can't sponge off of Steph and Brian forever."

"You could move in here." Surprised that the words had slipped out of his mouth, Eric suddenly realized that he meant it. The thought that this wonderful woman would disappear from his life made him miserable. "No commitment. No exclusivity, unless that's what you want." He moved on quickly. "You could have the same sort of setup here you had at the Carltons'."

Jessica grinned and squeezed Eric's hand. "Thanks for the offer, Eric, but the more I think about it, the more I realized that Ottawa feels like where I belong. This is an island, a refuge, but not a life, at least not for me."

"Don't go back to being Jessie."

Jessica leaned forward and kissed Eric warmly. "I'm not going back to being Jessie. I'm taking Jessica back with me."

"Shit, Jessica." Eric looked deeply unhappy. "What about us? I love you, Jessica. Very much."

"Whoa, Eric. I thought this was a non-exclusive, just-for-kicks thing between us. I love you in a very special way, but not the way I think you mean. The airplane is a terrific invention. I hope you'll visit me and I'll be here once or twice before the first of the year." Jessica winked. "Gary invited me to his party the first Saturday in October. I wouldn't miss that for anything."

Eric leaned forward and grasped Jessica's hand. "You're not getting my message. I love you."

Jessica pulled back, raised an eyebrow querulously, and smiled.

After a moment, Eric's shoulders relaxed and he smiled. "Okay, Jessica." He chuckled. "You're right. I guess I got a bit carried away but the thought of your leaving makes me sad."

"It makes me sad too, Eric. But I have a real life to lead and this just isn't it. Still, I also want you to be part of whatever comes after. Visit me. I'm just a quick plane flight away."

"And we have the rest of the summer."

Jessica's conversation with Cam was similar, and they also agreed to spend time together both in Harrison and in Ottawa.

"Jessica," Steph said one morning the following week. "I need to explain something to you and it's important that you understand."

"Okay. Shoot."

"I am going to be away next Friday night."

"And . . . ?"

"With a man you've never met."

"Oh."

"This is really weird, but I wanted you to understand something."

"Hey, Steph, it's okay. If you want to spend a weekend with some guy who lights all your bulbs, go ahead. This is Jessica, not the Jessie who arrived here a few weeks ago." Sometimes the changes that had occurred in such a short time amazed her.

"It's not just that." Steph shifted in her seat and stared at her hands.

"I'm totally puzzled." Jessica put her hand on her friend's shoulder. "We've shared fantasies, told our innermost secrets. What is making you uncomfortable?"

"Brian."

"I'm still confused."

Steph sat up straight and looked Jessica in the eye. "If you and he want to fool around while I'm away, I want you to know it's really okay with me." She let out a deep breath. "This is silly, you know." She took Jessica's hand. "I know that you turn Brian on. I also know that you are attracted to him but that you wouldn't do anything, even knowing our odd lifestyle. I want you to understand, deep down, that it is really all right with me. The thought of you two together, knowing you both as I do, is very delicious. I think you'd have a great time."

"You're right. This is weird. My best friend is giving me permission to go to bed with her husband."

Steph laughed. "Only in America."

"Have you discussed this with Brian?"

"I wanted to tell you first. If the situation arises, say yes or say no. But do it because it's what you and Brian want. Not for any reason that has anything to do with me. That's all I'm trying to say."

"And you know what I'm going to say? Let's go buy some new lingerie, for your weekend and for my whatever."

Later that afternoon, the two women arrived back at the Carlton house with their purchases. They carried their shopping bags up to Jessica's room and dumped the contents of the bags on the bed. "I love that little green thing you bought," Steph said, stretching out on the bed.

Jessica rummaged through the boxes, then held up a deep green lace bodysuit with a triangular cutout just above the breasts. "I got matching thigh-high stockings too, you know. And I have just the shoes."

"Try it all on," Steph said. "Let's see how it all goes together."

Jessica pulled the shoes out of her closet then, boxes in hand, went into the bathroom. She changed into the outfit, pulled on the stockings and slipped into a pair of four-inch-heeled black opera pumps. Then she looked at herself in the mirror over the sink. She grabbed a comb and teased her titian hair into a wild tangle around her face, then added dark green eye shadow, liner, and heavy black mascara. She applied a thick coat of deep coral lipstick, then opened the bathroom door.

"Holy shit," Steph said. "Brian would love you in that."

"You're serious, aren't you."

"I love Brian with all my heart and I love knowing he's having fun. That's all there is to it."

"You have no doubts about him."

"I set him free and he always comes back. He's his own person and I'm mine."

"Thanks, Steph," Jessica said, hugging her friend.

When Brian arrived home from work Friday evening, Jessica had prepared dinner. "I haven't cooked in so long that I wasn't sure I still could. I thought this would be nice." She had grilled a thick steak, made hash-brown potatoes, biscuits, and apple, celery and walnut salad and, while they ate, the two friends talked. As they pigged out on rum raisin ice cream, Brain asked about her plans.

"I'm leaving the day after Labor Day."

"I'll miss you like crazy, JJ. I've really enjoyed having you here."

"Me too," Jessica said, licking her spoon.

Brian took her hand. "You know Steph's away."

"Yes."

Brian kissed her fingers. "I want you."

"I know you do, Brian," Jessica said, gently disentangling her fingers from his. "And in some ways I want you too. But you're my friend. I'm very afraid that if we do end up in bed together part of our friendship will never be the same."

Brian looked crestfallen.

"And I understand what Steph said, and I know about your adventures at the party and all, but it just doesn't feel right to me. Not right, as in right and wrong, but right as in comfortable."

Brian sighed. "I'm disappointed."

"I'm sorry you are and in a way I am too." She picked up the ice cream bowls and put them into the dishwasher. "Let's go to the video store, rent a couple of old westerns, and make a bowl of popcorn."

As the credits rolled on the second John Wayne film, Brian looked at Jessica. "This has been a wonderful evening, JJ."

"For me too," Jessica said with a sigh.

"Steph never did get into old westerns."

"If your next remark is going to be 'My wife just doesn't understand me,' it won't float."

Brian's amusement was obvious. "You know, I must confess something. Part of me still wants to make long, leisurely love to you, but part of me has been making passes at you for so long it sort of got to be a habit."

"Well, don't break that habit," Jessica said, kissing him firmly on the lips. "One of these days I may just change my mind." They went to bed that night in their own rooms.

Jessica's remaining time in New York raced by. She spent evenings with Eric and Cam, and had a fantastic overnight with Gary in the special room. She especially enjoyed Steph and Brian's company, doing everything from crossing New York Harbor on the Staten Island Ferry to nude swimming in the Carltons' pool.

On the day after Labor Day, Steph and Brian drove Jessica to Newark Airport. The three friends hugged and finalized plans for Jessica to fly out for Gary's party in October. As her row number was called to board, Jessica kissed Steph. "We'll see you October sixth, right here. I'll miss you till then."

"Me too," Jessica said, turning to hug Brian.

"Maybe that weekend, JJ," Brian whispered, then nipped her earlobe.

"Maybe," Jessica said, grabbing her suitcase and almost running to the gate. She walked the length of the runway, boarded the 707, found her seat and stowed her small suitcase, glad she had packed several boxes and mailed them to herself at her office so she wouldn't have to check baggage. She was sad to leave Steph and Brian, but exhilarated to be returning to Ottawa.

She had called Viv and in response to Jessica's request, Viv had lined up several condos for her to visit, any one of which, according to Viv, would be perfect for her in her new life. She had appointments to see three of them the following morning. And she had a date with Steve over the weekend.

She realized she'd miss Eric and Cam. It wouldn't be as easy to see them and she had no real idea where she would find an outlet for her creative sexual energy, but if she had to, she'd suppress her libido until her next trip to New York. She snapped her seat belt, opened the new suspense novel she had bought the preceding day, and began to read.

"Terrible book," a deep voice said.

"Excuse me?"

"That's a terrible book. I read the first fifty pages and realized that if the hero just called the newspapers and told a bunch of reporters everything he knew, the whole plot would fall apart."

"Really?"

"Sorry, but I hate to see people waste their time."

Jessica closed the book. The man sitting next to her was pleasant looking, with toast-brown hair and deep blue eyes. "Well, that's that. I guess we'll have to talk. My name's Jessica. Jessica Hanley."

The man extended a large hand and engulfed hers in his warm grasp. "My name's David Scharff. And I was hoping you'd say that. You see, I hate flying."

Jessica noticed that his palms were damp. "I'm sorry. That must make this difficult for you."

"More than you know. I have to fly at least once a month on business."

Over the next hour, she found out that David lived in Joliet, a city between Chicago and Ottawa, was recently divorced, and worked as a salesman for a computer software company. When she mentioned Gary's name, the man's face lit up. "You actually met the elusive Mr. Powell? I'm impressed. He's a legend in the business. When he sold his company for all that money he dropped out of sight. Where is he now?"

"He lives north of New York City. He's a nice man with interesting hobbies and the money to enjoy them," Jessica said, smiling to herself.

As they fastened their seat belts for landing, David said, "Landing is the worst part for me. May I hold your hand? It helps."

"Sure," Jessica said. As she grasped David's hand and squeezed it tightly, she thought she felt a slight tremble that went beyond his nervousness about the flight. She slid her hand up and placed her palm over his wrist where it lay on the armrest. She pressed it down firmly and held it there, her fingers on his racing pulse.

David turned, gazed intently at her, then looked down at her hand. "Why are you doing that?" he asked, his voice a bit ragged.

"I thought it might help." She smiled as he adjusted his position to loosen his slacks. Amazing, she thought.

"It does."

Jessica leaned over and pressed her breast against his arm. Close to his ear, she said softly, "I'm sure it does. Tell me the truth. Are your pants getting a little tight?" When he remained silent, she said, softly, but strongly, "I asked you a question."

"Yes," he whispered, his voice now really trembling.

"Do you have to be home at any specific time?"

"No," he said.

Jessica looked at her watch, not releasing David's wrist. "It's almost five. Would you like to buy me dinner?"

David looked at her and smiled. "Very much." More softly but clearly audibly, he added, "Ma'am."

Jessica grinned as the wheels of the plane touched down. "You can call me JessicaLynn."

Slow Dancing

Chapter 1

"Maggie mine," Paul Crowley's voice echoed through the phone, "please marry me."

Maggie Sullivan's laughter warmed the miles of wire between them. "Paul, you're so sweet and you know I love you, but be real." She spread her voluminous purple silk robe out on the wide satin-covered bed and pressed the phone against her ear.

"I am being real. Marry me. Or, if not, let's run away together. We'll find an island with no one there but the two of us. We'll live on fish and mangos."

Maggie pictured Paul's deep brown hair and could almost feel its softness. He was in his midthirties and had a body that told everyone he worked out and prided himself on his physique. "Lord, after a bad day that's such a tempting offer." Maggie tangled her fingers in her black curls. As she twirled one strand around her index finger, she remembered when her hair had been that color without the help of her stylist. "But sweet, you're who you are and I'm what I am."

"That doesn't matter, Maggie mine. Let's forget all that and do what makes us happy for a change."

"Paul, we've been over and over this. I'm a prostitute. A hooker. Very high priced," she added, tucking the phone between her ear and her shoulder and leaning back against her collection of primary-colored pillows. She flipped one Mondrian-print curtain from in front of the air conditioner with her toe so the fan blew more cold air in her direction. "But still a hooker. And you're a banker. Very straight."

"I don't care. I just want you." She heard his sigh.

"And what about our ages. I'll begin to collect Social Security just about the time you reach forty."

"Sweet thing," he moaned. "We were just born at the wrong time. Anyway, what difference do a few years make?"

"What are you wearing, Paul?" Maggie purred, stretching her long, shapely legs and crossing her ankles. She spread the sides of the robe and looked at her body beneath it. Still slender, with muscular thighs from working out daily, and full breasts that sagged only a bit.

"What difference does that make?"

"I just opened my robe and underneath it I'm wearing a lilac teddy. It's a smooth satiny material and I'm running my palms up and down my side right now." Maggie's hands were, indeed, rubbing the slick material.

"Oh, sweet thing," Paul groaned.

"I had my nails done today, you know," Maggie said, gazing at her hands. "They're extra long and bright red now. The color's from a series called Romance. This shade is called Slow Dancing. Like we do when we're together. That's why I chose it. Now I'm running my nails over the front of my thigh. It feels really good."

Maggie could hear Paul drag air into his lungs. "The inside of my thigh is so soft, but I'm making bright red marks with my nails." She smiled. "Talking like this always makes me hot. I wish you were here." Paul was on a business trip and was calling Maggie in New York from his hotel room in Denver.

"I do too. But . . ."

"What are you wearing?"

"Jeans and a blue shirt."

"Take them off, baby. Please." She could hear his resigned sigh. Again she had deflected the conversation. Maggie could hear the rustling of Paul moving around his room.

"I'm pulling off my jeans and shirt even as we speak. You always do this. I propose and you reject me in the nicest way possible." There was a pause, then Paul said, "Now I'm only wearing my shorts."

"What color are they? I want to be able to picture you."

"Black. With a white waistband." Paul's voice was ragged.

"Is your cock big and hard?"

"Oh, Maggie," Paul groaned. "Why do you do this to me?"

Her smile broadened. "Because I love to make you hot. It's one of the things I do best and enjoy most. Now tell me. Is it hard?"

"Yes," he groaned.

"Do you want to touch it while we talk?"

Silence.

"Tell me, Paul. Do you want to touch it? Tell Maggie."

"Yes," he whispered.

"Wrap your fingers around it and I'll slip my fingers under the crotch of this teddy and rub all those spots you know I love. Come on, baby, do it for me." After a moment she continued, "Are you touching your cock through your tight black shorts? Does it feel good? Sort of muffled through the fabric?"

"Yes."

"I'm sliding my fingers over my slit. I'm very wet." Her fingertips danced over her skin as she pulled the thin strip of fabric aside and explored her wetness. "Ummm," she purred, "it feels so good. And I love knowing that you're touching yourself, too." She stroked her clit with her index finger, listening to Paul's heavy breaths. "Yes, baby. Do it to your hard prick while I rub myself." There was a long silence during which the only sound was rapid breathing. "Do you know what I'm going to do?" Maggie asked, opening the drawer of her bedside table.

"What?" His voice was raspy and hoarse.

"I'm getting that big dildo, you know the one, the really big one that fills my pussy almost as well as your cock does." She pulled a large, flesh-colored penis from the drawer. "I'm going to rub it over my pussy while you slide your hand under the cotton of your shorts and hold your naked cock in your hand." She rubbed the artificial cock over her wet skin. "Ooh, that's cold. I'm going to push it inside. Hold your beautiful prick while I fill myself. We can pretend that you're here beside me."

Maggie heard Paul moan softly and she pushed the dildo into her cunt. "So full," she whispered. "So full of your hard shaft." She rubbed her clit faster as she moved the dildo inside her body. "I'm so close. Are you close, too?"

"Yes. Oh, yes, sweet thing."

"I'm going to come soon," she purred. "Come with me. Soon. Soon." She felt her climax building, flowing up through her, curling her toes and arching her back. "Yes," she cried as the heat flooded her body. "Yes." She could feel the clutching movements of her muscles against the artificial phallus as waves of pleasure engulfed her. "Yes."

"Yes," Paul called. "Right now."

For a while the only sound through the phone lines was panting and a few low moans. Then Maggie slowly withdrew the dildo from her body, reveling in the soft relaxation that always followed a good, hard climax. "That was so good," she said, her heartbeat slowing. "Not as good as having you here, of course."

"Oh, shit, sweet thing. I got goo all over the bedspread."

Maggie giggled. "It probably isn't the first time. It will wash. Just leave the chambermaid an extra-big tip."

"It never ceases to amaze me how easily you do that to me."

"That's what I'm good for. I love giving you pleasure, but," she said, not allowing him to interrupt, "that's not what you build a marriage on. Good sex is wonderful, but it's not enough."

"Oh, Maggie mine, it's not just good sex. We have great times together."

"I've got to go now, Paul. Call me when you get back."

"I will. Good night, and please think about marrying me."

"Good night, Paul." Maggie placed the receiver on its cradle and sighed. Maybe if I'd found someone like Paul twenty years ago, she thought, but things are as things are. She rubbed the heel of her hand up and down her breastbone trying to ease the sudden feeling of pressure. But I'm truly happy, she thought. I have regrets as everyone who is human does, but I enjoy making love and I'm well paid for it. And why not?

Maggie took a hot shower then climbed into her wide bed, already wondering what Carl would enjoy the following evening. Carl had the most creative mind. Maybe she'd use the handcuffs and spreader bar. She fell asleep, unconsciously rubbing her breastbone.

Maggie was totally confused. She was standing in a large room, wearing now a soft, flowing white garment. "What the hell . . ."

"Not exactly," a voice said through the heavy white mist that covered the ground and swirled about her waist as Maggie took a step forward.

"What's all this?" Maggie asked, her arched eyebrows almost meeting the middle. This is a very strange dream, she thought.

"You like the mist?" the woman's voice continued. "We had it added a few months ago. Gives the place a bit of atmosphere, don't you think?"

Unable to make out the speaker, Maggie took another couple of steps forward. "Real nice," she said dryly. This is the most bizarre dream I've had in a long time, she thought.

"It's not a dream, Margaret Mary."

"Lord, I haven't been called Margaret Mary since grammar school."

"That's right. Forgive me," the voice said, sounding genuinely sorry. "Maggie. Right?"

"Yes. Maggie. I hate to ask the obvious, but where am I?"

"That's a bit hard to explain," the voice continued. It was soft, melodious, and somehow soothing.

Maggie thought she should be afraid, but somehow she wasn't. Maybe she should be angry at whoever was playing a joke on her. But instinctively she knew it was no trick. A dream, she told herself again. This is all just a dream.

"No," another, sharper, voice said. "It's not a dream. We're quite real. Well, not real exactly."

"Lucy," the soft voice said, "let me do this. You'll just confuse Margaret Mary unnecessarily. Sorry. I mean Maggie."

"According to the record, she's Margaret Mary Sullivan. We should call her by her true name."

"Don't pout, dear," the soft voice said. "Let's just get this done, shall we?"

"You know I hate it when you take over," Lucy said.

"I know you do, but when you do the introductions, you tend to get pushy and scare people to death, so to speak."

Maggie took another few steps and was finally able to make out the shapes of two women seated at a long table. "Maggie, my dear," the soft voice said, "do sit down."

The speaker was a blonde, with shoulder-length hair that waved softly around her ears. She was extremely attractive with a perfect, heart-shaped face, tiny, sloping nose, and beautiful lips. Her most arresting feature was her eyes, sky blue and fathomless, making Maggie suddenly picture calm seas or featureless blue skies. Those eyes should look cold and distant, Maggie thought, but they gazed almost lovingly at Maggie and made her feel warm, somehow. The woman motioned Maggie to a folding chair at the table, her long graceful fingers almost hidden beneath the sleeve of the diaphanous white gown she wore.

"Yes, yes, sit. Please." The harsher voice came from a dark-haired, dark-eyed woman, dressed in a tight black scoop-necked top that showed off her deep cleavage to its greatest advantage. She wore heavy makeup that accentuated the slight catlike tilt to her deep-set eyes. Her eyes, like her tablemate's, were her most amazing feature, so dark brown they were almost black, with long curling lashes and magnificently arched black brows. As Maggie looked into this dark woman's eyes, she fleetingly pictured a deep, bottomless well. "I'm Lucy," the dark woman said.

"She already knows that," the woman in white said gently but firmly to her neighbor. Then she turned to Maggie. "And I'm Angela."

Maggie took a seat at the table, and crossed her legs in a businesslike fashion. "How do you do. Now, if it's not too much trouble, would one of you two ladies tell me what this is all about?"

"Yes, yes," the one called Lucy said. "You see, you've presented us with a considerable problem."

"I'm afraid Lucy's right," Angela said. "A considerable problem." She checked the computer monitor at her elbow, pressed a few keys and continued. "Most people are easy. One or two keystrokes, a peek at their history and the decision's made. Actually, we're going to introduce a system whereby the computer actually makes most of the decisions. Very straightforward. Usually."

Maggie looked at the two women, so different, yet unconsciously mimicking each other's motions. Patience, she told herself. I will understand this eventually.

"You, on the other hand," Lucy said, clicking a few keys on her own console, "are a real dilemma."

"I'm really sorry about that," Maggie said, having no idea what was going on but willing herself to play along with this dream or hallucination or whatever it was.

"No, dear," Angela said, "it's not a hallucination either."

"No, no, of course not." Lucy turned to Angela. "I told you that the mist might be misunderstood. But no, you had to add it. 'Gives the place an ethereal air,' you said." Lucy grumbled, "Now you see? It just adds to the natural confusion."

"It might help if you'd begin," Maggie said, "by telling me where we are. That might end some of the confusion."

"That's a bit hard to explain right off," Angela said.

"Well, why don't you try," Maggie snapped, beginning to get a bit impatient despite all her best efforts.

"You won't believe it," Angela continued, shaking her head.

"Just get on with it, Angela," Lucy snapped. "Oh, never mind. Look, honey," she said, staring at Maggie, "you're dead."

"I'm what?" Maggie shrieked, jumping up from her seat.

"Lucy, don't do that," Angela said. "It just scares people unnecessarily. You have to break these things to them gently. How many times have I told you?"

"If you had it your way," Lucy said, "we'd be here for hours, breaking the news so gently that I'd starve."

"Ladies!" Maggie yelled. "Could you please stop arguing and just tell me what's going on."

"Of course, dear," Angela said. "Now sit back down and try to open your mind to new experiences."

Maggie dropped into the chair, her wobbly legs suddenly unable to hold her weight.

"Actually," Angela said, "although she said it crudely, Lucy is right. You are dead. You died quietly in your sleep of a massive heart attack."

Maggie tried to grasp what she was being told. "I did what?"

"It's always hardest to understand," Angela continued, "when you've had no warning. The chronically ill. They understand. They've been expecting it. But you. You appeared to be in perfect health."

"But your coronary arteries," Lucy said. "Shot. Too many french fries and rare steaks." She gazed at the ceiling. "Actually, right now, a thick sirloin with a baked stuffed potato. . . ."

"Dead?" Maggie whispered, unable to make any louder sound come out of her mouth. "I'm dead? Really, truly forever dead?"

"I'm afraid so, dear," Angela said. "Remember that pain right here?" She pointed to her breastbone. "Just before you went to bed that night?"

Numbly, Maggie nodded.

"Well," Lucy said, then snapped her fingers loudly. "That was the beginning of the end."

"But," Angela said, "being dead is not bad. Really."

"Dead," Maggie muttered. "And what is this place?"

"We call it the computer room. It's kind of a decision station," Angela said. "You know, up or down." She motioned with her thumb.

"You mean heaven, hell, that sort of thing?"

"Exactly," Lucy said.

"I'm finding all this a bit hard to believe," Maggie said.

"I can understand that," Angela said. "But I think we can convince you." Angela stood up and turned her back to Maggie. Two glittering white wings extended from her shoulderblades through an opening in her gown. "Angela, angel, you get it. Right?" The wings quivered and Angela rose about five feet, then gracefully settled back down.

Lucy stood up and turned. The tight black catsuit had a small opening just above her buttocks, through which a long sinuous black tail extended. "Lucy, Lucifer. Okay?" She extended her index finger and a narrow shaft of flame shot out, then, as quickly, was extinguished.

"Shit," Maggie hissed.

"Don't curse," Angela said.

"Let her say what she wants," Lucy snapped. "After all, it's her life, or death, as it were."

Slowly, Maggie was starting to accept the unacceptable. "Does everyone come through here? And what happens now? Do I meet someone like Mr. Jordan in that movie with Warren Beatty?"

"Ah, yes, *Heaven Can Wait*. That movie has led to more misunderstandings than anything in the last fifty years," Lucy said. "People expect some kindly old gentleman, a mixture of God, Santa Claus, and James Mason. Nope. No one like that. Just us."

"Actually," Angela said, "very few people get to see us at all." She clicked a few keys on her computer keyboard, then continued. "It's usually very easy. People die and the decision's already made. Good, bad, up, down. It's usually pretty straightforward."

"But, as we told you before," Lucy said, "you are a problem."

"Really," Maggie said dryly, staring at the two women clicking away at their terminals.

"We have a decision to make here that will affect you for all eternity," the women said in unison. "Heaven," Angela said. "Or hell," Lucy added.

"And what's it like," Maggie asked, looking into Lucy's deep black eyes, "down there? Is it like the movies, all fire and brimstone?"

"Nah," Lucy said, "actually it's been air-conditioned. The staff couldn't bear the heat any longer. It's not pleasant, however. Everyone has tedious tasks to perform, like the rock up the side of the mountain thing or cleaning up after the trolls or collating a thousand copies of my daily, hundred-page report.

"Or reading it," Angela said dryly.

Lucy glared at her, "Yes, lots of hard work and constant, blaring rock music." She rubbed the back of her neck. "And recently, we've added some rap. But you have the evenings off and the food's not half bad. Very hot, of course, vindalu curry and four-alarm chili at every meal." Lucy hesitated, then added, "What I wouldn't give for a steak, medium rare." She shook her head and grew silent.

"I see." Maggie turned to Angela expectantly.

"Oh, heaven's wonderful," she said, beaming beatifically. "There's sensational organ and harp music all the time, and we have little to do but relax on fluffy clouds and think wonderful thoughts. There is a constant supply of ambrosia to eat and nectar to drink and wonderful intellectual people to talk to." She sighed. "Ah, the talks we've had about the meaning of life and the future of mankind."

Maggie thought that hell sounded much more like her type of place, but she hesitated to say so in front of Angela. There was a lot at stake here. She waited for the two silent women to continue, but when long minutes passed, Maggie brought them back to the present. "And I'm a problem for you."

"Yes, yes, of course you are," Lucy said, her head snapping back to her console. "You're a prostitute, a hooker. You have sex with men for money. And you're unrepentant."

"I guess that's true," Maggie admitted. "I don't apologize for what I do." Suddenly a bit uneasy, she said, "Does that mean . . ." She made a thumbs-down signal with her right hand.

"It should," Lucy said. "It certainly should."

"But," Angela jumped in, "you're a truly nice person. Kind, considerate, loving. We checked your record." She turned the monitor on her computer toward Maggie and clicked a few more keys. "Remember Jake? It was just a month or so before you, er, died."

On the screen, Maggie could see a view of her apartment. Jake. She remembered that evening well as the scene played out.

The doorbell rang. Maggie rose gracefully from her chair, slid the crossword puzzle she had been working on under the seat cushion, straightened her simple yellow tennis sweater and rubbed her hands down the thighs of her jeans. "Coming," she called. She crossed the large living room and opened the door. "You must be Jake," she said, careful not to touch the young man who stood awkwardly before her. "Please come in."

She backed up and motioned for Jake to come inside, but the young man didn't budge. She looked him over quickly, noting his carefully combed sandy-brown hair and his gray tweed sport jacket and black slacks. She knew from his father that he was seventeen, but at that moment he looked about twelve, with large ears and skin deeply scarred from childhood acne. She tried not to smile at the nervous twining and retwining of his fingers and his deer-in-the-headlights expression. There had been so many similar young men over the years and most of them had looked like Jake.

"You don't look like . . ." Jake swallowed hard, his eyes uneasily flicking from her face to her breasts. "I mean . . . You look nice. I don't mean . . ."

"Jake," Maggie said, "I know exactly what you mean. Come inside. I promise it will be just fine." She reached for his arm, but he entered the lavish apartment without the need for her to touch him.

Jake stopped, standing restlessly in the center of the room. "This is really nice," he said, looking anywhere but at her.

"Thanks. I've collected lots of treasures over the years. I enjoy having things around me that have special memories." She crossed to a small white linen-and-lace butterfly that seemed to have settled in the corner of a framed photo of an old European village. "There's a town in Belgium called Bruges. It looks like it hasn't changed in four hundred years." Jake walked over and looked over her shoulder, and she sensed his effort not to let any part of his body touch hers. "Wonderful old buildings," she said softly, "churches that were old before our country ever thought about George Washington. I was there about six, no, seven years ago. They cater to tourists, of course, but the city is an old center for lace making and they still make some." She ran the tip of her finger over the butterfly's white lace wings.

"That's real nice," Jake said, tangling and untangling his fingers.

"And this," she said, pointing to a smoothly carved statuette of a seal perched on a rock, "is a soapstone carving that I got in Anchorage a few years ago." She picked up the six-inch-high stone piece and placed it in Jake's hand. "I liked the shape, but what sold me was the way it felt in my hand the first time I held it." She stroked the back of the seal. "Cool and so soft," she said as Jake imitated her movement without actually touching her hand. She took the seal from him and replaced it on the mantel.

"Come on, Jake, let's sit down. We can talk for a while. About anything you like." Deliberately, she sat in a chair rather than on the long sofa. She watched Jake's face relax as he sat on the end of the sofa nearest her chair, keeping his knees from touching hers. "Would you like a drink?" Maggie asked. "I have soda, wine, beer, whatever you might like."

"Could I have a beer?" he asked, then cleared his throat.

"Sure. I have Bud, Miller, Miller light, and Sam Adams." She grinned. "I sound like a waitress. Actually, to be honest, I did wait on tables many years ago."

"What are you having?" Jake said.

"I thought I'd have a Sam Adams," Maggie said.

Jake smiled tentatively. "Okay. Me too."

Maggie walked into the kitchen of the large Madison Avenue apartment, knowing that Jake was watching her retreating ass, which was barely contained in the tight jeans she wore. Not bad for a broad on the far side of fifty, she thought as she opened two beers. She placed them on a tray, pulled two mugs out of the freezer, balanced the tray on her palm and returned to the living room. "See," she grinned, holding the tray at shoulder level. "I used to be very good at this." She twirled the tray, set it down on the coffee table and deftly poured two beers.

She handed Jake his drink, took a swallow of hers and resettled in her chair. She smiled as Jake took several large gulps of the cold liquid. "Gee," he said, "this is nice."

"Tell me about you," Maggie said. "Your father tells me you're at Yale."

For the next fifteen minutes, as Jake visibly relaxed, they talked about Jake's classes, his plans for the future, his social life at school. When they had finished their first round, Maggie went into the kitchen for two more beers. "I guess I don't date much," Jake admitted as Maggie reentered the living room, the two fresh bottles on the tray, along with a large bowl of popcorn. "I'm not very good-looking either." He ran a finger over his chin and through a few deep pits on his jawline.

"You'll never be Paul Newman," Maggie said softly, putting the tray on the coffee table. She prided herself on never lying to anyone. "But you do have his eyes." Jake's eyes were sky blue, deeply set, with long sandy lashes.

"I do?" Jake said. Then ducked his chin and quickly added, "Don't bullshit me."

"I'm not," Maggie said, keeping her voice soft. "You've got beautiful eyes." She moved to sit beside him on the sofa. "Would you like some popcorn?" She picked a piece from the bowl and held it in front of her mouth. "It's very garlicky so I won't have any if you're not going to."

Jake reached out to take a piece of popcorn, but Maggie held the one in her hand out for him. "Here, take this one," she said.

He reached for it, taking it from her while barely skimming his fingertips over hers. He popped the piece of corn into his mouth. "This is really good," he said, reaching for a handful.

"Aren't you going to return the favor?" Maggie asked, raising one eyebrow. "You took my popcorn . . ."

Slowly he took a piece of popcorn from the bowl and held it out to her. She leaned over and took it from his fingertips with her teeth, nipping his index finger lightly. She watched him pull his hand back as though burned. "Do you know," she said, swallowing, "that I met your father through a few of his friends when he was in college?"

"You're kidding. That was a hundred years ago."

"I was in business even then, back in the dark ages. I fought dinosaurs with one hand while keeping track of my customers on clay tablets."

Jake looked sheepish. "I'm sorry."

Maggie laughed, no trace of scorn, only rich warm enjoyment. "Don't be. I know it seems like centuries, and maybe it was. But I did meet your father kind of like this."

"He never told me how he knew you. I guess I thought he met you after Mom died."

"He hadn't even met your mom when I first knew him. A few of his fraternity brothers were, let's just say, friends of mine. They dared him to visit me, even paid his way." Maggie sat back on the sofa and rested her head on the back. She kicked off her shoes and, at her glance, Jake did the same. She ran her long fingers through her tight black curls. "My hair was naturally this color back then," she remembered. "He was so cute. Scared to death, like you are now."

"I'm not scared," Jake protested.

"It's all right to be nervous," Maggie said. "I was living in a small apartment in Greenwich Village and he came to my place that first evening." She giggled. "He spilled an entire bottle of Scotch on my sofa, as I recall."

Jake laughed. "He did?"

"He offered to pour us each a drink, but his hands shook so much that he couldn't get the top off the bottle. He twisted one last time, the top came off in his hand and, of course, the bottle was upside down. It took weeks to get the smell out of the upholstery."

"I can't picture my dad as a nervous teenager."

"No one can picture others having the same fears, the same feelings of inadequacy they have. I remember a certain rock star who, well let's just say, couldn't get it up."

"Who?"

"I never reveal any of the secrets I learn," Maggie said. "But, if these walls could talk. . . ."

"What did he do?" Jake asked, his eyes widening. "The rock star, I mean."

"We sat and talked. Once he was comfortable with the fact I didn't want anything from him, that he could do what he chose, he relaxed." Maggie giggled. "We actually played spin the bottle. Then we made love. Several times, as I remember.'

"And my dad?"

"Uh, uh. No tales about anyone like that. How would you feel if I told him about you?"

Jake flinched. "Okay. Point made."

"Is it warm in here?" Maggie asked, pulling her sweater off over her head. She smiled as she felt Jake gaze at her erect nipples, clearly visible through her white stretch tank top. "Why don't you take off your jacket?"

Maggie didn't move while Jake removed his sport jacket, his eyes never leaving her ample breasts. Without lifting her head from the back of the sofa, she turned to Jake. "You know what I'd like to do? How about some slow dancing." She sat up and leaned forward, giving Jake a good view of her large breasts and deep cleavage. She reached for the remote control on the coffee table and pressed a button. As Michael Bolton's voice filled the room, Maggie stood up and held her hands out to Jake. "Come on. Dance with me."

Hesitantly, Jake stood up and walked around the coffee table. "I don't dance much."

"That's really too bad," Maggie said as she moved into Jake's arms, keeping space between them. "I love slow dancing. It's like making love to music."

Jake placed one arm gingerly around Maggie's waist and held her hand with the other. He slowly shifted his weight from one foot to the other.

"Relax," Maggie said, leading him, helping him to move more gracefully. "You're doing fine." She pressed her body closer, so the tips of her nipples brushed his shirtfront. She felt him shiver, his hands trembling. She hummed along with the music, slowly moving closer until her mouth was against his ear, her chest pressed fully against his. His excitement was evident against her lower body. "This is so nice," she said into his ear.

"Ummm," he purred, moving his feet with increasing sureness. "This *is* nice."

"And we're in no hurry," Maggie whispered. As the songs changed, the two moved around the living room, locked in each other's arms. She could feel his growing hunger and nursed it until she knew the time had come. "Would you like to kiss me?" she whispered, leaning away from Jake's body.

Unable to answer, Jake pressed his mouth hard against Maggie's.

"Soft," she murmured as she cupped her hands against his cheeks and pulled back slightly, gentling the kiss, her feet still moving in time to the music. Her lips whispering against his, Maggie said, "Kissing and dancing. So good. So slow and soft." She could feel his heavy breathing against her mouth and she kissed his cheek gently. She murmured soft nonsense words, kissed his face and ran the tip of her tongue over the skin of which he was so self-conscious. He tried to pull away, but her hands and the pressure of her body held him immobile.

Without breaking contact with his mouth, Maggie slid her hands between them, unbuttoned his shirt and pulled it off of his shoulders. His chest was hairless and surprisingly smooth as she slid her palms over his skin. "I know you would like to feel my breasts against your body." In one swift motion, she pulled her tank top over her head and, as they continued to dance, she rubbed her nipples over his skin. Minutes later, when she knew he was ready, she took his hands and placed them on her ribs. Her palms covering his, she guided his hands up her sides, to her breasts. "Yes," she purred. "Hold them, feel them. Yes. Like that."

His eyes watched his hands as his fingers played with her nipples, his breathing ragged, his feet still moving to the music. Maggie helped him, showing him where she wanted to be touched, how she liked to be pinched gently but firmly. Then she placed one finger under his chin and raised his face. She held his gaze and said, softly, "We will be a lot more comfortable in the other room."

Both naked to the waist, the two walked into Maggie's bedroom, Michael Bolton's voice following them through the apartment. The bedroom was large, dominated by a king-size bed covered with a soft off-white satin spread and a dozen pillows in bright reds, blues, and violets. The thick carpet was white, covered by an area rug of a bright geometric design in the same colors. There were two white leather side chairs with matching hassocks and a lounge chair with a chrome frame and black leather webbing. Jake's eyes widened. "I know," Maggie said, her arm around Jake's naked waist, "it's a bit flashy. But it makes me happy."

Jake turned to face the older woman. He tangled his fingers in her black curls. "You're quite something," he said. "And not what I expected at all." He pressed his lips to hers, now more sure in his motions. "I want you." He reached down and started to unzip his pants.

"Let me," Maggie said, running her fingernails down his chest and moving his hands aside. She deftly unfastened his pants and, in one motion, pulled down both his slacks and his shorts until he stood naked except for his socks. She knelt and pulled them off, her eyes level with the stiff, hard erection that stuck straight out from Jake's groin. She resisted the urge to take his hard cock into her mouth, knowing that their first time together should be plain vanilla. There would be time later to introduce Jake to the dozens of other pleasures she enjoyed.

"Would you like to undress me, or should I do it?" she asked.

Jake grinned and held his trembling hands in front of him. "I think you'd better."

Quickly she pulled off her jeans, panties and socks and led Jake to the bed. She stretched out on the spread and patted the space next to her. "Come here, darling. Let's try slow dancing this way." He lay beside her and she placed the soles of her feet against his insteps. Slowly she slid their feet over the satin spread, keeping the rhythm they had established in the living room. "Slow dancing isn't just for standing up." She wrapped one arm around him and took his hand with the other, holding him just as if they were dancing. She moved against him until the length of her body was against the length of his. Quickly she took a condom from the bed-table drawer and deftly unrolled it over Jake's throbbing cock. Then she maneuvered so her body was beneath his, her legs spread, the tip of his erection against the soaked folds of her entrance. "Yes?" she whispered. "Do you want me?"

"Oh, yes," he moaned.

"Then you know what to do."

He pushed his hips forward, sliding his cock deep inside Maggie's body. Maggie cupped his buttocks and held him still for a moment, then moved, still in the rhythm of the music. "Yes, sweet," she purred. "Dance with me. Do it. Make it feel so good."

It was only moments until Jake came, his hips pounding against Maggie's. "Oh, Maggie," he bellowed. "Oh, yes." He collapsed against her, then rolled onto one side, his cock sliding limply from her body. "Oh," he groaned, clutching her against him. "Too fast."

"Now comes the first lesson," she said, taking his hand and guiding it to her wet pussy. "You came, but I didn't. I need you to help me, to give me the same pleasure you just got."

Suddenly tense, he said, "I don't know how."

"Of course you don't," Maggie said. "How could you unless someone showed you?" She held one of Jake's fingers and rubbed it over her swollen clit. "This is where most of a woman's pleasure comes from. Rub like this." She showed him and found he was a fast learner. "Yes," she said, "like that." As she arched her back, she said, "Put two fingers of your other hand inside me. It will feel so good for me and you will feel what it's like when a woman comes."

Jake inserted his index and middle finger into Maggie's cunt and slowly stretched her hungry flesh. "Don't stop rubbing right here," she said, reminding his fingers where she got the most pleasure. "Yes," she purred. "And I like it if you suck my tit, too."

With his mouth on her nipple, his fingers filling her and his other hand rubbing her clit, Maggie could feel the familiar tightness start deep in her belly. "Yes," she said, "like that. Oh, baby, don't stop." The heat grew and filled her lower body until it exploded. "Feel what my body does when it comes," she cried. "Feel it. Share it." Waves of muscular spasms clenched at Jake's fingers.

"I've never felt anything like that," he said, his voice filled with wonder. "It makes me so hot. Can I fuck you again?"

"Of course," Maggie said, barely able to talk through the waves of pleasure. She felt him withdraw his fingers, put on a fresh condom and slide into her again. Still coming, the waves of orgasm engulfed both of them as Jake climaxed again.

Later, as they dressed, Jake said, "I never knew."

"I know, and that's what I love about doing this. I can introduce someone as sweet as you to a joy that will continue for the rest of your life. There's a lot more, too."

"I know. Can I see you again?"

"Of course," Maggie said. "Call and we'll make another date. And we can work out finances then."

"Thanks, Maggie," Jake said. "I never dreamed that this evening would be this wonderful and so," he winked, "educational. When he first approached me about this, I thought my dad was nuts."

"Give him my love," Maggie said as she guided Jake to the door.

"I will." Jake kissed her good-bye and grinned as she closed the door behind him.

"You see," Lucy said, looking up from her computer terminal. "You're a nice person. I hate that."

"But, you also have sex with married men for money," Angela said sadly.

"But I never do it without first suggesting that the men discuss things with their wives," Maggie said. "Men don't realize that their wives might be just as interested in some fun and games as they are." Maggie had little use for timid women who didn't understand the pleasures of lovemaking.

"I know that," Angela said. "But remember this evening? It was just last winter."

As Maggie stared, the monitor showed the face of Gerry O'Malley. A sales representative for a computer software firm, Gerry had been recommended to her by an old friend. She recalled their first evening together and how she had tried to convince him to share his fantasies with his wife. Adamantly refusing, Gerry and Maggie had made love in his hotel room, then arranged to meet there the following Wednesday. "I want something special," he had said, his hands clenched tightly, his fingers twined. "Dress up. Would you wear white . . . ?"

Chapter 2

Maggie had dressed in a white knit dress, short enough to show off her long, well-shaped legs and low cut enough to highlight the shadowed valley between her breasts. She added light gray thigh-high stockings, held up by elastic lace at the tops, and gold strappy sandals with four-inch heels. Long gold earrings that brushed her shoulders and a heavy gold necklace completed her outfit. She was not overly made up and her lipstick was soft pink.

Dressed in gray slacks and a light blue shirt, Gerry opened the door to his hotel room and stared, his face flushed. "You look wonderful," he said to Maggie. Gerry was medium height with thick brown hair with a hint of gray at the temples. Clean shaven, his jaw was tightly clenched and he stood filling the doorway.

Maggie smiled. "May I come in?" she asked, her voice soft and melodious.

Almost stumbling, Gerry backed away from the door. "I, uh, ordered some champagne," he said.

"Good. We both need to relax," Maggie said, patting Gerry on the arm. "It will all be fine. Really."

Almost bonelessly, Gerry dropped onto the sofa in the sitting room of the two-room suite. "I know."

With a practiced hand Maggie opened the champagne bottle and half-filled two flutes from the tray. "Here," she said, handing Gerry a glass, "sip this."

Gerry emptied the glass. "I guess it shows," he said. "That I'm really nervous. About this, I mean."

Maggie laughed. "It does show. But what are you so nervous about? We were together last week and it was very pleasurable."

"I want something different from what we did last week."

"That's fine with me. What would give you pleasure?"

Gerry took his wallet out of his back pocket and withdrew ten fifty-dollar bills. "I understand that I can pay extra for something special." He counted out four more fifties and handed all seven hundred dollars to Maggie. "I want to have you completely in my power. I want to feed you a potent sex drug. I mean," he hesitated, "I mean that I want to be able to do everything to you and have you beg for more." Maggie could see his throat muscles work as he swallowed hard.

"You do remember my rules. No real drugs and if you decide you want to have sexual intercourse, you will use a condom."

"Of course. I remember everything you told me last week and I will abide by your rules. No problem."

"And I get no pleasure from serious pain, so whips and things like that are not for me."

"I understand."

Maggie looked up at Gerry from beneath her long lashes. She smiled. "How will you give me this drug, or have you done that already?"

Gerry hesitated, then grinned and said, "Yes. Yes. I did give it to you already. It was in the champagne."

"Is that why I'm feeling so warm?" Maggie said, slipping into the role Gerry wanted her to play.

"It certainly is."

Maggie stretched out on the sofa and fanned herself with her hand. "I'm so hot, baby. So hot."

"Yes, you certainly are. Maybe you'd better take off your dress."

"Oh, yes," Maggie said, standing up and turning her back to Gerry. "Would you help me unzip? I seem to be all thumbs. I can't seem to make my hands work right."

Maggie could feel Gerry's cold fingers on her back as he fumbled with the zipper. As he slid the zipper down, Maggie began to move her hips. "I don't know what's wrong with me," she said, her voice low and breathy. "I can't seem to stand still." She wiggled out of her dress, let it fall around her feet and stepped out of it. Maggie had selected a pale pink satin bra and matching bikini panties. Although her age couldn't help but show, her frequent aerobic classes kept her figure tight. She rubbed her palms over the tips of her breasts. "God, I can't stand this. I'm so . . . I don't know."

Gerry stared at Maggie's breasts which more than filled the small cups of her bra. "Are you uncomfortable?" he asked with mock innocence.

"I don't know," Maggie answered, undulating her hips and rubbing her nipples. She watched Gerry's eyes, and from the gleam surmised that the fantasy was playing out to his satisfaction. "I just want something."

"I know exactly what you want and only I can give it to you."

"Please. Do it. Help me. I'm so hot."

"I know. You're hot all over, aren't you. Especially between your legs. Hot and itchy. Do you need to rub yourself?"

"Oh, yes," Maggie moaned.

When Maggie's fingertips started to slide under the elastic of her panties, Gerry pulled it back. "Well, you can't. Not yet. Not until I give you permission. Do you understand?"

"Yes. But . . ."

"No buts. You are mine to command and I say you may not have any relief yet."

Maggie played the game. "Please. Don't make me suffer like this. I need to rub and touch and stroke myself. I need to make myself come."

"I will let you when you've been a good girl and done your chores."

"What chores?"

"First you must undress me."

"Oh, yes. May I undress you very slowly? May I kiss and touch you, caress you and make you as hot as I am?"

Gerry spread his arms wide, wordlessly indicating she could begin. Maggie closed the distance between them and pressed the length of her body against his. Sinuously she rubbed her chest and thighs against his as she licked his lips. Then she unbuttoned his shirt, licking his chest as she exposed it. Slowly she pulled the tails from the waistband of his slacks, rubbing her pelvis against his erection as she did so. With her entire body pressed against his, she worked the shirt down over his arms and tossed it on a chair. Her hard nipples pressed against the fabric of her bra and she sensuously rubbed them across his lightly furred chest. "Oh, baby," she purred as she moved around behind him, constantly rubbing her body against his side, his arm, his back, stroking his skin with her satin-covered breasts and mound.

She moved completely around him until she was again in front of him. She knelt at his feet and put her fingers on his belt buckle. She gazed up at him, a silent question in her eyes.

"Say please," Gerry said.

"Oh, please. Let me." Slowly she pulled the end of his belt through the loops and unfastened the buckle. With fumbling fingers she unbuttoned and unzipped his fly. "Oh, baby," she purred. "You're not wearing anything underneath." Careful not to touch his large, fully erect cock, she pulled his slacks down and, at her signal, he stepped out of them.

"Are you hot enough to suck my cock?" Gerry asked.

"I don't have to be hot to want to suck such a beautiful cock," Maggie said, sensing these were the right words at the right time. She looked up at him. "Please. May I?"

Gerry wrapped one hand around his erect penis and aimed it at her mouth. His grin said that this was progressing exactly the way he had imagined.

"Do you have to touch it?" Maggie asked. "I want to hold it and suck it myself."

"Even better," Gerry said, his mouth open and his breathing quick.

Still kneeling at Gerry's feet, Maggie placed one finger on the tip of his cock and rubbed the tiny drop of pre-come around the head. "I want to taste you." She flicked the tip of Gerry's cock with the end of her tongue and watched him shiver. Afraid his knees would buckle, she said, "I would like to go into the bedroom, if that's all right with you."

"Yes," Gerry said, breathless. "Of course." Quickly they moved into the other room and Gerry stretched out on the bed on his back. "Now," he said, "continue what you were doing."

Maggie spread his legs, then climbed onto the bed and crouched between his thighs. "Right here," she said, wrapping her hand around the hard staff that stuck straight up into the air. "And right here." She licked the tip, then, making a tight ring with her lips, she sucked him into her mouth.

She looked toward his face and saw that his eyes were closed. "Look at me," she said, "and watch me suck your cock." She watched his eyes open and the glazed expression as he looked at her head, bobbing on his cock.

"Good," he moaned. "Good." It took only moments until he shot his come into Maggie's mouth. "Good," he yelled. "So good."

Maggie fingered his balls until he was completely drained.

Not even thinking about the fact that Maggie was unsatisfied, Gerry disappeared into the bathroom and Maggie heard the sound of the shower. "That was wonderful," he called from the bathroom. "I need to get cleaned up now." His tone was dismissive, so, with a sigh, Maggie dressed, wandered into the living room and poured herself another glass of champagne. It was far from the first time she had been asked to perform oral sex on a man who believed that it was such an onerous task that his wife wouldn't want to satisfy his hunger for fellatio. Nibbling on some of the peanuts from the champagne tray, she gathered Gerry's clothes and walked back into the bedroom. "I will leave now, unless there's something else you want." She folded his slacks and shirt and put them on the foot of the bed. She put his wallet on the dresser.

"No. That was fantastic."

Maggie counted out four of the fifty-dollar bills he had given her and put them on the dresser with his wallet. "It was wonderful for me, too," she said. "You know, oral sex isn't a chore at all. I really enjoy it."

"I guess your kind does."

Stung, but understanding, Maggie left the suite.

As the scene faded, Angela said, "See what I mean? He was a married man and you did what you did for money. That's adultery and it's a sin."

"Oh, lighten up, Angela," Lucy said, clicking the keys on her terminal. "Get real. It's done all the time. Sex is fun stuff and everyone should have his or her share."

"Yes. I suppose you're right to a point. I do take this sin thing a bit too seriously. But that still leaves us with a problem." She turned to Maggie. "You."

"Okay. So what does that mean exactly?" Maggie asked.

"Well," Lucy said, "I've talked Angela into giving you a way to help us make the decision. A task for you to do. Like the labors of Hercules and all that."

"Yes, Lucy did come up with an idea. We have someone for you to teach about sex. Someone who's so ignorant, it's shameful even to me."

Maggie grinned. "Teach some guy about sex? That's what I do best and enjoy the most."

"That's not exactly what we had in mind," Lucy said. "It's not a guy, it's a girl."

"I have to teach a girl about sex? A little girl?"

"A grown woman. Actually, she's thirty-one," Angela said. "And she's never had a good experience in bed. A few bad experiences since high school and no real boyfriends."

"Is she a nun? A total dog? Come on. Give me a break here."

"Actually," Lucy said, "she's a nice woman, which makes me dislike her from the start."

"She's sweet," Angela continued, "and she cared for her dying mother for eight years. During the final two, Barbara moved into her mother's house and tended to her almost nonstop. She had a nurse come in during the day while she was at work, but Barbara was with her mother almost every other minute."

"What does she do?"

"She's a secretary to a big-time lawyer type," Lucy said, "and she's half in love with him. But during all the time she lived with her mother, she had no time to consider dating. Now that Mom's no longer around, she has no clue where to start, and no self-confidence at all."

"And why do you two care?" Maggie asked.

"Well, actually it was her mother who got us interested," Lucy said. "She came through here about six months ago and asked us for help before we told her where she was to go." Lucy and Angela looked at each other and made the thumbs-up signal. "She was a good and caring woman and regretted what she had put her daughter through. Ugh. Self-sacrifice. I hate that, too." Lucy made a face.

"Anyway," Angela said, "we haven't done anything about it until now, but this seemed to be a great opportunity to put you to work to help us decide about which way you go, and do something for that nice mother, too."

"And," Maggie said, "put off the decision about me."

Lucy grinned. "And there is that as well."

"Okay," Maggie said. "If that's the only way to get a bit more time to play, it's okay with me. Do I get powers?"

"Powers?"

"Yeah. Like Michael Landon on *Highway to Heaven*. Remember, he had the *stuff*."

"The *stuff*? Oh, yes, I remember, Angela. He did little magic things. Tossed bad people into swimming pools and made flowers bloom for nice folks."

"I do remember." Angela sighed. "I always loved that show. Sent that nice Mr. Landon straight upstairs when he came through."

"Sorry but no *stuff*, Maggie. Only Barbara, that's her name by the way, only Barbara will be able to see and hear you. You can appear to her and converse with her when the two of you are alone. In public, she'll be able to see you, but no one else will."

"As to powers," Angela said, "I think not, although if we see that you're getting into trouble we may, and I emphasize *may*, help you out."

"This is sink or swim for you, girl," Lucy said. "If you succeed and help Barbara become a sexually whole person, you'll get to go up there." She raised her eyes heavenward.

"But," Angela said, "if you louse this up, it's . . ." She aimed her thumb at the floor and Lucy grinned.

"I'm not so sure where I want to be or, for that matter where I belong."

Maggie sighed. "Okay. Tell me more about this hardship case of mine."

Angela and Lucy looked at each other, then Angela began. "She's not a hardship case. She's a very nice woman who has just gone through some difficult times."

"I know. Her mother and all." Maggie tapped her foot on the soft floor. "So what's her problem. Men?"

"I guess that's the heart of it."

"Is she still in mourning for her mother?" Maggie asked. "That will make my job much harder, you know."

"She's not really in mourning," Angela said. "Her mother's death, when it finally came, was a blessing. It had been a long and very rough time."

"She lives in Westchester County," Lucy continued, "in the house that used to belong to her mother. Her father died when she was only four."

"No brothers or sisters?" Maggie asked.

"No. And no other close relatives either."

"How do I meet her?"

Lucy's fingers clacked the computer keys. She swiveled the monitor so Maggie could see. Slowly the picture crystallized. Maggie watched the image of a plain-looking woman materialize. "That's Barbara," Lucy said, "right now." There was momentary sound, but Lucy tapped what must have been a mute button.

Maggie looked at the screen. A nondescript-looking woman sat beside a desk, typing furiously on a laptop computer as the hunky-looking man behind the desk talked. She saw him pick up the phone on his desk, press the receiver against his ear and swivel his chair so his back was toward the woman, who continued to work on the laptop.

Maggie watched Barbara tuck an errant strand of her shoulder-length medium-brown hair behind one ear while her boss talked on. "Look at that woman," Maggie said. "She's not even wearing makeup. And that blouse . . ." Barbara was wearing an orangy-yellow blouse and a brown tweed skirt. "It's so wrong for her coloring. And sensible shoes, no doubt. Who's the guy?"

"That's Steve Gordon, one of the partners of Gordon, Watson, Kelly and Wise." Angela gazed at the screen. "He's rich, bright, successful, and very eligible. And as I said, she's crazy about him."

Maggie watched Steve hang up the phone and turn back toward Barbara. He opened a desk drawer, propped his feet on it and began to talk. Lucy tapped the button and the three women could hear the sound.

"That was Lisa," the man said. "Make me a reservation for eight o'clock tonight at Enrico's and send her a dozen roses. No, on second thought, make it just an arrangement."

"Of course," Barbara said. Maggie caught the heat of the woman's gaze as she looked at her boss, while he seemed oblivious.

"Well, that's your job, for starters," Lucy said, tapping the mute button again. "First a physical makeover, then the rest."

"Yes," Angela said. "I think she should end up with that gorgeous Mr. Gordon. I can see it. A large house in the country, kids, horses, dogs . . .'"

"Actually," Maggie said, "he reminds me of Arnie Becker on *LA Law*. A real ladies' man and just a bit sleazy."

"Yeah," Lucy said, "me too. But Barbara really likes him."

"She would," Maggie said, rolling her eyes.

"Well, I think he's perfect," Angela said.

"Does it have to end up with them together for me to succeed?" Maggie asked, thinking that Arnie was all wrong for Barbara.

"Oh, no, of course not," Lucy said. "Actually, I think she should get out, see the world, maybe end up like you did."

"Free will," Angela said. "That's what we advocate here. Her life is her choice. It's just that she has no real choices now. We want to grant her mother's request and see what happens."

"Do you think you're ready for the task?" Lucy asked.

"I guess so." Maggie shrugged her shoulders. What choice did she have? This was kind of like the Mad Tea Party in *Alice in Wonderland*, but her options were few. And, of course, this project did buy time for her back on earth. Wondering how long she could stretch this out, she uncrossed her legs and waited for the magical zap to transport her to meet Barbara.

"Well?" Angela said, raising an eyebrow.

"I'm waiting for the magic," Maggie answered.

Lucy motioned in the direction from which Maggie had entered the room. "The elevator's that way. Just press the ground-floor button."

"Oh," Maggie said, standing up. She looked down at her diaphanous white gown. "And do I get clothes? This is a bit overly dramatic, don't you think? I'll scare poor Barbara to death."

"Hmmm", Lucy said. "You're right. We'll see to it that there are proper clothes in the waiting room on the ground floor. It's on the right just this side of the front door. Change, then go out the door and you'll be just where you should be."

Maggie nodded, then turned toward the door. "Good luck," Angela and Lucy said in unison.

"Thanks," Maggie said over her shoulder. "I guess."

As the computer room door closed behind Maggie, Lucy held out her hand to Angela. "It's a bet?"

Angela took the proffered hand. "I firmly believe that Barbara will end up settled and happy in six months. Mrs. Steven Gordon. It has a nice ring to it, doesn't it."

"And I believe that once she discovers sex, there'll be no stopping her. Whoever invented it, it's the strongest drive we have, thank Lucifer. She'll get into no end of trouble and she'll love it. I'll bet on it."

"You know, people would never believe that you want anyone to be happy. You're supposed to represent misery, suffering, and hardship, and here you are betting on happiness of one sort or another."

"I know. But happiness isn't all it's cracked up to be either."

In the room on the ground floor, Maggie found a pair of well-washed jeans, a soft light gray turtleneck sweater along with underwear, socks, and slightly worn running shoes. She dressed, leaving the almost-transparent white gown on a hook behind the door. Then she left the room and walked across what appeared to be a marble lobby toward the revolving door. When she pushed the brass handle, the door turned and she exited on the other side, right into what she somehow knew was Barbara Enright's bedroom. Fortunately, Barbara wasn't in it at the time. Maggie could hear sounds from the kitchen below. "God," she muttered, recognizing the unmistakable sound of a food processor, "I'll bet she cooks, too." She shook her head, then crossed to the large walk-in closet, pulled the door open and flipped on the light.

Oh, Lord, she thought, riffling through a collection of slightly dowdy dresses, blouses, and suits. Way in the back, she found a soft chiffon dress in shades of blue. She lifted the hanger from the rod and held the dress at arm's length. It was slightly out of style, but beautiful nonetheless. "Now this is more like it," she said, putting the dress back where she had found it. "There's hope yet."

Suddenly she realized that she had been moving things and feeling things just like she had when she'd been alive. Phew. Been alive. That sounds awful. I don't feel dead. Actually, she thought, pinching her arm, I don't feel any differently than I did yesterday. She looked at the darkened window. It must be evening now, she thought, but I thought it was morning when I was with the gruesome twosome up there and I was on the phone with Paul last evening, I guess.

She looked at Barbara's bedside table and spotted the clock. "Five-thirty and it's pitch dark," she said aloud. "But it should still be light. It's midsummer." She crossed to the window and looked out. There were small areas of snow on the ground and the stars shone brightly in a blue-black sky. "I guess time doesn't work for the girls the way it works here on earth." She thought about Lucy and Angela and marveled at how sanguine she had become about something so impossible. "I feel like a character in a play and soon the curtain will go down or we'll break for a commercial and all this will all make sense." She shrugged again. "Oh, well." She crossed to the door and started down the stairs. "Better get this over with."

Dressed in a baggy sweat suit, Barbara Enright scooped the butter-and-garlic mix from the food processor and carefully spread it on the slices of French bread she had laid out on the cutting board. Meticulously she covered the bread to the edges so it would toast properly under the broiler. As she finished the second slice, she reached out and almost without looking swirled a spoon through the small pot of simmering marinara sauce. She popped the bread in the oven, then lifted a strand of spaghetti with the clawlike device and snipped off about an inch. She popped the piece in her mouth and chewed thoughtfully. Still just a bit too firm, she thought, remembering when she had to get it almost mushy so her mother could chew it.

As she mused, she realized that her mother's death didn't hurt anymore. With almost seven months gone by, she could remember the wonderful life her mother had led before the pain.

Barbara tucked a strand of hair behind her ear, stirred the sauce and checked on the bread. She pulled one of her mother's good Límoges plates from the closet, poured a Coke and set herself a place on the large kitchen table. With perfect timing born of years of cooking for herself and her mother, Barbara removed the bread from the oven, drained and served the spaghetti and poured sauce over the top. She flipped on the TV on the counter and watched *I Love Lucy* fade in from the darkness.

"Some red wine would really go better with that."

Barbara jumped and tipped over her chair at the sound of the voice behind her. With one hand reaching for the phone, her fingers ready to dial 911, she turned slowly. "Who the hell . . ."

"It's okay," the jeans-clad figure said. "It's really okay. I'm Maggie and we're going to be spending quite a bit of time together for a while."

"Get out before I call the police," Barbara said, trying to make her quavering voice sufficiently forceful.

"Don't do that or you'll look like a fool," Maggie said, crossing the kitchen and leaning over the pot on the stove. "Nice sauce. I always loved a good marinara sauce." She lifted a strand of spaghetti and dangled it over he mouth. Nipping off the bottom, she said, "Vermicelli. And properly al dente. Not many people know how to cook pasta correctly."

Barbara stood, mouth slightly open, with her hand on the phone. For some reason she couldn't quite fathom, she hadn't lifted the receiver yet.

"I know," Maggie said, picking up a slice of garlic bread, "this is something of a shock, but believe me, it's taking me a little while to adjust, too." She took a large bite and chewed thoughtfully. "You know, I don't even know whether I can eat." She swallowed. "I guess I can, but I'm not very hungry." She pulled out the chair opposite Barbara's and sat down. "Wouldn't you know it. I can probably eat what I want and not gain weight, but I'm not hungry."

"Would . . ." Barbara cleared her throat and tried again. "Would you kindly tell me what the hell you're doing here?"

"I'm not here to hurt you," Maggie said, swallowing the chewed mouthful. "But before I try to explain, you'd really better sit down."

Barbara thought she should be afraid, but she was more baffled than frightened. This woman had arrived in her kitchen unannounced and had made herself totally at home. She shook her head, righted her chair and dropped into it. The woman had, Barbara admitted, warm, honest eyes that looked directly at you when she spoke and an open, friendly smile. Wasn't that what made con artists so hard to resist? "Okay. Tell me what you're doing here. And if you're a salesman with a very peculiar way of getting my attention, I'm not buying."

"I'm not selling anything," Maggie said, "but if I were, you'd be buying. I've actually come to change your life."

"Out," Barbara said. "Get out. I don't know how you got in here with your 'I'm not selling anything' sales pitch, but if you don't leave I *will* call the cops." She reached over and moved the phone from the counter to the table beside her right hand. "Now get out."

"Hmm. How to explain? Let me begin by introducing myself. My name's Maggie Sullivan and I'm dead." She reached over and flipped off the TV.

Her mind whirling, Barbara reran all the six P.M. sales pitches she'd heard over the years. It had gotten so she didn't answer her phone between the time she got home from work and eight P.M. *Hi*, they all started, *my name is Maggie*. She'd heard them on the phone hundreds of times. She glared. "Sure. And your next line is 'And how are you this evening, Ms. Enright,'" she parroted as the last words of Maggie's speech penetrated, "'and I'm calling on behalf of . . .' You're *what*?" Had she heard correctly?

"I'm afraid you'll find this hard to believe, but I'm dead."

"Sure and I'm Minnie Mouse."

"You're not Minnie Mouse, but I *am* dead." Maggie hesitated. "How can I convince you? You know, I'm really new to this and I don't know what I can and can't do." She reached for the bread knife that Barbara had used earlier. "I hate this, but I think it just might work. I mean a dead person shouldn't be able to feel pain and I shouldn't bleed. Right?" To test the first part, Maggie pinched herself in the arm. Hard. "Well, I didn't feel that." She picked up the knife and held it poised over the index finger of her empty hand. "Do I really have to prove this to you? It may not be pleasant if I'm wrong."

Barbara raised one eyebrow. "This is certainly the most original pitch I've ever seen. I can't wait to see how you'll get yourself out of this." Strange, Barbara thought, but I actually rather like this ridiculous woman.

"Okay then," Maggie said. "Here goes." She took the knife and drew it slowly across the pad of her finger. "Amazing," she said. "I really didn't feel that at all." She held the finger toward Barbara. "See? No blood. And you can see I made a really deep cut."

Barbara could see that there was a deep cut across Maggie's finger that wasn't bleeding. "What's the gimmick? Are you selling artificial limbs? And why would that interest me?"

"Cut me some slack, will you?" Maggie said, putting the knife aside. "I'm really dead." She stood up. "Have you got any wine? I find I need something to fortify myself."

Barbara motioned toward a lower cabinet, and when Maggie opened the door she saw a reasonably well-stocked wine rack. "I guess it will have to be red since white wine should really be chilled." She pulled out a Chianti classico. "Corkscrew?" Numbly Barbara motioned to a drawer. While Maggie quickly removed the cork from the bottle, Barbara walked into the living room and returned with two glasses. Maggie quickly half filled the glasses and raised hers in silent toast.

As Barbara watched, Maggie took a sip, swished it around her mouth and swallowed. "Not bad, but a bit harsh. It really could have breathed for an hour or two, but it's okay." She waved at Barbara's glass. "Drink."

Barbara took a sip and swallowed. "I'm not much for wine, but my mom used to enjoy a glass with dinner." She put her glass down and took her seat. Maggie took a few more sips, then again sat opposite Barbara. "You know," Maggie said, "I don't even know whether I will have to pee as the evening progresses or whether this just goes into the ether somewhere. I have no blood, so I can't get tipsy. I wonder."

Without thinking, Barbara took another swallow. "Okay. You've been here fifteen minutes and I still have no idea why."

"I'm here for you. God, that sounds like a line from a bad sci-fi drama. Actually, I'm here because of your mother."

Barbara bristled. "What does my mother have to do with this? She died a while ago."

"I know. About seven months ago to be precise. And after she died, she asked a favor of two women I know. She wants you to be happy. Get out in the world. Date. Fuck. You know."

"I don't know anything like that at all and I'll thank you to leave my mother out of this."

"But she's an integral part of it." Maggie reached out to pat the back of Barbara's hand, but the younger woman pulled away. "Let me explain." Briefly Maggie told Barbara about her heart attack and how she had suddenly found herself in the Mad Tea Party with Lucy and Angela. "They can't decide whether I'm to go . . ." Maggie made a thumbs-up with one hand and a thumbs-down with the other. "So they gave me a project. You."

"I don't for a moment believe any of this," Barbara said, drinking more of her wine, "but why me?"

"I told you before," Maggie explained. "It was your mother. On her way through, she asked the girls to help you out." Maggie's head tipped to one side and she gazed into space. "Actually, I don't quite understand how your mother ended up in the computer room. According to Angela and Lucy, the interview process is only for the undecideds. Your mother's goodness seems to have left the girls little choice. Maybe it was a special request of some kind." She refocused on Barbara. "Anyway, I'm now here for you."

"Your reference to the Mad Tea Party is accurate. I still don't believe you."

"Well, that's neither here nor there, actually. I assume you want to get out more. Date. I saw the way you looked at your boss this afternoon."

Barbara's head snapped up. "How the hell do you know how I looked at my boss earlier?"

"The girls have a monitor and they can tune in on people. We watched you at work today so I would know who you were."

"This gets crazier and crazier," Barbara said. "Do you mean that they could be watching us right now?"

"Probably not. With the millions of people they have to check on as people come through for approval, I doubt whether they have time for idle peeping."

Barbara shivered. "It gives me the creeps nonetheless." She found she was actually playing along with this fantasy. Or was it a fantasy?

"So you're supposed to give me a makeover. What's this going to cost me?"

"Nothing. And it's more than a makeover, it's a whole change of attitude. According to your mother, you're ... How can I best say this? You're a bit of a prude."

"Nonsense. I'm just selective. Just because I don't let every Tom, Dick, and Harry into my bedroom doesn't make me a prude. Not in the least."

"Selectivity is good, Babs, but it's not life."

A handsome face suddenly flashed through Barbara's mind and her patience snapped. "Don't call me Babs. I hate it."

"All right. Don't get huffy."

"I'm sorry. I just really hate Babs. Anyway, you were telling me about my makeover."

Maggie sipped her wine. "Well, as I understand my job here, I'm supposed to teach you about yourself and sex and men and dating and all that. In the end, you're supposed to get out more, go dancing, make love."

Barbara toyed with her fork. "And what makes you such an expert?"

"I am, or was, a ... Again how to put this. I was an expert at making men happy. Let's just say I did it professionally."

The fork dropped out of Barbara's hand. "You were a hooker!"

"I prefer call girl. Very highly priced, I might add."

"But you look like you could be my mother."

Maggie winced. "Ouch. That hurt." She walked into the hallway outside the kitchen and looked at herself in the ornate mirror that hung just inside the entrance. She studied her face for a moment, then returned to the table and sat down. "I don't look that bad, despite my current circumstances, I'll have you know." She paused. "But I guess I am almost old enough to be your mother."

"So why would some man ... ?" Barbara suddenly realized that without being totally insulting she had no way to finish the sentence.

"Why would some man want to make love with me? Because I know how to make men happy, how to fulfill their fantasies, how to make them feel strong or weak, brave or pitiful, whatever they want. I'm damn good at what I do and I have a client list as long as your arm."

"What do you ... I mean, *did* you charge?"

"I was worth the five hundred a night that men paid me."

"Five hundred dollars? For one night?" Barbara's mouth literally hung open.

"Not the whole night, of course." Maggie ran her long fingers through her hair and fluffed it out at the sides. "And more if they want something special."

"I don't want to know about that part," Barbara said. "Look, I don't pretend to understand any of this, but I really don't need your help. I'm happy just the way I am." In response to Maggie's raised eyebrow, Barbara continued. "Really. My life is just what I want it to be. And I'm just the way I want to be."

"Sure," Maggie said, her voice dripping with sarcasm. "Listen. You've heard enough for one evening. You really need to take a day to digest all this. Let me run along now so you can think about what we've said." Maggie paused, then asked, "By the way, what day is it?"

"It's Tuesday," Barbara said, her head spinning. She was sitting in her kitchen having a conversation with a dead prostitute. She certainly did need some time to digest this. But she didn't need any help with her life. None. Absolutely not.

"What date? What year?"

"It's Tuesday, March 4, 1996. What did you think?"

"I'm totally disoriented. This bouncing from time to time. The last date I remember was July 18, 1995." Pain flashed across Maggie's face as she recalled Paul Crowley and their phone conversation that last evening. I wonder how he felt when he found out about me. "And where are we? It looks like New York, but everything wonderful looks like New York to me."

"We're about twenty miles north of the city, in Fleetwood."

"I know the town well." Paul lived in Bronxville, the next town up. With a sigh, she emptied her wineglass and shook off her negative feelings. "I'm not sure how this time thing will work, but I think I can manage to be here, same time tomorrow."

"I don't want to seem rude, but I don't want you to come back. Just go away and leave me alone."

"Sorry, but I can't. I have a job and my ultimate future depends on doing it well. And remember, this is what your mother wanted."

"I'm sure my mother didn't want some whore giving me makeup tips," Barbara snapped. Then her head dropped into her hands. "I'm sorry. That was uncalled for."

"Yes, it was. But I am what I am. I am—I was—a woman who made men happy for money. I did my job well, and got a lot of pleasure myself as well. And I was highly paid for my talents."

"I'm sorry. But this whole thing is so ridiculous."

"Just think about it. Consider what you have to gain. Think about looking appealing to your boss and having him ask you out. Dream about what your third or seventh date could be like. Think about all this and I'll see you tomorrow." Maggie crossed the room and walked into the hall.

Suddenly the house was silent. Having not heard the front door open, Barbara got up to be sure this crazy woman wasn't lurking somewhere waiting to pounce or something. "Maggie? Where are you?" She searched the house, but Maggie was nowhere to be found.

Chapter 3

Later that evening, Barbara lay on her bed, the romance novel she had been trying to read now discarded beside her. It had been foolish, she realized, to even try to think about anything besides the weird visit she had had with the ghost of a sort of motherly, utterly charming prostitute. Images had whirled in her brain as she had tossed her uneaten dinner in the trash and methodically washed the dishes and cleaned the kitchen.

She considered what Maggie had said. Her life wasn't dull, it was just predictable. She went to work five mornings a week, arriving in White Plains, barring car trouble, at almost exactly eight o'clock each morning. Gordon, Watson, Kelly and Wise was a small but elite firm, run by Mark Watson and John Kelly, two aging lawyers, and Steve Gordon, the thirty-five-year-old sexy-looking lawyer for whom Barbara worked. Barbara brought her half-sandwich and salad with her each day and ate her lunch at her desk. Steve Gordon Junior, son of one of the founding partners, wasn't overly dependent on her so Barbara usually left at four-thirty and was home before five.

Most weekends she did odd jobs around her two-story raised ranch. In the summer she mowed the lawn, in the winter she shoveled the driveway. Her kitchen and bathroom floors were clean enough to eat off of, and at the first sign of mildew she attacked her tub and shower with cleansers and brushes. She was an active member of her local church and could be counted to cook and bake for every benefit, chaperone the youth events and join parishioners in holiday visits to local nursing homes.

My life's not dull. It isn't. But when was the last time she had been out on a date? Carl Tyndell's face flashed again through her brain. He was the last, she realized, and that was … . She counted on her fingers. Let's see. Mom got really sick and moved in two years ago and it was a few months before that. Maybe more than a few months. Phew. Had it really been more than three years since she had had a date? Well, after that last debacle, it was just as well. Anyway, she was happy. Wasn't she?

She thought about Steve. He was almost six feet tall with piercing blue eyes and just enough gray at his temples to be distinguished and sexy. He had a strong jaw, and large hands with slender fingers and well-sculptured nails. Frequently Barbara would find herself watching his hands as he signed the correspondence she typed for him.

Was Maggie right? Barbara sighed and popped an M&M into her mouth from the open bag on her bedside table.

She slept little that night and, the next day since Steve was in court, she typed, arranged and organized several important briefs, two wills and a few mortgage documents. Without too much thought, she opened Steve's mail, dealt with the items she could handle herself and arranged the others in folders on his desk. She answered the phone, made and confirmed several appointments for her boss and gave him his messages and took copious notes about his responses each time he called in. She nibbled on her American cheese sandwich and salad at lunch and left the office at four thirty-five.

As she drove home, she realized that, although she had thought about her life and the things Maggie had said most of the day, she had made her decision the previous evening. If this whole thing wasn't an elaborate hoax or some kind of boredom-induced hallucination, she would go along with Maggie, at least for the moment.

When Maggie had walked out of Barbara's kitchen the previous evening she suddenly found herself back inside the revolving door. She pushed her way to the other side and stepped out, only to find herself walking back through Barbara's kitchen door.

"I didn't know whether you'd really be here," Barbara said as Maggie entered the kitchen.

"This is really disorienting," Maggie said, rubbing her forehead. The kitchen was different, with two plates on the table, each with hamburger on a toasted bun, mixed vegetables, and rice. "When am I?"

"That's an interesting takeoff on the typical question. It's almost six-fifteen. I wasn't sure you'd be back."

"Did we meet last evening or just a few minutes ago?"

"We met yesterday." Barbara sat at one end of the table and pointed to the second place setting. "I cooked some dinner for you, but I remember you told me you didn't get hungry. I can put it away and eat it for lunch tomorrow if you don't want it."

"This is all new to me, too," Maggie admitted. "I don't know exactly what I do and what I don't." She sat down and sniffed, enjoying the slightly charcoal smell of the grilled burger in front of her.

"Is this the first time you've helped someone?"

Maggie nodded ruefully. "I'm not like Michael Landon in *Highway to Heaven*. This isn't my job, you know. It's just a test to see where I go."

"I love *Highway to Heaven*. Michael Landon is so adorable."

Maggie raised an eyebrow. "Well, it's good to know you notice things like that." She picked up the burger and took a bite. "Delicious."

"Thanks. I did all the cooking for my mother and me until she died. Good wine and good food were her only pleasures toward the end, and I did what I could to make special things for her."

"Well," Maggie said, her mouth full, "this is really wonderful."

Barbara found herself delighted that Maggie liked her cooking. "What does an angel do all day? I mean, what did you do today?"

"I'm certainly not an angel as anyone who knew me in my old profession can tell you. That's the problem that puts me here with you. And for me, there was no today. I walked out of your kitchen and just walked back in." She blinked, then took another bite of her burger. "I guess I'll get used to it. Tell me what's been happening in the world since I left. Did the O.J. Simpson trial ever end?"

For the next hour Barbara caught Maggie up on what had occurred in the last eight months. Strangely, Barbara realized as she poured coffee for each of them, she had completely accepted the fact that Maggie was dead. She also realized that she hadn't enjoyed an evening this much in a long time.

"I think it's time we got down to business" Maggie said as she sipped her coffee. "I'm here to see that you get out, date, have some fun."

Barbara stretched her legs beneath the table and sighed. "It won't work. I am what I am."

"Do I hear self-pity? A bit of 'poor little me?'"

Barbara sat upright. "Not at all. It's just that you can't make something out of nothing."

"All right, let's get serious here. Do you have a full-length mirror somewhere?"

"I guess." Together the two women walked upstairs and into the guest bedroom. It was a simply decorated room with a flowered quilt, matching drapes, and a simple dresser. The room looked and smelled unused. Maggie walked behind Barbara and together they stood in front of the long mirror that hung on the closet door.

"Now, look at you," Maggie said, looking at Barbara's reflection over her shoulder. Barbara was wearing a pair of nondescript gray sweat pants and an oversize matching sweat shirt. "You look like you've just come from a ragpickers' convention."

"But this is just for comfort," Barbara protested.

"Comfort is one thing but dressing in sacks is another." Maggie grabbed a handful of the back of the shirt and pulled. The fabric stretched more tightly across Barbara's chest. "There's a body under this," she said. "Nice tits." She pulled the pants in at the seat. "And you've got nice hips, a small waist. Yes, there's actually a shape under all this material."

Barbara looked, but remained unconvinced.

"Look at your face," Maggie said, grabbing a fistful of hair and pulling it back, away from Barbara's face. "Nice eyes. Actually, *great* eyes. Good cheekbones, good shape. A definite nose, but not too much, and nicely shaped lips. Your skin's not great, but nothing that a decent foundation wouldn't cure." She released Barbara's hair and the two women stood, gazing into the mirror. "There's really a lot of potential. We just need makeup, a good hair stylist, and a new wardrobe."

"I don't need a new wardrobe," Barbara said, almost stomping toward her own room. She crossed to her closet, opened the door and flipped on the light. "Just look. There are lots of really nice clothes in here."

"Nice for a dowdy moderately shapeless old maid, but not for you. You need high shades, sapphire and emerald, deep claret and purple. Oh, you'd look sensational in eggplant."

"I have all the clothes I need."

"But not the ones you want. You seem to want to slide through life virtually unnoticed. Nonsense. Make a statement. Be a real person."

"I am a real person."

Maggie made a rude noise. "In attitude, you rate a D and in self-esteem you get an F. In looks, I'll give you a 'needs improvement.' And with the improvement will come a change in attitude as well. Are you game?"

Barbara dropped onto her bed. "I don't know, Maggie. Part of me wants to be adventurous, stick out in a crowd, have men notice me. But the rest is terrified. It's such a risk."

Maggie sat beside Barbara and put her arm loosely around the younger woman's shoulders. "Why is it a risk?" she asked softly.

"It just is."

"Think about the worst thing that could happen if you walked into a room in a bright red dress with black stockings and black high heels, with golden highlights in your hair and a 'here I am, come and get me' expression on your face. What's the worst thing?"

To her surprise Barbara burst into tears. Helpless, Maggie handed her a handful of tissues and, with her arms around Barbara's shoulders, let her cry it all out. It took fifteen minutes for Barbara to get calm enough for Maggie to attempt to talk to her again. "You have to tell me what's eating you."

Barbara wiped her face and shook her head.

"I can ask Lucy and she'll find out with that computer system of hers." Maggie explained Lucy's ability to replay events in her life at will. She had no idea whether she could even get to Lucy or whether Lucy could bring up bits of Barbara's past, but she thought it was a decent bluff.

"Oh, no. That would be too humiliating."

"Well, then, let me get us each a glass of wine and then you tell me what it is that frightens you so much. Where's the rest of the bottle we were drinking last evening?"

"In the closet next to the refrigerator, and the glasses are in the hutch in the living room."

"Lord. Unless I was entertaining I left dishes in the sink for days and in my drainer even longer. Okay. You think about how you're going to tell me the ugly details while I fetch for us." Maggie left the room.

Barbara listened to Maggie's footsteps on the stairs and slumped onto her back. Maybe I can just run away. Maybe I can tell her to go to hell. Maybe I can slit my wrists. She sighed. Maybe it will feel good to tell someone about Carl and Walt. But maybe Maggie would just give up on her if she did. Didn't that serve her purpose anyway, make Maggie go away? Too soon, Maggie returned and thrust a glass of wine into her hand.

"Drink this like it's medicine," Maggie said, brandishing the bottle and her glass in the other. "There's enough here for another half-glass for each of us."

Staying flat on her back on the bed, Barbara awkwardly emptied the glass, then held it out for Maggie to refill. Maggie emptied the bottle into Barbara's glass, then stretched out beside her on the bed. Softly she said, "Tell me about him."

"How did you know it was a him?"

Maggie chuckled. "When a woman has an ego that has been smashed as flat as yours it's always a man—or a woman. And from the way you gazed at that boss of yours yesterday, I assumed the asshole who flattened your self-esteem was a man."

"Oh, yes," Barbara said. "Carl Tyndell was definitely a man, and I guess an asshole, too."

"That's the attitude." Maggie stared at the ceiling, giving Barbara time to decide where to begin.

"I met Carl at a party. It was about four years ago and I had just had my twenty-seventh birthday. Notice I didn't say I celebrated, because, for some unknown reason, that birthday hit me very hard."

As she set the scene for Maggie, Barbara could almost see the room, hear the incessant babble of suburban conversation, smell the cold cuts on the dining-room table. A couple she knew slightly from her church had given the party to introduce some new neighbors. She had put her coat on the bed in the master bedroom and as she walked back down the stairs she saw a sensational-looking man talking in low whispers to Walt McCrory, a neighborhood bachelor whom she had dated a few times a few months earlier. The two men laughed loudly, then the stranger worked his way through the crowd and engaged her in conversation.

"I should have suspected something was up the way Walt leered at me," Barbara said.

"You and this Walt didn't part on good terms, I gather."

"We went out for a few weeks. We had dinner a few times, then one warm evening he invited me back to his place to check out his new above-the-ground pool. One thing led to another, but obviously not fast enough for Walt. After I told him I didn't want to be groped, he called me a cold bitch, incapable of giving a man a decent wet dream much less a hard-on."

"So he presumably talked this Carl person into picking you up."

"I guess that's true, but I was so naive that I didn't make the connection until much later."

"We never do," Maggie said sadly.

"Anyway, Carl and I made dinner plans for a few days later. We had a wonderful meal and a few too many drinks. He was attentive and seemed interested in everything I had to say. His eyes were so deep brown as to be almost black. His hair was also dark brown and he had nice hands. I'm a sucker for men with great hands."

"Me too." Maggie smiled, thinking about how many men's hands had touched her over the years.

"After dinner, Carl suggested a drive along the Hudson. We used my car, parked in a darkened area he knew about and kissed like teenagers. One thing led to another and suddenly my blouse was off and my bra was open. His mouth was on me and he was whispering, 'Babs, sweetie, oh, Babs.' Suddenly Walt pulled the car door open and snapped a flash picture of me, naked from the waist up.

" 'You win, Carl baby,' Walt said. 'I can't deny it when I have the proof and a great shot of Babs' tits right here.' I watched the picture spit out of the front of the camera and slowly appear before my eyes."

"Win what?" Maggie asked, annoyed by the pain inflicted by something that to those two probably amounted to nothing more than a prank.

"They had made a bet that Carl couldn't get my upper body exposed on the first date. Right there in the car Walt counted out a hundred dollars and handed it to Carl. Walt said that he didn't think anyone could get the ice bitch out of her clothes in under six months. They laughed, pounded each other on the back, then the two of them walked to Walt's car, and took off."

"Oh."

"Yes, oh."

"Well that wasn't the end of the world, was it?"

Barbara just stared at the ceiling. "I never told anyone about that night and, I guess, Walt never did either. I spent the next few weeks waiting for the picture or the story to circulate, but for some unknown reason, nothing happened."

"Did you ever see them again?"

"I never saw Carl again. He must have been 'imported talent.'" She said the phrase with a sneer. "I see Walt once in a while, but he's not a church type and I stick almost completely to church gatherings."

"Safe stuff. No risk of anyone getting sexual." Maggie took Barbara's hand. "Wouldn't you like to get him back sometime?"

Barbara smiled. "I'd love to, but there's no hope of that."

"I wouldn't be so sure. It just gives us another reason to make you over and get you some experience." She paused. "Are you a virgin?"

Barbara sat upright. "What a question."

"Well . . ."

"No. I've had relationships." She slumped back down onto her back. "But not recently."

"And Steve? Wouldn't you like him to notice you?"

"Of course."

"So you'll let me help you? For your mom and Steve and maybe even Walt and Carl."

Barbara sighed. She wanted to let Maggie help. It was all so bizarre but it was a chance to get some of the things she wanted. It might be her only chance. "I guess."

"Good," Maggie said. "First, call in sick tomorrow and we'll get your hair done, get someone to help you with your makeup and see what we can do about some clothes for you. I need to know something that's a bit embarrassing. Is money a problem? I'm a bit short of funds, you realize."

Barbara laughed out loud for the first time since Maggie had appeared the previous evening. "No. My job pays well and I don't spend much. I'm not Saks Fifth Avenue-well off, but we could certainly go to the mall and dent my credit card."

"Great."

"You know, it sounds like fun."

"It does, doesn't it."

"Will you be able to be here? I mean how do you just appear and disappear the way you do?"

Maggie thought, then answered, "I don't know how." She told Barbara about the revolving door. "I seem to be able to set some kind of clock, so I just come out of the door here at the right time."

"Do you have powers? Like moving stuff with your mind or walking through walls?"

"I don't think so, but Lucy and Angela seem to be in charge of that. They said I'd have what I needed when I needed it, so I'll just have to trust them." She stood up. "I've got to be going now." She cocked her head to one side. "I don't know how I know that, but I do." She walked toward the bedroom door, then turned. "Tomorrow. Ninish."

Barbara raised her hand and waved as Maggie walked through the bedroom door and vanished.

Barbara's dreams were troubled for the first part of the night. She was in the car with Walt and Carl, but the car was really the gaping jaws of a giant mythical beast and, as the two men jumped out, the jaws began to close on her naked, immobile body. Then she was walking down the aisle in church dressed in a bridal gown, with her mother holding her arm, ready to give her away to the man who stood beside the priest, his back turned to her. When she reached his side, he turned, but he had no face. She looked down and saw that he was a tuxedoed store mannequin with two poles holding him up where his legs should have been.

The following morning, Barbara called her office and told the woman who answered the phone that she had urgent personal business and wouldn't be in the office until the following day. She dressed in a man-tailored shirt and jeans, white socks and sneakers, grabbed a denim jacket and bounced down to the kitchen. Bounced, she thought, was a good word for the way she felt. Light. Elastic. Good!

She made a pot of strong coffee and toasted a bagel. She sat at the table munching and thinking about the day's activities. "Good morning," Maggie said from the doorway.

"Hi, Maggie," Barbara responded. "Coffee?"

"I guess. This time warp thing I'm in is still very confusing. It seems like only a moment ago I left you last evening."

"Nice outfit," Barbara said.

Maggie looked down, puzzled. "I didn't change clothes," she whispered. Last evening she had had on an outfit similar to the clothes Barbara was wearing this morning. But now Maggie was wearing a pair of wide-legged black rayon pants and a soft gray silk blouse. "Very disconcert-ing," she mumbled.

Barbara poured Maggie a mug of coffee and set it down beside a pitcher of milk and the sugar bowl. "Maggie," she asked as her friend dropped into a chair. "How did you become a . . . I mean . . . ?"

"Hooker?"

"Yeah. Well. . . ."

"You mean how did a nice girl like me end up entertaining men for money."

"You can't blame me for being curious."

Maggie grinned. "Of course not. And let's get this settled right now. I've said it before. I am proud of what I do, er . . . did. I had my own rules and I stuck by them at all times. My customers and I had fun. We were careful and honest."

"It's just difficult for me to believe in the hooker with the heart of gold. It's so clichéd."

"Heart of gold. I like that. I like that a lot. Anyway, you asked how I got started in my business. It began with my first divorce."

"You were married?" Barbara said, her eyes wide.

"Twice, but this is my story to tell. Anyway, Chuck and I married right out of high school in 1955 and stayed together for six years. The split was amicable. We just had nothing in common anymore. No kids, we both worked, our sex life was dull, dull, dull. He married again by the way, to a nice, mousey woman who seemed to make him happy. But that's another story.

"As a divorcee, I slept around. That was a very loose time, before AIDS, very into me first. I found that I loved sex. I enjoyed pleasing the men I was with and I had fun learning how to do it. I was still just begin-ning to learn about fantasy when I met Bob. He had a wonderfully cre-ative mind and taught me about all sorts of new things in the bedroom. When he suggested we get married, I thought I'd found my ultimate sex partner and in order to keep us together, I said yes."

"He sounds like a wonderful lover."

"He was and he taught me to be a giving, creative partner."

"But . . ."

"But I couldn't stand him outside of the bedroom. He and I were exact opposites. He was a neat freak, I'm a bit of a slob. He liked his meals at specific times, all organized, I like to scrounge for myself. You get it. So, after two fantastic years in the bedroom and two awful years everywhere else, we split, too. That was 1974, and it seems like forever ago. I was intensely glad when he left, but I was horny as hell. All the time. The one good thing about marriage is that you can usually have all the sex you want."

"That sounds terrible."

"It was for me. I still worked, of course. I was manager of the computer input department at a regional bank. I had very good people skills, as my boss called them, but I was bored. Bored, lonely and horny at home and bored, stressed, and frustrated at work. Not much of a life."

Barbara patted the back of Maggie's hand, well able to sympathize with the older woman.

"One evening I just couldn't bear to go home to that empty apartment so I stopped at a bar near work. I'd been sitting at the bar for about an hour, feeling sorry for myself, when a cute-looking guy sat down on the stool next to mine." Maggie closed her eyes and a smile changed her expression from despair to enjoyment as she remembered that evening. "I remember. I called myself Margaret at that time."

"Hi," the man said. "My name's Frank."

Maggie looked up, ready to brush the man off with a clever remark. But as she took in his charming smile, she changed her mind. "Hi. I'm Margaret."

"Glad to meet you, Margaret. I come in here whenever I'm in town but I've never seen you before."

"I've never been in here before," Maggie said.

Frank placed his elbow on the bar and leaned his chin on his hand, studying Maggie's face. "You know," he said after a moment, "you don't look like a Margaret."

Maggie sipped her white wine, unwilling to make any overt gestures of friendliness toward this stranger who was in the process of picking her up in a bar. "And how would a Margaret look?"

"Oh, let's see. Margaret is very serious. Tight bun. Thick glasses. Sensible shoes."

Maggie thought about that and realized that, in the months since she and Bob had gone their separate ways, she had become just what Frank pictured. No, she thought, I won't be that person. I'm only thirty-three. She took a large swallow of her wine and sat up a bit straighter. "Okay. I guess I can't be that kind of Margaret. What would you call me?"

"Well, Margie is young, pert, and too cute to be believed, so that's not you. And Peggy is an Irish lass with red hair and freckles."

"Okay. Neither of those sound like me. So who am I?"

"You look like a Maggie. Nice-looking. Interesting and interested. Open to new experiences."

"What a line you've got," Maggie said, realizing that, whether it was a line or not, this man had made her feel younger than she had in years. She lowered her chin and looked up at Frank through her lashes. "And I must say I like it."

Frank grinned. "Me too. And it usually works."

Maggie laughed. "You admit that it's a line? How original."

"The line's original, too," he said. "And you're the first woman who's picked up on it so quickly." He tried and almost succeeded in looking like a small boy with his hand in the cookie jar. It helped that he had medium brown hair naturally streaked with blond, wide blue eyes, and a fantastic mouth.

They talked for an hour, then went to a nearby French restaurant and shared a sumptuous meal which included a bottle of fine Chardonnay and a glass of sweet, golden dessert wine. She learned that Frank was divorced, in town from Dallas for a week for his firm's quarterly department meetings and that he was charming and sexy and determined to get her into his bed. As he dropped his credit card onto the check, he took Maggie's hand. As he held it across the table, his index finger scratched little patterns in her palm. "We could be good together," he purred.

She had to admit to herself that she was turned on. But this was a man who had picked her up, not someone she worked with or who had been introduced to her by friends. He was only in town for a short time. She couldn't even delude herself into thinking this was the beginning of a long-term relationship. But she wanted to go to bed with him nonetheless. "How can you be so sure?" she said.

"I can be very sure. I can see it in your eyes, your body, the way you smile, the way you can't quite sit still. You want this as much as I do. How do you like your sex?"

"Excuse me?"

"You heard me. How do you like your sex? Long and slow, with lots of kissing and stroking? Hard and fast, like the pair of animals we are? Standing up with your back pressed against the wall and your legs locked around my waist? In the shower under torrents of hot water? Tell me and I'll make it that way for you."

Maggie shrugged. She couldn't tell him how she liked her sex because she loved it all ways. "You tell me," she hedged. "How do you like it?"

"Oh, Maggie, I think I'd like it every way with you." He lifted her hand and nipped at her fingertips.

"No," she said, more seriously. "Tell me. How would you like to make love with me? Create the fantasy and let's see how we mesh."

"You're serious. You want me to tell you." When Maggie merely nodded, Frank said, "I see you slowly removing your clothes while I watch. I watch you reveal your body to me, one small piece at a time."

Silently Maggie reached up and unbuttoned the top two buttons on her blouse and parted the sides so the valley between her breasts was visible.

"Shit, baby. I'm hard as stone already."

Maggie raised an eyebrow but remained silent.

"Okay. I see you in your bra and panties." He looked around the tablecloth at Maggie's shoes. "Yes. Black high heels. I like that. You're not wearing pantyhose, are you?"

"I won't be," she said, contemplating a quick trip to the ladies' room. She watched the flush rise on Frank's face. She was turning him on. What a trip.

"You're walking toward me, then unzipping my pants."

Maggie was very turned on and more than a little drunk. Without changing her expression, she slipped one foot out of her shoe and stretched her foot across the space between them and rested her stocking-covered toes against the swelling in his crotch.

His startled look, followed by a shift of position to place her foot more firmly against his zipper, told Maggie exactly what she was doing to him. "Shit, baby, let's get out of here," he moaned.

"The waiter hasn't brought your credit card back," Maggie said, feigning an innocent expression. She wiggled her toes in his lap. "As I remember, I was unzipping your pants. Tell me more. I want to know exactly how you see this evening we're going to have."

She watched Frank take a deep breath. "I can't think when you do that."

Again she silently raised an eyebrow. She was in charge now, quite deliberately turning Frank on, a man she had met only three hours before.

His voice uneven, he continued. "You were unzipping my pants and taking out my cock. It's so hard it sticks up like a flagpole. You're wrapping your hand around it and licking your lips."

Maggie slowly ran the tip of her tongue across her upper lip. "Like this?"

At that moment, the waiter returned with Frank's charge slip, which he signed with an obviously shaking hand. As he wrote, Maggie moved her toes in his lap. As the waiter took the restaurant copy, Maggie asked, "Could I have just a bit more coffee?"

"Certainly, madame."

"But, Maggie, I thought we were going to my room." He was almost whining.

"We will. But I need just a bit more coffee and you haven't finished your story. I was holding your cock, as I recall. Squeezing it as it sticks up through the opening in your pants. Let's see, I'm wearing a black lace bra, bikini panties, and my high black shoes. Right?" Bob had taught her about the power of a well-set erotic scene and he had marveled at her ability to use words to turn him on. Now she was using all her skill to turn Frank on. And it was working better than she could have imagined.

Frank was again lost in his fantasy. "Right," he whispered.

"And I'll bet you want me to take your cock into my mouth and suck you."

"Oh, yes," he groaned as the waiter refilled Maggie's coffee cup. Without removing her hand from his, or her foot from his lap, she poured cream into her cup and stirred.

When he didn't continue, she said, "You want me to touch the tip of your cock with my lips, kiss it, lick it, make it wet." She deliberately slowed the cadence of her speech. "Then I can slowly suck it into my mouth. Very slowly. Pulling it deeper and deeper into that hot, wet cave."

Frank's eyes closed, obviously lost in the fantasy.

"Now I pull back, but I keep sucking so your cock pulls out so slowly. Down and up, my mouth is driving you crazy." She remembered a trick Bob had taught her. "But I wrap my fingers around the base of your cock so you can't come as I keep on sucking. I don't want you to come yet, baby."

"But I want to come."

"Not until we're both ready. So now I pull my panties off and rub myself. I'm very wet, you know. I let you lick my finger so you can taste me. Do I taste good?"

"Oh, yes."

"Good. Now I pull off your pants, but I leave your shirt on. It's very sexy for me to see you all dressed in your business shirt and tie while I slowly put a cold, lubricated condom over your cock. It feels tight, like it's hugging you. Now I push you down onto the bed, straddle your waist and use the tip of your slippery cock to play with myself." She looked at his closed eyes. "Can you see me?"

"Yes," he said, his voice harsh and almost inaudible.

"Let me take off my bra so you can watch my breasts as I play with your cock. I'm rubbing my clit now. It's hard and you can even feel it against your cock. And I'm so wet. Your hips are moving, trying to push your cock inside. Shall I let you?"

"Please."

"Yes, I will. I lower myself onto you, pulling you deep inside. You fill me up so well, baby. I raise up and drop, over and over, fucking you so good. Do you want to come now? I'm almost ready." With his eyes closed, Frank groaned. Maggie rubbed her foot along the length of his cock under the tablecloth.

"I'm almost ready. Almost. Wait for me, baby." Maggie was so turned on by her description of Frank's fantasy that if she reached under the table and touched herself, she would come. But she didn't.

"Yes, baby," she said. "I'm coming now. You can feel my pussy squeezing your cock. Come with me."

"Yes," Frank groaned. Then his eyes flew open. "No." He pushed Maggie's foot from his lap. "Not here."

"No. Not here," Maggie said. "But I need a trip to the ladies' room first." To remove her pantyhose. When she returned, Frank was waiting for her with her coat in his hands. "My hotel is just around the corner."

Maggie slipped her arms into the sleeves. "Good," she said. "I find I'm in a bit of a hurry."

"Are you sure you're not a professional at this? No offense."

"No offense taken. And no, I'm not a pro."

"Well, you should be. I've been with my share of professional entertainers and no one holds a candle to you."

As they walked out of the restaurant, Maggie asked, "You've been with call girls?"

"Sure. Sometimes the company provides entertainment for the out-of-town reps. And not one of them could come close to the way you turn me on. That little story back there . . ." He wrapped his arm around her shoulder. "Holy shit."

"I enjoy turning men on. I dated a lot before I met Bob, and then he taught me about fantasy and lots of variations on straight sex. I love it all."

"You should get paid for it."

"How much do call girls make?"

"The classy ones like you make hundreds a night."

"Hundreds of dollars?" Maggie gasped.

They turned the corner and approached Frank's hotel. "Sure. I know a few people and I could introduce you."

"Hmmm."

Maggie looked at Barbara. "The evening went exactly like the fantasy we had created." She took a drink from her coffee cup. "And he introduced me to someone who introduced me to someone else and, as they say, the rest is history."

"Wow."

"Yes. Wow. And I entertained men for twenty years."

"Did you ever have any bad experiences? You read about hookers getting beaten up and stuff."

"I had one or two men who didn't get the message when I told them to knock it off, but I know how to defend myself and I seldom take chances. All the men I entertain, er . . . entertained—it's so hard for me to think of myself in the past tense. The men I entertained were all recommended, lonely business types who just wanted someone to have some fun with. You know, do the things they wouldn't do with their wives."

"Like?"

"Mostly oral sex and anal sex. Some were into power fantasies, both giving and receiving and a few were into pain."

"You mean like whips?"

"I slapped a few men on the ass, but I never did whips because I can't get pleasure out of that. Heavy pain is such a turn-off for me that I made it clear I wouldn't play those games. But most other things were as exciting for me as they were for the men I was with."

"That's amazing."

Maggie looked at her watch. "It's getting late. Get your pocketbook and your credit cards and we're off to shop."

Barbara stood up. "I can't wait."

Chapter 4

"Now this doesn't mean I'm going to jump into someone's bed so fast," Barbara said under her breath as they walked into the Galleria Mall in White Plains. "You can't make a silk purse and all that."

"Let's first get you dressed and looking like the attractive woman you are," Maggie said. As they walked, the few shoppers they saw walked around Barbara but seemed unaware that Maggie was there. "You know," Maggie said, turning to stare at a woman with a stroller who had just missed bumping into her, "I don't think anyone can see me."

"But I can see you just fine," Barbara said.

They walked passed a large clothing store and paused in front of a mirrored section of wall. "I can see us both," Barbara said as Maggie dodged to avoid a mother pushing a blue-and-white stroller.

"It's really weird," Maggie said. "I'm here. I can see me." She rubbed her arms. "I can feel me, hear me. You can, too. But to judge by the people walking by, I don't exist."

"But you do exist," Barbara said.

"Mommy," a little girl said as she passed, "why is that woman talking to herself?"

"Let's go, darling," the mother said, hustling the tot off. "It's not nice to talk about . . ."

As the woman's voice faded, Maggie said, "We better be careful. People will think you're nuts."

As they strolled around the mall, getting the lay of the land, Barbara was careful not to speak to Maggie where anyone might overhear. Together the two women stopped periodically so Maggie could show Barbara outfits and shoes that would fit her new image. With Maggie steering, the two walked toward a hair salon called Expert Tresses. "We really should start with your hair."

"I like my hair," Barbara said, reflexively tucking a strand behind her ear. "It's easy and comfortable."

Maggie raised an eyebrow. "Easy and comfortable. Two of the most awful adjectives I can think of." She stopped and turned Barbara to face her. She peered at a section of hair just above her right temple. "What's this? The roots are white here."

"I was hoping we could overlook that. It's a white streak. My mother used to call it a witch's mark."

"You dye it?"

"My mother started doing that for me when I was a kid. It's just dyed to match the rest of my hair."

"It's sexy as hell. I want you to get someone to style this mop," Maggie said, staring at Barbara's soft, medium-brown hair. "And get the dye out of that section."

"But it's unlucky and creepy. I won't."

"Barbara, baby. It's unique and beautiful and it looks great. Your mother was a wonderful lady, but in this one instance, she was wrong. Please. Cooperate. Try this."

"No."

"Look," Maggie said, guiding Barbara into a small alcove. "Do this for me and for this project. Let someone do your hair. My way. Then give it one week. If you don't like it, you can dye it back. Okay? Please. I have a job to do here."

When Barbara hesitated, Maggie continued. "And get your nails done, too."

"But . . ."

Maggie put a hand in the small of Barbara's back and pushed, aiming her toward Expert Tresses. Since the salon was almost empty, three women walked toward her as she walked in. "May we help you?"

"I need a haircut," Barbara said.

"You want it styled," Maggie said, knowing that no one else could hear.

"I want it styled."

One of the women looked her over. "My name's Candy and I think you're mine this morning. Come on over here." The pink-smocked woman led Barbara to a chair at one side of the studio.

"I have a streak right here," Barbara said, fingering a section of hair as Candy covered Barbara's clothes with a plastic apron.

"Yes, I see," Candy said. "Why do you dye it?"

"It's a witch's mark."

"And it's so kinky." Candy lifted a strand of her long blond hair from her temple. "It wouldn't look as good on me," she said. She returned her attention to Barbara. "But on you . . ."

"Well . . ."

As they started to talk about styles, Maggie said, "She sounds like she knows what she's talking about, so let her do whatever she wants. I'll be back." Over her shoulder, she called, "And don't forget the nails."

Maggie left the salon and walked purposefully back to the mirrored section of wall. With people unable to see her, Maggie stood staring at herself. Since no one could hear her, she talked aloud to herself. "It's been six months since I, whatever, and my hair hasn't grown nor does it need to be colored." She looked down. "My nails are perfect and I don't look any older." She walked close to the mirror and stared at her skin. "No new lines. No signs of age. Nothing."

"And you won't age," a voice she recognized as Angela's said. "You'll just continue as you were on the day you died. That's one of the advantages of an assignment like this."

"Have you done this kind of thing often?" Maggie asked.

"Not really, but it does happen occasionally," Lucy said. "How's it going?"

"Don't you know?"

"Not really," Angela said. "We don't have the time to watch what's happening. We just drop in from time to time."

"Could Barbara hear you if she were here?"

"No," Angela continued. "Only you can hear us, and see us if it becomes necessary. But creating corporeal images on earth is very energy inefficient and in most cases unnecessary."

"How do you like Barbara?" Lucy asked.

"Actually, she's really nice. But mousy. She's got zero self-confidence. Even with a good hairstyle and attractive clothes, she's not going to be a beauty."

"You're not a Miss America candidate yourself," Lucy said.

"Oh now, Lucy," Angela said, "that's unkind."

"Look you two," Maggie said, "I know I'm not gorgeous, but I'm attractive. I use what I've got and I've never wanted for companions, paid and unpaid."

"That's the first lesson your friend Barbara has to learn," Angela said. "It's the gleam in the eye not the meat on the bones that makes a woman sexy."

"Listen, we've got other fish to fry, as it were," Lucy said. "Go pick Barbara up. She's waiting for you."

"But it's only been about five minutes," Maggie protested.

"You already know that time has little meaning in your existence," Angela said. "Go pick her up."

Her head now empty of voices, Maggie walked back to Expert Tresses and, sure enough, Barbara had just finished signing the charge slip. Maggie looked her friend over. The white streak was now prominent in Barbara's slightly darkened, carefully cut brown hair. Styled so it fell just at her shoulders, her hair curled up at the ends and moved gracefully as Barbara moved. She looked at Maggie and shrugged.

"You look just great," Maggie said. "What an improvement. And you've got makeup on."

Barbara stuffed the charge-card receipt into her wallet and walked out of the salon. "It's hard remembering not to talk to you where anyone might hear."

"Sorry."

"Candy gave me a few tips about foundation and eye makeup so I bought a few things and she and another woman helped me put this stuff on. Does it look okay?"

Maggie studied Barbara's light taupe shadow, soft brown liner, blush, and lipstick. "You really look nice. You'll need more for evenings, of course, but for day wear, it's just great."

Barbara stopped at the same mirrored section of the wall. "You really think so? It's so obvious. I look made up."

"You look like you took some time to enhance your looks. That's great. You don't always have to look like you got up late for work."

"I don't . . ."

"You do most of the time. There's nothing wrong with taking a little time to look good."

"It's vain."

"It's just good sense. Vanity in large doses is bad. Feeling good about the way you look is good. Let's see what we can do now about your wardrobe."

"After lunch. I'm starving."

"We just had breakfast."

Barbara looked at her watch. "That was almost five hours ago and I, for one, am famished."

In the food court, Barbara bought a corned beef sandwich with fries and a pickle. With her plate in one hand and a 7Up in the other, she found a small table off to one side of the seating area. She sat with her back to the other shoppers so she could talk to Maggie without everyone thinking she was nuts. As they talked, Maggie occasionally picked up a french fry and nibbled on it. Barbara wondered what others would see if they looked. Would a french fry just lift up into the air, then disappear?

The two women then spent the afternoon doing serious damage to Barbara's credit card. They bought several soft bright-colored silk blouses and two skirts, considerably shorter than Barbara had been used to. "You have great legs," Maggie said several times. "Show them off. You want to catch the eye of that boss of yours, don't you?"

Unable to argue without seeming like a nut, Barbara went along. In a shoe boutique, Maggie bullied Barbara into purchasing a pair of black, two-and-a-half-inch high opera pumps and a pair of knee-high brown butter-soft suede boots with stiletto heels.

As they started for the parking lot of the mall, Maggie spotted a Victoria's Secret store. "Let's go in," she said.

"I have underwear," Barbara said.

"I'll bet not the right kind."

Barbara had just about given up arguing so together the two women entered the store. Maggie all but dragged her friend to a display of lacy bra and panty sets. Both the bra and the panty were mostly net with flowers embroidered in strategic places. "Get the black one, the white one, and the light blue."

"But, Maggie," Barbara said, "they're so slutty."

A saleswoman whirled around. "Yes," she said, "can I help you? I'm sorry I didn't hear your last question."

"I wasn't talking to you."

The saleswoman looked around, then shrugged. "Those lace sets are on sale," she said. "It's buy two and get the third for a dollar."

"The black, the white, and the light blue," Maggie said, knowing she couldn't be heard by anyone but Barbara. "And don't argue. You know you want them and you don't ever have to wear them. Just indulge me."

"Okay," Barbara said, looking at the pleasant saleswoman. "I'll take the light blue and the white."

"A third set will only cost a dollar more."

Maggie tapped her foot and arched an eyebrow.

"Okay," Barbara agreed. "I guess I'll take the black as well."

"Good choice," the woman said. "And the size?"

"It's been a long time since I bought undies. Maybe I better try them on." She selected bras in three different sizes.

"Certainly," the woman said and showed Barbara to the fitting room.

In the tiny room, Barbara pulled off her shirt and bra and put the new white one on. Maggie appeared in the corner of the mirrored room and let out a low whistle. "You've got a great body, you know."

Barbara turned sideways, raised her rib cage and sucked in her tummy. "I could have if I never breathed again." When she relaxed, her belly bulged a bit and her diaphragm protruded.

"You've got a very nice figure," Maggie said. "And those bits of stuff you're wearing do wonders."

Barbara looked at the white lace bra she wore. She really didn't look half bad, she had to admit. The flowers woven into the fabric were designed so that leaves and blossoms covered her nipples but the rest was almost transparent.

"Very sexy," Maggie said. "Yes, very nice. I think your boss would approve."

Barbara blushed. "He will never see me like this," she said, replacing the silk with her serviceable cotton undies.

"He will if you want him to. He'll notice you and he'd be a fool not to be impressed. You will go into the office tomorrow a different woman."

Barbara smiled.

The following morning, Barbara showered and, when she returned to her bedroom, Maggie was sitting on her bed. "Wear that new cornflower blue blouse with the black skirt. And the light-blue bra and panties."

As Barbara reached for her traditional underwear, she asked, "What difference does it make what I wear underneath?"

"If you feel sexy under your clothes, it affects the way you behave. I want you to spend the day knowing that your breasts are being held by that wonderful erotic fabric."

"But . . ."

"Do what I ask, Barbara," Maggie said. "Trust me. You want him to notice you, don't you?"

"Well, yes."

"Good. So do it my way, just this once."

Barbara sighed and dressed as Maggie had suggested. After a quick breakfast, Barbara put on her coat. "Will you be at work with me today?"

"No," Maggie answered. "I'll see you here tonight and you can tell me all about it."

Barbara arrived at work at two minutes before eight, got her coffee and settled down to work. Her boss was in court that morning and wasn't due in until after lunch. Except for a quick trip to the ladies' room, Barbara stayed huddled at her desk all morning. The people who passed by noticed her new hairstyle and makeup and several commented cheerfully on how lovely she looked. One woman complimented her on the silver streak in her hair and a young male associate actually winked at her, something that had never happened before.

Throughout her almost solitary morning, she occasionally forgot her makeover, but then she would look down at her hands typing or dialing the phone and her nicely shaped nails, polished in a medium pink, reminded her again. Maybe Steve would notice her, like in one of those romantic movies. "Oh my goodness, Barbara," he would say, "I never realized." She smiled at the thought, then shook her head and got back to work.

As she usually did, Barbara ate lunch at her desk, then returned to work, her eyes glued on the screen of her word processor. At one-thirty, she jumped as her intercom buzzer sounded. She picked up the phone and her boss said, without preamble, "Barbara, I hope you finished the Sanderson documents. Mr. and Mrs. Sanderson are due here at two for the closing." Barbara realized that she had been so engrossed in hiding her new look that she hadn't even heard Steve come in.

She prided herself on her efficiency and always had documents completed long before they were needed. "Of course, Mr. Gordon, I've got them whenever you're ready."

"I wondered with that day off you took yesterday. Bring them in here, will you?"

"Certainly, Mr. Gordon." Barbara stood up, carefully arranged her black wool skirt and straightened the collar on her periwinkle blouse. As she walked into her boss's office, he was bent over, rifling through his briefcase which lay open on the floor beside his desk. "Damn," he swore, "I can't find a thing in here. Barbara, help me, will you?"

"What are you looking for?" Barbara asked, putting the documents she held on his desk.

"The Norton file. I had it just before lunch."

Barbara crouched, exposing a long expanse of thigh and began to systematically go through the contents of Mr. Gordon's briefcase. "It's right here," she said, quickly locating the missing file. As she looked up, she saw Mr. Gordon staring at her.

"What have you done with yourself?" he asked.

"I just got a few new things."

"And had your hair done, and got new makeup. Stand up."

Barbara stood, trying not the back up under his intense scrutiny. She watched his eyes travel from her hair to her heels and back up, several times. Then he released a long, low wolf whistle. "Not bad."

"Thank you, sir," Barbara said, straightening her shoulders. "I just felt I could use a lift."

"Well, you certainly got a lift." He stared for another full minute, then cleared his throat. "Okay. I see you have the Sanderson closing documents. I think everything should be in order. I have some notes from court this morning that need to be typed up."

Barbara sat in the small chair across from Steve Gordon's desk, smoothed her skirt and crossed her legs. As she arranged her computer on her lap, she caught Mr. Gordon staring at her knees. She sat, waiting for him to begin. "Mr. Gordon, I'm ready whenever you are."

"You know we've been together for how long? Almost two years?"

"Actually, it's almost six years."

"Well, don't you think it's about time you started calling me Steve?"

Totally taken aback, Barbara said, "I guess so, Mr. Gordon. I mean Steve."

"Good." He hesitated, then opened the folder in his hand. "I had a call from Mrs. Norton this morning. Take this down . . ."

At four-thirty, Barbara cleared the top of her desk, locked her laptop in her drawer and got her coat. As she was about to leave, Steve came out of his office. "Good night, Barbara," he said cheerfully. "And by the way, that silver patch of hair is very, well, very attractive. Have a nice evening. Got a date?"

"No, sir, I mean Steve. No date."

Steve put his arm around her waist and guided her toward the elevator. "Well then, maybe there will be time for me some evening."

Unable to breathe, Barbara merely nodded as the elevator doors opened.

"Well, have a nice evening."

"And he suggested that we might have dinner sometime," Barbara told Maggie several hours later. It was all Maggie could do not to swear when Barbara mentioned the whistle. He reminds me more and more of Arnie Becker, she thought.

"He looked at me," Barbara continued, unaware of Maggie's reaction. "I mean, really looked. He thought I looked good."

"Well, you do look good. Did work go well, too?"

"Sure. We did the Sanderson closing. I had caught a few minor errors and fixed them before they became problems. I also checked on the title insurance for him."

"What would he do without you?" Maggie said dryly.

"You're not happy for me, Maggie," Barbara said. "I don't understand."

"Sorry. I'm the one who helped you with the makeover and all and I'm glad you're pleased. It's just I have a basic dislike for men who only notice women when they're attractive."

"Oh, Maggie," Barbara said, sipping a glass of Chardonnay while she sautéed chicken and vegetables. Since Maggie's arrival, she was beginning to develop a taste for wine with dinner. "That's not really true. He always knew I was there. He just, well, you know. He's got other things on his mind."

Maggie patted Barbara on the shoulder. "I do know, baby. And maybe he'll ask you out. Is that what you want?"

"Oh, that would be wonderful. Dinner, maybe a little dancing."

"Ah, yes. Slow dancing. A wonderful way to make love standing up."

"You know, I never thought of it that way, but you're right. Making love standing up." Barbara placed the chicken mixture on two plates and sat across from her friend. In only two days it had become comfortable to have Maggie around. She had a friend.

"Do you like making love?" Maggie asked, anxious to move Barbara along to phase two of her makeover.

"It's not like it is in the novels I like to read, but the few times I did it it was tolerable."

"Tolerable. What a terrible way to think about making love. No bells? No stars? The earth didn't move?"

"That doesn't happen to people like me. That's for glitzy novels and X-rated movies."

"It can happen, and it does, and it should."

Barbara sipped her wine, her curiosity aroused. "Did the earth move for you?"

"You mean did I climax?"

Blushing slightly, Barbara nodded.

"No, not every time I made love. It takes a bit of effort and consideration on the part of both partners for orgasm to occur. But I did more often than not. I found that my men friends liked it when I came even though they were paying me to be sure *they* climaxed."

"But you only discovered good sex after your divorce."

"That's true and a bit sad. I regret that Chuck and I never found out what good sex was all about."

"Do you and he still see each other? I mean, did you? Does he know what you do, er . . . did?"

"Boy, tenses are a problem, aren't they. Anyway, no, I don't see Chuck anymore. He and his new wife moved to the West Coast many years ago. We had no kids, no ties, not much in common except a lot of history, and reminiscing wears thin very quickly."

"Can I ask you a question?"

"Sure." Maggie watched Barbara sip her wine as if searching for the right words. "Look, Barbara," Maggie said, "you can ask anything you want. I may choose not to answer, but please, we're friends and this is a really strange situation."

"As a, . . . let's say woman of the evening, you had to do all kinds of things with your customers. Is all that kinky stuff really fun?"

"You mean like oral sex and bondage?"

Barbara merely nodded.

"There are a thousand things people enjoy in the bedroom. Some enjoy plain straight sex, missionary position. Some enjoy telling stories in the dark, tying a partner up, spanking, anal sex. There are probably as many variations as you can dream of. Most I enjoy, a few I don't. But that's true with all things. I love almost all foods, but I hate liver and lima beans."

Barbara laughed. "What sex-type things don't you enjoy?"

"I already told you that I don't find pain pleasurable." Maggie thought a minute, then continued. "That's about all."

"Pain? That's sick."

"No, it's not. Listen, I hate to sound preachy, but I think this is very important. Anything that two consenting adults get pleasure from is none of anyone else's business and isn't sick. As long as both partners know it's important to say no if anything feels the least bit wrong, anything else is okay."

"I guess. How did you discover which things you enjoyed and which you didn't?"

"Trial and error. Lots of trial," Maggie grinned, "and a few errors."

"Errors?"

"Sure. I got myself into a few situations where I had to give someone his money back."

"Were they mad?"

"Not really. There was one guy from the Midwest. I won't go into details, but he wanted me to hurt him. Knowing that it would please him, I tried to do what he wanted, but I couldn't. However, I had a friend who was more into the pain side of pleasure than I was so I called her. He put on his clothes and hustled over to her house. He was so grateful that he called me the next day. He told me it had been everything he had ever fantasized about."

"No accounting for taste, is there?"

"No. And you may find as time passes that there are things you enjoy that you never dreamed of."

Barbara looked startled. "I'm not interested in kinky stuff. I don't mean to put you down, it's just that I'm not that type of person."

"You have no idea what type of person you are. I'll bet you have no real idea of what gives you pleasure."

"Of course I do." Barbara got a dreamy look in her eyes.

"You want romance, slow dancing, kissing and hugging. Long, slow sex with gentle penetration and a long rest period afterward."

"Sure. Why not?"

"No reason. But there's much more to good fucking than that."

"Fucking. Such a terrible word. It's so animal."

"That's what we are, animals. And human beings enjoy a good fucking as much as the average animal does. You know when you think of it, sex is a really awkward and embarrassing thing to do. It violates any feelings of personal space you might have, you get into lots of not-too-comfortable positions, and it's really messy."

"I never thought about it that way."

"So in order to create offspring, God, or Mother Nature, or evolution had to give the animals some reward for doing this ridiculous stuff. So that's where the pleasure comes in. I read somewhere that animals will go through much more maze-running and the like for sexual gratification than for any other reward."

"It's really pleasurable, isn't it?"

"It really is. I doubt you've ever experienced an orgasm."

"Of course I have."

Maggie raised an eyebrow and Barbara looked down and sipped her wine. "There's no shame in not having climaxed. It takes time and an understanding of your own body. You're not born knowing, you have to learn. Do you know where you like to be touched? What makes you hungry for more?"

Barbara continued to stare into her wineglass.

Maggie reached into her pocket and found the audiotape she had somehow known would be there. She pulled it out and stared at the label. "I don't understand how this got into my pocket, but there's a lot about my assignment I don't quite get yet. This is one tape in a series that a friend of mine made. He creates sensational erotica and has a soft, sexy voice, so he found this unique way to package his stories." She put the tape into Barbara's hand. "I'm going to give you an assignment."

Barbara looked up and giggled. "Homework?"

"Sort of. You must have a tape player." When Barbara nodded, Maggie continued. "I want you to fill the bathtub with nice warm water and play this tape. Just play it. If you're tempted to follow the instructions you'll be given, do it. No one will be watching, no one judging. Just you. Will you do that for me?" When her friend hesitated, Maggie said, "Please?"

"If it's important to you and your assignment."

"It is."

"Okay."

"Good." Maggie patted the back of Barbara's hand. "And find a new bar of soap, one you've never used of a different brand than your usual. You'll understand eventually. And I'll see you tomorrow evening."

Before Barbara could react, Maggie strode through the kitchen door and was gone.

An hour later, Barbara tidied up the kitchen and ran herself a bath. She had always loved the huge tub in the master bathroom. It was deep enough to fully cover her body almost to her shoulders. "This is pretty silly," Barbara said out loud as she plugged in an old cassette player she had recovered from the back of her closet. But if it was important to Maggie, it was important to her, she realized. In two short days she had gone from incredulity and scorn to friendship. She rummaged in the back of the bathroom closet and found a new bar of soap, then pressed the cassette machine's play button and stepped into the steamy water.

Music filled the bathroom, music with a quiet yet pulsing beat and a soft, slightly mournful clarinet and a baritone saxophone. The sounds that filled the room felt like soft summer nights with the sky filled with stars. Barbara thought of couples in open-topped cars staring down at city lights from darkened lover's overlooks. She rolled a small towel and placed it at the back of her neck and stretched out. She sighed deeply and relaxed.

"Are you all relaxed?" a soft, sensuous man's voice asked as the music faded slightly. "That's very good." Barbara started to sit up. "No, don't move," the voice said. "Just lie back and relax. Let the music fill you, create dreams, fantasies. Let it evoke pictures of teenagers in parked cars."

How did that man know what she was thinking? Barbara wondered. The music swelled again, and for several minutes the voice was silent. Then the music faded slightly and the voice returned.

"I hope you're naked, lying in a tub of warm water. The naked female body is such a wonder. It's so beautiful."

Yeah, right, Barbara thought. For all he knows, I'm a dog, a hundred pounds overweight with droopy boobs and three stomachs.

"Don't think like that. All female bodies are beautiful regardless of the way they actually look. Breasts are soft, firm, large or small. Nipples are chocolate brown or dark pink. Skin is deep ebony or almost transparent white. God, I love a woman's

breasts. And your bellies are concave, with prominent hipbones, or full and round. I love to feel the pulse in a woman's throat and know how it speeds up when she listens to me tell her how beautiful she is. Can you feel your pulse? Find it by stroking your throat. Go ahead. No one's watching."

Without really thinking, Barbara slid a wet finger up her neck and felt her pulsebeat.

"That's your life flowing throughout your body. You can feel it all over, in your wrist, in your foot, at your temple, in your groin. If I tell you that I want you to imagine me touching your breasts, does your pulse speed up? I love that I can do that for you."

Barbara felt her pulse. No silly man's voice was going to make her pulse beat faster. But it did.

"I want you to make your hands all soapy. Please, for me. Feel the soap, so smooth and slippery. Rub your hands over the bar, touching its contours. Close your eyes and just feel the soap as your hands caress it."

Barbara took the soap from the holder and rubbed it. She was strangely aware of the slick surface.

"Take the soap and make a rich lather, then slowly rub it on your throat. Feel the difference between the hard surface of the cake of soap and the soft, warm skin of your body. Move your hands around. Feel your jaw, the back of your neck. Now caress your cheeks. How smooth and soft they are through the lather. Keep your eyes closed and just feel. Feel rough and smooth spots, places that are warm and those that are cool. If you have fingernails, use them to scratch your shoulders, just lightly."

Barbara did, her eyes closed, her head resting against the towel on the rim of the tub.

"You need more lather, so rub the soap again. Can you smell the perfume? Does your soap smell like flowers or spice? Can you picture a field of summer blossoms or an Oriental harem?

*Maybe lemons or blackberries. Inhale deeply. Fill your lungs
with the scent and imagine."*

As the music filled the room, Barbara breathed deeply and saw a Pa-
risian boudoir with perfume bottles on a mirrored vanity. She vaguely
remembered her mother buying her this soap many years before. She lay
there seeing the boudoir. A woman sat at the vanity putting on makeup.
She was dressed in a filmy negligee, waiting for her lover. Barbara
opened her eyes. Now why had she created that scene? Waiting for her
lover, indeed.

*"I hope your eyes are still closed," the voice said softly. Bar-
bara snapped her eyes shut. "I want you to feel other places on
your body. Start with your breasts. Your soapy hands will feel so
good on your soft flesh. I want you to use the pads of your fingers
to stroke the flesh of your breasts, just around the outside. Press
a bit and feel. Are your breasts full, or small and tight? As I told
you, I like them all. Can you feel your ribs or is there deep softness? Please. I can't be there to feel your skin so you must do it
for me."*

Tentatively Barbara sat up slightly so the tops of her breasts were
above the waterline. She slid her soapy fingers over the crests, then
pressed her fingertips into the flesh. Deeply soft and pillowy, she
thought.

*"Find the areolas, just where the color changes, darkens.
Open your eyes if you must, then close them again. Run one fingertip over the slight ridge there, all around. Keep swirling
around that line. Can you feel your nipples tighten? No, not with
your fingers, but feel it inside. Don't look, feel. Can you feel your
nipples contract? Yes, I know they will."*

They did.

*"I wish I were there to touch your nipples. I would first swirl
my fingers around the outside the way you are doing it. Then I
wouldn't be able to resist sliding toward the tightened buds. I
want to feel them but I can't, so you will have to do it for me.
Touch. Squeeze. That's what I would do. I would squeeze those
tight nipples. It's hard to feel it when you touch lightly so make*

*yourself feel it. Do what you have to so that you know the touch
of your fingers. Pinch, use your nails."*

Barbara used her newly manicured nails to tweak the tips of her
breasts. She felt it, tight, slightly painful yet very stimulating.

*"I know you think this is strange and maybe you feel a bit
guilty, but it's your body and you are entitled to touch it. It's
God's creation and so beautiful. I know also that you're noticing
that you're not just feeling your fingers touching your breasts. You
are also starting to become aware of the flesh between your legs.
You're feeling full, maybe getting wet, not from your bath but
from your excitement."*

Barbara was aware of her groin. This is ridiculous, she thought, yank-
ing herself from her dreamy state. It's dirty.

*"I know you feel that what you're doing isn't what nice girls
are supposed to do, but that's nonsense. Feeling sexual and sensual is wonderful. It is what I would want you to be experiencing
if I were there. Relax. You and I are alone. No one will know, or
care, what you're doing. You are just making your body feel good.
What is wrong with that?"*

Nothing, Barbara thought, taking a deep breath. Nothing at all. He's
right. It is my body and I can touch it. That's why it was designed to feel
good.

*"I know you want to touch the flesh between your legs and
that's so good. I get so much pleasure out of knowing I excite
you. I know the water covers the parts of you that you want to
touch, but you must make your hands soapy and slippery anyway.
Do it for me since I can't caress you myself. Rub the soap while I
tell you what I'd like to be doing if I were there."*

Barbara picked up the soap and rubbed, closing her eyes as she did so.

*"If I were there with you I would cup your beautiful breasts
in my hands and lick the water off the tips with my rough tongue.
I would suckle and lick, and maybe nip the erect tip from time to
time with my sharp teeth. Can you feel me? I hope so. Don't*

touch yourself, just rub the soap and imagine my teeth and lips and tongue. Imagine what they are doing and how they make you feel. Are you getting tight between your legs? Do you want to touch? That hunger is what I want you to feel. Think of how my fingers would feel touching your ribs, your sides, your belly. If you're ticklish, I can touch you so it feels good, yet not make you laugh. I don't want you to giggle right now, although laughter is wonderful. Do you want me to touch you?"

The erotic music and the man's voice filled Barbara's ears, penetrating to her soul. Yes, she admitted, she did want him to touch her.

"I can't touch you, you know, and that makes me so sad. But you can touch all those places I cannot. Rub your palm over your belly. Scratch the skin on your sides. Now the insides of your thighs. Rub, caress, stroke. It's your skin and it feels so good."

Barbara had never touched herself like this before and it was a bit embarrassing. But it felt good and she didn't really consider stopping.

"Move your fingers closer to the center of all that you need. You want to touch. Do you know how? Do you know what would feel good? Well, I do. It would feel good if you rubbed the wet, slippery place. Find that place and know the difference between the water and your own slippery juices. Feel that slick, slithery substance? Your body is making that to make it easier for me to penetrate you, but, of course, I cannot. But you can.

"Have you ever wondered what you feel like inside? Under the water, make sure your fingers have no soap left on them. Then slide one into your passage. Touch the slick walls, rub all the places you can and find out which feels the best. I would learn that if I were there. I would know when you moan or purr, when your hips move to take me in more deeply, when you become wetter and more slippery. I would know the secrets of your pleasure, and you know them now, too. Run your fingers over the outside folds. Use the other hand if you like the feel of that finger inside you."

Barbara did have one finger inside her channel, in a place she had never touched before. It felt very good and she wanted more. She used the middle finger of her other hand to rub the deep crevices, moving from side to side, enjoying her own flesh.

"Have you found your clit? I would have by now. I would have rubbed up and down both sides, feeling the tight nub swell and reach for me. I would have put one finger on either side and rubbed. Oh, that does feel good, doesn't it. I can almost see your back arch, your eyes close, and your mouth open. Put a second finger inside your body to fill it up, and a third if that feels good. Rub your clit and all the places that feel as good."

Barbara was stroking her body, marveling at all the spots that gave her pleasure.

"If I were there, I would use my mouth now. No, it's not a bad thing. It's a beautiful experience. I would lick your clit, flick my tongue over the end, then wrap my lips around it and draw it into my mouth. Just a slight vacuum to suck it in and hold it while my tongue rubs the surface. Just don't stop what you're doing while I lick you."

Barbara filled her pussy with her fingers and rubbed her clit, feeling the pressure in her belly. This was dirty, but so good. She didn't want to stop, and she didn't. The words and the music and the rubbing and the fullness inside all drove her higher. She felt something build deep in her belly, then suddenly waves of ecstatic pleasure spasmed through her.

"Oh, yes, my wonderful girl," the voice said. *"Make it feel so good."*

Barbara continued as the clenching subsided.

"I will not talk anymore, but leave you to the music and to your pleasure," the voice said. *"Until the next time."*

"Oh," Barbara said, panting. "Oh."

Chapter 5

For the next several days, the tape was never far from Barbara's mind. She thought about that night in the tub and, with guilty pleasure, repeated the experience several times, twice while listening to the tape and, more recently, once while picturing Steve Gordon. That had happened at almost three in the morning when Barbara awakened from an erotic dream, a dream she couldn't remember but one that left her so excited that she had to reach beneath her nightgown and touch herself to relieve the tension. As she touched her body, now able to find the places that gave her pleasure, she thought about her boss, his slender hands with their long fingers and carefully trimmed nails. She could almost feel those hands on her body as she climaxed.

Maggie showed up at dinner time every two or three days and they talked about inconsequentials. Barbara was dying to ask questions about Maggie's life as a prostitute but never seemed to be able to work up the nerve.

One evening almost two weeks after Maggie's first visit, Barbara said, "There's an office party tomorrow night. It's a celebration for a big case the firm won, and they've invited all of their clients, all of the staff and who knows who else. Steve, Mr. Gordon, told me that he's looking forward to seeing me there. I think he might be ready to ask me to dinner."

"That's great. Will you go if he asks you?"

"Sure. It makes my palms sweat just thinking about it."

"I'm sure it does." Maggie grinned and arched an eyebrow. "So. He makes you hot, does he?"

"Maggie!" Barbara said. "That's not it at all. He's a very nice man and I'd like to get to know him better. That's all." The thought of her middle-of-the-night fantasies made her blush slightly.

"Okay. I won't tease. But being hot, horny, and hungry isn't a crime. As a matter of fact, it's delightful. It's a high, frustrating but delicious." Maggie hesitated. "I've been meaning to ask, did you like that tape?"

Barbara blushed several shades darker. "I'll get it for you. I'm sorry. I forgot to return it and now I'm not too sure where I put it."

Maggie reached out and covered Barbara's hand with her own, calming the nervous fingers. "Don't. Just don't. You and I both know you're lying. That tape is meant to do exactly what it did. It woke you up to things about your body you didn't know. That's why I gave it to you and that's why you can keep it. Sensuality is a joy and, once awakened, well, let's just say that it's very difficult to get the genie back into the bottle."

Barbara sighed. She couldn't hide anything from Maggie. The woman was too perceptive. And anyway, there was so much that Barbara didn't know. "Maggie, you're right. This is silly. But it's very difficult, after thirty-one years on this earth to admit that I'm such a dunce about sex."

"How are you supposed to learn?" Maggie said. "All those articles in *Cosmo?* How to have an orgasm any hour of the day or night. How to lure the man of your dreams into your camper. The things about men that women don't want men to know they know. Oh, please. Give me a break."

Barbara laughed. "I read those," she said.

"And many of them have good information. But many others are pure crap. How to climax seven times in three hours. Everyone in those articles is a stud, male and female. Let's hear it for people who like to make love, climax once or twice and cuddle. Sex is so much more than how many times a man ejaculates or a woman has an orgasm."

"It is?"

"Oh, Lord, darling," Maggie said. "Sex isn't the destination, it's the journey. It's how you get to that wonderful level of excitement that allows both partners to soar together, then relax. Did you even think that if it weren't for orgasm and the calm afterward, we'd be chasing each other all the time and we'd never get anything else done. Orgasm is the final chord in the symphony, but it's the music before that counts."

"Oh" was all that Barbara could say.

"I don't mean to preach, but I just love making love."

"But isn't there one right man, one person, who knocks your socks off? One man with whom you'd like to climb into bed for the next hundred years? What about your husband?"

"When Chuck and I were married I thought it was forever and I settled down, worked, fucked, and enjoyed. But even then I used to imagine handsome men adoring me, licking and touching me. I wasn't quite clear on exactly what they would be doing, just doing kinky things to my quivering body."

"Really?" Barbara said, grinning.

"Sure. Chuck and I had a good relationship, but it wasn't enough for either of us. He found his SueAnn. She's probably a lovely girl, and because of her I was pushed out of the plain-vanilla nest I had been in, into the world of Heavenly Hash." Maggie grinned. "And let's hear it for all twenty-eight flavors."

"There's no one special? No one man who you ever wished would take you away to a deserted cabin and keep you there forever?"

"Not really. I love the deserted cabin idea for a weekend, but one man? For life? I don't think so. Someone once said that if the plural of louse is lice, then the plural of spouse should be spice. I just happen to like lots of spice."

"Well, I'm not like you," Barbara said, somehow wondering whether what she was saying was entirely true. "I just want one man to love me and make a life with me."

"That's wonderful. Everyone should try to figure out what his or her dream is, then go for it. If that's what you want, then let's see what we can do to make it come true. Steve Gordon?"

Barbara's grin widened. "He could be the one."

"Why?" Maggie asked.

"Why?"

"Yes. What about him makes him the right one. I don't know him much at all. Tell me. Does he have a great sense of humor? Do you two share many common interests? Is he moody or more placid? Is he easy to be with?"

"Actually, I don't really know. I haven't spent much time with him. He's not too bad to work for. He understood about my mom and let me take time off when I needed it. And he depends on me to keep him going. I'm valuable to him."

"That's not a reason to make a life with someone. He has to be valuable to you as well."

"Of course he is," Barbara said. "He's wonderful."

"Okay, great." Maggie stood up. "What about this party? How dressed up is it?"

"It's cocktail dress."

"So. What are you going to wear? You want him to notice you, don't you?"

"I do. I mean, he does." Actually, he had noticed her the first few days after her dramatic makeover, but since then it had been business as usual.

Several of the other men in the office seemed to pay more attention to her new persona than Steve did. One man had actually asked her to dinner, but she had politely refused, preferring to meet with Maggie and concentrate on Steve.

"All right then, let's decide what you should wear. I saw a dress in the back of your closet the first night I was here."

The two women went upstairs and Maggie quickly pulled out the dress. "How about this?"

"Oh, Maggie. I bought that as a favor to my mom. It was one of the last shopping trips we took together before she became bed-ridden. I've never even worn it."

"Why not?"

"It's so, I don't know, obvious." She took the hanger from Maggie. The halter shaped chiffon bodice was soft blue with a full skirt that shaded from the pale blue of the top to a deep royal at the hem. She pointed to the low-cut back. "You can't even wear a bra. I couldn't wear this."

"Try it on for me," Maggie asked. "Come on, what will it hurt. Only I will see you."

With a deep sigh, Barbara stripped off her clothes and slipped into the dress. She adjusted the wide medium-blue belt and fastened the rhinestone buckle. While she was doing that, Maggie was rummaging around on the floor of Barbara's closet. Suddenly there was a triumphant "Taa Daa" and Maggie tossed out a pair of strappy black patent-leather sandals. "Put those on."

Barbara did, then the two women looked at Barbara in the full-length mirror. Maggie stood behind her and pulled her hair into an upswept mass, with a few strands artfully caressing her neck and the white streak prominently displayed. "God, I wish I had hair like this," Maggie sighed. "Mine's so tight and curly, I had to keep it short all the time."

"That's not me," Barbara said, looking at the striking brunette who looked back at her. "That dress and hairstyle are meant for a beautiful woman. And I'm certainly not beautiful."

"Not classically beautiful, no," Maggie said. "But a woman who looks comfortable in her skin, and particularly one who has that gleam of sensuality that you will have if I have anything to say about it, is attractive. And you are."

"Oh, Maggie. I couldn't." Could I?

"You can if you want to."

"Do you really think so? Could I knock 'em dead? Could I really get Steve to notice me?"

Maggie grinned. "I know so and I think maybe you're beginning to also."

Barbara suddenly realized things about herself she hadn't understood until that moment. She wanted to be that woman she saw in the mirror. Like Cinderella. No, not like Cinderella, she corrected herself. I don't want to be someone else for just one night. She thought about her new hairstyle and her new clothes. She realized, as she looked at herself, that in this dress she stood up straighter, looked herself in the eye. And she glowed.

"Maybe just a little," Barbara said.

"Good. That's all I ask. Enjoy the party, and don't dance only with Prince Charming. Cindy missed a lot of other really great folks at that ball."

The party was being held in the King's Room of a local hotel. Almost two hundred people were expected. When Barbara arrived, there was a four-piece dance combo playing innocuous music. Uniformed waiters and waitresses circulated with hot and cold hors d'oeuvres, glasses of red and white wine, and flutes of champagne. There was also an open bar for those who enjoyed soft drinks or hard liquor.

Barbara stood off to one side trying to figure out how to join one of the groups of laughing people. She searched the crowd for Steve, but could not find his familiar tall, slender shape. I wonder whether he's bringing someone, she thought. She looked down at the yards of bright blue skirt and thought about the hour it had taken for Maggie to fix her makeup and choose her accessories. As she moved her head, Barbara felt the large rhinestone earrings brush against her neck. Why had she allowed Maggie to talk her into those chandeliers? Why the wide bracelet? Why not her plain gold chain around her neck and her gold studs in her ears? She'd certainly feel more comfortable.

For want of something to do, she took a glass of white wine from one waiter's tray and a salmon puff from another.

"You've changed your hair," a voice said behind her. "I like it."

She turned and recognized Jay Preston, an investigator whom the firm employed for divorce work and other secret projects. "Thank you, Mr. Preston. I'm surprised you noticed." I never noticed how cute he is, she thought, still scanning the room for her boss.

"I have noticed a lot about you in the past few weeks. And it's Jay."

"I don't know what to say," Barbara said. God, he was sexy. Not handsome, Barbara thought, but the gleam in his deep gray eyes was directed entirely at her. His hair was almost black with just the beginnings of silver at the temples. Because Barbara wore two-inch heels she was only an inch shorter than he was, but he seemed to tower over her, making her think of some desert chieftain holding a sweet young woman captive. Now where had that thought come from? Barbara wondered.

"Don't say anything," Jay said. "Just tell me, are you alone tonight?"

"If you mean did I bring a date, the answer is no."

"Bring a date. You don't have to be a detective to know that that phrase means you're not married or engaged. This must be my lucky night." He took her elbow, his fingers on her naked skin causing shivers up her spine.

"You are a bit too fast for me," she said.

"I'm sorry. I just don't believe in wasting time when I see something I want."

Barbara took a step back. "It feels like you're using up all the air in here," she said honestly, sipping her wine.

Jay didn't try to close the distance between them. "Tell me about you. What do you do when you're not being Steve Gordon's Ms. Everything?"

They stood and talked for about half an hour, and found out they shared an interest in old TV comedies and cooking and abhorred partisan politics and snow. "I tried skiing once," Jay said, "and, well, I guess it's not macho to admit that after I fell more times than I could count, I took off my skis and walked down the baby slope."

Barbara laughed. "I never even tried. I had a few friends who invited me to go with them several years ago. I got there, put on boots that hurt my feet, took off the boots and spent the day in the lodge drinking hot chocolate and eating chili."

"Not together, I hope," Jay said.

"Not together, but I think I gained two pounds that day. So much for exercise."

Jay gave her an appraising look from her hair to her feet. "Not a problem," he said. "You look just right to me."

"Barbara," a familiar voice said, "there you are. I've been looking for you."

"Hello, Steve," Barbara said. "You know Jay Preston."

Steve nodded. "Preston." He turned to Barbara and put a friendly arm around her waist. "I wanted you to meet Lisa." He reached out and draped his other arm around the shoulders of a strikingly gorgeous woman. "Lisa, this is Barbara."

The woman smiled warmly and reached out a hand. "It's so nice to meet you. Steve talks about you so much."

Weakly, Barbara extended a hand. "It's nice to meet you, too." He didn't tell me much about you, she thought, and there was obviously a lot to tell. Lisa was a knockout in a long silver sequined gown.

"This is so great," Steve said. "My two girls." He hugged them both. "Dinner will be served soon. Will you sit with us?"

Jay put his arm around Barbara's shoulders. "I think Barbara intended to eat with me." He looked at Barbara and smiled.

"Yes, Steve," she said quickly. "Jay and I were just in the middle of something, if you don't mind."

"Of course not," Steve said. "Come on, Lisa. I see some people I want you to meet." The two walked away. As Barbara gazed after them, she felt a glass thrust into her hand.

"Have some champagne," Jay said. "It's good for what ails you."

"Does it show that much?" Barbara said, unable to pretend.

"Only to someone as perceptive as I am. And don't worry. I'm very good at cheering people up. I do limericks, bad jokes, and I promise not to sing while we dance."

"There's nothing between Steve and me, you know."

"I know. I do understand. And I'll leave you alone if you like. That business of sitting together at dinner was just for his benefit. Unless you'd like to."

Barbara turned from watching Steve and Lisa talk to one of the other partners and said, "I'd like that." She grinned and felt her shoulders relaxed. "This feels like a bad movie. Shunned by her boss, the heroine," she tapped her chest, "that's me, finally notices the handsome hero." She patted the lapel of Jay's tuxedo. "That's you. Then they fall madly in love and live happily ever after."

"Not *ever after*," Jay said, covering her palm with his. "I'm not that type of guy. I live for the now, not for next year. But, my love, I could definitely fall in lust with you."

"Excuse me?"

"Let me lay my cards on the table. I find you very attractive and you fit one of my favorite fantasies."

"Oh I do, do I?"

"Yes. I know more about you than you might wish. You're in love with your boss, or at least you think you are. You're an innocent, inexperienced woman who hasn't learned her own power yet. And you do have power. You radiate with it. But you don't understand it. I want to teach you so you can have anything you want."

"What power are you talking about? You're confusing me. This is some kind of line you use with people like me and I don't think I like it."

"It's not strictly speaking a line, because it's entirely honest. And you say you don't like it, but I have my fingers on your pulse and it's pounding right now. This whole thing excites you and you don't quite know what to do about it. I won't press you for the moment."

The doors to the dining room opened and Jay took Barbara's glass and put it down on a nearby table. "Will you sit with me?"

Barbara thought about how much this man was like Maggie. He was a free thinker, dangerous, charming, and totally unsuitable with goals that were completely different from hers. But she *was* terribly excited. She hesitated only a moment, gazed at Steve and the knockout, then back at Jay. It's time, she told herself. As a matter of fact, I'm long overdue. "I'd like that," Barbara said, taking Jay's arm as they joined the stream of people walking toward the dining room.

During the almost three-hour dinner, Jay was a perfect gentleman. They talked, laughed, and argued, with each other and with the other couples at their table. Between courses, they danced to the music of the combo, but Jay kept a discreet distance between them. After coffee was served, the place began to empty out. Steve and Lisa stopped at their table to say good night and Barbara smiled and wished them a good evening. The pain of seeing her boss with Ms. Knockout on his arm had diminished considerably.

As the band began a slow song, Jay took her hand and once again led her to the small wooden dance floor, now crowded with the few other couples still left. Jay took her in his arms and held her against him and their feet moved reflexively to the music. His mouth beside her ear, Jay said, "I've tried to give you some time to think about me as a real person, not as a lecherous private eye, but now the evening is almost over and I might not see you again, except in the office. I want to tell you again that I'm in lust with you and I want you in my bed. I want to lay you out on the sheets and touch you and lick you. I want to make you want me so badly you beg me to take you. I want to want you so badly that I do." He pressed his hand in the small of her back, leaning the bulge in his trousers against her belly.

Barbara couldn't speak. She was barely able to think.

"I want to do strange, unusual, extremely pleasurable things with you, things that will make you blush and scream and cry out in joy. But nothing long term. I live for now. Nothing exclusive. I love women and I love making love to them."

"Again I'm speechless."

"Let's dance for a few more minutes, then I'll take you to your car. I want you to think about everything I've said and I will call you tomorrow night. I want you to say yes, but on realistic terms. Will you think about it?"

"Will I think about anything else?"

Jay's warm chuckle tickled her ear. "Good."

Half an hour later, Jay dropped Barbara at her car. "I'll call you tomorrow, but if you haven't decided, I'll call you the following evening. Take as much time as you like. And understand that I do take no for an answer and I won't pressure you, except to promise you that it will be wonderful."

It was fortunate that, since the hotel was only two blocks from the office, Barbara had driven this route every day for many years, for she drove in a total fog. She knew what Jay was asking. He wanted to have an affair with her. A "no commitment, no tomorrow" affair. No, she told herself, It was impossible.

But God, how she was turned on. She didn't know what strange, unusual things he had in mind, but she was so curious. She wasn't stupid. She knew about oral sex, bondage, all the kinky things she had read about in novels, and she was fascinated. Isn't that how the cobra entices its victims? Doesn't he fascinate them until he can bite?

But what is the downside to all this? That nice girls don't? Is that a realistic reason not to do something that might be so good? She was so confused.

She wasn't at all surprised to see Maggie sitting in her kitchen when she arrived home. "How was it?" she asked, then hesitated. "Something happened. Did you spend the evening with Steve? Did he ask you out? Tell me everything."

Barbara did, with little comment from Maggie. "And Jay wants me to go to bed with him. No strings. No nothing. Just making love."

Momentarily Maggie thought about Angela's desires. "Get her married to that cute lawyer. Home, kids. . . ." If Maggie wanted to get to heaven, the best way was to do what Angela wanted, wasn't it? She should tell Barbara to reject Jay out of hand and concentrate on Steve. But she couldn't. Jay was right for Barbara now and what she wanted what was good for Barbara. "You have to do what you think is best," Maggie said. "But that's sometimes hard to sort out. I guess my philosophy would be, If it feels good and doesn't hurt anyone, do it."

"I keep thinking that going to bed with a man just for sex makes me a bad girl. What would my mother say?"

"From what I heard about your mother, both from you and from the girls . . ." She gazed at the ceiling, "I think she'd tell you to do what you want with none of the *good* and *bad* labels."

"I'm so confused."

"Sleep on it," Maggie said. "You don't have to decide tonight." As usual, to end the discussion, Maggie walked out the kitchen door and disappeared. Barbara went up to bed and, for the first time in her life, slept naked.

* * *

"I need to be honest with you, Jay," Barbara said into the phone the following evening. "I'm intrigued, but I'm scared to death, too. I don't know whether I want to have an affair with you that has no future. I wasn't brought up that way."

"Oh Barbara, you're wonderful. I completely understand. Look, how about this? Let me take you to dinner next Saturday. Just dinner. No commitment to do anything except enjoy each other's company."

"Well . . ." Barbara sat in the edge of her bed, playing with the hem of the pillowcase.

"We had fun together last evening and I'm not willing to let that go. Do you like Italian food? Not spaghetti, but real zuppe de peche, good osso buco with orzo. And they make the best tiramisù."

"Actually, I love Italian food." He's such a sweet man, she thought. And he seems to understand how I feel.

"As I remember, you told me you're a great cook, but let's let someone else do the cooking and we can get to know each other better. Please."

Barbara vacillated. She liked Jay a lot, but she wasn't ready for what he wanted, and she knew that hadn't changed. She didn't want a sleazy affair. Did she? "I did enjoy last evening a great deal." She took a deep breath. "All right. Just dinner."

"Great."

They made arrangements for Jay to pick Barbara up at her house the following Saturday evening.

"Maggie," Barbara said the following evening, "I'm really nervous about this dinner date."

"What are you afraid of exactly?"

Barbara sat at the dinner table, dirty dinner dishes spread around her, a cup of coffee cooling in her hand. "I've been trying to sort that out. I think I'm afraid that I'll be tempted to jump into bed with the guy. He's nice, warm, honest, and sexy as hell."

"And what if you do jump into bed with him?"

"I guess I'm afraid that I'll hate myself the next morning."

"You're right, that is a risk. So the question becomes, Is the risk worth the reward?"

"I never thought of it that way."

"Well, let's think of it that way now. If you do get involved with Jay, what's the reward?"

Barbara grinned. "He's a very sexy man and, to be perfectly honest, he turns me on. My insides get all squishy, my knees get weak, and well, I think it would be great."

"Okay, what's the reward if you tell him no."

Barbara considered for a few minutes. "I won't have any regrets the next morning."

"You won't?"

Barbara sipped at her cold coffee. "I will have regrets. I will regret all the things I didn't do."

"I think my job is to make you see all sides of this problem. You know what side I'm on. I think good sex is the best thing going. You're a big girl, and perfectly able to understand what you're getting yourself into, and you're no virgin. You understand, as I'm sure Jay does, about safe sex, condoms all that. You know how I feel, but it must be your decision."

Barbara pictured the scene, Jay stroking her hand at dinner, kissing her fingers. She'd read enough novels to know that once the hormones kicked in, resistance was futile. Then it wouldn't be her responsibility. "He'll convince me. I know he will and I'll do it."

But Jay didn't pressure her. Villa Josephina turned out to be a small Italian restaurant in Tuckahoe, with a round hostess who obviously knew Jay from frequent visits. They were seated at a table off to one side. Barbara took one look at the extensive menu and, her mouth dry and her appetite gone, she let Jay order for both of them. At first, Barbara was quite nervous and unable to do justice to a wonderful shrimp appetizer, but as the meal progressed she relaxed. Through the courses they talked. About everything but sex. Barbara began to feel like she was having dinner with an old friend, not a would-be lover. And, although he was a sensual man, he wasn't turning her on. As a matter of fact, she thought he was making an effort not to even indirectly refer to anything sexual. He had even dressed in a dark green flannel sport shirt and shaker sweater, muting any sensuality.

"I would offer you a brandy," Jay said to Barbara as the waiter brought small cups of strong espresso, "but I don't want alcohol to cloud your mind. Or mine, for that matter."

"Is that why you didn't order any wine?"

"I know what's going through your head. I know that this is a difficult decision for you, and I want you to be clear-headed." It was his first reference to the topic that had been so much on Barbara's mind. He took her hand across the soft blue tablecloth. "Whatever you decide is fine with me, but it must be your decision."

Barbara lowered her gaze.

"Okay," Jay said. "I understand."

He hadn't convinced her, pressured her or made her decision any easier. And without a push, she didn't think she could go through with it. She sipped her coffee. "Thanks. I think I'd like you to take me home," Barbara said.

Quickly Jay paid the check and drove Barbara back to her house in Fleetwood. He walked her to her door and said, "Do you think we might just have dinner together once in a while? I haven't enjoyed an evening this much in a long time." A boyish grin lit his face. "And maybe you'll change your mind."

"Kiss me," Barbara said, uncertain as to where the words had come from.

Jay looked startled, then put his hands on her shoulders. Drawing her close, he brushed his mouth across hers. He touched the tip of his tongue to the joining of her lips, then cupped her face with his hands.

Barbara placed her palms against Jay's chest and relaxed into the kiss. He was an expert, softly taking her mouth and possessing it. He explored and tasted until she parted her lips and allowed his tongue free access. Slowly she slid her hands up his chest to the back of his neck, holding him close. His fingers slowly slid up the sides of her neck and tunneled through her thick hair, caressing her scalp.

Finally he leaned back, his eyes caressing her face. "You kiss like an expert," he said. "I thought of you as being so innocent."

"I don't know where that came from. It must be that you do that to me," Barbara admitted.

Jay ran his fingers through her hair. "You know this silver stripe is incredibly sexy. Are you a witch?"

"No, of course not."

"What would you do if you were? Right now."

"That's an interesting question," Barbara said, smiling ruefully. "I think I'd make it tomorrow morning."

Jay cocked his head to one side. "Why?"

"Because tonight is causing me so much confusion. By tomorrow morning decisions would have been made."

"Do you want me to make the decision for you?"

"Yes." She paused. "No."

"What do you want?"

She looked into Jay's eyes and a slow smile spread across her face. "I want you to come inside with me."

Barbara watched Jay's eyes light up. "Are you sure?"

Barbara let go of Jay long enough to find her keys and unlock the front door. "Yes, I'm sure."

They walked into the house and Barbara put their coats in the living room. Then she slid back into Jay's arms and raised her face to his. He accepted the invitation readily. He brushed soft kisses on her eyes, her cheeks, her mouth, all the time keeping his hands on her back.

Barbara realized what she wanted. Her body was alive, impatient, unsatisfied. She ran her hands over the back of Jay's deep green sweater, then slid under it to touch his soft flannel shirt and the hard flesh beneath. She wanted, needed, him to make the next move. Push me, she cried. Seduce me. "Please."

"Oh, how I want you," he moaned, kissing her deeply again. When he pulled away, he looked around. "You know, living rooms are nice, but how about a nice horizontal surface? I want to make long, slow love to you, not paw and pet like teenagers."

Barbara motioned toward the stairs and together they walked up.

A small light was burning in the corner of the cozy room. Her bed was covered with a patchwork comforter, one pattern of which matched the curtains. Another of the patchwork fabrics covered the armchair on one side of the room, and the polished wood floor was covered with a multicolored braided rug.

This room is cleaner than it has been in weeks, Barbara realized as they entered. Maggie must have tidied up after I left for dinner. She glanced at the bed. Maggie had even changed the sheets. She had planned for this. She had known or hoped that Barbara would be here, like this, with Jay. Thanks, Barbara almost said aloud. She smiled silently as she watched Jay pull off his sweater. "Can I take that?" For want of something to do, she folded it and put it on a chair.

Jay came up behind her and slid his hands around her waist. "I know this is awkward for you," he said, his lips against the tender skin beneath her ear. "Let me lead. I promise you will like where we go together." He held her back against his hard chest and Barbara could feel the heat of his body against hers. He nuzzled her neck, planting small soft kisses on the skin he could reach. Then he turned her in his arms and again pressed his mouth against hers. She smelled his after-shave, spicy and mixed with the natural male smell of him.

Slowly the heat began to build. He kissed her over and over until all she was aware of was his mouth. She felt him press his lower body against hers so she could get used to his arousal. When he pressed, she found herself pressing back.

Jay stepped back and untied her scarf, then slowly unbuttoned her soft pink blouse. He pulled the blouse's tails from her burgundy skirt and slid the garment off her shoulders.

Barbara stood in a haze, wondering how Jay would see her, glad she had allowed Maggie to talk her into wearing her new, more daring, white lace underwear. She started to raise her arms to cover herself, but she heard Jay's voice. "Oh, my," Jay said, his eyes roaming over her body. "I expected you to have a nice figure, but you're really beautiful."

Barbara knew she weighed more than she should, but the look in Jay's eyes said he thought she was desirable. Her arms fell limply to her sides. Jay placed his hands on her ribs, then slowly slid them upward toward her breasts. "Your skin is so soft, like warm satin." His fingers reached Barbara's full breasts, still encased in the silk-and-lace bra. She felt him stroke her flesh softly, the touch muffled through the fabric. Go faster, she screamed in her mind. Push me onto the bed and fuck me. Get this waiting over with.

"No rushing," Jay purred as if reading her mind. "It's hard for me to wait, but this first time for us this night will live in my mind for a long time. I want it to be perfect. I want you to want me, not to get it over with but because your body feels empty, hollow, needy."

"But . . ."

He covered her protest with his lips, his thumbs now stroking her nipples through the cloth. Barbara knew how tight her nubs had become, and she felt the wet swelling between her legs. Jay kissed and rubbed, then held her tight while he found and opened the clasp of her bra. He let the garment drop to the floor and admired Barbara's firm breasts. He bent, touching the tip of his tongue to each crest in turn, until Barbara's knees threatened to buckle. She heard a low moan and realized that it came from her.

Jay knelt in front of her, unfastened her skirt and pulled it down. "Oh, honey," he said, seeing the matching panties and garter belt Maggie had insisted upon. "This is so sexy. I want to go slowly but you are making it very difficult." She wore the panties over the garters, so Jay lowered the tiny wisp of fabric until she could step out of it. Then he guided her to the bed with the stockings and garter belt still in place. "I think making love to a woman with stockings on like this is one of the sexiest things," he purred.

She stretched out on the bed, rubbing the sole of her nylon-covered foot over the quilt. She watched as Jay removed his shirt, then she looked at the body now revealed. He was tanned, but looked like he hadn't worked out in years. No perfect athletic body. Just a man's chest covered with tightly curled hair. Not intimidating, she thought. She saw that Jay had already removed his shoes and socks and was unzipping his pants. I wish I were brave enough, Barbara thought with the part of her brain still capable of thought. I would sit up and help him pull off his shorts. Maybe, she thought. Maybe.

Jay, now naked, stretched out beside Barbara on the wide double bed. He kissed her again, then bent down and licked a swollen nipple. "Oh, yes," Barbara purred. "Yes." Hesitantly she cupped the back of his head and held him as he suckled. Shivers echoed through her body, centering now deep in her belly. She felt herself getting wetter and wanted him to touch her. Soon, she thought. Soon I'll be brave, able to touch what I want. Able to ask, show, guide.

Jay placed the palm of his hand on her belly and, over the lace of the garter belt, lowered it to the thatch of springy hair below. "So hot," he purred. "So hungry." His fingers probed, finding her hard clit, her swollen lips, her wet center. "I want you to come for me, baby. I want to watch you as you take your pleasure." He rubbed, using all his senses to discover exactly what she liked, what sent her higher. "Oh," he said, "you like to be touched right here."

"Oh, yes," she moaned, now incapable of any thought. "Yes."

"Open your eyes and look at me. I want to see your eyes when you come."

It was difficult, but Barbara opened her eyes and looked at Jay. His concentration was complete. He was stroking, rubbing, probing, all the while not taking his smoky eyes from hers. Barbara spread her legs still more, making it easier for him to reach all the places she had learned about in the past week. She couldn't speak, so she tried to tell him everything with her body and he learned quickly. Slowly he insinuated one finger into her wet channel. "That feels good, doesn't it?" he said as she gasped.

"Oh, yes," Barbara said, her eyes closing.

"No baby," he said. "Don't close your eyes. Look at me."

Barbara forced her eyes open. "It's hard," she said.

"I know, but it makes you think about something other than my hand. I want my face to fill over your mind while I fill your body." Slowly a second finger joined the first, then his thumb began flicking over her clit. "Yes, I can watch your eyes glaze with the pleasure I'm giving you. You're so hot, so hungry. I like it that I can do that to you. I can fill you, stroke you." He leaned over and licked her nipple. "Even bite you." He lightly closed his teeth on her tender flesh, causing small shards of pain to knife through her breast. "But the slight pain is exciting, isn't it?"

It was, she realized. The combination of sensations was electric. "Yes. It's good."

"I knew it would be."

He dipped his head and, as his fingers drove in and out of her pussy, he spread her legs wide and flicked his tongue over her clit. "Oh, God," she cried, her voice hoarse, all but unable to drag air into her lungs. She came as only her own fingers had been able to make her come before. He kept pulling her along, bringing waves of pleasure to her entire body. As she continued to spasm, she felt his hand withdraw. With his mouth sucking at her clit, she felt him awkwardly move around the bed, then heard the tear of paper. Briefly he sat up and, as Barbara's body throbbed with continued pleasure, unrolled a condom over his erection. He crouched over her for just a moment, then drove his hard cock deep into her. "Honey," he cried as she twisted her stocking-covered legs around his waist. "Honey, now! Yes!"

His back arched and he groaned as he pistoned into Barbara's wet body. Harder and harder he pumped until, with a roar, he came deep inside her. Her legs held him tightly against her as the waves of orgasm claimed them both.

It took several minutes for their bodies to calm and for their breathing to slow. "Oh, honey," Jay said. "That was sensational. I didn't expect you to be so responsive. You are a very sexy lady."

Barbara preened. She was feeling like a sexy lady, and she wanted to be a sexy lady. She wanted to be able to do to a man what Jay had just done to her. She had never even considered anything like that before. Conservative, mousy Barbara. Not anymore.

Chapter 6

"It was like a revelation. I understood things. I want to be a sexually free woman. Not necessarily like you, Maggie," Barbara said the next morning as she devoured a piece of toast, "but I want to feel free to do anything sexually I want."

"That's quite a change from the frightened and uncertain woman who left here last evening."

Barbara's eyes sparkled, her skin glowed. "I know, and I have no idea where it came from. But as Jay and I were making love, I just knew. I want to learn. I want to experiment. I want to do things that I never even knew existed." She giggled. "I don't even know that those things are, I just know there's more to sex than I've ever imagined."

"What about Jay? Won't he teach you?"

"Of course and I want to learn with him, but now I want to know everything, taste everything. Taste everyone." She looked down, then laughed. "You know what I mean. I guess the genie's out of the bottle and I don't want her to go back inside."

Maggie's grin spread from ear to ear. "I'm so happy for you, Barbara. I just knew that once you discovered good sex, you'd be unstoppable." She'd known no such thing, but what the hell. She was winning and, although Angela wanted marriage and a home for Barbara, it was, after all, Barbara's decision. And it seemed she had made it. "So you and Jay had it good last evening."

"Oh Lord, it was cosmic. We made love, then talked for a while, then made love again." She smiled, remembering the second time.

"God Barbara it's such a turn-on to watch someone like you open up." It was about midnight and they lay side by side on Barbara's bed, the quilt thrown over them. It had only been an hour since her last orgasm, and already she was excited again. "I don't know how to express all the things I'm feeling."

"I can imagine," Jay said, his hand holding hers. "Your excitement is contagious. I'm not usually so quick to recover, but feel." He placed her hand on his again-erect cock. "Feel what you do to me."

"I like that. But I'm not responsible for your excitement."

"And who else is in this bed with me." He reached over and inserted one finger between her legs. She was wet. "And you are as excited as I am."

"It's just that we made love only an hour ago."

"And . . . ?"

"I should be lying here in some kind of afterglow, not lusting like an animal."

"I guess we're both animals then. And what are you lusting for?"

Barbara giggled. "I guess I have to admit that I want you again."

"I'm glad you do. What would you like?"

"You know."

"You want me to make love to you again." Jay raised himself up on one elbow and looked down at Barbara. She nodded almost imperceptibly. "Tell me," Jay urged. "Say yes."

"Yes."

"What would you like me to do? What gave you pleasure?"

Barbara pictured Jay's hands on her breast. And his mouth. That was what she wanted. But she couldn't say the words. "Everything you did gave me pleasure."

"Cop-out. Not an answer. What did you like best? When I nibbled your ear? When I stroked your tits? When I rubbed your cunt?"

Barbara's face went red. "Everything. Just love me."

"Maybe you need a lesson in words. Saying the words is very erotic. It's difficult and embarrassing, but it's also very exciting. Dirty words. Words your mother told you never to say. Words like 'fuck' and 'pussy' and 'dick.' Maybe you need a lesson on how to say those dirty words and ask for what you want." He placed his free hand flat on her belly and leaned his mouth against her ear. "What would you like this hand to do?"

Barbara was silent.

"Do you want it on your tits?"

She nodded slightly.

"Say it. Say, 'I want your hand on my tits.'"

"I can't say that," Barbara said, trying to contain the nervous giggle that threatened to erupt.

"Yes, you can and you will." He moved his hand upward until his fingers surrounded her breast. He moved his fingertips slightly, rubbing her ribs, nowhere near where she wanted his hands. "Say, 'Touch my tits.'"

"Touch me."

Jay shook his head. "Not good enough. Say 'tits.' Say it or I won't touch you."

His fingers were making her crazy. Her nipples were hard little buds aching for his hands and his mouth. She knew how good it had been just an hour before and she wanted it again. But could she say those words? She formed the word "tit" in her mind, then almost strangled on it. She couldn't get it out.

Jay's tongue was in her ear, licking and probing. Then he whispered, "Touch my tits. That's all you have to say."

His mouth was driving her wild. "Touch my . . . tits." There, she had said it.

"Such a good girl," Jay purred, his fingers squeezing her breasts and playing with her nipples. He pinched hard enough to make her gasp, but there was a stab of pleasure, too. "Now you probably want me to suck them, too. Tell me."

"Yes, please," she moaned.

"Say, 'Suck my tits.'"

"Suck my . . . tits." It was easier this time. "Please. I need your mouth."

"Oh, honey," Jay said, his mouth descending. He licked and sucked, and bit her. It was all ecstasy. For several minutes Jay played with her breasts, stroking, kneading, suckling. "God, you taste good," he purred. "But now it's time for more. You're hungry for me. You want my hands in your pussy. Say 'pussy.'"

Hearing the word made her back arch, the need almost overwhelming. "Jay, please touch me. I want you so much."

"I know you do. I know you want me enough to say the words. 'Touch my pussy.'"

"Touch my pussy. Jay, please."

"Oh, yes," Jay said, his fingers now busy driving her higher and higher. "Now I want something from you," Jay said. "Open your eyes." She did and saw his hand around his cock. "I want you to suck me the way I did it to you."

"I don't know how," Barbara said, suddenly cold and frightened. She had heard of women who "gave good head." There must be a knack to it. She couldn't, didn't know how.

"That's all right, I'll teach you." His hands still in her crotch, Jay turned, then knelt on the bed, his cock now only inches from her mouth. "Open your mouth. Just let me rub my cock over your lips so you get the feel of it." He stroked her lips with the velvety tip of his hard erection. "I'll teach you the best way. Do you want me to lick your pussy?"

"Yes."

He lay beside her, his head near her cunt, his cock only an inch from her mouth. His fingers continued to work their erotic magic. "Say 'pussy.' I know that as much as you deny it, saying those words makes you hot. Say it."

"Pussy," Barbara whispered.

"Such a good girl. Now I'm going to lick you. Try to duplicate what you feel with your tongue and my cock. If I lick slowly . . ." He gently licked the length of her slit. ". . . I want you to lick me slowly. Do it for me."

She used her fingertips to guide his cock close to her mouth. "Like this?" she whispered. She started about halfway down his shaft and licked to the tip as if her were a lollypop.

"Oh, God," he groaned. "Oh, honey."

Barbara was amazed at her ability to give him pleasure. She licked again and felt his sharp intake of breath.

Jay licked Barbara's clit lightly and she licked the tip of his cock the same way. Jay breathed hot air on Barbara's pussy and she breathed hot air onto his wet flesh. When Jay sucked her clit into his mouth, she was almost unable to think clearly enough to suck his cock, but when she did, she was rewarded with his moan. "Lady, you're a quick study."

Barbara could feel the vibrations of his voice against her hot flesh. "I hope so," she purred, hoping he could feel the same thing.

"You are a witch," he said, getting to his knees. He turned, put on a condom, crouched over her and plunged into her body. When his cock was deeply embedded in her cunt, he lifted and turned them both until she was straddling him. He held her hips and alternately lifted her and plunged her down onto his shaft. Harder and harder he drove into her, drove her onto him. "Say 'Fuck me good,'" he cried.

"Oh, Jay, fuck me good," she cried as she climaxed.

"Yessss," he hissed as he, too, came.

Barbara had been spending most of her weekends with Jay for more than a month before she saw Maggie again. One evening at the beginning of May, while Barbara was pouring herself a beer to go with the just-delivered pizza, Maggie walked into the kitchen.

"How have you been?" Maggie asked, dropping into a chair.

"Great. I've missed you." Barbara crossed to Maggie's chair and gave her a great bear hug.

"I haven't missed you, because, for me, I just saw you yesterday. How long has it been, and how is Jay?"

"It's the eighth of May and my dates have been great. We fuck like bunnies."

"Fuck. Such language." She tsk-tsked. "The Barbara I knew would never have used a word like that."

"I know, and I do keep it to a minimum except with you and Jay. But that's what it is, really. Wild, animal fornication, and it feels wonderful."

"That's terrific," Maggie said, taking a slice of pizza. She had discovered that she could eat what she wanted and food tasted great, although she had no concept of what happened after she swallowed. "I'm happy for you. Are you and Jay permanent? You know, forever?"

"Oh, Maggie," Barbara said, sitting across from her friend and taking a few large swallows of her beer. "I don't understand all this."

Maggie chewed, then said, "What's to understand? You said you guys were great together."

"I know, but it's not enough, somehow. I don't know. I've probably made love more in the past few weeks than I did in the previous thirty-one years. And I like Jay." As Maggie raised an eyebrow, Barbara continued. "I do. Really. It's just . . . Oh, forget it. I can't explain it."

"You know, I have no idea who decides when I appear, but whoever it is and however it's done, it seems you need someone to talk to right now. Try to explain."

Barbara took another long swallow of her beer and considered her words while Maggie devoured a slice of pizza. "Okay, let me put it this way. Jay's a real nice guy, but he's, how can I put this, predictable. We go to one of three restaurants for dinner. When I suggest somewhere else, he's willing but not anxious, so I don't pursue it. After dinner we go back to his place. We both love old movies, so we watch one of the tapes he has, usually an old John Wayne flick. We share some wine, get hot and make love. All fine, but . . ."

"Dull?"

Barbara sighed. "Yeah. Dull. After that first explosive night, when we made love twice, it's once, we doze, then he takes me home. That once is fantastic, don't get me wrong. But I thought that great sex like that first night was the answer to some question I didn't know I had."

"Great sex is just that, great, but it's also not life."

"I don't understand," Barbara said, startled. "Didn't you say that marriage was too predictable? That variation and hot sex was the answer for you?"

"I did, and I believe that. But from what you've told me, your sex life has become predictable. Dull."

"Yes, but . . ."

"There's lots of good stuff out there. Maybe it's time for you to spread your newly acquired wings and look around. See what's out there. There are lots of fish in the sea, my love."

"You mean men."

"I do. Look around. I'll bet there are guys who you see every day, and who you don't give a second look to who would be fun to fool around with."

"Fool around with?"

"Yeah. Get some experience. Steak is nice, but pizza is good sometimes, too." She lifted her slice in a mock salute. "You didn't cook tonight, I see."

Barbara laughed. "I've been spending more time thinking about life and less time cooking. There is more to life than gourmet meals that I prepare myself, for myself." She picked up a slice of pizza and took a large bite. Then she got up, crossed to her spice rack and returned with a jar of crushed red pepper. "Just a little spice to give my slice some pep."

"That's what your life needs, too," Maggie said. "There are as many pleasures as there are creative couples in the world."

"You're right. I want to experiment. I want to do everything."

"And what about Jay. Does he think you're exclusive?"

"Not at all. He's seeing at least one other woman. You know, when he told me, I thought I'd be jealous, but I'm not. We're having fun and he's having fun with Joyce. I keep waiting for misery, possessiveness, but I just don't feel that. I'm happy he's happy."

"Sounds healthy to me," Maggie said. "And what about Steve. Has he asked you out yet? Have you asked him?"

"He hasn't asked me and I haven't asked him."

"Why not? You want to be with him, don't you?"

"Yes. But I want to play for the moment and I don't want to complicate things with what might turn into something permanent." She sprinkled red pepper on another slice of pizza. "And anyway, he's still seeing that knockout. That Lisa person."

"Do I hear jealousy?"

"Maybe a little. It's not like Jay. Jay's a game. I want Steve to be serious. But not just yet. I have things to do and learn first, so we can be great together."

"I really do understand." Maggie remembered her first experiences after she and Chuck split. She had discovered that she loved sex. Good, rolling-in-the-hay, giggling, having-fun sex. "Remember the tape I gave you, the one that started all this?"

"Mmmm," she purred, "how could I forget?"

"Well, there are more in the series."

Barbara sat up, here eyes round. "There are?"

Maggie reached into her pocket and withdrew an audiotape. "This is another tape by the man who made that first one. These are erotic stories, published in an unusual way, using his bedroom voice. He's got a store in the city and sells them there and through the mail. Maybe you'll meet him sometime. He's a wild guy with a fantastic imagination." She placed the tape on the table between them. "That first one is unusual. Each of the remaining tapes is a story of people making love in new and exciting ways. Some you'll find exciting, some not. But the tapes will allow you to vicariously experience many of the things that couples do together. You can play them and see what turns you on, then go out and try to experience it."

Barbara took the tape.

"I'll be going, and you can play the tape at your leisure." Maggie stood up and walked toward the door. "How are they going to keep them down on the farm . . ." she said as she left through the kitchen door.

"How indeed," Angela said to Lucy as they flipped off the computer screen. "What did you get us into?"

"Be real, Angela," Lucy said. "You knew this might happen, and I'm glad it did. All that stuff about marriage. It's not right for Barbara, at least not yet. She's got some wild oats to sow."

"And this sudden need for her to get into kinky sex." Angela fixed Lucy with an icy stare. "Do you mean to tell me you had nothing to do with that?"

"It didn't take much." She grinned. "I guess the devil made me do it."

"Listen, I thought we had a deal here. There's a lot riding on how Barbara's life goes from here. We agreed that there would be no meddling."

Lucy looked only a bit chagrined. "I know. I couldn't help it. I just goosed her a little. I want to see her fly. I want to see her learn about good, hot sex. A good roll in the sheets beats anything going, including marriage and fidelity."

"What you want isn't the issue here. It's what she wants. Free will is everything. If humans lose that, decisions like Barbara's become meaningless."

Lucy sighed. "I know. I'm sorry. I just couldn't help myself."

Angela patted her friend's hand. "Okay. I guess I understand. It's hard to have any resistance to temptation where you come from. But promise me. No more."

"Okay. No more."

Barbara turned on the tap to run a tub full of hot water, sprinkled a handful of bath salts beneath the water stream, then undressed. All the while her gaze kept returning to the cassette player which already contained the tape Maggie had given her. When the tub was full, she turned off the water and stepped in. Before settling into the water, she pushed the play button. The familiar sensual wail of the saxophone filled the room. She rested her head against the rim of the large tub and closed her eyes.

> *As they walked, Jason and Carolyn felt the cool water wash over their burning feet. The sand was white and had soaked in the sun all day. Now, as the golden disk set, the sand radiated heat into the soles of their feet, up their legs and into their bodies. Gulls wheeled and dove into the surf hunting for their evening meal and crying their brief song over and over.*

The narrator's voice was sensual, soft, warm, like listening to warm heavy cream, Barbara thought as she listened. She let the voice and the story wash over her, as though she were there, seeing it, feeling it. It played like a movie in her head.

> *As they walked slowly along, Jason draped his arm over Carolyn's shoulder and slid his fingers down the edges of the top of her brief bikini. He allowed his fingertips to brush the swell of her lush breasts.*
>
> *Carolyn loved the look and feel of Jason's lean body. As she looked over at him, it seemed that the pink and orange light of the setting sun made Jason's skin glow as though lit from within. She wrapped her arm around his waist and felt his muscles move beneath his warm flesh as they walked along the deserted beach.*
>
> *"How did we get so lucky?" Jason said.*
>
> *"Fifteen raffle tickets and someone's lucky fingers," Carolyn answered.*
>
> *Surreptitiously Jason slid his fingers under one of the two tiny pieces of green fabric that made up the top of his wife's bikini and touched Carolyn's nipple. "Someone's fingers are still lucky."*
>
> *Playfully Carolyn batted Jason's fingers away. "Stop that, silly."*
>
> *"Why? This entire stretch of beach is deserted. All ours. 'Each cottage has its own deserted beach for lovers to share,' the brochure said."*
>
> *"I know, but it feels so public."*
>
> *Jason grinned. "I know. That's what's so erotic. Even though I know there's no one who can watch, it's like we're in public." With a gleam in his eye, Jason quickly untied the two knots that held Carolyn's top on and threw the fabric onto the sand. "Your breasts are so beautiful in the light of the setting sun."*

Carolyn was surprised at how sensuous and exciting it felt to be half naked with the evening breeze making her nipples tighten. With a brazenness she hadn't felt before, she turned to Jason and swayed from one foot to the other, rubbing her erect breasts against his chest.

Jason pulled the rubber band from the single braid that held Carolyn's long red hair and buried his hands in the luxuriant silken strands. He cradled her head, bent down and pressed his lips against hers, filling her mouth with his tongue. Her tongue joined his and they touched and explored.

"Ummm," he purred, "you taste salty. Are you salty all over?" He leaned down and licked the valley between her breasts.

"Oh, Jason, you get me so excited. But it's so exposed here."

"That makes me hotter." He licked first one breast, then the other. "You skin is so warm." He bent and filled his palm with the water that lapped around their feet. Slowly he trickled the cool liquid over Carolyn's chest, and before she could react to the cold, he licked the salty drops from her nipples.

Carolyn was getting very hungry and, somehow, the idea of making love in the open added to the appeal. What the heck, she thought. It's a deserted beach. "Two can play at that," she said, filling one hand with water and dribbling it over Jason's hot shoulders. She touched her tongue to a rivulet and followed the water's path through the downy hair on his chest and down his flat stomach. The water trickled to his navel, just above his tight elastic bathing suit and she dipped her tongue into the indentation.

Jason's head fell back as Carolyn swirled her tongue just above his throbbing erection. He reached down and pulled off the bottom of her bikini and his trunks. "I want to love you right here, with the calling of the gulls and the foaming water and the setting sun shining on your body."

Jason laid Carolyn on the sand and stretched out beside her, the waves lapping to their knees. He tangled his fingers in her pubic hair, feeling a wetness that had nothing to do with the ocean. "You're as anxious for me as I am for you," he murmured in her ear. "Open for me and let me love you." He felt her legs part.

Carolyn couldn't have kept her legs together had she wanted to, and she didn't want to. She needed Jason inside her so she pulled at his shoulder until he covered her body with his.

He filled her and let her slippery body engulf him. He moved in and out, feeling both her body and the play of the waves

*against his legs. He wanted her to climax, needed it so he could
come as well. He slid his fingers between their bodies and found
her swollen clit. "Yes," she purred, "rub it. Touch me while
you're inside me." His sentences were punctuated with sharp
intakes of breath. "Baby, yes." She reached between them and
placed her fingers over his, guiding them to the places she needed
to feel him. "Right there."*

*It took only a few strokes more until he felt the clenching of
her body around him and he could let his orgasm happen. And as
it did, he held his hips perfectly still letting the semen spurt from
his body into hers, experiencing her spasms of pleasure on his
cock.*

*"Oh, darling," he whispered, feeling the water swirl around
them. "That was unbelievable."*

*"Ummm, it was," Carolyn said. "And we still have three days
here. Let's go inside and take a shower together. I understand
that water can be very invigorating."*

Barbara was breathless, her fingers relaxing after a frantic orgasm.
As the music swelled, she thought about what she had heard. The woman
asked for what she wanted. And it seemed natural and right for her. And
it's right for me as well, Barbara realized.

The following Saturday, she and Jay had dinner at Villa Josephina
and, at Barbara's suggestion, had an after-dinner drink at a small club
around the corner. They danced on the tiny dance floor and, loose and
ready for something new, Barbara thought about the evening to come.
Yes, she thought, it was her turn to lead. "How about a bubble bath later?"
she murmured into Jay's ear as they danced.

"That's an interesting idea," Jay said. "But my tub isn't really big
enough for that."

"Mine is," Barbara said.

"You want to go to your house after?"

"That's what I had in mind."

"Ummm. I guess you've got a few ideas of your own. Sounds sensational."

Back at her house a while later, Barbara tuned her radio to an all-light
music station and, while Jay opened a bottle of champagne, she filled the
tub with hot water and placed several candles around the bathroom. As
she lit a match, she thought about all the wonderful things she had learned
in that tub. Tonight? More new experiences, this time with Jay.

"May I come in?" Jay said, standing in the bedroom doorway.

Quickly Barbara lit the candles and turned off the water. "Sure. I'm in here."

Jay walked into the bathroom with two flutes of champagne. "I love the atmosphere," he said, handing Barbara one of the glasses. He touched the rim of his glass to hers. "Here's to new adventures."

"New adventures," Barbara said. They undressed slowly, watching in the candlelight as each part of the other's body was exposed but not touching each other. "You're gorgeous," she said as she looked at Jay's naked body. She remembered the evening when, at the instructions of the man on the tape, she had discovered her own body in that tub. She wanted to get to know Jay's body as well. "I would like to touch you," Barbara said.

Jay stretched his arms out at shoulder level. "I would like that," he purred.

Barbara used her fingertips to touch places on Jay's body she had never explored before. She discovered that he was ticklish beneath his arms and down his sides. She found the almost downy texture of his chest hair a contrast to the wiry hair in his groin. She flicked his male nipples with a fingernail and watched them tighten. She turned him around and stroked his back with her palms, then scratched a thin line down his spine to a small patch of hair in the small of his back.

She had never taken the time to know his skin and what lay beneath, from his forehead to the soles of his feet. "You are a wonder," Jay said. "You make me feel sexy, yet soft and dreamy all at once. Strong and masculine, yet weak and almost submissive."

"I like that," Barbara said. "I like making you feel all different kinds of things." She took his hand and guided him to the tub. Together, holding hands, they stepped into the still-steamy water.

The tub was large enough that they could sink beneath the surface until only the tops of their shoulders and their heads were not submerged. "How do you feel under that water, I wonder?" she said, rubbing soap on her hands. Then she rubbed his chest, arms, and legs, again wondering at all the different textures. When she was content that she had touched all of Jay's body, she handed him the soap. "Touch me now," she said.

Smiling, Jay took the soap and used lathered hands to caress all of Barbara's skin, from her underarms to the back of her knees. He washed her fingers, sucking each into his mouth, then lathering and rinsing each. Then he did the same with her toes.

She giggled when he rubbed the sole of her foot and found that, rather than spoiling the mood, Jay shared the laughter. Then the laughter turned into a splashing contest and finally, when the bathroom was soaked, they got out of the tub and bundled each other in big fluffy towels.

"This wasn't what I expected," Barbara said as she rubbed her hair dry.

"What did you expect?"

"In the movies, the people always get very passionate in the tub. This was just sensual and fun."

"Hot water makes me less than passionate," Jay said. "I get the ideas in my mind, but my cock refuses to cooperate." He took the towel from Barbara and rubbed her hair. "Have you got a hairbrush?"

In the bedroom, Jay sat Barbara on the chair at her vanity then, from behind her, began to slowly brush her hair. Barbara closed her eyes and allowed the sensuous moment to engulf her. The mesmerizing strokes of the brush lulled her almost to sleep. "Open your eyes, sleepyhead," Jay said. "No nodding off here."

"Ummm. But it feels so good." She opened her eyes and looked in the vanity mirror. Jay stood behind her, his skin still glowing from the warm water, a towel fastened around his loins. Slowly she watched Jay remove the towel from around her shoulders. Then he took the brush and scratched the bristles along her collarbone.

"Hey," she said. "That hurts."

"No, it doesn't," Jay said. "It feels like it should hurt, but it doesn't. Watch what I'm going to do." He scraped the bristles across the flesh of her breast, then scratched the tip of one nipple. He repeated the action on her other breast, then down the center of her belly.

It didn't hurt. Quite the contrary. She felt her clit swell and her lips part and moisten. Two could play at that game, she thought. She took the brush from Jay's hand, then turned and rubbed the bristles through Jay's chest hair and down past his waist. She considered, then did it. She scratched Jay's semi-erect cock with the sharp spikes. Rather than being a turn-off, as she had feared, his cock jumped, getting harder while she watched.

She turned the brush in her hand so she could brush it up the inside of one of Jay's thighs, then scratch it over his testicles. Groaning, Jay grabbed her wrist and pulled her to a standing position. He took the brush, threw it into the corner, then dragged her to the bed.

"Not so fast," she said, laughing.

"Yes, so fast." He pushed her down on her back and, with one quick motion, unrolled a condom over his cock. Then he grabbed his erection in one hand. "You did this, now let me put it where it belongs." He crouched over her and with one thrust buried himself deep in her pussy.

Barbara wanted to feel him from a different angle, so she pushed at him until he was on his knees, her pussy still impaled on his cock. He supported her buttocks in his hands as she twined her legs around his waist. "Now, baby," she said. "Fuck me."

Her request was more than granted as he withdrew, then plunged in full length. She wanted, needed, stimulation for her breasts, but, rather than wait for Jay to touch them, she cupped her flesh and pinched her nipples. Because of their unusual position, Barbara's clit was completely exposed. She wanted Jay to touch it. "Rub my clit," she said, and Jay's fingers found her immediately. He rubbed and, as she pinched her hard nipples and Jay's long strokes filled her cunt, she came, hard, with a long, loud moan.

"Oh, Barbara," Jay said. "So good. So good." And with a scream, he came, too.

They lay silently side by side while their breathing returned to normal. "I can't believe how far you've come from that timid woman I first made love with," Jay said.

"I can't believe it either," Barbara said, pulling the quilt over them. "Thank you."

"Don't thank me," Jay said. "You are a wonderful partner. We fit so well together, in all ways."

Barbara giggled. "I love the way we fit together."

An hour later, as Barbara listened to Jay's car pull out of the driveway, she thought about what Jay had said. She was a different person and she liked the person she had become.

The following evening, Barbara was back in her tub with another of CJ's wonderful tapes. She settled back in the water, now confident that the tape was going to bring her at least one orgasm. The voice filled her head.

> *It was warmer than usual that evening in the health club so Jack removed his T-shirt and continued to lift. Twice twenty reps with a thirty-pound weight in each hand ought to finish it off. He glanced at the clock. Almost nine-thirty, he saw. He had had a business meeting so he had begun his workout later than usual. "I thought the club closed at nine," he muttered.*
>
> *Jack was well built with a smooth, muscular chest, well-developed arms and legs and an angular face. His short sandy beard covered a hard, granitelike chin. Long hair, slightly darker than his beard, was caught in a rubber band at the nape of his neck. His eyes were deep blue and a sheen of sweat covered his body as he lay on his back on the bench, lifting the barbell rhythmically. "Fifteen . . . sixteen," he counted.*
>
> *"It's way past closing time," a woman's voice said.*
>
> *"Seventeen, eighteen. Can I just finish?" he asked.*

"Sure," the voice said, and as he continued to lift, he thought little more about it. When he finished the first thirty, he rested for a few moments, then began on the second series. "You're taking advantage of my good nature," the voice said.

"I didn't realize you were still there," Jack said, almost dropping the weights. "I'm sorry if I'm inconveniencing you."

"You're the last one here," the voice said. "I'm waiting to close up."

As Jack started to sit up to return the weights to the rack, he looked behind him. She sat on another weight bench, wearing bicycle pants, a sports bra and a tight tee top with the name of the club across the front. He had never seen her here before. "I'm really sorry."

"How sorry?"

"I beg your pardon?"

The woman stared at Jack, her eyes never leaving his. "How sorry are you? I think you should make it up to me."

Was that an invitation? Jack thought. Is this beautifully built woman making a pass at me? He was certainly willing. "What did you have in mind?" he asked, looking over the woman's body. She was small, with tight breasts, slender, well-muscled thighs, and good definition in her upper arms. Her hair was cut very short, with tight red curls, and her eyes were green. She wore no makeup on her ivory skin and freckles dusted the bridge of her nose.

The woman stood up and walked over to the bench. She pushed her hand against Jack's chest until he was pressed back down onto his back. She put the weight Jack had been using on the floor beside his right hand. "Hold that and don't let go," she said. Jack wrapped his hand around the cold bar while the woman took the second hand weight and placed his left hand on it. "Don't let go or everything's over," she said.

Jack lay on his back on the narrow bench, his hands stretched toward the floor, his hard cock pressing upward against his shorts. God, he thought, is this really happening?

"My name's Nan," the woman said, "and I've been watching you. I think you'll be easy."

"Easy?"

"I think you will do anything I say, when I say it, and nothing more. I think you will do it all willingly because I'm going to do things to you and with you that we will both like. A lot. And you want me to do that, don't you?"

Jack could hardly catch his breath. "Yes," he whispered.

"Good. Here are the rules. You will keep your eyes on me at all times. Look nowhere else unless I tell you to. And keep those weights in your hands. If you let go, I will stop and leave at once. Do you understand the rules?"

Jack swallowed hard. "Yes," he whispered.

"Good. Let's see how hard you are already." She reached down and grabbed Jack's hard cock through the silky fabric of his workout shorts. "I knew you'd be easy. So hard." She grasped his cock and squeezed, moving her hand slightly up and down. "Too hard, I'm afraid. I don't know whether you will have enough self-control for me. Do you have self-control?"

"Yes," Jack said, barely able to breathe.

"We'll see. You are not to come. Period. If you do before I tell you to, I will leave. Immediately. Your cock is mine to control. Do you understand that?"

"Yes," Jack whispered, staring into the woman's deep green eyes. "Yes."

"All right. Let's test that control you say you have." Nan pulled off her tee top and bra and cupped her small tight tit with her hand. "I'm going to put my nipple into your mouth. You're not to suck, lick, or anything. Just keep your mouth open."

Jack opened his mouth and felt her large nipple between his lips. He wanted to suck, to caress the warm flesh with his tongue, but he thought of her warning and her challenge to his ability to master his desires. More intense than the urge to suck was his need for the woman not to leave. He kept his lips parted, her engorged nipple brushing his tongue. She moved, rubbing the nub against his lips, his cheeks, his chin. "Stick your tongue out, but don't move it."

He stuck his tongue out and she rubbed her nipple over the rough surface. He wanted to suckle, but he used all his concentration to keep his mouth still.

"Such a good boy," Nan said, and she straightened. "You might have more promise than I expected." She stepped out of her shorts, leaving herself dressed in only her sneakers and white socks. She straddled the bench with her back to him, and lowered her wet pussy to Jack's mouth. "The rules haven't changed. Do nothing." She wiggled her hips, and the aroma of her hot cunt filled Jack's nostrils. He licked his lips, but valiantly kept his tongue from caressing the swollen flesh so close.

*She lay down along his body, her cunt still less than an inch
from his mouth, her mouth close to his cock. Quickly she shifted
one leg of his shorts and pulled his cock free. It stood straight up
from his groin. "You can't see me too well from there," she said.
"Look in the mirror."*

*Jack had forgotten that one wall of the free-weight area was
mirrored. He turned slightly to his right so he could just see
around Nan's thigh. The sight was incredible. A naked woman
was lying along his body, her breasts caressing his belly, her
mouth just above his straining cock, her warm breath making him
quiver. Her smell filled him. Her weight pressed him down. His
hands gripped the weights until his knuckles went white, his muscles strained to push his cock into this woman's waiting mouth.*

*"You'll wait until I'm ready," she said. "Make me ready.
Lick me."*

*He did gladly, sliding his tongue over the length of her sop-
ping slit. He tried every trick he knew to give her pleasure, sucking her clit into his mouth, flicking the tip his tongue across her
then slowly laving the entire area. He pointed and stiffened his
tongue until his mouth ached, then stabbed it as far into her
pussy as it would go.*

*"My, my," Nan said, her breathing rapid, "you do good
work. I think you deserve a reward."*

*Jack felt her hot mouth draw his aching cock deep inside. It
would only take a moment of that level of intense pleasure for
him to come. "You'll make me come," he groaned.*

*"You better not come," Nan said. "You've got a job to do. If
you make me come first, then, and only then, will you be allowed
to climax. Do you understand that?"*

*Jack moaned and clenched his muscles tightly. "Yes," he
whispered, trying to concentrate on cold showers and snow-
covered mountains. He licked and sucked, his mind divided
between giving pleasure and trying to control his need to climax.
Slowly he felt Nan's thigh muscles tighten. He tried to concentrate
on which of the things his tongue was doing would make her
come. When he rubbed his lips over her clit, she quivered. When
he blew a stream of cold air over her swollen lips, her thighs
clenched around his head. Yes, he told himself, I can do it for her.
As he felt the ripples through her belly and the spasms of her vaginal muscles, he knew he could hold back no longer. He filled her
mouth with his semen, coming for what seemed to him like hours.*

It was several minutes before either of them moved. As Nan stood up, she said, "Damn, you're good. That was wonderful." She moved behind him.

Jack took a deep breath and let go of the weights. He flexed his aching fingers and picked up a small towel that lay on the floor. "Terrific." He sat up slowly, wiped his face, drying the sweat and enjoying the lingering smell of Nan's juices. "How about going back to my place? We can pick up a pizza and continue this when we recover." He took the towel away from his face and looked around in amazement. The gym was empty. Although he looked throughout the large facility, Nan seemed to have vanished.

Jack worked out late every night for several weeks, but eventually he had to admit that he would never see her again. But he had the memory of that one incredible night, a night he would never forget.

As the story ended, the room filled with the mellow tones of the saxophone, Barbara lay in the tub and rubbed her fingers furiously between her legs. When she came it was swirls of all colors, bright and silent.

As she relaxed, she lay in the cooling water thinking about the story she had just heard. There was so much out there, so much sexual fun for people to share. Next weekend she was seeing Jay again. Could she wait? She wanted to experience everything now. Right now.

Chapter 7

The following morning, Barbara showed up at work dressed in a soft rose knit suit. Although the line of the suit itself was quite conservative, the way it clung to her body as she moved was enough to ignite fantasies in a few of her office mates. And, for the first time, as she looked at the men she passed in elevators and hallways, she noticed the appreciative glances she received. Branch out, she thought. Date. Make love because it's fun and easy.

Midmorning she went to the ladies' room and looked at herself carefully in the full-length mirror. Not a raving beauty, not even conventionally pretty, she realized shaking her head, but there was a spark there now. She smoothed her skirt over her hips and adjusted the jacket's neckline slightly to reveal just a bit of cleavage. Not bad, she told herself. Not bad at all.

"Hi," a voice said as she walked back to her desk. "I don't think we've met. I'm Alex Fernandez. I'm from Gordon-Watson's West Coast affiliate."

"Nice to meet you," Barbara said, watching the man's eyes coolly appraise her. "I'm Barbara Enright."

"Well, Barbara Enright, I'm only here till tomorrow afternoon. I know I should take my time, but when I see something as delectable as you, I can't see beating around the bush. How about a drink after work?"

"You don't waste any time," Barbara said, grinning at the man's audacity. But he was gorgeous, medium height, with deep brown eyes and brown curly hair that looked like combing it was useless. He was wearing the office costume, dark suit and white shirt, but his tie was a wild print of orange and purple. Feeling bold, she reached over and touched his tie, pressing just hard enough so she knew he felt the slight pressure of her fingers. "Nice tie."

"Thanks. So how about that drink?"

She thought about it for only a moment. "I'd like that. Tonight?"

"If you're free," Alex said, his eyes holding hers. "Since I'm going back tomorrow, we don't have too much time. Listen, I have lots of work to do, but I can probably be out of here by seven."

"Let's see how the time works out as the day progresses," Barbara said.

About four-thirty Barbara found Alex in the law library. He had his head buried in a three-inch-thick tome and several others littered the table around him. "I have a few things to do. Why don't I stop back here around seven and we can see about that drink?"

Alex looked up and smiled slightly. "That'll be great," he said, looking at his watch. "Better make it about seven-thirty."

When Barbara got home, Maggie was waiting for her. As Barbara made coffee, she told Maggie about Alex. "I'm tingling all over," she said finally. "And I initiated it."

"Don't get carried away," Maggie said, then giggled. "Hey, listen to me. Which side of this am I on?"

"Oh, Maggie, I won't get carried away. It's just that this is so much fun. Flirting. Picturing every man I see without clothes. Wondering how he would be in bed."

Maggie patted the back of Barbara's hand. "I know, and I'm with you. Just be careful. Condoms and like that. And never do something that you don't want to do just because someone else wants you to."

Maggie looked at Barbara's watch. She had stopped wearing one because it never told the right time anyway. Whenever she went through the revolving room in the computer building, time got all shifted around. "It's getting late and you need to shower and make yourself gorgeous. Why don't you go meet Alex and let things flow from there." Maggie made a few suggestions about how to make the evening progress the way Barbara wanted it to, and Barbara listened carefully. Then she stood up. "I think I will do just what you suggested," she said. "And let the devil take the hindmost."

In the computer room, Lucy raised her arms in the air. "Yes," she hissed. "Right on, Barbara."

"Shut up," Angela growled.

It was almost eight when Barbara locked the office's heavy outer door behind her and dropped the keys back into her purse. She put her coat on her desk, then picked up the shopping bag she had brought with her and walked toward the library. About halfway down the hall she stopped. Could she do this? It had sounded like a fantastic idea when she and Maggie had talked about it, but now, in reality, she felt like she was about to make a fool out of herself. Alex probably wanted to talk to her about office politics or something.

Suddenly the door to the library opened. "Barbara," Alex said, seeing her standing in the hall. "I was beginning to think you'd stood me up." A grin lit his face.

"I'm sorry I'm late. I got held up." No, she wouldn't do it. She couldn't.

Alex walked toward her, then glanced down at the shopping bag. He peeked in the top, looked at her and smiled. "Champagne," he said, a slight catch in his voice. "Do some shopping on the way here? Is that a gift for someone?"

Now or never. "Actually, I thought you might be getting thirsty. All those books and all."

"What a great idea," Alex said, his eyes widening. "I was just going to get a soda, but this will go down much more easily. Got glasses?"

"I certainly do," Barbara said. As she slowly followed Alex back into the law library, she wondered whether he might have misunderstood. But what was there to misunderstand? An empty office. Champagne.

As Barbara closed the door behind her, Alex pulled the champagne bottle and two flutes from the bag. "What's this?" he asked, pulling out the tape player Maggie had placed there. She had included a tape Maggie had given her that contained just the erotic background music from the tapes Barbara had become so intrigued with. He put the tape in the player and pushed the play button. As he opened the bottle, the soft-summer-night wail of a saxophone filled the room.

"Great music," Alex said as he filled the two glasses. He handed one to Barbara and, with the music filling their ears, they clinked glasses. "Wonderful," he whispered, swallowing some of the bubbly liquid.

Nervously Barbara emptied the glass and Alex quickly refilled it. She sipped a bit more and looked at him standing in front of her. From the look in his eyes it was obvious that he wanted what Barbara wanted. But how to begin? As the hesitation lengthened, she decided she could make the first move. She could. Then she squared her shoulders, took a deep breath and said, "Dance with me?"

"Ummm, yeah," Alex said, putting his glass on the large oak table. "Good idea."

Barbara held on to her glass like some kind of security blanket as Alex took her in his arms. Their feet barely moved and his body pressed against hers. "I love slow dancing," she whispered into Alex's ear, alternately confident and terrified. "It's like making love standing up."

"I do too," Alex said, shaking his head. "But I don't believe this is happening. Things like this only happen in movies. And never to guys like me."

"Do you want it to happen?" Barbara asked.

"Oh, yes."

Barbara leaned back and gazed into Alex's eyes. "So?"

After a moment's hesitation, Alex's face softened and his mouth pressed against hers. The kiss was at first tentative, then deeper until Barbara felt her entire body fuse with his. When he took her in his arms, she could feel the drumming of his heart, and hers. She placed her mouth beside his ear and hummed a bit of familiar music.

Hungrily Alex placed a line of kisses from Barbara's ear, along her jawline, to her mouth. As his mouth covered hers, he took her glass and put it on the table. Then he laced his fingers with hers and held her hands against her thighs. They stood, their feet moving slightly to the deep rhythm of the music, their mouths fused, her nostrils filled with the smell of his aftershave.

Barbara was soaring. The music, which she had come to associate with erotic experiences, filled her soul, Alex's mouth teased, his tongue probing and filling, his hands holding hers immobile.

Alex slid their joined hands to the small of Barbara's back and pressed so her belly and mound were pressed intimately against his obviously hard cock. Barbara moved her hips slightly and heard Alex groan. She changed the position of the kiss slightly and tangled her tongue with his. He shuddered.

They danced until the backs of Barbara's thighs touched the edge of the large conference table. She boosted herself slightly until she slid onto the table, knees spread. Now she understood why Maggie had insisted that she change into a short denim skirt that zipped up the front. She wore a light green scoop-necked T-shirt and a denim vest that barely closed.

As Alex stepped between her knees, Barbara wrapped her legs around Alex's thighs and linked the high heels of her leather boots behind him. Between the effect of the music, the champagne, and the intensely hot look in Alex's eyes, she felt bold and daring. Her legs still around Alex's, she pushed books and papers aside until she could lie back on the cool wood.

With a groan, Alex pulled her shirt up so he could cover her lace-covered breasts with his hands. "Oh, sweet," he said, his voice hoarse. He found the clasp at the center front of her bra and deftly opened it.

"I knew you'd be gorgeous, but I had no idea . . ." he said as her breasts spilled out and filled his hands. He bent over and kissed her chest and ribs, finally covering her aching nipples with his wet mouth.

As he pulled and nipped, shafts of pure pleasure stabbed through her body. Unable to wait much longer, he grabbed the bottom of the skirt zipper and pulled it upward until the skirt was only held around her waist by a single button. "Oh, shit," he groaned when he discovered she wore lace garters to hold up her stockings but no panties. "Oh, shit." His eyes glazed as he stared at her naked pussy. "Oh, shit."

Quickly he pulled down his slacks and underwear. "Protection," Barbara said.

Alex pulled a condom from his wallet and opened the package. "Let me do that," Barbara said, standing up. She pushed Alex into a chair and unrolled the latex over the hard cock that stood straight up in his lap. When he started to rise, she said, "Let me do that, too." She straddled his thighs and slowly impaled herself on his erection.

"Oh, shit," Alex said again. "Yes, yes, yes."

When the length of him was inside her, she planted her feet firmly on the floor and levered herself up, almost off his cock, then allowed her body to drop again. Up and down, in and out, she established a carnal rhythm.

She allowed her head to fall back and surrendered herself to the music, the champagne, the heat of her desire. She reached between their bodies and rubbed her clit and the base of his cock. It took only another minute until Alex climaxed, and soon after Barbara reached her peak as well.

Panting, Barbara collapsed against Alex's chest, still covered with his white shirt and tie. "Making love half dressed is very erotic," he said. "I still have my shirt on and you're still almost wearing most of your clothes."

"God," Barbara said. "That was great." She rose and Alex quickly removed the condom with a wad of tissues. When he went to toss it into the wastebasket, she added, "Drop it into the bag. Why let anyone suspect what we've been doing?"

Alex tossed the tissues into the shopping bag as Barbara rose. She collected the champagne bottle and put it, the glasses, and the tape player into the bag.

"Leaving so soon?" Alex asked, picking up a few books and papers that had landed on the floor. "I'm running late, but we could have dinner in about half an hour."

As Alex pulled on his clothes, Barbara rezipped and tidied herself up. "I find that I'm not too hungry anymore," she said with a suggestive wink. "You satisfied my hungers just fine."

"Ummm," Alex purred, holding her and nibbling on her ear. "You aren't bad yourself."

"I'm going to catch a cab home and collapse from the pleasure of what we just did."

"I hope I'll see you before I leave."

"You might. And when you do, think about how good this was. And maybe next time you're on this coast we can do it again." Barbara picked up the shopping bag and looked around the library. "This room will never feel quite the same again," she said.

"I'll bet not," Alex said. "Sleep tight." He kissed her hard.

"Ummm," Barbara said. "Don't work too hard." As she opened the door, she looked back and marveled at the expression of pure satisfaction on Alex's face. She had put that there. Life was wonderful.

"Maggie, it was a trip," Barbara said the following morning as she poured coffee for herself and her friend. "It was sport fucking, it was no-strings lusting, it was more fun than I've had in years. And it was meaningless." Unable to sit still, Barbara paced the length of the kitchen, her cup in her hand.

"I know just how it makes you feel. Desirable, attractive, sexy."

"Yeah. All of that. No one has ever made me feel that way before. No, that's not really true. Alex didn't make me feel that way, *I* did. It's all inside me. Somehow I think it's always been there, that spark, that glow. It took you to make me see it." She walked up to Maggie, pulled her to her feet and gave her a giant bear hug. "I'm a sexy woman."

"That you are, yet you're also the same person you were three months ago, before we met."

"I feel like going to bars and picking up guys just to prove that I can do it. Then fucking their brains out, and mine, too, of course, just for fun."

"That's what sex is for. Fun. Sex with Chuck was never fun. It was okay, just not fun with a capital F. I never had fun like that until after my divorce."

Barbara sat down at the table and thought a moment. "Do you really mean that your marriage to Chuck was all bad?"

"Not bad, just boring."

"There wasn't anything good about it?"

"Marriage is for fools who are willing to settle for monotony and security."

"My parents had a good marriage, I think, until my father died. I think they were truly happy. I can remember that they used to disappear into the bedroom to 'go over finances.' They would close the door and giggle. Giggle. My mom and dad. They were truly happy."

"Maybe they were the one in a thousand," Maggie said.

"What about Bob? Wasn't that good?"

"Funny, it was the exact opposite of my marriage to Chuck. Hot sex but nothing else. It's impossible to have both hot sex and a good friendship in the same relationship."

"I hope you're wrong . . . Anyway, back to last night. Did I tell you about the tape? It was wonderful, so dreamy and erotic."

"Did you do some slow dancing? I always like to start an evening with a little concentrated body rubbing."

"Yeah, we did. And you're right about that. It is a great way to start things."

"But Alex is history?"

"He'll be in the office this morning, but I have several errands to run for Steve so I'll probably get to the office after he leaves to go back to the Coast. Anyway, seeing him the morning after would probably be a letdown." She took a swallow of her coffee.

"And Jay?" Maggie asked.

"Oh, no, he's still very much around. He's a nice man and I enjoy sex with him, even if it is a bit predictable."

"Why don't you initiate something new? Something that turns you on more than what you're doing."

Barbara looked surprised. "You know, old habits die hard. I guess I thought I could do new things with others, but I never thought of taking the initiative with Jay. Maybe I could. But I'm still such a dunce when it comes to creative stuff. I wouldn't know what to try." She raised her eyebrow a bit.

"Are you manipulating me?" When Barbara smiled, Maggie continued. "You want another of my tapes, don't you? You know you could buy some books of good erotica. They will be full of new ideas."

"I know, but those tapes turn me on. And I love both the music and the voice of the sexy man who reads the stories."

"That's my friend, the one who gave me the tapes in the first place. I think I told you that he runs an erotic boutique in the city. You should go there and meet him sometime."

"I think he'd intimidate me. He's sort of a professional at sex, and I'm such an amateur."

"He's a wonderful, creative lover with a marvelously devious mind. You shouldn't be afraid of him. You and he would make beautiful music together. I'll see whether I can get the two of you together. In the meantime . . ." Maggie reached into her pocket and pulled out another audiotape. "I want you to save this one for twenty-four hours. Put it on your dresser so you'll see it tonight when you get home from work. Think about it, but don't play it until tomorrow."

"Why?"

"It's a bit heavier than the ones you've listened to before and I want you to be really excited. So no touching, no sneaking, just let the excitement build till tomorrow. Okay?"

"If you want, Maggie. You haven't steered me wrong up to now."

Maggie looked at Barbara's watch. "Aren't you getting late for work?"

Barbara looked down. "Oh, damn," she said. "It's almost eight. I'm going to be late for the first time in years."

Since Maggie had given her the tape, Barbara had been intrigued. A bit heavier, she had said. The next night Barbara put the tape in the player and pushed play. There was music and that wonderful voice. She became wet just hearing it. I'm getting like Pavlov's dogs, Barbara thought. That man doesn't have to say anything dirty. He could read the telephone directory and I'd probably come. She stretched out on the bed, closed her eyes and listened.

> *His name was William Singleton and he had been working on the plan for months. First, he combed the city for just the right women, prostitutes to be sure, but women of beauty and refinement. Women who entertained men and didn't just fuck them. He paid them well and, telling them exactly what he intended, he invited the three he selected to his home.*
>
> *Over the following weeks, using exotic drugs and hypnosis, he trained the girls for many hours each day. Now he could show off his creations to his friends at a small exotic party he was throwing that evening.*
>
> *He checked the living room and the dining room. "Yes," he muttered as he rearranged a flower here and a napkin there, "everything's ready."*
>
> *He walked down the hall and opened the door to each of three special bedrooms. In each room, a girl lay sleeping, resting for the evening ahead. Reclosing the three doors, William went downstairs to await his guests. It would be a long evening.*
>
> *At eight o'clock, the doorbell rang for the first time, and by eight-fifteen there were four men in formal dress, including William, seated in the living room. Each held a drink in his hand; each talked nervously, anticipating the evening to come. Sir William Singletree was known for his erotic and highly unusual parties and his three best friends were anticipating a creative evening.*
>
> *At eight-thirty, the doorbell rang again. The butler, dressed in*

tailcoat and patent-leather shoes opened the door. The woman who swirled through the opening was beautiful. She shrugged out of her floor-length royal-blue velvet coat and left it with the butler. She was dressed in an ice-blue satin evening dress which was draped dramatically over her left shoulder. Her right arm and shoulder were bare, which showed off the wide diamond cuff bracelet that was her only piece of jewelry. Her meticulously arranged chestnut-brown hair swept up from her long, graceful neck.

She crossed the living room and offered a perfectly manicured hand to each of the gentlemen, greeting William last.

"My dear," he said as he took Sylvia's hand and kissed her cheek, "I think everything is ready for dinner now."

Without another word, she gracefully crossed the room and disappeared down the long hallway.

"Sylvia is looking magnificent as usual," Marshall said. He was in his midthirties and the star of a successful TV series. Tall, with dark and brooding good looks, his life was a continual battle to keep women from throwing themselves at him. But willing women bored him.

"Absolutely gorgeous," Samuel agreed. At almost fifty, he was the oldest man in the group. Gray hair and matching steel-gray eyes made him look the epitome of a business tycoon, which was exactly what he was.

"Yes," William said, taking obvious pride in the looks that his dinner companion got. "Sylvia is a beautiful and surprisingly resourceful woman."

Resourceful was a strange word to use for a woman, Paul, the third invited guest, thought. But leave it to William to use words in their most unusual connotations. Paul was about the same age and height as his friend Marshall but that was where the resemblance ended. Paul was a blue-eyed blond with hair slightly longer than was fashionable. A successful writer with three best sellers to his credit, he usually managed to look just a bit individual, and his sexual tastes were unusual as well.

William looked around at his three friends. Three totally different types, each with exotic sexual appetites like his own, but each with entirely different tastes. It would be interesting to watch how each one reacted to the evening's "entertainment."

Small talk continued to fill the living room until, about five minutes later, Sylvia returned, followed by three spectacularly beautiful women. Each was about twenty-five, one a blonde, one a brunette, and one a redhead. The women were dressed in identical evening dresses, strapless and unadorned, sweeping to the floor in a waterfall of silk. The only difference was that the blonde's dress was gold, the brunette's black, and the redhead's silver. Each was perfectly made up with an elaborate hairstyle that piled obviously long hair high on each woman's head.

The three guests stared. The women were all of medium height and well proportioned. "Good evening," they said, almost in unison.

"These are your dinner companions," William said. "Sylvia, introduce our guests."

Sylvia took the hand of the blonde in the golden dress and walked her over to where Marshall was standing. "Marshall, darling," she said, "I'd like you to meet Kitt. I think you and she will get along wonderfully."

Marshall took Kitt's hand as she murmured, "It's so good to meet you."

Sylvia then walked the brunette toward Samuel. "Samuel, you and Ginny have a lot in common, as I'm sure you'll find out."

"I've heard a lot about you," Ginny said, "and I've been looking forward to meeting you."

Paul walked over to the girl with the incredibly red hair. "I've always loved redheads," he said to the girl. "My name is Paul."

"This is Cynthia," Sylvia said. "She's to be your companion for the evening."

Almost immediately, William said, "Dinner is ready. Shall we eat?"

As dinner proceeded uneventfully, perfectly prepared dishes arrived one after another, accompanied by perfectly selected wines. The eight diners discussed politics, books, sports, any subject that anyone was interested in. Each man marveled at how perfectly the woman he was with fit his tastes, both in looks and in interests.

When coffee and brandy arrived at the table, William stood. Raising his brandy snifter, he said, "A toast to a splendid evening to come."

They all raised their glasses, then drank.

"Shall we go downstairs?" William asked.

They crossed the living room and walked down the great

curved staircase to the large well-carpeted area below. The three male guests had been in William's house many times before. His parties were legendary, and the best entertainment always took place downstairs.

The three couples settled themselves on large overstuffed sofas to wait for whatever entertainment William and Sylvia had planned.

The host and hostess crossed the room and, while Sylvia gracefully took her seat, William stood beside a table on which a line of glass bells of different sizes was arranged. With great ceremony, he took a small glass rod and tapped the bell at the near end of the row. A single clear note filled the room.

William looked at each of the three women. As he gazed, each man turned and looked at his companion. Each of the three identically dressed women stared into space, seemingly out of contact with the others in the room.

"Gentlemen," William said. "The ladies are unable to hear or see what's going on right now. They have been conditioned to the sound of these bells. When I ring this one, they all respond by going into a trance. When I tap the one on the other end," he tapped the bell, "they all return to us."

He looked at the three women. "Don't you, ladies?"

The women smiled and looked a bit confused, so Sylvia said, "You're feeling fine, aren't you, ladies?"

"Certainly, Sylvia," Kitt said. "We all feel wonderful."

William tapped the first bell and the three women again stared into space, their eyes distant and clouded over.

"Each one of these women has volunteered for a most amusing training program. Sylvia and I have spent weeks perfecting their behavior. We have done it as a present to each of you to thank you for your years of friendship and loyalty."

"You know you don't have to thank us," Samuel said. "We've always been there for each other."

"Well, I wanted to do this," William said, "so let's get on with it. Marshall, you get to go first."

Marshall looked a bit puzzled. "First for what?" he asked.

"I'll show you." William tapped a bell in the center of the row and said, "Kitt, take off your dress and show Marshall what is his for the evening."

Slowly Kitt rose. She looked into Marshall's eyes as she reached behind her and slowly unzipped her dress and gradually

allowed it to inch down her body. Proudly she displayed a sensa-
tional body, covered with a golden corselet that cinched in her
waist and cupped her breasts but left the nipples bare. Gold-
colored garters held up matching stockings. Her shoes were also
golden with high spike heels. She wore no panties and Marshall
could see her blond hair between the garters.

"What do you think, Marshall?" Sylvia asked.

"She's magnificent, Sylvia." He sounded hesitant.

"Say what you wish," Sylvia said. "She won't remember any-
thing we don't want her to."

"Well, you all know I don't like willing women. I like my
women to fight me."

Sylvia chuckled. "We know that, dear. We know all your
tastes. In our conversations with Kitt, we discovered that she has
a matching fantasy, one that she's been reluctant to discuss with
anyone. But we've used that desire to train her to fulfill your fan-
tasy, while fulfilling hers at the same time." She looked around
the room, catching Samuel's eyes, then Paul's. "The same is true
of your dinner companions, gentlemen. Your tastes match per-
fectly. Now, I hope you two don't mind waiting? We'd like to play,
one couple at a time."

The two others shook their heads. If William and Sylvia did
know all their tastes, it was going to be an evening worth wait-
ing for.

"Now, Kitt," William said, "listen to me. Marshall wants to
fuck you. Do you want him to?"

Kitt smiled and allowed her gaze to roam over Marshall's
body. "Yes. He's very sexy and I'm very hungry."

Sylvia said, softly, "The girls are all very hungry. Their bod-
ies have been conditioned to become physically aroused at the
sound of the bells." She looked at William, then at the three men.
"We have found that sexual excitement, like anything else, can be
conditioned. We have trained these girls to react in specific ways
to different sounds." She looked at Kitt, standing proudly and dis-
playing her shapely body. "How much do you want him? Tell
him."

A slow, erotic smile spread over her face. "I want you to
make love to me. I want you to fuck me now. Please fuck me."

Marshall looked disappointed. It was too easy.

"Don't worry," William said, "we understand." William
tapped Kitt's bell twice. Instantly, Kitt grabbed her dress and

held it in front of her as she backed away from Marshall. "I know who you are and what you want. You want to rape me." She licked her lips. "I've seen you looking at me all evening and I'm not going to give in. Don't you come near me," she snarled.

William looked at the smile that spread over Marshall's face. "Is this more to your liking?"

"Most certainly," Marshall said. "I've always had rape fantasies, but I would never actually commit rape, hurt anyone, you know. Are you sure that she really wants this?"

"You'll have to trust me. Each of these women has been selected for her sexual tastes and appetites. Don't worry. All of you," he looked around the room, "will get tremendous pleasure from what happens."

"If you're sure."

"I am. Now, she's all yours," William said.

Marshall stood and carefully removed his jacket and loosened his tie. He dropped the jacket on the sofa next to him but kept the tie in his hand. As he walked toward Kitt, he glanced around the room. Yes, he thought, there was everything he might need. He slowly stalked Kitt as she backed away from him. "Come here, Kitt, I won't hurt you."

"Stay away," she said.

"It will be easier for you if you hold still. I don't want to hurt you."

"I know exactly what you want, Marshall, and you won't get it from me without a fight." She continued to back away from him staying just out of arm's reach.

With sudden speed, Marshall took three steps, reached out and snatched the dress from Kitt's hands. Then, as she tried to scamper away, he snagged her wrist and pulled her to him. He twisted her arm behind her and tangled the fingers of his free hand in her hair.

Hairpins flew everywhere as long strands pulled free. Soon, still holding her squirming body, he wrapped a hank of long flaxen hair around his hand. He gently pulled her head back and pressed his lips against hers. She tried to twist away from his kiss, but his hand in her hair prevented her head from moving.

As he felt her press her lips together to keep his tongue out of her mouth, he said, "You aren't strong enough to resist me, you know."

Silently she glared at him, her lips sealed.

"Let me find out just how reluctant you really are," he said. He picked her up and dropped her on the nearest sofa. As she tried to twist away, he stretched his body on top of hers and reached his hand between her legs. He touched her pubic hair and slid a finger through her folds. He smiled. "You're soaking wet. You really do want me."

"Keep your hands off me!" she shouted.

Marshall hesitated.

"Marshall," William said, "just in case you need reassurance . . ." He tapped Kitt's bell. Instantly she was quiet. Looking puzzled about how she ended up on the sofa with her date's body stretched over hers, she gazed into Marshall's eyes and said, "Mmmm. You feel good against me. Are you going to make love to me?"

"Yes, darling, I am." Marshall nodded to William who tapped Kitt's bell twice. At the sound, she was a tiger again, squirming to get free of his hold. "God, I like it like this," Marshall said. He looked at Samuel and Paul. "Gentlemen, I could use a little help at this moment."

The two men got up and each held one of Kitt's arms. Marshall held both her legs and together they carried her over to a low table. Samuel and Paul each pulled off his tie. They stretched Kitt across the table, face up, her head hanging off the end. Using their ties and a soft rope that William provided, they tied her arms and legs to the table legs. Then they stood up and surveyed the scene. Kitt was still dressed in the corselet and stockings, but her cunt and nipples were exposed, offered to the men for their use.

"Yes," Marshall said, "that's very good." He paused, looking at her squirming body. "William," he said, "you said that she'd be enjoying this. I want you to release her so we can both enjoy."

William tapped her bell again. "Kitt," he said, "listen to me." Kitt's body went limp. "Marshall wants you to relax and be yourself. Do you understand?"

"Yes," Kitt said, testing her bonds, "I understand. But I can't move."

"No, you can't. Does that upset you?" When she hesitated, he asked again, his voice soft, "Does it?"

Kitt looked at Marshall. "No. I find it very exciting, being tied up like this. But it's hard for me to admit it."

"I understand. Do whatever you like. If you say stop, you can be sure that I will."

Kitt smiled and again pulled against the ties that held her. "I really am at your mercy. What are you going to do?"

"Pleasure us both, I hope," Marshall said. Then he walked around the table stroking and scratching Kitt's belly, thighs, nipples. "You're so beautiful."

Quickly he undressed and knelt at the head of the table so his hard, erect cock was level with her mouth. "I want you to suck it," he said.

Kitt opened her mouth, then paused. With a gleam in her eyes, she turned her head away, her lips firmly pressed together. "Oh, yes, baby, get into the game. Fight me."

Marshall twisted his hand in her hair and pulled her face around. "Open your mouth, bitch, and suck my cock!"

As she did as he said, he pressed his penis into her mouth. Suddenly Marshall knew she was enjoying what she was doing. He felt her lips tighten on his cock and her tongue slide over his skin. As he pulled back, he felt her create a vacuum in her mouth as she sucked. Still holding her head, he fucked her mouth until he came. Spurts of semen filled her throat and she swallowed, licking him clean.

As Marshall settled back on his haunches, he said, "What about her? She's so hot."

"What's your pleasure, gentlemen?" William asked.

"I'd like to watch one of the other girls get her off," Samuel said.

"Is that all right with you, Kitt?" Marshall asked.

"Would you like to watch?" she asked him.

"Oh, yes," he admitted.

Kitt smiled and nodded.

"That's a splendid idea," Sylvia said. "We haven't trained anyone specifically for that, so it will interesting to see how it works."

As William reached for another bell, Sylvia said, "Let me tell her. I think I'd enjoy doing that."

"Certainly," William said, tapping a different bell. A clear note, higher than any they had heard previously, sounded through the room. Ginny raised her dark-brown eyes and looked at William. "Ginny, you will listen to Sylvia like a good girl. You will hear only her voice and do whatever she says," William said.

Ginny turned toward Sylvia who said, "Dear, Kitt is so excited and she needs to come. I want you to pleasure her with your mouth."

William explained to the three men. "Ginny is our most adventurous woman. You must understand that I never ask any woman to do anything that is outside her nature."

During William's explanation, Ginny had sat quietly, not yet obeying Sylvia's instructions.

"Has she ever had any lesbian experiences?" Samuel asked.

"Several, according to her, and she enjoys it tremendously," Sylvia said, turning to the girl. "Ginny, I told you to do something."

"Tell me exactly what you want me to do," Ginny whispered. "I want to hear the words."

"All right, my dear. I want you to do whatever I tell you." Sylvia smiled. "Now, get up and go over to the table."

Marshall was holding Kitt's head in his hands, stroking her face. "We'll both enjoy what's going to happen," he whispered to her.

Ginny approached and, at Sylvia's instruction, knelt beside Kitt. "Now suck her nipples," Sylvia said. "Take one into your mouth and suck it, hard. Tug at it with your teeth."

Ginny bent over Kitt's body and began to suck her breasts, exposed above the corselet.

"Use your hands. Pull her tits out and caress them with your hands."

Marshall could hear slurping sounds as Ginny sucked.

"Now the other one," Sylvia said. Obediently Ginny switched to the other breast.

Kitt's hips thrust upward, reaching for something, a cock, a tongue. "She needs you, Ginny. She needs your mouth on her pussy to make her come. Lick and suck her pussy, Ginny, like a good girl."

Ginny moved around the table and tentatively touched the tip of her tongue to Kitt's cunt lips. "Lick the whole length of her slit," Sylvia said, "then flick your tongue over her clit. Good. Now stick your tongue inside and pull it out. Lick. Nibble at her clit."

Sylvia walked over and placed her hand on Kitt's belly, just above her pubic hair. "I can feel her hips moving," she said. "Lick faster. Flick your tongue over her clit, then pull it into your mouth. Yes. Make her come. I can feel it coming. Don't stop."

There was a moment's pause, then Sylvia yelled, "Now! Suck hard now."

Marshall reached down and felt the tiny, compulsive movements of Kitt's hips. As she came, he pressed his mouth against hers and probed with his tongue. He thrust his tongue in and out of her mouth in the rhythm he could feel with his hand. Her climax seemed to go on for hours. When she calmed, Marshall untied her and cradled her in his lap.

As Ginny finished licking Kitt's body, Samuel stood up, unzipped his pants and pulled out his erect cock. He had to have her now. On a side table there was a jar of lubricant and he spread a handful on his cock. "Tell her to let me fuck her my way."

"She already knows," Sylvia said, "and she loves it that way. Offer Samuel what he wants, Ginny."

Ginny flipped her dress up over her back, raised her ass in the air and, still licking Kitt's pussy, parted her ass cheeks with her hands. All anyone could see were the same garters and stockings that Kitt was wearing, except Ginny's were black to match her dress.

Samuel found his cock getting even harder at her eagerness to give and take pleasure. God, he wanted her tight ass. He rubbed his lubricated fingers over her entire rear, then pressed the tip of one finger against her hole.

"Oh, yes, darling," Ginny said, holding very still. Samuel's finger pressed and released. Slowly, the pushing became a bit harder and the tip of his finger penetrated. Deeper and deeper his thrusting finger went, rhythmically forcing itself into her.

As the finger continued its assault, her hips began to thrust backward. "That feels good, doesn't it, Ginny. It's tight, but it makes your pussy hot." He reached around and fingered her sopping cunt with his other hand. "So wet. You're so wet."

Samuel stroked her pussy with one hand and fucked her ass with the other. When he felt she was ready and he could wait no longer, he lubricated his hard cock and pressed the tip against her puckered hole, then thrust deep into her.

"It feels so good, darling. Do it harder," she screamed.

Samuel kept massaging her cunt and soon felt her rear muscles relax and her hips begin to buck. "Yes," he said, establishing his own rhythm, "move your hips while I fuck your ass and finger your cunt. Move with me."

"Oh, God," she screamed, "I'm going to come."

"We're both going to come, Ginny."
He fucked her ass and rubbed her pussy until they both came and collapsed on the floor.

Barbara stopped the tape and, panting from her orgasm, she went into the bathroom and got a glass of water. That I could get so hot from just a story . . . she thought. No wonder people buy dirty books and magazines. Then she stopped herself. Not dirty. Erotic. Delicious. She made a mental note to find a bookstore or newsstand and do a little shopping. When she was calmer, she lay back on the bed and pressed play again and the story resumed. She was instantly back in the basement with William and Sylvia.

William crossed to the bar and poured Sylvia and the three men a drink. They untied Kitt and put robes on the two spent girls. Then they sat them on the sofa and put them back into their trance.

William looked at Paul. "Yours is yet to come. I just want everyone a bit rested to watch the show."

Paul smiled and rearranged his clothing over his hard cock. After what he had already witnessed, whatever William and Sylvia had in store for him would be worth any amount of inconvenience.

After they had rested for a short while, William said, "Your treat is a bit different, Paul. Cynthia has been trained for a new experience. When she hears her bell she will listen only to my voice and she will feel exactly what I tell her to feel." William tapped a bell with a lower, more mellow tone. Cynthia sat up.

"Cynthia," William said, "it's very warm in here, isn't it?"

"Yes," she said. "Very warm."

"So warm that you think you'll never be able to get cool."

Cynthia started fanning herself with her hand. Her face began to flush and she blew a stream of cool air on her chest.

"That air you're blowing is hot and it's making you hotter. Even though this room is full of important people and you will be very embarrassed to do so, you have to pull the top of your dress down to get cool."

Cynthia looked around at the "important people" and looked very uncomfortable. "I'm so hot," she murmured, "I have to get cool." She pulled the top of her dress down and, like the other girls, she was wearing a corselet that bared her nipples, hers in silver.

"You're still so hot," William continued. "That's not helping.

Your nipples are the center of the heat. They're so hot they're on fire. You have to cool them off. Your whole tit is so hot." Cynthia *pulled her breasts out of the corselet, looked frantically around the room and spotted the ice in Paul's drink. She grabbed the glass, pulled out an ice cube and rubbed it over her breasts. "Yes, that feels better, doesn't it?"*

"Yes." The word came out like a hiss. "Better."

"The ice is getting hotter from the heat of your breast. It's not cooling anymore. You need something else."

"What?" she asked, dropping the ice cube.

"Paul's mouth. That's the only cool thing in the room. But he might not want to suck your tits and cool them. You have to ask nicely."

"Please cool my tits," she said, offering her breasts to him. "Please."

Paul blew a stream of air across her nipples. "Yes," she purred, "that's cool. But I need your mouth."

Paul smiled and said, "You'll have to force them into my mouth." This was his oldest fantasy coming true.

She climbed into his lap and forced her swollen buds into his mouth. She pulled at his hair and his ears as she tried to force her whole breast into his mouth at once. He sucked and was in heaven.

"Now the other one, Cynthia. Let Paul's mouth cool it."

Paul alternated between Cynthia's pillow-soft, white breasts, filling his mouth and his hands with her flesh.

"Your tits are getting cool now," William said, "but the heat is traveling to your mouth. It's your mouth that is hot now."

Cynthia opened her mouth and panted, trying to draw in cool air. Then she picked up Paul's drink and took an ice cube into her mouth.

"That ice is still hot, Cynthia," William said. "There's only one thing here that's cool." She looked at him, puzzled. "Paul's cock. It's the only cool thing in the room."

Frantically Cynthia pulled at Paul's zipper until she could pull his pants aside and take out his cock. It was huge. Paul loved to have it sucked, but it was too big for most women.

"It's a huge ice cube, Cynthia," William said. "If you take it into your mouth it will cool you, but only where it touches. The rest of your mouth will still be hot."

Cynthia wrapped her hand around Paul's erection and opened her mouth as wide as she could. She took Paul's entire cock into her mouth, her tongue and hands moving ceaselessly. She bobbed her head, moving the "cold" cock around to cool each part of her hot flesh.

For five minutes, everyone watched as Cynthia sucked Paul's erection until it was hard for him not to come. "Make her stop," he cried. "I want to come in her pussy."

"The heat in your mouth is subsiding now, Cynthia." Cynthia's body slowly relaxed and she sat up. "Your body is warm again all over. You'd better take off your dress."

Cynthia pulled off the dress that had been bunched around her waist.

"That's better," William said. "Now the heat is flowing back, this time in your pussy. It's like hot honey running down inside your belly and flowing out of your cunt, making it warmer and warmer."

Cynthia spread her legs as she "felt" the honey flow. "Spread your legs as the honey streams down your thighs. You need something cool. The honey is making you hot. Paul's cock is still the only cool thing in the room. Sit on it. Take it inside you."

Cynthia climbed onto Paul's lap and impaled herself on his cock. "Move it around to cool your entire cunt," William said. "Up and down so it cools the sides of your passage. There's cool juice inside that prick. Tighten your muscles to squeeze out the cool juice. Squeeze and relax, squeeze and relax. That's the best way."

Paul could take no more. With a scream he came deep inside her. "Yes, you did well," William said. "Cold juice is spurting into your pussy and putting out the fire. But you must hold Paul's cock inside you or you'll get hot again."

Paul looked at William, exhausted. He had no idea what William had in mind, but he was spent.

"Have you ever felt a woman come?" Sylvia asked Paul. "Really felt it? Well, we've always thought that we could make one come just from the sound of William's voice. The only way we'd be sure is if she came while your cock was still inside and you could feel her climax. Are you game?"

Paul looked at Cynthia still sitting in his lap. He knew she couldn't hear him or Sylvia. "Yeah, sure. I'm game. But I don't think you can do it. Orgasm isn't trainable."

"We think it is. Let's put it to the test. I'll let the other women listen, too. You can all enjoy your date's excitement."

He tapped another bell. All the women looked at William.

"Now, ladies, don't move any part of your body, just listen to my voice. You will feel exactly what I tell you to feel. Do you understand?"

Cynthia and the other women nodded. "I understand."

"You feel hands on your breasts. One hand on each breast is kneading your flesh. It feels so good. Lean forward just a bit so your breasts will press into the caressing hands." Paul felt her strain forward. *"That's good. The fingers are twisting your nipples now. It's painful, but it is also exciting. The pinches have taken on a rhythm, first one side then the other. They are pulling at your nipples, milking your breasts. Those hands are making you so excited."*

Paul could feel Cynthia's body swaying with the sound of William's voice. The voice was so exciting that each of the other two men were playing with the breasts of the women now sitting on their laps.

"The fingers are creating tiny electrical charges that are sparking through your tits. Hot electrical sparks that excite you and make your pussy wetter. You can feel the sparks through your ribs and your belly. Tiny pinpoints of pain and pleasure are traveling over your skin, lower and lower through your belly and now over the insides of your thighs.

"The sparks are tiny caresses now, flicking soft touches up the insides of your thighs. Now those flickers are on your pussy, pulsing over your clit."

Almost simultaneously the other two men entered their women and began pumping in sync with William's voice.

"Your clit is pulsing with the sensation. You can feel the tightness grow in your belly as your climax approaches. That tightness is traveling to your pussy."

Paul could feel his cock swell as he tried to remain still. He could feel Cynthia's juices soaking his thighs.

"Feel those pulses all over your body, in your breasts, in your mouth, in your ass. Those pulses are your orgasm approaching. You want to resist but you can't. The pull of the pulses is too strong. The pulses are pulling your orgasm from you.

"Tell me, are you going to come?"

"Yes," each woman screamed. *"I can feel it . . . right now."*

"Then come now. Let the orgasm come. Let the pulses flow through your cunt."

Paul screamed as he felt Cynthia's climax suck at his cock. He couldn't keep his own orgasm back and he climaxed again.

No one was sure how much later, William tapped the bell that released the women from their trances. He and Sylvia tossed blankets over the exhausted couples and turned down the light.

"Good night, everyone," William said. "Sylvia and I are going upstairs."

Chapter 8

It was several weeks before Barbara saw Maggie again. She had dated Jay frequently and had had dates, and been to bed, with three other men—one from her office, one a neighbor, and one a man she had met at the supermarket. She had also played the tapes frequently and found that, thanks to the attitudes of the people in the stories, she had become accepting of sex in all forms, and was able to suggest games and activities that proved both stimulating and rewarding.

In mid-June, Barbara arrived home from work one evening to find Maggie in her kitchen, cooking. After long, almost tearful hugs, Barbara stepped back, looked at her friend and said, "It's been such a long time and I've missed you. God, things smell good in here."

"I've missed you, too," Maggie said. "And I'm making corned beef and cabbage. I couldn't resist."

"You must have shopped. How did you do that? Could people see you?"

Maggie looked shocked. "They must have been able to, but I have no clue how. I never even thought about it. I just went to the supermarket and picked up a few things." She shook her head. "People must have seen me. The woman checked me out without a blink. And I had money in my wallet."

"But in the mall, no one could see you but me."

"Things in this plane of existence work strangely to say the least. When is this?"

"It's June."

"It looked springy," Maggie said. "But I cooked this anyway. It was in my mind when I arrived at the A&P."

Barbara lifted a piece of cabbage from the pot and tasted. "Wonderful. I'm glad you did. And I'm incredibly glad to see you."

Maggie hugged Barbara again. "Me too, although I just left you a few moments before I showed up at the supermarket."

Barbara opened the refrigerator door and spied a six-pack of Sam Adams. She looked toward Maggie questioningly. "My favorite. One for you?" At Maggie's nod, she pulled out two bottles.

"Sure." She pushed a long fork into the slab of meat in the pot. "Let's give this about fifteen more minutes."

The two women sat at the kitchen table and each poured a beer. "How have you been, Barbara?" Maggie asked.

"I've been great," Barbara said. "Lots of dates, lots of good healthy sex."

"Steve?"

"No. Not him. Despite all the great clothes and keeping myself looking good, he pays almost no attention to me, except as a very useful piece of furniture."

"Have you asked him out?"

"No. We did have dinner one evening, but it was with a client and his wife. I guess Lisa, Ms. Knockout, isn't the kind you take to dinner with a guy with oodles of old money. You should have seen his wife. Her jewelry was older than I was."

"And nothing remotely date-like from Steve?"

"Not a whisper. He didn't even take me home, just put me into a hired car and told the driver to take me wherever I wanted to go."

"We really have to do something about that, don't we?"

"Yes, we do. But I have another request first. Those tapes?"

"I gave you all I had," Maggie said.

"You told me that the man who made them has a store in the city. I think, well . . ."

"Yes? Out with it."

"Well, I'd like to meet him."

"His voice really gets to you, doesn't it?"

"His voice fills my erotic dreams, which, of course, I'd never admit to having except to you. What's he like?"

"He owns an erotic toy, book, and what-have-you store in the Village. He's a free spirit with a great understanding of the secret desires everyone has. And he exploits that knowledge in his stories and the items he sells in the shop. He's wonderfully creative in everything he does. And I do mean everything."

"You've been to bed with him?"

"Beds, boats, tables, CJ makes love wherever the fancy strikes him. But yes, I've been with him many times."

"Was he a customer?"

"He doesn't ever have to pay for it. He has whatever he wants, whenever he wants it. And frequently he wanted me. And I wanted him. So we did. I met him when I first went into his shop to buy a few things."

"I don't want to make love with him, I just want to see the man who goes with that incredible voice."

"The shop is called A Private Place." Maggie wrote down the address on a piece of paper. "Take one of the tapes as sort of an introduction. And keep an open mind and be ready for anything, that is, if you're so inclined."

"Oh, Maggie," Barbara said. "That's not why I want to meet him."

"Whatever you say." She took a long drink of her beer and the conversation shifted.

The storefront was unremarkable, a large window with a display of erotic books, but nothing overt enough to offend any passers-by. The words *A Private Place* were lettered on the window in ornate gold script, and there was a small sign in the corner of the window that proclaimed *C. J. Winterman, Prop.* CJ. Yes, that voice. Hours 11:00 to 5:00 Tues., Thurs., and Sat. He certainly works only when it suits him, Barbara thought.

That Saturday afternoon, as she stood looking in the window, Barbara rubbed her sweating palms together. She was nervous as a teenager, yet she dearly wanted to meet the man who had been part of her fantasies since Maggie gave her the first tape. She took a deep breath, inhaling late spring air, then glanced at her watch. Almost five o'clock. Only a few minutes until closing, but the sign read Open. She pushed open the door and heard a small bell jingle.

The store was well lit, with racks and shelves filled with sex toys, erotic games, books, greeting cards, everything the creative lover might want. She slowly toured the shop, pausing to giggle at several get well and birthday cards, then trembled a bit in front of a display of bondage equipment. As she crossed the front sales area, she overheard a young couple discussing which vibrator they should purchase.

"Do you think that's powerful enough?" she said.

"I don't want the kind that plugs in," he responded. "You're limited by the length of the cord."

"I like this one. It has a clit tickler," she said.

"If you like it, then we'll get it." The man handed a woman behind the counter a credit card as Barbara looked over a display of whips and leather harnesses.

"These are cleverly arranged so that you can strap on a dildo leaving your hands free for other pleasures," a voice behind her said.

It was his voice, the voice from the tapes. It hummed through her, making her knees weak and her pussy wet. She swallowed and turned slowly. He was about her age, average height with very curly brown hair and a sweet, almost cherubic face. His smile was open and warm. No wonder people buy stuff here, Barbara thought. He seems so innocent, as though everything in here must be ordinary. "You must be CJ," she said.

"Is that a guess from the sign in the window, or have you been here before?"

That voice. That incredible voice.

"Actually neither. I know your voice from some tapes I've been listening to." She withdrew a tape from her pocketbook and showed it to him.

"Oh." His face lit up as he grinned. "Yes. But these are part of the special edition, ones I made up for my friends." He pointed to the gold rim around the label. "See. This is how you tell. Where did you get this one?"

"That's a bit of a long story. Let's just say I got a few of them from a wonderful woman named Maggie."

"I haven't seen Maggie in a long time. I miss her. How is she?"

How to handle this one? Barbara wondered. "Actually, Maggie passed away last summer."

"I am so sorry. She was an amazing woman. Were you good friends?"

"Oh, yes, very good friends. But that was long ago."

"And were you and she kindred spirits?"

Barbara knew exactly what he was asking. Was she a hooker? "We weren't in the same line of work," she answered. "But we shared a lot of the same feelings." Was that an invitation? She hoped so. Much as she had denied it to Maggie, she had to admit that she wanted this man as she had never wanted anything.

"And what can I do to help you?" CJ asked.

"CJ," a voice called, postponing her answer. "It's after five and my husband's waiting outside. Unless you need me, I'm leaving."

"Have a nice evening, Alice," CJ called. "And turn the sign as you leave."

"I guess you're closing now," Barbara said, unable now to ask for what she wanted. The moment was gone. "I'll be leaving, too."

"Since you're a friend of Maggie's, you're welcome to wander as long as you like. Were you looking for anything special?" He placed his hands on her shoulders and turned her toward the display of leather-and-metal harnesses. "These are usually bought by dominants, for training sessions with their subs. Do they interest you?" He spoke with his mouth close to her ear, his breath warm, his hands on her shoulders.

"Yes," she whispered.

"You're trembling. Tell me what has you so excited. The idea of wearing one of those and doing deliciously evil things to someone?" When she remained silent, he continued. "Or maybe having someone wear a harness like that and overpower you."

Barbara couldn't move, couldn't speak. She was unable to control any parts of her body. All her thoughts were concentrated on his hands, his mouth, and her aching pussy.

"Did you want to buy one for your lover? Male or female?"

"Not for a lover," she croaked.

"For yourself?"

"For you." The words slipped out, but she was glad she had said them.

"Ah." His breath was warm against her ear. "You have a fantasy about me. Maybe in the fantasy I am wearing something made from heavy leather straps with metal rings and buckles, holding you down while I violate your body." Barbara couldn't answer. "You are helpless, unable to prevent me from doing whatever I want to you. Is that what you want?" Silence. His mouth remained against her ear, his tongue licking the edge. His arm slipped across her upper chest and pressed her back tightly against his chest. "Is it?"

"Yes," she whispered.

"Good girl," he purred. "Don't move." He nipped at her ear with his teeth, then left her. She heard him pull down the shades and put the chain on the door. He returned to stand behind her. "Now no one can come in and disturb us. Come with me."

Barbara moved like an automaton, following his slender frame through a curtain and into the back of the shop. They passed through a storage area and into another room. CJ closed the door and slid a bolt home. "Now we are truly alone. You are here of your own free will, are you not?"

"Yes," she whispered.

"Do you understand about safe words?"

Barbara remembered that Maggie had explained that if anyone used the pre-agreed safe word during any bondage session, everything stopped. She nodded.

"I use a slightly different system." He placed a Ping-Pong ball in Barbara's hand. "If you drop this, I will stop anything and everything, no questions asked. Do you understand?"

Barbara looked down at the small white ball in her hand. "Yes," she said, unable to say anything more even if she wanted to. The inside of her mouth felt like cotton, her knees were jelly, and her insides were trembling so hard it was difficult to concentrate on anything else. But she was so turned on, she felt as if she could come on command.

"And do you promise me you will drop that if anything, and I do mean anything, bothers you? It's most important that I have your word on that."

"You have my word," she said.

"Good." CJ flipped a switch and the room filled with the music that formed the background on the tapes. Then he opened a small closet in the corner of the room, grabbed some clothes and stepped behind a shoulder-height screen. "Get undressed," he said, his head above the top of the screen. "I want you completely naked." When she hesitated, he snapped, "Now!"

Barbara put the ball down, quickly removed her clothes, put them on a chair and picked up the ball again.

"Let me see you," CJ said, still behind the screen. "Stand up straight, stretch your arms up over your head and spread your legs."

Barbara separated her feet slightly and raised her arms.

"Wider," he snapped.

Barbara spread her feet wider and stared at CJ's face, the only part of him she could see.

"Nice," he said, obviously fumbling with clothes behind the screen. "Good legs, nice hips. Show me your tits."

"What?" Barbara said.

"Put the ball down and hold those tits for me so I can see how full they are." When her hands remained in the air, he said, "Do it now or leave."

Barbara put the ball on the small chair at her side, then cupped her breasts. The room was warm but she was shivering, from need, from lust, and from a sliver of fear. What had she gotten herself into?

"Pinch the nipples and make them hard. Show them to me."

Embarrassed but so aroused, she pinched her nipples until they swelled.

"Nice titties," CJ said. "Big and soft. You'll do nicely." When she went to put her feet together, he said, "Not in my presence. Your feet will always be apart, your body ready for me. Do you understand? Get the ball, then come here."

He stepped from behind the screen, now dressed in a deep brown harness. Wide straps of what appeared to be hard, unyielding leather crossed his bare chest and a leather pouch cupped his penis and testicles. He wore leather sandals that laced up his slender, yet muscular legs. He wore wide silver cuffs around his biceps and a leather collar around his neck. Whatever led me to see him as an angel? Barbara wondered. In this outfit, he was all power and control.

Holding the Ping-Pong ball, Barbara crossed the room and stood before CJ. He stared at her legs and glared. She looked down, then separated her feet.

"Stand with your chest against the wall."

She moved so she stood facing a bare wall, then felt his hand on her back, pressing her tightly against the cold surface. He raised her arms above her head, spread about as far apart as her feet. "How much of this do you want?" he asked. "I can make you cry or beg, I can hurt you or just control you. What do you want? This is the last decision you will make."

Barbara thought. She wanted to try everything. She didn't know whether pain would be a turn-on, but she had the ball in her hand and she trusted CJ completely. "Everything," she whispered. "I want to try it all."

"Good girl," he said. Then she felt the snap as cold metal cuffs were locked onto her wrists and ankles, then CJ attached the cuffs to the wall. She couldn't move. Then CJ placed cotton balls against her eyes, and covered them with a blindfold. She could see nothing.

"Now," he said, "we begin." He inserted his finger in her slit. "Such a hot slut," he said. "So wet. Let's cool you down a little."

Barbara heard noises, then jumped as something very cold pressed against her heated lips. The frozen object was inserted into her channel. "Some ice should cool you off a bit. You're much too excited." He rubbed another ice cube over her slit, numbing her flesh, yet heating her belly.

"God, that's too cold," she said.

"You will say nothing, or I'll gag you, too." When she shuddered, she felt a wad of cloth stuffed into her mouth, then another cloth stretched between her teeth and tied behind her head. Then he rubbed her clit and laughed. "You want this. Your body tells me everything."

She did want it. She wanted to give everything over to this man with the magic voice. He could do everything to her, all the things she had only dreamed about. Cold water trickled down her inner thigh but she couldn't move to wipe it off. Her mind traveled to the ball in her hand. She wouldn't drop it. Not yet. Maybe not at all.

"Now, let's see how you like this part." Suddenly she felt a hard slap on her right buttock. Then one on her left.

She groaned, making strange strangled sounds around the gag in her mouth. Again and again, his hand landed on her heated flesh. She burned. She throbbed, yet she was also incredibly turned on. The music filled her mind and the pleasure/pain filled her body. She could control her body no longer and she climaxed. Without anyone touching her pussy, without being filled with anything but an ice cube.

"No self-control," he said, laughing again. "I like that, but you're much too easy. Maybe now that you've come once, you'll be more of a challenge." Barbara felt CJ rub some lotion on her hot buttocks, kneading and caressing her skin from the small of her back to her cheeks. Some of the liquid trickled into her slit, oozing over her asshole and joining with the water still running from her icy cunt.

When her flaming ass was a bit cooler, CJ unclipped her cuffs from the wall and led her across the room. He placed her hands on a table of some kind, then pushed her so she was bent over the soft leather cover, her feet on the floor, her upper body cradled in the soft fabric, her arms hanging down. Still holding the Ping-Pong ball, her hands were cuffed to the front legs of the table and her ankles to the rear two. There were openings in the table so her breasts hung freely.

She felt fingers pulling on her nipples, then lightweight clips attached to the hard, erect flesh. "Just so you won't forget your tits," the wonderful voice said. Then he continued. "I know you can't talk, but shake your head. Have you ever been taken in the ass?"

Barbara shook her head.

"Oh, a virgin. That's wonderful."

He left her lying across the table, unable to move, her blindfold and gag in place, tits hanging, with the clips attached. Although it was difficult, Barbara used the moment to catch her breath and come down from the earth-moving climax that had ripped through her while he was spanking her. But although she had come once, hard, she knew she was close to coming again.

Then she felt his mouth beside her ear. "I have a dildo in my hand. It's quite slender, but wide enough to fill your ass. Remember the ball in your hand. I will know if it falls."

Barbara felt him stroke her back, then press his hand against her waist. "I'm going to rub some lubricant on now." The sound of his voice, telling her what he was going to do was unbelievably erotic. "Your ass will feel so filled, so fucked. It will feel strange, but wonderful." He rubbed cold, slippery gel over her ass, sliding his finger in just a tiny amount. Then he slowly inserted a slender plastic rod into her previously unviolated rear.

"No," she tried to say around the gag. "Don't." But she didn't drop the ball from her hand. "No."

"Oh, yes," he purred, slowly driving the rod deeper into her body. When it was lodged inside her, he stopped and left it there.

"Oh, God," she mumbled. Then his finger was rubbing her clit and she came again. She couldn't help it. The orgasm ripped through her, making her entire body pulse.

"Such a good slut, but again too easy. But it's my turn now." A moment later, he said, "I just want to assure you that I'm using a condom, so you don't have to worry." His cock rubbed against her cunt, moving the dildo that still filled her ass. His hips and groin pressed against her burning ass, forcing the dildo still deeper into her ass. He plunged his cock into her pussy and she came yet again, her spasms clutching at him. It took only a few thrusts for him to bellow his release.

A while later, CJ released Barbara's wrists and ankles, then removed the blindfold and gag. "You're so receptive. It makes me crazy when you come like that."

"So good for me, too," Barbara said, her breathing still ragged. "It's never been any better."

The silence broken only by the music, they dressed. There was no talk of dinner. She realized they had never even kissed. "Please come to my store again," CJ said as he opened the outer door. "There are several more things I can show you and some I'm sure you could show me."

"Maybe," she said, not being coy, just unsure whether she would repeat the experience. "I don't really know."

"That's fine," he said. Then he placed two tapes in her hand. "For another time," he said. "I just made these recently and they both focus on performing for an audience. If you're ever interested in living out this type of fantasy, let me know." With the tapes she saw that he had handed her his business card. "CJ Winterman A Private Place Unusual Items and Entertainments of All Sorts." It contained the store's address and a phone number. "The number rings here in the store and in my apartment upstairs."

Barbara put the tapes and the card in her pocket. "Thank you," she said, walking toward the door. "For everything."

That night Barbara lay in bed and put the tape into the player. The expected music filled the room and CJ's voice, a voice she could now put a face and a body to, began to spin his latest tale. She let herself drift into the story.

>   *The club was warm and the lights low as the music began for the last show of the evening. Marianne stood at the side of the small stage, ready for her first effort at entertaining the patrons at the Exotica Club, a totally nude review club a few miles from her home. She had practiced her act and thought she could give them a good show. After all, she had watched the performing often enough.*
>   *It had all begun a year earlier when the club first opened. Her husband Matt had frequented a similar club in the city before their marriage and had often told her about the wild dancing at the storefront club he had gone to. When the Exotica Club opened, she and Matt had been among its first patrons. A bit raw at first, the club's entertainment had improved. The comedians had become increasingly talented, the singers more professional,*

and the dancers more skillful in their movements. Now, a year later, shows were sold out weeks in advance and lines formed early in the evening to get the few tables or spots at the bar that might become available.

Thursday night had evolved into Talent Night, when anyone could sign up for a spot on the program and, after much urging from Matt, Marianne had finally listed herself among the performers. As she stood in the wings watching the first woman take her turn, she looked into the audience. Matt sat at a table right in front and Marianne watched him gazing at the slender, small-bosomed woman who strutted around the stage to "The Stripper." She removed her clothing slowly but a bit awkwardly, Marianne thought. The next act was a new, young comedian whose routine was filled with expletives and was quite funny. He was followed by a male dancer and a woman in a slinky dress who sang several erotic songs.

Finally, as a couple performed a tango, almost copulating right on the stage, Marianne realized that she was next, and last, on the program. The couple's performance was followed by cheers from the audience. As she looked past the lights, she could see several couples engaged in sexual play, hands in crotches rubbing, caressing. She took a deep breath and squared her shoulders. You ain't seen nothin' yet, she thought.

The lights dimmed and a stagehand pushed a large washtub onto the center of the stage and set a short stool beside it. Marianne picked up a basket of old clothes and, as the lights brightened and some soft music began, she walked slowly to the center of the stage. She was wearing a small pinafore that barely concealed her breasts and covered the front of a short skirt that came only to midthigh. She was barefoot, her long blond hair was braided, and she wore almost no make up.

As background music played, she put her basket down, sat on the stool, her knees widely spread so the audience could see the crotch of her white panties, and took a pair of men's brief's from the basket. She glanced at Matt and saw him grinning from ear to ear. She knew how much he loved watching her and, although there were probably almost a hundred people watching, Marianne performed for him alone.

She took an old-fashioned wash board and started to scrub the pants, sloshing water everywhere, including all over herself. After a moment, she stood up and tried to sluice the water from the top of her pinafore. All she succeeded in doing was wetting the entire front so her breasts were easily visible. "Oh, my," she said, looking innocently into the audience. "Oh, my." She covered her breasts and giggled, then looked into the laundry basket. She found a white T-shirt she had put there because not only was it too tight but it had been washed so many times it was almost transparent.

She turned her back to the audience, took off the pinafore and put the T-shirt on. "Better?" she asked softly as she turned back to the gathering. Her breasts were clearly visible and her dark nipples were pressing against the front.

"Yeah," some yelled.

"Take it all off," yelled others.

"I couldn't do that," she said sweetly, batting her eyelashes. "I'm not that kind of girl."

There were whistles and groans, cheers and calls of, "Yeah, right."

"I have to get back to work," she said and sat back on the stool, giving the audience another clear view of her crotch. Again she washed an item and again sloshed water everywhere. By now, whatever had been partially hidden by the T-shirt was fully revealed and her skirt was soaked as well. "Oh, my," she said again, holding her skirtfront and squeezing water from the fabric. "Oh, my."

The watchers silenced, waiting for her to remove more clothing. She turned her back to the audience and unbuttoned her skirt, letting it fall around her feet. All the while, soft music played in the background. Finally she turned back to the sea of eyes watching her, now wearing only the soaked T-shirt and a pair of tiny white panties.

"Oh, yeah, lady. Right on."

Again she sat and washed another garment, now soaking herself. "Oh, my," she said as she stood up and watched water run from her body. "Oh, my." She slowly ran her hands over her skin, ostensibly scraping the water from her legs and belly. Then she wrung out the front of her T-shirt, smiled sweetly to the audience and shrugged. With agonizing deliberation, she pulled the soaked shirt off, eventually revealing her white skin, her breasts, and dark, dusky nipples. She appeared to try to cover herself, then shrugged and apparently gave up. Then she slowly she removed the ribbons that held her hair and fluffed it free. It fell almost to the small of her back and she slowly ran her fingers through it, arranging it so it flowed down her chest, and almost, but not quite, covered her breasts.

Now, as she sat on the stool, she was only clad in her panties and her hair. She picked up another piece of wash and sloshed it around in the tub. Now her panties were almost transparent, allowing the audience only a partially screened view of her blond bush. "Oh, my," she said, standing again and looking at her panties. The audience roared and screamed, then silenced as she looked at them. They could see that this was more than just a strip show. She was letting them peek at an embarrassed girl, making them delighted voyeurs.

She slowly slid the panties down her legs, bending so those in the audience couldn't see her crotch. She remained crouched and looked at the faces of the crowd. Then she looked at Matt, who was quite obviously rubbing the bulge in the front of his trousers. She could feel an answering tingle in her pussy. "Oh, my," she said again, then stood up, allowing the people to see her nude body. "Oh, my," she said again as she looked around. The audience was strangely silent, as if not wanting to disturb the sweet young girl and her laundry. Although several couples were making love and one woman knelt with her partner's cock in her mouth, all eyes on the show. Wow, Marianne thought. This is great. I can turn people on. I love this and it makes me so hot.

Giving the audience a good view of her bush, she once more sat down and dropped the another piece of laundry into the water. Water flew everywhere until she was dripping. She stood up and rubbed her body to remove the water. Then she rubbed her crotch as if to remove the last of the water. "Oh, my," she said, rubbing her flesh. "Oh, my."

As she had planned, water had splashed on several people in the front of the audience, including her husband. As faces peered up at her, she walked to the edge of the stage, then slowly made her way down to the level of the tables, a small towel from the laundry basket dangling from one hand.

Several large men stood around the periphery of the room watching to see that everyone followed the club's rules. A performer could do anything to anyone in the audience. Those watching could do nothing to or with a performer without being invited.

She and Matt had discussed things that might happen and

*they had agreed that Marianne could do anything the mood com-
pelled her to. Matt would enjoy watching her antics. He knew
that she loved to play and that she would end the evening with
him. He also knew that she loved him totally. That was enough
reassurance for him. She could play to her heart's content.*

*She made her way to Matt and sat on his lap. "Oh, my," she
said, wiping water from the front of his shirt. Then she wiped the
front of his slacks, pressing all the places she knew would delight
him. Under her breath, she asked, "Still all right with this?"*

"Oh, yes, baby. Have fun."

*Marianne stood up and moved to another man, who stared at
her in rapt attention. "Oh, my," she repeated, wiping the man's
face and shirt. As she rubbed his pants, she felt his hard cock.
Slowly she crouched between his spread knees and unzipped his fly.
With little urging, his cock sprung forth. "Oh, my," she said, clear
appreciation in her voice. She curled her fingers around his large
erection and rubbed, watching small drops of fluid ooze from the
tip. "Mmmm," she purred, and she continued to caress his staff.*

"You don't know what you're doing to me," he groaned.

*"I certainly do," she said as semen erupted into her hand.
"Oh, my." Minutes later, she wiped her hand and moved away.
Two women were stretched out on a double lounge chair at one
side of the room. As Marianne watched, they rubbed breast to
breast, their hands working in each other's pussy. She walked
over and tweaked two nipples, then inserted fingers of both hands
into two wet pussies.*

*For several more minutes she wandered around the room,
touching, rubbing, caressing, then she walked back up on the
stage. She splashed water onto her face and allowed some to
dribble onto her breasts. Her right hand rubbed her clit while her
left palm slid over her nipples. She sat on the stool, her legs
spread, her head back, so everyone could watch her stroke herself. And she did, she watched Matt out of the corner of her eye.
He was really excited, she realized, and so was she. It had
stopped being just a show. If she rubbed in just the right
place . . . She stroked and caressed and then inserted two fingers
into her pussy. Men and women were watching while sucking and
fucking each other and Matt had his naked cock in his hand. All
eyes were on her.*

She moaned. "Oh, God," she yelled. "Oh, now."

As she came, a small part of her still watched Matt and the others, all approaching or just past orgasm. "Yes," she groaned as she climaxed, her juice running down her fingers. She sat for long moments as the audience remained almost completely silent. Then it erupted in applause and calls of "Way to go, baby" and "Lemme have some." Several husky men surrounded the stage to prevent anyone from getting too close.

Slowly the lights dimmed and Marianne left the stage, her breath slowly returning to normal, her knees still weak. Matt found her in the dressing room, tossed her onto the floor and drove his cock into her, unable to stop until he erupted inside her slippery pussy.

"Oh, my, baby," he said later, as he lay beside her. "Oh, my."

Barbara lay on her bed as the music filled the room. She had just climaxed for the third time during the story, glad she had learned to masturbate for lengthy pleasure and multiple orgasms, not just to scratch her itch. She thought back on what had excited her the most about the story. Performing? Giving a stranger a hand job? No. What had driven her quickly over the edge was the picture that formed in her mind of the two women.

The following evening, Maggie and Barbara sat in the living room sipping wine. "I know I sound like a commercial, but I have to say it. You've come a long way," Maggie said.

"Yes, I'm a very different person that I was when we first met."

"Are you happy?" Maggie asked. "Or at least happier?"

"I'm having so much fun, but I don't know whether it's a life."

"I don't quite understand."

"Neither do I right now, but I do know that this is an interlude, a time of change. I'm not the person I was, but this isn't the person I will be eventually either." When Maggie looked at her questioningly, Barbara continued. "Sport fucking is wonderful for right now. I'm learning about sexuality and sensuality, but not really about relationships. I don't love any of these men I'm with. I lust for them and it's exciting to be together, but none of them are people with whom I could spend a life. There's not a lot outside of the bedroom."

"I had love. It isn't much either," Maggie said, a bit of bitterness in her voice.

"What did you have exactly? With your husband, I mean. Weren't there any good times? What did you two have in common?"

"Sure there were good times. We played golf together, and tennis. We liked pizza and Kentucky Fried. We were both rather nonpolitical, but once a guy ran for the state assembly we really believed in. We campaigned, went door to door." Maggie gazed into space. "Yeah, there were good times."

"The sex was always bad?"

"It was nothing."

"Even at first? You told me yourself that first times are the best. Wasn't that true with your husband? Do you remember the first time you and he ever made love?"

Maggie smiled. "Yeah, I do. It was in my living room. I still lived at home and my parents were out. Chuck and I sat on the sofa supposedly watching TV. He touched me and kissed me until we were both crazy."

"Were you a virgin?"

"I was, believe it or not. I was almost eighteen and still untouched."

"And Chuck?"

"Oh, he had been with a few girls. But he didn't know very much."

"So it was lousy?"

Maggie considered Barbara's question for a long time. "No, actually it was cosmic. It's been so long that I guess I had forgotten. If I must be honest, it was pretty good for the first few years. Then along came," she deepened her voice like a radio announcer, "*the other woman*. I was really angry."

"And why not? He didn't tell you anything about it."

"Actually, he did. He felt so guilty that he confessed all. They had been friends for several months at work, then he got snowed in at the office. She lived nearby and offered to let him stay on her sofa. One thing led to another and that was that for my marriage."

"Did he want to leave you or did you throw him out?"

"A bit of both. We were both bored and, if I have to be brutally honest, we were both ready to move on."

"So it wasn't as one-sided as you led me to believe."

"Maybe not. I'm not ready to admit all that just yet."

In the computer room, Lucy snapped off the computer screen. "You goosed her, didn't you. You helped her to remember how it really was in her marriage. That's cheating."

"It is not," Angela snapped. "I just prodded some actual memories. I didn't create anything that wasn't already there. I wouldn't cheat. After all, look at who I represent."

"You cheated."

"And you didn't, goosing Barbara into believing free sex is fun just for itself."

"Well, it is."

"That's neither here nor there. We still have a bet, and Maggie's future will depend on the next few weeks."

A lanky, angular man walked into the computer room. "Hey. What is this place?" he asked.

"Well that's a change from 'Where am I?'" Lucy said, returning to her seat and changing the focus of her computer to the life of the newcomer. "And this place is a little hard to explain."

Chapter 9

It was several days before Barbara had the time and sexual energy to play the second of the two tapes CJ had given her. The story was, if anything, more erotic for her than any of the ones she had heard so far.

It was to be an initiation of sorts, several men to be accepted as full members of the exclusive Hathaway Group, a collection of wealthy men in their twenties and thirties who spent one evening a month at a retreat, devoting themselves to pleasures of the flesh. The annual initiation ceremony was eagerly anticipated by both the initiates and the existing members of the Group. Although several of the women at the meeting were hired, many were volunteers who had enjoyed the hedonistic activities of the Group at previous gatherings. In all, there were almost thirty men and more than a dozen women.

Although all the women would have their share of sexual fun, Scott Hathaway, the leader of the group, had selected one to take the central part in the initiation ritual. The Carnal Sacrifice she was called. As all the men stood around the raised platform, Scott extended his hand and led the honored woman to the stage.

Alyssa walked forward and took Scott's hand, her diaphanous white gown flowing around her long, shapely legs. Her breasts, barely covered by the sheer fabric, were high and full and her almost white hair flowed down her back like a pale curtain. Her face was carefully made up and she had applied perfume to all the erogenous zones of her body. She climbed the two steps to the platform and turned to face the audience. Men dressed in flowing black robes with crimson cowls stood with

*arms draped over the shoulders of bare-breasted women. Four
men were bareheaded, and would receive their ceremonial cowls
when they had completed the ritual. Everyone stared at the dais
with lust-clouded eyes.*

*On the stage was a velvet bench, specially designed for the
men's pleasure. And, after bowing to the crowd, Alyssa allowed
Scott to remove her gown, leaving her gloriously naked. She
stretched out on the bench on her back, her arms at her sides, her
legs spread. Scott slowly rotated the table so the audience could
see every aspect of the woman spread invitingly before them.
Mirrors reflected from above and around the dais, and several
video cameras projected images on large screens around the
room. The room lights dimmed and spotlights brightened to illuminate the body on the stage. Alyssa was surprised at the heat
that raced through her as one spotlight was adjusted to shine
directly on her open pussy lips.*

*As the group watched, Scott tied Alyssa's wrists and ankles
to rings in the bench with soft velvet strips. Then he released a
section of the table so her head fell back, and adjusted the bottom of the bench so her legs were still more widely spread.*

*"Let the initiates come forward," Scott said, and the four
would-be group members climbed the two steps. "Disrobe," Scott
said and the men removed their robes. They were nude beneath
and all had hard erections. "Take your places."*

*Each man moved to a different spot, one to her head, one to
each side, and one between her thighs. Each man unrolled a condom over his cock. "Each of you will have the advantage of the
condom, which mutes the sensation. The one who comes first will
have to spend another year as an initiate, as Barry has had to do
this year." He patted the shoulder of the man who stood at the
woman's head. "Actually, Barry, I don't think you minded at all,
going through all the training for a second time. As a matter of
fact, I think you might have lost on purpose." Everyone, including
Barry, laughed.*

*"Now, you all know the rules. First you will rub oil into
Alyssa's skin, all over her body. Then each of you will slowly take
Alyssa, one in her mouth, one in each hand, and one in her pussy.
Then you will remain unmoving while Alyssa does whatever she
can to make you climax." He looked down at the men and women
in the crowd below. "Those of you who want to copulate while
you watch what is happening may certainly do so. 'Whatever
gives pleasure' is our motto. And, gentlemen," he said, speaking*

to the four initiates, "if you can make our Carnal Sacrifice come, without coming yourself, then you all pass the initiation test automatically. But once you are inside her, you cannot touch her."

Alyssa lay on the bench, listening to the leader give his speech. Last year she had watched from the audience. The man she had been with had pointed out each man and how he was pleasing the woman on the stage and how he was being pleased as well. As they watched, she had become hungrier and hungrier until she begged the man to take her right there on the floor. Now she was on the stage ready for the ultimate pleasure.

"Gentlemen," Scott said, giving each man a bottle of oil, "you may begin."

Alyssa closed her eyes as eight hands rubbed warm oil on her belly, her breasts, her thighs. Hands kneaded, stroked, fondled, and pinched. Several fingers invaded her pussy, opening her, readying her for what was to come.

"Enough," Scott said. "Enter her."

And she was filled. One cock slowly thrust into her mouth, the latex not diminishing her pleasure. One cock was pressed into each waiting hand and she closed her fist around each. And finally one slowly filled her pussy. Then each man stood completely still and Scott said, "The job of the Carnal Sacrifice is to make them come."

Alyssa smiled inwardly and licked the cock in her mouth. Since she couldn't move her hands because of the bonds, she squeezed her fingers, one after another, to pump those two cocks, and she clamped her vaginal muscles to squeeze the cock so deep in her pussy. She was so excited it was hard to concentrate on making the men come, without coming herself. She wanted to lie there and revel in the sensation of being so full. So many men were part of her at one time.

She opened her eyes and saw that Scott was moving around the table with a video camera in his hand, taking close-up shots of the cocks. She discovered that she could see the TV screen on which the images were projected in the mirror on the ceiling above her.

It was so erotic, the vision of her body invaded by so many men. She watched the men in the mirror, their eyes closed, concentrating on not allowing their body the freedom to come. As she sucked, she heard the man whose cock had penetrated her mouth hiss. Yes, she realized, he was close. But so was she. Although the *excitement was almost unbearable, she couldn't come yet, not until one of the men came first.*

She increased the movements of her hands, her mouth, her pussy muscles. She hummed softly so the buzzing was echoed in the cock in her mouth. Then the man between her legs blew on her clit. That was enough. Her back arched and she came. Almost simultaneously, both the cock in her mouth and the one in her right hand erupted as well. Only moments later, while the spasms still filled her belly, the other two men came, their groans and howls filling the room.

Now that the contest was over, the cock in her cunt pumped hard, hips slamming into her groin. The men at her sides bent over and each took a nipple in his mouth. The man at her head cupped her head in his hands, holding her still and pumped into her throat. Several people in the audience moaned as they came as well. The room smelled of sex and sweat and animal lust.

Alyssa came and came and came, unwilling to allow the pulses that throbbed through her body to end. Over and over cocks invaded her, men moving around the table taking additional pleasure from her mouth, her hands, and her cunt. It was an orgy of sensation she prayed would never end.

When the men were spent, they withdrew and Scott said, "Since it was impossible to tell who came first, I will declare all the men members of the Group. And I will take my turn with our carnal sacrifice." He pulled off his robe and, unrolling a condom over his large cock, he moved between Alyssa's legs. She watched as he adjusted the leg sections of the table until her legs were in the air, her bottom exposed.

"You know what happens now."

"Yes, my lord," she said, her body throbbing with both echos of her climax and her need for more.

"Only one part of you remained uninvaded. That part is mine. Do you agree?"

"Yes, my lord."

"Yet you are willing?"

"Oh, yes, my lord."

Someone else held the camera so Alyssa could see the tip of

*Scott's finger slowly enter her tight hole. The feeling of fullness
was both unpleasant and wildly erotic. Part of her wanted to
expel the invading finger, part wanted to drive it deeper. Slowly,
as she watched the monitor in the mirror, the finger went deeper
and deeper, stretching and oiling her for the eventual penetration.
Scott withdrew the finger, then used his thick thumb to open her
still further.*

*She had been anxious to try this type of sexual fun, yet had
been a bit unsure as well. She was no longer doubtful. It was
magnificent. "My lord, I am ready for you," she cried.*

*As he held the tip of his cock against her puckered opening,
he rubbed her clit with his other hand. Then in a single, slow
stroke, he filled her. She came with the first stroke, screaming her
pleasure for all to hear. Scott pulled back, then thrust into her
again. Over and over he filled and emptied her ass until he, too,
succumbed to the pleasure of the fucking.*

*As he left her body, someone announced that anyone who
wanted any part of the carnal sacrifice's body could take it. Many
did, in her mouth, in her hands, her pussy, her ass. She lost track of
the number of times she came or the number of men she pleasured.*

*Later, she was released from the bench and given a cooling
drink. Then two women lovingly massaged her body to relax and
refresh her. Finally, when she was ready, she rose and walked
through the room to the applause and cheers of all assembled.
She had given and taken the ultimate pleasure, and that, of
course, was what the group was all about. "Alyssa," Scott said as
he handed her a glass of champagne, "you were wonderful. I
don't know when we've had a better initiation ritual."*

"Thank you," Alyssa said.

*"Would you consider being the Carnal Sacrifice again next
year?"*

Alyssa smiled. "It would be my ultimate pleasure."

Barbara thought about the most recent tapes for the next few days,
imagining herself on stage like Marianne, performing for a bunch of
strangers. Could she do that? It was an intriguing possibility. And, of
course, she did want to see CJ again. And this was, after all, no-holds-
barred sex. A week after she left the store, she called CJ.

"Well, hello, hot woman," CJ said. "I have been hoping all week that
I'd hear from you."

"I just thought I'd call and thank you for the tape. I really liked that
club scene."

"Do you think you could dance like that?"

"I don't know. It's an intriguing thought, but I think I'd chicken out at the last minute."

"You're an honest woman, Babs."

Barbara reacted automatically to hearing the name that Walt and Carl had called her all those years ago. The humiliation of the situation, the flash of Walt's camera. She could almost smell Carl's All Spice aftershave. But this was CJ's voice, a voice that had come to mean hot, erotic sex, and the sound of it made her wet. Should that experience have felt all that terrible or was it just that she didn't have a life then? She didn't have any idea what good sex was all about. But then neither did Carl or Walt. All these thoughts flashed through her mind in an instant. "I like to think so," she said into the phone.

"I have a group of friends who get together once a month, sort of like the Hathaway Group in the story. Women are invited to participate in the various activities. There's a party next weekend and I wondered whether you'd like to come."

Barbara hesitated. What CJ was describing sounded like an orgy. Was this what her sexuality was leading her to? Was this the culmination of her months of learning about herself? Voices filled her head. Do it, it will be fun. It's a sin. Enjoy. You'll be punished.

"If I can chicken out at any time, I think I'd like to."

"I promise you that any time you say so, I will take you home. Instantly. No questions asked, no recriminations."

"It sounds very interesting."

As arranged, Barbara arrived at CJ's shop at five the following Saturday afternoon, prepared for anything. CJ had promised her that nothing would happen without her permission, but, if she were willing, all kinds of new experiences awaited her. As she walked into A Private Place, his assistant was just leaving and CJ was finishing with his last customer. She stood, gazing at the bondage equipment while the customer debated whether to buy a green or a red dildo.

"Barbara, come over here and help us," CJ said loudly. When she approached the counter, he asked, "Which do you like better?"

Barbara looked at the two dildos on the counter, then at the display beneath the glass. "Actually, just to confuse you, I like that black one. It looks dangerous and erotic, and makes me think of black lace underwear and high heels."

The man who stood beside her looked at her, then said, "I'll take the one the lady likes. If my girlfriend glows like this lovely woman does at the thought of that black dildo, I'll be a lucky man."

Barbara grinned as CJ wrapped the dildo in red lace gift paper. With a thank-you, the man put the package into his pocket and left. As the customer closed the shop door behind him, CJ locked it. He walked to Barbara, placed his hand on the back of her neck and kissed her softly. "Welcome. This is going to be one wonderful night." He placed her hand against the crotch of his black jeans, cupping his hard cock. "I'm looking forward to it."

His voice turned her on like few things in the world. Without hesitation, Barbara placed CJ's hand against the crotch of her jeans. "Feel the heat? I'm looking forward to tonight, too."

CJ laughed. "You're quite a brazen bitch," he said. "Come into the back." He led her into a room she hadn't been in the last time, invited her to sit down and poured her a glass of white wine. Then he deftly opened a dozen oysters for each of them, and served them with lemon and a cocktail sauce spiced with lots of horseradish. "They say wonderful things about oysters, but I don't believe that nonsense. I just like them. We'll be eating quite a bit later, but I thought this would hold us for now."

Barbara picked up a shell and, with loud slurping noises, slid an oyster into her mouth. "I love them, too," Barbara said. She licked her lips with exaggerated movements of her slender tongue.

"The way you eat those makes me want to fuck you right here, right now. But there's a long evening ahead of us and anticipation makes it that much better."

They chatted amiably, ate and drank and, by the time they had finished, Barbara was no longer turned on. She merely felt warm and comfortable.

"As I told you, I would like to dress you up for the evening," CJ said finally. "But first, I have a question for you. Have you ever thought about shaving your pussy?"

Barbara thought for a moment. "I haven't, but I wouldn't mind, if you'd like me to."

"I'd like to shave you myself. It's very sexy for a man to look at a shaved pussy. It's so brazen somehow, so inviting and obvious. It would be perfect for this evening. If you don't ever want to do it again, you can let it grow. I will warn you, it might be a bit itchy as it grows out."

"I'll risk it. It sounds kinky."

CJ beamed. "Great. Take your jeans and panties off and sit here," he said, indicating a leather director's chair.

Slightly embarrassed at casually undressing before a man that, despite their previous activities, she hardly knew, Barbara removed her jeans, panties, shoes, and socks. She sat in the chair and CJ draped her legs over the arms so her pussy was exposed and vulnerable. Then CJ brought a pair of scissors, pan of warm water, soap, a razor, and a handful of towels.

While Barbara watched, he cut her pubic hair very short, then rubbed the short stubble and 'accidentally' brushed her now-exposed clit. From not turned-on to ravenous in only a moment, she thought. Barbara swallowed hard but tried to look as casual as CJ. Then he made lots of soapy lather and rubbed it over her pubis. Slowly and with infinite care, he shaved off all the hair, his probing fingers and the gentle rub of the razor making Barbara tremble with need.

He washed the area with a soft cloth, then smoothed on some antiseptic lotion. Then he rose and returned with a large mirror that stood on a wooden stand. "Look at your wonderful pussy," he said, adjusting the mirror so Barbara could see her hairless mound. CJ was right. It was obvious and erotic, like an opening begging to be filled. CJ stroked one finger along her naked slit. "It makes you hot looking at yourself, doesn't it?"

"Yes," she breathed, her voice barely audible.

"Then you need to be filled." CJ disappeared, then returned with a dildo like the one she had recommended to the customer. "Remember how Alyssa could watch the men as they fucked her? Now, watch in the mirror while I fuck you with this." He held the dildo against her opening, then slowly, while Barbara watched, fascinated, slid it into her body.

Barbara was shaking from the intensity of the twin sensations, watching herself being fucked with the dildo and the feel of the large member penetrating her. "May this be the first of many tonight," CJ said, kneeling between her legs and tonguing her clit until she came, her juices trickling over her now-exposed skin. "You are the most responsive woman," CJ said, rubbing her clit and thrusting the dildo in and out as tremors shook her. "And you are so beautiful when you come."

Unable to speak, Barbara just moaned.

A while later, CJ stood up and said, "If you're calmer now, we can get you dressed for the party." He looked at his watch. "It starts in an hour."

Barbara took a deep breath and took her legs from the arms of the chair. Smiling, she said, "What would you like me to wear?"

CJ reached for a box on a table and handed it to her. "The idea of presenting you to my friends wearing this makes me hot, but it will only work if it turns you on as well." Barbara opened the box. Inside was a black latex body suit with long legs, long sleeves, and openings where her breasts and pussy would be. "Picture yourself in that," CJ purred. "You would look amazing. Are you game?"

Barbara gazed at the garment. Her large breasts and now-hairless crotch would be exposed, but the rest of her body would be tightly encased in the stretchy fabric. It sounded delicious. She nodded and CJ smiled. "You delight me," he crooned, handing her the suit. "I need to change, too."

While CJ was in another room changing for the party, Barbara slowly wiggled the tight suit on over her skin. Zippers tightened the sleeves and legs until, when it was in place, it fit like her skin, with only her breasts and pussy exposed. She looked at herself in the mirror and was amazed at the wanton woman who looked back at her. "Oh, Lord," she said to her reflection. "Barbara, what have you done to yourself?"

"Made yourself into the most desirable woman I've ever seen," CJ said from behind her. She turned and saw that he was dressed in a similar black latex outfit, only his had short sleeves, thigh-length pants, and a full crotch. His swollen shaft beneath was hard to miss. "The feel of the latex hugging my cock keeps me erect all night." When he placed her hand between his legs, she felt something around the base of his cock. To her puzzled expression, he said, "I wear a cock ring to keep me from coming before I'm ready."

"Oh," Barbara said.

"Now, sit back here," CJ said, motioning her to the leather chair. "I want to do your finger-and toenails."

With great care, CJ polished her now-long fingernails and her toenails with polish that was almost black. Then he asked her to close her eyes while he applied additional makeup and arranged her hair over her shoulders. She could feel him stroke the silver streak.

When he was done, he angled the mirror so she could look at herself. She opened her eyes and stared. He had used deep green shadow, heavy mascara, and deep, almost-black lipstick. She looked like an animal on the prowl. Where's the woman who Maggie met that first night? she wondered. Gone for now, she answered herself.

"Do you approve?"

"Very much," she said.

He handed her a pair of calf-high, black patent-leather boots, with spike heels. "I think these should be about your size," he said, and she slipped them on and stood up.

"Oh, yes," he said, slowly lowering himself until he was crouched at her feet. "Mistress."

Mistress. He was inviting her into his fantasy, she realized. He wanted her to control him. Did she know how? Her confusion must have shown on her face. "You'll learn how, if you're willing," he said. "There will be many there willing and able to teach you. And I will serve you." He got a cloak from the closet and draped it around Barbara's shoulders, carefully arranging her hair over the collar. "If you will allow me to lead," he said.

"Yes," Barbara said, standing up straight, now taller than he was in her high heels. "Do that."

In silence, they took a taxi across town to an old loft building in Soho. Although the taxi driver gave them a few odd looks, the trip was uneventful. CJ paid the driver and opened the door for her. They entered an old elevator and ascended two floors. When the doors opened, Barbara looked around, her eyes widening.

The room took up more than half of the loft and was furnished with tables and chairs, single and double lounges, and soft sofas. There were benches with straps and rings attached, stocks, and items that Barbara could only imagine uses for.

There were about two dozen couples, a few dancing, several sitting around tables, others in various stages of copulation. Music played in the background, similar to the music on CJ's tapes, with deep, pulsing rhythms that echoed in Barbara's soul.

As CJ removed Barbara's cloak, two men got up and walked over to them. "Who is this goddess?" one asked.

"My mistress," CJ said.

"And she allows you to speak on your own?"

"Occasionally," CJ said. "When I have pleased her sufficiently. Her name is Barbara."

"Good evening," she said, slowly getting acclimated to her surroundings and trying to figure out exactly how to behave.

"Good evening, Mistress Barbara," the two men said.

"CJ. It's good to see you," a woman called, motioning them over. The men led CJ and Barbara to a small table. "My name's Pam," the woman said as Barbara sat down. "And this is Tisha," she said, indicating the other woman at the table. "You're new to our little group."

"Yes, I am," Barbara said.

"My mistress is new to everything about this," CJ said. "But she wants to learn."

"Wonderful," Tisha said. A tiny blonde, she wore a genuine-looking policeman's uniform, with a pair of handcuffs dangling from a clip on her wide leather belt. "Let me show you what wonderful things my pet can do." She snapped her fingers and spread her legs. Barbara saw then that, like her outfit, the crotch of Pam's navy-blue pants was missing. "I like my men to be able to service me whenever I like." One of the men who had greeted her now knelt between Tisha's legs and began to lick her pussy. Tisha picked up her glass and sipped, trying unsuccessfully to look unaffected. "He's gotten too good at this," she said, panting. "Shit," she yelled, and Barbara watched as waves of orgasm overtook her.

Pam laughed. "He seems to be able to bring her off with almost no effort. I don't know whether she's that hot all the time, or he's that good." It was all Barbara could do not to stare at the woman speaking. She wore a kelly-green lace teddy that barely covered any of her athletic, ebony body, with thigh-high, green lace stockings and green satin heels. She also wore dark-green, elbow-length fingerless gloves. Even sitting down, Barbara could tell that she had to be over six feet tall. And gorgeous.

"She certainly seems to enjoy it," Barbara said.

"And why not," Pam said. "It's the best. I understand you're new to this type of fun and games."

"Yes," Barbara said, not sure what she was supposed to do.

"Watch what goes on around you and do what you think will give you and CJ pleasure."

"God, that was good," Tisha said, rejoining the conversation. "Get me something to eat," she said to the man who was now sitting on the floor at her feet.

"Yes, Mistress," he said, rising and moving to the buffet table. Pam looked at the man beside her and he quickly got up and followed.

Barbara looked at CJ. "I'm hungry, too," she said in what she hoped was a sufficiently authoritative tone. "Get me something."

CJ tried not to smile. "Oh, yes, Mistress," he said, and left the table.

"CJ's never brought a mistress here before," Pam said. "Usually he's the dominant one."

"How can someone be dominant one time and like that another?" Barbara asked.

"Many people enjoy both sides of dominant/submissive behavior. Others only enjoy being in charge, or surrendering." She smiled, encouraging Barbara to trust her. "What do you usually enjoy?"

"I don't really know. I've been tied up and I loved that. I've also listened to a lot of CJ's tapes and all the stories really turn me on. But I've never actually been in anything like this before, on either side."

"How wonderful to explore," Pam said. "To try it all out for the first time. I envy you. First times are so hot."

"I like to run the show," Tisha said. "I can't get into letting someone else tell me what to do."

"And I love it when someone tells me what to do," Pam said. "It's so liberating. I don't have to think about anything. Just do as I'm told."

Tisha gazed at Pam, her eyes wandering over the other woman's lush body. "Maybe I'll take you up on that offer before the evening is done," she said. She looked at Barbara, and the heat in her gaze made Barbara look down. "You, too, love."

The three men returned with plates of food and, as Barbara watched, Tisha held out a bit of meat and the man at her feet ate it from her hand. "Oh, this is Pet. That's what I call him since that's what he is."

"Hello," Barbara said.

Pet inclined his head, but said nothing.

"And this is Mack," Pam said, patting the man at her side on the head. "He's such a good boy."

"Thank you, ma'am," the man whispered, obviously pleased at the compliment.

Barbara took a shrimp and offered it to CJ. He stared at her, the heat in his gaze almost stinging her naked nipples. Then he took the shrimp from her fingers with his teeth.

Together, the three couples ate and talked. Actually, the women talked, the men remained silent, eating only when a morsel of food was handed to them.

Despite the thoroughly bizarre situation, Barbara was surprised at how much she liked the two women. They were honest, sexually open, and easy to talk and listen to.

When they finished, a man in a tuxedo walked to the center of the dance floor and announced the entertainment for the evening. Several men danced Chippendale-style, and a woman did amazing things with two thick candles. There was a Don't Come contest during which three men were teased until finally one erupted onto the floor. After he cleaned up the mess, he was escorted into another room by his mistress for what Barbara was told would be suitable punishment for his lack of self-control.

Then a naked man was led to the stage and his arms and neck were locked in a set of wooden stocks. Women from the audience used hands, paddles, and a hairbrush to spank his ass until it was bright red.

When the lights rose again, several couples moved toward a door at the far end of the room. "They are going to have ceremonial whippings and other heavy pain games. Some people like that sort of thing, but since many do not, whippings and things like that are held at in another, sound-proof room. Not my thing," Pam said.

Barbara didn't think she would enjoy watching or participating in pain for pleasure games. "Me neither," she said, glad she wouldn't lose her new-found companions.

"Barbara," Tisha said, "I can see that CJ is enjoying being the bottom, the submissive, but you don't seem comfortable with the role of top."

Barbara sighed. "I guess I'm not. I'm just not used to giving orders."

She turned to CJ. "I'm really sorry. I know that having me control you would turn you on, but, well . . ."

"Don't apologize," CJ said. "Something that doesn't turn you on, no matter how much the thought of it might excite me, won't make me happy."

"Would you like to be the one controlled?" Tisha asked.

Barbara felt heat rise and thought she might actually be blushing. "I don't know."

"Yes, you do," Tisha said. Then she quickly changed the subject. While they sipped club sodas, the women made small talk. Barbara felt the heat of Tisha's stare frequently over the next half hour. At one point Tisha spent several minutes staring at her nipples. Barbara felt her nipples tighten and her pussy get wet from the heat of Tisha's gaze. "Excuse me," she said, disappearing to the ladies' room.

When she returned, she saw CJ whispering in Tisha's ear. "Barbara, CJ tells me that he would love to watch you make love to Pam. Under my orders, of course. I think you want that." Tisha stared at Barbara. "Sit down!" she snapped. Barbara sank into a chair.

"Spread your legs!" Seemingly without any control from her brain, her knees parted. "Wider." She spread her knees farther.

"Good," Tisha said, smiling. "And, if I'm so inclined, I might even let the men join you later. If they are very good, that is."

Oh God, what had she gotten herself into? Barbara wondered. But she flashed back to the scene in on of CJ's tapes. The dancer who had been able to make two women so hot that they made love in public. She shivered.

Tisha leaned toward Barbara. "The safe word is Cease. Do you understand?"

Barbara remembered the ball she had held when she and CJ had played the last time. She nodded.

Tisha took a police whistle from around her neck and blew into it. "I think we need an audience." Several other couples brought chairs and surrounded the table. "Now, Pam, kiss her."

Obediently Pam turned and cupped Barbara's face in her hands. Softly she brushed her lips across Barbara's, her tongue teasing and probing. Barbara sighed, closed her eyes and relaxed. This was very strange, but arousing. She allowed herself to be pulled into the situation. She touched Pam's cheeks with her fingertips, just brushing the soft skin. She moved her mouth and pressed it more firmly against the other woman's. The smell of Pam's musky perfume filled her nostrils.

Pam leaned forward and rubbed her lace-covered breasts against Barbara's naked nipples. Tit against tit, the two women slowly stood up, their bodies intertwined.

"Massage each other's tits," Tisha said. "Tweak those titties."

As Barbara's hands rose to touch Pam's breasts, she felt Pam's large hands on her bare flesh. "Barbara, pull out Pam's tits." Barbara pulled the cups of Pam's teddy aside and filled her hands with warm flesh. She had never felt anything like this before. Soft hands on soft breasts. Hers. Pam's. White fingers on black skin. Black fingers on white skin. Her knees almost buckled from the heat of it all.

She heard movement around her and opened her eyes to find a lounge chair now beside her. "Barbara, sit there," Tisha said, and Barbara gladly collapsed into the chair.

With a few snaps of her fingers, Tisha moved Pet to one side of Barbara and Mack to the other. "Suck," she said, and suddenly two mouths suckled at Barbara's breasts.

"Do her, Pam," Tisha said, and Pam laid, her chest on the bottom of the lounge chair, her mouth on Barbara's clit. "Look, Barbara. See what's happening." When Barbara's eyes remained closed, Tisha said, "I said, open your eyes!"

Barbara opened her eyes.

"That's better. But don't come," Tisha said. "Don't you dare!"

Barbara looked down. She was still tightly encased in the latex suit, the black rubber shining under the lights. Sweat pooled beneath her arms and on her belly, but the feeling was sensual, not uncomfortable. Two men suckled at her breasts, their fingers kneading her flesh. She could see Pam's face, turned up to her, her tongue dancing over Barbara's naked pussy.

Tisha didn't want her to come. But how could she keep the orgasm from building in her belly? She gritted her teeth and tried to fight the myriad of sensations trying to control her body.

"Stop!" Tisha's order could not be disobeyed.

Barbara took a deep breath as the mouths left her. Tisha looked at her. "Get up." When she did, Tisha ordered, "Pam, you sit there." Once Pam was stretched out in the lounge chair, her thighs spread wide, one leg on either side of the chair, Tisha leaned over and removed the crotch of Pam's teddy. "So wet," she said, then snapped her fingers, and the men resumed their places, now sucking Pam's nipples.

"Now, Barbara, lick her the way she licked you. Do it while we all watch."

Could she lick a woman's pussy? Ordinarily, Barbara thought in a small, conscious place in her mind, no. But she was so hot that anything was possible. She knelt at the foot of the lounge chair, lay on the bottom section and pressed her aching breasts against the rough fabric. She rubbed like a cat, trying the relieve the itching hunger in her swollen nipples. As her face neared Pam's steamy pussy, the odor of the woman's excitement surrounded her. She looked at Pam's shaved mound and saw the swollen outer lips, parted to reveal the hard clit between. She pointed her tongue and licked, marveling at the shudder that ran through Pam's body. She tasted Pam's juices. So this is what I taste like, she thought, filling her mouth with the salty tang.

Feeling increasingly brave, she explored every fold, each hollow. Using the things she understood about her own body, she quested the spots that would give Pam the most pleasure. "Finger-fuck her, Barbara. Make her come." She inserted one finger into Pam's sopping pussy, smiling at the moans and animal cries that Pam couldn't control. A second finger joined the first and, knowing what she herself enjoyed, Barbara spread the two fingers, stretching Pam's channel.

Suddenly something was behind her and there was a hand in the small of her back pressing her against the chair. She felt something slippery being spread on her ass and cunt.

"Is she hot?" Tisha asked.

Someone at her back rubbed her opening. "Soaked. Hot enough to fire."

"Do it."

As Barbara fingered Pam's pussy, she felt something rammed into her ass. A dildo? A cock? She couldn't tell. Then there was a mouth on her cunt. Whose mouth, whose cock? She had no idea. Nor did she care.

"Don't you dare come until Pam does." Tisha said, swatting her ass hard, once. "And Pam, don't you come until Barbara does."

Barbara needed to come. She was trying to concentrate on making Pam climax and not on her own needs screaming inside her. Not yet, she told herself as her mouth worked on Pam's clit and her fingers fucked her cunt. Just a little more. She used the index finger of her other hand to rim Pam's asshole. As she slowly circled, she could feel the tiny spasms that heralded the woman's climax. But she felt her own orgasm building as well.

"Ah!" Pam screamed as she came, and Barbara's orgasm erupted seconds later. Wave upon wave of electric pleasure washed over her. She put her head on Pam's belly and allowed her fingers to softly caress Pam's calming body. Now her cunt and ass were empty, but she felt someone press against her from behind.

She turned and watched CJ rub his latex-covered cock between her spread ass cheeks, his head thrown back, his hips bucking. Tisha reached down the front of his tight bicycle pants and quickly removed the cock ring CJ had put on earlier. It took only a moment until, rubbing against Barbara's ass, he screamed loudly and he came, his cock still inside the latex shorts.

Barbara rested, then, through a haze, she felt herself guided to her feet and her cloak replaced around her shoulders. She vaguely realized that she was being told how much everyone enjoyed her presence and she numbly said good night to the people she had met.

CJ directed the taxi to her car, and then, while Barbara dozed, he drove her home to Bronxville, Tisha and Pet following in their car. He kissed her firmly at her door. "They are waiting for me. I'll call you."

"Mmmm," Barbara said, opening her door. "It was amazing. I've never experienced anything like this."

"I'm glad. It was great for me, too. I never know where these parties will lead, but it's always wonderful. Tonight was particularly terrific because I know how much you enjoyed it, too."

"You weren't disappointed because I couldn't . . . you know."

"Whatever you enjoy is great, and the things you find you don't, we won't do. It's really quite simple."

"Thank you," Barbara said, kissing him again.

"Good night." CJ climbed into the waiting car and Barbara closed the door behind her and went to bed.

Chapter 10

"I think I reached the ultimate of something last evening," Barbara said the following morning as she and Maggie sat over coffee. "It's the best time I've had in maybe forever, but after I got home I thought a lot about it, and about me."

"Thinking's always dangerous," Maggie said dryly, "but tell me about it."

"I think that I understand myself a lot better than I did a few months ago. Last evening was wonderful, but that was outside of the real world. It's not life."

"And what is life."

"For me, life is having mad, wild sex with one person, someone I know and like. Someone who pleases me inside and outside of the bedroom. CJ is a wonderfully creative lover, but that's all. He's sort of out of context." Barbara slumped. "This is really hard to explain."

"I think I understand."

"But your life with Chuck wasn't life either. What I need is equal parts friend and lover. What's depressing me is that I'm not sure something like that really exists."

"I'm not sure either," Maggie said, lacing her fingers. "But all you can do is try."

"Which do you think comes first, the friendship or the sex?"

"I think for there to be really good sex, there has to be a level of trust and friendship, a desire to please the other person. It can develop over a period of months or just in a day. Take you and Jay. From what you told me, you started the relationship for sport fucking, but it was a lot more than that from the start."

Barbara looked puzzled. "But I wasn't in love with him nor he with me. And we weren't and aren't exclusive by any means."

"All that is true, but there was a lot of genuine caring and concern, each for the other. No one was taking anything at the expense of the other. Right?"

Barbara cocked her head to one side. "Right."

"That's not love, but it's the kind of caring necessary for really good sex."

"I never thought about it that way."

"Actually, neither did I until now," Maggie admitted. "But as I think back to my good and bad bed partners, it's true."

"I guess Jay and I did have a lot of mutual respect and caring. Just not enough to build a life on. So then, what is love?"

"You think I know? I haven't a clue. To be completely honest, I think I have been in love a few times. Not just in lust, but really in love. Caring about someone else's happiness more than my own. Maybe it was that way when Chuck and I were first married." Then she thought about Paul and their last phone conversation the night of her heart attack. "And there was a guy who wanted to run away with me. He was a banker type and twenty years my junior. It never would have worked, but I did love him, in my own way."

"I've never felt that, and I want it. I guess I'll just have to keep looking."

"What about Steve."

Barbara smiled. "Maybe it's time I found out what Steve is really like. I've been in love with him from a distance, whatever that means, for a long time. But, what I understand now is that from a distance is easy. It's the up-close-and-personal stuff that's hard."

"And it's more difficult with someone who you're going to see every day, whether it works out or not."

"I know. I keep wondering whether it's worth it. It doesn't seem so important or intense now."

"Do you want to find out?" Maggie asked.

"I think I do."

Later that morning, Maggie left the kitchen and, as she had dozens of times before, found herself in the revolving door. Instead of pushing to see when she would emerge, she stopped in the dark and said aloud, "Lucy, Angela, I think we need to talk."

"Push the door," a voice said and, when she did, she found herself in the computer room. "Yes?" Angela said.

"I was wondering what there is left for me to do. Barbara has discovered herself and I think she's a happier, more complete woman. She's going to ask Steve to dinner and maybe they will end up together, just like you wanted. So what more is there?"

Lucy looked at her. "Do you think Steve is right for her?"

"How should I know?" Maggie snapped. "I'm trying to do what you asked me to do when you gave me this assignment."

"I still think Steve is perfect for Barbara," Angela said.

"Not a chance," Lucy said. "And Maggie, there are still one or two things left that Barbara will need your help with."

"If you say so," Maggie said, turning toward the door. "I just want to do the best job I can, you know."

"Of course. Just a few last loose ends. We'll send for you when we know the outcome."

"Hers or mine?" Maggie said.

"Both," the two women said in unison.

Barbara arrived at Gordon-Watson at her usual time the following Monday morning. She had taken particular care with her wardrobe, selecting a sheer white blouse and short tan linen skirt. She topped the blouse with a brown linen vest so that the sheerness of the blouse and the lacy bra she wore beneath were only evident when she unbuttoned or removed the vest. She wore sheer stockings and brown suede pumps. She took care that her makeup was sexy yet understated, then applied a new, musky perfume behind her ears and in her cleavage.

She settled at her desk and by nine-thirty was deep into a will she was assembling from a set of stock paragraphs. "Good morning, Barbara," Steve said as he approached her desk.

She looked up and held his gaze just a bit longer than usual. "Good morning, Mr. Gordon."

"What's on my calendar for today?" he said, breezing past her desk.

Barbara picked up her laptop, then followed him into his office. She settled into a soft leather chair, crossed her legs and slipped one shoe off then lifted it with her toe. Then she clicked a few keys on her computer. "You've got the Harris deposition at ten-thirty, lunch with Jack Forrester at twelve-thirty, and, if the deposition doesn't go too late, you can go over Mr. Carruthers's will and the McManister closing documents for tomorrow. And, whenever you have time, I have a list of phone calls you need to make." As she looked up, she saw Steve gazing at her swinging foot. She smothered a smile as she shifted in her chair, moving so her skirt rode up to midthigh. "Do you have anything for me?" she asked with mock innocence. When he didn't answer immediately, his eyes following her foot and the dangling shoe, she said, "Mr. Gordon?"

"Yes?"

"Did you hear me?" Barbara asked.

Obviously snapping back to reality, Steve said, "Of course." He picked up a pencil from his desk and tapped it on the arm of his chair. "Barbara, I've been meaning to talk to you. You've seemed different recently."

"Different?" She slowly unbuttoned her vest and allowed the sides to part.

"More . . ." He looked her over from head to toe, his gaze lingering on her breasts. "More, I don't know. Just more."

She lowered her head so she looked up at him through her lashes. "I hope I can take that as a compliment."

"You can." He looked her over again. "Listen, maybe we can have dinner sometime."

"Are you asking me out on a date?"

Steve hesitated, then said, "I guess I am."

"Well, I'd love to have dinner with you, Mr. Gordon." Barbara giggled. "I guess I should call you Steve now."

"I guess you should." He stood up and walked around and positioned himself behind Barbara's chair. She could feel him touch her hair. "You know," he said, "you're quite something. I'm surprised at myself for not really noticing before now."

Delighted that they were finally going to get to spend some time together, Barbara said, "Shall we say Saturday?"

She could feel Steve playing with the silver streak in her hair. "Saturday sounds great. How about Indian?"

Afraid she would spoil the mood but unwilling to eat very hot food, Barbara said, "I'm not a big fan of curry. How about sushi?"

"Raw fish?" He made a face. "I know a great steak place."

Barbara grinned. "That sounds wonderful." She was glad they had found common ground.

"And Saturday I have tickets for the City Center Ballet. I was going to ask my mother to join me, but I'd much rather have you by my side."

Barbara remembered several trips to the ballet with her mother years before. She had found it stultifying. "The ballet might be nice, and if you already have the tickets . . ." She wondered whether the gorgeous Lisa enjoyed the ballet.

"I try to get there every week or so during the season, but I can tell from your voice it isn't your idea of an enjoyable evening. I'll just give the tickets to my mother and we can go wherever you like." He sat down on the chair beside her and placed a hand on her knee. "Where would you like to go?" He gazed deeply into her eyes. "I mean, if you could go anywhere."

Barbara thought. She had read the entertainment section of *The New York Times* just yesterday. "There's a Woody Allen film festival."

"Oh," Steve said, taking a deep breath. "That would be fine."

Barbara could tell he viewed Woody Allen the way she viewed the ballet. "Maybe just a small, intimate place where we could talk," she said quickly. "We could take some time and get to know each other. And maybe do some slow dancing."

Steve's face brightened. "That sounds wonderful. But I have to warn you, I don't dance."

Barbara stared at Steve. She had been in love with him for so long. But in love with what? He was handsome, well dressed, and very intelligent. But what did they really have in common? "What do you enjoy doing? Tennis? Golf?"

"Actually, I love swimming and I lift weights. And, of course, I really like sports. But you already know that."

She had gotten enough last-minute tickets for sporting events over the years for him that she should. But she had never made the connection. "That's right. Of course. You particularly like boxing."

"I love a good heavyweight match," Steve said, taking her hand. "I guess you probably don't like that sort of thing, but you could learn. It's an acquired taste, like anchovies."

"I hate anchovies, and I think the idea of watching two men beat each other's brains out for money is barbaric." She pulled her hand back.

"We don't have to like the same things, do we?" He cupped her chin and pulled her face toward him. He kissed her softly on the lips. "I'm sure there are some things we will enjoy doing together very much."

She closed her eyes and leaned into the kiss. His lips were warm and moist and his tongue slipped between her teeth to caress her. Suddenly she felt his hand on her breast, squeezing and kneading her tender flesh like bread dough. His other hand began to unbutton her blouse. "No," she said, leaning back. "I don't think this will work."

"But, baby . . ." Steve said, reaching behind her neck to cradle her head. He kissed her harder, forcing her head back.

She placed her palms against his chest and pushed him back. "Steve, Mr. Gordon, I don't think this will work at all. I'm really sorry. It was a mistake." She stood up, put the laptop onto Steve's desk and rebuttoned both her blouse and vest. "This was really a big mistake."

"Oh, baby, don't say that. I'm sorry. This shouldn't have started in the office. Not here where there's no privacy. I understand. Let's talk about it Saturday."

"No, Mr. Gordon, let's not. Let's not see each other Saturday. This isn't going to work. I'm really sorry."

"But . . ."

"Look. We've worked well together for all these years. This is just going to spoil it. Let's just keep this as a business relationship. I like working here and I do the work well. Let's just leave it at that."

Steve stood up and heaved a deep sigh. "I think you're underestimating how good we could be."

She floundered for the right words to tell him to go away without losing her job. "Maybe I am, Mr. Gordon, but I'd rather keep a good relationship here in the office than spoil it with a extracurricular fling, no matter how good it might be." Or how awful.

"I'm disappointed."

"So am I, but I think it's for the best." She retrieved her laptop. "Did you have anything more for me or should I begin placing those phone calls? We can probably get a few things done before the deposition."

Steve looked Barbara over from head to toe. "Well, maybe you're right." Slowly Barbara left the office and walked toward her desk. Then she turned, looked at the sign beside the door. Steven Gordon. She shrugged, then grinned.

"Babs," a voice cried from the end of the soup-and-canned-vegetable aisle in the supermarket a few weeks later. Barbara had stopped in after work to pick up something for dinner. "Babs," the voice said again. "Imagine running into you here."

She looked around for the source of the slightly louder than necessary voice. Striding toward her was a person she hadn't been able to forget. "Hello, Walt," she said softly.

"Babs, you look terrific," Walt said, leaning forward and grasping Barbara by the shoulders. He looked her over from left and right, then from head to toe. "I haven't seen you in a long time. You've changed." He reached over and fingered the streak of white hair above her ear. "And this is very sexy."

Barbara gritted her teeth and tried not to glower at the man whose face she had last seen in the glare of a camera's flash bulb. I certainly have changed, she said, trying not to let all the humiliation rush back. "I haven't seen *you* in a long time."

"What have you been doing with yourself?" he asked, his smarmy smile trying to give the impression that they were old friends.

In as few words as possible, Barbara told him that she was still work-ing at the same place and that her mother had died more than a year ago. "Nothing much else has changed." At least nothing she wanted to discuss with him.

He flashed his most charming smile. "Well, I think you look wonder-ful. Why don't we have dinner some evening and catch up on old times?"

"I'm really quite busy these days," Barbara said, her fingernails dig-ging into her palms.

"If you're still at the same place, I must still have your number. I'll give you a call. I'm sure we can work something out. I really want to see you."

I don't want to see you, she thought. "I don't think it will work out," she said, turning her back and pushing her shopping cart toward the front of the store.

"Good, I'll call you."

"You know, Maggie, almost every sentence began with 'I.' He's such a prick."

"I wouldn't insult wonderful erect pricks like that," Maggie said with a twinkle in her eyes.

Barbara burst out laughing. "Thanks for that," she said. When she could talk again, she said, "I needed you to put everything back into per-spective. God, he's such a jerk."

"He certainly sounds like one. But he did notice how wonderful you look." She winked. "He's obviously a very perceptive guy."

Barbara giggled as she considered how far she'd come. "I don't think I look that different," she said, "but I feel so differently about myself."

"That's so much a part of how you look. Confidence, a positive image of yourself, and, don't overlook the sensuality that's so much a part of you now."

"I guess Walt saw that," Barbara said. "He looked me over like I was the blue plate special. It made me want to punch his lights out, then take a shower."

"But does it still hurt? Think before you answer."

Barbara considered, then said, "Yes, I guess it does. But I'm so dif-ferent now. It shouldn't hurt anymore, but when I saw him in the market, my stomach clenched and it was as though that evening happened only a day ago."

"Maybe you need to exorcize the evil spirits."

"I'd love to. But how?" Barbara asked, flexing her fingers to try to work out the sudden stiffness.

"Revenge is good for the soul occasionally," Maggie said. "Women have weapons, you know."

"I couldn't," Barbara said, her brain suddenly scrambling, searching, planning. Maggie raised an eyebrow and Barbara smiled. "Could I?"

"This has to be your decision," Maggie said.

Barbara knew that this was, indeed, her decision. Could she do it? Even the few moments she had spent with Walt had done a job on the self-confidence she had built up over the last months. She thought about the men she saw now on a regular basis, Jay, CJ, and the others. What did they see when they looked at her?

The two women were silent for a long time, then Barbara sighed and silently nodded. She was not the same person Carl and Walt had humiliated that night years ago. She was happy, and, although she had yet to find someone who gave her everything she wanted in life, she knew that finding him was possible. And in the meantime she was having fun.

She nodded more strongly, then grinned. "I want to smash the slimy son of a bitch into pulp," Barbara said. "Starting with his overactive cock." She was quiet again, then said, "And I think I have the germ of an idea. Will you help me?"

"Do you need to ask?" Maggie said, her grin widening. The two women talked for hours until they had every aspect covered. All that remained was for Barbara to pick up a few items on her next visit to CJ's store.

The following evening Walt called, as Barbara had known he would. "Babs, I have been thinking a lot about you since we ran into each other the other day."

"And I've been think about you too, Walt," Barbara said, her voice soft and mellow.

"I was wondering about dinner on Saturday. I happen to be free and I thought we could talk about old times."

Old times indeed. The bastard acted as though they had had a wonderful, but unfortunately interrupted, dating relationship. She was spending the evening with CJ on Friday, so Saturday would work fine. "That should be all right for me," she said.

Walt sounded a bit taken aback as he said, "Sure. Great. I wasn't sure you'd be available."

"Well, you're in luck, Walt. How about the Peachtree Lounge?" she said, selecting the most expensive restaurant she could think of. She could almost picture Walt considering whether she might be worth a hundred-and-fifty-dollar dinner.

"Uh . . . okay. That's sounds fine."

He was hooked. "Can you pick me up about seven?" Barbara suggested. "You remember where I live, I'm sure. And will you make the reservation?"

"Of course. The man should make the reservations anyway. And let's make it seven-thirty on Saturday. I'll be looking forward to it."

Barbara bit the inside of her mouth to keep from laughing. Seven-thirty. She suspected that Walt had to make a point of making the decisions. "That's fine. I'll see you then."

On Saturday afternoon, Barbara settled into the tub and pulled out one of her favorite tapes. She played it and masturbated to several satisfying orgasms. As she dried herself off, her sensual awareness was at its height. She selected a new, basic black dress with deceptively sexual lines and spread it out on the bed. Surprised that Maggie wasn't here to help her, she picked out a black satin-and-lace teddy, thigh-high black stockings, and high-heeled black shoes. Heavy silver earrings and several bangle bracelets completed her outfit. She brushed her hair, then arranged it so, although it was high on her head, it was held with only three combs that could easily be removed. She used a curling iron so that the silver streak curved against her jaw and caressed her neck as she moved.

As she looked at herself in the full-length mirror, she knew she had created exactly the image she wanted. And without any help from Maggie. "Nice work," she told herself.

Walt rang the bell right on time. She opened a second-floor front window and called down, "The door's open. Make yourself comfortable and pour a drink if you like. I'll be down in a few moments." Although she was completely ready, she sat in her bedroom for almost half an hour. As she finally walked downstairs, Walt was pacing the living room. As he turned and saw her, his expression turned from annoyance to appreciation. "My God," he whispered. "Babs, you look . . ."

"Thanks," she said as she handed Walt her light jacket so he could drape it around her shoulders. She leaned back into him just slightly so he could inhale the exotic scent she had carefully applied behind her ears.

"I never imagined you could look like that," Walt said. "It's amazing."

"I thought a lot about you after we met last week and I realized that you never got to know the real me." She walked out the front door and locked it behind her. Walt walked around and got into the driver's seat of his Ford while Barbara opened her door and got into the passenger seat. As she fastened her seat belt, she allowed her skirt to slide up her thigh. She patted Walt's leg. "I think we're going to have an interesting evening."

They drove the short distance to the restaurant in silence. At the entrance, a valet opened her door and assisted her out, with an appreciative look. They entered the large room with a soft blue, nineteenth-century southern decor and were seated side by side on a blue-and-white patterned banquette. As they settled, Barbara reached over and grasped Walt's thigh, just above his knee. "I'm glad this evening is finally here."

Walt blinked his eyes several times and leered at her as the waiter arrived to take drink orders. "We would like a bottle of wine," he said without consulting Barbara. "White."

"I'd like to see the wine list," Barbara said.

"Of course, madam," the waiter said. "I'll send the sommelier over."

"I didn't know you knew anything about wine," Walt said.

Barbara thought about the financial analyst who had taught her to appreciate fine wine. And a few other things as well. "There's a lot about me you don't know," she purred, wondering whether Walt would be sickened by the incredibly predictable dialogue.

He leaned forward, hanging on her every word. Beneath the table-cloth, he reached over and placed his hand on her stockinged knee. Rubbing her index finger up and down his inner thigh, she glared at him until he removed his hand. It had become clear that she could do what she wanted, but he had to keep his hands to himself. Slowly, she allowed herself a slow smile. "Later."

When Walt placed both his hands on the table, Barbara saw they were shaking.

"The wine list," the sommelier said, handing her a leather-covered tome.

"Goodness, this is quite a list," she said. She leaned forward so Walt could get a good view of her cleavage. "Walt, are you having beef, fish, chicken, what?"

She could see his gaze reluctantly rise from the shadowed valley between her breasts. "I thought I'd have a steak," he stammered.

"Good." Still caressing his thigh with one hand and holding the wine list with the other, she discussed the wine selection with the sommelier for almost five minutes.

"You have wonderful taste, madam," the sommelier said as she finally selected a 1984 California Cabernet from an obscure vineyard. "I'll get that right away."

As he disappeared, Barbara returned her attention to Walt. She licked her lips and watched his eyes follow the path of her tongue. "I hope you don't mind, but I found a wonderful wine at a ridiculous price. I'm sure it was a mistake on the list. Only thirty-five dollars. It should have been at least fifty."

Walt was in a daze and seemed not to hear anything Barbara said. Barbara talked and Walt listened through the pouring of the wine. Since Walt seemed incapable of concentrating, Barbara ordered the meal: a creamy carrot soup, sirloin steaks medium-rare with baked potatoes and sour cream, broccoli, and green salads with the house vinaigrette dressing.

During the meal, Walt spoke very little, totally distracted by the frequent presence of Barbara's hand on his leg. Her hands, her looks, her very posture were designed to keep him off-balance. Sensual, inviting, yet taking charge at every opportunity, she was creating exactly the atmosphere she wanted.

As the plates were cleared and the last of the wine poured, Walt said, "How about we go back to my place after? We could continue this wonderful evening there. I even put clean sheets on the bed."

Barbara bit her lip to keep from laughing. *He still thinks he's choreographing this evening.* "I have a better idea," she said. "I have some wonderful things to play with at my house."

"Oh" was all Walt could say.

"But let's have coffee first." Barbara let the tension build for another half an hour before she signaled for the check. Moments later, Walt signed the credit card slip.

They waited only a moment outside the restaurant as the valet got Walt's car. As the valet started to hand Barbara into the passenger side, she walked around to the driver's seat. "I think I'll drive. Okay, Walt?"

"Sure," Walt said hesitantly.

Barbara got behind the wheel and saw that Walt hadn't fastened his seat belt. "Here, let me help you." She leaned across Walt's body and, as Walt gazed down the front of her dress, she grasped the seat belt and pulled it across his chest and snapped it into place. "There," she said, patting his chest.

"But I'm caught," he said, realizing that his arms were trapped.

"I know," Barbara said, and tapped him on the chest again, "and I like it that way." She pressed her lips against his, licking the surprised 'O' his lips formed. He stopped trying to free his arms from beneath the belt, the tent in his slacks growing each minute.

Again in silence, they drove to Barbara's house and she let them in the front door. She remembered the first evening she had had a man in her house, her first evening with Jay. So much had changed. "Come upstairs with me," she said, "and let's have some fun."

Eagerly Walt followed her up the stairs and into her room. "Now," Barbara said, "I really like to play. And I think you do, too."

"Oh, I do," Walt said, unbuckling his belt.

"Not so fast," Barbara said, slapping his hands hard. "In here we do things my way." She watched Walt consider the situation. Would he go along? To increase his incentive, she licked her lips slowly, then reached out and squeezed the hard ridge in his pants. "It will be wonderful. I promise."

Walt dropped his hands to his sides. "I'm sure it will."

She was in control. When she had first thought up this idea, she had wondered whether she could pull it off. She had been very reluctant to assume control at CJ's party, but now it seemed comfortable. Different situations, different views, I guess. "Good boy," she said. "Now that we understand each other, strip."

"What?"

"You heard me. Strip."

"But . . ." He stared at her, obviously unsure.

Barbara met his eyes and tapped her toe on the carpet until Walt's gaze dropped to her shoes.

Awkwardly, without a word, Walt quickly pulled off all his clothes until he stood in the middle of Barbara's bedroom naked. He's actually not badly built, she thought, but she also noticed that his erection had softened. She wanted to keep him continually hard so he would do anything she wanted. She pulled the combs from her hair and shook out the dark mass, allowing it to fall around her face. She separated out the silver strands with her fingers and twisted them around her pinky.

"Let me give you a taste of what's to come," she said then. Still fully clothed, she quickly knelt at his feet and sucked his semi-erect cock into her mouth. He was hard again instantly.

After only a moment, she stood again and lifted her skirt. She motioned him to his knees and pulled the crotch of her teddy to one side. "Now lick me."

Eagerly he licked at the hot, wet places between Barbara's legs. Although he seemed to pay no attention to what pleased her, he did lick many of the places she enjoyed. She'd get hers this evening, she vowed, in more ways than one. "Use your hands, too," she said and felt his fingers probe her pussy. As she wiggled, his fingers slipped toward her anus. "Umm," she said, "I like it back there, too."

As she took her pleasure, she looked down and saw that Walt had one fist around his erection. She leaned over and slapped first his hand, then his cock. "Mine," she snapped. "And don't forget again."

"But . . ."

"No buts. Your hands and your cock are mine. Unless you want to leave, of course."

Walt groaned "No," and his shoulders sagged. He was hers.

"Good. Get on all fours. I like the feel of my pussy on your back."

Reluctantly Walt knelt on his hands and knees and Barbara stepped over him and rubbed her wet pussy on his spine. "It's like horseback riding," she said as she settled her weight on his back. "It always gets me hot." She had never been on a horse in her life, but it sounded good. "Move underneath me," she said. He moved a bit and she purred, "Mmmm, that's good." Slowly he seemed to get into the game and began to arch his back and wiggle his hips so his spine rubbed against Barbara's wet lips.

"You are very good at this," she said. She dismounted, reached beneath him and squeezed his cock. "And you certainly seem to enjoy it." She left for a moment, and returned with a tube of lubricant. "I love hard cocks," she said, rubbing the cold gel all over his erection and balls. "You feel so hot, so hard. I've never known anyone so hard."

She watched him preen, the oily bastard. Still rubbing his cock with one hand, she slid one finger of the other to the sensitive area behind his balls and stroked. Gradually, her caresses worked her fingers closer to his anus. "So hot, baby," she purred as she rubbed his puckered hole. She had no idea whether he'd ever done anything like this before, but whether or not he was experienced, he seemed to be enjoying her ministrations. She lightened her touch on his cock so he wouldn't come just yet.

"A horse needs a tail," she said, "and I have just the thing." She quickly found an anal plug with a slender neck just below the flange and a dozen strands of leather attached to the base. She imagined that some used the dildo end as a handle for the whip, but she knew what she wanted to do with the device.

Still on all fours, Walt looked at the item in Barbara's hand. "You're not going to hurt me with that, are you?" he said.

"No, baby," she said, rubbing her slippery hand over the flesh-colored plastic handle. "I am going to fill you as you may never have been filled before."

"I don't know," he said.

Barbara looked at his cock, now harder than ever.

"Yes, you do. It's dirty and evil, but the idea of having something invade your ass excites you." She leaned beneath his groin and rubbed his swollen cock. "You can't fool me, so don't try. Just be quiet and let me do this."

Walt shuddered but remained silent. Gently Barbara massaged Walt's rear hole with the tip of the dildo, then pushed it inch-by-inch into his rear passage. When it was deep inside, held by his tight sphincter, the leather strips made it look as though her horse indeed had a tail.

Again Barbara straddled Walt's back, undulating so her pussy rubbed against his heated flesh. "Such a good mount," she said, gazing off into the corner. She reached into her crotch and fingered her clit. "Ummm," she purred loudly. "Good horsy. Buck for me, horsy."

Walt arched his back and, with only a few more strokes, Barbara came, her wetness soaking Walt's skin.

"When does it get to be my turn?" he moaned.

Barbara caught her breath, then stood up and crossed the room. She pressed a few buttons on a small remote control, then flipped on the TV. "We'll see what you want after you've watched this hot video." She pressed the remote's rewind button then pressed play.

After a moment of snow, the image of Walt on his knees before Barbara filled the screen. Staring at the sight of his head moving against her crotch and hearing the sounds of her purrs and his pleased grunts, Walt stood up and walked, naked, toward the TV. As Walt watched himself get down in his hands and knees, he growled, "You taped the entire thing?" He reached behind him and yanked the dildo from his ass, his face turning bright red.

"The entire thing," Barbara said. She pressed fast-forward, then slowed the picture again as a clear shot of Walt, with the tail hanging from his rear, filled the screen. The camera zoomed in on the dildo in Walt's ass.

"How did you get it to zoom like that? Shit. Someone must have been holding the camera."

Maggie had been controlling the camera at that moment, but Walt would never know or understand that. Barbara let the tape play for another few moments. Then she said, "Now, go home."

Walt's breathing was raspy and his entire body shook. His eyes wildly searched the room. "How? Why?"

Barbara slowly shook her head. "You poor, stupid bastard. You don't even remember the trick you and your friend Carl played on me several years ago. The car? The camera?" She watched as recognition slowly changed his expression. "Good. I see you remember now. That was me. And you humiliated me in ways you couldn't even imagine." She smiled ruefully. "And you didn't even remember it."

"Okay. I'm sorry," Walt said as he pulled on his pants. "Really. I am. Now give me that tape." He prowled the room looking for the camera.

"I'm sure you are sorry. Now. But sorry isn't enough. Be a good boy and get out of here."

"Not without that film"

"The film is only part of it. The friend who helped me with the camera also took lots of still pictures. Like the ones you took of me that night. Those photos of you and your lovely tail are long gone." There were no such pictures, but Walt would never know that.

Walt stopped searching the room and pulled on his shirt and jacket. "What are you going to do with them?"

"Actually, nothing." She retrieved the camera from its hiding place behind some ferns on her wardrobe and pulled out the cassette. "You didn't do anything with the photos you took that night, so here . . ." She handed the cassette to Walt. "I'll hold on to the stills. Just having them is a symbol of something for me."

"You won't show them around?" Walt said, stuffing the cassette into his jacket pocket.

"No. Unless you get out of line, that is. So run along. Go home." She thought about the condition of his deflated cock and what she hoped were very uncomfortable balls. "And jerk off."

Walt stared at her for a long moment, then shook his head. "Amazing," he said. "Just amazing." She left, and Barbara heard him pound down the stairs and slam the front door behind him.

"It's all gone," Barbara said to Maggie later that evening. "All that leftover anger and frustration are gone. I don't even hate the poor slob anymore."

"I'm glad. Did he believe you about the still pictures?"

"He did. Just like I expected him to. Thanks for aiming the camera for me. I didn't even mind it that you were watching."

"I only watched for a few minutes." She patted Barbara's hand. "You were great."

"It all felt good. And maybe Walt will think twice before he plays tricks on women again."

"I hope so. What's up for you now?"

"Just more of life, I guess," Barbara said, stretching out of the bed in her bathrobe. "I saw a T-shirt recently. It said, 'So many men and so little time.'"

Maggie laughed. "Well, babe, I've got to go."

"Okay. See you soon."

"Yeah," Maggie said, knowing it was a lie.

Maggie pushed through the revolving door and, as she thought she would, ended up in the computer room, wearing the soft white gown she had been wearing on her first visit. This was it, she knew. Up or down. And how had she done? She didn't really know.

"And we don't know either," Lucy said, as always reading her mind.

"Yes, we know you did your job," Angela said.

"And you did it well," Lucy chimed in.

"But the outcome is not quite what either of us anticipated," Angela added.

"Outcome?" Maggie said, making herself comfortable in a chair facing the women's desk.

"Oh, that's right," Angela said. "You left Barbara after her evening with Walt."

"That was seven months ago," Lucy said.

"Seven months? Oh," Maggie said. "It's funny. I miss her even though it seems only a moment ago."

"Well, once we knew you were gone permanently, we fixed it so she wouldn't miss you."

"Fixed it?"

"We erased you," Lucy said.

"You what!" Maggie yelled, jumping from her chair. "You erased me?"

Angela walked around the desk and patted Maggie's shoulder, pushing her back down into her chair. "Lucy's got the tact of a wart hog, and that's an insult to wart hogs. But try to understand." A chair appeared beside Maggie and Angela sat down, arranging her wings carefully behind her. "We couldn't let her remember you. She had come so far and missing you would have only depressed her. And she needed to remember all her changes as her own doing. It was the final step in her lessons."

"And after all," Lucy said, "how could she have explained you?"

"But . . ."

"Sweetie," Angela said, still patting Maggie's shoulder. "You really do understand."

Maggie sighed. "I guess I do. It just makes me sad." She sniffed and a lace hanky appeared in her hand.

"I know," Angela continued. "But she's doing so well now."

"Really? What's she doing?"

Lucy picked up the story. "She's got a boyfriend. Full time. They are thinking about moving in together. Barbara met him just after that evening with Walt. He's a banker and went to her boss about some legal matters. They met and hit it off immediately, both as friends and hot lovers. For a long while they dated, but continued to see other people. Now they've become exclusive and they're very happy."

"That's wonderful." Maggie wondered why she felt so empty. It was nice when Barbara needed her, looked to her for guidance, learned from her. Now her job was done and it was a letdown. She blew her nose.

"I know it's a letdown," Angela said, "but you can relish the fact that you did a super job."

"Would you like to see them, her and her boyfriend?" Lucy asked. "I can tune you in if you like."

"Not in the bedroom," Maggie said, curious to see the ending to Barbara's story. "I don't want to eavesdrop."

Lucy's fingers danced over the computer keyboard. "Not at all. They're out for the evening at a little place they frequent." She turned the monitor so Maggie could see.

In the picture, a couple danced, their bodies close. Barbara leaned against the man who held her, her mouth beside his ear. "I just love slow dancing," she whispered. "It's like making love standing up."

They turned so Maggie could see the man's face. "That's Paul!" she cried. "That's the guy I was on the phone with that last night. That's my Paul."

"That's her Paul now, and they're blissfully happy," Angela said.

Maggie caught her breath. Paul. She had really loved him, she realized. She gazed at him for a while, getting pleasure from the obvious joy on his face. Maggie sighed and smiled. "We could never have been happy together," she said. "He was a banker and I was a prostitute. It would never have worked." She watched the screen.

Paul spoke into Barbara's ear. "You know, every time you talk about slow dancing, I remember a woman I once knew. Her name was Maggie and it was very long ago. I loved her."

"Do you still love her?" Barbara asked.

"She's been dead for a couple of years. I just remember her fondly. She always liked slow dancing."

"I vaguely remember someone named Maggie in my past, too. I don't remember when I knew her, but I get warm feelings when I think of her."

Paul pressed his hand into the small of Barbara's back, moving his body still closer to hers. "I like warm feelings. Let's go back to your place and feel warm all over."

As Lucy turned off the image on the computer screen, Maggie brushed a tear from her face. "I'm happy for them. I really am."

"I know you are, dear," Angela said, rising and circling the desk again. "But that still leaves us with the problem of what to do with you."

"Yes," Lucy said. "We're still confused."

"We had a bet about how this would end up."

"And we can't even decide who won."

Lucy leaned over and whispered animatedly to Angela. Although Maggie couldn't hear the words, it was obvious from the body language that the two women were arguing. Hands flew through the air, Lucy's tail swished, and at one point Angela's wings flapped and she rose several feet into the air.

Finally Lucy said, "That's the only answer."

"I think so."

"Well," Maggie said, realizing that her fate for the remainder of all time was being decided, "have you figured it all out?"

"Actually, no," Angela said. "But what about you? Where do you think you belong?"

"I don't know either. Heaven sounds real nice, I guess, but maybe a bit dull."

"Well, I have no complaints," Angela said, looking offended.

"I didn't mean to be insulting," Maggie said quickly. "I'm sure it's a lot of fun once you get used to it. But I'm not accustomed to sitting around all day discussing philosophy."

"See, I told you," Lucy said. "My place is much more interesting."

"Yes, I'm sure it is, but I'm not sure I want to associate with the people who go . . ." Maggie pointed her thumb downward.

"Shows you have good taste," Angela said. "And I think Lucy and I have arrived at a solution, at least for the short run."

"How would you like to be an operative for us?" Lucy continued. "You would just do more of what you did with Barbara. Fix up people's lives."

"Like Michael Landon in *Highway to Heaven*?"

Angela nodded. "Maybe, but on a more earthy level. You know, teaching people to love making love."

"Teaching people to love to fuck," Lucy said, turning to Angela, a mischievous grin on her face.

Angela hurumphed, and looked seriously at Maggie. "Would you do that? We've got a lot of cases like Barbara's waiting for someone like you."

Maggie swallowed her tears and thought about Barbara and Paul. Then she considered the offer for only a moment. "I think I'd like that."

"Good," Angela and Lucy said simultaneously.

"Okay. And this time, how about giving me some powers. You know, like *the stuff* Michael Landon had."

"We'll see as the situation arises," Angela said.

"Now, come over here. I want to show you a woman named Pam." Lucy's fingers flew over the keyboard. "She's a tough one."

Maggie swiped a tear from her cheek. The girls were right. Barbara and Paul would be so good together. But it was hard to grasp that that part of her life was over. Maggie circled the table and stood behind Lucy. "That's her?"

"That's Pam. She's almost forty, divorced and dumpy."

"She must weight over two fifty."

"Aren't you the one who believes that sensuality is as much a product of the look in the eyes as the body behind it?"

Maggie drummed her fingers on the back of Lucy's chair. "I hate hearing my own words thrown back at me," she said, "and you're right, of course. Anyone can be sensual."

"She really needs your kind of help," Angela said.

Maggie took a deep breath. "Okay, when do I start?"